Raves for ~~David Zindell's~~
Neverness

"~~N~~ot just a brilliant novel, but a strong and serious view of human potential . . . as I read it I heard Zindell say things I had tried to say in many of my own works, but never did, not this clearly, not this fully. . . . I have read Zindell's book, and I want to *know* what he knew that allowed him to tell this tale."
—Orson Scott Card,
author of *Ender's Game*, *WYRMS*,
and *Speaker for the Dead*

"Talented, ambitious . . . thoughtful philosophic concepts and challenging writing, recalling early John Barth."
—*Publishers Weekly*

"Zindell's heady prose opens a gateway to a world of rich imagination."
—*Library Journal*

Neverness

A Novel by
David Zindell

SPECTRA

BANTAM BOOKS
NEW YORK · TORONTO · LONDON · SYDNEY · AUCKLAND

This edition contains the complete text
of the original hardcover edition.
NOT ONE WORD HAS BEEN OMITTED.

NEVERNESS

A Bantam Spectra Book / published by arrangement with
Donald I. Fine, Inc.

PRINTING HISTORY

Donald I. Fine edition published May 1988
Bantam edition / July 1989

For Melody

I

Journeymen Die

On Old Earth the ancients often wondered at the origin of life, and they created many myths to explain the mystery of mysteries. There was Mumu the mother goddess who swallowed a great snake which multiplied inside of her and whose nine billion children ate their way through her belly into the light of day and so became the animals of the land and the fishes of the sea. There was a father god, Yahweh, who created Earth and the heavens in six days and who called forth the birds and the beasts on days five and six. There was a fertility goddess and a goddess of chance named Random Mutation. And so on. And so on. The truth is, life throughout the galaxy was everywhere seeded by a race known as the Ieldra. Of course the origin of the Ieldra is unknown and perhaps unknowable; the ultimate mystery remains.

> —from *A Requiem for Homo Sapiens* by
> Horthy Hosthoh, Timekeeper and Lord
> Horologe of the Order of Mystic Mathematicians
> and Other Seekers of the Ineffable Flame

There is infinite hope, but not for Man.
> —Frank Kafka, Holocaust Century Fabulist

Long before we knew that the price of the wisdom and immortality we sought would be almost beyond our means to pay, when man—what was left of man—was still like a child playing with pebbles and shells by the seashore, in the time of the quest for the mystery known as the Elder Eddas, I heard the call of the stars and prepared to leave the city of my birth and death.

I call her Neverness. The founders of our Order, so the Timekeeper once told me, having discovered a neighborhood of space where the pathways through the manifold twist and loop together like a hard knot of string, decided to build our city on a nearby planet named Icefall. Because such knots of space were once thought to be rare or nonexistent—the cantors now call them thickspace—our first Timekeeper declared that we could fall through the galaxy until the universe collapsed inward upon itself and never find a denser thickspace. How many billions of pathways converge around our cool yellow star no one knows. There are probably an infinite number of them. The ancient cantors, believing that their theorems proved the impossibility of an infinite thickspace, had predicted that our pilots would never find the topological nexus that they sought. So when our first Lord Pilot had fallen out of the manifold above the small, cold, mountainous island that was to shelter our beloved and doomed city, he named her Neverness, in mockery of the nay-saying academicians. Of course to this day the cantors call her the Unreal City, but few pay them much attention. I, Mallory Ringess, whose duty it is to set forth here the history of the golden age and great crisis of our Order, shall follow the tradition of the pilots who came before me. Neverness—so I knew her as a child when I entered the novitiate such a short time ago; Neverness I call her now; Neverness she will always remain.

On the fourteenth day of false winter in the year 2929 since the founding of Neverness, Leopold Soli, my uncle and Lord Pilot of our Order, returned to our city after a journey lasting twenty-five years—four years longer than I had been alive. Many pilots, my mother and Aunt Justine among them, had thought him dead, lost in the inky veils of the manifold or perhaps incinerated by the exploding stars of the Vild. But he, the famous Lord Pilot, had fooled everyone. It was the talk of the city for eighty days. As false winter hardened and the light snows deepened, I heard it everywhere whispered, in the cafes and bars of the Farsider's Quarter as well as the towers of the Academy, that there would be a quest. A quest! For journeymen pilots such as we were then—in a few more days we would take our pilot's vows—it was an exciting time, and more, a time of restlessness and excruciating anticipation. Within each of us stirred a dreamlike but deeply felt intimation and fear that we would be called to do impossible things, and soon. What follows, then, is a chronicle of the impossible, a story of dreams and fears and pain.

At twilight of the evening before our convocation, my fat, lazy friend Bardo and I devised a plan whereby we—I—could confront the Lord Pilot before the next day's long, boring ceremony. It was the ninety-fourth of false winter. Outside our dormitory rooms, a soft snow had recently fallen, dusting the commons of the pilot's college with a veil of cold white powder. Through our frosted windows, I saw the towers of Resa and the other colleges gleaming in the light of the setting sun.

"Why do you always do what you're not supposed to do?" Bardo asked me as he stared mournfully at me with his large brown eyes. I had often thought that the whole of his complicated character and cunning intelligence was concentrated in his great, bulging forehead and in his deep-set, beautiful eyes. Apart from his eyes, though, he was an ugly man. He had a coarse black beard and bulbous red nose. His gaudy silk robe spilled over his mountainous chest, belly and legs, onto the seat of the immense, padded chair on which he sat, next to the window. On each of his ten fat fingers he sported a differently colored jeweled ring. He had been born a prince on Summerworld; the rings and the chair were articles of great value he had imported from his family's estate, reminders of the riches and glory that could have been his had he not renounced (or tried to renounce) worldly pleasures for the beauty and terror of the manifold. As he twined his long mustache between his thumb and forefinger, his rings clicked together. "Why do you want what you can't have?" he asked me. "By God, where's your sense?"

"I want to meet my uncle, what's wrong with that?" I said as I pulled on my black racing kamelaika.

"Why must you answer a question with a question?"

"And why shouldn't I answer a question with a question?"

He sighed and rolled his eyes. He said, "You'll meet him tomorrow. Isn't that soon enough? We'll take our vows, and then the Lord Pilot will present us our rings—I hope. We'll be *pilots*, Mallory, and then we can do as we damn please.

Tonight we should smoke toalache or find a couple of beautiful whores—a couple apiece, I mean—and spend the night swiving them until our blood's dry."

Bardo, in his own way, was wilder and more disobedient than I. What we *should* have been doing the night before taking our vows was to be practicing zazen, hallning and fugue, some of the mental disciplines needed to enter—and survive—the manifold.

"Last seventyday," I said, "my mother invited Soli and Justine to dinner. He didn't have the decency to answer the invitation. I don't think he wants to meet me."

"And you think to repay his rudeness with greater rudeness? If he wants to waste away drinking with his friends, well, everyone knows how Lord Soli likes to drink, and why. Leave him alone, Little Fellow."

I reached for my skates and pushed my feet into them. They were cold and stiff from lying beneath the drafty window too long. "Are you coming with me?" I asked.

"Am I coming with you? Am I coming with you? What a question!"

He belched and patted his rumbling belly as he looked out the window. I thought I saw confusion and indecision rippling in his dark, liquid eyes.

"If *Bardo* doesn't come with you, you'll go alone, don't tell me you won't, goddammit!" Like many of the princely caste on Summerworld, he had the pretentious habit of occasionally speaking of himself by his own name. "And what then? *Bardo* will be to blame if anything happens to you."

I tightened the laces of my skates. I said, "I want to make friends with my uncle, if I can, and I want to see what he looks like."

"Who cares what he looks like?"

"I do. You know I do."

"You can't be his son, I've told you that a hundred times. You were born four years after he left Neverness."

It was said that I looked enough like the Lord Pilot to be mistaken for his brother—or son. All my life I had endured the slander. My mother, so the gossips prattled, had long ago fallen in love with the great Soli. When he had spurned her in favor of my Aunt Justine—this is the lie they tell—she had searched the back streets of the Farsider's Quarter for a man, any man, who looked enough like him to father her son. To father me. Mallory the Bastard—so the novices at Borja had whispered behind my back, and some of them, the bolder few, to my face. At least they had until the Timekeeper taught me the ancient arts of wrestling and boxing.

"So what if you *do* look like him? You're his nephew."

"His nephew by marriage."

I did not want to look like the famous, arrogant Lord Pilot. I hated that the signature of his chromosomes was seemingly written upon my own. Bad enough to be his nephew. My great fear, as Bardo knew, was that Soli had returned in secret to Neverness and had used my mother for his own selfish purposes or. . . I did not like to think of other possibilities.

"Aren't you curious?" I asked. "The Lord Pilot returns from the longest journey in the three thousand years of our Order, and you aren't even curious to know what he's discovered?"

"No, I'm not afflicted with curiosity, thank God."

"It's said that the Timekeeper will call the quest at the convocation. Don't you even want to know?"

"*If* there's a quest," he said, "we'll probably all die."

"Journeymen die," I said.

Journeymen Die—it was a saying we had, a warning cut into the marble archway above the entrance to Resa that is meant to terrorize young journeymen into leaving the Order before the manifold claimed them; it is a saying that is true.

"'To die among the stars,'" I quoted the Tycho, "'is the most glorious death.'"

"Nonsense!" Bardo shouted as he slapped the arm of the chair. He belched and said, "Twelve years I've known you, and you're still talking nonsense."

"You can't live forever," I said.

"I can damn try."

"It would be hell," I said. "Day after day, thinking the same thoughts, the same dull stars. The same faces of friends doing and talking about the same things, the relentless apathy, trapped within our same brains, this negative eternity of our confused and painful lives."

He shook his head back and forth so violently that drops of sweat flew off his forehead. "A different woman each night," he countered. "Or three very different women each night. A boy or an alien courtesan if things got too boring.

Thirty thousand planets of the Civilized Worlds, and I've seen only fifty of them. Ah, I've heard the talk of our Lord Pilot and his quest. For the secret of life! Do you want to know the secret of life? Bardo will tell you the secret of life: it's not the amount of time we have, despite what I've just said. No, it's not quantity and it's not even quality. It's variety."

As I usually did, I had let him blather, and he had blathered his way into a trap.

"The variety of the bars in the Farsider's Quarter," I said, "is nearly infinite. Are you coming with me?"

"Damn you, Mallory! Of course I am!"

I put on my racing gloves and clipped in the blades of my skates. I walked towards the heavy mahogany door of our room. The long racing blades left dents in the alien-woven Fravashi carpet. Bardo bellowed as he stood up and followed behind me, smoothing out the dents with the balls of his black-slippered feet. "You've no respect for art," he said as he put on his skates. He fastened his black shagshay fur cape around his neck with a gold chain and opened the door. "Barbarian!" he said, and we skated out onto the street.

We sped between Resa's Morning Towers tucked low and tight with our arms swinging and our skates clacking mechanically against the smooth red ice. The cold wind against my face felt good. In no time at all we shot past the granite and basalt towers of the high professionals' college, Upplysa, and passed through the marble pillars of the west gate of the Academy, and there she was.

She shimmers, my city, she shimmers. She is said to be the most beautiful of all the cities of the Civilized Worlds, more beautiful even than Parpallaix or the cathedral cities of Vesper. To the west, pushing into the green sea like a huge, jewel-studded sleeve of city, the fragile obsidian cloisters and hospices of the Farsider's Quarter gleamed like black glass mirrors. Straight ahead as we skated, I saw the frothy churn of the Sound and the whitecaps of breakers crashing against the cliffs of North Beach and above the entire city, veined with purple and glazed with snow and ice, Waaskel and Attakel rose up like vast pyramids against the sky. Beneath the half-ring of extinct volcanoes (Urkel, I should mention, is the southernmost peak, and though less magnificent than the others, it has a conical symmetry that some find pleasing) the

towers and spires of the Academy scattered the dazzling false
winter light so that the whole of the Old City sparkled. The
streets, as everyone knows, are colored ice. Throughout the
city, the white shimmer is broken by strands of orange and
green and blue. "Strange are the streets of the City of Pain,"
the Timekeeper is fond of quoting, but though indeed colorful and strange, they are colorful and strange to a purpose.
The streets—the glissades and slidderies—have no names.
Thus it has been since our first Timekeeper announced that
young novices could prepare their brains for the pathways of
the manifold by memorizing the pathways of our city. Since
he understood that our city would grow and change, he
devised a plan whereby returning pilots who had been away
too long might still be able to negotiate the ice and not lose
their way. The plan is supposed to be simple. There are two
main streets: the Run, colored blue, which twists from West
Beach across the long sleeve of the peninsula where it meets
the foothills of Attakel and Urkel, and the Way, which is laid
straight from the Hollow Fields to the Sound. Any orange
sliddery intersects—eventually—the Way. Any green glissade
intersects the Run. The glidderies, colored purple, join with
glissades, and the red lesser glidderies give out onto the
slidderies. I should not confuse matters by mentioning that
there are two yellow streets running through the Pilot's
Quarter, but there are. No one knows how they came to be
there. A joke, no doubt, on our first Timekeeper.

We turned onto the Way at an orange and white checkered intersection about a mile west of the Academy. The
street was crowded with harijan and wormrunners and other
farsiders. We passed and bowed to the eschatologists, cetics,
akashics, horologes, the professionals and academicians of our
Order. (We did not come across any other pilots. Although
we pilots—some will deny this—are the very soul of our
Order, we are outnumbered by the scryers, holists, historians, remembrancers and ecologists, by the programmers,
neologicians and cantors. Our Order is divided into one
hundred and eighteen disciplines; there are too many disciplines, more disciplines, it seems, every year.) There was
excitement in the air, as well as the alien scent of a couple of
Friends of Man, who had their trunks lifted as they talked to
each other, spraying out their foul speech molecules. Next to
us skated an expensively dressed Alaloi—or rather a man

whose flesh had been sculpted into the thick, powerful, hairy body of an Alaloi. This kind of artificial return to the primitive form had been a fashion in the city for years, ever since the famous Goshevan of Summerworld had tired of his human flesh and had gone to live with the Alaloi in their caves on the islands to the west of Neverness. The false-Alaloi, who was wearing too much purple velvet and gold, pushed one of the slender, gentle harijan out of his way and shouted, "Watch out, stupid farsider!" The bewildered harijan stumbled, made a sign of peace across his shiny forehead, and slunk off into the crowd like a beaten dog.

Bardo looked at me and shook his head sadly. He had always had a strange empathy for the harijan and other homeless pilgrims who come to our city seeking enlightenment. (And too often, they come seeking riches of a more mundane nature.) He smiled as he edged closer to the barbaric Alaloi. He insinuated his thick tree-trunk of a leg between the purple-covered legs of the unsuspecting man. There was a ringing of steel against steel, and steel grinding against ice, and suddenly the man pitched forward to the street with a slap and a crack. Bardo shouted, "Excuse me!" Then he laughed, reached back and grabbed my forearm, and pulled me through the crush of skaters who were jostling one another and vying for position in their hurry to reach their favorite cafes or kiosks for their evening meal. I looked back through the crowd, but I could not see the man whom Bardo had tripped.

"On Summerworld," Bardo said to me between gasps of air, "we brand dung like him with red-hot steel."

We crossed into the Farsider's Quarter and came to the Street of the Ten Thousand Bars. I have said that the streets of Neverness have no names, but that is not entirely true. They have no *official* names, no names that are marked on buildings or posted on street signs. Especially in the Farsider's Quarter, there are many nameless streets that are named according to the prevailing enterprise transpiring along its convolutions of colored ice. Thus there is a Street of Cutters and Splicers, and a Street of Common Whores, as well as a Street of Master Courtesans. The Street of the Ten Thousand Bars is actually more of a district than a street; it is a maze of red lesser glidderies encompassing tiny bars that cater to the unique tastes of their patrons. One bar will serve only toalache while another might specialize in cilka, the pineal gland of the thallow bird which induces visions in small quantities and is lethal in larger ones. There are bars frequented only by the alien Friends of Man, and there are bars open to anyone who writes haiku (but only Simoom haiku) or plays the shakuhachi. Near the edge of the district, there is a bar where the eschatologists argue as to how long it will be before the exploding Vild destroys the last of the Civilized Worlds, and next door, a bar for the tychists who believe that absolute chance is the fundament of the universe, and that most probably some worlds will survive. I do not know if there are as many as ten thousand bars or if there are many more. Bardo often joked that if one could imagine a bar existing, it must exist. Somewhere there is a bar, he claimed, where the Fravashi analyze the anguished poetry of the Swarming Centuries and another bar where their criticisms are criticized. Somewhere—and why not?—there is a bar for those wishing to talk about what is occurring in all the other bars.

We stopped in front of the black, windowless master pilots' bar, or, I should say, the bar for master pilots *recently* returned from the manifold. The sun had set, and the wind moaned as it drove flowing, ghostlike wisps of snow down the darkened gliddery. In the dim light of the street globes—when for a moment the wind suddenly pulled away the ragged, drifting snow shroud—the ice of the street was blood red.

"This is an ugly place," Bardo said, his voice booming from the stone walls surrounding us. "I have a proposition. Since I'm in a generous mood, I'll buy you a master courtesan for the night. You've never been able to afford one, have you? By God, it's like nothing you've ever—"

"No," I said as I shook my head.

I opened the heavy stone door, which was made of obsidian and so smooth that it felt almost greasy to the touch. For a moment, I thought the tiny room was empty. Then I saw two men standing at the dark end of the narrow bar, and I heard the shorter one say, "If you please, close the door, it's cold."

We stepped over to the bar, into the flickering light of the marble fireplace behind us. "Mallory," the man said, "and Bardo, what are you two doing here?"

My eyes adjusted to the dim orange light, and I saw the

master pilot, Lionel Killirand. He shot me a swift look with his hard little eyes and contracted his blonde eyebrows quizzically.

"Soli," he said to the tall man next to him, "allow me to present your nephew."

The tall man turned into the light, and I looked at my uncle, Leopold Soli, the Lord Pilot of our Order. It was like looking at myself.

He stared at me with troubled, deep-set, blue eyes. I did not like what I saw in his eyes; I remembered the stories my Aunt Justine had told me, that Soli was a man famous for his terrible, unpredictable rages. Like mine, his nose was long and broad, the mouth wide, firm. From his long neck to his skates, thick black woolens covered his lean body. He seemed intensely curious, scrutinizing me as carefully as I did him. I looked at his hair; he looked at mine. His hair was long and bound back with a silver chain, as was the custom of his birth planet, Simoom. He had unique hair, wavy black shot with red, a genetic marker of some Soli forebear who had tampered with the family chromosomes. My hair, thank God, was pure black. I looked at him; he looked at me. I wondered for the thousandth time about my chromosomes.

"Moira's son." He said my mother's name as one says a curse word. "You shouldn't be here, should you?"

"I wanted to meet you," I said. "My mother has talked about you all my life."

"Your mother hates me."

There was a long silence broken by Bardo who said, "Where's the bartender?"

The bartender, a tonsured novice who wore the white wool cap of Borja over his bald head, opened the storage room door behind the bar. He said, "This is the master pilot's bar. Journeymen drink at the journeymen's bar, which is five bars down the gliddery towards the Street of Musicians."

"Novices don't tell journeymen what to do," Bardo said. "I'll have a pipe of toalache and my friend drinks coffee— Summerworld coffee if you have it, Farfara if you don't."

The novice shrugged his skinny shoulders and said, "The *master pilots* don't smoke toalache in this bar."

"I'll have a tumbler of liquid toalache, then."

"We don't serve toalache or coffee."

"Then we'll have an amorgenic. Something strong to send the hormones gushing. We've a busy night ahead of us."

Soli picked up a tumbler of a smoky colored liquid and took a sip. Behind us a log in the fireplace popped and fell between two others, scattering glowing cinders and ashes over the tiled floor. "We drink liquor or beer," he said.

"Barbaric." This came from Bardo who added, "I'll have beer, then."

I looked at my tall uncle and asked, "What liquor are you drinking?"

"It's called skotch."

"I'll have skotch," I said to the novice, who filled two tumblers—a large one with foamy beer and a smaller one with amber skotch—and set them in front of us atop the rosewood bar.

Bardo gulped his beer, and after I had taken a sip of skotch and coughed, he asked, "What does it taste like?" I handed him my tumbler, watching as he brought it up to his fat red lips. He, too, coughed at the fire of the burning liquid and announced, "It tastes like gull piss!"

Soli smiled at Lionel and asked me, "How old are you?"

"Twenty-one, Lord Pilot. Tomorrow when we take our vows, I'll be the youngest pilot our Order has ever had, if I may say that without sounding like I'm bragging."

"Well, you're bragging," Lionel said.

We talked for a while about the origins of such immense and fathomless beings as the Silicon God and the Solid State Entity, and other things that pilots talk about. Soli told us of his journey to the core; he spoke of dense clusters of hot new stars and of a great ringworld that some god or other had assembled around Betti Luz. Lionel argued that the great and often insane mainbrains (he did not like to use the word "gods") roaming the galaxy must be organized according to different principles than were our own miniscule minds, for how else could their brains' separate lobes—some of which were the size of moons—intercommunicate with others across light-years of space? It was an old argument. It was one of the many bitter arguments dividing the pilots and professionals of our Order. Lionel, and many eschatologists, programmers, and mechanics as well, believed the mainbrains had mastered nearly instantaneous tachyonic information flow. He held that we should seek contact with these beings, even though such

contact was very dangerous and might someday force the
Order to change in ways repugnant to older and more
old-fashioned pilots such as Soli.

"Who can understand a brain encompassing a thousand
cubic lightyears of space?" Soli asked. "And who knows about
tachyons? Perhaps the mainbrains think slowly, very slowly."

To him, the origin and technology of the gods were of
little interest. In this he was as stodgy as the Timekeeper,
and like the Timekeeper, he thought that there were certain
things that man was not meant to know. He recited a long list
of pilots, the Tycho among them, who had been lost trying to
penetrate the mystery of the Solid State Entity. "They
overreached themselves," he told us. "They should have
been aware of their limits." I smiled because this came from
the tight lips of a man who had reached farther than any
other, a famous pilot whose discovery would provoke the
great crisis of our Order.

It was a heady drug, to talk to master pilots as pilots, as if
we had long ago taken our vows and proved our mastery of
the manifold. I drank my skotch and gathered up my courage, and I said, "I've heard there will be a quest. Will there
really be?"

Soli glared at me. He was a sullen man, I thought, with a
sad, faraway look to his sea-blue eyes, a look that hinted of
freezing mists and sleepless nights and fits of madness.
Though his face was young and smooth, as young as mine, it
had recently been as old and deeply seamed as a face could
be. It is one of the peculiarities of the manifold that a pilot
sometimes ages, intime, three years to every year on
Neverness. I imagined, for a moment, that I had the powers
of a cetic and that I could see the wrinkled, ancient Soli
through the taut olive skin of his new body, in the same
manner one envisions a fireflower drying to a brittle black, or
the skull of death beneath the pink flesh of a newborn baby
boy. A master horologe, whose duty it was to determine the
intime of returning pilots according to complicated formulae
weighting einsteinian time distortions against the unpredictable deformations of the manifold, had told me that Soli had
aged one hundred and three years this last journey and would
have died but for the skills of the Lord Cetic. This made my
uncle, who had been brought back three times to his youth,
the oldest pilot of our Order.

"Tell us about your discovery," I said. I had heard a wild rumor that he had reached the galactic core, the only pilot to have done so since the Tycho, who had returned half-insane.

He took a long drink of skotch, all the while watching me through the clary bottom of the tumbler. The poorly dried firewood hissed and groaned, and from the street came the humming and steaming of a zamboni as it hovered over the gliddery, melting and smoothing the ice for the next day's skaters.

"Yes, the impatience of youth," he said. "You come here disrespecting the needs of a pilot for privacy and the company of his friends. In that, you're much like your mother. Well, then, since you've gone to so much trouble and endured the vileness of skotch whiskey, you'll be told what happened to me, if you really want to know."

I found it irritating that Soli could not simply say, "*I'll* tell you what happened to me." Like most others from that too-mystical planet, Simoom, he usually observed their taboo against using the pronoun "I."

"Tell us," Bardo said.

"Tell us," I said, and I listened with that strange mixture of worship and dread that journeymen feel toward old pilots.

"It happened like this," Soli said. "A long time had passed since my leaving Neverness. We were deep in dreamtime and fenestering inward toward the core. The stars were dense. They shined like the lights of the Farsider's Quarter at night, yes, a great burning fan of stars disappearing into the blackness at the fan's pivot point, at the singularity. There was the white light of dreamtime—you young pilots think instantaneity and stopping time are all there is to dreamtime, and you have much to learn—there was a sudden clarity, and voices. My ship told me it was receiving a signal, intercepting one of a billion or so laser beams streaming *out* of the singularity."

He suddenly slammed his empty tumbler on the bar and his voice rose an octave. "Yes, that's what was said! *From* the singularity! It's impossible, but true. A billion lines of infrared light escaping the black maw of gravity." To the novice he said, "Pour some skotch in here, please."

"And then?"

"The voices, the ship-computer receiving half a trillion bits per second and translating the information in the laser beams into voices. They, the voices, claimed to be—let's call them the Ieldra. Are you familiar with that term?"

"No, Lord Pilot."

"It's what the eschatologists have named the aliens who seeded the galaxy with their DNA."

"The mythical race."

"The hitherto mythical race," he said. "They have—and many refuse to believe this—they've projected their collective selfness, their consciousnesses, into the singularity."

"Into the black hole?" Bardo asked as he pulled at his mustache.

I looked at Soli carefully, to see if he was having a joke with us. I did not believe him. I looked down at his tense hands and saw that he was carelessly ungloved. Plainly, he was an arrogant man who had little fear of contagion or that his enemies might make use of his plasm. His knuckles were white around the curve of his refilled tumbler. The black diamond of his pilot's ring cut into the skin of his little finger. He said, "The message. The white light of dreamtime hardened and crystallized. There was a stillness and a clarity, and then the message. 'There is hope for Man,' they said. 'Remember, the secret of Man's immortality lies in your past and in your future'—that's what they said. We must search for this mystery. If we search, we'll discover the secret of life and save ourselves. So the Ieldra told me."

I think he must have known we did not believe him. I nodded my head stupidly while Bardo stared at the bar as if the knots and whorls of the rosewood were of great interest to him. He dipped his finger into the foam of his beer, brought it to his lips, and made a rude sucking sound.

"Young fools," Soli said. And then he told us of the prediction. The Ieldra, he said, understanding the cynicism and doubtfulness of human nature, had provided a surety that their communication would be well received, a prediction as to part of the sequence of supernovae in the Vild.

"How can they possibly know what will occur according to chance?" I asked.

"*Do* the Vild stars explode at random?" Lionel broke in.

"Ah, of course they do," Bardo said.

In truth, no one knew very much about the Vild. Was the Vild a discrete, continuous region of the galaxy expanding outward spherically in all directions? Or was it a composite of many such regions, random pockets of hellfire burning and joining, connecting in ways our astronomers had not determined? No one knew. And no one knew how long it would be before Icefall's little star exploded, along with all the others, putting an end to such eschatological speculations.

"How do we know what we know?" Soli asked, and he took a sip of skotch. "How is it known the memory in my brain is real, that there was no hallucination, as some fools have suggested? Yes, you doubt my story, and there's nothing to prove to you, even if you are Justine's nephew, but this is what the Lord Akashic told me: He said that the auditory record was clear. There was a direct downloading from the ship-computer to my auditory nerve. Perhaps you think my ship was hallucinating?"

"No, Lord Pilot." I began to believe him. I knew well the power and skills of the akashics. A short half year ago, on a bitterly cold day in deep winter, having completed my first journey alone into the manifold, I had gone before the akashics. I remembered sitting in the Lord Akashic's darkened chamber as the heaume of the deprogramming computer descended over my head, sitting and sweating and waiting for my memories and mappings of the manifold to be proved true. Though there had been no cause for fear, I had been afraid. (Long ago, in the time of the Tycho, there had been reason to be afraid. The clumsy ancient heaumes, so I understand, extruded protein filaments through one's scalp and skull into the brain. Barbaric. The modern heaume—this is what the akashics claim—models the interconnections of the neurons' synapses holographically, thereby "reading" the memory and identity functions of the brain. It is supposed to be quite safe.)

Bardo, as was his habit when he was nervous or afraid, farted loudly, and he asked, "Then you think there will be a quest for this . . . this, uh, *secret* of the Ieldra? Lord Pilot?"

"The eschatologists have named the secret the 'Elder Eddas,'" Soli said as he backed away from him. "And yes, there will be a quest. Tomorrow, at your convocation, the Timekeeper will issue his summons and call the quest."

I believed him. The Lord Pilot, my uncle, said there would be a quest, and I suddenly felt my heart beating up through my throat as if it were fate's fist knocking at the doorway to my soul. Wild plans and dreams came half-formed into my mind. I said quickly, "If we could prove the Continuum Hypothesis, the quest would be full of glory, and we'd find your Elder Eddas."

"Don't call them *my* Elder Eddas," he said.

I should admit that I did not understand the Lord Pilot. One moment he proclaimed that there were things man was not meant to know, and the next moment he seemed proud and eager to go off seeking the greatest of secrets. And yet a moment later, he was bitter and appeared resentful of his own discovery. In truth, he was a complicated man, the second most complicated man I have ever known.

"What Mallory meant," Bardo said, "was that he admires— as we all do, as we all do—the work you've done on the Great Theorem."

That was not at all what I had meant.

Soli looked at me fiercely and said, "Yes, the dream of proving the Continuum Hypothesis."

The Continuum Hypothesis (or, colloquially, the Great Theorem): an unproved result of Lavi's Fixed-Point Theorem stating that between any pair of discrete Lavi sets of point-sources, there exists a one-to-one mapping. More simply, that it is possible to map from any star to any other in a single fall. It is the greatest problem of the manifold, of our Order. Long ago, when Soli had been a pilot not much older than I, he had nearly proved the Hypothesis. But he had become distracted by an argument with Justine and had forgotten (so he claimed) his elegant proof of the theorem. The memory of it haunted him. And so he drank his poisonous skotch whiskey, to forget. (The powers of a pilot's mind, Bardo reminds me, crescendo at an early age. It is a matter of dying brain cells, he says, and the rejuvenation we pilots undergo is imperfect in this respect. We grow slowly stupider as we age, and so why not drink skotch, or smoke toalache and lie with whores?)

"The Continuum Hypothesis," Soli said to me as he spun his empty tumbler on top of the bar, "may very well be unprovable."

"I understand you are bitter."

"As you will be if you seek the unobtainable."

"Forgive me, Lord Pilot, but how are we to know what is obtainable and what is not?"

"We grow wiser as we grow older," he said.

I kicked the toe of my boot against the brass railing at the foot of the bar. The metal rang dully. "I may be young, and I don't want to sound like—"

"You're bragging," Lionel said quickly.

"—but I think the Hypothesis is provable, and I intend to prove it."

"For the sake of wisdom," Soli asked me, "or for the glory? I've heard that you'd like to be Lord Pilot someday."

"Every journeyman dreams of being Lord Pilot."

"A boy's dreams often become a man's nightmares."

I kicked the railing, accidentally. "I'm not a boy, Lord Pilot. I take my vows tomorrow; one of my vows is to discover wisdom. Have you forgotten?"

"Have *I* forgotten?" he said, breaking his taboo and flinching as he shouted out the forbidden pronoun. "Listen, *Boy, I've* forgotten nothing."

The word "nothing" seemed to hang in the air along with the hollow ringing of the railing as Soli stared at me and I at him. Then there came too-loud laughter from the street outside, and the door suddenly opened. Three tall, heavy men, each of them with pale yellow hair and drooping mustaches, each of them wearing light black furs dusted with snow, ejected their skate blades and stomped into the bar. They came up to Lionel and Soli and grasped each other's hands. The largest of the three, a master pilot who had terrorized Bardo during our novice years at Borja, called for three mugs of kvass. "It's spiky cold outside," he said.

Bardo leaned over to me and whispered, "Time to go, I think."

I shook my head.

The master pilots—their names were Neith, Seth and Tomoth—were brothers. They had their backs to us, and they seemed not to have noticed us.

"I'll pay for six nights of master courtesans," Bardo mumbled.

The novice banged three mugs of steaming hot black beer down on the bar. Tomoth backed a few steps closer to the fire and shook the melting snow from his furs. Like some of the older pilots who had gone blind from old age, he wore jeweled, mechanical eyes. He had just returned from the edge of the Vild, and he said to Soli, "Your Ieldra were right, my friend. The Gallivare Binary and Cerise Luz have exploded. Nothing left but dirty hard dust and light."

"Dust and light," his brother Neith said, and he burned his mouth with hot kvass and cursed.

"Dust and light," Seth repeated. "Sodervarld and her twenty millions caught in a storm of radioactive dust and light. We tried to get them off but we were too late."

Sodervarld orbits Enola Luz, which is—had been—the star nearest the Gallivare Binary. Seth told us that the supernova had baked the surface of Sodervarld, killing off every bit of life except the ground worms. The small master pilot's bar suddenly seemed stultifyingly tiny. The three brothers, I recalled, had been born on Sodervarld.

"To our mother," Seth said as he clinked mugs with Soli, Lionel and his brothers.

"To our father," Tomoth said.

"*Freyd.*" This came from Neith who inclined his head so slightly that I was not sure if he had actually nodded or if his image had wavered in the firelight. "To Yuleth and Elath."

"Time to go," I said to Bardo.

We made ready to leave, but Neith fell weeping against Tomoth, who turned our way as he caught his brother. His jeweled eyes gleamed in the half-light when he saw us. "What's this?" he shouted.

"Why are there *journeymen* in our bar?" Seth wanted to know.

Neith brushed yellow hair from his wet eyes and said, "My God, it's the Bastard and his fat friend—what's his name?—Burpo? Lardo?"

"*Bardo*," Bardo said.

"They were just about to leave," Soli said.

I suddenly did not feel like leaving. My mouth was dry, and there was a pressure behind my eyes.

"Don't call him 'Bardo'," Neith said. "When we tutored him at Borja, everyone called him Piss-All Lal because he used to piss in his bed every night."

It was true, Bardo's birth name was Pesheval Lal. When he first came to Neverness, he had been a skinny, terrified, homesick boy who had loved to recite romantic poetry and who had pissed in his bed every night. Half of the novices and masters had called him "Bardo," and the other half, "Piss-All." But after he had begun lifting heavy weights above his head and had taken to spending the nights with bought

women so that he wet his bed with the liquids of lust instead
of piss, few had dared to call him anything but "Bardo."

"Well," Tomoth said as he clapped his hands at the novice
behind the bar. "Piss-All and The Bastard will toast with us
before they leave."

The novice filled our mugs and tumblers. Bardo looked at
me; I wondered if he could hear the blood pounding in my
throat or see the tears burning in my eyes.

"*Freyd*," Tomoth said. "To the dead of Sodervarld."

I was afraid I was about to cry from rage and shame, and
so, looking straight into Tomoth's ugly metal eyes, I picked
up my tumbler and tried to swallow the fiery skotch in a
single gulp. It was the wrong thing to do. I gagged and
coughed and spat all at once, spraying Tomoth's face and
yellow mustache with tiny globules of amber spit. He must
have thought that I was mocking him and defiling the memory of his family because he came at me without thought or
hesitation, came straight for my eyes with one hand and for
my throat with the other. There was a ragged burning beneath my eyebrow. Suddenly there were fists and blood and
elbows as Tomoth and his brothers swept me under like an
avalanche. Everything was cold and hard: cold tile ground
against my spine, and hard bone broke against my teeth;
someone's hard nails were gouging into my eyelid. Blindly, I
pushed against Tomoth's face. For a moment, I thought that
cowardly Bardo must have slipped out the door. Then he
bellowed as if he had suddenly remembered he was Bardo,
not Piss-All, and there was the meaty slap of flesh on flesh,
and I was free. I found my feet and punched at Tomoth's
head, a quick, vicious, hooking punch that the Timekeeper
had taught me. My knuckles broke and pain burned up my
arm into my shoulder joint. Tomoth grabbed his head, dropping to one knee.

Soli was behind him. "Moira's son," he said as he bent
over and reached for the collar of Tomoth's fur to keep him
from falling. Then I made a mistake, the second worst
mistake, I think, of my life. I swung again at Tomoth, but I
hit Soli instead, smashing his proud, long nose as if it were a
ripe bloodfruit. To this day, I can see the look of astonishment
and betrayal (and pain) on his face. He went mad, then. He
ground his teeth and snorted blood out of his nose. He
attacked me with such a fury that he got me from behind in a

head hold and tried to snap my neck. If Bardo had not come between us, peeling Soli's steely hands away from the base of my skull, he would have killed me.

"Easy there, Lord Pilot," Bardo said. He massaged the back of my neck with his great, blunt hand and eased me toward the door. Everyone stood panting, looking at each other, not quite knowing what to do next.

There were apologies and explanations, then. Lionel, who had held himself away from the melee, told Tomoth and his brothers that I had never drunk skotch before and that I had certainly meant them no insult. After the novice refilled the mugs and tumblers, I said a requiem for the Sodervarld dead. Bardo toasted Tomoth, and Tomoth toasted Soli's discovery. And all the while, our Lord Pilot stared at me as blood trickled from his broken nose down his hard lips and chin.

"Your mother hates me, so there should be no surprise that you do too."

"I'm sorry, Lord Pilot. I swear it was an accident. Here, use this to wipe your nose."

I offered him my handkerchief, but he pretended not to see my outstretched hand. I shrugged my shoulders, and I crumpled the linen to sponge the blood out of my eye. "To the quest for the Elder Eddas," I said as I raised my tumbler. "You'll drink to that, won't you, Lord Pilot?"

"What hope does a *journeyman* have of finding the Eddas?"

"Tomorrow I'll be a pilot," I said. "I've as much a chance as any pilot."

"Yes, chance. What chance does a young fool of a pilot have of discovering the secret of life? Where will you look? In some safe place, no doubt, where you've no chance of finding anything at all."

"Perhaps I'll search where bitter and jaded master pilots are afraid to."

The room grew so quiet that I heard the spatter of my uncle's blooddrops against the floor.

"And where would that be?" he asked. "Beneath the folds of your mother's robes?"

I wanted to hit him again. Tomoth and his brothers laughed as they slapped each other on the back, and I wanted to break my uncle's bleeding, arrogant face. I have always felt the hot pus of anger too keenly and quickly. I wondered if it *had* been an accident that I had hit him; perhaps it was my

fate (or secret desire) to have hit him. I stood there on
trembling legs staring at him as I wondered about chance and
fate. The heat of the glowing fire was suddenly oppressive.
My head was pounding with blood and skotch, and my eye
felt like molten lava, and my tongue was like syrup as I made
the worst mistake of my life. "No, Lord Pilot," I blurted out.
"I'll journey beyond the Eta Carina nebula. I intend to
penetrate and map the Solid State Entity."

"Don't joke with me."

"I'm not joking. I don't like your kind of jokes; I'm not
joking."

"You *are* joking," he said as he stepped closer to me. "It's
just the silly brag of a foolish journeyman pilot, isn't it?"

Through the haze of my good eye, I saw that everyone,
even the young bartender, was staring at me.

"Of *course* it was a joke." Bardo's voice boomed as he
farted. "Tell him it was a joke, Little Fellow, and let's leave."

I looked into Soli's intense, fierce eyes and said, "I swear
to you I'm not joking."

He grabbed my forearm with his long fingers. "You swear
it?"

"Yes, Lord Pilot."

"You'll swear it, formally?"

I pulled away from him and said, "Yes, Lord Pilot."

"Swear it, then. Say, 'I, Mallory Ringess, by the canons
and vows of our Order, in fulfillment of the Timekeeper's
summons to quest, swear to my Lord Pilot I will map the
pathways of the Solid State Entity.' Swear it to me!"

I swore the formal oath in a trembling voice as Bardo
looked at me, plainly horrified. Soli called for our tumblers to
be filled and announced, "To the quest for the Elder Eddas.
Yes, my young fool of a pilot, we'll all drink to that!"

I do not remember clearly what happened next. I think
that there was much laughter and drinking of skotch and
beer, as well as talk about the mystery, the joy and agony of
life. I remember, dimly, Tomoth and Bardo weeping, locking
wrists and trying to push each other's arm to the gleaming
surface of the bar. It is true, I now know, that liquor obliter-
ates and devours the memory. Bardo and I found other bars
that night serving skotch and beer (and powerful amorgenics);
we also found the Street of the Master Courtesans and
beautiful Jacarandans who served our lust and pleasure. At

least I think they did. Because it was my first time with a skilled woman—women—I knew very little of lust and pleasure, and I was to remember even less. I was so drunk that I even allowed a whore named Aida to touch my naked flesh. My memories are of heavy perfume and dark, burning skin, the blindly urgent pressing of body against body; my memories are murky and vague, spoiled by the guilt and fear that I had made enemies with the Lord Pilot of our Order and had sworn an oath that would surely lead to my death. "Journeymen die," Soli said as we left the master pilot's bar. As I stumbled out onto the gliddery I remember praying that he would be wrong.

2

A Pilot's Vows

*Strange, though alas! are the Streets of the City of
Pain ...*

—Rainer Maria Rilke,
Holocaust Century Scryer

We received our pilot's rings late in the afternoon of the next
day. At the center of Resa, surrounded by the stone dormitories, apartments and other buildings of the college, the
immense Hall of the Ancient Pilots overflowed with the men
and women of our Order. From the great arched doorway to
the dais where we journeymen knelt, the brightly colored
robes of the academicians and high professionals rippled like
a sea of rainbow silk. Because the masters of the various
professions tended to cleave to their peers, the rainbow sea
was patchy: near the far pillars at the north end of the Hall
stood orange-robed cetics, and next to them, a group of
akashics covered from neck to ankle in yellow silk. There were
cliques of scryers berobed in dazzling white, and green-robed
mechanics standing close to each other, no doubt arguing as
to the ultimate (and paradoxical) composition and nature of
the spacetime continuum, or some other arcanum. Just below
the dais was the black wavefront of the pilots and master
pilots. I saw Lionel, Tomoth and his brothers, Stephen
Caraghar and others that I knew. At the very front stood my
mother and Justine, looking at us—I thought—proudly.

The Timekeeper, resplendent and stern in his flowing red
robe, bade the thirty of us to repeat after him the vows of a
pilot. It was good that we knelt close together. The warm,
reassuring bulk of Bardo pressing me from the right, and my

friend Quirin on my left, kept me from pitching forward to the polished marble surface of the dais. Although that morning I had been to a cutter who had melded the ragged tear of my eyelid and had taken a purgative to cleanse my body of poisonous skotch, I was ill. My head felt hot and heavy; it seemed that my brain was swollen with blood and would burst my skull from inside. My spirit, too, was burning. My life was ruined. I was sick with fear and dread. I thought of the Tycho and Erendira Ede and Ricardo Lavi, and other famous pilots who had died trying to pierce the mystery of the Solid State Entity.

Immersed as I was in my misery, I missed most of the Timekeeper's warnings as to the deadliness of the manifold. One thing he said I remember clearly: that of the two hundred and eleven journeymen who had entered Resa with us, only we thirty remained. *Journeymen Die,* I said to myself, and suddenly the Timekeeper's deep, rough voice vibrated through the haze of my wandering thoughts. "Pilots die too," he said, "but not as often or as easily, and they die to a greater purpose. It is to this purpose that we are gathered here today, to consecrate..." He went on in a like manner for several minutes. Then he enjoined us to celibacy and poverty, the least in importance of our vows. (I should mention that the meaning of celibacy is taken in its narrowest sense. If it were not, Bardo could never have been a pilot. Although physical passion between man and woman is exalted, it is the rule of our Order that pilots not marry. It is a good rule, I think, a rule not without reason. When a pilot returns from the manifold years older or younger than his lover, as Soli recently had, the differential aging—we call it crueltime—can destroy them.) "As you have learned and will learn, so must you teach," the Timekeeper said, and we took our third vow. Bardo must have heard my voice wavering because he reached over and squeezed my knee, as if to impart to me some of his great strength. The fourth vow, I thought, was the most important of all. "You must restrain yourselves," the Timekeeper told us. I knew it was true. The symbiosis between a pilot and his ship is as profound and powerful as it is deadly addictive. How many pilots, I wondered, had been lost to the manifold because they too often indulged in the power and joy of their extensional brains? Too many. I repeated the vow of obedience mechanically, with little spirit or enthusiasm. The Timekeeper paused, and I thought for a moment he was going to look at me, to chasten me or to make me repeat the fifth vow again. Then, with a voice pregnant with drama, in a ponderous cadence, he said, "The last vow is the holiest vow, the vow without which all your other vows would be as empty as a cup full of air." So it was that on the ninety-fifth day of false winter in the year 2929 since the founding of Neverness, we vowed above all else to seek wisdom and truth, even though our seeking should lead to our death and to the ruin of all that we loved and held dear.

The Timekeeper called for the rings. Leopold Soli emerged from an anteroom adjacent to the dais. A frightened-looking novice followed him carrying a velvet wand around which our thirty rings were stacked, one atop the other. We bowed our heads and extended our right hands. Soli proceeded down the line of journeymen, slipping the spun-diamond rings off the wand and sliding them onto each of our little fingers. "With this ring, you are a Pilot," he said to Alark Mandara and Chantal Astoreth. And to the brilliant Jonathan Ede and the Sonderval, "With this ring you are a pilot," on and on down the line of kneeling journeymen. His nose was so swollen that his words sounded nasal, as if he had a cold. He came to Bardo, whose fingers were bare of the jewelry he usually wore and instead encircled with rings of dead white flesh. He removed the largest ring from the wand. (Though my head was supposed to be bowed, I could not resist peeking as Soli pushed the gleaming black ring around Bardo's mammoth finger.) Then it was my turn. Soli bent over me, and he said, "With this ring you are a . . . *pilot*." He said the word "pilot" as if it had been forced out of him, as if the word were acid to his tongue. He jammed the ring on my finger with such force that the diamond shaved a layer from my skin and bruised my knuckle tendon. Eight more times I heard "With this ring you are a pilot," and then the Timekeeper intoned the litany for the Lost Pilot, and said a requiem, and we were done.

We thirty *pilots* left the dais to show our new rings to our friends and masters. A few of the wealthier new pilots had family members who had paid the expensive passage to Neverness aboard a commercial deep ship, but Bardo was not one of these. (His father thought him a traitor for abandoning the family estates for the poverty of our Order.) We mingled with our fellows, and the sea of colored silk engulfed us. There were shouts of happiness and laughter and boots stamping on the tiled floor. My mother's friend, the eschatologist Kolenya Mor, indecently pressed her plump, wet cheek next to mine. She hugged me as she bawled, "Look at him, Moira."

"I'm looking at him," my mother said. She was a tall woman and strong (and beautiful), though I must admit she was slightly fat due to her love of chocolate candies. She wore the plain gray robe of a master cantor, those purest of pure mathematicians. Her quick gray eyes seemed to look everywhere at once as she tilted her head quizzically and asked me, "Your eyelid has been melded. Recently, hasn't it?" Ignoring my ring, she continued, "It's well known what you said, the oath you swore. To Soli. It's the talk of the city. 'Moira's son has sworn to penetrate the Solid State Entity,' that's all I've heard today. My handsome, brilliant, reckless son." She began to cry. I was shocked, and I could not look at her. It was the first time I had ever seen her cry.

"It's a beautiful ring," my Aunt Justine said as she came up to me and bowed her head. She held up her own pilot's ring for me to look at. "And well deserved, no matter what Soli says." Like my mother, Justine was tall with slightly grayed black hair pulled back in a chignon; like my mother she loved chocolates. But where my mother most often spent her days thinking and exploring the possibilities of her too-ambitious daydreams, Justine liked to socialize and skate figures and perform difficult jumps at the Ring of Fire, or the North Ring, or one of the city's other crowded ice rings. Thus she had retained the streamlined suppleness of her first youth at the expense, I thought, of her naturally quick mind. I often wondered why she had wanted Soli for a husband, and more, why the Timekeeper had allowed these two famous pilots a special dispensation to marry.

Burgos Harsha, with his bushy eyebrows, jowls and long black hairs pushing out of his piglike nostrils, approached us and said, "Congratulations, Mallory. I always expected you to do something extraordinary—we all did, you know—but I never dreamed you'd break our Lord Pilot's nose the first time you met him and swear to kill yourself in that nebula known colloquially—and, I might add, quite vulgarly—as the

Solid State Entity." The master historian rubbed his hands together vigorously and turned to my mother. "Now, Moira, I've examined the canons and the oral history of the Tycho as well as the customaries, and it's clear—I may be wrong, of course, but when have you known me to be wrong?—it's clear that Mallory's oath was a simple troth to the Lord Pilot, not a promissory oath to the Order. And certainly not a solemn oath. At the time he swore to kill himself—and this is a subtle point, but it's clear—he hadn't taken his vows, so he wasn't *legally* a pilot, so he was not *permitted* to swear a promissory oath."

"I don't understand," I said. From behind me came singing, the swish of silk against silk, and the chaotic hum of a thousand voices. "I swore what I swore. What difference does it make who I swore it to?"

"The *difference*, Mallory, is that Soli can release you from your oath, if he wants to."

I felt a squirt of adrenalin in my throat, and my heart fluttered in my chest like a nervous bird. I thought of all the ways pilots died: They died fenestering, their brains ruined by too-constant symbiosis with their ship, and they died of old age lost in decision trees; supernovae reduced their flesh to plasma, and dreamtime, too much dreamtime, left them forever staring vacantly at the burning stars; they were killed by aliens, and murdered by human beings, and minced by meteor swarms, and charred by the penumbras of blue giant stars, and frozen by the nothingness of deep space. I knew then that despite my foolish words about death among the stars being glorious, I did not want glory, and I desperately did not want to die.

Burgos left us, and my mother said to Justine, "You'll talk to Soli, won't you? I know he hates me. But why should he hate Mallory?"

I kicked the heel of my boot against the floor. Justine traced her index finger along her eyebrow and said, "Soli's so difficult now. This last journey nearly killed him, inside, as well as out. Oh, I'll talk to him, of course, I'll talk on until my lips fall off as I always do, but I'm afraid he'll just stare at me with his broody eyes and say things like, 'If life has meaning, how can we know if we're meant to find it?' or, 'A pilot dies best who dies young, before crueltime kills what he loves.' I can't *really* talk to him when he's like that, of course, and I think it's possible that he thinks he's being noble, letting Mallory swear to die heroically, or perhaps he really believes Mallory will succeed and just wants to be proud of him—I can't tell *what* he thinks when he's all full of himself, but I'll talk to him, Moira, of course I will."

I had little hope that Justine would be able to talk to him. Long ago, when the Timekeeper had let them marry, he had warned them, "Crueltime, you can't conquer crueltime," and he had been right. It is commonly believed that it is differential aging, the alder, that kills love, but I do not think this is entirely true. It is age and selfness that kill love. We grow more and more into our true selves every second that we are alive. If there is such a thing as fate it is this: the outer self seeking and awakening to the true self no matter the pain and terror—and there is always pain and terror—no matter how great the cost may be. Soli, true to his innermost desire, had returned from the core enthralled by his need to comprehend the meaning of death and the secret of life, while Justine had spent those same long years on Neverness living life and enjoying the things of life: fine foods and the smell of the sea at dusk (and, some said, her lovers' caresses), as well as her endless quest to master her waltz jumps and perfect her figure eights.

"I don't want Justine to talk to him," I lied.

My mother tilted her head and touched my cheek with her hand as she had done when I was a boy sick with fever. "Don't be foolish," she said.

A group of my fellow pilots led by the immensely tall and thin Sonderval, diffused like a black cloud through the professionals around us and surrounded me. Li Tosh, Helena Charbo, and Richardess—I thought they were the finest pilots ever to come out of Resa. My old friend, Delora wi Towt, was pulling at her blonde braids as she greeted my mother. The Sonderval, who came from an exemplar family off Solsken, stretched himself straight to his eight feet of height, and said, "I wanted to tell you, Mallory. The whole college is proud of you. For facing the Lord Pilot—excuse me Justine, I didn't mean to insult—and we're proud of what you swore to do. That took courage, we all know that. We wish you well on your journey."

I smiled because the Sonderval and I had always been the fiercest of rivals at Resa. Along with Delora and Li Tosh (and

Bardo when he wanted to be), he was the smartest of my fellow pilots. The Sonderval was a sly man and I sensed more than a bit of reproach in his compliment. I did not think he believed I was courageous for swearing to do the impossible; more likely he knew that my anger had finally undone me. He seemed very pleased with himself, probably because he thought I would never return. But then, the exemplars of Solsken always need to be pleased with themselves, which is why they have bred themselves to such ridiculous heights.

The Sonderval and the others excused themselves and drifted off into the crowd. My mother said, "Mallory was always popular. With the other journeymen, if not his masters."

I coughed as I stared at the white triangles of the floor. The singing seemed to grow louder. I recognized the melody of one of Takeko's heroic (and romantic) madrigals. I was filled instantly with despair and false courage. Confused as I was, vacillating between bravado and a cowardly hope that Soli would dissolve my oath, I raised my voice and said, "Mother, I swore what I swore; it doesn't matter what Justine says to Soli."

"Don't be a fool," she said. "I won't have you killing yourself."

"But you'd have me dishonor myself."

"Better dishonor—whatever that is—than death."

"No," I said, "better death than dishonor." But I did not believe my own words. In my heart, I was all too ready to accept dishonor rather than death.

My mother muttered something to herself—it was a habit of hers—something that sounded like, "Better that Soli should die. Then you'd suffer neither. Death nor dishonor."

"What did you say?" I asked.

"I didn't say anything."

She looked over my shoulder and frowned. I turned to see Soli, tall and somber in his tight black robe, pushing his way through the sea of people. He was leading a beautiful, eyeless scryer by the arm. I was struck immediately by the contrast of white and black: The scryer's black hair hung like a satin curtain over the back of her white robes, and her eyebrows were bushy and black against her white forehead. She moved slowly and too carefully, like a cold, marble statue brought to sudden—and unwelcome—life. I took little notice of her heavy breasts and dark, large nipples so obvious beneath the

thin silk; it was her face that fixed my stare, the long aquiline
nose and full red lips, and most of all, the dark, smoothly
scarred hollows where her eyes used to be.

"Katharine!" Justine suddenly exclaimed as they came
closer. "My darling daughter!" She threw her arms around
the scryer and said, "It's been so long!" They embraced for a
while; then Justine wiped her moist eyes on the back of her
gloves and said, "Mallory, may I present your cousin, Dama
Katharine Ringess Soli."

I greeted her and she turned her head in my direction.
"Mallory," she said, "at last. It's been so long."

There have been moments in my life when time came to a
stop, when I felt as if I were living some dimly remembered
(though vital) event over again. Sometimes the sound of
thallows screeching in winter or the smell of wet seaweed will
take me instantly back to that clear night long ago when I
stood alone on the desolate and windy beach of the Starnbergersee and gave myself over to the dream of mastering the
stars; sometimes it is a color, perhaps the sudden orange of a
sliddery or a glissade's vivid greenness that transports me to
another place and time; sometimes it is nothing at all, at least
nothing more particular than a certain low slant of the sun's
rays in deep winter and the rushing of the icy sea wind.
These moments are mysterious and wonderful, but they are
also full of strange meaning and dread. The scryers, of
course, teach the unity of nowness and thenness and times
yet to be. For them, I think, future dreams and self-
remembrance are two parts of a single mystery. They, those
strange, holy, and self-blinded women and men of our Order,
believe that if we are to have visions of our future, we must
look into our past. So when Katharine smiled at me, and the
calm, dulcet tones of her voice vibrated within me, I knew
that I had come upon such a moment, when my past and
future were as one.

Although I knew I had never seen her before, I felt as if I
had known her all my life. I was instantly in love with her,
not, of course, as one loves another human being, but as a
wanderer might love a new ocean or a gorgeous snowy peak
he has glimpsed for the first time. I was practically struck
dumb by her calmness and her beauty, so I said the first
stupid thing which came to mind. "Welcome to Neverness," I
told her.

"Yes, welcome," Soli said to his daughter. "Welcome to the City of Light." There was more than a little sarcasm and bitterness in his voice.

"I remember the city very well, Father." And so she should have remembered since, like me, she was a child of the city. But when she was a girl, when Soli had gone off on his journey to the core, Justine had taken her to be raised by her grandmother on Lechoix. She had not seen her father (and I thought she would never see him again) for twenty-five years. All that time she had remained on Lechoix in the company of man-despising women. Although she had reason to be bitter, she was not. It was Soli who was bitter. He was angry at himself for having deserted his wife and daughter, and he was bitter that Justine had allowed and even encouraged Katharine to become a scryer. He hated scryers.

"Thank you for making the journey," Soli said to her.

"I heard that you had returned, Father."

"Yes, that's true."

There was an awkward silence as my strange family stood mute in the middle of a thousand babbling people. Soli was glowering at Justine, and she at him, while my mother stole furtive, ugly glances at Katharine. I could tell that she did not like her, probably because it was obvious that I did. Katharine smiled at me again, and said, "Congratulations, Mallory, on your . . . To go off exploring the Entity, that was a brave . . . we're all very proud." I was a little irritated at her scryer's habit of not completing her sentences, as if the person she was talking to could "see" what was left unsaid and skip ahead to the crest of her rushing thoughts.

"Yes, congratulations," Soli said. "But the pilot's ring seems a little small for your finger. Let's hope your pilot's vows aren't too great for your spirit."

My mother cocked her head as she pointed at Soli's chest and said, "What spirit remains? Within the Lord Pilot? A tired, bitter spirit. Don't speak to my son of spirit."

"Shall we speak of life, then? Yes, we shall speak of life: Let's hope Mallory lives long enough to enjoy the life of a new pilot. If there was a tumbler of skotch at hand we'd toast to the glorious but too short lives of foolish young pilots."

"The Lord Pilot," my mother said quickly, "is too proud of his own long life."

Justine grasped Soli's arm while she brought her full,

pouting lips up to his ear and began whispering. He broke away and said to me, "You were probably drunk when you swore your oath. And your Lord Pilot was certainly drunk. Therefore, my lovely wife informs me, we've only to announce that the whole thing was a joke, and we are both finished with this foolishness."

Beneath the silk of my robe, I felt hot sweat running down my sides in rivulets as I asked, "You would do that, Lord Pilot?"

"Who knows? Who knows his fate?" He turned to Katharine and asked, "Have you seen his future? What will be done with Mallory? Should he be kept from his fate? 'To die among the stars is the most glorious death'—that's what the Tycho said before *he* disappeared into the Solid State Entity. Maybe Mallory will succeed where our greatest pilot failed. Should he be kept from fate and glory? Tell me, my lovely scryer."

Everyone looked at Katharine as she stood there calmly listening to Soli. She must have sensed their stares because she put her hand into the side pocket of her robe, "the pocket of concealment," where the scryers keep their rub of blacking oil. When she removed her hand, her forefinger was covered with a cream so black that it shed no light; it was as if she had no finger, as if a miniature black hole existed in the space that her finger occupied. According to the custom of the scryers she daubed the oil into the hollows of her eyepits, coating the scars with concealing blackness. I looked at the hollows above her high cheekbones; it was like looking down two dark, mysterious tunnels into her soul where windows should have been. I looked at her for only a moment before I had to look away.

I was about to tell my sarcastic, arrogant uncle that I would do as I had sworn no matter what he decided when Katharine let out a clear, girlish laugh and said, "Mallory's fate is his fate, and nothing can change . . . Except, Father, that you *have* changed it and always will have . . ." And here she laughed again, and continued, "But in the end we choose our futures, do you see?"

Soli did not see, and neither did I nor anyone else. Who could understand the paradoxical, irritating sayings of the scryers?

Just then Bardo ambled over and thumped me on the back. He bowed to Justine and smiled before quickly looking away. Bardo—he had always tried to keep it a secret, but he could not—lusted for my aunt. I did not think that she lusted for him, nor did she quite approve of his brazen sexuality, though in truth, they were alike in one certain way: They both loved physical pleasure, and cared little for the past, nothing at all for the future. After being introduced to Katharine, he bowed to Soli and said, "Lord Pilot, has Mallory apologized for his barbaric behavior last night? No? Well, I'll apologize for him because he's much too proud to apologize, and only I know how sorry he really is."

"Pride kills," Soli said.

"'Pride kills,'" Bardo repeated as he smoothed his black mustache with the side of his thumb. "Of course it does! But where does Mallory get his pride from? I've been his roommate for twelve years, and *I* know. 'Soli is mapping the core stars,' he used to say. 'Soli almost proved the Great Theorem.' Soli this, and Soli that—do you know what he says when I tell him he's insane for wasting time practicing his speed strokes? He says, 'When Soli became a pilot, he won the pilot's race, and so shall I.'"

He was referring, of course, to the race between the new pilots and the older ones held every year just after the convocation. For many, it is the high point of the Tycho's Festival.

I was sure that my face was red. I could hardly bear to look at my uncle as he said, "Then tomorrow's race should be challenging. No one has beaten me for..." His eyes suddenly clouded, and his voice trembled, slightly, and he continued, "for a long time."

We spent a short while debating the aerodynamics of racing. I held that a low tuck was more efficient, but Soli pointed out that in a long race—as tomorrow's race would be—a low tuck quickly burned-out the muscles of the thigh, and that one must practice restraint.

Our conversation was cut short when ten red-robed horologes marched out onto the dais and took their places by the Timekeeper, five to either side. In unison they sang out, "Silence, it is time! Silence, it is time!" and there was a sudden silence in the Hall. Then the Timekeeper stepped forward, and he announced his summons and called the quest for the Elder Eddas. "The secret of Man's immortality," he told us, "lies in our past and in our future." I felt Katharine's

shoulder brush my own, and I was shocked (and excited) to
feel her long fingers quickly and secretly squeeze my hand. I
listened to the Timekeeper repeat the message that Soli had
brought back from the core; I listened and for a moment I
was enraptured with dreams of discovering great things.
Then I happened to look at Soli's brooding eyes, and I did
not care if I did great things. In my single-minded way I
cared about only a single thing: that I should beat Soli in the
pilot's race. "We must search for the mystery," the Timekeeper continued. "If we search, we will discover the secret of life
and save ourselves." At that moment I did not care about
secrets or salvation. What I wanted, simply, was to defeat a
proud, arrogant man.

I had resolved to return to my room and to sleep until the
sun was high above the slopes of Urkel, but I had not
counted on the excitement that the Timekeeper's summons
would arouse. The halls of our dormitory—and indeed, all of
Resa—rang from the happy cries and shouts of pilots and
journeymen and masters. Against my wishes, our rooms
became a nexus for the night's celebrations. Chantal Astoreth
and Delora wi Towt arrived with three of their neologician
friends from Lara Sig. Bardo distributed pipefuls of toalache,
and the revelry began. It was a wild, magic night; it was a
night of tremulously announced plans to reach Old Earth or
to map the Tycho's nebula, to fulfill our vow to seek wisdom
as befitted our individual talents and dreams. Soon our two
adjoining rooms were thick with blue smoke and carpeted
from wall to wall with excited pilots and various other professionals who had heard about the party. Li Tosh, who was a
gentle man with bright, quick almond eyes, announced his
plan to reach the homeworld of the trickster aliens, the
Dharghinni. "It's said that they've studied the history of the
nebular brains," he told us. "Perhaps when I return, I'll have
enough courage to penetrate the Entity, too." Hideki Smith
would sculpt his body into the weird, cruel shape of the
Fayoli; he would journey to one of their planets and try to
pose as one of them in hope of learning their secrets. Not
to be outdone, red-haired Quirin proposed to journey to
Agathange, where he would ask the porpoise-like men—who
had long ago broken the law of the Civilized Worlds and had
carked their DNA so that they were now more than men—he

would ask the wise Agathanians about the secret of human life. I must admit that there were many skeptics such as Bardo who did not believe that the Ieldra possessed any great secret. But even the most skeptical of these pilots—Richardess and the Sonderval came immediately to mind—were eager to be off into the manifold. To them the quest was a wonderful excuse to seek fame and glory.

Around midnight my cousin Katharine appeared in our outer room's open doorway. How she had found her way blind and alone across the confusing streets of the Academy she would not say. She sat next to me cross-legged on the floor. She flirted with me in her secretive, scryer's way. I was intrigued that an older, wiser woman paid me such attention, and I think she must have realized that I found her tantalizing. I told myself that she, too, was a little in love with me, although I knew that scryers often act not to satisfy their passions but to fulfill some tenuous and private vision. In many barbaric places, of course, where the art of genotyping is primitive, cousin marriage (and mating) is forbidden. One never knows what sort of monsters the mingling of the germ plasm will produce. But Neverness was not one of those places. That we were so closely related seemed only slightly incestuous and very exciting.

We talked about what she had said earlier to Soli about fate, in particular about my fate. She laughed at me as she stripped the black leather glove from my right hand. She slowly stroked the lines of my naked palm and foresaw that the span of my years would be "measureless to man." I thought that she had a keen sense of humor. When I asked if her words meant that my life would be very long or absurdly short, she turned to me with that beautiful, mysterious smile the scryers affect, and she said, "A moment to a photino is infinite, and to a god, our universe has lived but a moment. You must learn to love the moments you have, Mallory." (Towards the early part of morning, she taught me that moments of sexual ecstasy and love can indeed be made to last nearly forever. At the time I did not know whether to ascribe this miracle to the time-annihilating training of the scryers, or if all women had such power.)

It was a night of sorrowful goodbyes, as well. At one point Bardo, his weepy eyes electric with toalache, pulled me away from Katharine and said, "You're the finest friend I've ever

had. The finest friend *anyone* has ever had. And now Bardo
must lose you because of a stupid oath. It's not fair! Why is
this cold, empty universe, which has bestowed upon us what
we so laughingly call life, why is it so barbarically unfair? I,
Bardo will shout it across the room, shout it to the Rossette
Nebula and to Eta Carina and to Regal Luz: It's unfair! Unfair
it is, and that's why we were given brains, to cozen and plan,
to circumvent and cheat. It's to cheat death that I'm going to
tell you what I'll tell you. You won't like this, my brave, noble
friend, but here it is: You've got to let Soli win the race
tomorrow. He's like my father, he's proud and vain, and he
hates for anyone to beat him. I'm a keen judge of character,
and I know. Let him win the race and he'll let you take back
your oath. Please, Mallory, as you love me, let him win the
stupid race!"

Late the next morning, I pulled on my racing kamelaika
and met my mother for breakfast at one of the cafes that line
the Run opposite the flowing Hyacinth Gardens. "You're
racing Soli today, and you didn't sleep last night, did you?
Here, drink this coffee. It's Farfara prime. I've taught you
strategy since you were four years old, and you didn't sleep
last night?"

"Bardo thinks I should let Soli win the race."

"He's a fat fool. Haven't I told you that for twelve years?
He thinks he's clever. Clever he's not. I could have taught
him cleverness. When I was four years old."

From a delicate blue pot, she poured coffee into a marble
cup and slid it across the table. I sipped the hot, black coffee,
totally unprepared for what she said next. "We can leave the
Order," she whispered, tilting her head as she quickly glanced
at the two master mechanics sitting at the table next to us.
"The new academy, the one on Tria, you know what I'm
saying don't you? They *need* pilots, good ones like you. Why
should our Order tyrannize the fallaways?"

I was so shocked that I spilled coffee on my lap, burning
my leg. The Merchant Pilots of Tria—those wily, unethical
thingists and tubists—for a long time had tried to break the
power of our Order. "What are you saying, Mother? That we
should be traitors?"

"Traitors to the Order, yes. Better for you to betray a few
hastily given vows, than to betray the life I gave you."

"You always hoped I'd be Lord Pilot someday."

"You could be a merchant prince. Of Tria."

"No, Mother, never that."

"It would surprise you. That certain pilots have been offered middle estates on Tria. Certain programmers and cantors, too."

"But no one has accepted, have they?"

"Not yet," she said, and she began drumming her fingers against the table top. "But there is more dissension among the professionals than you know. Some of the historians like Burgos Harsha think the Order is stagnating. And the pilots. The rule against marriage is almost as hated as marriage is hateful." Here she paused to laugh at her little joke, then continued, "There is more disorder in the Order than you'd dream." She laughed again as if she knew something I didn't, and she sat back in her chair, waiting.

"I'd rather die than go to Tria."

"Then we'll flee to Lechoix. Your grandmother will welcome us, even if you are a bull."

"I don't think she will."

My grandmother whom I had never met, Dama Oriana Ringess, had brought up Justine and my mother—and Katharine—properly. "Properly" in the Lechoix matriarchy meant an early introduction into the feminine mysteries and severe language rules. Thus men are despised and are referred to as "bulls," or "gamecocks," or sometimes "mules." Desire between man and woman is called "the sick heat," and marriage, heterosexual marriage, that is, is "the living hell." The High Damen, of which my grandmother is one of the highest, abhoring the belief that men make better pilots than women, support the largest and best of the Order's elite schools. So it was that when my mother and Justine arrived at Borja long ago having never seen a man, they were shocked—and in my mother's case, hateful—that such young beasts as Lionel and Soli could be better mathematicians than they were.

"Dama Oriana," I said, "would do nothing that would shame the Matriarchy, would she?"

"Listen to me. Listen! I won't let Soli kill my *son*!" She said the word "son" with such a wrenching desperation that I felt compelled to look at her, even as she burst into tears and sobbed. She nervously pulled her hair from the chignon's binding leather and used the shiny strands to dry her face.

"Listen, listen," she said. "Brilliant Soli returns from the manifold. Brilliant as always, but not so brilliant. I used to beat him. At chess. Three games out of four before he quit playing me."

"What do you mean?"

"I've ordered you bread," she said as she held up her hand and motioned to the domestic. It rolled to the table where it placed before me a basket of hot, crusty black bread. "Eat your bread and drink your coffee."

"You're not eating?"

Usually she had bread at breakfast; like her sisters on Lechoix she would eat no foods of animal origin, not even the cultured meats favored by almost everyone in our city.

I reached for one of the small, oblong loaves. I bit into it; it was delicious. As I chewed the hard bread, she removed a ball of chocolate from the blue bowl in front of her and popped it into her mouth.

"What if I succeed, Mother?" I asked. She stuffed three more balls of chocolate into her mouth, staring at me.

Her reply was barely comprehensible, a burble of words forced through a mouthful of sticky, melting chocolate: "Sometimes I think Soli's right. My son is a fool."

"You've always said you have faith in me."

"Faith I have; blind faith I have not."

"Why should it be impossible? The Entity is a nebula much like any other: hot gases, interstellar dust, a few million stars. Perhaps it's mere chance that the Tycho and the others were lost."

"Heresy!" she said as she picked apart a chocolate ball with her long fingernails. "Haven't I taught you better? I won't have you saying that word. It's not *chance*. That killed the Tycho. It's She."

"She?"

"The Entity. She's a web of a million meshing biocomputers the size of moons. She manipulates matter. And She plies energy. And She twists space to Her liking. The manifold inside Her is known to be strange, hideously complex."

"Why do you call her 'She'?"

My mother smiled and said, "Should I call the greatest intelligence, the holiest life in our universe 'he'?"

"What of the Silicon God, then?"

"Misnamed. By certain of the older eschatologists who

divide essences into male and female. She should be called the 'Silicon Goddess.' The universe gives birth to life; the essence of the universe is female."

"And what of men?"

"They are repositories for sperm. Have you studied the dead languages of Old Earth as I've asked you to do? No? Well, there was a Romance expression: *instrumenta vocalia*. Men are tools with voices. Magnificent tools they are. And sometimes their voices are sublime. But without women, they're nothing."

"And women without men?"

"The Lechoix Matriarchy was founded five thousand years ago. There are no patriarchies."

I sometimes think my mother should have been an historian or a remembrancer. She always seemed to know too much of ancient peoples, languages and customs, or at least enough to turn arguments her way.

"I'm a man, Mother. Why did you choose to have a son?"

"You're a foolish boy."

I took a long sip of coffee, and I wondered aloud, "What would it be like for a man to talk with a goddess?"

"More foolishness," she said. And then, "I've made our decision. We'll go to Lechoix."

"No, Mother. I won't be the only man among eight million women who prize cunning above faith."

She banged her coffee cup down on the table. "Then go to your race. With Soli. And be thankful your mother's mother taught me cunning."

I stared as she stared at me. We stared at each other for a long time. As a master cetic might, I tried to read the truth from the flickers of light reflecting from her bright irises and from the set of her wide mouth. But the only truth that came to me was an old truth: I could no more read her face than I could descry the future.

I sucked the last drops of coffee from my cup and touched my mother's forehead. And then I went out to race Soli.

The race of the Thousand Pilots is not supposed to be a serious affair. (Neither do as many as a thousand pilots ever take part in the festivities.) It is, essentially, a somewhat farcical pitting of old pilots against the new, a symbolic rite of passage. The master pilots—usually there are about a hundred or so—gather in front of the Hall of the Ancient Pilots, and, as is their wont, they drink mugs of steaming kvass or other such beverages, all the while slapping shoulders and hands to give each other encouragement while they shout and jeer at the smaller group of new pilots. That afternoon there were mobs of brightly furred academicians, high professionals and novices crowding the ice of Resa Commons. There were wind chimes tinkling and journeymen whistling to the wormrunners as they held up their gloved hands to place their illegal bets. From the steps of the Hall came the piping of the clarinas and shakuhachis. The high, keening notes seemed to me like an anguished plea full of desperation and foreboding, at odds with the gaiety all around us. Bardo, too, must have felt the music inappropriate because he came up to me as I tested the edges of my skates with my thumbnail, and he said, "I detest mystical music. It makes me feel pity for the universe and arouses certain other feelings I'd rather not have aroused. Give me horns and drums, and by the way, Little Fellow, could I offer you a pinch of fireweed to get the blood singing?"

I refused his red crystals, as he must have known I would. The race master—I saw to my surprise that it was Burgos Harsha, wobbling on his skates because he had no doubt been drinking kvass since the morning's preparations—called the two groups to our starting places. We crowded along the red checkered line where the lesser glidderies gave out onto the white ice at the edge of the Commons. "I had something important to tell you, but I've forgotten what it was," he cried out. "And when have you ever known me to forget anything? Now what was I saying? Does it matter? Well, then, may you pilots not lose your way and may you return soon." He reached for the white starting flag that a novice held out to him and managed to entangle his forearm in the cotton fabric. The novice pressed the short, wooden staff into his grasping fingers, and he waved the flag back and forth in front of his face, and the race began.

I shall mention only a few details of what happened on the streets of my City that day, because due to the peculiar nature and rules of the race, that is all a single pilot can do. The rules are simple: A pilot may choose any path through the four quarters of the city so long as she or he passes in sequence through one of the various checkpoints such as

Rollo's Ring in the Farsider's Quarter, or the Hofgarten between the Zoo and the Pilot's Quarter. The theory is that the smartest and most cunning pilot will win, the pilot who had best memorized the streets and shortcuts of our city. In practice, though, speed is at least as important as brains.

Bardo bellowed and stroked as he pushed between a cluster of master pilots who were blocking his way. (Such shoving, I should add, is permitted if the pilot first shouts out a warning.) Blond-haired Tomoth, who stroked furiously in a high tuck, almost fell as Bardo's elbow caught him on the shoulder. Then Bardo shouted out, "First among equals!" and he disappeared around the curve of the gliddery.

We caught up to him at the Rose Womb Cloisters, that jumble of squat buildings at Resa's western edge housing the tanks in which we had floated for a considerable portion of our journeyman years. He was skating raggedly as we passed him. He had pulled the hood of his kamelaika away from his dripping head. "First among . . . equals," he said wheezing and gasping for air. "At least . . . for a . . . quarter mile."

At the west gate of the Academy we dispersed. Fifteen pilots turned onto the southernmost of the orange glidderies that lead to the Way while eight master pilots and six pilots—Soli and myself among them—chose a lesser gliddery through the gleaming Old City in order to avoid the arterial's heavier traffic. And so it went. The sky above us was deep blue, the air dense and cold. In front of me Soli's steel skates striking smoothly against the ice and the shouts and laughter of the onlookers lining the narrow street were like a racy music. I tucked low and turned as I cradled my right arm against the small of my back, and suddenly I was alone.

I saw other pilots only a few times during the rest of the race. I did not want to make a false analogy between the streets of Neverness and the pathways through the manifold, yet I could not help thinking about the similarities: to suddenly pass from the cold, shadowed, red lesser glidderies onto a sliddery and then to the brilliantly illuminated Way was like fenestering, falling from the manifold into the bright light surrounding a star. As a pilot far from our city segues into a decision tree where he must choose the correct pathway or perish, so we racers had to match our memories of the branching streets against the reality of the tangled knots of glissades and glidderies, or lose. And if dreamtime can be said to be the most important and pleasurable of a pilot's mindsets, then the ecstasy of cool wind and intensely focused vision was what we felt, at least for the first five miles or so. Thus when I entered the checkpoint of the Winter Ring deep within the Farsider's Quarter, and I saw Soli and Lionel ten yards in front of me and other racers skating onto the opening of ice behind me, I had enough breath and enthusiasm to call out, "Five miles alone on the city streets, and here we gather, as if we were stived around the fixed-points of a star!"

As Soli turned to answer me, the features of his face narrowed into a mask of fierce concentration. He was breathing deeply, and he said, "Beware exploding stars!" And then he was gone, speeding down one of the lesser glidderies connecting to the dangerous Street of Smugglers.

I did not catch up to him until near the end of the race. I circled the spouting Silver Spume in the Zoo, where Friends of Man and Fravashi and two races of aliens I had never seen before looked on at the curious spectacle that we provided them. At North Ring the race officer shouted, "Soli first followed by Killirand a hundred yards followed by Ringess one hundred fifty yards followed . . . ," and at the great circle outside the Hofgarten, where the Run intersects the Way, I heard, "Soli first followed by Ringess fifty yards followed by Killirand three hundred . . . ," and so it went. At the last checkpoint, which was in the Pilot's Quarter, I saw my uncle a mere twenty yards ahead. I knew I would not see him again until I crossed first into the Commons and Burgos Harsha pronounced me the winner.

I was wrong.

I was skating west on the Run, cleverly—or so I thought—doubling back along the northern edge of the Old City so that I could cut along a little gliddery I knew of that led straight to the Academy's north gate. The blue ice was crowded with novices and others who had somehow guessed that a few of the racers might choose this unlikely route. As I was congratulating myself and envisioning Burgos pinning the diamond victory medal to my chest, I glimpsed a streak of black through the press of skaters in front of me. The crowd shifted, and there was Soli calmly stroking close to the red stripe separating the skating lane from the sled lane. I was considering shouting out a challenge when I heard raucous laughter behind my back. I turned my head midstroke and

saw two black-bearded men—wormrunners I guessed from
the flamboyant cut of their furs—elbowing each other, clasp-
ing hands, and alternately whipping each other ahead by
snapping their arms. They were much too old, of course, and
the street was much too crowded for a game of bump-and-
skate. I should have perceived this immediately. Instead, I
completed my stroke because I was determined to give Soli
no warning as I passed him. All at once the larger wormrunner
smacked into Soli's back, propelling him across the warning
strip into the sled lane. There came the sudden thunder of a
large red sled as he stutter-stepped on his skates with his
arms outstretched. He performed a desperate dance to avoid
the sled's hard, pointed nose, and suddenly he was down.
The sled rocketed over him in a tenth of second. (Though it
seemed like a year.) I crossed the warning stripe and pulled
him to the skating lane. He pushed me away with an astonishing
force for someone who so nearly had been impaled. "Assassin,"
he said to me. He grunted and tried to stand.

I told him that it was a wormrunner who had pushed him,
but he said, "If not you, then your mother's hirelings. She
hates me because she thinks you'll be held to your oath. And
for other reasons."

I looked at the circle of people standing over us. Nowhere
could I see the two black-bearded wormrunners.

"But she's wrong, Moira is."

He held his side and coughed. Blood trickled from his
long nose and open mouth. He beckoned to a nearby novice
who approached nervously. "Your name?" he asked.

"Sophie Dean, from The Nave, Lord Pilot," the pretty
girl answered.

"Then," he said, "your Lord Pilot in the presence of the
witness Sophie Dean releases Mallory Ringess from his oath
to penetrate the Solid State Entity."

He coughed again, spraying tiny red droplets over Sophie's
white jacket.

"I think your ribs must be broken," I said. "The race is
over for you, Lord Pilot."

He grabbed my arm and pulled me closer to him. "Is it?"
he asked. Then he coughed as he pushed me away and began
skating towards the Academy.

I stood there for a moment staring at the drops of blood
burning tiny holes into the blue ice. I did not want to believe

that my mother had sent assassins to murder Soli. I could not understand why he had released me from my oath.

"Are you all right, Pilot?" Sophie asked.

I was not all right. Though my life was saved, I felt sick to my stomach, utterly wretched. I coughed suddenly and vomited up a chyme of black bread and black coffee and bile.

"Pilot?"

Sophie blinked her clear blue eyes against the sudden wind cutting beneath my garments, and in my mind was a knowledge, a complete and utter certainty that I would keep my oath to Soli and my vows to the Order no matter the cost. Each of us, I realized, must ultimately face death and ruin. It was merely my fate to have to face them sooner than most.

"Pilot, shall I call for a sled?"

"No, I'll finish the race," I said.

"You're letting him get a lead."

It was true. I looked down the Run as Soli turned onto the yellow street leading to my secret shortcut to the west gate.

"Don't worry, child," I said as I pushed off. "He's injured and full of pain, and he's coughing blood. I'll catch him before we get halfway to Borja."

I was again wrong. Though I struck the ice with my skates as fast as I could, I did not catch him as we passed the spires of Borja, and I did not catch him as we circled the Timekeeper's Tower; I did not catch him at all.

The wind against my ears was like a winter storm as we entered Resa Commons. The multitudes cheered, and Burgos Harsha waved the green victory flag, and Leopold Soli, barely conscious and leaking so much blood from his torn lungs that a cutter later had to pump plasma into his veins, beat me by ten feet.

It might as well have been ten light-years.

3

The Timekeeper's Tower

The goal of my theory is to establish once and for all the certitude of mathematical methods . . . The present state of affairs where we run up against the paradoxes is intolerable. Just think, the definitions and deductive methods which everyone learns, teaches and uses in mathematics, lead to absurdities! If mathematical thinking is defective, where are we to find truth and certitude?
— David Hilbert, Machine Century Cantor, from "On the Infinite"

The days following the pilot's race and Leopold Soli's near-murder passed quickly. The clear, dry, sunny weather gave way to winter's deep powder snows that continually fell on the glissades and kept the zambonies busy. Soli's would-be assassins were never caught. Though he made full use of the Order's resources, and the Timekeeper set his spies to listening at doorways and peeking in windows (or whatever it is that spies do), our Lord Pilot could do little more than rage and demand that my mother be brought before the akashics. "Lay her brain bare," he thundered at the pilot's conclave, "expose her plots and lies!" It was a measure of his vast reputation that the pilots, many of whom had grown to adulthood and had taken their vows during his long journey, voted to try my mother.

On fourthday she submitted to the review of Nikolos the Elder. With his computers he painted pictures of her brain as vivid as a Fravashi frescoe. But the plump, little Lord Akashic

45

pronounced that he could find no memory inside her of a plot
to kill Soli.

That night, in her little brick house in the Pilots' Quarter,
she said to me, "Soli goes too far! Nikolos proclaims my
innocence. What does Soli say? He says, 'It's well known that
the matriarchs of Lechoix keep drugs that destroy specific
memories.' Destroy! As if I'd destroy part of my *brain*!"

I knew how my mother treasured the hundred billion
neurons that made up her brain. I did not believe that she, as
those of the aphasic sect often did, had taken an aphagenic to
destroy her memory; neither could I trust that she was
innocent, not after what she had said to me the day of the
race. (Even supposing she *had* used such a drug, I could not
very well ask her if she had. Such is the nature of the
induced micro-brain lesions that she would have no memory
of her crime, nor of having dissolved the memory of her
crime.) I was angry and my voice quavered as I asked, "How
did you fool the Lord Akashic?"

"My son doubts me?" she said as she slumped against the
bare brick wall of her sleeping room. "How I hate Soli! The
Lord Pilot returns. To take away what I love most. And so I
went to the Timekeeper. And lied, yes I admit I lied. I
begged him to ask Soli. To release you from your oath."

"And the Timekeeper listened to you?"

"The Timekeeper thinks he's cunning. But I told him we
would go to Tria. To become merchant pilots, if he didn't talk
to Soli. The Timekeeper thinks he's fearless, but he fears
such a scandal."

"You told him *that*? He must think I'm the worst kind of
coward."

"Who cares what he thinks? At least I've saved you. From
a stupid death."

"You've saved me from nothing," I said as I walked toward
the door. "Don't ever lie on my behalf again, Mother."

I told her I had resolved to keep my oath, and she began
to cry. "How I hate Soli!" she said as I opened the door to the
street. "I'll teach him about hate."

I spent the next few days in final preparation for my
journey. I consulted eschatologists and other professionals,
hoping to glean some bit of information as to the nature and
purpose of the impossible being known as the Solid State
Entity. Burgos Harsha told me that Rollo Gallivare had

discovered the first of the mainbrains, and that he believed them to be aliens from another galaxy. "It is recorded in the apocrypha of the first Timekeeper that the Silicon God appeared within the Eta Carina nebula toward the end of the Swarming Centuries. And in the chronicles of Tisander the Wary, we find a similar assertation. But when have those sources ever been accurate, I ask you? In the history of the Tycho, Reina Ede holds that the brains evolved from the seed of the Ieldra, as did Homo Sapiens. What do I believe? I don't know what I believe."

Kolenya Mor thought that the Ieldra, before they melded their consciousnesses with the bizarrely tortured spacetime of the core singularity, must have closely resembled the Solid State Entity. "As to the Entity's purpose, why, it's the purpose of all life, to awaken to itself." We talked for a long time, and I told her that many of the younger pilots denied that life *had* a purpose. She looked at me with her horrified little eyes and exclaimed, "Heresy! *That* ancient heresy!"

I was not the only one, of course, called to quest. The whole of our Order seemed afire with the dream of finding Soli's Elder Eddas. What indeed *was* the secret of man's immortality? "Find out why the goddamned stars are exploding," Bardo said, "and you'll find your secret." Of course, he was a pragmatist whose mind did not often turn towards esoteric problems. Others believed that the secret of the exploding Vild would be only the first part of the Elder Eddas. (Albeit a vital part.) Where should we look for this secret? Why hadn't we discovered it long ago? Phantasts and tinkers and pilots—many of us felt that despite the three millenia in which our Order had spent accumulating knowledge, we might have overlooked an important, perhaps vital thing. Historians begged the Timekeeper for permission to leave Neverness, to raid the library on Ksandaria for clues to the mystery. Neologicians and semanticists locked themselves in their cold towers as they set to creating and discovering new languages, lost in their certitude that the secret of the Elder Eddas—and every other kind of wisdom—was to be found in words. The fabulists spun their fictions, which they claimed were as real as any reality, and declared that the Elder Eddas is that which we create. And who was to say they were wrong? And the pilots! My brave, fellow pilots: Richardess and the Sonderval, went forth into the manifold, seeking lost planets and strange new alien races. Tomoth and a hundred other master pilots would try to map the Vild. Soli himself would attempt to penetrate the inner veil of the Vild, while Lionel devised yet another plan to find Old Earth. Even cowardly Bardo would make a journey, even if he proposed nothing more daring than his own, private expedition to Ksandaria. Although a few cynical professionals like my mother had no intention of chancing their lives on such a dream, it was an exciting time, and more, a glorious time we would never see again.

The day before my departure, a day of fierce, sudden gales and stinging ice-powder, the Timekeeper summoned me to his tower. As I skated between the dark gray buildings separating Resa from the great tower, I shivered beneath my too-thin kamelaika. I wished that I had either greased my face or worn a mask against the freezing wind. It would be an insult, I thought, to appear before the Timekeeper with patches of white, frostbitten skin blighting my face. It was good to enter the warm tower, good, even, to stand impatiently in an anteroom below the top of the tower as I stamped my boots on the red carpet and waited for the master horologe to announce my arrival.

"He is waiting for you," the horologe said in a voice almost breathless from his climbing up and down the stairs into the Timekeeper's chambers. "Be careful," he said, "he's in an ugly mood today," and then he ushered me up the winding stairs into the circular sanctum of the tower where the Timekeeper stood waiting.

"So, Mallory," he said, "the pilot's ring looks good on your hand, eh?"

The Timekeeper was a grim-faced man with a mane of thick white hair erupting from his taut skin. Most of the time he seemed very old, though no one knew just how old he was. When he frowned, which he often did, the muscles of his jaws stood out like knots of wood. His neck was thick and popping with tendons, as was the rest of his tense, large-boned body. I stood in the spacious, well-lighted room, and he stared at me as he always did when I came to see him. His eyes were black and fathomless like chunks of barely cooled obsidian hammered into his skull; his eyes were hot, restless, angry and pained.

"What would it take to kill you?" he asked me.

The muscles of his bare forearms tensed and relaxed, tensed and relaxed. Once, when I was a novice, when he had taught me leverage grips and killing holds and other wrestling skills, I had had occasion to view the powerful body beneath the long red robe he always wore. His torso and legs were etched with scars; a fine network of hard, white cicatrices more intricate and convoluted than the glidderies of the Farsider's Quarter began at his neck, twisted through his dense, white, body hair, and ran down his groin and muscular legs to his feet. When I had asked him about the scars, he had said, "It takes a lot to kill me, you see."

He motioned for me to sit in an ornate, wooden chair facing the southern window. The tower, a monolith of white marble imported from Urradeth at extraordinary cost, overlooked the whole of the Academy. To the west were the granite and basalt arches of the professionals' colleges, Upplyssa and Lara Sig; to the north, the densely clumped spires of Borja, and looking south towards Urkel, I saw my beloved Resa. (I should mention that the tower windows are made of fused silica, and calcium and sodium oxides, a substance the Timekeeper calls glass. It is a brittle substance given to shattering when the gales of midwinter spring come roaring across the Starnbergersee. Nevertheless, the Timekeeper, who is fond of archaisms, claims that glass allows in a cleaner light than does the clary used in all the buildings of the Civilized Worlds.)

"Do you hear the ticking, Mallory, my brave, foolish, *young* pilot? Time—it ticks, it runs, it twists, it dilates, shrinks, and kills, and one day for each of us, no matter what we do, it stops. Stops, do you hear me?"

He pulled up a chair identical to mine and rested his red-slippered foot on the seat. The Timekeeper—afraid perhaps that if he ceased his restless motions, *his* internal clock might stop—did not like to sit. "You're the youngest pilot in history. Twenty-one years old—a nano in the life of a star, but it's all the time you've had. And the clock beats; the clock tolls; the clock ticks; do you hear it ticking?"

I heard it ticking. All around us, in the Timekeeper's circular tower, were clocks ticking. Interspersed with the curved panes of glass around the circumference of the room, from the fur-covered floor to the white plaster ceiling, were wooden shelves upon which sat the clocks. Clocks of every conceivable design. There were archaic weight-driven clocks and spring clocks encased in plastic; there were wood-covered pendulum clocks, electric clocks and quartz crystal clocks; there were bio-clocks powered by the disembodied heart muscles of various organisms; there were quantum clocks and hourglasses filled with cobalt and vermilion sands; I saw three water clocks and even a Fravashi driftglass, which measured the time since the drifting super-galactic clusters had erupted from the primeval singularity. As far as I could determine, no two of the clocks told the same time. On top of the highest shelf was the Seal of our Order. It was a small glass and steel atomic clock which had been set on Old Earth the day the Order was founded. (The largest clock, of course, was—is—the tower itself. Far below, set into the circle of ice surrounding it, twenty rows of granite radiate outward and mark the passing of the sun's shadow. This giant sundial, inaccurate though it may be, is theoretically the only clock in the city by which we citizens can direct our activities. The Timekeeper abhorred the tyranny of time, and so he long ago ordered all clocks banned. This prohibition has proved a boon to the wormrunners who make fortunes smuggling in Yarkona pocket watches and other contraband.)

A clock gonged, and he gripped his forearms, one in either hand. He said, "I've heard that Soli has dissolved your oath."

"That's true, Timekeeper. And I wish to apologize for my mother. She had no right to come to you, asking you to talk to Soli in my behalf."

With his foot he pushed back the chair as he kneaded the tight muscles of his forearms. "So, you think I ordered Soli to release you from your oath?"

"Didn't you?"

"No."

"My mother seems to think—"

"Your mother—forgive me, Pilot—your mother often thinks wrongly. I've known you all your life. Do you think I'm stupid enough to believe you'd desert the Order to become a merchant pilot? Ha!"

"Then you didn't speak to Soli?"

"You question me?"

"Excuse me, Timekeeper." I was confused. Why else would Soli have released me from my oath, unless it was to shame me before all my friends and masters of the Academy?

I confided my doubts to the Timekeeper who said, "Soli has lived three long lifetimes; don't try to understand him."

"It seems there are many things I don't understand."

"You're modest today."

"Why did you send for me?"

"Don't question me, damn you! I've only so much patience, even for you."

I sat mutely in the chair looking out the window at Borja's beautiful main spire, the one the Tycho had built a thousand years ago. The Timekeeper circled around to my side so that he could look upon my face as I stared straight ahead. It was the traditional position of politeness between master and novice that I had been taught when I first entered the Academy. The Timekeeper could search my face for truth or lies (or any other emotion) while preserving the sanctity of his own thoughts and feelings.

"Everyone knows you intend to keep your oath," he said.

"Yes, Lord Horologe."

"It seems that Soli has tricked you."

"Yes, Lord Horologe."

"And your mother has failed you."

"Perhaps, Lord Horologe."

"Then you'll still try to penetrate the Entity?"

"I'll leave tomorrow, Lord Horologe."

"Your ship is ready?"

"Yes, Lord Horologe."

" 'To die among the stars is the most glorious death,' is it not?"

"Yes, Lord Horologe."

There was a blur from my side and the Timekeeper slapped my face. "Nonsense!" he roared. "I won't listen to such nonsense from you!"

He walked over to the window and rapped the glass pane with his knuckles. "Cities such as Neverness are glorious," he said. "And the ocean at sunset, or deep winter's firefalls—these things are glorious. Death is death; death is horror. There's no glory when the time runs out and the ticking stops, do you hear me? There's only blackness and the hell of everlasting nothingness. Don't be too quick to die, do you hear me, Mallory?"

"Yes, Lord Horologe."

"Good!" He crossed the room and opened a cabinet

supporting a jar of pulsing, glowing red fluid. (I had always presumed that this evil-looking display was a clock of some sort, but I had never had the courage to ask him exactly what sort.) From the cabinet's dark interior—the wood was a rare ebony and so dully black that it shed little light—he removed an object that appeared to be an old, leather-covered box. I soon saw that it was not; when he opened the "box," that is to say, when he turned back one section of the stiffened pieces of the brown, cracked leather, there were many, many sheets of what seemed to be paper cleverly fastened to the middle section. He came closer to me; I smelled mildew and dust and centuries-old paper. As his fingers turned the yellow sheets he would occasionally let out a sigh or exclaim, "Here it is, in ancient Anglish, no less!" Or, "Ah, such music, no one does this now, it's a dead art. Look at this, Mallory!" I looked at the sheets of paper covered line after line with squiggly black characters, all of which were alien to me. I knew that I was looking at one of those archaic artifacts in which words are represented symbolically (and redundantly) by physical ideoplasts. The ancients had called the ideoplasts "letters," but I could not remember what the letter-covered artifact itself was called.

"It's a *book*!" the Timekeeper said. "A treasure—these are the greatest poems ever dreamed by the minds of human beings. Listen to this . . . ," and he translated from the dead language he called Franche as he recited a poem entitled, "The Clock." I did not like it very much; it was a poem full of dark, shuddering images and hopelessness and dread.

"How is it that you can interpret these symbols into words?" I asked.

"The art is called 'reading,'" he said. "It's an art I learned long ago."

I was confused for a moment because I had always used the word "read" in a different, broader context. One "reads" the weather patterns from the drifting clouds or "reads" a person's habits and programs according to the mannerisms of his face. Then I remembered certain professionals practiced the art of reading, as did the citizens of many of the more backward worlds. I had even once seen books in a museum on Solsken. I supposed that one could read words as well as say them. But how inefficient it all seemed! I pitied the ancients who did not know how to encode information into ideoplasts and directly superscribe the various sense and cognitive centers of the brain. As Bardo would say, how barbaric!

The Timekeeper made a fist and said, "I want you to learn the art of reading so you can read this book."

"Read the book?"

"Yes," he said as he snapped the cover shut and handed it to me. "You heard what I said."

"But why, Timekeeper, I don't understand. To read with the eyes; it's so . . . *clumsy.*"

"You'll learn to read, and you'll learn the dead languages in this book."

"Why?"

"So that you'll hear these poems in your heart."

"Why?"

"Question me again, damn you, and I'll forbid you to journey for seven years! Then you'll learn patience!"

"Forgive me, Timekeeper."

"Read the book, and you may live," he said. He reached out and patted the back of my neck. "Your life is all you have; guard it like a treasure."

The Timekeeper was the most complicated man I have ever known. He was a man whose selfness comprised a thousand jagged pieces of love and hate, whimsy and will; he was a man who battled himself. I stood there dumbly holding the dusty old book he had placed in my hands, and I looked into the black pools of his unfathomable eyes, and I saw hell. He paced the room like an old, white wolf who had once been caught in a wormrunner's steel trap. He was wary of something, perhaps of giving me the book. As he paced, he rubbed the muscles of his right leg and limped, slightly. He seemed at once vicious and kind, lonely, and bitter at his loneliness. Here was a man, I thought, who had never known a single day's (or night's) peace, an old, old man who had been wounded in love and cut in wars and burnt by dreams turned to ashes in his hands. He possessed a tremendous vitality, and his zest and love of life had finally led him to that essential paradox of human existence: He loved the air he breathed and the beating of his heart so fully and well that he had let his natural hatred of death ruin his living of life. He brooded too much about death. It was said that he had once killed another human being with his own hands to save his own life. There were rumors that he used a nepenthe to ease the panic of lapsing time and to forget, for a little while, the pains of his past and the angry roar of pure existence. I looked at the lines of his scowling face, and I thought the rumors might be true.

"I don't understand," I said, "how a book of poems could save my life." I began to laugh.

He stopped by the window, smiling at me without humor. His large, veined hands were clasped behind his back. "I'll tell you something about the Entity that no one else knows. She has a fondness for many things human, and of all these things, she likes ancient poetry the best."

I sat quietly in my chair. I did not dare ask him why he thought the Solid State Entity liked human poetry.

"If you learn these poems," he said, "perhaps the Entity will be less likely to kill you like a fly."

I thanked him because I did not know what else to do. I would humor this somewhat deranged old man, I decided. I accepted the book. I even turned the pages, carefully, pretending to take an interest in the endless lines of black letters. Near the middle of the book, which contained thirteen hundred and forty-nine brittle pages, I saw a word that I recognized. The word reminded me that the Timekeeper was not a man to be laughed at or mocked. Once, when I was a young novice, the horologes had caught a democrat with a laser burning *written words* into the white marble of the tower. The Timekeeper—I remember his neck muscles writhing like spirali beneath his tight skin—had ordered the poor man thrown from the top of the tower in antonement for the dual crimes of destroying beauty and inflicting his ideas on others. Barbaric. According to the canons of our Order, of course, slelling is supposedly the only crime punishable by death. (When slel neckers are caught stealing another's DNA they are beheaded, one of the few ancient customs both efficient and merciful.) We hold that banishment from our beautiful city is punishment enough for all other crimes, but for some reason, when the Timekeeper had seen the graffito, FREEDOM, etched into the archway above the Tower's entrance, he had raged and had discovered an exceptionary clause in the ninety-first canon permitting him, so he claimed, to order that: "The punishment will fit the crime." To this day, the graffito remains above the archway, a reminder not only that freedom is a dead concept, but that our lives are determined by sometimes capricious forces beyond our control.

We talked for a while about the forces that control the universe, and we talked about the quest. When I expressed my excitement over the possibility of discovering the Elder Eddas, the Timekeeper, ever a man of contradictions, ran his fingers through his snowy hair as he grimaced and said, "I'm not so sure I want man saved. So, I've had enough of men—maybe it's time the ticking stopped and the clock ran down. Let the Vild explode, every damn star from Vesper to Nwarth. Saved! Life is hell, eh? and there's no salvation except death, not matter what the Friends of Man say." I waited for his breath to run out as he ranted about the pervasive—and perverse—effect that the alien missionaries and alien religions had had upon the human race; I waited a long time.

The sky had long since grown dark and blackened when he hammered the edge of his fist against his thigh and growled out, "Piss on the Ieldra! So they made themselves into gods and carked themselves into the core? They should leave us alone, eh? Man's man, and gods are gods, each to his own purpose. But you've sworn your silly oath, so you go find them or their Eddas or anything else you think you can find."

Then he sighed and added, "But go carefully."

It is strange how often the smallest of events, the most trivial of decisions, can utterly change our lives. Having said goodbye to the Timekeeper, I reached the ice beneath the Tower, and I stole another look at the book he had given me. Poems! A simple book of clumsy, ancient poems! There on the gliddery, which was dark and bare, I stood for a long time wondering if I shouldn't throw the book into our dormitory room's fireplace; I stood there brooding over the meaning of chance and fate. Then the icy, damp wind off the Sound began to blow, carrying into my bones the chill of death— whose death I did not then know. The wind drove hard snowflakes across the ice, stinging my face and scouring the windows of the tower. The soft sound of ice brushing against glass was almost lost to the tinkling of the wind chimes hanging from the Tower's window ledges. Shrugging my shoulders, I pulled the hood of my kamelaika over my head. The Timekeeper wanted me to read the book. Very well, I would read the book.

My hands were numb as I slipped it into the pack I wore at the small of my back. I struck off down the gliddery in a hurry. Bardo and my other friends would be waiting dinner for me, and I was hungry and cold.

I spent most of my last night in the city making my various goodbyes. There was a dinner in my behalf in one of the smaller, more elegant restaurants of the Hofgarten. As was the custom of the scryers, Katharine refused to wish me well because, as she said, "my destiny was written in my history," whatever that meant. Bardo, of course, alternately wept and cursed and blustered. He had, perversely, taken a liking to heated beer, and he drank copious amounts of the foamy yellow liquid to ease his fear of the uncertain future. He made toasts and speeches to our friends, reciting sentimental verses he had composed. He lapsed into song, until Chantal Astoreth, that wry, dainty lover of music, pointed out that his voice was slurry with drink and not up to its usual fine quality. Finally, he fell stupefied into his chair, took my hand in his, and announced, "This is the saddest day of my damned life." And then he fell asleep.

My mother said a similar thing, and she barely kept herself from crying. (Though the corner of her mouth twitched uncontrollably as it did when she was full of strong emotion.) She looked at me, with her crooked, dark eyebrows and her nervous eyes, and she said, "Soli severs your oath because your mother went begging to the Timekeeper. And how do you repay me? You cut my heart."

I did not tell her what the Timekeeper had said to me earlier that day in the tower. She would not want to know how easily he had seen through her lies. She drew on her drab fur, which was shiny gray in patches where the fine shagshay hairs had worn off. She laughed in a low, disturbing manner as if she had a private joke with herself. I thought she would leave then without saying another word. But she turned to me, kissed my forehead, and whispered, "Come back. To your mother who bleeds for you, who loves you."

I left the restaurant before dawn (I didn't sleep that night), and I skated down the deserted Way to the Hollow Fields. There, at the foot of Urkel, even in the coldest part of morning, its acres of runs and pads were busy with sleds and windjammers and other craft. Thunder shook the ice of the slidderies, and the air was full of red rocket tailings and sonic booms. High above, the feathery lines of contrails glowed pink against the early blue sky. It was very beautiful. Although I had come here often on duties at this time of day, it occurred to me that I had always taken such beauty for granted.

Beneath the Fields, the Cavern of the Thousand Light Ships opened through a half mile of melted rock. Although there were not nearly so many as a thousand ships—and have not been since the Tycho's time—there were many more than the eye could take in at a glance. Near the middle of the eighth row of ships, I stood chatting with an olive-robed programmer beside my ship, the *Immanent Carnation*. While we debated a minor augmentation in the ship's heuristics and paradox logics, someone called out my name. I looked down the walkway where the row of sleek, diamond hulls disappeared into the depths. I saw a long shape limned by the faint light of the luminescent lichen covering the Cavern's walls. "Mallory," the voice rang out, echoing from the dark, curving ceiling above us. "It's time to say goodbye, isn't it?" The walkway sang with the slap of heavy boots against reverberating steel, and then I saw him clearly, tall and severe in his black woolens. It was Soli.

The programmer, Master Rafael, who was a shy, quiet-loving man with skin as smooth and black as basalt, greeted him and hastily made an excuse for leaving us alone together.

"She's beautiful," Soli said, scrutinizing the lines of my ship, the narrow nose and the swept-forward wings. "That has to be admitted. Outside she's lithe and balanced and beautiful. But it's the *inside* that is the soul of a lightship, isn't it? The Lord Programmer told me you've played with the Hilbert logics to an unusual degree. Why so, Pilot?"

For a while we talked about the things that pilots talk about. We debated the paradoxes and discussed my choosing of Master Jafar's ideoplasts. "He was a great notationist," he said, "but his representation of Justerini's omega function is redundant, isn't it?"

He suggested certain substitutions of symbols that seemed to make great sense, and I could not keep the note of surprise from my voice as I asked, "Why are you helping me, Lord Pilot?"

"It's my duty to help new pilots."

"I thought you wanted me to fail."

"How could you know what was wanted?" He rubbed his temples as he looked into the open pit of my ship. He seemed agitated and ill at ease.

"But you tricked me into swearing the oath."

"Did I? Did *I*?"

"And then you released me. Why?"

He reached out and touched the hull of my ship, almost as one would stroke a woman. He did not answer my question. Instead he pressed his lips together, and he asked me, "Then you really will journey into the Entity?"

"Yes, Lord Pilot, I've said I would."

"You'll do it freely, of your own will?"

"Yes, Lord Pilot."

"Is that possible? You think you can bend yourself to your own will, that you're free? Such arrogance!"

I had no idea of what he was leading up to, so I recited the usual evasion, "The holists teach that the apparent dichotomy between free will and forced action is a false dichotomy."

He pulled at his chin and said, "Holists and their useless teachings! Who listens to holists? The question is this: Does *your* will impel you to your death, or will it be blamed on your Lord Pilot?"

Of course I blamed him; I blamed him so fiercely I felt the bile souring my stomach and spreading hotly through my veins. I wanted badly to tell him how much I blamed him, but instead I stared at his dull reflection in the hull of my ship. I looked at his black-gloved hand resting against my ship. I said nothing.

He removed his hand, rubbed his nose, and said, "When your time comes, when you're close to it and have the choice between blaming me or not, please remember you tricked yourself into failure."

My muscles were hot and tight, and without really thinking about it, I punched the hull of my ship where his face wavered in the gleaming blackness. I nearly broke my knuckles. "I . . . won't . . . fail." I let the words out slowly, to keep from screaming in pain. I could hardly bear to look at him, with his long nose and his shiny black hair shot full of red.

He bowed his head quickly and said, "All men fail in the end, don't they? Well, then. Goodbye, Pilot, we wish you well." He turned his back abruptly and walked away, into the depths of the Cavern.

There is not much more I wish to tell of that unhappy morning. Master Rafael returned accompanied by the usual cadre of professionals, journeymen and novices that attend a pilot's departure. There was an orange-robed cetic who pressed his thumbs against my temples and examined my face for illness. There were journeymen tinkers who lifted me into the darkened pit of my ship, and a horologe to seal the ship's clock. And others. After what seemed like days (already the distortions were working on my time sense), I "faced my ship," as the master pilots say; I interfaced with the deep, profound neurologics that are the soul of a lightship. My brain was now two brains, or rather, a single brain of blood and neurons which had been extended and melded into the brain of my ship. Reality, the lesser reality of sights and sounds and other sensual impressions, gave way to the vastly greater reality of the manifold. I plunged into the cold ocean of pure mathematics, into the realm of order and meaning underlying the chaos of everyday space, and The Cavern of the Thousand Light Ships was no more.

There was, of course, a brief moment of impatience as my ship was lifted to a surface run, the boredom of rocketing through the atmosphere and falling into the thickspace above our icy planet. I made a mapping, and a window into the manifold opened to me. Then our star, the little yellow sun, was gone, and there were an infinite number of lights and beauty and terror, and I left Neverness and my youth far behind me.

4

The Number Storm

*In the beginning, of course, there was God. And
from God arose the Elder Ieldra, beings of pure light
who were like God except that there was a time
before their existence, and a time would come when
they would exist no more. And from the Elder Ieldra
arose the Ieldra, who were like the elder race except
they had substance and flesh. The Ieldra seeded the
galaxy, and perhaps many galaxies, with their DNA.
On Old Earth, from this godseed evolved the primitive algae and bacteria, the plankton, slime molds,
worms, fishes, and so on until ape-Man stood away
from the trees of the mother continent. And ape-Man
gave birth to cave-Men, who were like Men except
that they did not have the power to end their own
existence.*

*And from cave-Men at last arose Man, and Man,
who was at once clever and stupid took to bed four
wives: The Bomb; The Computer; The Test Tube;
and Woman.*

—from *A Requiem for Homo Sapiens*,
by Horthy Hosthoh

It is impossible to describe the indescribable. Words, being
words, are inadequate to represent that for which there are
no words. Having said this, I shall attempt an explanation of
what occurred next, of my journey into the nameless pathways of the manifold.

I made my way along the glittering, spiral Sagittarius arm
of the galaxy. I progressed outward in good style across the

lens of the Milky Way, though there were of course times when I was forced to loop back across my pathways, kleining coreward towards the hellishly bright and dense stars of the central bulge. This part of my journey, I knew, would be easy. I followed pathways that the Tycho and Jemmu Flowtow had long ago discovered. To fall from a red giant such as Gloriana Luz to one of the hot blue stars of the Lesser Morbio is easy when the mapping of the respective point-sources in the neighborhood of the two stars has long ago been made (and proved to be simply connected). So easy is it that the cantors have given these known pathways a special name: They call them the stellar fallaways to distinguish them from that part of the manifold that is unmapped, and quite often, unmappable. Thus, to be precise I should say I began my journey through the fallaways, fenestering at speed from window to window, from star to star in my hurry to reach the Solid State Entity.

I spent most of this time floating freely within the darkened pit of my ship. For some fearful pilots—such as the failed ones who guide the deep ships and long ships that ply the trade routes of the fallaways—the ship's pit can be more of a trap than a sanctuary in which to experience the profounder states of mind; for them the pit is a black metallic coffin. For me, the pit of the *Immanent Carnation* was like a gentle, comfortable heaume surrounding my whole body rather than just my head. (Indeed, in the Tycho's time the ship's computer fit tightly over the pilot's head and extruded protein filaments into the brain, in the manner of the ancient heaumes.) As I journeyed through the near stars, the neurologics woven into the black shell of the pit holographically modeled my brain and body functions. And more, the information-rich logics infused images, impulses and symbols directly into my brain. Thus I passed the stars of the Nashira Triple, and I faced my ship's computer and "talked" to it. And it talked to me. I listened to the soundless roar of the ship's spacetime devouring engines opening windows to the manifold, and I watched the fire of the more distant nebulae as I proved my theorems—all through the filter of the computer and its neurologics. This melding of my brain with my ship was powerful but not perfect. At times the information flooding within the various centers of my brain became mixed-up and confused: I smelled the stars of the Sarolta being born and listened to the purple sound of equations being solved and other like absurdities. It is to integrate this crosstalk of the mind's senses that the holists evolved the discipline of hallning; of a pilot's mental disciplines I shall later have much to say.

I entered the Trifid Nebula, where the young, hot stars pulsed with wavelengths of blue light. At those times when my ship fell out into realspace around a star, it seemed that the whole of the nebula's interior was aglow with red clouds of hydrogen gas. Because I needed to pass to the nearby Lagoon Nebula, I crossed the Trifid at speed, fenestering from window to window so quickly that I had to hurry my brain with many moments of slowtime. For me, with my metabolism and my mind speeding from the electric touch of the computer, since I could think much faster, time paradoxically seemed to slow down. In my mind, time dilated and stretched out like a sheet of rubber, seconds becoming hours, and hours like years. This slowing of time was necessary, for otherwise the flickering rush of stars would have left me too little time to establish my isomorphisms and mappings, to prove my theorems. Or I would have dropped into the photosphere of a blue giant, or fallen into an infinite tree, or died some other way.

At last I passed into the Lagoon. I was dazzled by the intense lights, some of which are among the brightest objects in the galaxy. Around a cluster of stars called the Blastula Luz, I prepared my long passage to the Rosette Nebula in the Orion Arm. I penetrated the Blastula and segued to the thickspace at its nearly hollow center. This thickspace is called the Tycho's Thick, and though it is not nearly so dense as the one that lies in the neighborhood of Neverness, there are many point-sources connecting to point-exits within the Rosette Nebula.

I found one such point-source, and the theorems of probablistic topology built before my inner eye, and I made a mapping. The manifold opened. The star I orbited, an ugly red giant I named Bloody Bal, disappeared. I floated in the pit of my ship, wondering how long I would fall along the way from the Lagoon to the Rosette; I wondered—and not for the last time—at the very peculiar nature of this thing we call time.

In the manifold there is no space, and therefore there is no time. That is to say there is no *outtime*. For me, inside my lightship, there was only shiptime or slowtime, or dreamtime, or sometimes quicktime—but never the realtime of the outer universe. Because my passage to the Rosette would probably be long and uneventful, I often quieted my brain with quicktime. I did this to ward off boredom. My mentations slowed to a glacial pace, and time passed more quickly. Years became hours while long segments of tedious nothingness were shrunken into the moment it took my heart to beat a single time.

After a while I tired of quicktime. I thought I might as well drug my mind with sleep, or drug it with drugs. I spent most of my passage in the more or less normally alert state of shiptime examining the book that the Timekeeper had given me. I learned to read. It was a painful thing to do. The ancient way of representing the sounds of speech by individual letters was an inefficient means of encoding information. Barbaric. I learned the cursive glyphs of that array known as the alphabet, and I learned how to string them together linearly—linearly!—to form words. Since the book contained poems written in several of the ancient Old Earth languages, I had to learn these languages as well. This, of course, was the easier of my tasks since I could infuse and superscribe the language and memory centers of my brain directly from the computer's store of arcana. (Though few of these poems were composed in ancient Anglish, I learned that oldest of tongues because my mother had long nagged me to do so.)

When I had learned to scan the lines of letters printed across—and, sometimes, down—the old, fibrous pages of yellowed paper, learned so well that I had no need to sound out the individual letters in the inner ear of my brain but could perceive the units of meaning word by word, I found to my astonishment that this thing called reading was pleasurable. There was pleasure in handling the cracked leather of the cover, pleasure too in the quiet stimulation of my eyes with black symbols representing words as they had once been spoken. How simple a thing reading really was! How strange I would have appeared to another pilot, had she been able to watch me reading! There, in the illuminated pit of my ship, I floated and held the Timekeeper's book in front of me as I did nothing more than move my eyes from left to right, left to right, down the time-stiffened pages of the book.

But it was the poems themselves that gave me the greatest pleasure. It was wonderful to discover that the ancients, in all

their stupendous ignorance of the immensity of spacetime
and the endless profusion of life that fills our universe, knew
as much of the great secret of life—or as little—as we know
now. Though their perceptions were simple and bold, it
seemed to me they often perceived more deeply that part of
reality directly apprehensible to a mere man. Their poems
were like hard diamonds crudely cut from some primal stone;
their poems were full of a pounding, sensual, barbaric music;
their poems sent the blood rushing and made the eyes focus
on vistas of untouchable stars and cold, distant, northern
seas. There were short, clever poems designed to capture
one of life's brief and sad (but beautiful) moments as one
might capture and preserve a butterfly in glacier ice. There
were poems that ran on for pages, recounting man's lust for
killing and blood and those pure and timeless moments of
heroism when one feels that the life inside must be rejoined
with the greater life without.

My favorite poem was one that the Timekeeper had read
to me the day before my departure. I remembered him
pacing through the Tower as he clenched his fists and recited:

> Tyger! Tyger! burning bright
> In the forests of the night,
> What immortal hand or eye
> Dare frame thy fearful symmetry?

"It is important," he had told me, "to rhyme 'symmetry'
with 'eye.'"

I read the poems over and over; after a time, I could
repeat some of them without looking at the book. I said the
poems out loud until they echoed inside, and I could hear
them in my heart.

And so I fell out in the Rosette Nebula, which lies at the
edge of the expanding star-blown region known as the Vild. I
looked out into the glowing hell of hard light and ruined stars
and dust, and I heard myself say:

> Stars, I have seen them fall
>   But when they drop and die
> No star is lost at all
>   From all the star-sown sky.

(When I say I "looked out" at the Vild, I mean, of course, that my ship illuminated my brain with models of the Vild that it had made. So far away was the Rosette from the Vild in realspace—in light-years—that the light from most of the exploding stars had not yet reached the Rosette.)

In contrast to the ugliness of the dying Vild, the Rosette was beautiful. It was a giant star-making womb whose new-born suns flashed and pulsed with such violent energies that the shock waves and pressures of light had swept away the whole of its interior, leaving the nebula hollow like a ruby and diamond-studded eggshell. It was around the famous Siva Luz, brightest of that splendid, rosy sphere of lights, that I began the first of the mappings that would lead me to the doorway of Eta Carina and the Solid State Entity.

I continued my journey along the most ancient route of the manswarm. I fell out around stars whose planets were thick with human beings (and beings who were less and more than human). Rollo's Rock, Wakanda and Vesper—these old planets I passed by as quickly as I could. And Nwarth and Ocher, Farfara and Fostora, where, it was said, the men had long ago learned the art of carking their selfnesses into their computers. (It was also said that the Fostora women, disdaining the transfer of human mind into "machine," had ventured forth in long ships until they came to the planet they called Lechoix. Whereupon they founded the oldest of the matriarchies. The historian Burgos Harsha, however, gives a different explanation of their origin. He holds that Lechoix was colonized by a renegade deep ship full of nubile girls bound for the sun domes on Heaven's Gate. Who really knows?)

After a long time, I passed into that portion of the fallaways little touched by either the second or third waves of the Swarming. Here were planets so old—Freeport and New Earth and Kaarta among others—that they had been peopled long before man had come to formulate the laws of civilization. Here were women and men who had carked their DNA, tampered with their chromosomes and changed their flesh in many horrible ways to fit their new habitats as a drillworm fits the hole it chews into a living skull.

Darrein Luz was a yellow star, beyond which lay others for which there existed no known mappings. It was my task, as a pilot, to discover new mappings, to set up the isomorphisms and prove my theorems, that or die. And though as a

journeyman I had made such mappings of the manifold near
our city's little sun, I had never made so many nor journeyed
so far.

At first it was easy. With zazen I emptied my mind of
everything except mathematical thoughts. I was alert and
open to the manifold's undulations and sudden deformations.
Various spaces folded and re-folded around me. I was afraid as
I entered a torsion space, but I found a little theorem that let
me make sense of the writhing tunnels threatening to devour
me. "The faithful mathematician must use his will to achieve
insight from pattern"—so the cantors say. My will was strong
at first, and with each successful mapping I made, it grew
stronger still. Sixty-eight stars beyond Darrein Luz, I was so
puffed-up with pride I plunged into what I thought would be
a rather simple thickspace.

It was nothing of the sort. The point-sources were indeed
stived as densely as lice on the head of a harijan, but I could
find no mappings to the point-exits in the nebula which lay
before me, the nebula called the Solid State Entity. I wondered why. It seemed beyond all chance that there should be
no mappings. Because I could go no further, I fell out into
realspace above a ringed planet. I felt alone and lost, and so I
named the faint, yellow star nearest the thickspace "Perdido
Luz." I vowed I would master the thickspace even if it took
me forty days of realtime.

I do not know how long I spent, intime, scurfing the
windows of the thickspace. Certainly it was much longer than
forty days. It was truly a bizarre thickspace, riddled with too
many zero-points and embedded spaces. Often I had trouble
fixing points; often I tunneled from one dark window to
another only to find the windows fixed in a closed ring. The
usual rules of interfenestration seemed not to hold. I must
have mapped sixty-four thousand point-sources, and not one
of them could I prove to be simply connected with any other
among the stars of the Entity. Once, I laughed so hard my
jaws almost popped out of joint; then in despair I bit my lip
until I tasted the hot salt of blood. The very existence of this
impossible thickspace mocked my faith in the trueness of the
Great Theorem. I was almost certain that *no* mapping from
Perdido Luz to the Entity could be found. I was ready to give
up when I stumbled upon a beautiful, discrete set of point-
sources, all of which connected to a single white star in the

outer envelope of the Entity. I had only to make the mapping, open a window, and I would be the first pilot in five hundred years to dare the fickle, whirlpool spaces of a living nebula.

I made the mapping and fell out around the star. So, I thought, *this* is the group of stars that has terrorized the pilots of my Order; well, it is not so terrible after all. I told myself there was no reason for fear. Then I looked out on the glowing hydrogen clouds, and I was not so sure. The whole nebula seemed dark and strange. There were fewer stars than I had thought there would be, perhaps as few as a hundred thousand. The interstellar dust was too dense, scattering and obscuring the light of even the nearer stars. Grains of graphite and silicates and ices, and iron particles, too, reddened and polarized the dim starlight. Some of the individual dust particles were so gigantic that they seemed not to be dust at all but rather the fragments of planets which had been pulverized and torn apart. Why, I wondered, would the Entity need to tear planets apart? To gather the mass—the food—for Her fabled moon-sized brains? Or perhaps it wasn't *She* who had stripped of planets almost every star I came across; perhaps it was some other natural, if deadly, phenomenon?

The mechanics say that intelligence can warp and shape the fabric of spacetime. I now know this is true. As I set out and fenestered inward toward the heart of the Entity, the manifold within the nebula changed in subtle ways. I found myself too often kleining back upon my pathways. Once, like a worm swallowing its tail, I thought I was caught in an infinite loop; I worried that I would die of old age or lose my mind among the incomprehensible pathways that bunched and writhed and led onwards and back, and through and in, into the twisting of this unknown portion of the manifold. Another time I lost the theme of a theorem I was proving. Usually such a trifling, momentary distraction would not have mattered, but I was in the middle of a wildly segmented space the like of which I had never seen before. I began slipsliding off my normal fenestering sequence. I had the strangest feeling that the Entity Herself was perturbing the spaces before me, measuring my mathematical abilities, testing me as pilot and man.

Suddenly the segmented space snapped like twig, and I

fell out into realspace. I nearly scudded into the gravity well
of a neutron star. There was blackness all around me. There
were unusual black globules of matter half a mile in diameter
floating in the blackness of space. These black bodies—there
were millions of them—must have been the handiwork of the
Entity. I could only guess what they were. Because they were
so black that they did not reflect any of the milky starlight or
any other radiation, I had to deduce their presence from their
gravity fields. They had crushingly powerful gravity fields,
though not so powerful as the neutron star they orbited. Why
they were not sucked down the star's gravity well I could not
say.

Were these black bodies pieces of manufactured matter
which somehow regulated the flow of information within the
Entity? Were they tachyon machines or some other unnatural
engine for producing particles traveling faster than light? Or
were they perhaps cancerous growths, some type of wild,
unstable matter left over from the Entity's experiments in
shaping the universe to Her whims? I did not know. I
wondered if the eschatologists were wrong after all; perhaps
the Entity's brain was composed of black bodies much smaller
than moons. Could it be that I was looking at the fount of
intelligence of a goddess?

I had no time to explore this fascinating discovery because
the intense magnetic field of the star—it was a thousand
billion times stronger than that of Icefall's—was ruining my
ship. The star's densely packed neutrons, probably the core
remnants of an ancient supernova, were spinning rapidly, and
they had conserved the magnetic field of the original star. I
had to make an instant mapping, but at least I escaped being
crushed and pulled apart like a seashell. I fell at random into
the manifold, and I was lucky I did not fall into an infinite
decision tree.

There were other dangers and escapes I will not mention.
And wonders, too. I discovered the first of the Entity's brain
lobes in a region of the nebula where the underlying manifold
was rich with tunnels and point-sources winding through and
connecting with every other part. There was a star pumping
out light in measured, intense bursts every nine-tenths of a
second. It was a little pulsar which reminded me of the
beacon atop Mount Attakel warning the windjammers away
from its dark, frozen rocks. But it was much, much brighter.

In time with the beating of my heart, it pulsed with the
energy of a thousand suns. With every pulse, it illuminated
the silver moon orbiting it half a billion miles away. I saw this
through my ship's telescopes, which were my ears and eyes. I
watched the fabled moon-brain of the Solid State Entity as it
absorbed energy and spun on its axis and thought its
unfathomable, infinite thoughts, or whatever it was that a
goddess did to fulfill her existence.

Of course, it was a mystery what the Entity did with all
this energy. I saw that She used energy faster than a starving
hibakusha could swallow a bowl of milk. And, as long as I am
speaking of my ignorance, I should mention that I did not
really know if the Entity's brain was solid state or if it was put
together of some bizarre type of manufactured matter. (I
thought of the black bodies I had seen near the neutron star,
and I wondered.) Certainly Her brain was not solid state in
the sense that it was composed of silicon crystals or germanium or other such semiconductors. Long ago, during the
lordship of Tisander the Wary, the eschatologists had found a
single, dead mainbrain out near the stars of the Aud Binary.
When they dissected the moon-brain—it was really only the
size of a large asteroid—they discovered billions of layers of
ultra-thin organic crystals, a vast latticework of interconnecting
proteins which jumped to the touch of an electric current.
The latticework was much like the neurologics that the
tinkers grow inside the lightships—but infinitely more complex. It was so complex that the programmers had never
decoded a single one of the mainbrain's programs, not even
the simple survival programs which must have been hardwired into the protein circuits. They had remained as ignorant of the mainbrain's purpose (and cause of death) as I was
of the living brain orbiting the pulsar.

I found a point-to-point mapping and fell to within half a
million miles of the moon. Though I made such analyses and
tests as I could, I discovered little about its composition. That
it really was a brain and not a natural moon I did not doubt. I
had never seen a natural moon so featureless and uncratered.
Its surface was as smooth and satiny as the skin of a Jacarandan
whore. And as I have said, the manifold nearby was distorted
in ways explicable only by the presence of a huge intelligence. But what was the *nature* of this intelligence? However
desperately I wanted to know, I could not seriously consider

landing on the moon's surface to drill a core sample for analysis. It would have been a crude, barbaric thing to do, and futile, like drilling into the pink brain of an autist in an attempt to map his inner world of fantasy. And it would have been dangerous beyond thinking. Already, I knew, I had been lucky to survive the dangers of the manifold. If I were stupid enough to perturb the Entity, as She perturbed the manifold by Her mere presence, I did not think I would be lucky much longer.

I should have fled homeward immediately. I had fulfilled my vow to penetrate the Entity, and I had mapped at least a part of Her. I probably should not have tried to communicate with Her. Who is man to talk with a goddess? It was foolish—so I thought—to bombard the moon with information written into laser beams, to bathe her silvery surface with radio waves carrying my inquisitive voice and the coded greeting of the ship-computer. But I did it anyway. Once in a lifetime a man must chance everything to experience something greater than himself.

The Entity, however, did not seem to be aware of my existence. To Her my laser beams must have been as unfelt and unheeded as is the "ping" of a single photon striking a man's calloused palm. My radio waves were like drops of water in the ocean of radio waves emitted by the pulsar. I was nothing to Her, I thought, and why should I despair that I was nothing? Was I aware of a single virus tumbling through the capillaries of my brain? Ah, I told myself, but a virus has almost no consciousness, whereas I was a man aware of my own awareness. Shouldn't a goddess, in some small way, take notice of that awareness? Shouldn't she be aware of me?

Of course it was vain of me to think this way, but I have never been a humble man. It is one of my worst flaws. Vain as I was, though, I knew there was nothing I could do to apprehend this fantastic, glistening, alien intelligence. I was in awe of Her—there is no other word. With lasers I measured the diameter of her moon-brain and found that it was a thousand and forty miles from pole to pole. If I could reproduce my brain a trillion times over, I thought, and a billion times again, and glue the sticky, pink mass all together, it would still not be as great as hers. I realized that any bit of her neurologics was a million times faster than my own sluggishly firing neurons, and that within the nebula, around bright stars tens of light-years distant, there floated probably millions of moon-sized brain lobes, each pulsing with intense intelligence, each interconnected in unknown ways with every other across and through the rippling tides of space.

Because I was curious and as convinced of my own immortality as all young men are, I set off to map the Entity more completely. I fell out around hot red giant stars and discovered many more moon-brains. As many as a hundred moons orbited some of the stars. There the manifold was warped and hideously complex. There I segued into dangerous decision trees and segmented spaces even wilder than the one I had first encountered. It was during this long journey inward through the Entity's brain that I first felt confident of my pilot's skills, that I really *became* a pilot. Sometimes I was overly confident, even cocky. Where was another pilot, I wondered, who had had to learn so much so quickly? Could Tomoth or Lionel—or any other master pilot— have threaded the torsion spaces as elegantly as I did?

I wish I had room here to catalog all the wonders of that unique nebula, for they would fascinate many, not just our Order's astronomers. Most wondrous of my discoveries, other than the wonder of the nebula Herself, was the planet I found orbiting a red star named Kamilusa, named not by me but by the people living on the planet. People! How had they come to be there, I wondered? Had they fallen through the manifold as I had? Were they perhaps the descendents of the Tycho and Erendira Ede or other pilots lost in the Entity? I was astonished that *people* could live inside the brain of a goddess. Somehow it did not seem right. I thought of them as parasites living off the light of their bloody sun, or as drillworms who had somehow chewed their way into the brain of an incomprehensibly greater being.

After greeting the people by radio, I made planetfall on one of the broad, western beaches of the island continent called Sendai. It was very warm so I opened the pit of my ship. The sun was a hot, red plate above me, and birds resembling snow gulls swooped and sloshed along the currents of the moist wind, which stank of seaweed and other vegetation. Everything, even the air itself, was too green.

To the naked people lining the dunes of the beach, I must have looked very alien as I stood on the packed, wet sand, sweating in my black boots and kamelaika. My beard had grown out during the long days of my journey, and my body was slightly wasted from too little exercise. When I bowed to the people, my back muscles quivered with the strain. Naturally I had asked to speak to the lord of the planet. But the people had no lord—nor masters, sensei, matriarchs, kings, protectors or anyone else to direct their day-to-day activities. They were anarchists. As I learned, they were probably the descendents of hibakusha who centuries ago had fled the oppressive hierarchies of the Japanese Worlds. However, they seemed to have only the sketchiest memories of their passage through the Entity. No one could tell me how they had once piloted their deep ships and scurfed the windows of the manifold because no one remembered. And no one cared. They had lost the noblest of arts, and most other arts as well. The planet's few hundred thousand people were barbarians who spent their long days eating, swimming, copulating and roasting their bodies brown in the sun's red oven. The society of Kamilusa was one of those stale utopias where robots did the work of man's hands and made more robots to do ever more work. And worse, they had programmed their computers to direct their robots, and worse still, they had let their computers do all their thinking for them. I spent five hundred-hour days there, and not once did I find a woman or man who cared where life had come from or where it was going to. (Though many of the children possessed a natural, soon-to-be-crushed curiosity.) Remarkably, no one—except perhaps the computers—seemed to realize that Kamilusa lay within the brain of a goddess. I record the following conversation because it is representative of others that I had during those stifling, hot nights and days.

One evening, on the veranda of one of the villas built on the beach dunes, I sat in a plush chair across from an old woman named Takara. I had learned a dialect of New West Japanese just to talk to her. She was a tiny, shriveled woman with wispy strands of hair growing in patches from her round head. Like everyone else, she was as naked as an animal. When I asked her why no one wanted to know about such wonders as the construction of my ship, she said, "Our computers could design a lightship, if that was our desire."

"But could they train pilots?"

"Hai, I suppose." She took a drink of a clear blue liquid

one of her domestic robots had brought her. "But why should we want to train pilots?"

"To fall among the stars. There are glories that only pilots—"

"Oh, I don't think so," she interrupted. "One star is much like any other, isn't it? Stars give us their warmth, isn't that enough? And also, as you admit, your travel from star to star is too dangerous."

"You can't live forever."

"Hai, but you can live a long time," she said. "I, myself have lived . . ." and here she spoke at one of the computers built into the sandstone veranda. It spoke back, and she said, "I've lived five hundred of your Neverness years. I've been a young woman, oh, perhaps . . ." and she spoke to the computer again. "I've been young ten times; it's wonderful to be young. Maybe I'll be young ten more times. But not if I do dangerous things. Swimming is dangerous enough, and I don't do that anymore even though the robots keep the sharks away. Hai, I could always take a cramp, you know. It's well known how the dangers build over the years. There is a word for it, oh . . . what is it?" When her computer had supplied her with the word, she said, "If there is a certain *probability* that I will die in any year, then the *probability* grows greater every year. It *multiplies*, I think. The tiniest risk becomes riskier as time goes on. In time, if there is the slightest risk of death, then death will occur. And that is why I do not leave my villa. Oh, I used to love to swim, but my fourteenth husband died when a bird dropped a conch shell on his head. Ashira—he was a beautiful man—he used to shave his head. He was bald as a rock. The bird must have thought his head *was* a rock. The conch shell broke his skull, and he died."

As if she were ever wary of bizarre accidents, she looked up into the starry sky to look for birds. She pointed to the robot lasers lining the veranda's high walls, aimed at the dark sky, and she said, "But I'm not afraid of birds any longer."

What she had said was of course true. Life is dangerous. Because of the laws of antichance, pilots—and everyone else in our Order—almost never lived as long as Soli had. Which explains why the younger pilots called him "Soli The Lucky."

"It's a dangerous universe," I said. "And mysterious, but there are beauties—you admit you're a student of beauty."

"What do you mean by *beauty*?" she wanted to know as she placed her hand between her breasts, which were brown and withered as old leather bags. She sniffed the air in my direction and wrinkled her tiny nose. Plainly, she did not like the wooly smell of my sweat-stained kamelaika. It was annoying that she looked at me as if *I* were the barbarian, not she.

I pointed to the moon shining above us. I told her that the moon was really a huge bio-computer, the brain and substance of a goddess. "It shines like silver, and that's beautiful," I said. "But it shares its shining intelligence with a million other moons, and just to imagine the possibilities... that's a different, higher kind of beauty."

She looked at me as a logician looks at a babbling autist and said, "I don't think the moon is a computer. Why should you lie to me? Computers aren't beautiful, I don't think."

I said, "I wouldn't lie to you."

"And what do you mean by *goddess*?"

When I had explained to her about higher intelligences and the classifications of the eschatologists, she laughed at me and said, "Oh, there's *God*, I suppose. Or there used to be—I can't remember any more. But to think the moon *thinks*, well that is insane!"

Suddenly she glared at me with her old, old eyes and shook like a tent in the wind. It must have occurred to her that if I were insane, I might do something risky and was therefore a threat to her longevity. When she looked at me again, I noticed that the robots were pointing their lasers at me. She spoke to her computer and said, "The moon is made of... of *elements*: carbon, hydrogen, oxygen, and nitrogen."

"The elements of protein," I said. "The neurologics of computers are often made of protein."

"Oh, who cares what things are made of? What matters is peace and harmony. And you are dangerous to our harmony, I think."

"I'll leave, if that's what you want."

In truth, I couldn't wait to leave that hot, stifling planet.

"Hai, you must leave. The longer you stay, the more dangerous you become. Please, tomorrow will you leave? And please, do not talk to the children anymore. They would be frightened if they thought the moon was alive."

I abandoned the people to their pleasures and their decadent harmonies. In the middle of the long night, I rocketed away and fell again into the manifold. Again I fenestered inward towards the center of the Entity's brain. I was more determined than ever to seek the nexus of her intelligence, if indeed such a nexus existed. The further I fell, the more moon-brains I discovered. Near one hot, blue giant star, there must have been ten thousand moons clumped together like the cells of an embryo. I had an intense feeling that I was witnessing something I was not meant to see, as if I had caught my mother naked in her morning bath. Were the moons somehow reproducing themselves, I wondered? I could not tell. I could not see into the center of the clump because the space there was as black as a black hole. Even though I knew it would be chancey to fall any further, I was afire with the *possibilities* of new, godly life, so I made a point-to-point mapping into the center of the gathered moons.

Immediately, I knew that I had made a simple mistake. My ship did not fall out into the center of the moons. Instead, I segued into a junglelike decision tree. A hundred different pathways opened before me, dividing and branching into ten thousand others. I was sick with fear because I had only instants to decide upon the correct branching, or I would be lost.

I reached out with my mind to my ship, and slowtime overcame me. My brain rushed with thoughts, as snowflakes swirl in a cold wind. As my mentations accelerated, time seemed to slow down. I had a long, stretched-out instant in which to prove a particularly difficult mapping theorem. I had to prove it quickly, as quickly as I could think. The computer modeled my thoughts and began infusing my visual cortex with ideoplasts that I summoned up from memory. These crystal-like symbols glittered before my inner eye; they formed and joined and assembled into the proof array of my theorem. Each individual ideoplast was lovely and unique. The representation of the fixed-point theorem, for instance, was like a coiled ruby necklace. As I built my proof, the coil joined with feathery, diamond fibers of the first Lavi mapping lemma. I was thinking furiously, and the ideoplasts froze into place. The intricate emerald glyphs of the statement of invariance, the wedgelike runes of the sentential connectives, and all the other characters—they formed a three-dimensional array ordered by logic and inspiration. The quicker I thought, the quicker the ideoplasts appeared as if from nothingness and found their place in the proof array. This mental manipulation of symbol into proof has a special name. We call it the *number storm* because the rush of pure mathematical thinking is overwhelming, like a blizzard in midwinter spring.

With the number storm carrying me along toward the moment of proof, I passed into dreamtime. There was an indescribable perception of *orderedness*; there was beauty and terror as the manifold opened before me. The number storm intensified, nearly blinding me with the white light of dreamtime. I wondered, as I had always wondered, at the nature of dreamtime and that wonderful mental space we call the manifold. Was the manifold truly deep reality, the reality ordering the shape and texture of the outer universe? Some cantors believe this (my mother is not one of these), and it is their faith that when mathematics is perfectly realized, the universe will be perfectly understood. But they are pure mathematicians, and we pilots are not. In the manifold there is no perfection. There is much that we do not understand.

I was deep in dreamtime when I realized I did not understand the type of the decision tree branching all about me. I was close to my proof—I needed only to show that the Lavi set was embedded in an invariant space. But I could not show this, and I did not know why. It should have been a simple thing to do. When the tree divided and split into a million and then a billion different branches, I began to sweat. Dreamtime intensified into that terrifying, nameless state I thought of as "nightmaretime." Suddenly I proved that the Lavi set could *not* be embedded in an invariant space. My heart was beating like a panicked child's. With my panic came despair, and my proof array began to crash, to shatter like ice crystals ground beneath a leather boot. There would be no proof, I knew. There would be no mapping to a point-exit in real space. I would not fall out around any star, near or distant. I was not merely lost in a hideous decision tree, I had stumbled—or been propelled—into an infinite tree. Even in the worst of decision trees, there is a probability that a pilot will find the correct branch among the billion billion branchings. But in an infinite tree, there is no correct branch, no branch leading to an exit into the warm sunlight of realspace. The tree spreads outward, one branch growing into another, and into ten centillion others, on and on, dividing and redividing into infinity. From an infinite tree there is no escape. My neurons would gradually disassociate, synapse by synapse, leaving me to play with my toes as a child plays with the beads of an abacus. I would be insane, blinded by the number storm, frozen in forever dreamtime, forever drooling into infinity. Or, if I turned away from my ship-computer and let my mind go quiet, there would be nothing, nothing but an empty black coffin carrying me into the hell of the manifold.

I knew then that I had lied to myself utterly. I was not ready to chance everything to experience a goddess; I was not ready to face death at all. I remembered I had chosen my fate freely. I could only blame myself and my foolish pride. My last thought, as a scream formed up on my lips and I began hearing voices inside me, was: Why is man born to self-deception and lies?

5

The Solid State
Entity

If the brain were so simple we could understand it,
we would be so simple we couldn't.
                    —Lyall Watson, Holocaust Century
                                        Eschatologist

Somewhere it is recorded that the first man, Gilgamesh, heard a voice inside him and thought it was the voice of God. I heard voices reverberating through my inner ear, and I thought my fear of the infinite tree had driven me insane.

Why?

It is a sign of insanity when a man hears voices born not of lips but of his own loneliness and longings. Unless, of course, it is the voice of his ship stimulating his aural nerves, suffusing sounds directly into his brain.

Why is man?

But a ship-computer has little free will; it cannot choose what words or what tone of voice to speak within a pilot. It is possible for it to receive signals from another ship-computer and to translate these signals into voices, but it is not programmed to generate its own signals.

Why is man born?

I knew my ship-computer could not be receiving signals from another lightship because the propagation of signals through the manifold was impossible. It *was* possible, I told myself, that some of my ship's neurologics had weakened and died. In that case, my ship was insane, and as long as I remained interfaced with it, so was I.

Why is man born to self-deception and lies?

If I did not like the way my ship was echoing my deepest

thoughts, it terrorized me when it began speaking in voices, in a hodgepodge of the dead languages of Old Earth. Some of these languages I understood from my learning to read; others were as alien to me as the scent language of the Friends of Man is to human beings.

Shalom, Instrumentum Vocale, la ilaha il ALLAH tat tvam asi, n'est-ce pas, kodomo-ga, wakiramasu? Hai, and thereto haddle he riden, no man ferre, poi s'ascose nel foco che gli affina which he called the stars of the Solid State Entity und so wir betreten, feuer-trunken—Ahnest du den Schopfer? It is I, Mallory Ringess.

So, I thought, this is insanity, to greet myself as a tool with a voice, to speak of entering the Entity "drunk with fire," whatever that meant. I recognized the phrase, *Ahnest du den Schopfer.* It was a line of a poem written in Old High German which meant something like, "Do you sense your creator?" I "sensed" that my ship and myself had gone completely mad, either that or it really was receiving a signal through the warped manifold of the Entity. And then I heard:

> *If thou beest born to strange sights,*
> *Things invisible to see,*
> *Ride ten thousand days and nights,*
> *Till age snow white hairs on thee.*

So, the Entity did like ancient poetry. If any signal were being sent through the manifold, I thought, it must be coming from Her. The voices began to modulate and resonate into a single voice. In a way, it was a feminine voice, at once seductive and lonely, beatific and sad. It was a voice uncertain as to whether or not it would be understood. Hearing this lovely voice echo the dead languages of Old Earth made me guess that She was probing to discover my milk tongue. But I was mistrustful of this thought the moment it entered my mind. Perhaps I desired too ardently to speak with Her; perhaps I was only speaking with myself.

No, Mallory, you are speaking with me.

—But I'm not speaking at all; I'm *thinking.*

Do not flatter yourself that what occurs in your mind is true thought.

—How can you read my thoughts . . . my *mind,* then?

You are inside of me and I am inside of you. Yin-yang,

*lingam-yoni, outside-inside. I am an entity, but I am not
solid. Not always.*

—What are you?

*I am the frenzy; I am the lightning; I am your refining
fire.*

—I don't understand.

*You are a man. Verily, a polluted stream is man. What
have you done to purify yourself?*

So, I thought, I had longed to experience a greater being,
and she spoke to me in riddles. Quickly I turned my mind
away from the manifold and the infinite tree. I tested the
ship's neurologics. But they were healthy and sound, and
nowhere could I find the source of the Entity's signal.

*There is no signal, as you think of signal. There is only
perception and touch: I look into the electric field of your
ship's logics and reach out and jiggle the electrons to change
the hologram. And so your computer runs my thoughts and
suffuses my voice into your brain. I would touch your brain
directly but that would frighten you.*

Yes, yes, it would have. I was already frightened enough.
I did not want anything alien to "jiggle" the electrons in my
brain, to fill me with its images and sounds, to make me see
and hear and touch and smell things which did not exist, to
change my very perception of reality. With this thought came
a much more disturbing thought: What if the Entity already
were jiggling my brain's electrons? Perhaps She only wanted
me to *think* that the voice I heard came from the computer. I
did not know what to think. Was I really thinking my own
thoughts? Or was the Entity playing with me, making me
doubt that I was thinking my own thoughts? Or worse still,
what if it all was a nightmare of madness? Maybe my ship had
disintegrated; maybe I was experiencing a final moment
before death, and the Entity—for whatever reasons—had
reached into my brain to create an illusion of sane existence.
Maybe I was dead or just dreaming; maybe I, whatever "I"
was—was entirely the Entity's dream creation. Everyone, of
course, has these thoughts and fears, but very few have had a
goddess speak to them. When I thought of Her being inside
my mind, I was dizzy with a sense of losing my self. My
stomach churned with a sick feeling that I had no free will. It
was an awful moment. I thought that the universe was a
terribly uncertain place where I could be certain of only a

single thing: that in the realm of my mind, I wanted no thoughts other than my own to alter my thinking.

Because I was full of fear and doubt, the Entity explained how she manipulated matter through the layers of the manifold. But I understood only the smallest part of the physics, the simplest of ideas. She had created a new mathematics to describe the warp and woof of spacetime. Her theory of interconnectedness was as beyond me as a demonstration of the different orders of infinities would be to a worm. Ages ago, of course, the mechanics had explored the paradoxes of quantum mechanics. For example, they had shown that both photons in a pair of photons are connected in fundamental ways no matter how far the two particles are separated in realspace. If two photons fly away from a light source towards the opposite ends of the universe, each will "know" certain of its twin's attributes, such as spin or polarization, no matter how far apart they are. And they will know it instantaneously, as if each instantly "remembered" it should be polarized horizontally, not up and down. From this discovery the mechanics theorized that it is possible to transmit information faster than light, though to their disgrace they have never succeeded in doing so. But their brains are small where the Entity's is measureless. It seemed She had found a way not only to communicate but to instantaneously touch and manipulate particles across and through the reaches of space. How She did so, I still do not understand.

—I don't understand your definition of a correspondence space; is it isomorphic to what we call a Lavi space? I can't see . . . if only there was more time!

At the beginning of time all the particles of the universe were crushed together into a single point; all the particles were as one, in the singularity.

—And I don't remember the derivation of your field equation. It must be—

Memory is everything. All particles remember the instant the singularity exploded and the universe was born. In a way, the universe is nothing but memory.

—The correspondences are superluminal, then? The correspondence scheme collapses? I've tried to prove that a hundred times but—

Everything in the universe is woven of a single superluminal fabric. Tat tvam asi, that thou art.

—I don't understand.

You are not here to understand.

—Why do you think I've crossed half the galaxy, then?

You are here to kneel.

—What?

You are here to kneel—these are words from an old poem. Do you know the poem?

—No, of course not.

Ahhh, that is a shame. Then perhaps you are here to die as well as kneel.

—I'll die in the infinite tree; there's no mapping out of an infinite tree.

Others have come before you; others are lost in the tree.

—Others?

Suddenly the voice of the goddess grew as high and sweet as a little girl's. Like the piping of a flute, the following words spilled into my brain:

> *They are all gone into a world of light!*
>   *And I alone sit lingering here;*
> *Their very memory is fair and bright,*
>   *And my sad thoughts doth clear.*

You must die. Deep inside you know this. Don't be afraid.

—Well, pilots die—or so they say. I'm not afraid.

I am sorry you are afraid. It was that way with the others.

—What others?

Eight pilots of your Order have tried to penetrate my brains: Wicent li Towt, Erendira Ede and Alexandravondila; Ishi Mokku, Ricardo Lavi, Jemmu Flowtow and Atara of Darkmoon. And John Penhallegon, the one you call the Tycho.

—Then you killed them?

What do you know about killing? As an oyster, to protect itself, encapsulates an irritant grain of sand with layer upon layer of pearl, so I have confined all but one of these pilots to the branchings of a decision tree.

—What's an oyster?

The Entity reached into my computer's thoughtspace and placed there an image etched in light and touch and smell. By means of this forbidden telepathy—forbidden to us pilots—I experienced Her conception of oyster. In my mind I saw a soft, squishy creature which protected itself with a hinged shell that it could open or close at will. My fingers closed almost against *my* will, and in my hand I felt gritty sand against a scoop-shaped, hard, wet shell. My jaws moved of their own, moved my teeth against a tender meat which suddenly ruptured, filling my mouth with living fluids and salt and the taste of the sea. I smelled the thick, cloying perfume of naked proteins and heard a sucking sound as I swallowed the gobbet of raw, living flesh.

That is oyster.

—It's wrong to kill animals for their meat.

And you, my innocent man, are a pretty pearl in the necklace of time. Do you understand the time distortions? The other pilots are alive, as a pearl is alive with luster and beauty, yet they do not live. They have died, yet they remain undead.

—Again, you speak in riddles.

The universe is a riddle.

—You're playing with me.

I like to play.

Before my mind's eye, a transparent, glowing cube appeared. The cube was segmented into eight other stacked cubes, each of which flickered with confusing images. I looked inward at the cubes, and the images began to coalesce and harden. In each cube, except the one on the lower right, a disembodied head floated within its prison, as a pilot floats within his ship's pit. Each face was scarred with the rictus of terror and insanity. Each face stared open-mouthed at me— stared through me—as if I were air. I recognized the faces, then. The historians had taught me well. They were the faces of Wicent li Towt, Ishi Mokku and the others who had come before me.

What is death, Mallory? The pilots are each lost in a dividing branch of the decision tree. They are as lost and forgotten as the poems of the Aeschylus. But someday, I will remember them.

I wondered how she had encapsulated the pilots (and myself) in the infinite tree. There are ways, of course, to open a window into the manifold at random, to send a pilot unmapped and unprepared into an infinite tree. But She had used none of these ways. She had done something else, something marvelous. How was it possible, I wanted to know? Had Her consciousness really molded the shape of the manifold, twisted the very strands of deep reality, much as a child braids together ropes of clay?

I did not know. I could not know. I had seen less than a millionth part of her, and She had probably needed only the tiniest portion of that part to speak with me mind to mind. I was like a grain of sand trying to understand an ocean from a few eddies and currents sweeping it along; I was like a flower trying to deduce space travel from the faint tickle of starlight upon its delicate petals. To this day I search for words describing my impression of the Entity's *power*, but there are no words. I learned—if that is the right word for knowledge which comes in a sudden flash of insight—I was given to understand that She manipulated whole sciences and thought systems as I might string words into a sentence. But her "sentences" were as huge and profound as the utterances of the universe itself. She had reached truths and ways of knowing far beyond even the meta-philosophies of the alien Fravashi. She, a goddess, played with concepts which could remake the universe, concepts unthinkable to the mind of Man. While most of my race lived out their days muddled and confused in darkness, She had solved problems and found new directions of thought which we had never dreamed of, and worse, She had done so as easily as I might multiply two times one.

The mechanics often bemoan their oldest paradox, which is this: The strings weaving the fabric of the universe are so infinitessimal that any attempt to study them will change their properties. The very act of observation perturbs that which is observed. On Old Earth, it is said, there was a king who carked the atoms of everything around him so that all he touched turned into gold. The fabled king could neither eat nor drink because his food and wine tasted of nothing but gold. The mechanics are like this king: Everything they "touch" turns into ugly lumps of matter, into electrons, quarks, or zeta-neutrinos. There is no way for them to perceive deep reality except through the golden, distorting lenses of their instruments or through the touch of their golden equations. In some unfathomable way, the Entity had transcended this prison of matter. To see reality directly, as it really is—this, I thought must be the privilege of a godly intellect.

Do you see the pilots, Mallory Ringess?

I saw insanity and chaos. I stared into the cube containing the undead pilots. The black, sharp face of Jemmu Flowtow was leaking drool from its narrow lips.

—You trapped the pilots; then you could free them. And me.

But they are free. Or will be free when the universe has remade itself. What has been will be.

—That's scryer talk.

The time distortions: When the universe has expanded outward so that the closest two stars are as far apart as the Grus Cloud of galaxies is now from the Canes Venatici, after billions of your years, the pilots will be as you see them, frozen into forever nowness. It is easier to stop time, is it not, than to restart it? To kill than create? But creation is timeless; creation is everything.

—The pilots... in the tree where the infinities branch into insanity, have you seen their insane frozen faces, then?

There is no help for insanity. It is the price that some must pay.

—I feel like I'm going insane now down the branching of this tree where it splits into two and two into for insanity you say there's no helping me escape from infinity and stop playing games with my mind!

You, Mallory, my wild man, we will play together, and I will teach you all there is to know of instantaneity, and perhaps insanity, too. Will you join the other pilots? Watch carefully, the empty cube is for you.

I noticed then what I should have seen immediately: that eight pilots had been lost within the Entity, but only seven of the ghastly death's-heads floated within the cubes. In none of them did I see the huge, walruslike head of the Tycho.

—What happened to the Tycho?

I am the Tycho; the Tycho is me, part of me.

—I don't understand.

The Tycho exists in a memory space.

Inside my mind the little girl's voice returned, only it was no longer quite so sweet, no longer quite the voice of a little girl. There were sultry, dark notes coloring the innocent fluting and I heard:

But oh! that deep romantic chasm which slanted
Down the green hill athwart a cedarn cover!
A savage place! as holy and enchanted
As e'er beneath a waning moon was haunted
By woman wailing for her demon lover!

He was a savage man beneath his silken robes, a lovely
man, a demon lover of a man. When I saw what a wild
intelligence he had, I severed his brain from his body, and I
copied it synapse by synapse into a tiny pocket of one of my
lesser brains. Behold John Penhallegon.

Suddenly, within the pit of my ship, an imago of the
Tycho appeared. He was so close to me that I could have
touched his swollen red nose as one reaches for a snow apple.
He was—had been—a thick-faced man with yellowish incisors
too long for his blubbery lips. He had a mass of shiny black
hair hanging in clumps halfway down his back; his jowls hung
from his bristly chin halfway to his chest. "How far do you
fall, Pilot?" he asked in a voice thick with age, repeating the
traditional greeting of pilots who meet in faraway places. His
voice rang like a bell through the pit of my ship. Apparently
the Entity could generate holograms and sound waves as
easily as She could jiggle electrons. "Shalom," he said. With
his red, sweaty fingers he made the secret sign that only a
pilot of our Order would know.

"You can't be the Tycho," I said aloud. The sound of my
own voice startled me. "The Tycho is dead."

"I'm John Penhallegon," the imago said. "I'm as alive as
you are. More alive, really, because I can't be killed so
easily."

"You're the voice of the Entity," I said as I wiped the
sweat from my forehead.

"I'm both."

"That's impossible."

"Don't be so certain of what's possible and what's not.
Certainty can kill, as I know."

I rubbed the side of my nose and said, "Then the Entity
has absorbed the Tycho's memories and thoughtways—I can
believe that. But the Tycho can't be *alive,* he can't have free
will, can he?...can *you?* If you're part of the whole...Entity?"

The Tycho—or the imago of the Tycho, as I reminded

myself—laughed so hard that spit bubbled from his lips. "Nay, my Pilot, I'm like you, like all men. Sometimes I have free will, and sometimes I don't."

"Then you're *not* like me," I said too quickly. "I've freedom of choice, everyone does."

"Nay, was it freedom of choice made you break your Lord Pilot's nose?"

It scared and angered me that the Entity could pull this memory from my mind, so I angrily said, "Soli goaded me. I lost my temper."

The Tycho wiped the spit from his lips and rubbed his hands together. I heard the swish of skin against skin. "Okay. *Soli* goaded you. Then *Soli* was in control, not you."

"You're twisting my words. He made me so mad I wanted to hit him."

"Okay. *He* made you."

"I could have controlled myself."

"Is that so?" he asked.

I was angry, and I huffed out, "Of course it is. I was just so mad I didn't care if I hit him."

"You must like being mad."

"No, I hate it. I always have. But then that's the way I am."

"You must like the way you are."

I closed my eyes and shook my head. "No, you don't understand. I've tried... I *try*, but when I get mad, it's ...well, it's *part* of me, do you see? People aren't perfect."

"And people don't have free will, either," he said.

My cheeks were hot and my tongue was dry. It seemed that the Tycho, too, was trying to goad me into losing my temper. As I breathed rhythmically, struggling for control, I looked at the phased light waves composing the imago of the Tycho. His robe was like glowing smoke in the black air.

I asked, "Does a goddess, then? Have free will?"

Again the Tycho laughed, and he said, "Does a dog have Buddha nature? You're quick, my Pilot, but you're not here to test the goddess. You're here to be tested."

"To be tested... *how?*"

"To be tested for possibilities."

As I was soon to learn, the Entity had been testing me since I first crossed the threshold of her immense brain. The torsion spaces and the ugly segmented spaces that had almost

defeated me—they were her handiwork, as was the infinite
tree imprisoning me. She had tested my mathematical prowess, and—this is what the Tycho told me—She had tested my
courage. Not the least of my tests had been my ability to
listen to Her godvoice and not lose myself in terror. I had no
idea why She would want to test me at all, unless it was just
another of Her games. And why should She use the Tycho to
test me when She could look into my brain to see all of me
there was to see? No sooner had I thought this when the
godvoice rolled through my head like thunder:

*Thousands of years ago your eschatologists mapped the
DNA molecule down to the last carbon atom. But they still
search for the rules by which DNA unfolds life and codes for
new forms of life. They are still learning DNA's grammar. As
with DNA, so it is with the unfolded brain. Imagine a baby
who has learned the alphabet but who has no idea what
words mean or the rules for putting them together. To understand the brain from its trillions of synapses would be like
trying to appreciate a poem from the arbitrary twistings of
individual letters. You are that poem. There are infinite
possibilities. You, my Mallory, will always be a mystery to me.*

—I don't want to be tested.

Life is a test.

—If I succeed, will you free me from the tree?

*Like an ape, you are free at this moment to escape your
tree.*

—Free? I don't know how.

*That is too bad. If you succeed, you are free to ask me
three questions, any questions. It is an old, old game.*

—And if I fail?

*Then the light goes out. Oh, where does the light go when
the light goes out?*

I tightened my fists until my fingernails cut my palms. I
did not want to be tested.

"Well, my Pilot, shall we begin?" It was the Tycho
speaking as he scratched his jowls.

"I don't know."

I will not record here in detail the many tests that the
Tycho—the Entity—put to me. Some of the tests, such as the
Test of Knowledge, as he called it, were long, meticulous and
boring. The nature of other tests, such as the Test of Chaos, I
hardly understood at all. There was a Test of Reason and a

Test of Paradox, followed, I think, by the Test of Reality in which I was made to question my every assumption, habit and belief while the Tycho bombarded me with alien ideas that I had never thought before. This test nearly drove me mad. I never understood the need to be tested at all, not even when the Tycho explained: "Someday, my angry Pilot, you may have great power, perhaps as Lord Pilot, and you'll need to see things through multiplex eyes."

"I'm rather fond of my own eyes."

"Nevertheless," he said, "nevertheless..."

Suddenly, within my head, echoed the teachings of the famous cantor, Alexandar of Simoom, Alexandar Diego Soli, who was Leopold Soli's long-dead father. I was immersed body, mind and soul in the belief system of the strange Friends of God. I saw the universe through Alexandar's dark, gray eyes. It was a cold universe in which nothing was certain except the creation of mathematics. Other forms of creation did not really exist. Yes, there was man, but what was man, after all? Was man the creation of the Ieldra, who had in turn been created by the Elder Ieldra? And if so, who had created *them*? The Very Elder Ieldra?

And so I learned this strange theology of Alexandar Diego Soli: It was known that the first Lord Cantor, the great Georg Cantor, with an ingenious proof array had demonstrated that the infinity of integers—what he called aleph null—is embedded within the higher infinity of real numbers. And he had proved that *that* infinity is embedded within the infinities of the higher alephs, a whole hierarchy of infinities, an infinity of infinities. The Simoom cantors believed that as it is with numbers, so it is with the hierarchies of the gods. Truly, as Alexandar had taught his son, Leopold, if a god existed, who or what had created him (or her)? If there is a higher god, call him god^2, there must be a god^3 and a god^4, and so on. There is an aleph million and an aleph centillion, but there is no final, no highest infinity, and therefore there is no God. No, there could be no true God, and so there could be no true creation. The logic was as harsh and merciless as Alexandar of Simoom himself: If there is no true creation then there is no true reality. If nothing is real, then man is not real; man in some fundamental sense does not exist. Reality is all a dream, and worse, it is less than a dream because even a dream must have a dreamer to dream it. To assert otherwise is nonsense. And to assert the existence of the self is therefore a sin, the worst of sins; therefore it is better to cut out one's tongue than to speak the word "I."

As this reality gripped me, I was transported in space and time. I shivered and opened my eyes to the mountain mists settling over Alexandar's stone house on Simoom. I was in a tiny, bare, immaculate room with gray slate walls, and I looked at a young boy kneeling in front of me. I was Alexandar of Simoom, and the boy was Soli.

"Do you see?" the Tycho asked me. And he placed in my mind Alexandar's memory of his son's austere, bitter education:

"Do you understand, Leopold? You must never say that word again."

"What word, Father?"

"Don't play games, do you understand?"

"Yes, Father, but please don't slap me again."

"And who do you think you are to be worthy of punishment?"

"Nobody, Father . . . nothing."

"That is true, and since it is true, there is no reason for you to be spoken to, is there?"

"The silence is terrible, Father, worse than being punished. Please, how can you teach me in silence?"

"And why should you be taught anything at all?"

"Because mathematics is the only true reality, but . . . but how can that be? If we are really nothing, we cannot create mathematics, can we?"

"You have been told, haven't you? Mathematics is not created; it is not a thing like a tree or a ray of light; nor is it a creation of mind. Mathematics is. It is all that is. You may think of God as the timeless, eternal universe of mathematics."

"But how can it . . . if it is . . . I just don't under—"

"*What* did you say?"

"*I* don't understand!"

"And still you profane. You won't be spoken to again."

"I, I, I, I, I . . . Father? Please."

I did not understand how the Entity had acquired the memories of Alexandar of Simoom. (Or perhaps they were Soli's memories?) Nor did I learn how She knew so much of the even stranger realities of the autists and the brain-maiming aphasics. Strange as these realities were, however— and it was very strange to enter the internal, self-painted thoughtscapes of an autist—they were human realities. Human thought is really all the same. Thoughts may differ from person to person and from group to group, but the *way* we think is limited by the deep structures of our all too human brains. This is both a curse and a blessing. We are all trapped within the bone coffins of our same brains, imprisoned in thoughtways evolved over a million years. But it is a comfortable prison of familiar white walls, whose air, however stale, we can breathe. If we would escape our prison only for an instant, our new way of seeing, of *knowing*, would leave us gasping. There would be glories and excruciating beauty and—as I was soon to learn—madness.

"Okay," the Tycho said to me, "you grasp Alexandar of Simoom and Iamme, the solipsist. And now, the alien realities."

The Tycho—or rather the phased light waves that were the Tycho—began to blur. The redness of his round nose deepened into violet as the nose itself broadened into a bristly snout. Like a piece of pulled clay, the snout stretched out into a long, supple trunk. His forehead bulged like a bloodfruit swollen with rotten gases, and his chin and jowls hardened into a boxlike organ lined with dozens of narrow, pinkish slits. Suddenly, his robe vanished like smoke. His naked body began to change. Balls of round muscle and brown and scarlet fur replaced the Tycho's gray, sagging flesh. His ponderous testes and membrum withered like seaweed and shrunk, vanishing within the red fold of skin between the thick legs. I waited and stared at the alien thing being born within the pit of my ship. Soon I recognized her for what she was: an imago of one of that gentle (if cunning) race known as the Friends of Man.

The alien raised her trunk, and the pink slits of her speech organ vibrated and quivered, releasing a rank spray of molecules. I smelled esthers and ketones and flowers, the stench of rotting meat mingled with the sweetness of snow dahlia. In a way, with her trunk entwined with the blue helix of a master courtesan, she reminded me of Soli's friend (and, some said, mistress) Jasmine Orange.

Behold Jasmine Orange.

I beheld Jasmine Orange through her own eyes: I became Jasmine Orange. I was at once Jasmine Orange and Mallory Ringess, looking at an alien through human eyes and, through my trunk, smelling the essence of a human being. Suddenly, my consciousness left my human body altogether, and there

were no colors. I watched the scarlets and browns of my fur
fade to light and dark gray. I looked across the pit of my ship
and saw a bearded, young, human pilot staring at me; I saw
myself. I listened for the sound of the Entity's voice, but
there was no sound inside or out because I was as deaf as ice.
I did not really know what sound was. I knew only smell, the
wonderful, mutable world of free-floating scent molecules.
There was jasmine and the tang of crushed oranges as I spoke
my lovely name. I curled my trunk, sucking in the fragrance
of garlic and ice-wine as I greeted the human, Mallory
Ringess, and he greeted me. How alien, how bizarre, how
hopelessly stupid seemed his way of representing single units
of meaning by a discrete progression of linear *sounds*, whatever sounds really were! How limited to put *sounds* together,
like beads on a string! How could human beings think at all
when they had to progress from sound to sound and thought
to thought one word at a time like a bug crawling along the
beads of a necklace? How very *slow*!

Because I wanted to speak with the pilot Ringess, I raised
my trunk and released a cloud of pungent odors that was to a
human sentence what I supposed a symphony must be to a
child's jingle. But he had no nose and he understood so little.
Yes, Ringess, I told him, the scent-symbols are not fixed as,
for example, the sounds in the word "purple" are fixed; they
do not always mean the same thing. Isn't meaning as mutable
as the smells of the sea? Can you sense the configuration of
the minute pyramids of mint and vanilla bean and musk in
this cloud of odors? And the meanings—do you know that the
smells of jasmine and olathe and orange might mean, "I am
Jasmine Orange, the lover of Man," or, "The sea is calm
tonight," depending on the arrangement and the proximity of
the unit pyramids to the other molecules of scent? Can you
grasp meaning as a whole? And the logic of structure? Do you
understand the complexities of language, my Ringess?

Ideas blossom outward like arctic poppies in the sun
growing into other ideas crosslinked and connected by pungent association links, and link to link the smells of roasting
meat and wet fur flow outward and sideways and down, and
blend into fields redolent with the sweet perfume of strange
new logic structures and new truths that you must inhale like
cool mint to overwhelm and obliterate your bitter, straightfor-
ward ideas of logic and causality and time. Time is not a line;

the events of your life are rather like a jungle of smells forever preserved in a bottle. One sniff and you'll sense instantly the entire jungle rather than the fragrances of individual flowers. Do you understand the subtleties? Do you dare open the bottle? No, you have no nose, and you don't understand.

He understands all that the structure of his brain will let him understand.

I understood that a man who dwelt too long inside an alien brain would go mad. I closed my eyes and shook my head as I pinched my nostrils shut against the mind-twisting smells flooding the pit of my ship. *My* eyes, *my* nostrils! —when I opened them, I was human again. The alien imago was gone, though the aftersmells of vanilla bean and worm-wood remained. I was alone inside my sweaty, hairy, human body, inside my old brain which I thought I knew so well.

—Their logic, the truth structures . . . it's so different; I never knew.

The deep structure of their brain is different. But at a deeper level still, the logic is the same.

—I can't understand this logic.

Few of your Order have understood the Friends of Man.

Like everyone else, I had always been suspicious of these exotic, alien whores. I had supposed they seduced men with their powerful, aphrodisiacal scents in order to proselytize them when they were drugged with sex, to slyly persuade them to the truth of their mysterious alien religion. Now I saw—"saw" is not the right word—I *perceived* that their purpose was much deeper than merely changing mankind's beliefs; they desired to change mankind itself.

But it is the hardest thing to change the mind of a man. You have such a small sense of yourselves.

—A man must know who he is, as Bardo says.

And what is a Bardo?

While I snorted and tried to rid my nose and mind of disturbing smells, I thought about Bardo and how he had always had a clear, if flamboyant, sense of who he was: a man determined to experience pleasure as no other man ever had or ever would.

Your Bardo defines himself too narrowly. Even he may have possibilities.

During the tests which followed, by implication and deduction, I learned much about the Entity's sense of Herself. Each moon-brain, it seemed, was at once an island of consciousness and part of the greater whole. And each moon could subdivide and compartmentalize at need into smaller and smaller units, trillions of units of intelligence gathering and shifting like clouds of sand. I supposed only the tiniest part of one of Her lesser moons was occupied with testing me. And yet I was given to understand that, paradoxically, all of Her was in some small way inside my brain, as I was inside hers. When I joked about the strange topologies involved in this paradox, Her thoughts drowned out my own:

You are like the Tycho, but you are playful where he is savage.

—Am I? Sometimes I don't know who I am.

You are that you are. You are a man open to possibilities.

—Others used to say I thought too many things were possible. A wise man knows his limits, they said.

Others have not survived the Test of Realities.

I was delighted that I would have to suffer no more alien realities and more than a little pleased with myself, a pleasure lasting no longer than it took for me to draw in a breath of air.

There will be one last test.

—What test?

Call it the Test of Fate.

The air in front of me flickered, and there appeared an imago of a tall woman wearing a white robe. Her straight black hair shined and smelled of snow dahlia. When she turned to me, I could not take my eyes off her face. It was a face I knew well, the aquiline nose and high cheeks and most of all, the dark, smoothly scarred hollows where the eyes should have been; it was the face of my beautiful Katharine.

I was angry that the Entity would pull this most private memory from my mind. When Katharine smiled at me and bowed her head slightly, I hoped that the Entity would not overhear the words to an ancient poem which formed unspoken on my lips:

> *I love, pale one, your lifted eyebrows bridging*
> *   Twin darknesses of flowing depth.*
> *But however deep they are, they carry me*
> *   Another way than that of death.*

* * *

In a voice mysterious and deep, a voice which was a weird blend of Katharine's compassionate forebodings and the calculated words of the Entity, the imago tensed her lips and said, "There is another way, my Mallory, than that of death. I'm glad you like poetry."

"What is the Test of Fate?" I asked aloud.

As I stared into the caverns beneath her black eyebrows, flickers of color brightened the twin darknesses. At first I thought it was merely an aberration of the imago's phased light waves. Then the wavering blueness coalesced and stilled, filling her vacant eyepits as water fills a cup. She blinked her newly grown eyes, which were large and deep and shined like liquefied jewels. She looked at me with those lovely, blue-black eyes and said, "Because of you, I renounce the greater vision for . . . Do you see your fate? Now I have eyes again I'm blind, and I truly can't see what will . . . Your face, you're splendid! I'd preserve you if I could! If only . . . the Test of Fate; the Test of Whimsy or Caprice. I will recite words from three ancient poems. If you can complete the unfinished stanzas, then the light burns on."

"But that's absurd! Should my life depend on my knowing a stupid poem, then?"

I chewed the edges of the mustache that had grown over my lip during my long journey. I was furious that my fate—my life, my death—should be decided by so arbitrary a test. It made no sense. Then I remembered that the warrior-poets, that sect of assassins which infect certain of the Civilized Worlds, were rumored to ask their victims the lines of a poem before they murdered them. I wondered why the goddess would practice the custom of the warrior-poets? Or perhaps She had originated the custom eons ago, and the warrior-poets worshipped Her and all Her practices? How could I know?

"And the Tycho," I said. I ground my teeth. "He didn't know any of your poems, did he?"

Katharine smiled the mysterious smile of the scryers as she shook her head. "Oh, no, he knew each poem but the last, of course. He chose his fate, do you see?"

I did not see. I was rubbing my dry, hot eyes, trying to understand when she sighed and said in a sad voice:

The many men, so beautiful!
And they all dead did lie:

She looked at me as if she expected me to immediately
complete the stanza. I could not. My chest was suddenly
tight, my breathing ragged and uneven. Like a snowfield, my
mind was barren.

The many men, so beautiful!
And they all dead did lie:

I was empty and sick because I knew I had "read" those
words before. They were from a long poem three quarters of
the way through the Timekeeper's book. I closed my eyes,
and I saw on page nine hundred and ten the title of the
poem. It was called, "The Rhyme of the Ancient Pilot." It was
a poem of life and death and redemption. I tried to summon
from my memory the long sequences of black letters, to
superimpose them against the white snowfield of my mind,
even as the poet had once written them across white sheets of
paper. I failed. Although at Borja, along with the other
novices, I had cross-trained in the remembrancers' art (and
various others), I was no remembrancer. I lamented, and not
for the first time, that I did not possess that perfect "memory
of pictures" in which any image beheld by the living eye can
be summoned at will and displayed before the mind's eye,
there to be viewed and studied in vivid and varicolored
detail.

Katharine's skin took on the texture of Urradeth marble as
she said, "I shall repeat the line one more time. You must
answer or . . ." She put her hand to her throat, and in a voice
as clear as Resa's evening bell, she recited:

The many men, so beautiful!
and they all dead did lie:

I remembered then that the Timekeeper had told me I
should read his book until I could hear the poems in my
heart. I closed my mind's eye to the confusion of twisting
black letters I was struggling to see. The remembrancers
teach that there are many ways to memory. All is recorded,
they say; nothing is forgotten. I listened to the music and

rhyme of Katharine's poem fragment. Immediately distinct words sounded within, and I repeated what my heart had heard:

The many men, so beautiful!
And they all dead did lie:
And a thousand slimy things
Lived on; and so did I.

The Katharine imago smiled as if she were pleased. I had to remind myself that she wasn't really Katharine at all, but only the Entity's recreation of Katharine. Or rather, she was my imperfect *memory* sucked from my mind. I realized that I knew only a hundredth part of the real Katharine. I knew her long, hard hands and the depths between her legs, and that she had a submerged, burning need for beauty and pleasure (to her, I think, they were the same thing); I knew the sound of her dulcet voice as she sang her sad, fey songs, but I could not look into her soul. Like all scryers she had been taught to smother her passions and fears within a wet blanket of outer calm. I did not know what lay beneath, and even if I had known, who was I to think I could hold the soul of a woman within me? I could not, and because I could not, the imago of Katharine created from my memory was subtly wrong. Where the real Katharine was provocative, her imago was playful; where Katharine loved poems and visions of the future for their own sake, her imago used them for other purposes. At the core of the imago was a vast but not quite omniscient entity playing with the flesh and personality of a human being; at the core of Katharine was . . . well, Katharine.

I was still angry, so I angrily said, "I don't want to play this riddle game."

Katharine smiled again and said, "Oh, but there are two more poems."

"You must know which poems I'll know and which I won't."

"No," she said, "I can't see . . . I don't know."

"You must know," I repeated.

"Can't I choose to know what I want to know and what I don't? I love suspense, my Mallory."

"It's foreordained, isn't it?"

"Everything is foreordained. What has been will be."

"Scryer talk."

"I'm a scryer, you know."

"You're a goddess, and you've already determined the outcome of this game."

"Nothing is determined; in the end we choose our futures."

I made a fist and said, "How I hate scryer talk and your seemingly profound paradoxes!"

"Yet you revel in your mathematical paradoxes."

"That's different."

She held her flattened hand over her luminous eyes for a long moment as if their own interior light burned her. Then she said, "We continue. This simple poem was written by an ancient scryer who could not have known the Vild would explode:"

> *Stars, I have seen them fall,*
> *But when they drop and die . . .*

And I replied:

> *No star is lost at all,*
> *From all the star-sown sky.*

"But the stars *are* lost, aren't they?" I said. "The Vild grows, and no one knows why."

"Something," she said, "must be done to stop the Vild from exploding. How unpoetic it would be if all the stars died!"

I brushed my hair out of my eyes and asked the question occupying some of the finest minds of our Order, "Why is the Vild exploding?"

Katharine's imago smiled and said, "If you know the lines to this next poem, you may ask me why, or ask me anything you'd like . . . Oh, the poem! It's so pretty!" She clapped her hands together like a little girl delighted to give her friend a birthday gift. And words I knew well filled the air:

> *Tyger! Tyger! burning bright*
> *In the forests of the night,*

I was free! The Solid State Entity, through the lips of a

simple hologram, had spoken the first two lines of my favorite poem, and I was free. I had only to repeat the next line, and I would be free to ask Her how a pilot could escape from an infinite tree. (I never doubted She would keep Her promise to answer my questions; why this is so I cannot say.) I laughed as beads of sweat formed up on my forehead. I recited:

Tyger! Tyger! burning bright
In the forests of the night,
What immortal hand or eye
Could frame thy fearful symmetry?

"It is important," I said, "to rhyme 'symmetry' with 'eye.'" I laughed because I was as happy as I had ever been before. (It is strange how release from the immediate threat of death can produce such euphoria. I have this advice to offer our Order's old, jaded academicians so bored with their daily routines: Place your lives at risk for a single night, and every moment of the next day will vibrate with the sweet music of life.)

Katharine's imago was watching me. There was something infinitely appealing about her, something almost impossible to describe. I thought that this Katharine was at peace with herself and her universe in a way that the real Katharine could never be.

And then she closed her eyes and said, "No, that is wrong. I gave you the lines to the poem's last stanza, not the first."

It is possible that my heart stopped beating for a few moments. In a panic, I said, "But the first stanza is identical to the last."

"No, it is not. The first three lines of either stanza are identical. The fourth lines differ by a single word."

"In that case, then," I asked, "how was I to know which stanza you were reciting? Since, if the first three lines are identical, so are the first two?"

"This is not the Test of Knowledge," she said. "It is the Test of Caprice, as I have said. However, it is *my* caprice," and here she smiled, "that you be given another chance." And, as her eyes radiated from burning cobalt to bright indigo, she repeated:

Tyger! Tyger! burning bright
In the forests of the night,

I was lost. I clearly—very clearly, as clearly as if I *did* possess the memory of pictures—I remembered every letter and word of this strange poem. I had recited correctly; the first and last stanza *were* identical. And I heard again:

Tyger! Tyger! burning bright
In the forests of the night,
What immortal hand or eye . . .

"What is the last line, Mallory? The one the poet wrote, not the one printed in your book."

I wondered if the ancient academicians, in their transcribing the poem from book to book (or from book to computer), had made a mistake? Perhaps the mistake had occurred during the last days of the holocaust century. It seemed likely that some ancient historian, in her hurry to preserve such a treasure before the marrow-death rotted her bones, had carelessly altered a single (though vital) word. Or perhaps the mistake had been made during the confusion of the swarming centuries; perhaps some revisionist, for whatever reason, had objected to the single word and had changed it.

However the mistake had been made, I needed desperately to discover—or remember—what the original word had been. I tried my little trick of listening for the words in my heart, but there was nothing. I applied other remembrancing techniques—all in vain. Far better that I should guess which word had been changed and pick at random a word—any word—to replace it. At least there would be a probability, a tiny probability, that I might pick the right word.

Katharine, with her eyes tightly closed, licked her lips then asked, "What is the last line, Mallory? Tell me now, or must I prepare a pocket of my brain in which to copy yours?"

It was the Timekeeper who saved me from the Entity's caprice. In my frustration and despair, as I ground my teeth, I happened to think of him, perhaps to revile him for giving me a book full of mistakes. I remembered him reciting the poem. At last, I heard the words in my heart. Had the Timekeeper spoken the true poem? And if he had, how had he known the more ancient version? There was something

very suspicious, even mysterious, about the Timekeeper.
How had he even chanced to speak the same poem as the
goddess? Had he, as a young man, journeyed into the heart
of the Entity and been asked the very same poem? The
poem, which had passed from his mouth like a growl, was
indeed different from the poem in the book, and it differed
by a single word.

I clasped my hands together, took a deep breath, and said:

Tyger! Tyger! burning bright
In the forests of the night,
What immortal hand or eye
Dare *frame thy fearful symmetry?*

"*Dare* frame," I repeated. "That's the altered word, isn't
it? *Dare* frame."

The imago of Katharine remained silent as she opened her
eyes.

"Isn't it?"

And then she smiled and whispered:

'Tis evening on the moorland free,
The starlit wave is still.
Home is the sailor from the sea,
The hunter from the hill.

"Goodbye, my Mallory. Who dares frame *thy* fearful
symmetry? Not I."

As soon as she said this her hologram vanished from the
pit of my ship, and I was alone. Oh, where, oh, where, I
wondered, does the light go when the light goes out?

You are almost home, my sailor, my hunter of knowledge.

—The poem . . . I remembered it correctly, then?

You may ask me three questions.

I had passed Her tests and I was free. Free!—this time I
was certain I was free! In my mind, one hundred questions
danced, like the tease of a troupe of scantily dressed Jacarandan
courtesans: Is the universe open or closed? What was the
origin of the primeval singularity? Can any even number
be expressed as the sum of two prime numbers? Had my
mother really tried to kill Soli? How old was the Timekeeper,

really? Why was the Vild exploding? *Where does the light go when . . . ?*

The light goes out.

—That was not my question. I was just thinking . . . wondering how—

Ask your questions.

It seemed I had to be very careful in asking my questions, else the Entity might play games with me. I thought for a long time before asking a question whose answer might hint at many other mysteries. I licked my dry teeth and asked aloud a question which had bothered me since I was a boy: "Why is there a universe at all; why is there *something* rather than nothing?"

That I would like to know, too.

I was angry that She hadn't answered my question, so without thinking very carefully I blurted out, "Why is the Vild exploding?"

Are you certain this is what you really want to know? What would it profit you to discover the "why," if you do not know how to stop the Vild from exploding? Perhaps you should recast your question.

—All right, how can I—can anyone—stop the Vild from exploding?

Presently, you cannot. The secret of healing the Vild is part of the higher secret. You must discover this higher secret by yourself.

More riddles! More games! Would She answer any of my questions simply, without posing riddles? I did not think so. Like a Trian merchant-queen guarding her jewels, She seemed determined to guard Her precious wisdom. Half in humor, half in despair, I said, "The message of the Ieldra—they spoke in riddles, too. They said the secret of man's immortality lay in the past and in the future. What did they mean? Exactly where can this secret be found?"

I did not really expect an answer, at least not an intelligible answer, so I was shaken to my bones when the godvoice sounded within me:

The secret is written within the oldest DNA of the human species.

—The oldest DNA of . . . what is that, then? And how can the secret be decoded? And why should it be—

You have asked your three questions.

—But you've answered with riddles!

Then you must solve your riddles.

—Solve them? To what end? I'll die with my solutions. There's no escaping an infinite tree, is there? How can I escape?

You should have thought to ask me that as your last question.

—Damn you and your games!

There is no escape from an infinite tree. But are you sure the tree is not finite?

Of course I was sure! Wasn't a pilot weened on the Gallivare mapping theorems? Hadn't I proved that the Lavi set could not be embedded in an invariant space? Didn't I know an infinite tree from a finite one?

Have you examined your proof?

I had not examined my proof. I did not like to think that there could be a flaw in my proof. But neither did I want to die, so I faced my ship-computer. I entered the thoughtspace of the manifold. Instantly there was a rush of crystal ideoplasts in my mind, and I began building the symbols into a proof array. While the number storm swirled, I made a mathematical model of the manifold. The manifold opened before me. Deep in dreamtime, I reconstructed my proof. It was true, the Lavi set could *not* be embedded in an invariant space. Then a thought occurred to me as if from nowhere: Was the Lavi set the correct set to model the branchings of the tree? What if the tree could be modeled by a *simple* Lavi set? Could the simple Lavi set be embedded in an invariant space?

I was trembling with anticipation as I built up a new proof array. Yes, the simple Lavi could be embedded! I proved it could be embedded. I wiped sweat from my forehead, and I made a probability mapping. Instantly the trillions of branches of the tree narrowed to one. So, it was a finite tree after all. I was saved! I made another mapping to the point-exit near a blue giant star. I fell out into realspace, into the swarm of the ten thousand moon-brains of the Solid State Entity.

You please me, my Mallory. But we will meet again when you please me more. Until then, fall far, Pilot, and farewell.

To this day I wonder at the nature of the original tree imprisoning me. Had it *really* been a finite tree? Or had the Entity somehow—impossibly—changed an infinite tree into a finite one? If so, I thought, then She truly was a goddess worthy of worship. Or at least She was worthy of dread and terror. After looking out on the warm blue light of the sun, I was so full of both these emotions that I made the first of the many mappings back to Neverness. Though I burned with strange feelings and unanswered questions, I had no intention of ever meeting Her again. I never again wanted to be tested or have my life depend upon chance and the whimsy of a goddess. Never again did I want to hear the godvoice violating my mind. I wanted, simply, to return home, to drink skotch with Bardo in the bars of the Farsider's Quarter, to tell the eschatologists and Leopold Soli, and the whole city, that the secret of life was written within the oldest DNA of man.

6

The Image of Man

For us, humanity was a distant goal toward which all men were moving, whose image no one knew, whose laws were nowhere written down.
— Emil Sinclair, Holocaust Century
Eschatologist

My homecoming was as glorious as I hoped it would be, marred only by Leopold Soli's absence from the City. He was off mapping the outer veil of the Vild, so he could not appreciate my triumph. He was not present in the Lightship Caverns with the other pilots, cetics, tinkers and horologes as I emerged from the pit of my ship. How I wish he had seen them lined up on the dark, steel walkway along the row of ships, to see their shocked faces and listen to their furious, excited whispers when I announced that I had spoken with a goddess! Would he have clapped his hands and bowed his head to me as even the most skeptical and jaded of the master pilots did? Would he have honored me with a handshake, as did Stephen Caraghar and Tomoth and his other friends?

It was too bad he wasn't there when Bardo broke from the line of pilots and stomped towards me with such reckless enthusiasm that the whole walkway shook and rang like a bell. It was quite a moment. Bardo threw out his huge arms and bellowed, "Mallory! By God, I knew you couldn't be killed!" His voice filled the Caverns like an exploding bomb, and he suddenly whirled to address the pilots. "How many times these past days have I said it? Mallory's the greatest pilot since Rollo Gallivare! Greater than Rollo Gallivare, by

God if he isn't!" He looked straight at Tomoth who was watching his antics with his hideous, mechanical eyes. "*You* say he's lost in dreamtime? *I* say he's schooning, scurfing the veils of the manifold, and he'll return when he's damn ready. *You* say he's lost in an infinite loop, snared by that bitch of a goddess called the Solid State Entity? *I* say he's kleining homeward, tunneling with elegance and fortitude, returning to his friends with a discovery that will make him a master pilot. Tell me, was I right? Master Mallory—how I like the sound of it! By God, Little Fellow, by God!"

He came over to me and gave me a hug that nearly cracked my ribs, all the while thumping my back and repeating, "By God, Little Fellow, by God!"

The pilots and professionals swarmed around me, shaking hands and asking me questions. Justine, dressed sleekly in woolens and a new black fur, touched my forehead and bowed. "Look at him!" she said to my mother, who was weeping unashamedly. (I felt like weeping myself.) "If only Soli could be here!"

My mother forced her way through the swarm, and we touched each other's forehead. She surprised me, saying, "I'm so tired. Of these formal politenesses." Then she kissed me on the lips and hugged me. "You're too thin," she said as she dried her eyes on the back of her gloves. She arched her bushy eyebrows and wrinkled her nose, sniffing. "As thin as a harijan. And you stink. Come see me. When you've shaved and bathed and the akashics are through with you. I'm so happy."

"We're all happy," Lionel said as he bowed, slightly. Then he snapped his head suddenly, flinging his blonde hair from his eyes. "And I suppose we're fascinated with these words of your goddess. The secret of life written in the oldest DNA of man—what do you suppose She meant by that? What, after all, is the oldest DNA?"

Even as the akashics dragged my grimy, bearded, emaciated body off to their chamber to de-program me, I had a sudden notion of what this oldest DNA might be. Like a seed it germinated inside me; the notion quickly sprouted into an idea, and the idea began growing into the wildest of plans. Had Soli been there I might have blurted out my wild plan just to see the frown on his cold face. But he was off trying to penetrate the warped, starblown spaces of the Vild, and he probably thought I was long dead, if he thought about me at all.

I was not dead, though, I was far from dead. I was wonderfully, joyfully alive. Despite the manifold's ravaging my poor body, despite the separation from my ship and the return to downtime, I was full of confidence and success, as cocky as a man can be. I felt invincible, as if I were floating on a cool wind. The cetics call this feeling the testosterone high, because when a man is successful in his endeavors, his body floods with this potent hormone. They warn against the effects of testosterone. Testosterone makes men too aggressive, they say, and aggressive men grasp for success and generate ever more testosterone the more successful they become. It is a nasty cycle. They say testosterone can poison a man's brain and color his judgments. I believe this is true. I should have paid more attention to the cetics and their teachings. If I hadn't been so full of myself, if I hadn't been so swollen with tight veins and racing blood and hubris, I probably would have immediately dismissed my wild plan to discover the oldest DNA of the human race. As it was, I could hardly wait to win Bardo and the rest of the Order over to my plan, to bathe myself in ever more and greater glory.

During the next few days I had little time to think about my plan because the akashics and other professionals kept me busy. Nikolos the Elder, the Lord Akashic, examined in detail my every memory from the moment I had left Neverness. He copied the results in his computers. There were mechanics who questioned me about the black bodies and other phenomena I had encountered within the Entity. They were properly impressed—astounded is a more accurate word—when they learned that She had the power to change the shape of the manifold as She pleased. A few of the older mechanics did not believe my story, not even when the cetics and akashics agreed that my memories were not illusory but the result of events that really happened. The mechanics, of course, had known for ages that any model of reality must include consciousness as a fundamental waveform. But Marta Rutherford and Minima Jons, among others, refused to believe the Entity could create and uncreate an infinite tree at will. They fell into a vicious argument with Kolenya Mor and a couple of other eschatologists who seemed more interested that people lived within the Entity than they were in the esoterics of physics. The furor and petty antagonisms that my discoveries provoked among the professionals amused me. I was pleased that the programmers, neologicians, historians, even the holists, would have much to talk about for a long time to come.

I was curious when the master horologe, with the aid of a furtive-looking young programmer, read the memory of the ship-computer and opened the sealed ship's clock. Although there is a prohibition against immediately telling a returning pilot how much inner time has elapsed, it is almost always ignored. I learned that I had aged, intime, five years and forty-three days. (And eight hours, ten minutes, thirty-two seconds.) "What day is it?" I asked. And the horologe told me that it was the twenty-eighth day of midwinter spring in the year 2930. On Neverness, little more than half a year had passed. I was five years older, then, while Katharine had only aged a tenth as much. Crueltime, I thought, you can't conquer crueltime. I hoped the differential ticking of Katharine's and my internal clocks would not be as cruel to us as it had been to Justine and Soli.

Later that day—it was the day after my return—I was summoned to the Timekeeper's Tower. The Timekeeper, who seemed not to have aged at all, bade me sit in the ornate chair near the glass windows. He paced about the bright room, digging his red slippers into the white fur of his rugs, all the while looking me over as I listened to the ticking of his clocks. "You're so thin," he said. "My horologes tell me there was much slowtime, too damn much slowtime. How many times have I warned you against the slowtime?"

"There were many bad moments," I said. "I had to think like light, as you say. If I hadn't used slowtime, I'd be dead."

"The accelerations have wasted your body."

"I'll spend the rest of the season skating, then. And eating. My body will recover."

"I'm thinking of your mind, not your body," he said. He made a fist and massaged the knuckles. "So, your mind, your brain, is five years older."

"Cells can always be made young again," I said.

"You think so?"

I did not want to argue the effects of the manifold's time distortions with him so I fidgeted in my hard chair and said, "Well, it's good to be home."

He rubbed his wrinkled neck and said, "I'm proud of you, Mallory. You're famous now, eh? Your career is made. There's talk of making you a master pilot, did you know that?"

In truth, my fellow pilots such as Bardo and the Sonderval had talked of little else since my return. Even Lionel, who had once despised my impulsive bragging, confided to me that my elevation to the College of Masters was almost certain.

"A great discovery," the Timekeeper said. He ran his fingers back through his thick white hair. "I'm very pleased."

In truth, I did not think he was pleased at all. Oh, perhaps he was pleased to see me again, to rumple my hair as he had when I was a boy, but I did not think he was at all pleased with my sudden fame and popularity. He was a jealous man, a man who would suffer no challenge to his preeminence among the women and men of our Order.

"Without your book of poems," I said, "I would be worse than dead." I told him, then, everything that had happened to me on my journey. He did not seem at all impressed with the powers of the Entity.

"So, the poems. You learned them well?"

"Yes, Timekeeper."

"Ahhh." He smiled, resting his scarred hand on my shoulder. His face was fierce, hard to read. He seemed at once kindly and aggrieved, as if he could not decide whether giving me the book of poems had been the right thing to do.

He stood above me and I looked at my reflection in his black eyes. I asked the question burning in my mind. "How could you know the Entity would ask me to recite the poems? And the poems She asked—two of them were poems you had recited to me!"

He grimaced and said, "So, I couldn't know. I guessed."

"But you must have known the Entity plays riddle games with ancient poetry. How could you possibly know that?"

He squeezed my shoulder hard; his fingers were like clutching, wooden roots. "Don't question me, damn you! Have you forgotten your manners?"

"I'm not the only one who has questions. The akashics and others, everyone will wonder how you knew."

"Let them wonder."

Once, when I was twelve years old, the Timekeeper had

taught me that secret knowledge is power. He was a man who kept secrets. During the hours of our talk, he secretively moved about the room giving me no opportunity to ask him questions about his past or anything else. He ordered coffee and drank it standing as he shifted from foot to foot. Frequently, he would pace to the window and stare out at the buildings of the Academy, all the while shaking his head and clenching his jaws. Perhaps he longed to confide his secrets with me (or with anybody)—I do not know. He looked like a strong, vital animal confined within a trap. Indeed, there were some who said that he never left his tower because he feared the world of rocketing sleds and fast ice and murderous men. But I did not believe this. I had heard other gossip: a drunken horologe who claimed the Timekeeper kept a double to attend to the affairs of the Order while he took to the streets at night, hunting like a lone wolf down the glissades for anyone so foolish as to plot against him. It was even rumored that he left the City for long periods of time; some said he kept his own lightship hidden within the Caverns. Had he duplicated my discoveries a lifetime ago and kept the secrets to himself? I thought it was possible. He was a fearless man too full of life not to have needed fresh wind against his face, the glittering crystals of the number storm, the cold, stark beauty of the stars at midnight. He, a lover of life, had once told me that the moments of a man's life were too precious to waste sleeping. Thus he practiced his discipline of sleeplessness, and he paced as his muscles knotted and relaxed, knotted and relaxed; he paced during the bright hours of the day, and he paced all the long night driven by adrenalin and caffeinated blood and by his need to see and hear and be.

I felt a rare pang of pity for him (and for myself for having to endure his petty inquisitions), and I said, "You look worried."

It was the wrong thing to say. The Timekeeper hated pity, and more, he despised pitiers, especially when they pitied themselves. "Worry! What do you know of worry! After you've listened to the mechanics petition me to send an expedition into the Entity's nebula, then you may speak to me of worry, damn you!"

"What do you mean?"

"So, I mean Marta Rutherford and her faction would have

me mount a *major* expedition! She wants me to send a deepship into the Entity! As if I can afford to lose a deepship and a thousand professionals! They think that because you were lucky, they'll be, too. And already, the eschatologists are demanding that if there *is* an expedition, *they* should lead it."

I squeezed the arms of the chair and said, "I'm sorry my discovery has caused so many problems." I was not sorry at all, really. I was delighted that my discovery—along with Soli's—had provoked the usually staid professionals of our Order into action.

"Discovery?" he growled out. "What discovery?" He walked over to the window and silently shook his fist at the gray storm clouds drifting over the City from the south. He didn't like the cold, I remembered, and he hated snow.

"The Entity . . . She said the secret of life—"

"The secret of life! You believe the lying words of that lying mainbrain? Goddledygook! There's no secret to be found in 'man's oldest DNA,' whatever *that* might be. There's no secret, do you understand? The secret of life is life: It goes on and on, and that's all there is."

As if to punctuate his pessimism, just then the low, hollow bell of one of his clocks chimed, and he said, "It's New Year on Urradeth. They'll be killing all the marrow-sick babies born this past year, and they'll drink, and they'll couple all day and all night until the wombs of all the women are full again. On and on it goes, on and on."

I told him I thought the Entity had spoken the truth.

He laughed harshly, causing the weathered skin around his eyes to crack like sheets of broken ice. "Struth!" he said bitterly, a word I took to be one of his archaisms. "A god's truth, a god's lies—what's the difference?"

I told him I had a plan to discover man's oldest DNA.

He laughed again; he laughed so hard his lips pulled back over his long white teeth and tears flowed from his eyes. "So, a plan. Even as a boy, you always had plans. Do you remember when I taught you slowtime? When I said that one must be patient and *wait* for the first waves of adagio to overtake the mind, you told me there had to be a way to slow time by skipping the normal sequence of attitudes. You even had a plan to enter slowtime without the aid of your ship-computer! And why? You had a *problem* with patience. And you still do. Can't you wait to see if the splicers and imprimaturs—

or the eschatologists, historians or cetics—can discover this oldest DNA? Isn't it enough you'll probably be made a master pilot?"

I rubbed the side of my nose and said, "If I petition you to mount a small expedition of my own, would you approve it?"

"Petition me?" he asked. "Why so formal? Why not just ask me?"

"Because," I said slowly, "I'd have to break one of the covenants."

"So."

There was a long silence during which he stood as still as an ice sculpture.

"Well, Timekeeper?"

"Which covenant do you want to break?"

"The eighth covenant," I said.

"So," he said again, staring out the window to the west. The eighth covenant was the agreement made three thousand years ago between the founders of Neverness and the primitive Alaloi who lived in their caves six hundred miles to the west of the City.

"They're neandertals," I said. "Cavemen. Their culture, their bodies . . . so old."

"You'd petition me to journey to the Alaloi, to collect tissues from their living bodies?"

"The oldest DNA of man," I said. "Isn't it ironic that I might find it so close to home?"

When I told him the exact nature of my plan, he leaned over and gripped my wrists, resting his weight on the arms of the chair. His massive head was too close to mine; I smelled coffee and blood on his breath. He said, "It's a damn dangerous plan, for you and for the Alaloi, too."

"Not so dangerous," I said too confidently. "I'll take precautions. I'll be careful."

"*Dangerous*, I say! Damn dangerous."

"Will you approve my petition?" I asked.

He looked at me painfully, as if he were making the most difficult decision of his life. I did not like the look on his face.

"Timekeeper?"

"I'll consider your plan," he said coldly. "I'll inform you of my decision."

I looked away from him and turned my head to the side.

It was not like him to be so indecisive. I guessed that he agonized between breaking the covenant and fulfilling his own summons to quest; I guessed wrongly. It would be years, however, before I discovered the secret of his indecision.

He dismissed me abruptly. When I stood up, I discovered the edge of the chair had cut off my circulation; my legs were tingly and numb. As I rubbed the life back into my muscles, he stood by the window talking to himself. He seemed not to notice I was still there. "On and on it goes," he said in a low voice. "On and on and on."

I left his chamber feeling as I always did: exhausted, elated and confused.

The days (and nights) that followed were the happiest of my life. I spent my mornings out on the broad glissades watching farsiders fight the thick, midwinter snows. It was a pleasure to breathe fresh air again, to smell pine needles and baking bread and alien scents, to skate down the familiar streets of the City. There were long afternoons of coffee and conversation with my friends in the cafes lining the white ice of the Way. During the first of these afternoons, Bardo and I sat at a little table by the steamed-over window, watching the swarms of humanity pass while we traded stories of our journeys. I sipped my cinnamon coffee and asked for the news of Delora wi Towt and Quirin and Li Tosh and our other fellow pilots. Most of them, Bardo told me, were spread through the galaxy like a handful of diamonds cast into the nighttime sea. Only Li Tosh and the Sonderval and a few others had returned from their journeys.

"Haven't you heard?" he asked, and he ordered a plate of cookies. "Li Tosh has discovered the homeworld of the Darghinni. In another age it would have been a notable discovery, a great discovery, even. Ah, but it was his bad luck to take his vows at the same time as Mallory Ringess." He dunked his cookie in his coffee. "And," Bardo said, "it was Bardo's bad luck to take them then, too."

"What do you mean?"

As he munched his cookies, he told me the story of his journey: After fenestering to the edge of the Rosette Nebula, he had tried to bribe the encyclopaedists on Ksandaria to allow him into their holy sanctum. Because the secretive encyclopaedists were known to be jealous of their vast and precious pools of knowledge, and because they hated and feared the power of the Order, he had disguised himself as a prince of Summerworld, for him not a very difficult thing to do.

"One hundred maunds of Yarkona bluestars I paid those filthy tubists to enter their sanctum," he said. "And even at that skin price—you'll forgive me, my friend, if I admit that, despite our vow of poverty, I had hoarded a part, just a small part of my inheritance—ah, now where was I? Yes, the encyclopaedists. Even though they gouged a fortune from me, they kept me from their sanctum, thinking that an ignorant buffoon such as I would be content to fill my head from one of their lesser pools of esoterica. Well, it did take me a good twentyday before I realized the information I was swallowing was as shallow as a melt puddle, but I'm not stupid, am I? No, I'm not stupid, so I told the wily master encyclopaedist I'd hire a warrior-poet to poison him if he didn't open the gates to the inner sanctum. He believed me, the fool, and so I dipped my brain into their forbidden pool where they keep the ancient histories and Old Earth's oldest commentaries. And . . ."

Here he paused to sip his coffee and munch a few more cookies.

"And I'm tired of telling this story because I've had my brains sucked dry by our akashics and librarians, but since you're my best friend, well, you should know I found an arcanum in the forbidden pool that led right to the guts of the past, or so I thought. On Old Earth just before the Swarming, I think, there was a curious religious order called arkaeologists. They practiced a bizarre ritual known as "The Diggings." Shall I tell you more? Well, the priests and priestesses of this order employed armies of slave-acolytes to painstakingly sift layers of dirt for buried fragments of clay and other relics of the past. Arkaeologists—and this was the prime datum from the forbidden pool—were, and I quote: 'Those followers of Henrilsheman believing in ancestor veneration. They believed that communion with the spirit world could be made by collecting objects which their ancestors had touched and in some cases, by collecting the corpses of the ancestors themselves.' Ah, would you like more coffee? No? Well, the arkaeologists, like all orders, I suppose, had been riven into many different factions and sects. One sect—I think they

were called aigyptologists—followed the teachings of one
Flinders Petr and the Champollion. Another sect dug up
corpses preserved with bitumen. Then they pounded the
corpses to a powder. This powder—would you believe it?
—they consumed it as a sacrament, believing as they did that
the life essence of their ancestors would strengthen their
own. When generation had passed into generation, on and
on, as the Timekeeper would say, well, they thought eventually man would be purified and they'd be immortal. Am I
boring you? I hope not because I must tell you of this one
sect whose high priests called themselves kurators. Just before the third exchange of the holocaust, the kurators, and
their underlings, the daters, sorters and the lowly acolytes,
they loaded a museum ship with old stones and bones and
the preserved corpses of their ancestors that they called
mumiyah. It was their ship—they named it the *Vishnu*—
which landed on one of the Darghinni worlds. Of course, the
kurators were too ignorant to recognize intelligent aliens
when they saw them. Sad to say, they began delving into the
dirt of that ancient civilization. They couldn't have known the
Darghinni have a horror of their own past—as well they
should. And *that*, my friend, is how the first of the Man-
Darghinni wars really began."

We drank our coffee and talked about this shameful,
unique war—the only war there had ever been between
mankind and an alien race. When I congratulated him on
making a fine discovery, he banged the table with his fat hand
and said, "I haven't finished my story! I hope you're not
bored because I was just about to tell you the climax of my
little adventure. Well, after my success with the encyclopaedists—
yes, yes, I admit I was successful—I was filled with joy. 'The
secret of man's immortality lies in our past and in our
future'—that was the Ieldra's message, wasn't it? Well, I'm
not a scryer, so what can I say about the future? But the past,
ah, well, I thought I'd discovered a vital link with the past.
And as it happens, I have. My mumiyah may prove to contain
some very old DNA, what do you think? Anyway, the climax:
I was so full of joy, I rushed home to Neverness. I wanted to
be the first to return with a significant discovery, you see. You
must visualize it: I would have been famous. The novices
would have stumbled over each other for the privilege of
touching my robes. Master courtesans would have paid *me* for

the pleasure of discovering what kind of man lives beneath these robes. How pungent my life would have been! But Bardo grew careless! In my hurry through the windows, I grew careless."

I will not record all of my friend's words here. In short, while fenestering through the dangerous Danladi thinspace he made a mistake that would have made the youngest of journeymen blush. In his mapping of the decision-group onto itself, he neglected to show the function was one-to-one, so he fell into a loop. Now any other pilot would have laboriously searched for a sequence of mappings to extricate himself from the loop. But Bardo was lazy and did not want to spend a hundred or more days of intime searching for such a mapping. He had an idea as to how he might instantly escape the loop, this lazy but brilliant man, and he played with his idea. After a mere seven hours of intime, he tasted the pungent fruit of genius. He proved that a mapping of points present to points past always exists, that a pilot could always return to any point along his immediate path. Moreover, it was a constructive proof; that is to say, not only did he prove such a mapping existed, he showed how such a mapping could be constructed. Thus he made a mapping with the star just beyond Ksandaria's. He fell out into the fallaways, into the familiar spaces he had recently passed through. And then he journeyed homeward to Neverness.

"I'm sought after, now," he laughed out. "It's ironic: I, in my stupidity, I stumbled into a loop but I've proved the greatest of the lesser unproved theorems. Bardo's Boomerang Theorem—that's what the journeymen have named my little mapping theorem. There's even talk of elevating me to a mastership, did you know that? I, Bardo, master pilot! Yes, I'm sought after now, by Kolenya and others with their luscious lips and beautiful, fat thighs. My seed flows like magma, my friend. I'm famous! Ah, but not as famous as you, eh?"

We talked all afternoon until the light died from the gray sky and the cafe filled with hungry people. We ordered a huge meal of cultured meats and the various exotic dishes favored by Bardo. He poked his finger into my ribs and said, "You've no meat on your skinny bones!" He praised me again for my discovery, and then I told him about my new plan.

"You want to do *what*?" he said, wiping meat jelly from

his lips with a cloth. "To journey to the Alaloi and steal their DNA? That's slelling, isn't it?" Realizing he had spoken that awful word too loudly, he looked around at the other diners and lowered his voice conspirationally. He leaned across the table, "We can't go slelling the Alaloi's DNA, can we?"

"It's not really slelling," I said. "It's not as if we'd use their DNA to tailor poisons or clone them or—"

"Slelling is slelling," he interrupted. "And what about the covenants? The Timekeeper would never allow it, thank God!"

"He might."

I told him about my petition, and he grew sullen and argumentative.

"By God, we can't just take a windjammer and land on one of their islands and ask them to drop their seed in a test tube, can we?"

"I have a different plan," I said.

"Oh, no, I don't think I want to hear this." He ate a few more cookies, wiped his lips and farted.

"We'll go to the Alaloi in disguise. It shouldn't be too hard to learn their customs and to scrape a few skin cells from the palms of their hands."

"Oh, no," he said. "Oh, too bad for Bardo, and too bad for you if you insist on this mad plan. And how do you think we could disguise ourselves? Oh, no please don't tell me, I've had enough of your plans."

I said, "There's a way. Do you remember the story of Goshevan? We'll do as he did. We'll go to a cutter and have our bodies sculpted. The Alaloi will think we are their cousins."

He farted again and belched. "That's insane! Please, Mallory, look at me and admit you know it's insane. By God, we can't become Alaloi, can we? And why should you think the Alaloi's DNA is older than any other? Shouldn't we concentrate our efforts on the main chance? Since I've discovered mumiyah from three thousand years before the Swarming, why don't we—you, I and Li Tosh, mount an expedition back to the Darghinni? After all, we *know* there are the remains of a museum ship on one of their worlds."

I coughed and I rubbed the side of my nose. I did not want to point out that as of yet, we had no idea where to look for the wreckage of the museum ship. I said, "The Alaloi DNA is probably fifty thousand years old."

"Is that true? We don't know anything about the Alaloi except that they're so stupid they don't even have a language!"

I smiled because he was being deliberately fatuous. I told him everything known about the Alaloi, those dreamers who had carked their humanness into neandertal flesh. According to the historians, the Alaloi's ancestors had hated the rot and vice of civilization, any civilization. Therefore, they had fled Old Earth in long ships. Because they wanted to live what they thought of as a natural life, they back-mutated some of their chromosomes, the better to grow strong, primitive children to live on the pristine worlds they hoped to discover. In one of their long ships, they carried the frozen body of a neandertal boy recovered from the ice of Tsibera, which was the northernmost continent of Old Earth. They had spliced strands of frozen DNA; with the boy's replicated DNA they performed their rituals and carked their germ cells with ancient chromosomes. Generations later, generations of experiment and breeding, the cavemen—to use the ancient, vulgar term—landed on Icefall. They destroyed their ships, fastened their hooded furs, and they went to live in the frozen forests of the Ten Thousand Islands.

"That's interesting," Bardo said. "But I'm bothered by one thing. Well, I'm bothered by everything you've said, of course, but there is one thing that bothers me stupendously about this whole scheme of searching for man's oldest DNA."

He ordered some coffee and drank it. He looked across the cafe at a pretty journeyman historian, and he began flirting with his eyes.

"Tell me, then," I said.

He reluctantly looked away, looked at me, and said, "What did the goddess mean that the secret of life is written in the oldest DNA of the human species? We must think very carefully about this. What did She mean by 'old'?"

"What do you mean, 'what did She mean by old?'"

He puffed his cheeks out and swore, "Damn you, why do you still answer my questions with questions? Old—what's old? Does one race of man have older DNA than another? How can one living human have older DNA than another?"

"You're splitting words like a semanticist," I said.

"No, I don't think I am." He removed his glove, fingered

his greasy nose and said, "The DNA in my skin is very old stuff, by God! Parts of the genome have been evolving for four billion years. Now that's *old*, I think, and if you want me to split words, I shall. What of the atoms that make up my DNA? Older still, I think, because they were made in the heart of stars ten billion years ago."

He scraped along the side of his nose and held out his finger. Beneath the long nail was a smear of grease and dead, yellow skin cells. "Here's your secret of life," he said. He seemed very pleased with himself, and he went back to flirting with the historian.

I knocked his hand aside and said, "I admit the Entity's words are something of a riddle. We'll have to solve the riddle, then."

"Ah, but I was never fond of riddles."

I caught his eyes and told him, "As you say, the genome has been evolving for billions of years. And therefore any of our ancestors' DNA is older than ours. This is how I'll define old, then. We'll have to start somewhere. The Alaloi have spliced DNA from a body fifty thousand years old into their own bodies. We can hope this DNA—and the message *in* the DNA—hasn't mutated or degraded."

"But the Alaloi are not our ancestors," he said.

"Yes, but the neandertals of Old Earth *were*."

"No, by God, they weren't even members of the human species! They were slack-jawed, stoop-shouldered brutes as dumb as dodos."

"You're wrong," I said. "Their brains were *larger* than those of modern man."

"Larger than *your* brain, perhaps," he said. He tapped his bulging forehead. "Not larger than Bardo's, no, I can't believe that."

"We evolved from them."

"Now there's a revolting thought. But I don't believe you. Does Bardo know his history? Yes, I think I do. But why should pilots argue history?" He held his head up, stroked his beard and looked at the historian. "Why not let an historian settle an historical argument?"

So saying, he excused himself, belched, stood up, brushed cookie crumbs from his beard and squeezed by the crowded tables. He approached the historian and said something to her. She laughed; she took his hand as he guided her back toward our table.

"May I present Estrella Domingo of Darkmoon." Estrella was a bright-looking journeyman and nicely fat, the way Bardo liked his women to be. He introduced me, then said, "Estrella has consented to resolve our argument." He pulled up a chair so she could sit down. He poured her a cup of coffee. "Now tell us, my young Estrella," he said. "Were neandertals *really* our ancestors?"

In truth, I do not think Bardo had any hope of winning his argument. After a while, it became obvious that he had invited this pretty, impressionable girl from Darkmoon to our table not to listen to a history lesson, but to seduce her. After she had patiently explained that there were different theories as to man's recent evolution and told him, yes, it was most likely that the neandertals *were* our direct ancestors, he exclaimed, "Ah, so my friend is right once again! But you must admit, it's too bad that man once looked like cavemen. They're so ugly, don't you agree?"

Estrella did not agree. She coyly observed that many women liked thick, muscular, hairy men. Which was one of the reasons it had become fashionable years ago for certain professionals to sculpt their bodies into the shape of Alaloi.

"Hmmm," Bardo said as he twisted his mustache, "that *is* interesting."

Estrella further observed that the difference between neandertals and modern man was not so great as most people thought. "If you look carefully," she said, "you can see neandertal genes in the faces of certain people on any street in any city on any planet of the Civilized Worlds." (As I have said, she was a nice, intelligent young woman, even if she had the irritating habit of stringing together too many prepositional phrases when she spoke.) "Even you, Master Bardo, with your thick browridges above your deepset eyes surrounded by such a fine beard—have you ever thought about this?"

"Ah, no, actually I never have. But it would be interesting to discuss the matter in greater detail, wouldn't it? We could scrutinize various parts of my anatomy and determine those parts which are the most primitive."

After Bardo and she had made plans "to discuss the

matter in greater detail," she returned to her table and whispered something in her friend's ear.

"What a lovely girl!" he said. "Isn't it wonderful how these journeymen acquiesce to established pilots?" And then, "Ah, perhaps the neandertals were our ancestors ... or perhaps not. That's still no reason to sculpt our bodies and live among cavemen. I have a better plan. We could bribe a wormrunner to capture an Alaloi. They poach shagshay, don't they? Well, let them poach a caveman and bring him back to the city."

I took a sip of coffee and tapped the bridge of my nose. "You know we can't do that," I said.

"Of course, all the wormrunner would really need is a little blood. He could render a caveman unconscious, bleed him a little, and return with a sample of his blood."

I sloshed the coffee around in my mouth. It had grown cold and acidy. I said, "You've always accused me of being too innocent, but I'll admit that I've thought about doing what you suggest."

"Well?"

I ordered a fresh pot of coffee and said, "One man's blood would not be enough. The neandertal genes are spread among the Alaloi families. We have to be sure of getting a large enough statistical sample."

He belched and rolled his eyes. "Ah, you always have these *reasons,* Little Fellow. But I think the real reason you want to make this mad expedition is that you *like* the idea of sculpting your body and living among savages. Such a romantic notion. But then, you always were a romantic man."

I said, "If the Timekeeper grants my petition, I'll go to the Alaloi. Will you come with me?"

"Will I come with you? Will I come with you? What a question!" He took a bite of bread and belched. "If I *don't* come with you, they'll say Bardo is afraid, by God! Well, too bad. I don't care. My friend, I'd follow you across the galaxy, but this, to go among savages and slel their plasm, well ... it's insane!"

I was not able to persuade Bardo to my plan. I was so full of optimism, however, so happy to be home that it didn't matter. As a returning pilot I was entitled to take a house in the Pilot's Quarter. I chose a small, steeply roofed chalet heated by piped-in water from the geyser at the foot of Attakel. Into the chalet I moved my leather-bound book of poems, my furs and kamelaikas and my three pairs of skates, my chessboard and pieces, the mandolin I had never learned to play, and the few other possessions I had accumulated during my years at Resa. (As novices at Borja, of course, we were allowed no possessions other than our clothes.) I considered ordering a bed and perhaps a few wooden tables and chairs, such minor tubist indulgences being at that time quite popular. But I disliked sleeping in beds, and it seemed to me that chairs and tables were only appropriate in bars or cafes, where many could make use of their convenience. Too, I had another reason for not wanting my house cluttered with things: Katharine had begun spending her nights with me. I did not want her, in her world of eternal night, tripping over a misplaced chair and perhaps fracturing her beautiful face.

We kept our nightly trysts a secret from my mother and my aunt, and from everyone else, even Bardo. Of course I longed to confide in him; I wanted to tell him how happy Katharine made me with her hands and tongue and rolling hips, with her passionate (if anticipated) whispered words and moans. But Bardo could no more keep a secret than he could hold his farts after consuming too much bread and beer. Soon after our conversation in the cafe, half the Order, it seemed—everyone except my cowardly friend—wanted to accompany me on what would come to be called the great journey.

Even Katharine, who had seen enough of the future not to be excited, was excited. Long after midnight on fiftieth night, after a night of slow, intense coupling (she seemed always to want to devour time slowly, sensuously, as a snake swallows its prey), she surprised me with her excitement. She lay naked in front of the stone fireplace, flickers of orange and red playing across her sweating, white skin. She smelled of perfume and woodsmoke and sex. With her arms stretched back behind her head, her heavy breasts were spread like perfect discs against her chest. Eyeless as she was, she had no body shame, nor any appreciation of her beauty. At my leisure I stared at the dark, thick triangle of hair below her rounded belly, the long, crossed legs and deeply arched feet. She stared upward at the stars, scrying. That is, she *would* have stared at the stars if she had had eyes, and if the skylight between the ceiling beams hadn't been covered with snow. Who knows what she saw gazing down the dark tunnels to the future? And if she had suddenly been able to see again, I wondered, could the sparkle of the milky, midwinter stars ever have pleased her as much as her own interior visions?

"Oh, Mallory!" she said. "What a thing I've . . . I *must* come with you to your Alaloi, do you see?"

I smiled but she could not see my smile. I sat cross-legged by her side, a fur thrown over my shoulders. With my fingers, I combed her long, black hair away from her eyepits and said, "If only Bardo had your enthusiasm."

"Don't be too hard on Bardo. In the end, he'll come, too."

"Come too? Come where?" I wasn't sure which disturbed me more: her descrying the future or her insistence I take her with me to the Alaloi. "What have you seen?"

"Bardo, in the cave with his big . . . he's so very *funny*!"

"You can't come with me," I said. "I'm sorry."

"But I *must* come with you! I will come because I have . . . Oh, Mallory?"

Of course, it was impossible for her to come with me. I told her it was impossible. I said, "The Alaloi leave their crippled and blind out on the ice when it blizzards. They kill them." I had no idea, really, if this were true.

She turned toward me and smiled. "You're not a very good liar," she said.

"No, I'm not, am I? But I don't understand why you would want to come with me."

"It's hard to explain."

"Tell me."

"I'm sorry, Mallory, but I can't tell you."

"Because of your vows?"

"Of course, but . . . but more because the words don't exist to describe the future."

"I thought you scryers had invented a special vocabulary."

"I wish I could find the words to tell you what I've seen."

"Try," I said.

"I want to grow eyes again so I can see the faces of your . . . it's there, on the ice in deep winter you'll find your . . . Oh, what should I call it, this thing I see, this *image*, the image of man? I'll break my vows, and I'll grow eyes to see it again for a while before I . . . before I *see*."

Silently I rubbed the bridge of my nose while I sat sweating in front of the crackling fire. Grow eyes indeed! It was a shocking thing for a scryer to say.

"There," she sighed. "You see, I've said it so badly."

"Why can't you just say which events will occur and which will not?"

"Swee Mallory, suppose I had seen the only event which really ma   rs. If I told you that you must die at a certain time, every moment of your life would be agony because . . . you see, you'd always dwell on the moment of . . . it would rob every other moment of your life of happiness. If you *knew*."

I kissed her mouth and said, "There's another possibility. If I knew I had a hundred years before I died, I'd never be afraid of anything my whole life. I could enjoy every instant of living."

"Of course, that's true," she said.

"But that's a paradox."

She laughed for a while before admitting, "We scryers are known for our paradoxes, aren't we?"

"Do you see *the* future? Or do you see possible futures? That's something I've always wanted to know."

Indeed, most pilots—and everyone else in our Order— were curious to know the secrets of the scryers.

"And seeing the future," I said, "why not change it if you wish?"

She laughed again. At times, such as when she was relaxed in front of the fire, she had a beautiful laugh. "Oh, you've just stated the first paradox, did you know? Seeing the future of . . . if we then act to change it, and *do* change it . . . if it's changeable, then we haven't really *seen* the future, have we?"

"And you would refuse to act, then, merely to preserve this vision of what you'd seen?"

She took my hand and stroked my palm. "You don't understand."

I said, "In some fundamental sense, I've never really believed you scryers could see anything but possibilities."

She dragged her fingernail down my lifeline. "Of course . . . *possibilities*."

Because I was frustrated, I laughed and said, "I think it's easier to understand a mechanic than a scryer. At least their beliefs are quantifiable."

"Some mechanics," she said, "believe that each quantum event occurring in the universe changes the . . . They've quantified the possibilities. With each event a different future. Spacetime divides and redivides, like the branches of

one of your infinite trees. An infinity of futures, these parallel
futures, they call them, all occurring simultaneously. And so,
an infinity of parallel *nows,* don't you see? But the mechanics
are wrong. Nowness is . . . there is a unity of immanence . . . oh,
Mallory, only one future can ever *be.*"

"The future is unchangeable, then?"

"We have a saying," she told me. "We don't change the
future; we *choose* the future."

"Scryer talk."

She reached up to me. She ran her fingers through my
chest hair and made a sudden, tight fist above my heart,
pulling at me as she said, "I will have gone to a cutter
named . . . He'll grow me new eyes. I want to see your face
when you . . . *one* time, just the one time, is that okay?"

"Would you really do that?" I wondered aloud. "Break
your vows? Why?"

"Because I love . . ." she said. "I love you, do you see?"

During the next few days I could think of little else except
this strange conversation. As a returning pilot I was required
to teach, so I agreed to tutor two novices in the arts of
hallning. I must admit I did not perform my teaching duties
with as much attention as I should have. Early one morning
in the classroom of my chalet, as I was supposedly demon-
strating simple geometric transformations to little Rafi and
Geord, I found myself thinking back to my journey to the
Entity, remembering how the imago of Katharine had grown
eyes and looked at me. I wondered: Had She known what
Katharine would one day say to me? I was mulling over the
implications of this while I showed the novices how it is
impossible to rotate a paper, two-dimensional tracing of a
right-handed glove to match and fit the tracing of a left-
handed glove, if the motion was restricted to rotations within
a plane. I failed to notice they were bored. I picked up one of
the glove tracings from the wooden floor, flipped it over and
placed it on top of the other tracing. I said, "But if we lift it
off the plane like so and rotate it through space, it's trivial to
match the two tracings. Similarly—"

And here the gangly, impatient Rafi interrupted me,
calling out, "Similarly, it's impossible to rotate a three-
dimensional left glove into a right-handed glove. But if we
rotate the glove through four-space, it's simple to superimpose the two gloves. We know that, Pilot. Are we done now?

You promised to tell us about your journey to the Alaloi—remember? Are you really going to drive dogsleds across the ice and eat living meat?"

My distractions, I saw to my dismay, had apparently infected even the novices. I was a little annoyed at Rafi, who was too quick for his own good. I said, "True, the gloves can be superimposed, but can you *visualize* the rotation through four-space? No? I didn't think so."

Two days later I took them to a cutter who modified their lungs, and then down to the Rose Womb Cloisters. I put them into the hexagonal attitude chamber, which occupied most of the rose-tiled tank room. There they floated and breathed the super-oxygenated water while performing the day's exercises. With their sense of right and left, and up and down, dissolved by the dark, warm, salty water, they visualed four-space; they rotated the image of their own bodies around the imaginary plane cutting through their noses, navels and spines. They were trying to rotate themselves into their own mirror images. Even though it is really a simple exercise, akin to reversing the line diagram of a cube by staring at until it "pops," I should have paid them close attention. But again, I let my mind wander. I was wondering if Katharine would be able to find a cutter to make her new eyes when I happened to look through the wine dark water at the novices. Rafi, I noticed, had his arms wrapped around his knees, and his eyes were tightly closed as he breathed water. How long had I left him like this? If I left him too long in the fetal attitude, he would build a dependency on sightlessness and closure. I reminded myself that he was to be a pilot, not a scryer, so I removed him from the tank.

"The exercise was . . . too easy," Rafi said. He stood there naked, beads of water dripping off him. Due to his altered lungs, he was having trouble breathing. "Once one *sees* one transformation, the others are easy."

"That's true with geometric transformations," I said. "But the topological transformations are harder. I remember when Lionel Killirand made me reverse the tube of my body, inside out. Now *that* was a horrible exercise. Since you've found today's exercise so easy, perhaps you'd like to play with the topological transformations, then?"

He smiled a haughty smile and said, "I'd rather play at a *real* transformation, like you, Pilot. Are you really going to sculpt yourself? Is that as severe a transformation as altering one's lungs? Would you take a novice with you, to the Alaloi? Could I come?"

"No," I said, "you're just a boy. Now, shall we practice motions through five-space? I don't think you'll be able to visualize five-space so easily."

The excitement that my proposed journey provoked throughout the Order was not wholly surprising. Man is man, and even civilized man—especially civilized women and men—will sometimes long for simplicity. In each of us, there is the lure of the primitive, an atavistic desire to experience life in its rawest form; there is a need to be tested, to prove our worth as natural (and ferocious) animals in a natural world. Some said the Alaloi led a truer, more purely human life than could any modern man. Too, the story of Goshevan and his marrow-sick son, Shanidar, had fired the imagination of an entire generation. To return to nature as strong, powerful, natural men—what could be more romantic than that? No day passed that some semanticist didn't offer advice as to the complexities of the Alaloi language or a fabulist recite the epic of Goshevan's doomed journey to live among the cavemen; no night ended without one pilot or another drugging himself with toalache and begging to accompany me to the Alaloi.

Toward the end of that brilliant, happy season of romance and deep snows and plans, I was elevated to my mastership. Strangely enough, although I was by far the youngest pilot ever to become a master, I no longer took pride in my relative youth. Having aged five years intime on my journey, I suddenly felt ageless, or rather, old—as old as the glazed ledges of the Hall of Ancient Pilots where the master pilots welcomed me to their college. I remember waiting for their decision at the far side of the Hall, near the dais where Bardo and I had received our rings. I tapped my boot against the cold floor, listening to the sound vanish into the arched vault above me. I examined the conclave room's long, black doors, which were made of shatterwood and carved in bas-relief with the faces of Rollo Gallivare and Tisander the Wary, the Tycho and Yoshi, all three hundred and eighty-five of our Lord Pilots since the founding of our Order. Near the center of the left door, I found Soli's hard profile, with the long, broad nose, the hard chin and the combed hair bound in its silver chain. I wondered if my own profile would ever be carved in the old, brittle wood, and if it were, I wondered if anyone would be able to distinguish it from Soli's. Then the doors opened, and the ancient Salmalin, who was the oldest pilot next to Soli, pulled his white beard and invited me into the circular conclave room, and I no longer felt very old. I sat on a stool at the center of a huge, ringlike table. Around the table sat Tomoth, Pilar Gaprindashavilli, the dour Stephen Caraghar, as well as Lionel and Justine and the other master pilots. When Salmalin stood up to welcome me to the master's college, all the pilots stood and removed the gloves from their right hands. In that simplest and most touching of all our Order's ceremonies, I went around the table shaking hands. When I took Justine's long, elegant hand in my own, she said, "If only Soli had been here to see this, I'm sure he would have been as proud as I am."

I did not remind her that if Soli had been present, he would probably have vetoed my elevation.

After she and Lionel (and others) congratulated me, my mother met me outside the conclave room. We walked through the almost deserted Hall together. "You're a master now," she said. "The Timekeeper will have to pay more attention to your petition. And if he approves it, we'll sculpt our bodies. And go to the Alaloi where there will be fame and glory. No matter what we find or don't."

I thought it was funny that even my mother had been infected with the general excitement. I bit my lip, then said, "You can't seriously think of coming with me, Mother."

"Can't I? I'm your mother. Together we're a family. The Alaloi would regard us as a family—what could be more natural?"

"Well, you can't come."

"I've heard that to the Alaloi, family is everything."

"The Timekeeper," I said, "will probably deny my petition."

She cocked her head and laughed, almost to herself. "Can the Timekeeper deny you this chance? I feel not. We'll see, we'll see."

Later there was feasting and drinking. Bardo was so happy for me that he practically cried. "By God!" he said. "We'll celebrate! The City will never be the same!"

His words, along with my mother's instincts, would prove to be curiously prophetic. (Sometimes I thought my mother was a secret scryer.) Two days after my elevation, on eighty-fifth day, a day of cold, mashy snow and deep irony, Leopold

Soli returned from the Vild. He was enraged to find me
alive—so it was rumored. Out of spite and revenge—Bardo
told me this—he went to the Timekeeper to demand that my
petition be denied. But the Timekeeper fooled him. The
Timekeeper fooled everyone, and fooled me most of all. He
granted my petition, but added a proviso: I could mount an
expedition to the Alaloi provided I took my family, my
mother and Justine and Katharine, along with me. And Soli,
too. Soli, who was my uncle, must come or else there would
be no expedition. And since Soli was Lord Pilot, Soli must
lead the expedition—this was Timekeeper's galling, ironic
proviso. When I heard this news I could not believe it. Nor
did I suspect that Bardo was right, that as a result of our
expedition, the City would never be the same.

7

Rainer's Sculpture

*I was an experiment on the part of Nature, a gamble
within the unknown, perhaps for a new purpose,
perhaps for nothing, and my only task was to allow
this game on the part of primeval depths to take its
course, to feel its will within me and make it wholly
mine. That or nothing!*
—Emil Sinclair, Holocaust Century Eschatologist

I spent the next few days sulking about my house. I am
ashamed to admit this, but the truth is the truth: I brooded
like a boy upon learning of the Timekeeper's proviso. I told
Katharine to stay away; I told her I was angry with her for not
warning me the Timekeeper would humble me with his
proviso. (This was a lie. How could I be angry with a
beautiful scryer sworn to keep her visions secret?) I read my
book of poems or split firewood or set up my wooden chess
pieces, replaying the games of the grandmasters, all the while
cursing Soli for ruining my expedition. That Soli had persuaded the Timekeeper to allow him to steal the leadership from
me, I could not doubt.

Soon after his return, Soli came to visit me, to discuss
plans for the expedition and to gloat—or so I thought. I
received him in the fireroom in front of the cold, blackened
fireplace. He immediately noticed the minor insult of the
unlit fire, but he could not appreciate the greater insult, that
I invited him to sit atop the same furs on which I had swived
his daughter. I shamelessly savored the knowledge of this

insult. As Bardo often reminded me, I had a cruel vein running into my heart.

I was surprised at how much Soli had aged. He sat cross-legged on the furs, touching the new lines on his forehead, pulling at the loose flesh below his long chin. He looked twenty years older. I had heard that he had almost penetrated the inner veil of the Vild. But the price he had paid for attempting those impenetrable spaces was time, crueltime. His voice was older, deeper, cut with new inflections. "There should be congratulations on your journey," he said. "The College did well to make you a master."

I had to admit he could be gracious when he wanted to be, even though he was obviously lying. I wanted to tell him not to waste his breath lying. But I remembered my manners and said, "Tell me about the Vild."

"Yes, the Vild. There's little to tell, is there? The stars flare, then die. The Vild grows. And the rate that it grows, grows. What do you want to know? That it's impossible to map those spaces? That a pilot must use slowtime almost continuously in the Vild? Look at me, then, and you'll see that that is so."

We talked of our respective journeys; I thought he was bitter that I had succeeded where he had failed. And then he surprised me, congratulating me again for the mappings I had made through the Entity. "That was elegant piloting," he said. Pointedly, however, he refrained from mentioning my discovery.

I offered him coffee but he refused, saying, "Coffee speeds the brain, and there's been enough of that, hasn't there?"

"Would you like some skotch, then?"

"No thank you, Pilot," he said. "There's no joy drinking skotch in front of a dead fireplace, is there?"

"I could light the fire, if you'd like."

"Please."

I heaped some green logs onto the grate and lit the fire, and he came to the purpose of his visit. "It seems there will be an expedition to your Alaloi after all."

"And you're to lead it?"

"Yes."

I ground my teeth, then said, "I understand. You want the glory."

"Is that true? No, you don't understand. The Timekeeper orders me to lead it."

"Why?"

"Who knows what his reasons are?"

Liar, I thought, liar!

"I'll speak to the Timekeeper," I said.

"You'd question him?"

"It was my discovery. The Alaloi . . . my plan. It's my expedition."

He bowed his head and said, "Yes, it's clear, you want the glory."

"No, I want the knowledge."

"So you tell yourself," he said, and he sipped from the tumbler of skotch I had handed him.

"It would weaken the expedition if you come." I looked at his long nose, the nose I had broken. "There's blood between us," I said.

He rubbed the bridge of his nose. He said, "No, you're mistaken. There's no blood between us."

I gulped a quarter of my own tumbler of skotch. My eyes were burning from the piney smoke escaping into the room. I said, "If the Timekeeper doesn't rescind his proviso, I'll withdraw from the expedition. I won't go with you."

Soli smiled and told me, "Yes, your pride is hurt. But you don't have a choice."

"What do you mean?"

"This is the reason for my visit; you must be told: The Timekeeper orders you to come with me."

"Orders me?" I half-shouted. "Ten days ago, he wasn't even going to allow an expedition!"

"The Timekeeper," Soli said, "apparently has changed his mind. Don't ask me why." He sipped his skotch, then continued, "There will be six of us. Justine and Bardo, your mother, too, are ordered to accompany us."

"That's only five."

His voice was unnaturally calm as he said, "The sixth will be Katharine. The Timekeeper has ordered my daughter to grow new eyes and come with us."

So, I thought, Soli must have gone to the Timekeeper and asked that his wife and daughter come with him. How gratified he must have been that Katharine would renounce her scryer's vows and grow eyes, he who despised scryers! I could not understand, though, why my mother and Bardo had been included in the expedition's roster, unless it was to appease me and keep me from doing something foolish, such as breaking my vow of obedience and running off to the Alaloi on my own. Then, by way of explanation Soli said, "We'll pose as distant relatives of the Devaki tribe of the Alaloi. The Timekeeper believes we'll have a better chance if we pretend to be an extended family. And since some of us are really related, it should be that much easier of a deception."

Yes, I thought, Soli was indeed a deceitful man.

I said, "Let me guess; we'll pretend that Bardo is your son, and my cousin."

"No," he said, "that's not the plan." His face suddenly turned sour as if he had swallowed gull piss, not skotch. He seemed very unhappy. "You're to pose as my son."

"What? That's impossible!"

"As my son," he repeated quietly, "since you look so much like me. Katharine will be your sister."

"That's insane! It won't work!" I was suddenly on my feet, fingers clenched, shaking my fists on either side of my head. "You and I . . . we'd fight and what would the Alaloi think? The whole plan . . . Katharine my sister, insane! I'll break down the doors of the Timekeeper's tower if I have to but I won't let him order this insane plan!"

"Again, you must be reminded, you have no choice. Sorry."

Indeed, I had no choice. I was furious because I had no choice. I was a pilot who had taken vows—so I reminded myself while pacing through the fireroom after Soli had left me. Later that day I called for an audience with the Time-keeper, but he would not see me. In a bare anteroom, I waited all afternoon playing over chess games in my head to calm myself, to keep myself from breaking into his chambers. Finally, he sent a journeyman horologe to inform me that he was meeting with a merchant prince from Tria and would not be able to see anyone for a good tenday.

I did not believe him. The Timekeeper was testing my obedience, I thought, and humbling me because he was jealous of my discovery. Bardo, too, shared this opinion. Around midnight we met in the master pilot's bar. He was drunk, and oddly, for him, quite subdued. His bearded head was loose on his shoulders as he kept dipping his lips into his beer. "It's a pity," he said. "It's a very pity. By chance you didn't ask the Timekeeper to . . ." He belched and continued, ". . . to order me on this mad expedition, did you? Oh, of

course you didn't, stupid of me for even suspecting. Where's
my damn faith in friends? Oh, too bad, where's my faith in
anything? You're always saying success begets success but I
think not. You and your damn testosterone high! You come
back famous, full of pride and seed, ready for anything, but
that's not the reality, oh, no. Shall I speak in metaphor? I
shall, I shall: We're like thallows, you and I, the higher we
soar, the greater the fall when the wind turns against us. I
have a bad feeling about this expedition, Little Fellow."

Bardo, of course, had bad feelings about anything which
put his life at risk. He was a natural pessimist always waiting
for calamity to occur, and the greater his happiness, the
greater his fear it might momentarily be taken away from
him. Thinking to soothe him (and myself), I drank more
skotch, threw my arm around him, and said, "It will be all
right."

"No, no, Little Fellow, I think I'll die out on the ice, yes,
I'm sure of it."

"I didn't know you were a scryer."

"Well, it doesn't require any special vision to see I'm
doomed." He pulled a small mirror from his pocket and held
it in front of his face. With drunken fingers, he wiped beer
foam from his mustache as he spoke to himself: "Ah, Bardo,
my friend, what's happened, what's to become of you? Oh,
too bad, too bad!"

Despite Bardo's foreboding and my maimed pride, despite Soli's and my antipathy for each other, despite everything, the initial planning for the expedition went well. Each
of us, except Bardo, took on a different task. Lionel, who was
miffed at not being included in the expedition, nevertheless
helped us learn to handle the sled teams. Soli prepared his
inventories of the spears, furs, oilstones, icesaws and krydda
spheres, all the hundreds of tools and things we would need
to pose as Alaloi (and, if need be, to survive). Justine and my
mother consulted the akashic records and histories, learning
as much as they could of the culture of the Devaki tribe. It
was my task—and it was clever of Soli to assign me this
crucial, delicate task, a sop to my pride—to hire and super-
vise the cutter who would sculpt our bodies into the shape of
neandertals.

On the tenth day of false winter I made arrangements
with a Mehtar Hajime, whose shop was the largest and finest

on the Street of Cutters. (Which is itself one of the straightest
and broadest streets in the Farsider's Quarter.) The shop front
was jacketed with sheets of rare, blue obsidian carved with
bizarre shapes, some of which were human—though barely
so—and others bearing as little resemblance to humans as
humans do to monkeys. There were grotesque bearded men
whose parts had been broadened and lengthened until their
membrums hung pendulously almost to their knees, and there
were others as tall and thin as exemplars. There seemed to be
no pattern or logic to the placement of the figures: A cluster of
the double-sexed in orgy was set next to a breastless madonna
wearing the binding fiber of a Vesper priestess around her
elongated head. Bizarre, how bizarre and barbaric! The largest
of the figures, I saw, was melted into the stone above the
doorway. It advertised the type of sculpting for which Mehtar
was most famous: An Alaloi man, with his thick jaw firmly set,
held a spear and stood with his arm cocked as he sighted on
the eye of an enraged, charging mammoth. I recognized the
sculpture of Goshevan, he who had heroically killed a mammoth with a single stroke of his spear. Mehtar took obvious
pride that it had been a cutter much like himself who had once
made Goshevan into an Alaloi.

I knocked at the door, and a domestic opened it and led
me through the stone hallway into the warm, disgustingly
plush tearoom, where I sat at the single table. It served me a
fair coffee that I could not quite identify. I drummed my
fingers against the table top, all the while examining the
expensive wall tapestries, the many expensive objects atop
the polished furniture. I was annoyed because this venal
cutter, whoever he was, was not there to meet me.

"Many pay well to be more than they were born to be," I
heard someone say. I looked up to see a man who must have
been Mehtar standing in the doorway leading to his changing
rooms. He looked as much like a caveman as any Alaloi. He
was thick and obviously powerful, with great bunches of
muscles gathering beneath his hairy skin. His browridge
jutted so far out from his forehead that I could barely see his
quick brown eyes. He looked very familiar; I was almost
certain I had seen him before, though I could not remember
where. With the flat of his palm, he thumped his chest and
said, "Do you see this magnificent body? As I've done for
myself, so I can do for you."

I sipped my coffee (it was Solsken coffee, I guessed, which

is treasured more for its rarity than taste), and I asked him, "How do you know I haven't come to have my nose shortened?"

"You're the master pilot Mallory Ringess," he said. "And I know why you've come to me." He took the chair opposite mine and sat stroking his heavy jaw. He looked at me as if he were appraising a piece of art. Abruptly he said, "Look at the Fravashi tondo," and he pointed to the wall behind me.

I turned to look at the tondo. The alien painting, a culture of variegated, programmed bacteria pressed between two sheets of clary, mutated and shifted colors and shape as I watched. The pretty, flowing colors depicted the epic of Goshevan of Summerworld and the birth of his son, Shanidar; it was an impressive display. Of course, private possession of such technology was illegal, but I said nothing.

"A famous castrato who had lost his voice—I'm sure you know his name—gave me this painting in trade for his restoration. Restore him I did! I cut at his larynx until he sang like a bell, and to prove my good will, I stitched new testes into his empty ball sacks for free. So that he could be a man again while he sang with a young boy's voice! No, I'm not a venal man, no matter what my enemies say."

I explained what I needed, and he closed his nostrils and said, "The price will be six thousand city disks, a thousand for each body I sculpt and—"

"You're joking! Six *thousand* city disks?"

"Have some more coffee," he said, pouring the pungent liquid into my mug. "The price is high because I am who I am. Ask any cutter or splicer on the street, and they'll tell you who is the best. Did you know I apprenticed to Rainer? The cutter who sculpted Goshevan?"

He was lying, of course. I had consulted the City archives before choosing a cutter. Mehtar, although he looked decently old, was really quite young, much too young to have been Rainer's apprentice. He had come to Neverness as a young boy having witnessed the death of his planet, Alesar, in one of those rabidly hateful religious wars which occasionally destroy isolated societies. His family had belonged to a schismatic sect of spiritualists—I do not recall the exact nature or substance of their belief—and he had watched them die the marrow-death as he vomited blood and swore he would never again put his faith in ideals he could not see or feel or possess. He had come to Neverness determined to enrich himself while wreaking vengeance on any flesh that came his way. Therefore in little time he had become the best—if strangest—cutter in the City.

"Six thousand disks!" I repeated. "Nobody needs access to that much information. It's indecent."

"You won't buy my services by insulting me, Pilot."

"We'll pay you a thousand disks."

"That's not enough."

"Two thousand."

He shook his head and made a tisking sound with his tongue. "That will buy you the services of Alvarez or Paulivik, any of the lesser cutters. Maybe you should go to them."

"Three thousand, then."

"I don't like amounts containing the number 'three.' It's a superstition of mine."

"Four thousand," I said, realizing that I should have persuaded Bardo to come with me. I had rarely paid money for anything in my life, while he had a lifetime of experience arguing over the value of land or haggling with whores over the price of their bodies.

"I can sculpt four of you for that price."

"Five thousand city disks. Five *thousand*."

"No, no, no, no, Pilot."

I slapped the table so hard that my mug rattled and coffee slopped over the rim. I muttered, "You would think you'd sculpt us for free. Doesn't the quest mean anything to you?"

"No, it doesn't, Pilot."

"Well, five thousand is all I can pay." I was certain that if I had brought Bardo with me, he would never have agreed to pay the six thousand disks that Mehtar had originally asked for.

"If that is all you have," he said, "that is all you have. But you will never know how fine it feels to wear an Alaloi's body, how good it is to be strong." So saying he grasped his empty mug with his hand and squeezed. It shattered into crumbs and slivers, one of which drove through his palm. He held his hand up so I could watch him slowly draw the bloody white sliver from his punctured flesh. At first the wound spurted blood in rhythmic pulses, and Mehtar said, "Clearly, I've sliced the artery." He closed his eyes, and the muscles of his upraised hand began to tremble. The pulses of red slowed to a steady flow and then to a trickle. When he opened his eyes, the bleeding had stopped altogether. "I can give you powers over your sculpted body as well as strength. There are hormones to keep your balls overflowing with seed, or a neurotransmitter wash to dissolve your need for sleep. And, more practically, with a little splicing, various of your tissues can be programmed to pump out glycopetides, to keep your flesh from freezing on your expedition. I, Mehtar Constancio Hajime can do this. My price will be six thousand one hundred city disks."

"Six thousand . . . *one hundred?*"

He pointed to the pieces of the mug scattered across the table. "I must factor in my advertising costs. They blow these mugs on Fostora, and you must know, it was precious."

I pounded the table with the edge of my fist and felt porcelain crumbs grinding into the thin leather of my glove. "You're a filthy, greedy tubist," I said.

He looked at me quickly as his nostrils opened and closed. "A tubist, you call me. Yes, it's true, I serve myself, and why not? I used to serve my God, but He betrayed me." He pointed to the tondo and at the case of priceless Darghinni jewelry standing next to it. "Now I collect things. Things do not betray."

"Too many things," I said. "You're a thingist *and* a tubist."

"And why not? Certain things possess a luster and beauty that do not fade with age. We arise in the morning to greet our things, a place for each finely made thing, and each thing in its special place. We buy things, perhaps a chair carved of fine-grained shatterwood or a beautiful Darghinni hangnest, and we can be certain that the having of it will increase our worth."

"I don't believe that."

He smiled and said, "Nevertheless, it's true. When we own many things, we may trade them to acquire more things, each more beautiful, each more precious, each containing real value against the day of disaster when things will have to be traded to preserve that most precious thing of all: our precious lives."

"Nobody lives forever," I said. I stared at the silvery strands of the hangnest glittering in its case. I thought of the thousands of Darghinni nymphs who must have died when their nest was stolen. "Maybe you value yourself too much."

"Well, Pilot, this flesh I wear, it's all I am. What should I value more? Six thousand one hundred city disks—a heavy sum, but there's never enough to insure the sanctity of a man's flesh. Never, never enough."

In the end I paid the amount he asked. It was bad enough having to deal in *money*; it was far worse to argue over it. The next day when I told Bardo the details of our arrangement he was aghast. "By God, you've been plundered! I really should have come with you. What did the Timekeeper say? He's a miserly old wolf and... ahhh, he doesn't know, does he?"

"He won't know unless the master bursar tells him."

"Good, good." And then, "Do you really trust this Mehtar Hajime to sculpt us?"

Did I trust the cutter? How could one trust a man who wore smuggled shagshay furs stolen from the flayed body of a once-living animal? "I trust his greed," I said. "He'll do what we pay him to do on the hope that our friends will come to him for sculpting."

Four days later I was the first to lie beneath Mehtar's lasers. I was surprised to learn that the difference between an Alaloi and a full human was really very little. Unfortunately, these little differences had to be added or deleted from every part of my body. He remade me from inside out, leaving no part of me untouched. He did the bone work first, thickening and strengthening one hundred and eighty of my body's bones. It was during this period, which lasted a couple of tendays, that I felt the worst pain of the entire procedure. Whistling to himself and occasionally telling me bad jokes, Mehtar would lay open layers of skin and muscle and cut among the plates and spicules of a bone's honeycombed interior as I clamped my jaws shut and sweated. He steened the walls with new bone and strengthened the shafts and tendon attachments. "Bone pain is deep," he said, all the while opening and closing his nostrils as he drilled down the length of my thigh bone. "Deep and hot but it doesn't last long."

There were a few times when my pain blocks failed and Mehtar had to render me unconscious. I suspected he used these times to introduce colonies of illegal, programmed bacteria into my body. The bacteria—I was never able to prove this—found their way into those parts of my bones Mehtar could not reach with his drills. There some of the bacteria disassembled and ingested my natural bone while others manufactured and spun out a webwork of collagens and mineral crystals, layer upon layer of new bone with a tensile strength greater than steel. Once, when I hinted how afraid I was of this technology, Mehtar laughed and said, "You should think of the bacteria as tools, tiny machines, infinitessimal robots programmed to a certain biochemical task. Do machines rebel? Can a computer take charge of its own programming? No, no, no, Pilot, there's no danger in these tools, but of course, all the same, I would never employ them because to do so would violate your City canons, archaic as those canons are."

I rubbed the glued skin of my arm—he had been working on the humerus that day—and I said, "No one likes to be colonized by bacteria, especially intelligent bacteria."

"Oh, noble Pilot, even if I was one of those cutters who ignore your foolish laws, I would program the bacteria to die after they had completed their task, of course I would! You have my promise!"

Somehow his promises did not reassure me. I said, "And what of Chimene and the April cluster, then?"

"Those names mean nothing to me."

I told him that Chimene was one of those planets where a colony of bacteria had mutated and escaped, consuming all life in the biosphere, disassembling and totally remaking the planet's surface into a mat of purplish-brown, hugely intelligent bacteria—all in a matter of days.

"And the eschatologists think it only took a few years for them to infect the whole April cluster," I said. "Ten thousand stars swarming with your harmless bacteria." Of all the gods in the galaxy, the eschatologists feared the April colonial intelligence the most.

"Ancient history!" Mehtar scoffed. "Such carelessness could never happen today. Who would permit it? Again, I assure you, you have nothing to fear."

While I was healing, he worked on the others in succession. Soli was the second to feel the marrow-pain, followed by Justine, Katharine and my mother. Bardo, wanting to see the results of as many sculptings as he could, went last.

"I've heard terrible things about these cutters," he confided to me one day in the changing room. "Aren't I thick enough that he could leave my bones alone? No? By God, I wish he'd avoid the spine—so many delicate nerves there.

What if he sneezes at the wrong moment? One little slip of the laser and Bardo would never mount another woman. I've heard of it happening. Can't you imagine: Bardo's mighty pole rendered as limp as a soba noodle because of a sneeze?"

To help him relax and block his nerves, I massaged the heavy, fanlike muscles at the top of his spine. I tried to reassure him, pointing out that many people underwent cuttings much more extensive solely for the sake of fad or fashion. I did not tell him my suspicions about Mehtar's bacteria.

"Well, this *may* be a minor alteration," he admitted after we had talked about certain pilots who had found it useful to pose as one or another species of alien. "But there's another thing. Doesn't this cutter look like that rude Alaloi I tripped the day you broke Soli's nose? Do you remember?"

Suddenly, I did remember. Suddenly, I knew where I had seen Mehtar before. To reassure Bardo, I said, "I'm sure this isn't the same man." It was a lie, but what could I do?

"Ah, but what if you're wrong? Suppose he remembers me? Suppose he *dis*members me, forgive the pun, out of vengeance, do you know what I mean?"

It seemed, though, that Mehtar did not remember him. Either that, or he did not hold a grudge. If anything, Mehtar did his smoothest work on him, probably because he had had all the rest of us to practice on. Bardo, of course, was not satisfied until he had tested his virility on his whores. Everything must have functioned properly because he claimed he had swived twelve whores in a single evening, which was a record, even for him.

The work on my face began soon after this, in late false winter. Mehtar built me a new jaw filled with larger teeth. The enamel of the molars was thick and layered; the jaw itself was massive and jutting in order to provide greater leverage for the toughened jaw muscles. I would be able to crack baldo nuts or gnaw bones without trouble or pain. The work was delicate, especially around the eyes. Because my entire face, as seen from profile, projected at a greater angle from my skull, Mehtar needed to sculpt great browridges to protect the vulnerable eyes. This he did slowly, taking great care with the optic nerves. I was blind for the better part of two days. I was afraid I would never see again, and I wondered how

Katharine made her way through the black prison surrounding her head.

When the cutter finished this painstaking procedure and I could see again, he held a silver mirror in front of me. "Behold," he said. "You are magnificent, yes? Note the nose, which I broadened while you were pain-blocked and blind. Note the flaring nostrils. Wiggle them for me, please. Very good, open, now close, and open again. A protection against the cold," he said proudly, all the while opening and closing his own nostrils. "This planet is so cold."

I looked at the reflection in the mirror; it was not really like looking at myself. Or rather, it was like looking at some mutation of myself composed of two thirds Mallory Ringess and one third beast. My face was strong and well proportioned, at once primitive and as expressive as any human face. My ancestors on Earth, I thought, must have looked as I did. I could not decide if I was handsome or ugly (or neither). I placed my fingertips on my forehead feeling the browridge; it was like the overhang of a cliff. I was not used to seeing myself in a thick beard, nor could I keep my tongue from probing the slippery contours of my huge, new teeth. For a moment I was disoriented and despondent. I had a feeling of intense depersonalization, as if I didn't know who I was, and worse, as if I didn't really exist. Then I looked at my eyes, and though they were set deeply into my skull, I saw that they were my same blue eyes, the eyes I knew so well.

I must admit that no one else suffered this same sense of loss of identity as I did. My mother and Justine, and of course, Soli, had more than once experienced the shock of having their old bodies made new. This is not to say they each were wholly pleased with Mehtar's sculpting. In particular, Soli hated it that after so many drastic alterations, we still nearly resembled each other. (Though as usual, he kept his silence.) Justine hated everything about her new self. When she saw what Mehtar had done to her, she said, "Oh, no, look at me! They'll laugh at me when I skate at the Hofgarten, and as for *that*, look how my weight has been redistributed, I've lost my center and I'm so *ungainly*!" and she sulked for three days. When Soli told her that the Alaloi would consider her beautiful, she asked him, "And do *you* think I'm beautiful?" And Soli, who like to pretend he was a truthful man, said nothing.

Just before the first storm of midwinter spring, we underwent changes not quite so severe. Mehtar stippled our skin, cutting away many of our sweat glands so we would not soak our furs and freeze to death encased in a sheath of ice. He also stimulated the individual hair follicles, and we each of us, the women as well as the men, sprouted a forest of hair from neck to ankle. (For some reason Mehtar could not explain, thick sprigs of black hair erupted from between Bardo's toes and along the tops of his feet. As Mehtar said, there are some genetic quirks beyond the control of the finest cutters.) During this time we lifted stones and performed vigorous exercises to stimulate muscular growth. Mehtar took us into his weight chamber and rubbed our limbs as he subjected us to the Fravashi deep-space method of locally inducing supergravities along the muscles of our arms and legs. Soli hated this as much as he hated it whenever Mehtar touched him. "If this continues," he said, flexing the great ball of muscle of his upper arm, "I'll be as bulky as Bardo."

There were thought exercises as well. One by one, we visited an imprimatur who made us visualize the coordinated firing of individual muscle fibers. She imprinted our neural pathways with certain skills we would need to pose as Alaloi. Thus, for instance, we learned how to flake a blade of flint without ever touching hand to stone. And where the Alaloi men practice for a decade before they can hit their marks with their spears, we learned this art in a single day.

There was one minor surgery I have neglected to mention. The Alaloi, it seems, with their sharp flakes of flint mutilate the membrums of their male children at the onset of manhood. The tribal elder slices off the foreskin covering the bulb of the membrum, and he makes tiny cuts in the delicate skin along the shaft. Into these cuts he rubs ashes and salt and colored powders. The wounds fester and scar, and the man—the boy who has become a man—is left with rows of minute, multicolored keloids decorating his membrum from base to bulb. Naturally, Bardo was terrified when he learned Mehtar would have to duplicate the effects of this barbaric ritual. (I had withheld the foreknowledge of it until the last possible moment.) I, myself, was a little apprehensive, especially when Mehtar grasped my membrum and joked that if he ruined it beyond repair, he could easily transform me into a woman, and no one I met would be the wiser. Again, everything went smoothly, though for days afterward

I could not bear to look down when I stood up to piss.

The last thing Mehtar did, or so I thought at the time, was to make Katharine new eyes. He implanted them in the vacant hollows beneath her dark, enlarged brows. They were beautiful eyes, eyes that I had seen before in dreams; they were the eyes of the Entity's Katharine imago, deep and lovely like blue-black, liquefied jewels. I held a mirror to her so she could see her eyes, but she pushed my hand away, saying, "I've looked inside for so long; now I want to look at *things.*"

Like a child gazing through a telescope for the first time, she took joy in examining the things of Mehtar's changing room: the hard white tile, the intricate tubular microscopes, the lasers, pessaries, and other gleaming instruments. When I took her to the Hofgarten to watch the skaters, she sighed and said, "Oh, it's good to see again! I'd forgotten how deeply colored the ice is, the blueness."

The next day, in the privacy of my house, she probed my body with her hands as well as her eyes. With her hot, dry hands, she grasped my membrum, running her fingers over the colored bumps along the shaft. It excited her, I think, and I wondered if the Alaloi decorate their membrums in order to please their women. (Though my studies of their culture indicated that little the Alaloi men did was solely for the pleasure of their women.) Later as we panted and pushed our thickened loins against each other with zest and abandon, at our moment of ecstasy, she opened her eyes and looked at me as if she were seeing me for the first time.

"Your face," she said after we had separated. "It was like the face of a rutting... It was so *bestial.*"

I rubbed my beard and felt my huge jaw, and I told her that indeed I now possessed the face of a beast.

But she said, "No, you don't understand. I've seen something I haven't realized since I was a little girl. All men are beasts if you look at them just right."

During the days that followed we were very busy. It was not enough, of course, that we merely sculpt our bodies to look like Alaloi. We had to *become* Alaloi, which meant learning their language and imprinting millions of bits of specialized knowledge. The correct method of slitting a snow hare's belly, the aligning of one's head towards north during sleep, the words and intonations for the burial of the dead—all must be learned before we could pose as cavemen. The language of the Devaki, the tribe of Alaloi we planned to join, proved more difficult than I had imagined. I do not mean that it was difficult to learn or articulate. It was not. My mother discovered that the akashic's computers had once laid bare the mind of the Alaloi named Rainer and had recorded his thought, deeds and memories. It was a simple thing to infuse our memories with his, with the words and grammatical rules of the Devaki language. It was a simple thing to find our lips smoothly articulating the soft, round vowels, to listen to the liquid consonants rolling easily off our skilled tongues. To be sure, the mastering of the tones took a little time. A few of the Devaki words were distinguishable from each other solely by the tones of their vowels. For instance, *sura* might mean either "purple" or "lonely," depending on whether the first vowel was pronounced in a sing-songy, rising tone, or in a low, falling tone. But in the end, everyone except Bardo found these few words simple to memorize. What was not simple was the understanding. The morphology, particularly of the Devaki verbs, proved to be subtle and complex. The verbs were not inflected according to our basic notions of past, present and future tense, because the Devaki do not understand time as we do. (As I was to learn later, the Devaki deny the existence of past and future.) How do the Devaki inflect their verbs? They inflect them according to the state of consciousness of the speaker. Thus a man full of fear might scream, *Lo mora li Tuwa*, I killed the mammoth!, while a man deep in dreamtime—what the Devaki call dreamtime— will say, *Lo morisha li Tuwa*, which means something like: I, in the ecstasy of the eternal Now-moment, am joined by the spirit of the mammoth who opened his heart to my spear. There are one hundred and eight verb inflections, each corresponding to a different emotion or state of mind. What worried me was that at least seven of these states were alien to me and would be incomprehensible to any woman or man of our Order. How could we choose the correct word forms, how could we understand primitives who sliced up and understood reality in ways very different from ours?

My mother and I, Justine too, spent much time discussing the problem with the semanticists. Yannis the Elder, who was taller than any man I have ever know, as thin and fragile-looking as an icicle, suggested that the Friends of Man might help us to duplicate these incomprehensible states of mind. "I understand you have achieved a partial understanding of the aliens' scent language," he said to me, referring to my experiences within the Entity "Now to understand alien thinking, which I *think* we understand the Devaki mindsets to be, why not approach *true* aliens as to their understanding of thoughtways which may, or may not, be considered by them to be understandable to anyone who understands that that which *cannot* be understood, cannot be understood solely on account of the context of the misunderstanding." (That is how the master semanticists, those miserable, pedantic seekers of word-meaning often talk. I am not joking.) In the end, his suggestions were of little help. When deep winter came and hardened, smothering the City in a sea of almost liquid air, we were forced to break off our research into these esoteric matters. There was only so much we could learn of the Devaki language and customs. Some things, it seemed, would have to be faked.

Leopold Soli, however, was not pleased with this fakery. In his own way he was a careful, meticulous man, despite the fantastic chances he had taken on his journeys into the manifold. As the time of our departure drew nearer, he became increasingly critical of my planning and preparations. We argued over a hundred little things, from the number of dogsleds we should take to my insistence that one radio would be enough to summon help from the City if we found ourselves stranded or otherwise needed rescue. We argued important questions, too. It was our argument over one vital, blindingly important question that nearly wrecked the expedition before it began.

At the very edge of the high professionals' college, Upplyssa, is a row of buildings known as the Brain Boxes. The pink granite buildings—there are seven of them—are squat and low, roofed with triangular panes of glass. On snowfree days, the interiors of the buildings are bright with a clean, natural light. Before all such enterprise had been moved to the factories south of Urkel, in the time of Ricardo Lavi, the tinkers and programmers had grown the neurologics for their computers in these seven buildings. During the winter before our expedition, the huge, enclosed spaces were given over to journeymen who sculpted great blocks of ice and others needing (or wanting) to manipulate material things. In the fourth and third buildings the fabulists created their three-dimensional tone poems while in the second building, certain historians were reconstructing in miniature the underground cities of Old Earth. Soli had chosen the empty seventh building to store the equipment for our expedition. Along the bare wall nearest the Academy's west gate were stacked long, heavy mammoth spears, bales of silky white shagshay furs, leather straps and slats of supple wood which could be bent into long skis or fashioned into the chassis of our sleds. There were strips of raw, frozen meat wrapped in oilskins, and snow goggles, oilstones, heaps of flint, and a hundred other things.

On sixtieth day, early in the morning, I was alone in the cold building making harnesses for the dog teams. Because Soli did not trust our hasty imprinting, he had suggested that we practice working leather or flaking flint and other Devaki skills. I sat punching holes in a stiff piece of leather with a bone awl. Next to me crouched a sleek, beautiful sled dog named Liko. I had made friends with this intelligent beast, and he liked to watch me work, even as he licked and worked at the clean marrow-bone I had given him. I was talking to Liko—and occasionally running my fingers through the gray fur covering his broad head—when he cocked his ears and let out a whine. There came the grinding speed-stop of a skater from the gliddery outside. The doors opened with much creaking and scraping against frozen snow, and the dark figure of Soli stood limned in the soft light streaming in from the street. Despite the bitter cold, he wore only a kamelaika and a thin wool jacket. His sculpted head was bare. For all the weight of the new bone grafted onto his face, he held himself rigidly erect. As he crossed the building his steps were measured, full of grace—I will admit that—but full of a dangerous new power as well.

"It's early," he said, picking up a chisel and laying out a mammoth tusk. He stroked his beard, which was black and thick and shot with stiff red hairs. His eyes were deeply pouched as if he had not slept well; he looked worn and middling old. He was too thin from having eaten too little. He whistled at Liko and watched me as I punched a hole, and he said, "That's no way to hold an awl. Careful you don't punch a hole in your leg."

We worked for a while in silence. The only sounds were the scraping of flint against wood, and the soft popping of the awl punching through leather. (And the clack of Liko's teeth as he munched his bone.) Occasionally Soli would shrink his neck down into his wool collar and let out a huff of steamy air. When I told him he was foolish for exposing his naked head to the wind, he asked, "Is it stupid to prepare for the deep cold of the Ten Thousand Islands? To toughen ourselves, to plan for the worst? *You* seem to be afraid of planning."

"What do you mean?" I ground my teeth and punched a hole in the cold leather.

He examined my handiwork and said, "Careful you space your holes evenly. We don't want the Devaki to think we do careless work." He shook his head at me, then said, "Your plan to collect tissue samples—it's really no plan at all, is it?"

Again I asked, "What do you mean?"

I had planned to collect Devaki nail clippings and strands of hair and other bits of cast off tissue in the hope of deciphering the Elder Eddes from their plasm—as circumspectly as possible. This was the Timekeeper's ruling: The Devaki must never know we were breaking the covenant between the founders of Neverness and the tribes of the Alaloi; they must never know who we really were.

"Your plan is careless," Soli said. "It may not be as easy as you think to gather up skin scrapings and the like."

"And you have a better plan, then?"

"There is a better plan. It's the women's plan; it's not my plan." He shivered violently and rubbed his hands together. His teeth chattered as he fitted the long bone runner to the wood chassis he held clamped in his white hand.

"Tell me about this plan," I said.

He rubbed the side of his nose and told me, "It's simple: The Devaki are known to be promiscuous in their sex. As Justine has pointed out, it would be a simple thing for our women to collect samples of the Devaki's semen."

"But that would be adultery!" I shouted. "Justine and you . . . and if you think my mother will swive—"

"Neither your mother or Justine will collect the semen. No one could ask your mother to do the impossible, and Justine, well it would be unseemly for a married woman to do that, wouldn't it? No, as Justine reminds me, the semen must be collected by an unmarried woman. And that's why Katharine will collect the semen."

"Katharine!"

"Yes."

"Your *daughter*? You'd make your daughter into a whore?"

"It was Katharine who suggested the plan."

"I don't believe you!"

He shot me a swift look, and I realized I had protested too strenuously. Until that moment, he probably had not suspected I had a passion for Katharine. I clamped my jaws shut and gripped the awl tightly. The hardness of it hurt my fingers.

"My daughter?" He smiled and I wanted to push the sharp tip of the awl into the black spot at the center of his eye. Never had I struggled so hard to swallow my rage and restrain myself. "Yes, she was my daughter, wasn't she?"

"I don't understand you."

He felt the sled's runner with his thumb tip; he stared at it with unfocused eyes as if he were examining a cast-off piece of his life rather than a material thing made of wood and bone. How I hated this inwardness of his! I hated that he found in every person or problem or thing an excuse to guiltily examine the scars and contours of his soul.

"It used to be," he said slowly, "when Katharine was a little girl, we could understand each other just by looking at each other. She was wise beyond her years, a beautiful, beautiful girl. But when she became a scryer, not a pilot according to my will, but a damned scryer—when she took her scryer's vows it was impossible to look at her eyes because she had plucked them out. No, Katharine left me long ago."

I told him I could not believe that a woman of the City—my cousin, especially—would willingly lie with the Devaki men, though in truth it was all too easy for me to imagine her coaxing the liquids of life from the membrums of brutal, rutting cavemen.

"Perhaps she's tired of the arms of civilized men," he said. I thought he was looking at my knotted hands, at my trembling arms. "Or perhaps she's just curious—she was always a curious girl."

I pushed hard with the awl, careless of what I was doing. There was a sharp, hot pain in my thigh; I yelled and looked down to see the bone point puncturing my woolens. A dark, widening circle of blood spread out from the hole. Liko, who had been anxiously worrying his bone, was up on his legs whining, sniffing, and looking back and forth between Soli and me.

Soli shook his head, all the while watching me peel back the fabric from the edge of my wound. "Do you need help,

Pilot?" he asked. "So careless," and he came over to me and reached for my leg.

"Damn you!" I shouted. I stood up and grabbed his forearms as he grabbed me. Hot trickles of blood ran down my leg, and Liko was barking because he didn't know what to do. "Damn you!"

We stood there for a moment, grappling. I felt the power of his new body running along the muscles of his forearms. I fought to get a hand free so I could dig my fingers into the soft area beneath his ear, to rip his jaw away from his face. But he held me as tightly as I held him. I could see in his frosty eyes a knowledge, an utter certainty, that with our toughened ligaments and new, popping tendons, we could destroy each other. We could pull each other apart, snap each other's bones, pulp each other's precious brains. Strong men can quickly kill strong men—I knew this suddenly; suddenly I was certain that he could see the knowledge in my eyes. We let go of each other at the same moment. Never again, I knew, could I touch him in anger unless I was prepared to kill him.

I withdrew the awl from my thigh and threw it at the bale of shagshay furs. It bounced twice across the topmost fur, leaving red skidmarks on the stretched, white leather. I tried to stop the flow of blood much as Mehtar had stanched his bleeding hand. The mind *can* control the body, I thought; how wonderful that brain is the master of muscle. I was trying to remember this, trying hard to quiet my raging muscles when Soli patted Liko on his head, nodded at me and said, "It must hurt you bad."

I did not know if he was referring to my wounded leg or to my outrage at Katharine's planned infidelities. He never said another word about either. (Nor would Katharine answer me when I demanded to know if she had really volunteered to collect the semen samples.) Ten days later, before dawn on the first of deep winter's dead days, Bardo and the members of my unhappy family drove our three loaded sleds out of the building. We paraded through the streets of the Academy down to the Hollow Fields where a windjammer was waiting to carry us six hundred miles over the western ice.

8

Kweitkel

And so Man dropped his seed into the Test Tube, and from the artificial wombs came many races of men, and races that were men no longer. The Elidi grew wings and the Agathanians carked their bodies into the shape of seals and dove beneath the waters of their planet; the Hoshi learned the difficult art of breathing methane while the Alaloi rediscovered arts ancient and ageless. On the Civilized Worlds there were many who sought to improve their racial inheritance in some small way. The exemplars of Bodhi Luz, for example, desired children of greater stature and so, inch by inch, generation by generation, they bred human beings ten feet tall. Chaos reigned as human beings from different planets found that they were unable to mate and bear children in the natural manner. Thus Man formulated the third and greatest of his laws, which came to be called The Law of the Civilized Worlds: A man may do with his flesh as he pleases but his DNA belongs to his species.

—from A Requiem for Homo Sapiens,
by Horthy Hosthoh

The Thousand Islands is a vast archipelago scattered across four thousand miles of ocean. In a broad crescent the islands reach from Landasalia in the uttermost west, to Neverness in the southeast. Although there are many more than a thousand islands, many, many more, most of them are small, volcanic upspillings worn almost flat by wind and ice and the pull of gravity; they are barren wastes of tundra and sedge and wind-packed snow. (In fact, the name "The Thousand Islands" is a mistranslation of the Devaki, *helahelasalia,* which means, "The Many, Many Islands." The Devaki, indeed all the tribes of the Alaloi, have no expression other than *hela* for quantities greater than twenty.) It is on the larger islands that the thirty-three tribes of the Alaloi make their homes. The islands of the southern group, which are called the *Aligelstei* (or "God's Glittering Jewels"), teem with life. They are very beautiful. There the Alaloi hunt shagshay and trumpeting mammoths through the evergreen forests; there they shield their eyes from the colors and brightness of the snowfields, and at night, they huddle in their snowhuts and caves drinking their blood tea and wondering at the light of the stars.

The sixteenth island is called *Kweitkel,* named for its great white peak rising fifteen thousand feet above the sea. According to my mother, who had imprinted the more relevant of the Alaloi Rainer's memories, we would find the Devaki gathered in a cave below the southern foothills of Kweitkel. Every winter, when the sea freezes fast, the scattered families of the tribe drive their dog teams across the open ice. They come from nearby islands such as Waasalia and Jalkel and Alisalia, and other islands, Sawelsalia and Aurunia, which are not so near. They come together to find wives for their sons and to perform their ceremonies of initiation into manhood; they come to tell stories and give gifts to each other, and they come because the dark of deep winter, when the air is so cold it sucks the soul from your breath, is a terrible time to be alone.

Our plan was to approach Kweitkel from the south, a single family group seeking our ancestral home. Here was the ruse toward which all our fakery had been aimed: We would pretend to be the descendants of Senwe, a brave man who had left the Devaki four generations ago to found a tribe of his own. (I hoped that the memory of Rainer *was* clean and true, that there had actually been a man named Senwe. Had he really ventured across the southern ice seeking *Pelasalia,* the fabled Blessed Islands? There are, of course, no islands to the south of Kweitkel, blessed or otherwise. Senwe, if he had really set out to the south, had no doubt died long ago when the pack ice broke up under false winter's harsh sun; he and his doomed family had most likely been sucked down into the cold, fathomless sea.) Under the shroud of darkness we would set down ten miles from the southern shore of Kweitkel. There, where the wind roars unceasingly and unhindered over thousands of miles of ice, we would harness our dogs and fasten our furs and make the short journey to our new home.

We left the City in the hold of a silvery windjammer, and we rocketed across the six hundred miles separating Neverness from the first of the Outer Islands. Two generations ago Goshevan had come this way, alone on the ice miles below us. Our journey was far easier and much quicker than his had been. In little time we passed over the fifteen Outer Islands, a famous poaching ground for wormrunners who risk death by laserfire in their lust to smuggle priceless, real furs to the tubists of the City. Below us, covered by the ink of night, were forested mountains and herds of white shagshay. Below us—again I had to rely on Rainer's memory—was the ancestral home of the Yelenalina and Reinalina, two of the largest families of the Devaki tribe.

We landed to the south of Kweitkel, according to our plan. At least, I believed we landed there. We had to rely on the navigation skills of a Markov Ling, a journeyman pilot fresh out of Borja. (It is ironic that we pilots, who easily journey from Urradeth to the Gelid Luz, are notoriously inept at the much simpler task of flying a windjammer.) In near silence we unloaded our three sleds and our fifteen whining dogs. We worked quickly so Markov could be off before the sun rose to expose our fakery to anyone who might be watching from the distant shore.

It was cold and black as I fumbled with the harness traces; the starlight was too faint to fully illumine my snarling dogs. But I could hear them growling and snapping at each other, biting at the freezing leather straps binding them. The wind blew dark, flowing sheets of spindrift over them, and they began to snort and sneeze and shiver. Next to me Bardo cuffed his lead dog, Alisha, with his open hand. With the hood of his shagshay fur pulled tightly around his head, he looked like a great white bear. He cursed and spoke to Justine; I could not make out what he said because the wind rose like a howl and blew his words out across the ice. Soli, who seemed immune from the wind, harnessed his dogs and bent low to check his load. The women, according to the Alaloi custom, helped where they could. But Justine grew careless. She pulled the harness too tightly around my third dog, Tusa's, chest. He slashed at her, nearly tearing her mitten from her hand. Instantly my mother fell upon the vicious dog with a leather whip. She lashed his hindquarters until he yelped and pushed his belly down against the snow. "That Tusa is a beast," she said into the whistling wind. She turned to me. "Didn't I tell you? That we should have used bitches instead of males?"

All this time Soli was staring at her, although it was too dark to see the expression on his face. He said simply, "Males are stronger," and he signaled to Markov that we were ready to be off. Markov, who never left the warmth of the ship, made a sign to Soli and fired the rockets. With a roar, the windjammer shot forward and angled upward into the dark eastern sky. The thunder echoed across the ice, then died.

I did not remember ever having felt so alone as I did that morning upon the sea. I, who had journeyed far into the manifold, billions of miles from another human being, stood to the east watching the red rocket tailings of the windjammer. To be alone inside a lightship—or any ship—was to be not really alone. There was the security of the womblike pit, the reassuring and familiar touch of the neurologics, the safety of human design. On the ice there was only bitter wind and cold so thick it was like liquid in my eyes and nose; on the ice there were things that kill, no matter the help of family or friends. For the first time in my life I would be intimately close with the things of life. I would kill animals for food and make my clothes from their bloody skins; I would fashion blocks of hard-packed snow into a house to keep from freezing to death. The wind cut beneath my parka, and I suddenly knew, in a tangible, immediate way, just how delicate my skin really was, despite its coverings of black hair and white fur. Ice-powder stung my greased face, and I listened to the moaning wind; I listened to the wind moaning from my chilled lungs and felt tiny needles of ice fracturing and reforming inside my nose with every breath taken and released. I wondered, neither for the first nor last time, if what I would find on the island of Kweitkel would be worth the price of aching teeth and frozen flesh.

After a while, Soli whistled to his lead dog, and I realized it was time to go. Since I was pretending to be an Alaloi, I thought I should practice their rituals. I turned to the four points of the world, giving thanks for the morning. In the east there was a low, red light the color of glowing blood where the ice joined the sky. Wisps of pink and gray hung from the blue-black dome, illuminated by the sun beyond the curve of the world. To the south, gray mist and endless ice. The west was dark, the outline of Sawelsalia still lost into the fold of night. I bowed to the north, and there was Kweitkel rising in the distance like a massive, white god. (The word "kel," which means mountain, is also the Devaki word for god.) Its lower slopes were green and dark white, almost slaty against the sky, but the snowfields of the upper cone glared orange in the streaming light. *"Kweitkel, nu la lurishia,"* I whispered, hoping no one would overhear me greeting the mountain. *"Shantih, shantih."*

We pointed our sleds north and whistled four short low notes followed by a long, keening, high note, that peculiar tiralee by which the Devaki urge their dogs forward when they wish to spare the lash. The dogs, with their black noses and lolling pink tongues, leapt at their harnesses and dug their feet into the snow. Soli drove the lead sled followed by Bardo. Most of the time the women rode in the beds of the sleds. At least twice that morning, though, my mother pestered me to take the rails of my sled. But I would not let her. Devaki women, I told her to her annoyance, do not drive sleds. I had the rear sled, which was the easiest to handle for two reasons: firstly, my lead dog, Liko, was by far the smartest and strongest of the dogs, and secondly because I had only to follow the track already broken by Soli and Bardo. The snow itself was hard-packed and clean; the iced runners of our sleds glided smoothly in their parallel grooves. The Devaki call such snow *safel*, fast snow, and fast it was. By midmorning we had covered most of the distance to the island, and we would have gone even further but for the ragged and pitiful condition of the dogs.

I must admit here that I was to blame for starving the dogs. From the first, this cruelty was my plan. Of all the hurtful things I have done in my life—and there have been many things, many—in some ways I regret this torture of innocent beasts most of all. It was necessary, so I told myself and the others, necessary that we put forth the *appearance* of having traveled a great distance. If we had really crossed a thousand miles of ice, as we were pretending we had, our dogs would be thin with toil and hungry from eating half rations for too many days. To this end, against Soli's wishes, I had demanded that the dogs be fed very little. Furthermore, I had—I myself did this—before we left the City I had rubbed salty, frozen slush into their paws until they bled and froze. As they whined and looked at me with their trusting eyes, I had starved and maimed them; I did this so the Devaki would accept us as brothers, and we might discover the secret of life. (I am not, I know, forgiven this barbarity merely because I starved myself. The others did the same. What is man but that being who can stand any barbarity, misery or pain?)

It was a pity, too, that Bardo and I had to whip the dogs. All the way to the island, Bardo used his whip freely. He shouted and cursed and flailed at the hindquarters of his rear dog. Curiously, Soli, whose dogs had the task of breaking trail, did not use his whip. He had learned another trick from Lionel, learned it better than Lionel himself. I remember how Soli's clear whistle pierced the morning air. It was a beautiful whistle, full of music; to this day I can hear the keening of his whistle. There was an urgency in the clean, high notes and also an understanding, as if Soli well knew the agony of shrunken bellies and freezing, bleeding paws. He whistled over and over the short tiralee, and his dogs panted and pulled hard at their traces. Soon, I hoped, if our luck held, they would be rewarded with a roaring fire and bloody hunks of fresh-killed meat.

Thus we approached the rocky shore of the island. There was a thrilling spray of wind, the scrape and glide of the sled over the snow. My face was so numb from the cold I could barely speak. But there was little to say and much to listen to: the yelping of the dogs and Bardo's blustering voice; the screams of the thallows as they dove from the cliffs beyond us and beat their wings against the wind; the ice particles etching the rock promontories rising out of the sea; and when the wind died and the living things were quiet for a moment, the sudden rush of silence, vast and profound.

About a mile from the shore, I saw that there would be difficulty with our landfall. The southern coast of Kweitkel was broken with high cliffs; spires of volcanic rock pushed out

of the coastal waters like great, ragged, black fingers eaten
away by a disease of salt and snow. At the high strand, the sea
was frozen upon the rocks, the ice crusty and folded and
thick, glazed ripples running across the beach in uneven
bands of white and blue. I thought we would do better to
circle the island and drive our sleds up the gentle slope of the
western coast. When we stopped for our midday meal of
baldo nuts and cold water, Soli disagreed, saying, "If we
pretend we're of the far south, we must be seen to approach
from the south."

"But the western slope would be quicker," I said in a
voice slurry with cold.

"You're always hurrying, aren't you?"

"Perhaps the Devaki have been watching us approach," I
said. "They've had the whole morning to watch us." I looked
at the stark southern cliffs, and I felt a rawness in my throat, a
presentiment of disaster and doom. But I was no scryer, so all
I said was, "I don't like these cliffs."

I wondered how our three sleds would have appeared as
seen from the ridge above the Devaki cave. There could be
nothing as tiny and insignificant as men and the artifacts of
men moving against the spread of the endless ice. Three tiny
lines strung out across infinite whiteness, creeping more
slowly than a snow worm—that, I imagined, is what anyone
would have seen looking out to sea.

Soli tightened his lips, which were shiny with grease.
"The universe doesn't turn around Mallory Ringess or any of
us." As if to reassure himself, he looked at Justine, who was
sitting on his sled's bed. "Why should the Devaki be watching
us?"

I rubbed the side of my nose; the hardened grease was
sticky and cold. I said, "If we take our dogs up through the
cliffs, they'll think we're stupid."

"No, that's not so." He held his hand over his brows,
squinting as he picked apart sections of the beach with his
hard eyes. He pointed at a break in the sea cliffs where the
beach rose up to meet the forest. "There," he said, speaking
the Devaki language as if born to it. "We will drive our sleds
along the tongue of ice where it licks the edge of the
forest."

"It will be hard going."

"Yes, that is true," he said.

That afternoon we performed the hardest work of our

lives. Near the island, the sea was frozen into a patchwork of green and blue ice blocks, a jungle of crystals the size of a house, of cracks and humps and jagged spears of ice which snagged the harnesses, almost impaling the dogs. There were moments when the sleds jammed against the fissures and folds of the ice ridges, or worse, dangled over the edge while the dogs howled in frustration and fear. At least three times we had to unharness the dogs and stand at the top of a ridge, pulling hand over hand at the leather traces, hauling our loads up and over. Once we had to unload the sleds completely. Bardo, of course, hated effort of any sort which did not occur in bed, and at every opportunity he bellowed and cursed the instance of his birth. Each of us, in his or her own way, reacted according to type: Justine sang a cheerful little tune and laughed at every difficulty just because she loved being outside in the snow next to her husband; Katharine, distracted and disassociated from her labor, was fascinated by the ice's glitter and the texture of the distant forest, and she could not stop looking all around at the things of the world; Soli seemed to relish problems of any sort, probably as a test of his cleverness and ability to endure pain. Only my mother—and here was one of the great surprises of my life—seemed at ease with the muscle-popping work. She moved across the dangerous ice crusts lithely and surely; she seemed to relish the strength of her new, Alaloi body. This newfound pleasure of being was apparent in the relaxed way she pulled at the harness traces and leaned into the wind, driving forward with her hips as she set her boots against the slippery ice; it was apparent in the set of her sculpted face, which, for all its thickness of nose and jaw, was very beautiful.

It was late afternoon when we reached the edge of the forest. The muscles along my forearms were swollen and burning. I had strained my knee when Katharine lost her footing and slipped, and the whole weight of the near-dangling sled had fallen upon me. I had slipped too, twisting the joint with ligament-tearing force. I owed it to Mehtar, I knew, that the ligaments had held. I limped along the snowline where the beach gave way to the dark forest, and I found myself—absurdly—giving thanks to the tubist cutter that I was not a cripple.

Bardo, who pretended to be crippled with exhaustion, sat on a rock holding his head in his hands as he moaned, "By

God, I'm tired! See my hands? Why can't I close them? This is madness. Ah . . . but it's cold, cold enough to freeze your piss before it hits the ground as I'd show you if I weren't too tired to stand. Goddamn Shiva Lal and goddamn Drisana Lal for spreading her legs and having him and having me. Damn Govinda Lal and damn Timur, too, and Hanif and . . ." He went on in this manner cursing his ancestors for inflicting upon him the pain of living; he went on for quite a while. The princes of Summerworld, I knew too well, had an excellent memory of their lineage. He cursed his great-grandfather's grandfather, and he cursed the unreasonableness of water for permitting itself to freeze into the greenish-white icicles hanging down his mustache. At that moment I did not pity him, even though I knew that before coming to Neverness he had never seen snow or ice.

While my mother took one of the dogs and went into the woods on skis to survey the terrain, Justine began wrapping skins around the other dogs' bloody paws. Katharine, I noticed with a mixture of annoyance and wonder, bent over a bristly bush, holding her naked hands spread above the petals of a fireflower. "It's warm," she said. "The colors, look how they change, red into burning carmine, carmine into . . ."

Soli crunched up the beach over to me, and we immediately started to argue. I was eager to drive on to the Devaki's cave, but he shook his head and said, "It's late. The forest is no place to be at night."

"By nightfall," I said, "we'll be in the Devaki's cave. There's only four miles of easy forest ahead."

"Yes, if Rainer's memory is true."

"Don't you have faith?" I asked him slyly.

"Faith!" he said, and he knocked the snow from his boots. "We've two hours before twilight."

"Do we, Pilot?"

I looked to the west but we were too near the base of the cliff to see the position of the sun. I wished we had brought a clock with us. It would have been an easy thing to do. I remembered seeing in the Timekeeper's Tower a clock no bigger than the nail of my little finger. (The nail of my little finger, that is, before Mehtar carved my hands.) The clock was a wafer of some alive substance which glowed and shifted colors to mark the passing of the seconds and hours, much as Katharine's flowers mutated from magenta to flame-purple. If

I had hidden one of these wafers in my furs, I could have predicted the moment when the turning edge of the world would obliterate the sun.

"We could have had the tinker attach a clock to the radio," I said, reopening the old argument. "But you wouldn't break the Timekeeper's edict."

The radio itself was hidden inside the false bottom of Soli's sled along with the spheres of krydda we would need to preserve the culled Devaki tissues. Of course, it was not easy to get at the radio; we would use it only to signal the windjammer when we had finished this dangerous business of posing as cavemen.

It seemed that Soli regretted he had not broken the Timekeeper's edict against clocks. It must be difficult, I thought, to be the Lord Pilot. He stared at the base of the cliff, at the banded layers of rock; it was as if he were staring through ancient marls and sediments down to the heart of the world. "The Timekeeper is right, isn't he, to hate time? Why should we care what time it is? Why do we need a clock when we have Mallory Ringess to reassure us we have two hours before the light dies?"

When my mother returned to report that the way through the woods was clear and not very steep, our decision was made. "There's deep snow," she said. "But the crust is thick. Look at Ivar. With his hard, little paws—he didn't break through the crust."

It was while we were harnessing the dogs for our final run through the forest that a terrible thing happened. I should have been forewarned because Katharine suddenly dropped the traces, stood erect and gazed off into the sky as if she were looking at a painting. But I was tired, too busy with Liko to realize she was gazing at the reenactment of a past vision. I was pulling the harness around Liko's deep chest when there came a flurry from behind a rock near the edge of the forest. A snow hare, its ears laid back flat, bounded across the snow in a wild zig-zag. Liko let out a tremendous bark, and before I could grab hold, he bolted after the hare.

What happened next is difficult to tell. Difficult not only because my memory is disturbed and opaque but because the telling of it hurts. Liko sprinted across the snow, a blur of near-white against white pursuing a bounding ball of white.

Bardo was up off his rock, looking skyward, shouting, "By God, look at it!" There came another blur from over the lip of the cliff. The hare hopped nearer to the forest, and I looked up to see a great blue shape spread against the blueness of the sky. It was a thallow with its talons pointed, diving toward the hare, diving toward Liko, diving toward one or the other—I did not know which—but diving fast and true, its rear talon pointed like a falling spear. It drove the talon into Liko's neck. There was a terrible high cry. Or perhaps it was the mingling of two cries: the victorious cry of the great bird joining Liko's terrified yelp—I do not know. The dog dropped to the snow, squealing, working his jaws. I was running toward him, and I wondered why he didn't try to escape the thallow. I was running toward him, too blind from the dazzling snow and fear to realize that the thallow had probably broken his neck. While I was running toward him, intent on pulling the wings from the thallow and breaking *its* neck, the bird looked at me with its bright eye as it dug its talons into Liko's side. It turned its head as if puzzled, and then it dipped its hooked beak into Liko's frothy mouth. There was another terrible scream, and then silence. The thallow held its head up—and all this time, which was almost no time, I was running—the thallow held Liko's pink tongue in its beak. It snapped its head suddenly, swallowing the bloody tidbit, and it fixed me with its eye. It dipped its beak again, as if it had endless time to perform this violation. I heard myself scream, and the tip of the beak tore into Liko's eye, which all the time had been open and alive with terror. I beat the air with my fists; the thallow threw back its head and opened its throat, and then, looking almost leisurely at me, it sprang into the air with a cry and a thunder of wings and soared off into the sky.

I stood over Liko, opening and closing my hands, helpless.

Soli came over to me, and Bardo, and the others came too. Soli looked at Liko, who was whimpering, and he said, "Can't you see he's dying?"

I was silent, staring at the red stains on the snow.

"Your dog, Pilot, he's your dog."

The bloody slush froze while I watched, and Soli said, "You'll have to kill him."

No, I thought, I can't kill Liko, my lead dog, my friend.

"Do it now, Pilot. Quickly."

"No," I said. "I can't."

Soli, who rarely cursed, shouted, "Damn you!" and he bent quickly as he whipped his balled fist with a terrible force against Liko's head. I heard the skull crack, and Liko was still, a piece of fur and meat lying dead against the snow. Soli cursed again, and he bowed his head and pressed the flat of his hand against his temple as he walked away.

Bardo came over to me, and I said, "Liko's dead."

He draped his heavy arm around my shoulders and squeezed. "Little Fellow," he said.

I tried to look at Liko but I could not. "He was alive," I whispered, "and now he's dead."

Bardo dropped to his knees. He removed his mitten and felt beneath Liko's fur for a heartbeat. "Too bad," he muttered as he shook his head. "Too bad."

I wanted to throw my arms around Liko, to touch his fur, to hold my hand against his freezing nose. But I could not touch him. He was not an alive being to be touched; he was a thing of fur and hardening blood and bone, and soon, when the thallow returned or the wolves worked at his meat, he would be nothing more than a stain on the snow.

"He was so pretty," Justine said. And then, so softly her words were nearly lost to the wind, she said, "Liko, *mi alasharia la shantih*," which is the Devaki prayer for the dead.

I tried to repeat the prayer, but I could not make my lips form the words. I had never before seen an animal die. I did not believe that Liko's spirit would rest in peace on the other side of day. "There's no glory when the ticking stops," the Timekeeper had told me. "There's only blackness and the hell of everlasting nothingness." I looked at the dog's body, and I saw nothingness. The wind roared in my ear and rippled through his fur like waves upon false winter's sea, and I remembered I had seen death before. Once, when I was a boy on the beach outside the Hofgarten, I had seen a seagull pecking the corpse of one of his brothers. I remembered this first vision of death very well: the torn, oily feathers dirty with seafoam and sand, the bright red jewels of meat holding my fascinated stare. And later that same day, the day I had ended my solitary walks on the beach, I had seen the skeleton of a beached whale revealed by the ebb-tide as it withdrew into the sea. I remembered the great fingers of white bone curving upward from the wet sand as if to grasp the wind's breath from the sky. Yes, I had seen death before, but never the dying, never. The broken, seagull's wings, the whale's naked ribs—these were *things* capriciously cast upon the beach, bone reminders that there was a horror and final mystery to be avoided at any cost. I looked at Liko's fine body, the thick neck, the deep chest, and I saw that he was at once a thing and something more; he was a unique being I had watched pass from life into death. It was this passage that terrified me. It was the dying that made my teeth ache and robbed my muscles of will. I looked at Liko and felt tears freezing in my eyes; I looked at Liko and I despised myself because I realized he was far beyond my pity or pain.

I would have buried him but the snow was too hard for digging. Down the beach, Soli whistled to his dogs, a reminder that soon the forest would be dark, that we had no time for burials. Justine, that innocent, beautiful woman who thought she could never die, said a few foolish words of consolation to me and went to join him. My mother stood over Liko, rubbed her heavy eyebrows and cocked her head. "He was only a dog," she said. "What is left to bury? We should go back to the sleds. Before it's too dark." She left me there, too. I watched her unharness Tusa and put him at the lead of the sled in Liko's place.

"Barbarians!" Bardo shouted at them. "By God, look at this poor dog!" He lifted his head to the sky and let loose a thunderous curse. He cursed the thallow for killing Liko, and he cursed the gods for letting him die; he cursed Liko's sire and dame for whelping him; he cursed Soli and last of all he cursed me. He bent low to the beach, cursing, and in his arms he hefted a granite boulder which he placed over Liko's body. I lifted a rock, a smaller rock, and did the same. In this manner, working like madmen, we quickly built a cairn over the dog.

When we were finished, Katharine came over with handfuls of fireflowers she had picked in the woods. She laid them atop Liko's grave. "I'm sorry, Mallory," she said.

"You saw the thallow, didn't you? In a dream—you knew this would happen."

"I saw . . . possibilities. I knew but I didn't . . . There's no way I can make you see it, is there?"

I watched the flowers shrivel and lose their red fire; it only took a few moments for the light to die.

"You should have warned me, what you saw. I could have saved him."

"I'm sorry."

"I don't think you are."

"I'm sorry for you."

There is not much left to tell of our long day's journey to the Devaki's cave. Our passage through the forest was as quick and easy as I had hoped. I remember that the island was beautiful. The green trees against the soft, white slopes, the white and green hills where they touched the blue sky—curiously this perfection of colors comes instantly to mind whenever I recall the tragic events of our journey. (I do not mean the death of Liko; I am referring to the tragedies which were soon to come.) Our dogs pulled us gliding over the gentle, gradually rising upland. It was not so cold as it had been out on the ice, but it was cold enough to crack trees. A few times we passed the shredded, fallen corpses of the shatterwood trees half-buried in the snow. Though we never saw one explode, the thunder of dying trees reverberated from hill to hill. There was wood-dust and long white splinters driven into the drifts; I saw that Soli was right, that the forest was no place to be at night.

At last, as the light faded and our shadows grew almost as long as trees, we came around the curve of a small hill. Before us was a larger hill, and set into its northeast face like a black mouth was the cave of the Devaki. Above us, to the north above both hills, high above the lesser undulations of the world stood Kweitkel, vast and white and holy—or so the Devaki believe. But standing there in the half-light and stillness, looking up into the depths of the cave I did not feel holy at all; I felt tired, desecrated, and very, very profane.

9

Yuri the Wise

From Man and the Bomb were born the Hibakusha,
the worlds of Gaiea, Terror, Death, and the First
Law of the Civilized Worlds, which was that Man
was forbidden to explode hydrogen into light. And
the Hibakusha fled and took to bed Law, and so were
born the Aphasics, the Friends of God, the Astriers,
Autists, Maggids and Arhats of Newvania. And Ter-
ror wed Death, and so were born the Vild and the
great Nothingness beyond. And Terror wed Law as
well and begat the Hive Peoples, who valued life less
than Order, and so they surrendered their Free Will
to the lesser god of Order. Of the Hive Peoples we
know almost nothing.

—from *A Requiem for Homo Sapiens*,
by Horthy Hosthoh

Our entrance to the cave was a confusion of barking dogs
and shouts and children running between our sleds. With
their little hands they peeled back the sled covers to see if we
had brought with us mammoth tongues or shagshay liver or
any other of the Devaki's favored delicacies. They rapped the
leather barrels of baldo nuts and shook their heads, disappointed that our only remaining food was so meager and poor.
They seemed not to suspect that we were not their distant
cousins but civilized people come to steal their plasm. We
stood near our sleds waiting as their parents emerged from
the mouth of the cave. I turned my face to the entrance fires
and let the heat melt the ice from my beard. There were

babies crying, the smell of roasting meats as well as the stench of wet fur and rotting blood. I was unready for this stench, and it made me sick. The cloying thickness of old piss sprayed on rocks, the woodsmoke and cut pine, the reek of skin oils and baby vomit wafting from the furs of the curious Devaki women—though Rainer's memory had proven accurate it seemed that it was also incomplete; I had no memory in my mind of these terrible smells. (This, I believe, is a flaw in the workings of the akashic computers. The memory of smells is captured deep within the limbic brain, sometimes too deep for the akashics to reach.) The area between the firepits was strewn with gnawed bones and pieces of hide and flesh; I had to step carefully lest I squash one of the numerous, half-frozen piles of dog dung atop the snow. The men of the Devaki—thick, rude men dressed as we were in shagshay furs—surrounded us, touching our furs, touching our sleds, touching each other as they spoke their words of welcome, *ni luria la Devaki, ni luria la*. Then Soli, who was patting the head of one of the children, said, "I am Soli, son of Mauli who was the son of Wilanu, the Whalekiller, whose father was Rudolf, son of Senwe who left the Devaki many years ago to seek the Blessed Isles." He turned to me and put his arm around my shoulders. "This is my son Mallory; we are the people of Senwe, who was the son of Jamaliel the Fierce."

I hated the touch of Soli's hand on my shoulder; I hated having to pose as his son. I hated the stench of the cave and the running wounds on the blunt hands of the men, and I hated the crush of stinking bodies pressing me, the odor and intimations of disease and death. I hated all these things and more, but I had little time to savor my hatreds because Soli's recitation of our fake lineage had aroused great excitement. There were laughs and shouts and gasps of astonishment. A huge, one-eyed man limped forward and cupped his hand around the back of Soli's neck. He did the same to me and said, "I am Yuri son of Nuri who was the son of Lokni the Unlucky." Yuri, with his bristly gray beard and weathered skin, was past middling old and taller than any of the forty men of the cave except Bardo. He had a huge, high nose cutting between his prominent cheekbones. While he spoke to us, he turned his head back and forth like a thallow, his single eye scrutinizing our sleds and our gaunt, growling dogs. He seemed to be searching for something he could not find. He continued, "Lokni's father was Jyasi, son of Omar son of Payat, who was Senwe's older brother and Jamaliel's son." He threw his arms around Soli, pummeling his back with his fists. "We are near-brothers," he said, and his great brown eye glistened in the light of the fires. *"Ni luria, ni luria, Soli wi Senwelina."*

He led us inside the entrance to the cave. Thirty feet from the fires there were two snow-huts, small domes made of cut snow blocks carefully trimmed and fit together. The small hut nearest the rear of the cave had a hole in the wall big enough to stick a head through. The other hut, which was pitted with the shallow pockmarks of dripping water, was even smaller. After Soli introduced my mother and Bardo as his sister-by-marriage and nephew (this, too was part of our deception), Yuri stared at them with his eye and told them that they were welcome to share the smaller hut. He came up to Bardo and he squeezed his upper arm and felt the muscles of his chest. He said, "Bardo is a strange name, and you are a strange man, I think, strange but very strong." He looked my mother up and down as if doubting that she was Bardo's mother, and told her, "You should have named him *Tuwa*, the mammoth." He indicated that Soli and I, and Justine and Katharine, were to share the larger hut. I thought I had misheard him. Surely he could not really expect all of us to cram into such a tiny space? I looked through the hole in the wall but it was too dark to see anything. The smells of rotting fish and piss made me want to kick the hut in. "You may lay your sleeping furs and patch the hole, and you will be warm," Yuri said. "Now, I will show you the cave of Jamaliel son of Ian whose father was Malmo the Lucky, son of . . ." and as we went deeper into the cave, he recited our line of ancestry halfway back to the mythical Manwe, who was the son of Devaki, mother of the people. (According to the myth, the god Kweitkel thrust the tip of his cone inside Devaki where it erupted, thus filling her womb with Yelena and Reina and Manwe, and the other sons and daughters of the world.)

The cave was a lava tube opening seventy yards into the depths of the hill. It had been formed, no doubt, when some gigantic bubble of gas was trapped within a pocket of molten lava flowing from one of Kweitkel's erupting vents. (The real Kweitkel, I mean, not the god.) The lava had cooled and the gases had bled away through cracks in the hardened rock. At some time in the distant past, a quake had fractured the end of the tube, opening the cave to wind and snow, and to the tiny band of Alaloi who had made it their home. Opposite our two snow-huts, but deeper inside the nearly cylindrical cave, were the huts of one of the smaller families of the tribe, the Sharailina. Midway into the cave—it was difficult to see very much—a pendant of cooled lava hung from the ceiling to the cave floor. The lava, perhaps molded and shaped by the pressures of the wild, primal gases, had cooled unevenly; if one looked at the pendant from behind, facing the entrance fires, the bulges of rock and shadowy indentations took on the profile of an old man smiling.

"He is the Old Man of the Cave," Yuri told us, "and he is smiling because deep winter has come and all his children have returned to him." We went deeper into the cave, past the huts of the Reinalina and Yelenalina families, until we came to the Manwelina's six huts, as deep as I thought we could go. Then I heard a baby squalling, and Yuri pointed into the darkness. "Deeper still are the birthing huts; it is my granddaughter you hear crying."

We sat on the dirty furs laid between the huts of the Manwelina family. Strictly speaking we were not of the Manwelina because our pretend ancestor, Senwe, had left the family to form one of his own. Nevertheless, Yuri welcomed us as family. He motioned for Liam and Seif, his two huge sons, to sit with us while his wife served us bowls of hot soup. Her name was Anala, which means "lifefire," and she was a stout, well-formed woman with gray hair hanging to her waist. She smiled too readily and too much, and I did not like it when she immediately befriended my mother. I was suspicious of the way they hugged each other and alternately cupped their hands and whispered in each other's ear. My mother, I thought, had become a Devaki woman a little too quickly.

Yuri said, "My wife is happy to meet her near-sister, and who can blame her?" Then he looked into the sick yellow glow of the burning oilstones as if *he* were not happy at all. Plainly, he did not like my mother. To Soli he said, "Tell us of your journey, tell us of *Pelasalia*, the Blessed Isles."

While Soli told the carefully forged lies, the fake story of our "miraculous" journey, the people of the Devaki gathered around us. Where they could not sit, they stood with necks stretched and ears turned toward Soli, hoping to hear his memorable words. When he had finished, there were surprised gasps and cries of woe. Wicent, who was Yuri's younger, shaggy brother, said, "It was a great tell. A sad tell, but a great tell. We will pray for the spirits of our near-mothers and fathers and children who died on the frozen sea."

What Soli had told them was that Senwe had *not* found the Blessed Isles, that he had found instead a frozen, barren waste where the living was hard and grim. Soli's ancestors, he lied, had neither prospered nor multiplied. When his father, Mauli, had died, Soli said he had determined to return the survivors of the family to their ancestral home. "But Mallory's wife, Helena, and my three grandchildren took a fever and died on the journey. And Bardo's wife died in childbirth before we ever set out."

I rubbed the side of my nose in embarrassment because it was hard to listen to such a fraudulent story. To my surprise (and, I suppose, satisfaction), the Devaki seemed to believe every word of it.

"We will pray for the children especially," Yuri said. "When you arrived without your children I was afraid to ask you what had happened."

With feigned bitterness Soli rubbed his temples and said, "The Blessed Isles are a dream. To the south there is nothing but bare rocks and ice; the ice goes on forever." He told them this, as we had planned, so that none of the Devaki would kill themselves journeying south, seeking a dream.

But Liam, whose blue eyes were wild with bravery and dreams, said, "You should have gone farther south instead of returning to Kweitkel. South, where the ice is not endless but gives way to the Blessed Isles. The air is so warm, snow falls as water from the sky."

"There is only ice and death to the south," Soli said.

Liam looked at Katharine as she threw back the hood of her furs, and he mumbled, "Perhaps it is good that you came north."

I did not like the pugnacity of his strong face; I did not like the way he looked at Katharine as she brought the bowl of soup to her lips and blew on the steaming broth. Even by civilized standards of beauty he was too handsome a man, with his straight nose and long, pretty eyelashes. His hair and his luxurious beard were golden, a color I never liked to see on a human being. I suppose he had a charming smile—everyone said he did—but when he opened his mouth to smile at Katharine, all I could think was that his teeth were too large and fine, his lips too red, too full, too sensual.

"To the south," I said, for once agreeing with Soli, "There is only ice and death. Only a fool would seek death by ice."

"It is said, what is foolishness to a weak man, a strong man does bravely."

"After you've crossed a thousand miles of ice," I said, "and had to kill your lead dog, then you may speak of bravery."

Liam looked at me quickly, as if realizing he could achieve more with flattery than insults. "Of course all the Senwelina were strong and brave to cross the frozen sea. To survive the storms, the cold of the Serpent's Breath. My near-brother, Mallory, is very brave, and my near-sister is very brave and beautiful. It is good you have returned home so that such a beautiful woman does not have to marry Bardo, her brave cousin."

I hated the way Katharine smiled at him as he said this. It was a bold smile, an intimate smile laden with curiosity. I hated having to pose as her brother. I wanted to grab Liam by the collar, to shake him, to tell him that *I* was Katharine's cousin, not Bardo. I wanted to tell him, to tell everybody that as soon as we returned to the City, Katharine would marry her cousin, her real cousin. Instead I clamped my jaws shut and said nothing.

Yuri got up and walked to the front of the cave. He removed several ropes of meat hanging from the spit above the fire. He carried these back to us slung over his arm, careless of the juices leaking from the cracks in the blackened flesh. One of these ropes he presented to Soli, while he kept one and handed the remaining one to his brother.

"We watched you coming from the south," Yuri said. "It has been a poor year; the shagshay and the silk belly have fled to the Outer Islands, and Tuwa is so sick with mouthrot and his numbers so diminished that we may not hunt him." He brought the charcoaled meat to his nose and sniffed. "We've had to hunt *Nunki*, the seal. But his numbers too are diminished because the fish do not swim as they used to. *Nunki* does not leap to our spears. This seal meat is the last of our meat. Liam would have eaten it for breakfast, and who could blame him? But we saw you coming from the south, and we knew that if you were men, not spirits as Wicent said you must be, you would have a hunger for meat."

So saying he threw back his head and opened his mouth. He dipped the meat rope in and severed a section of it with his strong, white teeth. The meat, I saw to my horror, was raw beneath the black crust. Yuri bit and chewed quickly and swallowed and bit again; he swallowed and chewed and blood from the near-living meat ran over his red lips. As he chewed he made a sucking, slobbering sound as of wetness being slapped against wetness. He chewed with his mouth open, gustily pulping the tough meat.

Soli watched him carefully and then did as the old man did, devouring the meat like a beast. Yuri ate a few more mouthfuls of meat, and he passed what was left to his oldest son, Liam. Soli, with his face held rigidly impassive as his jaws worked, offered me the disgusting, mutilated rope of meat. But I could not touch it. I, who had so eagerly planned this romantic quest for the secret of life—I was sickened and frozen by the piece of life dangling from Soli's greasy fingers.

Liam looked at me as he tore at his meat. Yuri, too, had his eye turned to me, obviously wondering why I did not accept the meat. "It is good, fat meat," he said as he winked at me and licked his mustache. "I hate to kill Nunki, but I love the taste of his meat."

Soli was staring at me, and Wicent and his sons, Wemilo and Haidar, were staring too. My mother and Katharine and a hundred curious Devaki men and women—everyone was staring at me. Bardo, sitting cross-legged next to me, nudged me with his elbow. I reached out to take the meat. It was still warm from the fire, hard on the surface, hot and soft and yielding within. I held it lightly, as if afraid my nervous fingers would bruise the meat. Greasy juices oozed from the broken crust, running over my hands. I felt hot juices squirt inside my mouth, the sudden hot nausea deep in my throat. The smell of roasted meat made me want to retch. I turned my head, swallowing saliva, and I said, "I should give this meat to my cousin, Bardo. He is bigger than I and hungrier than a bear at the end of midwinter spring."

I glanced at Bardo, who was indeed eyeing the meat as he chewed his mustache. Bardo, I thought, despite his layers of acquired culture and taste, despite the deep repugnance of a

civilized man for anything other than cultured meat, despite
the sheer *barbarity* of eating living meat, Bardo if he were
hungry enough would eat anything.

But Yuri shook his head back and forth and said, "Does a
son refuse the life his mother and father gave him? No, and
so he may not refuse the meat his father offers him nor the
drink his mother makes. Are you sick, Mallory? Sometimes
the cold and wind make a man so sick with hunger he cannot
eat. Then his hunger dies and *his* meat falls away from his
bones, and his hungry ghost is too eager to see the other side
of day. I think you are a hungry man who has denied his
hunger too long: This a blind man could see. Shall I send
Anala to make some blood tea? To awaken your hunger?"

I held the rope of meat in my hands and I swallowed back
my vomit and I said, "No, I will eat the meat." From the lore
of Rainer's akashic records I suddenly remembered the reci-
pe for blood tea. Great as my disgust was at the eating of
meat, I had a greater horror of drinking the tea, an unbelievable mixture of seal's blood, urine, and the bitter root of the
shatterwood tree. I tilted my head back and dangled the meat
above my mouth. I took a bite of meat.

I will not pretend the meat tasted very different from the
cultured meats my mother had made me eat as a child. It did
not. True, the meat was fattier and rimed with char and
much, much rarer than any meat should be. But it was still
meat. "Meat's meat," Bardo said, stuffing himself with meat
after I had eaten my share. No, it was not the taste of meat
that bothered me; it was the idea of chewing flesh that had
once jumped to the command of a living brain, flesh that had
been alive. I chewed and swallowed slimy proteins little
different from those cloned from de-brained muscle cells and
cultured in vats. I ate my portion of meat horrified yet
fascinated at this need of life to feed from other life. The
tastes of iron and salt filled my mouth, and my cold, exhausted
body awakened to its urge to life. I took another bite of meat
and then another, and still another. It tasted good. I was so
hungry I filled my mouth with bloody gobbets; I chewed so
quickly I bit my cheeks. I swallowed my own blood along
with that of the seal's and ate until I felt the urge to vomit.
When I could eat no more I handed the meat to Bardo.

The rest of our meal was even more disgusting. And
worse, the old, decayed foods Anala and the women brought

forth did not even taste good. The Devaki men and women, their children too, cracked baldo nuts between their teeth. They ate the plump nut-meats, which were yellow and moldy, covered with a white fuzz. Wicent's wife, Liluye, a skinny, nervous woman with stumpy yellow teeth, prepared us a soup of rotten thallow eggs. The big blue eggs had incubated too long, but the Devaki ate them anyway, straining out only the eyes of the embryos. (They did this because thallows are blind at birth, and they did not wish to acquire this blindness.) There were other foods as well, foods I could not believe a human could eat: raw chunks of seal fat swallowed as my mother would a ball of chocolate; the raw intestines of thallows and other birds; year-old mammoth bones which had been buried and allowed to soften and rot; and of course, the ever-present bowls of reeking blood tea. (I do not mean to imply that the Devaki took no care of the substances they swallowed. This was not so. Curiously, they would drink no water containing the tiniest particle of dirt. And as to the aforementioned foods, they ate them only because they were hungry. Hunger is the great spice of life. Later that winter, when we were nearly starving, worse horrors were to come.)

After we finished our meal, Yuri massaged his belly and said a prayer for the souls of the animals we had eaten. "The winter has been cold and hard," he said. "And last winter was hard, and the one before that. And the winter before, when Merilee died, that was a bad year. But if you had come five winters ago you would have feasted on mammoth steaks." He yawned and squeezed Anala's thigh. She sat next to him searching through his head hair with her fingers. "But tomorrow Tuwa is sick with the mouthrot and the Devaki are hungry, and so we hunt the seal." Anala removed an insect—I think it was a louse—from the gray hair above his ear. She crushed it between her dirty fingernails and swallowed it. Yuri motioned to Soli, Bardo and myself. "Are the men of the Senwelina, who are Devaki as I am Devaki, are they too tired to hunt the fat, gray seal with us tomorrow?"

I should have let Soli answer since he was the supposed head of our family. But I was full of seal meat and horror, and I could not bear the thought of murdering so intelligent an animal as a seal. "We are tired," I blurted out. "We are tired and our dogs need rest."

Soli flashed me a fierce look as Liam rubbed his greasy hands over the face of his younger brother, Seif. (Was this a protection against the cold? A barbaric benediction? I searched my mind, but I had no memory of such a custom.) With a broken fingernail Liam pried a strand of meat from between his teeth. "You were not too tired to eat the seal," he pointed out.

He bent over me suddenly, and I smelled his thick reek as he ran his calloused hand under my furs and tested the muscles of my neck and back. How I hated the Devaki customs! I hated this intimate touching; I hated the cold, greasy touch of a strange man's hands, the horror of another's skin touching mine. "Mallory is thin but still strong," he announced. "Strong enough to hunt the seal, I think. But he is tired; perhaps he should rest in his furs while his near-brothers bring him fat-rib and tenderloin and other delicate pieces of meat."

I twisted away from him. How easy it would be, I thought, to grab his windpipe and tear it from his throat. I twisted and I pulled my collar tight around my neck, and then I said a thing that made Bardo and Soli, and the others from the City, look at me strangely.

"We are tired," I said, "but not too tired to hunt. On the southern ice there are no mammoth so we hunt the seal often. I have killed many seals; tomorrow I shall kill a seal for Liam and give him the liver."

As I said this I was reminded of my brag to penetrate the Entity. But where that brag had been impulsive and had nearly cost me my life, to Liam I had bragged to a purpose. I would kill a seal. Somehow I would kill a noble animal. I would do this in order to shame Liam into silence and to gain approval for my "family." Then, I thought, we might more quickly find what we were looking for and leave this filthy, barbaric place.

We sat there on the furs for a while telling stories—false stories—of hunting seals on the southern seas. Anala's pretty daughter, Sanya, served blood tea, which the Devaki slurped noisily, smacking their lips and tongues. Later I was shocked to see Sanya's baby sucking milk from her nude, blue veined breast. Everything seemed to shock me that night, especially the uninhibited cries of delight coming from the nearby huts of the Yelenalina. I overheard a woman gasping out intimate instructions to her husband—I hoped it was her husband—and I listened to the ragged breathing and rustling furs, the sounds of human beasts rutting. Immersed as I was in these new sensations, I hardly noticed Yuri moving closer to me. I stared at the faint petals of fire fluttering above the oilstone in front of me, and I was shocked when he softly said, "You should not kill the seal. Nunki is your *doffel*. That is why you had trouble eating seal meat—I should have seen this immediately."

The Devaki, I remembered, believe that every man's soul is mirrored in the soul of a particular animal, his *doffel*, his other-self whom he may not hunt.

I looked around quickly, but no one was paying us any attention. Soli and Justine had returned to our hut. My mother and Katharine sat with Anala while Bardo entertained— if that is the right word—the others with a song he composed as he sang it.

I turned to Yuri and said the first thing that came to mind, "No, *Ayeye*, the thallow is my doffel. My grandfather told me so when I became a man."

He grabbed my arm suddenly, looking at me with his sad eye as he said, "Sometimes it is very hard to determine which animal holds our other-self. It is hard to see and mistakes are made."

"My grandfather," I lied, for I had no grandfather whom I knew, "was a very wise man."

Just then everyone started laughing because Bardo had mispronounced two words of his song, which had completely changed their meaning. He had meant to sing:

I am a lonely man from the southern ice
Searching for an elegant wife.

But he had gotten the vowels all wrong, and the lines came out as:

I am a purple man from the southern ice
Searching for an elegant lice.

He seemed not to notice his mistake, not even when Anala cackled like a snow loon, slapped her thighs and started searching through Liam's blonde hair to see if she could find Bardo any "elegant lice." Apparently, everyone thought his mistake was intentional, that he was a great wit, not just a silly buffoon.

Yuri smiled and gripped my arm more tightly. His hands were as huge as Bardo's but harder, toughened by years of work and cold. "Sometimes," he said—and there was a peculiar urgency to his voice—"sometimes grandfathers, who are very near to their grandsons, cannot see the soul hiding behind the eyes. And you have difficult eyes, a blind man could see that. They are blue and fierce as an ice-mist, and they look far away. Can you blame your grandfather, Mauli, for mistaking your soul for the angry soul of the thallow? But Ayeye is not your doffel, I need only a single eye to see that. Nunki the seal, who loves the taste of sea-salt and the ocean's cold peace—he is your doffel."

It is impossible to explain here the beliefs of the Alaloi. There is no space to record the rich mythologies, the totem system devised to commune with the spirits of animals and with what they call the World-soul. (In any case I am not sure I really understand the concept of telepathic communications with trees and thallows and seals, even rocks. I do not understand—even now, after all that has happened—how the Alaloi creates the world moment by moment in the trance of the eternal Now-moment.) It is a complicated system and old, so old the historians have no record of its beginnings. Burgos Harsha believed the original Alaloi had borrowed piecemeal bits of Sufi mysticism and other ancient philosophies that would suit their new environment. They had also adopted, he thought, the totem system and dreamtime of Old Earth's ancient Strailia tribes. There, in the deserts of that isolated continent, man had had fifty thousand years of solitude to develop this system of symbol and thought. It was an elaborate system, logically consistent, dependent on strange hierarchies of thought and mind. There were rules by which men and women lived their lives. A man's method of building a fire, the direction in which he pisses (to the south, always to the south), the times he is permitted copulation with his wife—every aspect of life is determined by this refined system. No matter how primitive and naive it seemed to me, it represented the longest unbroken intellectual scheme in man's history. And since Yuri, as eldest of his tribe, was a master of this system, I should have accepted that he could determine the one animal I was not permitted to hunt. But I did not accept this and I said, "Tomorrow I shall hunt Nunki as I said I would."

Yuri shook his head back and forth. He whistled the long, low note the Devaki whistle when they mourn for the dead. "It is sad," he said. "It is not well known that once in a great while a man is born who does not accept his other-self. And not accepting this he is vulnerable because the other-self will seek to destroy him rather than be left alone forever. For him there can be no joining, no unity. And so he must kill, he is doomed to kill this half of himself—do you understand? If he does not do this, the remaining half—the deathless-self—can never grow to fullness. It is very painful and hard, and I must ask you: Are you willing to be a murderer?"

We sat there talking for a long time, gazing at the cave's walls. All the others had long since gone to bed, and there I sat listening to the words of a superstitious old man. Yuri had a richly resonant voice. With the intonation of a master storyteller—or shaman—he held me with his voice, speaking on and on, far into the night. His words contained echoes of arcane philosophies and mysteries. His words were too simple to be taken seriously, yet they disturbed me even so. He told me that the fear of this self-murder would make me sick; he prophesied that a day would come, and soon, when my courage would flee like a snow hare into the forest, a day when I would gnash my teeth and cry: All is false! "For what is the *great* fear?" he asked me. "It is not the dread of cold nor of the white bear's teeth. These are fears of flesh, fears we forget sitting by the warm fire or playing with our wives. It is not even the fear of death because we know that if the tribe prays for our ghosts we will live forever on the other side of day. No, the great fear is the fear of the self inside. We fear becoming this deathless-self. To discover the unknown within is like jumping into the mouth of the volcano. It burns the soul. If you kill your doffel, you will come to know this fear. And you must understand, this is pain without measure or end."

I finally limped back to our hut in a state of utter exhaustion. It had been the longest day of my life. (Excluding, of course, those days in the manifold—they were not really *days*—spent in slowtime.) I crawled through the entrance tunnel into the hut's glowing interior and found that someone had laid out my sleeping furs on a bed of snow. I climbed into

them. The pain of my knee and the other pain made me lie
uneasily. The oilstones were burning and they cast a warm
yellow light over the sleeping figures on their snow beds.
Katharine lay next to me, her breathing as even and gentle as
the lapping waves of the sea. Soli, I noticed to my astonishment, was holding Justine in his arms as he slept fitfully. (I do
not know which was the greater shock: this tenderness of his
or to see that he, the broody Soli, was actually capable of
sleep.) I was exhausted but I was also trapped in that overly
stimulated state of wakefulness beyond exhaustion. I thought
about Yuri's words. I could not sleep. Soli's grinding teeth,
the plip-plop of water falling from the roof in syncopation
with the overly loud beats of my heart, the hissing of the
wind through the ice-patched hole in the wall—these sounds
kept me awake. The snow walls were too good of an insulation against the cold. The hut was too warm and it stank. The
heat of the sleeping bodies brought out the reek of rotting
piss and my own sour sweat and other odors I could not
identify. So awful was this reek that I could hardly breathe.
The air smothered me like an old fur soaked with vomit. I felt
a sickness and dread in the pit of my stomach. I flung off the
furs, dressed quickly and ran from the hut to the mouth of the
cave where I spewed my feast onto the snow. I thought of my
promise to murder a seal the next day, and I retched until my
stomach was knotted and dry. As I stumbled outside the cave
a dog growled and snapped, and then another and another. I
turned in a half-crouch back toward the cave. There, in the
ragged, orange light, against the flickering tongues of fire, the
dogs were leaping at their leashes. Tusa, and Nura, Rufo and
Sanuye, my poor, starved sled dogs, fought among themselves, snapping up half-digested pieces of seal meat from the
pink slop steaming on the snow. Tusa growled and slashed at
gentle Rufo, who yelped and contented himself with lapping
up one of the smaller puddles of vomit. Then Tusa ripped
open Nura's ear, and Sanuye ate the slushy snow red with
Nura's blood.

I pulled the dogs apart. There was a jumble of snapping
muzzles and barks and surging fur. One of the dogs bit me. I
tied them tighter to their stakes, and I scooped mounds of
snow over the mess I had made.

What a terrible thing true hunger was! How wrong I was
to have starved the dogs! My bleeding hand burned as I

thought about this, and there was a pain in my empty stomach. Was this life, then? Was this emptiness inside and desire for food the price of living? No, I thought, it is too terrible a price, and I wondered at the vanity which had brought me to the Devaki seeking the meaning of life. The secret of life—could it really be embroidered upon the chromosomes of these filthy, blood-drinking people? Could their ancestors really have captured within their DNA the mystery of the Ieldra?

I imagined I had the skills of a splicer and an imprimatur, that I could unravel the strands of Yuri's DNA as an historian, in his search for knowledge, might pull apart an ancient tapestry. Would I find coded among the twisting sugars and bases information that the Ieldra had woven long ago? Was there some message coiled within the testes of Wicent or Liam, some secret of meaning, a right way of living for all mankind? And if this message existed, why should it be shrouded in mystery? If the Ieldra could tell us to look in our past and future for the secret of life, why couldn't they tell us what this secret was?

Why couldn't the gods, if they were gods, simply talk to us?

I looked up at the stars, at the bright triangle of Wakanda, Eanna and Farfara twinkling above the eastern horizon. Beyond them the core of the galaxy was streaming with laser pulses in a way the mechanics could not explain. If I opened my eyes as wide as I could, would they burn with the light of the gods? If I turned my face to the distant solar wind of the core stars, would I hear the gods whispering in my ears?

I listened but the only sound was the sigh of the wind sifting through the forest below. From the western slope of Kweitkel came the howl of a wolf calling out to the sky. I stood there for a while listening and watching, watching and waiting. After a while I turned back to the cave. Tomorrow I would kill a seal and perhaps understand, if not the secret of life, the meaning of death.

10

The Aklia

Man cannot bear too little reality.
—Saying of the cetics

Early the next morning I awoke to a chorus of coughing and
spitting, the sounds the women and men of the Reinalina
family in the huts across the cave made as they hawked up
clots of phlegm and cleared their sore throats. My throat, too,
was raw from the intensely cold air of the previous day's
journey. (Was it only a day ago, I wondered, that the thallow
had killed Liko? It seemed like a year.) Dressing was painful.
My leg was so stiff I could hardly straighten it. Although I
was very hungry, I could not eat the nuts Justine offered me.
"*All* our throats are sore," she said while she roasted nuts
over the fire at the center of the hut. "It hurts to swallow
them, I know, but they don't taste bad if you chew them
quickly, and you'll need your strength if you're really going to
hunt a seal. Are you?"

Katharine, who was on her knees dressing, looked at me
as if she knew exactly what I would do. She said nothing. Soli
sat by the oilstones scraping ice from his furs. I marveled at
how erect and straight he could hold himself even when
sitting—and this despite the pain of his newly sculpted spine.
(For some reason, Soli had taken longer to heal than the rest
of us. Mehtar had hypothesized that there was a limit to the
resiliency of rejuvenated cells and that Soli, who had thrice
been brought back to youth, was close to that limit.) He
looked up, and for a moment his eyes moved over the objects
and features of the hut: the rectangular block of snow used to

stop the tunnelway against the drilling wind, the cracked, peeling drying rack above the oilstones, the long, serrated snow-knife, the hide-scrapers, spears, bowls, drills and other tools stacked against the curving walls, the soft, still-warm sleeping furs atop the snow bed on which he and Justine had so recently lain. He said, "Yes, Mallory will hunt the seal."

I looked at him and lowered my voice, "We spent half a year planning this expedition but we forgot one thing."

He contracted his black eyebrows and stroked his beard. "What thing?"

"Coffee," I said, feeling the ache in my head. "I'm dying for the taste of coffee."

"You're hungry," he said. "That's why your head aches."

"I didn't say my head aches."

"You didn't have to say anything." And then, "Do you think you're the only one who craves coffee?"

I coughed and looked at Katharine combing her long, black hair. I said, "Perhaps this journey was a stupid idea."

"Eat some nuts," Soli said. "Eat; don't think about coffee or your stupidity. You'll have time enough for both when we return to Neverness."

I picked up a handful of nuts and popped them in my mouth. They tasted dry and bitter.

"You have to chew them," Justine said. To Soli she held out a bowl of roasted nuts, which he took in the following manner: He placed his long hands over hers and watched her eyes as she slowly drew her hands away, slowly allowing him to take the weight of the bowl. With this intimate gesture they touched each other's skin and caressed with their eyes. Obviously, despite their very different motivations and dreams, despite years of mutual neglect and rancor, despite the bitterness of crueltime, they loved each other deeply. It was a love, I thought, renewed by their sense of isolation, by the clarity of frozen ice and open sky. And how not to love the beautiful Justine with her endless optimism, her zest and happiness at merely being alive? Yes, I could see why Soli loved her, because we all loved her; what I could not understand was why she loved him.

After we had munched down our breakfast, Bardo and my mother crowded into our hut to drink a few bowls of herb tea. What a strange little group we were, sitting elbow to elbow in a circle, hunched over, sipping from our bone bowls, pretending

to be Alaloi! What a miracle that we had fooled the Devaki
into believing we were their near-brothers! In a way, I was
glad enough to be posing as Soli's son. Everyone had accepted Soli as my father, whereas Liam had make jokes about
Bardo's conception.

"I don't like that man," Bardo said to me, all the while
rubbing the sleep from his large, brown eyes. (It was a pity, I
thought, that Mehtar had little altered the ugliness of his
great bulging forehead or his bulbous nose.) "Did you hear
what Liam said? He said your mother shouldn't be left alone
when we go hunting, or else she might be raped again by a
bear and give birth to another Bardo. What a joke!"

I was glad none of the Devaki knew I was my mother's
son, not Justine's. If they had known, they probably would
have joked that Soli had raped my mother. "If they knew my
mother," I whispered to Bardo, "they'd feel sorry for any
bear—or anyone else—who tried to rape her." As far as I
knew, my mother had lain with a man only once in her life,
the night she had conceived me.

Soli finished his tea and announced it was time to go. He
reached for his seal spears. "Yuri and his family will be
waiting." He was frowning, looking at Katharine when he
said, "We'll leave you women to do your. . . women's work."

Somehow I did not think Soli was referring to the sewing
of skins or the suckling of babies, the everyday work of the
Devaki women. Clearly, he suspected that Katharine and I
were lovers. Clearly, he wanted to torment me with thoughts
of her lying beneath the Devaki men. Either that or he
wanted to torment himself—I am not sure which. But I did
not think Katharine would have much of a chance to "do her
work" that day. Most of the men would be away hunting, and
I did not think she would have any luck collecting semen
from young boys.

As we put on our furs, my mother was looking from me to
Soli to Katharine, and then back at me. I did not like the
way she looked at Katharine. It was a look, I thought, of envy,
probably because Katharine was capable of work that she was
not. "Go hunt your seals," my mother said. "And while you
are gone we *women* will prepare your beds. To lie in when
you return."

We joined the other men and boys of the Manwelina
family at the entrance of the cave. The many teams of dogs

gobbled their food as the men laid out the harnesses and iced the runners of their sleds. The work was cold and painful in the pink light of the dawn. Beneath ice-glazed boulders and fir trees heavy with snow, Yuri and Wicent, and Liam, Seif, Haidar, Jinje and the other men of the Manwelina, had their sleds belly-up towards the still dark sky. Since ice would not adhere directly to bone, they plastered a paste of vegetable muck and pulverized dirt mixed with water and urine over the runners, repairing the nicks and divots with a thick shoeing of frozen mud. The morning air was so cold that the paste froze immediately upon contact, making it difficult to shape and smooth. It was frustrating work. I expected to hear grumbling and curses, but the Devaki men joked and laughed, all the while dipping their fingers into the bag of warm mud they wore inside their furs next to their skins. Quickly, precisely and quickly, they daubed blobs of mud over our bone. Ten feet from me Liam artfully smoothed over a divot with his fingers and then quickly stuck them in his mouth so they wouldn't freeze. The air was thick with little shouts and puffs of steam and muddy spittle as the men sucked their fingers and laughed and talked and spat. Bardo was having a difficult time with his sled, and so was I. He moved over next to me and muttered, "Isn't it romantic? The cold, clear air, the lonesome cry of the wolf, peace, nature's sweet kiss, serenity — and the taste of pissy muck. Thank you, Little Fellow, for bringing me to this enlightened place."

I watched Liam spray lukewarm water from his mouth. He smeared the quickly freezing liquid over the mud shoeing. In little time, the runners of his sled glistened with layers of ice. I looked around the clearing. Yuri's cousins, Arani and Bodhi, and their sons, Yukio, Jemmu and Jinje were spraying their sleds, too.

Bardo shook his head at Jaywe and Arwe, who were also Yuri's cousins, and he said, "They've had a lifetime of this stinking work. How do they stand it?" Then he bent and spat water along the runners of his sled, doing as he saw the others do, binding ice to frozen mud. "This is what I truly hate," he said as he hefted his waterskin. "I loathe having to carry this bag of water next to my belly. What is man—a heat machine to keep water from freezing? The damn sloshing galls me, by God!"

Soli saw us whispering and strode over to us. "Quiet," he

said. And then, "*Silu wanya, manse ri damya,*" which might be translated as: Children complain; men restrain (themselves).

We loaded the sleds and harnessed the dogs, and Yuri gathered his family around him. He said, "Mallory has promised to take a seal, and so Mallory must tell us where Nunki is waiting."

The men looked at me, and I remembered that among the Alaloi promises to take meat are not made lightly. A hunter may promise a kill only when he perceives that his meat animal is ready to "leap to his spear." To do this he must fall into the state of *auvania*, or open-waiting, a sort of trance state in which he feels wild and fey and can see through the black sea of death to the other side of day. Such visions he may not seek; they are a gift of the to-be-slain animal's living spirit, his anima. I faced Kweitkel's white cone and let my eyes focus on infinity. I tried to practice this seeing, tried to *askeer,* as the Alaloi say; I tried too hard. No vision came to me. But the men were waiting, so I pretended the seal's anima had appeared before me. I said—I lied: "*Lo askaratha li Nunki, mi anaslan, lo moratha wi Nunkiyanima.*" I sagely pointed west because the western islands, Takel and Alisalia, seemed like golden mountains of snow and I felt an urge to be closer to them.

Yuri nodded his head and turned his eyes east to greet dawn. "*Lura sawel,*" he said, and we repeated after him, "*Lura sawel,*" all the time standing in that curious position in which the Alaloi do reverence to the sun: Like insects I had once seen in the zoo, we stood with our arms together and raised to the sun, our fingers closed and pointed towards the snowy ground. With our heads bowed, we stood on one leg, the other leg bent up behind. We stood in this ridiculous position for a long time because the great Manwe, on the tenth morning of the world, had so honored his uncle, the sun. Then Yuri grasped the rails of his sled, whistled to his dogs and we were off.

The day broke cold and calm with the hills smothered in near-silence. The only sounds were the schussing of the sleds and the snow loons' warbling as they glided and circled, circled and dived, looking for their morning meals. On the far ridges the shagged limbs of the fir trees stood out clearly, so clearly I could almost distinguish the separate needles. We drove straight down the gently sloping forest to the sea. The

land was folded and in places cut with ravines and granite
cliffs. I was wary of those cliffs because thallows made their
aeries there, above the dark green trees. There were no
thallows that day, however, even though the snow hares and
sleekits were busy digging for berries. Once I saw an arctic
fox, and more than once we came upon wolf tracks frozen in
the snow. But they were old tracks; most of the wolves, Yuri
said, had abandoned the island to follow the shagshay herds.

When we reached the sea there was some trouble crossing the frozen breakers, though far less than we had encountered
the previous day on the ragged southern shore. By late
morning we were free of the icy jungle, running fast over the
cotton cake snow of the Starnbergersee. About five miles
from land I nodded to Yuri and we scattered. I say "about"
because the air was heavy as liquid over the ice, a huge, blue
lens distorting distances, making far things seem near. Four
sleds glided northwest towards Alisalia, which wavered on
the horizon across miles of white ocean; nine sleds—Yuri's
and Liam's among them—headed in the direction of Jakel
and Waasalia. We fanned out over a circle of ice perhaps two
miles in diameter. I halted my sled at a likely spot. I
presumed all the other hunters did the same. I unharnessed
Nura, who had been trained to sniff out seal holes. To the
north, some fifty yards away, Bardo had his seal dog leashed,
though it was not clear who was leading whom. The powerful
Samsa pulled Bardo in jerks across the snow, trotting this way
and that, occasionally sticking his black nose in the snow and
blowing out a cloud of white powder. To the south was Soli,
and to the west, across the brilliant ice, Yuri and his sons had
apparently found their holes and were cutting snow blocks to
build a wall against the wind.

The Alaloi call the seal's hole the *aklia*. I held Nura on a
leash of braided leather as he pawed the snow and sniffed,
searching for his *aklia*. He seemed happy to be free from the
sled; twice he lifted his leg and yellowed the snow just for the
fun of it. Then he caught a scent, let out an excited bark, and
lunged at the leash. He started digging at the snow. After
marking the spot with a stick, I dragged the disappointed dog
downwind and staked him to the ice. I did the same with my
other dogs, Rufo, Sanuye and Tusa. Seals are practically blind
but their sense of hearing is extraordinarily keen, and I did
not want the dogs' barks to alert my seal. I returned to the

aklia carrying my feeler-stick and ice-saw, and other more murderous gear.

Seals, being earth-type mammals, cannot breathe water, as can certain peculiar orders of carked mammals bred to the seas of Agathange and Balaniki and other watery worlds. They must have air, and so each seal keeps many holes in the ice open throughout the winter. A bull seal—and perhaps a cow—will bob up and down in the water as the ice crusts are forming in early winter, breaking and rebreaking the thin, frozen sheets as the ice builds and builds around the aklia. He visits his many holes, bobbing up and plunging down, breaking through to the air, breathing and swimming on to his next hole. When winter deepens to its longest, coldest days, the walls of the hole are nearly ten feet thick. As the snows fall and blow and freeze and melt and refreeze, a snowbridge forms over the hole, obscuring it from the eyes of the hunter, but not from the dogs' sensitive noses. Beneath the snowbridge, the seal comes up to sit on the sloping ice ledges on either side of the hole. There, under the arch of packed snow, in midwinter spring, the cows give birth to their furry pups. There the seals huddle and play, safe from the wind and drowning and the teeth of the killer whales— but not safe from men.

I took my curved feeler-stick and pushed it down through the snowbridge, down into the hole I could not see. By rotating it around in a circle I felt-out the size of the hole and determined its center. Then I lifted my face to the north wind, which stung me even through layers of grease. It was cold, not so cold as deep cold, but colder than blue cold. My eyes watered and my toes were a little numb. I thought it might be a long wait for the seal, so I cut blocks of snow and built a wall around the north rim of the aklia to shield against the killing wind. Next I slid my wooden marker-bob down through the center of the hole until it touched the water. As the seal came up to breathe, he—I prayed it would be a bull because I dreaded killing a pregnant female—he would displace a large quantity of water, causing the marker to bob up. When it sank, I would know the water had fallen back to the ocean's surface and the seal had risen.

"*Lo luratha lani Nunki,*" I prayed, and I spread a square of silk belly fur in front of the hole. I stood on it wiggling my stiff toes, hoping its insulation would keep my feet from freezing like blocks of ice. The last thing I did was to rest my harpoon across two forked sticks that I shoved into the crusty snow. The detachable head of the harpoon, the wickedly sharp, barbed, murderous head, was made of whalebone and had a carved ring at its base. Knotted to this ring was a long, braided leather cord. I wrapped the end of the cord around my hand and watched the marker-bob. When it rose I would pick up my harpoon, and when it fell—when the seal had risen and the marker fell—I would thrust the harpoon into the center of the aklia. I would do this murderous thing because in my jealousy and pride I had promised to do so.

And so I waited. Precisely how long I waited I do not know. What is time without a clock with which to measure it? How long did I stand in that difficult attitude of the hunter, feet together, buttocks high, looking down, always down, watching the marker-bob in the seal's hole? How long, *pela Nunki*? How long must a hungry man wait until his emptiness is filled?

"Three days," Yuri had told me the night before. "Three days is not too long to wait because Nunki has many holes. At the last moment his anima might be too frightened to make the great journey, and so he will make the shorter journey to another hole."

I watched and I waited bent over like a crippled old man. I stood absolutely still while the muscles along the back of my legs began to knot and burn; I waited a long time.

It is said that patience is the supreme virtue of the hunter. Very well, I told myself, I would be patient. I listened to the wind slash across the ice; I listened to the individual whorls and eddies which flowed together into gusts and then nearly died before building and surprising me with stronger, colder blasts. Occasionally the wind would die altogether, and there would be silence. These long spells filled me with unease and restless anticipation. I did not want to hear the murmur of my own heart, nor was I eager for the explosive rush of air when the seal came up to breathe, when he came, if he came at all. There were many things I did not want to hear. I knew that the great white bears hunted seals and hunted humans, too. According to Yuri, *Totunye* liked to sneak up close to an aklia, to lie in wait before pouncing and bashing in the hunter's head with his murderous paw. When stalking across the snowdrifts the bears are impossible to see, and they make

almost no noise. I listened for the swish of bear fur against
ice, waiting. From the north there came a distant moan. It
was the wind again, and it swelled into a low howl, whipped
across the ice and began to roar. I waited a long time and I
was very cold. My bladder filled. Far above me the yellowish
glare off the icefields vibrated against the blueness of the sky.
The Devaki call this cold shimmer of yellow-chrome an
iceblink, I suppose because the brightness makes them blink.
I blinked my eyes, all the while staring at the marker-bob set
into the aklia. I thought of the pain in my bladder and the
pain of the bear's teeth, and other pains. I tried to concentrate. I imagined the seal's anima was whispering in my ears,
calling out to me, but it was only the wind. The wind cut my
face, and I waited, and I blinked my eyes, and . . .

The marker-bob rose.

I picked up my harpoon, waiting for the marker-bob to
fall. As it disappeared into the aklia, with both hands I
grasped the long harpoon high above my head. I drove it
down into the snow. It slid easily through the crust, and
then there was the sickening resistance of the harpoon's barb
piercing the seal. A deep, anguished bellow resounded beneath the snow as the seal called to me. I shouted, *"Lo moras
li Nunki!"* and I gripped the leather cord attached to the
harpoon's head. There was a violent pull which nearly jerked
me off my feet. I dug my heels into the snow, leaning
backward, straining against the cord while I wrapped it
around my back.

"Mallory *moras li Nunki!"* I heard Bardo call out. And
then, echoing across the ice from aklia to aklia, growing ever
fainter, the cry: Mallory *moras li Nunki!"*

I heaved backward trying to pull the seal from his hole.
There was a stab of pain in my sore knee. I gained a few feet.
And then, forward again as the seal fought me and backward,
and suddenly, beneath the snowbridge, the seal surged with
life and pulled me off my feet. I slid toward the aklia with my
face and chest scraping the snow. If I did not let go, the seal
would pull me down through the crumbling snowbridge,
down into the killing sea. I gripped the cord more tightly. I
tried to flip onto my back and rotate my heels forward, to dig
them into the snow. But I fouled my legs on the cord even as
the snowbridge began to buckle and collapse. I was helplessly
ensnarled by the tightening cord.

"Let go!" a voice boomed out. But I could not let go. Then the cord tightened behind me. I turned to see Bardo, with his eyes bulging and his fat red cheeks puffed out, heaving against the cord. "Pull, damn you!" he shouted.

I found my feet and pulled at the cord. I stared down into the open aklia. From beneath the blocks of snow floating and bobbing atop the churning sea there emerged a great, black seal. High on his side, above the flipper, the base of the harpoon's head stuck out of a bloody hole in his skin. I heaved so hard I thought the harpoon would pull free. But it held, and foot by foot we hauled the seal out of the aklia onto the snow. I was horrified because the old bull was still alive. He let loose a cough that sounded like an exhausted sigh, and bright arterial blood sprayed from his mouth onto the snow.

"Mori-se!" I said to Bardo, *"kill him!"*

But Bardo shook his head and pointed north at Yuri and Liam, who were running to help us. It was my privilege and duty to kill the seal, as cowardly Bardo reminded me. I had promised to do so, but I could not.

"Ti Mori-te," Bardo said, and he handed me a stone maul. "Quickly, Little Fellow, before I start crying."

I swung the maul in an arc down against the seal's forehead. There was a thwack of granite against flesh and a whoosh of air as if the seal were expressing gratitude at being released from his agony. And then silence and stillness. I looked into the seal's dark, liquid eyes but the life was gone.

Yuri and Liam stopped at the edge of the aklia. They were puffing for air. Yuri examined the seal and immediately prayed for his spirit. *"Pela Nunkiyanima,"* he said, *"mi alasharia la shantih Devaki."* He turned to me and said, "Look at him, Mallory! Never have I seen such a seal! He is a grandfather of a seal, a great-grandfather of a seal! It is a miracle that you and Bardo alone could pull him from his hole."

Soli came running to us, as did Wicent and the rest of the Manwelina family. They surrounded the seal, nudging his blubber with the toes of boots and touching his dark skin. Liam pulled at his thick lower lip and said, "This is a four-man seal. Once, when I was a boy, my father and Wicent and Jaywe pulled up a three-man seal, and that was the largest seal I have ever seen." He looked at Bardo and me with a mixture of envy and awe and asked, "How did two men pull up a four-man seal?"

Yuri turned his eye to his son and explained simply, "Bardo is as strong as two men, I think, and today Mallory killed his doffel, and so you must not wonder how two men pulled a great-grandfather of a four-man seal from the sea." But for a long time he looked at the huge carcass lying on the snow as if *he* wondered how we had done such a thing.

I had killed a seal.

I scooped a handful of snow into my mouth. I leaned over and opened the seal's mouth. His smell was fermy and strong. From my lips, I let a stream of cold water trickle into his mouth, giving him a drink so he would not be thirsty on his journey to the other side.

Soli caught my attention and gave me a slight nod. Among the Alaloi it is a given, the most basic thing, that hunters who have taken an animal will immediately eat their fill. Since I had killed the seal, it was my privilege to begin the butchering. But I hesitated so long I could almost feel Soli's eyes drilling into me. Then I picked up my knife. I split the seal's belly open, and I cut around the liver. It was bloody, horrifying work. To Liam, as I had promised, I handed the purple, steaming liver. He sullenly cut it into strips and distributed them among the other hunters. "Mallory was lucky," he said.

I ate a piece of liver. The taste was rich and steely and good. I could hardly believe I had killed a seal.

"Mallory Sealkiller has brought us luck," Yuri said. "Bardo the Strong and Mallory Sealkiller, they have brought us luck. Tomorrow, I think, there will be many seals."

Almost everyone was smiling and seemed happy. There was one man, however, Yuri's cousin's son, who was not so happy. His name was Jinje, and he was a stocky, ugly man with a crooked leg. He had frozen his feet waiting for his nonexistent seal. Yuri helped him get his boots off, then held him while he stuck his ugly, hairy, white, frozen feet into the seal's carcass to thaw them. Then Liam cut him a piece of liver which he gulped as if he were a dog.

The men fell on the seal with their knives, hacking out choice organs and cuts of meat. Wicent's youngest son, Choclo, opened the stomach and found it full of notothins and ice perch and other fish. With his impish, beardless face and his small hands, he was really more of a boy than a man, but he was an expert with his fish knife. In no time at all he scaled an ice perch, gutted it and found yet a smaller fish in

its stomach. After cutting off its head and scales he swallowed
it whole. All around me the other men were busy cutting and
swallowing. The snow near the seal was slippery with fat and
spattered blood. It was a terrible thing, this hunger of men.
Their bellies groaned and rumbled while their teeth tore at
huge chunks of meat. It was astonishing how much meat a
single man could eat. I myself ate most of the heart because
that is where Alaloi believe the soul dwells. We fifteen
hunters, our bellies bloated and our beards crusty with frozen
blood, must have eaten a hundred pounds of meat. It was a
serious business, this devouring of ready flesh, and we ate
without pause or conversation. The only sounds were the
cracking of our jaws and smacking lips, and the fatty belches
of Bardo and Choclo competing to see who could let loose
the loudest. Like beasts we first ate the choicer cuts of meat
and then put our teeth to less desirable tidbits. Liam, perhaps impatient with the pace of the feast, tore out a rib which
he broke apart with his fine teeth. He sucked down the
marrow as a baby does milk. We ate for a long time, stopping
only because dusk was approaching and it would be deadly to
be caught in the open after dark.

The men of the Manwelina returned to their aklias to
build snowhuts for the night. After moving our sleds and dogs
closer, we fed the whining beasts a slop of intestines, blubber
and lungs. Then Soli and I built ourselves a hut near the
aklia. I cut blocks of snow which Soli stacked one atop the
other, filling in the chinks with ice-powder. Bardo held his
belly and belched, watching us work. "Oh, my poor stomach," he moaned, "what have I done to you!" To Soli he said,
"It's selfish of me, I know, to watch while you work, but you're
doing so well without me."

Indeed, Soli *was* doing well, trimming out the hut and
fitting the key block as expertly as any Alaloi. Soon the hut
was done and we flopped our sleeping furs inside. The north
wind blew a continuous sheet of spindrift across the darkening
sea. In silence we each turned to the south and performed
our "piss-before-sleeping." Bardo went to bed while Soli and I
staked Tusa near the tunnel of the hut. We hoped he would
let out a howl or bark in case a bear sniffed out the seal's
carcass and came to explore.

For a while we watched the stars wink into brightness in

the sky. Soli drew the hood of his parka tightly over his head. "You were lucky to kill the seal—such extraordinary luck."

So, I was lucky to have killed a great, noble animal.

"You can't always count on luck," he said. "One day the weight of antichance will fall against you. You'll be standing under a building at the wrong time or perhaps one night on a back gliddery you'll cross paths with a poor harijan only to find he's a slel necker come to steal your plasm. Or perhaps you'll try to pierce the Vild's inner veil and lose yourself—"

"I don't believe in chance," I said.

"Yes, how forgetful of me, Mallory must pursue his *fate*."

"Don't you think it's strange beyond coincidence that the seal chose my aklia?"

"Yes," he mocked, "the seal's anima sought your hole so you could grasp your fate. Well, how does it feel to be a killer?"

I wiped the water from my nose and said, "It feels... natural." In truth, it did feel natural, although I did not tell him how I dreaded taking my place in the natural order of things.

"Is that true?" he asked me.

I placed my mittens over my face to warm the muscles. Talking was difficult and my words were coming out like slush. I did not want to discuss my fears with him so I said, "You're a tychist, aren't you?"

"You think so?"

"It's the creed of older pilots, I've heard."

He rubbed his temples and said, "Yes. Those pilots who rely on possessing a fate grow careless and do not grow old."

"But you've taken greater chances than I have. 'Soli the Lucky' the journeymen used to call you when I was at Resa."

"Calculated chances, every one."

"But chances, nevertheless."

I think he smiled then, but it was already so dark I could not be sure. He stomped his boots against the snow, trying to keep warm. "One day the weight of antichance will fall against me, too." And again he mocked me, saying, "It's my fate."

I worked my jaws silently before asking him, "You don't believe it could be a man's fate to be lucky, then?"

"No," he said, "not forever."

Then he yawned, knocked the spindrift from his furs, and

entered the hut to sleep for the night. I stood looking at the purple-black mountains of Alisalia outlined against the glowing horizon.

It was my fate to have killed a great, noble seal.

At last the wind found me beneath my furs, and I began to shiver. I crowded into the small hut and collapsed next to Bardo, who was snoring loudly. I lay stiffly awake for a long time before the warmth of my furs lulled me and I slept. But I did not sleep soundly. It was a night of twisting and sweating, a night of dreams. One of my dreams I remember well: I dreamed I killed a great seal; I dreamed that the seal's son and daughters, not wanting to be alone, leapt to our spears so they could join their father on the other side of day.

The next morning we killed nine seals, and Soli said that we were very lucky.

11

The Old Man
of the Cave

Live? Our servants can do that for us.
—from *Axel*, by Villiers de L'Isle Adam, Machine
Century Fabulist

The Devaki say the firefalls is the most beautiful sight in the
world. It is a wall of light created by the excitation and
discharge of oxygen atoms high in the atmosphere. (The
Devaki, of course, do not know this. They believe the pale,
ghostly fire is alive with the spirits of their ancestors. Sometimes they whistle to the cold lights, hoping to draw them
nearer.) On certain nights in deep winter the firefalls hangs
from the northern sky like a luminous curtain of green and
rose. It has a delicate, almost other-worldly beauty. But there
is beauty and there is beauty. The Devaki have two words for
beauty: *shona,* which they use to describe sunsets and mountains and trees fresh with snow, and *halla,* which has a
different meaning altogether. In essence a thing—or event—
is halla if it is in harmony with nature, more precisely, if it
"sees the intention of the World-soul." Thus it is halla for the
Devaki not to slaughter sick mammoths, just as it is halla to
die at the right time. Almost anything can be halla. A spear, if
properly balanced and well-made, is also halla. The Devaki
have come to call halla many things that would not at first
thought seem to possess beauty of any kind. Being human,
they often confuse the World-soul's intention with their most
basic desires. Even though the scooped-out carcass of a seal is
the ugliest of sights, I have heard Yuri declare it halla. Does
not a single seal feed the entire Manwelina family for three
days? And is it not the World-soul's intention that the Devaki

194

nourish themselves and thrive? So a gutted seal is halla, and ten seals laid out on the sleds of returning hunters are *hallahalla* because in reality nothing is more beautiful to the Devaki than the sight of fresh meat. The night of our lucky hunt we unloaded our sleds near the entrance fires, and the whole cave emptied of women, men and children, each of them touching the seals and crying out, *"Losna halla! Li pela Nunki losna-nu hallahalla!"* Only one of them, an old woman named Lorelei, happened to notice the firefalls shimmering in the north. *"Loshisha shona,"* she said, looking at the lights, which that evening were like an evanescent, scarlet robe. *"Lo morisha wi shona gelstei."*

While we were dividing up the beautiful seals, Yuri came up to me and said, "I must find someone to take a meat offering to the Old Man of the Cave."

I looked deeply into the cave, at the lava pendant almost lost in the shadows. I was confused because I thought the Devaki did not make offerings to idols or to natural rock formations accidentally shaped in the image of an old man. "I do not understand," I said.

He rubbed his forehead with his bloody fingers. He said, "There is one of the Devaki who lives alone in a chamber off the side of the cave. He is your great near-uncle, and I must ask you, since you killed the first seal and it is your privilege, will you do the honor?"

"Why does he live alone?"

"He lives alone," Yuri said, "because he committed a great crime long ago, and no one wishes to live with him. He is the other 'Old Man of the Cave.'"

"Did he murder someone?" I asked.

"No, it is worse than that. He lived when he should have died. When it was time for him to make the great journey, his father became filled with the volcano spirit and saved him from the death-by-ice. And is it not said that many try to die too late but few too soon? We are obliged, are we not, to die at the right time? Well, this man did not die at the right time. He was born a *marasika* without legs, and when the midwife tried to smother him, his father beat her and stole his son back to life."

Yuri's story seemed achingly familiar. I tried to ignore the shouts of all the happy people kicking up the snow and swarming around the meat, and I asked, "What is this man's name?"

And he covered his eyes with his scarred hand as he said, "His name is Shanidar, son of Goshevan. Goshevan, who killed my grandfather, Lokni, for trying to prevent this crime. Goshevan came to the Devaki to live, but when his son was born without legs, he stole Shanidar away across the eastern ice to the Unreal City where the shadow-men made him new legs. And when Shanidar had grown to be a man, he returned and said, 'I am Shanidar, and I have come to live with my people.' But everyone knew it was too late for him to live, and so my father, Nuri, told him he could spend the rest of his days in the chamber off the side of the cave."

We walked into the cave and he pointed at a long, dark gash in the cave's wall behind the huts of the Sharailina family. I assumed it was a side vent leading to Shanidar's chamber. He blinked his eye and said, "Now he is an old man who cannot kill his own meat. And who can blame him? He is a little crazy from the hell of the living-death, this poor, lonely man named Shanidar."

I nodded my head as if it all made sense.

"Meat must be taken to Shanidar so that he does not make the double crime of dying too soon."

I nodded my head that this was so.

"Shanidar would be eager to hear the story of your journey across the southern ice because he himself has made a long journey."

I nodded my head very slowly and asked, "There is no one else to fetch his meat?" I did not want to see this old man who had once known the cutting shops—and other sights—of the City.

Yuri sighed. "The honor usually falls to Choclo. But tonight, I must ask you: Will you take Shanidar his portion of this beautiful meat?"

I tried looking through the side vent into Shanidar's chamber, but I saw nothing except blackness. "Yes," I said, "I will take Shanidar his meat."

I piled some hunks of meat together and wrapped them in a skin. Through the side vent of the cave I climbed, stumbling against blocks of rock projecting from the upward-sloping, black floor. The walls were cold and close around me. I bumped my head on a blade of rock and cursed. Ahead of me and above was a faint yellow glow, as of coldflame

lighting a distant window. Somewhere water was dripping;
the plip-plop was too loud and very near. I smelled wet rock
and a sickly, sweet aroma that made my throat gag and
clutch. From the walls of rock surrounding me reverberated a
moaning that was at once full of irony and sorrow, pity and
pain. Occasionally the moaning would break into a high-
pitched ululation and then soften to a sing-song gurgle. I
drove myself upward towards this pitiful, demented wailing,
dreading what I would find. I wondered that the fabulous
Shanidar should still be alive. He must be very old, I
thought, very old.

But what can a young man understand of old age? How to
understand the aches and fears, the nostalgic looking backward to the days of youth? Although I had been among many
old men—Soli and the timeless Timekeeper came immediately to mind—their oldness had been transmuted by the arts of
civilization; they were old souls brought back to young, vital
flesh, men who had tasted little of decrepitude or helplessness.
And I, too, was a civilized man—of the slow death of shaking
limbs and cankers and sudden lapses of memory I had no
wish to know.

I had never before seen a truly old man.

He was sitting cross-legged in the middle of a stone
chamber so small that two men would have had trouble lying
lengthwise, toe to head. In front of him burned a small, wood
fire, which sent plumes of smoke curling up toward a crack in
the ceiling high above. I could see him plainly, holding his
frail, bony hands in front of the fire, watching me approach.
"Mallory Sealkiller," he said. He smiled at me nicely, but he
had no teeth. "*Ni luria, ni luria.* I am Shanidar."

"*Ni luria,*" I said, and I dumped the meat onto a slab of
rock next to the fire. "How did you know my name?"

"Choclo, my little near-grandson, visits me often, you
know. Yesterday morning, before the hunt, he told me that
men had come across the ice. Such a tale he told me. Of
course, he himself likes to hear tales of the Unreal City, even
though he doesn't believe me when I say the shadow-men
build boats that sail among the stars. Who could believe such
a thing, hmmm? Nevertheless, it's true. I have seen it with
my eyes."

He carefully touched his temples and smiled again. The
skin around his eyes was inelastic and heavy, drooping so

much that he seemed sleepy. The eyes themselves were of some indeterminate bluish color and milky with cataracts—I did not think he could have appreciated the silvery lines of a lightship with those eyes, though perhaps they were still sensitive to the rhythms of light and dark. He was an old, old man whose wasted lower jaw met the upper without the interference of teeth. The effect of this mutilation was to foreshorten his face so that his chin nearly touched his nose. It was an ugly thing. His cheek skin, I noticed, hung from his face bones in loose, white, wrinkled sheets; his skin was thin and delicate and shot with a webwork of ruptured blood vessels. I did not like to look at him, but the sheer grandeur of his ugliness made me stare.

He saw at once—if "saw" is the right word—he detected my horror and fascination, and he said, "The shadow-men of the Unreal City trap their spirits inside young flesh, you know, you know, and so their animas are very old when they make the journey to the other side of day. Did you bring me meat? I'm sorry: too old, you know. It's said that there is a barren island on the other side where these spirits howl with outrage because they are so old—old, old, old, old—they have been cheated their enlightenment. Seal meat isn't it? They won't be redeemed from time, of course you know that—listen I must interrupt myself often because I'm afraid if I don't then I'll forget something important—they won't be redeemed so they'll wander their lifeless island stuck in the eternal Then-moment. The pity—that's the real hell. We must grow old, and we must die at the right time. That's the key, did you know?" And then, "Seal meat is full of life, hmmm? Will you be kind and cut me a small piece of blubber?"

I did as he asked and he popped the cube of fat into his mouth. I did not like it that he spoke so often of the Unreal City, and so I repeated the skeptical (and wishful) saying of the Devaki: "I had a dream that shadow-men live in a city under the silver fog of dawn, unreal, unreal. I had a nightmare and when I awoke the city was gone, unreal, unreal."

He ate another piece of blubber while he stared in my direction with his cloudy eyes. "That is good," he said. "Will you cut me some meat? Cut the pieces small, you know, I have to swallow them whole. This is good meat—did you know the meat in the Unreal City grows in ponds? I have seen it with my eyes. But this meat tastes better—careful, you know, cut the pieces smaller or I'll choke." He laughed and said, "And that would be an undignified way to go over, you know, choking with a throat full of seal meat. Of course, there are some who will tell you I should have gone over long ago, when I was a baby born without legs. But my father had a dream and brought me to the Unreal City which I have seen with my own eyes. My father, whom I loved, had a dream."

As he rambled on about his father's dream of escaping the nightmare of civilization, I cut tiny cubes of seal meat and glanced about the chamber. I was surprised that the grooved and rippled walls were covered with paintings. How he had acquired the magenta, pink and green pigments to color his paints I could not guess. Along one wall, the silvers and reds and purples flowed together in a brilliant fusion of colors. I had the impression he had tried to capture a vision of his Unreal City. It was beautiful, if inelegant work. The paintings on the other wall were quite different; the other wall ran with ochers and dark greens and puce. The light in the chamber was poor, but I saw that Shanidar had daubed red splotches everywhere, seemingly at random. They could have been anything: a predator's eyes peering from behind a mottled curtain of vegetation or expanding red giant stars gone nova—or drops of blood. The splotches—indeed, all the rest of the paintings—were very disturbing. He must have known what I was looking at because he said, "You see my glories? You see? You see?"

I saw that this old man was neither truly civilized nor savage. I thought his paintings were mirrors for both the terrors of the primitive world and the (to him) marvels of civilization. Here, in a dark crack in the ground, he lived apart from other men, an outsider who had no home. (I did not consider his stinking chamber, with its piss-soaked furs and neat, conical piles of dung, to be a home.) I pitied him, but as we talked it became clear that he had little pity for himself. "How I love the taste of seal meat!" he exclaimed. "It was better, you know, when I had teeth to release the juices, but it is still very good. Mallory Sealkiller—it is said that Nunki is your doffel and you killed him, is that true?"

"Yuri believes the seal is my doffel."

"He is a wise man, it is said."

"My grandfather told me Ayeye, the thallow, is my doffel."

"And who was your grandfather?"

I recited my fake lineage, and he confided, "When I was a boy I had no grandfather to name my doffel. So I had to discover it for myself. Could you cut me more meat, hmmm? Cut the pieces small, you know. That way you release more juice. Ah, that's good! Such a taste—I love the taste of Nunki, who doesn't?"

"Would you like some more blubber?"

"When I was a young man I crossed the eastern ice from the Unreal City—yes, blubber tastes good, hmmm?—I crossed the ice. Why do I remember every crevasse and snowstorm of that journey when I cannot remember young Choclo's birth, which happened only thirteen winters ago? Or was it twelve? But I remember my doffel." He grinned and looked at me expectantly.

"And who is your doffel, then?"

I cut him a handful of diced meat and gave it to him. He rolled the meat around in his mouth, swallowed, and said, "I've lived such a life. There is nothing like the taste of seal meat, is there? I've lived alone and apart but I've lived a rich life, no man richer. Sometimes a man must live apart from his brothers, outside of his family's cave. It is a hard life then, you know, but rich and beautiful because living apart is like being a mountain above hills, like being a god among men. The glories! On the top of a mountain there is loneliness and terror, but there are glories, too. The drop is terrible, but the view, oh, the glorious view! And you know this, so why listen to an old man? Because you are kind—Mallory the Kind I will call you. It will be our secret, you know. Now will you cut me some of this delicious seal meat? It is delicious, isn't it, this meat of Nunki's, who is my doffel, too. Did Yuri tell you that? When I was younger, one time I killed a seal just to see if I could. Yuri thought I would be too afraid, but I killed him just the same."

I cut him slices of meat, all the while wondering how I could run from his chamber without offending him. I did not want to agree that the seal was my doffel. I hated that there should be a correspondence of any sort between us. I did not want to share the infamy of having killed our mutual doffel, nor did I desire the lonely kinship of men who must stand apart from other men. What I wanted, simply, was to discover the secret of life so I could live it more fully in the company of other women and men.

The Old Man of the Cave ate as he waited for my reply. He slurped his meat into his toothless mouth and swallowed it unchewed. He consumed so much meat I thought his old, shrunken belly would burst. As I watched, his skin took on ugly sallow tones as if his bile were poisoning him. He began to cough. His stomach rumbled and he farted so loudly even Bardo would have been impressed. "It is too much, you know. Oh, the pain, it cuts like ice through my bowels." He hunched forward on his hands and knees, gasping, trying to stand. "A man should not eat his meat like a dog." he said. And then, "Help me."

I helped him to his feet. I hated touching him; I hated the frailness of his thin, birdlike bones, the obscene feel of the hump between his shoulders where the spine had cracked and bent with age. He opened his lips to thank me, and I could not help looking into his mouth. His mouth was a horror. The tongue was coated and thickened, and his gums were bleeding, covered with sores. The odor was like nothing I had ever smelled before. He hobbled to the end of the chamber where he carefully vomited over one of the piles of excreta. When he returned to the fire, his skin seemed white, almost translucent like glacier ice. He took my arm in his cold, wilted hands. "Nunki's meat is good but it is tough, you know? Oh, I think you are smiling because you still have all your teeth. They are strong, aren't they, hmmm? Will you be kind enough to chew my meat for me with your strong teeth?"

I did not want to chew his meat for him. I was full of meat; the thought of chewing more meat made me sick.

"Choclo sometimes chews my meat, you know. Such a kind boy."

I could not bear to watch him place a meaty wad moist with my saliva into his mouth. "I can't," I said.

"Please, Mallory, I'm hungry."

I quietly cursed and bit off a chunk of meat. I chewed it thoroughly. As I spat out the brownish-red mass into my hand, he said, "You know, I used to chew my father's meat when he was old." He scooped up the contents of my hand with his own and gobbled it down. "That's good, very good. But you don't have to chew it so much. You'll chew out the juices if you are not careful, and meat is best when it is juicy, hmmm?"

He reached out feeling the meat I had brought him, kneading his hands through the seal blubber. With his greasy fingers he rubbed his face thoughtfully and then returned to his explorations. "What's this?" he cried out. "Under the ribs—it feels like liver!"

"Yes, I've brought you some liver," I said. "I thought you might like it."

"But I may not eat liver, don't you know?"

"Is it too rich?"

"It *is* too rich and that is why I may not eat it. Yuri says liver must be reserved for the hunters and pregnant women. And sometimes the children. They need its richness more than I do, you know."

"It's just a little liver," I said. "Would Yuri deny you a taste of liver?"

"Listen, he would deny me more than that, of course. Before you came I had not eaten much for twelve days. When times are hard, you know. . . well, I am old and the children must eat, hmmm?"

I did know about this cruel custom of the Alaloi's, and thoughtlessly, I said, "Children must eat, then, but it is evil for a man's family to make him starve."

In truth, I did not really think it was evil that the old should die so the young could live. But that the Alaloi should have to live so close to life—and death—*that,* I thought, was somehow evil.

"Evil, hmmm . . . would you cut me a piece of liver, please?" He stared at the fire for a long time, pulling at the loose skin of his throat. Orange fingers of light played across his greasy face. With his scrawny neck and toothless, puckered mouth opening and closing in anticipation of his dessert, he looked like a hellish, glowing bird. "What is evil, hmmm? What is good? Do you know?"

He turned around and rummaged in a pile of decaying offal and old bones. He grunted, turned back to me, and held up a piece of organ meat. "This is the stomach of Ayeye, the thallow who flies above—did you know Yuri hates me because I once freed a young thallow from one of his traps?—the thallow flies above mountains, and it is bad to eat Ayeye, but Yuri wanted the thallow for Liam's initiation, not for eating.

But I freed the bird anyway because I pitied him, you know? Of course I would have freed him even if Yuri had been hungry and wanted to eat him because it is wrong to eat—do you see the stomach of this thallow that Choclo has brought me, that my hungry people have eaten?"

"I see it," I said. "Put it away, it stinks."

He jabbed his pale, crooked finger through the lower opening of the stomach. As one puts on a glove, he pulled the glistening muscle in folds down around his hand until the finger emerged from the upper opening. He wriggled his finger and said, "Death is evil, do you think? You know, we are worms in the belly of God, and so we perceive only two of God's attributes, hmmm? Like a worm," and here he again wriggled his finger inside the bird's stomach, "one part of us looks up through the throat and mouth of God into the light, and we call this good—did you know that Yuri's doffel is the thallow?—we look into the light of life and call it good while our other part crawls down into God's bowels, down into blackness and dung and evil. You know, most people, caught in the stomach of God as they are, tend to see these two attributes only, but there are many more beyond our comprehension. Can you please slice me another piece of liver?"

I cut him a piece of liver and said, "Try to eat it slowly. Else you'll waste it, and that *would* be evil."

"Thank you. That was good, hmmm? Good for an old man to eat the tender liver of the seal, but not so good for Nunki, hmmm? If Nunki could talk, he might even say it was evil that he should go over to the other side while still so young and full of life? But what can an animal know? What does a man know? Listen, little Choclo likes to talk to me—shall I sing the song I taught him?—he talks about what he sees, you know, and he said that Mallory Sealkiller looks at his sister, Katharine, the way Liam looks at Katharine. And that is wrong, he says, that is evil, but what can he know of either? He thinks he knows good and evil, of course, but I did not tell him that some men, men who stand apart high on mountain tops, some men can imagine what it is like to leave the belly and view the whole body of God. I myself have almost seen it once or twice. It is a mighty thing, you know, with a golden beak and silver wings stretching across all the universe until the tips touch at the far side. I heard its cry once or twice as a child so I can tell you the deepest thing I know: The nature of God is beyond good or evil."

I smiled as I sliced soft, jellylike pieces of liver. I remembered that the Alaloi believe God is a thallow so great it can devour the world as easily as a loon swallows a berry; they believe that God and the universe are one. I chewed quickly and spat a purple bolus of liver into my hand. Because I doubted that any man could know the true nature of God, be it a thallow or a ball of light or an ultimate system of describing the infinite structures of the manifold (as certain pilots believe), because I doubted many things, I said, "Perhaps your vision of the thallow was only a dream. Dreams can sometimes seem real. But most dreams are false, aren't they?"

He snapped the liver from my hand and ate it. "You men of the southern ice have strange dreams, hmmm? False dreams, too, I see. You know, you are a kind man but sometimes your words cut like the wind. I will tell you the simplest thing I know, hmmm? A hungry man is not more certain of the existence of hot meat that I am of God."

Thus I passed most of the evening, feeding him as a beast feeds its young. We talked about many things, but most of all we—I should say Shanidar—talked about good and evil. I was surprised that he talked so freely with me, but then the Alaloi are natural philosophers and they love to talk. Also, I think he was too aware of his own mortality; he must have been desperate for companionship of any sort, even mine. It puzzled me, though, that he seemed to like me, because I did not like him. I pitied him, especially when he reached out to grasp my hand, and he said, "Once at night, years ago, I dreamed of having a son but none of the Devaki would marry a man who had not died at the right time, you know? I had a dream at night—Listen, the lights in the sky are the eyes of God watching us. The lights in the midnight sky are stars, and there real men live in the radiance of God's eyelight, though no one believes me that this is so. If I had been blessed with a son I would have taught him the truth—Listen, there is something I want to ask you, hmmm? When it is time for me to go over—clearly it is not time yet because this liver lies so cleanly in my belly—when it is time, just before I—Listen, don't let Yuri know you brought me the seal liver because he would think I am stealing it from the mouths of the mothers, and if it were true that would be evil, hmmm?—When it is time for God to devour *my* meat, would you carry me out of the cave so I can sit beneath the night? I want to feel the starlight once more before I make the great journey."

I promised to do as he asked and he squeezed my hand. He thanked me for bringing him enough meat so he could go to bed and not lay awake thinking about his hunger. He patted his belly, smiling. I was glad to be done with my loathsome task and I smiled too. We smiled together. It should have been a good moment, with both of us smiling, but it was a moment of horror. I was seized with a sudden, inexplicable panic. The cave walls drowning in vivid colors, the fiery logs crackling and spitting cinders, the putrid smells of blood and breath, Shanidar's too-familiar smile—all these sensa filled me with a deep fear of my own existence. The sheer hopelessness of life terrified me. Shanidar smiled at me from across the fire, and it seemed as if his head were floating above a sea of orange flames. I could see only his head, sunken in flesh and the folds of time, smiling as I smiled. I stared at his eyes, at the lenses frosted and white with the ice of cataracts. I stared through my eyes at eyes similar to mine. All men, I realized, would come to have such eyes if only they lived long enough. I was shaken with the fear, the bone knowledge, the utter certainty that the shape of Shanidar's smiling face was the shape of my own. No skill or force could keep me from this fate should the ticking of my inner clock slow down as his had slowed for him. I was young now, but soon, very soon according to the measure of universal time, I would be old. My fear was so great that I felt an overwhelming urge to scream for help. There was no escape, I thought, and my stomach knotted and I began to sweat. No matter the arts of the cutters and the cetics—they could fold flesh back to youth a few times, perhaps even many times, but they could do nothing to prevent the mutability of one's selfness and soul. There was no way I could keep myself young, no way to stop myself from changing inside, where it mattered. It was my fate to change, as it was everyone's fate. Shanidar smiled, and he had no teeth, and I realized that the whole of my life until this moment had been false. I looked at the solid walls of rock running with paints, and I squeezed my aching knee, and everything at once, the rocks and blood and bones seemed utterly unreal.

As if he could hear my thoughts, he turned his head in my direction and suddenly stopped smiling. "You know, even kind men such as you and I must grow old, hmmm? That is why we must go over at the right time. Otherwise there is no peace forever."

He talked about the peace and enlightenment awaiting on the other side of day, and he talked about his love for his people who had almost completely rejected him. I must admit I paid him little attention. I wanted to run back into the main cave, to find Soli and the others, to make them understand that our quest for the secret of life was stupid and meaningless. There was no secret; there was only the crushing bondage of being, and finally when it was time to be no more, nothingness.

I stood up abruptly, nearly ignoring the Old Man of the Cave as he said, "There is one thing I should tell you before you leave, hmmm? I forgot to tell you this, but you should know. God's wings touch at the far end of the universe—did I tell you this before?—his wings are silver and they touch, but his eyes are closed because he himself is sleeping. Listen, one day God will wake up and be able to see himself as he really is. I can almost hear his scream, the beating of his wings. But until then, good and evil will not exist because only God can truly see what is good and what is not. And this is the thing that I wanted to tell you: Men such as you and I, kind men who kill their own doffels, we must do as we will because for us all things are permitted. But there is always a price, hmmm?" He ran his trembling finger along the gums inside his mouth and repeated, "The price must be paid."

I returned down the rock vent as fast as I could. I wanted to find Katharine, to stroke her hair, to ask her what she had *seen*; I wanted to make her tell me what I would be like when I had grown old. As I hurried through the dark passageway, the Old Man of the Cave began to sing a mournful song, and I tried not to listen.

12

The Little Death

*What an extraordinary thing, that the ripples in the
spacetime continuum should ripple in such a way
that the ripples could control their own rippling!
That energy captured and bound should lead to
greater concentrations of energy instead of gradually
bleeding away into the heat death and universal
calm! How mysterious that consciousness should lead
to greater consciousness and life beget life greater
and more complex!*

—from *A Requiem for Homo Sapiens*,
by Horthy Hosthoh

When I returned to the main cave, the Devaki and my
"family" were feasting on seal meat. Obsessed as I was with
thoughts of decay and death, I was unprepared for joy, the joy
of a hundred and twenty happy people filling themselves with
their beautiful meat. It was a feast of flesh, a celebration of
love and life with little respite or pause. Everyone except the
unweaned babies and children gorged on roasted seal steaks
and blubber. (At first, of course, many were so impatient and
hungry they ate their meat raw.) The cave was alive with the
smell of burning sweetbreads and the happy chatter of the
children as they licked down fingers of grilled liver dipped in
melted fat. Yuri and the rest of the Manwelina were glad to
share the food with the Yelenalina and Reinalina families.
Their hunters had returned earlier that day from their shagshay
hunt with empty sleds, but Yuri announced they would fill
their bellies anyway because he knew that in the next hunt

207

the luck might go the other way. Even the Sharailina, who possessed the lowest status of all the families due to an unfortunate and unsavory accident that happened years ago, even the lowly Sharailina partook of the rich meat. Around all the huts the cave floor was littered with cracked bones; the bloated, distended bodies of those who had eaten too much (nearly everyone) were sprawled in front of the fires. There were grunts and belches and moans. And to my surprise, many of the Devaki were telling lewd jokes and touching each other openly. I stalked through the cave, and I saw a nubile Yelenalina woman—I think her name was Pualani—giggling and whispering something in young Choclo's ear. They fondled each other and disappeared into one of the Yelenalina's huts. All around the oilstones, in the soft, flickering light, it seemed the men and women were pairing and touching, quietly vanishing into the darker recesses of the cave. I found Bardo with his arms thrown across the backs of two pretty Senwelina girls as he sat between them singing. I walked closer to huts noisy with gasps of passion, and he winked at me and bellowed, "Two's not too many for one, but it's too few for two such men as we! But when Bardo is content, Bardo is willing to share." And then, "Where have you been? You look white as bird puke."

"Where's Katharine?" I asked him.

"Forget about Katharine," he said, pulling at his beard. "Why do you care where she is?"

I did not think it was a good time to tell him that Katharine and I were lovers, though from the look in his crafty brown eyes, I think he must have guessed the truth well before we had left Neverness.

"Have you seen her?" I asked.

He licked his lips, ignoring my question. He nuzzled the neck of the youngest girl, the one with the small nose and beautiful high laugh. He said, "Her name is Nadia, daughter of Jense. She's curious, she tells me, to see if the spear of Mallory Sealkiller is long and straight enough to pierce *her* aklia."

Nadia giggled again and seemed disappointed when I shook my head. "I have to find Katharine," I said.

"Ah, too bad." He shook himself free of the girls, stood up, and took me aside. "What's wrong with you?"

I started to tell him about my visit with Shanidar, but I

found myself biting my lip instead. All I could force out was: "This expedition, the quest . . . everything, it's all meaningless."

"Of course it is. And that's why you should live while you can. Life is boring and meaningless, but when you explode inside a woman, for a moment your boredom dies and—am I boring you?—and you feel like you could die from the pleasure, or from anything else, and not care a damn. When you die the little death and she screams and claws your back because she's dying, too—well, is there anything better than that?"

I tried to tell him that the problem was much more complicated than he thought. But he just stood there, squeezing my shoulder and shaking his head. "How hard I've tried to educate you!" he said. "All in vain, all in vain!" In a low voice he said, "But thank you, Little Fellow, for bringing me to this enlightened place."

When I warned him of the dangers of swiving ripe, young women, he pulled his beard thoughtfully. He had always feared fathering children. It was a bizarre, irrational fear: He had half-convinced himself that if his seed ever sprouted inside a woman, then somehow he would have fulfilled his purpose in life and would therefore be obsolete and liable to death. "It's too bad," he said, "that I can't train my sperm to die the instant they leave my body. But if I . . . ah, that is to say, if one of these hairy women *did* become pregnant, who could ever know who the father was?"

He sighed, then licked his mustache as he turned back to the girls. For men such as Bardo, I am afraid, lust will always conquer fear.

I stalked through the cave looking for Katharine but I did not find her. No one could tell me where she was. I returned to our hut and almost embarrassed Soli and Justine in the middle of their loveplay. Quietly, I limped away toward the huts of the Manwelina. I saw my mother and Anala sitting together. They were scraping seal skins, talking and laughing. I overheard Anala bragging about her son Liam's virility. He would make any young woman a good husband, she said. I remembered that in my wanderings in the dark I had not seen Liam either. From the soft, round, glowing hut behind them came a rhythmic gasping and sudden, private cries. I ground my teeth and leaned against the cold cave wall, wondering why this contagious communal passion had been no part of Rainer's memory.

What occurred that night and for the next two days was not precisely an orgy. As far as I could tell, the Devaki did their sex in couples and as privately as possible. With one exception (I shall discuss Bardo's peccadillos and exploits presently), there were no groupings of three or more, no voyeurism or drunken perversions. The Devaki, it seemed, knew little of the failed arts of civilization. But they were very familiar with promiscuity, or I should say, they practiced a zestful coupling that was free and wild within a rigid system of rules and taboos. (No man or woman, for instance, could lie with another's mate, and sex among family members was an abomination.) The young and unmarried "shared the volcano's explosion" often and with many different partners. Especially when they had eaten great heaps of meat and the blood grew hot and full, they sought each other in the darkness of the cave and furiously coupled and feasted and found another with whom to share their fire. They did this, Yuri told me, because eros was the gift of Devaki to the god Kweitkel and should be practiced with energy and passion until the wombs of the women (or the girls who had thus become women) were full of new life.

"Do not wait too long for your spear to rise," he warned me around midnight, when he found me sitting with the dogs by the entrance fires. "Soon the young women's aklias will be exhausted and you will have missed your fun." He threw some wood on the fire and sighed as it began to crackle and roar. "Perhaps you are thinking how hard it was to kill your doffel, and who could blame you? But it is not good for a man to think too much." With his huge finger, he tapped his forehead above his eye socket and admonished, "In you I think there is too much distraction, too many voices inside. You must quiet the word storm in your head, and what better way than to lose yourself in a woman? Haven't you seen how the Sharailina girls, Mentina and Lilith, look at you?"

What better way indeed! How I envied Yuri his purity and innocence! He knew nothing of contagion or the diseases that had ruined many of the Civilized Worlds. He was ignorant of the touch of slel neckers who tailor genotoxins to rob a man of his selfness and soul. I desperately wanted to lose myself in a woman, to lose myself in *something*, anything to drown out Shanidar's quavering old voice, to extinguish his image burning within me. But I was a civilized man, despite my primitive body. I dreaded intimately touching these un-washed, lice-ridden women. How could I explain this to Yuri? How to explain that I, who sought the secret of life, was afraid of life?

There was one Yelenalina woman, however, who seemed different than the others. Her name was Kamalia, and she was beautiful. Her hair seemed less full of grease than that of her cousins and near-sisters; her teeth were white and not so worn. After Yuri had gone off to bed with Anala, she sat with me by the fire. She smiled at me coyly, covering her pink lips with her hand. She began pulling at my furs, and I found her thick odor somehow pleasant, intoxicating even. The fire was hot on my face, the air full of sweet smoke and Kamalia's laughter. Suddenly I was tired of searching, tired of thinking, tired of everything but the touch of Kamalia's clever little hands. I nuzzled her neck (the Devaki do not practice the barbaric art of kissing, thank God!), and we found an empty hut in which to do our sex. We swived each other to exhaustion and slept and awoke and swived some more. I died the little death. I felt wild and pure and invulnerable. I swived her four times during the day that followed, trying to escape boredom and fear of living. I swived her, and it was good. But it was not enough, and I sought out her younger sister, Pilaria, and I swived her as well, and she screamed and clawed my back, and it was very good, but it was not enough to soothe me. I was hungry so I ate some meat and found myself in Arwe's hut where I coaxed shy Tasarla into sex play. Later that day—I did not care what day it was—I swived Mentina, who hummed a little melody as she massaged my chest and rocked back and forth astride me, back and forth, rubbing and humming. When Bardo learned of my private quest to find oblivion, he spread the rumor that I, too, was a great hunter of women and very skilled with my spear, which was long and thick, if not quite so long and thick as his. (But then, whose was?) I swived women whose names I have forgotten or never learned. They were each beautiful in their own way, even cross-eyed Mentina and Lilith, with her fishy smell and crooked teeth. I took great pleasure with them, but it was not enough, never enough to silence the noise inside my head.

Early in the third night of this revelry, during a rare
moment of sleep, Kamalia and I were awakened by the cries
and bellows echoing from the hut next to us. I listened to a
long, barbaric rondo of moans and giggles and belches, an
obscene symphony of unrestrained squeals of delight. "Ten!"
a voice called out, and I recognized Bardo's basso profundo
booming beneath a waterfall of high-pitched, girlish laughter.
And later, "Eleven!" and later still, "Twelve and thirteen!" I
heard low sighs, the voices of different women. "Fourteen!"
Bardo cried, and I realized he was—stupidly—keeping a
count of his copulations. When he reached the number
"nineteen," towards dawn, I was afraid he would have to
lapse into civilized language because, as I have said, the
Alaloi have no numbers for quantities greater than twenty. (It
would be ridiculous, I thought, for him to call out *hela*, or
"many," after each woman he swived.) Kamalia and I shared a
piece of seal meat as we waited for him to breach his
twentieth woman. But he never called out number twenty.
Instead there was a long silence, broken when he shouted,
"By God, what trick is this? What poison?" And then, "It
won't go down!" He called out my name, and there was panic
and desperation in his voice. I smiled at Kamalia, quickly
dressed and went into Bardo's hut.

"Mallory," he gasped, "look at it, it won't go down!"

He paced helplessly at the center of the hut, entirely naked.
On one of the snow beds two women half-covered with furs sat
watching him. They held hands, giggling and pointing at his
enormous, rigid membrum, which stood out beneath his
round belly like the spout of a teapot. "*Bardo wos Tuwalanka!*"
one of the women said as she held her hands spread in front
of her, "*Tuwalanka!*" (It was true, Bardo *did* have the "spear"
of a mammoth. So large was his membrum, in fact, that when
he was younger, he used to fear that the blood needed to
engorge it would be diverted from his brain, robbing it of
oxygen and thus damaging that most precious of organs.)

I told the women to dress, and I shooed them from the
hut. "What's wrong?" I asked.

"I don't know," he said. He grasped the shaft of his
membrum, pulling it horizontal. "I won't get soft. Ah, I don't
know—it must be poison, this has never happened before."

"You've merely overstimulated yourself."

"No, no, Little Fellow."

"Six or seven women in three days has drugged your body with adrenalin and sex." In truth, I, too, felt insatiable and prepotent—who would not with a succession of young women eager to rouse one's spear?

"Eleven women and I don't think that's it at all. I feel the hormones gushing inside. It's poison, by God!"

From a distance I examined his membrum. I noticed a curious thing. On the underside of the shaft, the small, round multicolored keloids scarring his "mammoth spear" did not seem to be arranged at random. The red dots twisted among the green and blue, forming a familiar pattern. I moved closer and half-squatted, peering at the ugly patch of skin just beneath the bulb. I remembered the verses and the dead languages of the Timekeeper's book of poems, and the pattern became clear: The red dots formed the ancient Japanese pictogram for the word "revenge." Mehtar, that cunning pointillist, had tattooed Bardo's membrum with what he had obviously believed to be an undecipherable message. So, Mehtar *had* remembered Bardo, after all. The wily cutter had revenged himself for Bardo's pushing him to the ice the day we had met Soli in the master pilot's bar. Most likely he had implanted timed hormones in Bardo's flesh, afflicting him with unending tumescence. It was a cruel thing he had done, a nasty joke. It was cruel and treacherous and distressing, but it was also, for some reason I could not quite understand, hilariously funny.

"What do you see?" he asked me.

"I don't know."

"Don't lie to me, Little Fellow."

"You'll be fine," I said.

"Mallory!"

"It's nothing, really," I reassured him, and I began to laugh.

"Tell me, by God!"

I laughed for a while as his face reddened and his membrum grew even stiffer. I laughed until the tears ran from my eye; I laughed so hard I began to hiccup and cough.

"Oh, you're cruel," he said. "You're a hard man."

I calmed myself and explained what I thought Mehtar had done. He said, "I've heard of such things. He's altered my chemistry, by God! I'm being killed by poisons from the gonads! Revenge is it? When we return to the City I'll show him revenge! I'll cut off his pissroot and nail it to the sign above his shop, by God I will!"

"Shhh, keep your voice low!" I said.

"No one can hear me!"

But obviously someone had heard him. Either that or the two women had spread the news of his turgid condition throughout the cave. Yuri and his brother Wicent entered the hut and looked at Bardo in astonishment. "We heard your shouts," Yuri said. I will never forget the helpless expression on Bardo's face as Yuri examined his membrum, freely feeling the shaft with his greasy fingers. "Whoever initiated you was very careful," Yuri said. "A great shaman made these scars, but then he had a great spear to carve on. Truly, Bardo has a mammoth spear, Seratha and Oma did not exaggerate."

Bardo pulled away from him and began putting on his furs. His face was as red as a bloodfruit.

"The women are curious to view such a spear," Yuri said. "And who could blame them?" He leaned closer to Bardo, speaking in a low, confidential voice. "They are too curious, I think. We would not want the married women sneaking into your hut to verify the greatness of your spear, would we? That would cause disharmony. You must satisfy their curiosity now while they are sick of sex and men's spears. What is seen and known often creates less desire than the hidden. Come outside the hut; Anala and Liluye are waiting."

Bardo stared at him and did not move.

"Quickly now, before it softens like a worm."

Bardo looked at me as an array of emotions crossed his face. One who did not know him would have thought he was too modest to expose himself to the women's stares. But he was not a modest man. He was afraid, I thought, that Soli and the others would view his engorged membrum and thus witness Mehtar's humiliating revenge. It seemed unlikely, though, that anyone except me, and possibly my mother, had studied ancient Japanese. I nodded to him reassuringly. He must have somehow understood because he shrugged and said, "I hope they don't faint at the sight of this," and he backed out of the hut. With a shagshay fur thrown like a cape across his massive shoulders, he strode nearly naked among the glowing huts, stopping to pose and preen in front of the Old Man of the Cave. The Devaki women—there must have been fifty of them—surrounded him. (I should add that the

men were also very curious. They stood peering from behind
the women's shoulders, plainly envious.) A few of the more
fascinated women, Anala and nervous Liluye among them,
pointed and gasped and vied with one another to grasp his
membrum, as if to palpably verify its size. A sea of snakelike
arms reached out for him, touching, fondling. Most of the
women, however, groaned and sadly shook their heads and
looked away. Bardo ignored them. He paraded around making obscene thrusting motions with his hips as he announced,
"Tuwa the mammoth does not have a bigger spear. Behold!"
And then he recited a little poem that was a favorite of his:

> *Short and thin*
> > *Has little in;*
> *It's long and thick*
> > *That does the trick.*

Muliya, who was Mentina's fat, cross-eyed mother, laughed
and asked, "Does a woman lie down with a beast?"

Anala stroked her gray hair and said, "You are supposed to
make fire inside a woman, not kill her with your spear." And
everyone, including Bardo, laughed.

"Ah, but it's cold," he said, all the while strutting with his
hands on his hips.

"So cold," someone called out, "that your spear is frozen."

This seemed to remind him of the seriousness of his
condition. "Ah, yes... frozen. Too bad." He winked at me,
shivered, and returned to the hut to fetch his clothes.

The men and women joked for a while and went back to
their feasting and sleeping. Yuri caught me by the arm and
said, "Bardo is a strange man. All the men of the southern
ice—you sons of Senwe are strange. Brave and strong, but
strange."

I didn't say anything because I was worried Bardo's
obscene antics, and perhaps my own foolish inhibitions, had
caused him to suspect our civilized origins. But he continued
and it was clear that Bardo and I weren't the only ones he
considered strange: "Soli, too, is a strange man. Never have I
seen anyone take so little joy from living. He loves Justine
like the sun loves the world, but when he discovers she
cannot reflect the wholeness of his radiance, he grows cold as
a star. He forgets that such love is the soul's hopeless attempt

to escape its own loneliness. Strange. And you, Mallory, the strangest of all—you have murdered your own doffel. What strangenesses will come of all this?" He looked at me with his deep, single eye, plainly worried. "I do not know," he said, "I do not know."

I stared over his shoulder at the huts of the Manwelina. As he spoke, Liam emerged from the nearest hut. He combed back his long, blond hair and went over to the meat pit where he picked up an axe and hacked at a piece of seal meat. Moments later Katharine backed out of the hut's tunnelway. She stood up and smiled at him in a way that made me want to grind rock between my teeth. She began walking toward the entrance fires. I stepped into the shadow of the Old Man of the Cave so she wouldn't see me. I quickly looked back at Yuri. "I don't know either," I said. "I don't know."

I followed Katharine back to our hut. I didn't want her to think that I was a spy, so I waited a while before joining her inside. As silently as I could, I crept through the dark, icy tunnelway. When I reached the main chamber, all the oilstones were lit and the interior was awash in a sea of golden light. Soli was gone, probably out feeding the dogs or skiing through the forest, which he liked to do at daybreak. I did not know where Justine could have been. I pushed my belly close to the snow, watching. Katharine was kneeling above her snowbed, looking around at the white, curving walls as if to examine them for flaws. She lifted back the fur draped over the edge of the bed, exposing the bare, packed snow. She began to dig. It was so quiet I could hear her deep breathing above the sounds that her fingers made scooping out clumps of snow. In little time she had excavated a hollow perhaps two feet deep. She pulled her head back—despite my jealousy I could not help thinking how beautiful she was—she looked around the hut once more before reaching into her secret crypt. One by one she removed five krydda spheres, which were each a translucent green and slightly smaller than a snow loon's egg. She opened the first sphere carefully. Very carefully, from the inner pocket of her fur, she removed a snipping of blond hair. She twisted it into a golden ball and pushed it into the sphere. She performed a similar procedure with the other spheres in turn, storing in them nail parings, a child's tooth, and, amazingly, the blackened, amputated little

toe of Jinje, whose flesh had run to gangrene after his feet
had thawed. The last thing she did I could not see clearly
because she was squatting with her back to me. She reached
down into her furs below her stomach and removed something. I guessed it was a pessary, no doubt full of Liam's seed. I
think she emptied it into the last sphere. When she finished
this private work, she replaced the spheres and closed the
hole beneath her bed.

I was so angry I forgot that I was not supposed to be
spying on her. I stood up and said, "I hope you have enough
samples."

She jumped suddenly; her whole body contracted at once
as it sometimes did at night when she lay near me in that
floating state of consciousness just before sleep. "Oh," she
said, "I didn't know you were . . ." She pulled the fur over her
handiwork and sat on the bed. She thrust her hands beneath
her crossed arms to warm them.

I wanted to take her cold hands in mine, to let the flush
and heat flow into them. But I was very angry so I asked,
"How many samples do you have?"

"I'm not sure I know."

"You've had three days to skulk about the cave," I said.
"How much longer do you think you'll need?" Originally, we
had planned to take at least twenty samples of the Devaki's
plasm and tissues, five from each of the four families. According to the master imprimatur, that should have contained a
sufficient expression of the tribe's chromosomes.

"I'm not sure," she repeated.

"Why don't we count the samples, then?"

"Why are you always so obsessed with numbers?"

"I'm a mathematical man."

She rubbed her naked hands together and blew on them.
The air was steamy with her breath. "You mean to ask how
many men I've been with—not enough, do you see?" And
then, that infuriating saying of the scryers: "What will happen
has happened; what has been will be." She flexed her
intertwined fingers and said, "I'm not Bardo; I haven't counted
my—"

"How many?" I asked.

She looked straight at me. "It would be cruel of me to tell
you," she said.

"How many men?" I asked. "Seven? Eight? The barbaric orgy lasted three days."

"Fewer than you might think. I don't like men as well as you or Bardo like women."

I crossed the space between us and grasped her hands. "Two? Three? I couldn't find you for days," I said. "How many?"

She smiled sadly as I held her hands. "There was only one *man*, don't you see?"

I did see. All at once the hateful images of her and Liam naked together came unbidden into my mind. I tried to think of other things, but I could not. My beautiful Katharine lying beneath him, pulling at his buttocks with her hands—this image burned inside me. It was an obscene image, like the lewd and colorful flesh frescoes which writhe beneath the pale skins of farsider whores. I clenched my teeth and asked, "You spent all your time with Liam? Why?"

"It's best I don't tell you," she said. "It would be cruel of me to tell . . ."

It was stupid of me to insist that she tell me, but I was stupid that day, so I repeated, "Why?"

She twisted her hands away and said, "Liam . . . he's different than other men, different than *civilized* men."

"Men are men," I said, rubbing my nose. I was thinking furiously. I asked, "Different how?"

"When I'm . . . when he's . . . when *we're* together, he isn't thinking of diseases or of other men I've been with or the consequences of . . . he isn't always *thinking*, don't you see? Do you know what it's like to be with someone who exists in the moment solely with you? Solely *for* you?"

"No," I said truthfully. "What is it like?"

"Ecstasy," she said.

I was silent and I stared into her eyes. "Ecstasy," I repeated. I was so sick with jealousy the veins in my neck ached.

"With Liam, it's as natural as breathing . . . he's *patient*, do you see?"

Ecstasy. I closed my eyes, and I could see it all too easily, this ecstasy of Katharine's. I saw her with her eyes tightly closed, with her head thrown back, lost in pleasure. Perversely, my jealousy began to change into desire even as my anger gave way to the quick swelling of lust. There was a pressure all through my body, the heaviness of pounding blood. Despite the excitement of the past three days, perhaps because of it, I was eager to swive her; I was dying to swive her. I found myself whispering apologies in her ear while I lost my hand in the raw silk of her hair. Barbarically, I kissed her neck. And all the while—even as I pulled the furs from her—she stared at me with eyes both open and blind. She nodded suddenly as if she had seen a clear and vivid image of her own. She pressed her palms against my cheeks and slowly said, "It's . . . so . . . dangerous!" But I didn't care about danger just then; I trembled with a need to act and do, so I threw off my furs and began caressing her. "You don't see," she murmured, "you don't . . ." She lay back against the bed, and like a farsider whore, she threw her arms up above her head and bent her knees to reveal the dark wedge of hair between her legs. The tendons strained beneath her skin, and she smelled of sex. "Mallory," she said, and I rested my knees between hers, and I did not care that I heard scraping sounds outside the hut; I did not care at all.

How can I explain this mysterious impulse that overcame us every time we were alone? We used to joke that although we often didn't like each other, the cells of her body loved the cells of mine. It was love, I like to think, that drove us together that day in the hut. We rutted quickly like beasts, and it was an artless but ecstatic copulation. Unlike most women, Katharine was quick and easy to arouse. However, once her blood was hot she liked to spread her pleasure out for hours, savoring each moment one by one. This had often annoyed me because I was always eager for the finish, for that blinding moment when our ecstasy crescendoed and we died the little death together. I was eager for ecstasy, and we had only a few moments, so we thrust furiously, in rhythm, pushing and panting and sweating. Her heels were hard against the backs of my legs as she urged on and on. I must have kicked aside the old furs covering the floor because I felt my naked toes gripping and digging into the snow. I was dying to be done, and I moved faster, moaning like a beast. "No, wait," she said, and I opened my eyes, and she opened hers, staring through me into herself, into her luminous, crystalline interior where she could view her own pleasure as a voyeur peers at a rutting couple through a crack in an icy wall. But I was dying and I couldn't think of waiting; I couldn't think of anything at all. I gasped to feel myself hot and alive inside her, burning drops of life leaving me in spasms. We gasped together too loud and too long, but I did not care.

Afterwards she lay still for a long time, clutching the back of my neck, opening and closing her fingers. She seemed both sad and amused; her face was open with resignation and anxiety, but with happiness, too. "Oh, Mallory," she said, "poor Mallory." I wondered if what we had done had happened against her will, but then I remembered she was a scryer who denied her individual will. "It's all so *intense* for you, isn't it?" she said. When she held her hands over her eyes and shook with both laughter and tears, I realized that I would never understand her.

She separated from me and stood up to dress. She turned to me, whispering her scryer's whisper: "How I loved the memory of the last you; how I always shall." Then she fled from the hut, leaving me to renew the oilstones' flames, which had burned too brightly and were pale yellow and dim.

13

Hunger

If we become too many, we will kill all the mammoth and have to hunt silk belly and shagshay for food. And when they are gone, we will have to cut holes in the ice of the sea so to spear the seals when they come up to breathe. When the seals are gone, we will be forced to murder Kikilia, the whale, who is wiser than we and as strong as God. When all the animals are gone, we will dig tangleroot and eat the larvae of furflys and break our teeth gnawing the lichen from the rocks. At last we will be so many, we will murder the forests to plant snow apple so that men will come to lust for land, and some men will come to have more land than others. And when there is no land left, the stronger men will get their sustenance from the labor of weaker men, who will have to sell their women and children so that they might have mash to eat. The strongest men will make war on each other so that they might have still more land. Thus we will become hunters of men and be doomed to hell in living and hell on the other side. And then, as it did on Earth in the time before the Swarming, fire will rain from the sky, and the Devaki will be no more.
—from the *Life of Lokni the Unlucky*, as told by Yuri
the Wise

A few days later I confessed everything to Bardo. Because he was as terrified of his own mortality as anyone I have ever known, he pretended to boredom and a false calm when I told him of my experience in Shanidar's chamber, my great "vastation," as he called it. But he was more than curious to hear the details of my tryst with Katharine. Upon learning that we had been lovers since the night we received our pilot's rings, he was full of advice.

"Your jealousy unmans you, Little Fellow. Let her swive as many men as she needs to—why else did we come here? A man should love women, of course, but he should not love *a* woman too well. It poisons him to do so." We were standing in the woods outside the cave, drilling yellow holes in the snow as we performed our "piss-after-drinking-the-morning-tea." The wind was up, blowing in gusts from the south. This made our urination awkward and perilous, because as I have said, the Devaki must always face south when they relieve themselves. Bardo shook himself dry and said, "By God, it's cruel the way this wind blows down the trousers." And then, "Poisons! I should tell you this poison of Mehtar's is peculiar, indeed. Here, look at this," he said showing me his membrum, which was limp and wrinkled, though still very large. "Who ever heard of such a poison? During the day it hangs like the hammer of a bell, and there is nothing I or these hairy women can do to make it rise. But at night—ah, at night it splits the air, so what else is there to do but find a woman to drain it dry? You should be glad the Devaki share their sex so freely, my friend. Do you want some advice? I will give you some advice: Let Katharine collect her samples, and then we'll go home."

Katharine, I should mention, was not the only one who managed to collect bits and pieces of Devaki flesh. As head of our family, Soli was called to help hold Jinje when Yuri decided that his frozen, rotten toes must come off. I was not present at the amputation so I never learned how Soli pocketed one of the toes and smuggled it to Katharine for storage in her krydda sphere. And of course I was not allowed near Marya at the rear of the cave when she gave birth to her baby boy. The men, being men, were forbidden to witness this deepest of feminine mysteries. But my mother was there helping (I would not doubt that she took charge of the entire labor), and she returned to our hut with a small section of Marya's afterbirth. Even though I had instigated, had once believed in this expedition, I found it difficult to think there could be any great secret hidden in the slelled tissues of an afterbirth. Surely, I thought, the Entity had deceived me. Surely it was all a joke, or perhaps a game in which we were pieces to be moved, frozen, starved or sliced into parts at the caprice of the goddess or according to the whimsy of the greater gods. Surely there was no secret at all.

Our life among the Devaki soon settled into a routine. After we had finished the last of the seal meat, every morning the men would arise, ice the sleds, and go off hunting on the ice or skiing through the dark forest. Although we had bad luck with the animals, I came to cherish these moments of clean air and exhilaration away from the smoky cave, away from Katharine's nightly forays into the huts of different Devaki men. Out on the ice there was peace and privacy, even in waiting for the seals that never came. And in the forests where the shagshay used to herd, I came to love the hunters' keen whistles ringing across the ridges; I loved the feel of the silky snow beneath my skis; I loved the silence of the morning trees, the greenness against the quiet white, and above the trees and the snow and the silence, the blue window of the winter sky. I often think of those rugged hills beneath Kweitkel, for it was there that I first began to see the Devaki for what they were. To watch Yuri stalking an arctic fox or setting his snares for the eiders and other birds was to appreciate the *care* which attended every aspect and moment of the hunt. The Devaki were neither wanton murderers nor butchers, nor did they do their killing without thought. When a seal was taken, water had to be passed from the hunter's lips into the seal's mouth, or else his anima would have to go over to the other side thirsty. A kittiwake's eyes had to be rubbed with ice, and so on. There were a hundred rituals to be performed, one for each of the different animals. The Devaki, I realized, did not really see the animals as meat at all, at least not as long as their spirits remained to be honored. They loved the animals; they could not conceive of life or the world without animals; they even thought of themselves as animals, or rather, as spirits who had duties and responsibilities to the spirits of each of the animals they hunted. They were intimately connected to the world of animals, and to the world itself, in countless different ways.

Once, on a cold day near the end of deep winter when we were all a little hungry, I watched Yuri let a white bear escape from the ring of spears pointed at her chest. Why did he do this? Because, as he observed, the bear's third claw on the right paw was broken, and everyone knew (or should have known) that such bears were *imakla,* magic animals who may not be killed. Killing, I discovered, was not the real purpose or end of the hunt. This was a hard lesson for me to learn. I spent many bad moments hating that I must kill to live. Most of all I hated the rush of intense aliveness which pumped through me like a drug whenever I speared an innocent animal and I saw the spurting of his blood as drink that would soon quicken my own. The Devaki did not share my hatred, although I believe they never felt so alive as when they were close to killing their prey. I do not claim I was ever able to enter into the hunter's mindset, but I think I glimpsed at least a portion of their worldview: To hunt was to absorb the wind's myriad sounds or the distant smell of the mammoths, to see the patterns in the ermine's droppings and scratchings in the snow, to see patterns in the folds of ice and in the undulations of the land and sky and world; to hunt was to be a part of this pattern, just as the rocks and trees and birds were parts, too. Nothing was so important as the perception of this pattern, of the beauty that is the intention of the World-soul. And nothing the hunter said or thought or did should disturb this beauty, this halla.

"It is better to go over to the other side hungry," Yuri said as he watched the bear disappear into her snowcave, "than to go over deranged and drunk with the blood of an imakla bear blinding our souls."

This attention to the interconnectedness of all the animals, events and things of their world was not a question of morality, but of survival. The Devaki believe they can only survive moment by moment, generation by generation, if they pay attention to what the world requires of them. And by behaving, by learning to perceive what is halla and what is not. I do not mean that any of the Devaki learned this art perfectly. There were always imperfections, uncertainties and little evils in their everyday life. Someone, I remembered, had killed Shanidar's thallow for food even though all thallows were imakla. Certain of the Devaki, although they knew the rules of impeccable behavior, could not conceive of a world in which they had to starve while the thallows soared free. How could such a world be halla? And so they killed the sacred birds, or killed imakla bears, or, rarely, they killed seals or other animals which happened to be their doffels.

In truth, the Devaki never really starved. The forest was
not really empty, but rather like a cafe which had run out of
the choicer foods. When we were hungry we began eating
those disgusting things we had so far disdained. We ate—I
should say the Manwelina and the other families bolted down
this slime, for we of the City held back as long as we
could—we ate unbelievable things. Wicent and his son Wemilo
uncovered a cache of fish heads they had buried during the
previous false winter. The sharp bones had decayed to a
dead, grayish-white and were as soft as flesh. Liluye collected
the rotten bones in a bowl and kneaded the reeking mass into
a paste from which she made small round cakes, flipping
them back and forth between her nervous little hands. She
baked them in the glowing coals of the fire, and the men ate
them slowly as if they were being forced to eat dirt. Other
foods were worse. The dogs were fed slime scraped from old
hides stinking of the putrefied brains used in the tanning
process. Yuri killed a silk belly, and with his single eye half
shut and twitching, he gobbled down the contents of the
stomach, all the while smacking his lips and insisting, for the
benefit of the children, that the goo tasted sweet as roasted
nuts. The children often foraged through the snow for whatever they could find. Often they ate sleekit droppings, which
they munched like berries. Yuri's cousin, Jaywe, split apart
years-old mammoth bones swarming with maggots. Jaywe, a
short, funny man whose peculiar palate had led him to savor
the slip of birds' eggs, licked his lips and sucked down
handfuls of squirming white maggots and said that they were
more delicate than year-old snow loon embryos. I did not
doubt him. Thereafter the rest of his family jokingly referred
to him as Jaywe Maggoteater. I myself ventured to eat thawed
oysters. The squishy blobs of meat ruptured inside my mouth;
the squirt of juices and salt instantly reminded me of my
experiences inside the Entity. I marveled that the taste of
real oysters was exactly the same as the taste the Entity had
placed inside my mind—just as real and just as bad.

In truth, the Devaki were—and are—a smart, resourceful
people. They are tough and hard to kill. During our brief stay
in the cave, I heard tens of stories of resourcefulness and
survival. Yuri once told me that when he was a boy, his
immediate family had almost been exterminated while crossing the ice in early false winter.

"When I was five years old," Yuri told me, "my father and my mother decided to make the pilgrimage to Imakel, where my mother's ancestors are buried. But one night the ice opened unexpectedly, as it sometimes does. We lost one of our sleds, and all of our harpoons, furs, oilstones, spears—everything. And we lost most of our dogs, too. My father had only his snowknife, and my mother—her name was Eliora—had nothing but her teeth and a few old sealskins. We had no way to spear seals, to hunt, or even to make a fire. I was afraid, and who could blame me? But my mother and father never lost their courage."

I will not relate the whole story here because it is too long. But briefly, Nuri, who was Yuri's father, fished his dead dogs out of the sea (his heavy sled had sunk like rock), and he and his family and the remaining dogs ate them. Somehow they managed to reach the nearest island, which was so small and barren that it had no name. With his snow-knife Nuri cut blocks of snow and built a hut. Somehow, Nuri and Eliora made new weapons and tools from the poor materials they found on the island. Nuri hunted and Eliora skinned the animals he killed, and she made their clothing. They ate snow hare and sleekits, and kittiwakes, gulls and chinocha—anything they could find. They fed themselves, and they fed their dogs; Yuri grew quickly and one of the dogs bore a litter the following false winter. The two of them, husband and wife, over the course of that winter and the winters that followed, re-created from almost nothing most of the tools and artifacts of their culture. It took them three years of collecting pieces of driftwood and saving bones to gather together the materials to build a new sled. They improvised and invented new ways of putting together hides and bones, and when they were done, they did not return to Kweitkel. They continued on to Imakel, completing their pilgrimage. They placed fireflowers on the grave of Eliora's grandfather and grandmother. They visited with Eliora's family. And when Eliora's father, Narain, offered to give them a sled for their journey home, Nuri pointed at his patchwork creation and told him, "Thank you, but you see, the Manwelina know how to build sleds." And everyone laughed because his sled could not have carried them another mile, let alone the two hundred miles back to Kweitkel.

I often thought that this ability to shape random materials

into useful things lay at the heart of the Alaloi's culture. Given the requirements of their world, there was nothing they could not make. If a tool or item of clothing required a particular combination of flexibility, strength, texture or insulative properties, they would experiment until they discovered the right combination. Their knowledge of the things of the world was detailed and precise: Lubricants were extracted from the shagshay hoof because they had discovered the fats in the joints furthest from the body froze at lower temperatures; they made the windows of their huts (when they desired windows) from the tough, translucent intestines of the bearded seal; shagshay horns were flexible and so were bent into the side prongs of fish spears; and so on. They were geniuses at making things, the women as much so as the men. Among other things, the women were responsible for making and caring for that most vital of all survival tools: the marvelous Alaloi clothing.

At night after hunting—and this, too, was part of our daily routine—we would sit around the oilstones, eating what food we had, talking, watching the women making our clothes. The women's mouths were always busy because they were either chatting about the events of the day or chewing skins with their stubby, worn teeth. Their teeth were tools, and they used them effectively, to soften the frozen parkas of their husbands and to work new skins into leather. By early midwinter spring, with the first storms of the new year blowing outside the cave, my mother and Justine, Katharine too, had become used to this grueling work. They had also become experts at sewing waterproof sealskins into boots, or making waterproof kamelaikas, or tailoring the ruffs of the shagshay parkas with wolf fur, a fur which would shed the ice crystals condensed from one's breath. With their bone needles and sinews they made their precise stitches, stitches which would swell when wet, keeping cold and moisture from entering the clothing. I was glad they had imprinted these skills because an Alaloi hunter is utterly dependent upon the women in his family. As my mother put it one night, holding a half-made kamelaika up to my shoulders, "Where would Yuri be today? If not for the skills of his mother? If not for the clothes she made, the fish spears, the oilstones, if not for her milk, the very flesh of his flesh? Is there anything a woman cannot make?"

There was one part of our daily routine I wish I could forget. During this cold, hard time of hungers and chilblain and petty miseries, I began suffering another misery, in some ways the most miserable misery of all. I discovered I had lice. The hair of my body and head and pubes was crawling with these tiny, flat insects. It was the price of swiving dirty, savage women, I thought, and I twitched and scratched until I bled, and I rubbed ash mud over my body from ankle to neck, but nothing helped until I submitted to my mother for what would come to be the nightly delousing. Every night, I would rest my head on my mother's lap while she danced her fingers through my hair, searching for lice. She had sharp eyes, my mother did, to pick them out with only the oil-stones' dim light illuminating my black hair. I felt her sharp fingernails like a tweezers crushing the lice and, occasionally, plucking from my itchy scalp a few hairs which she said were as gray as Yuri's.

Her grooming did little good, however, because the cave and all the furs were full of nits waiting to hatch. The other members of my family became infested as well, although they seemed to have fewer lice and a greater tolerance for this petty torture than I did. (Bardo, for some inexplicable, unjust reason—he ridiculously claimed that the poisons from his gonads had soured his skin, rendering him unappealing to crawling insects—remained free of lice.) It was not the prickling pain or itch that bothered me; it was the *idea* of the lice thrusting their tiny mouthparts into my skin that sent me shuddering and twitching. I loathed the *idea* of insects drinking my blood, of life living off other life. I considered shaving my body with sharp blades of flint. But I did not do so. I recalled that there were whole segments of humanity out towards Gamina Luz who had purged their systems of bacteria and other parasites only to discover they had to enclose themselves in made-worlds lest they contaminate their sterile bodies with the dirt of civilization. This isolation, however, had weakened their immune systems, leaving them vulnerable to bizarre diseases. Who knew what natural balances I might disturb if I did not live as the Alaloi lived? There was another reason, too, why I did not shave myself: The flint flakes we made were so sharp I might easily cut my skin, opening it to infection. And infection among the Alaloi, as Jinje had proven with his rotting toes, could be very bad.

Of all the triumphs of civilization I sometimes think the greatest and most sublime was the invention of the hot bath. How I longed for soap and hot water! How I missed the joy of soaking my cold limbs, of letting the wet heat lull me and warm me from skin to bone! How badly I wanted to be clean! I missed the sounds and smells and comforts of the City and found myself thinking about her all the time. Why had I left her? Why had I come here seeking nonexistent secrets, killing seals, feeding toothless old men, disturbing the harmony of the Devaki families? How could I have believed a civilized man could live as a savage? From where had I acquired such arrogance?

One night over a mug of tea, Bardo confessed that he, too, missed the comforts of our city. "I would advise that we leave here as soon as Katharine has collected her samples," he said to me. "We don't want to starve, do we? How long can it take her to swive a few men? Excuse my candor, Little Fellow, but I don't understand why she has ignored so many, ah . . . *possibilities?*"

Of course, he hadn't had the slightest thought of leaving so long as he could fill his belly with meat every night, and every night fill one or more women with his seed. The others, though, were not so eager to leave as I would have hoped. Soli welcomed the hardships of our primitive life and seemed to be enjoying himself, if that dour man was capable of joy. Justine found everything about her new existence "fascinating," as she put it, while my mother reveled in her power to make her living directly from the things of life. And as for Katharine, she seemed to be biding her time, to be waiting for some important event that she would not reveal.

As the storms of the new year grew more frequent, I gradually became aware that the Devaki had not completely accepted us. I do not mean that they necessarily suspected our civilized origins. But many of them, not just Yuri, thought that we were strange, and worse than strange. Because of the storms, the hunting became more difficult and dangerous. Our hunger deepened. Sometimes there were grumblings and complaints and petty arguments over the division of the meat. More than once I heard the men grumble that my killing my doffel had brought them bad luck, not good. There was a rumor going about the cave that I had fed Shanidar half of the beautiful liver of a snow loon. (In truth, ever since my encounter with the Old Man of the Cave, I had been smuggling him choice cuts of meat, to keep him alive. It was wrong of me, I know, but what else could I do?) And there was other gossip, vicious talk the women spread among themselves that gradually reached the ears of their husbands. I should have been warned something was wrong when Piero of the Yelenalina family and Olin of the Sharailina began threatening to leave Kweitkel for the islands of the west. I thought they were just crabby with hunger, but I soon discovered they had other complaints.

One late afternoon after a long, fruitless day of hunting, Yuri caught me aside in the forest outside the cave and said, "Piero is wrong to blame you for our hunger. If Tuwa was not sick with mouthrot, we would have plenty to eat."

I agreed that it was so.

"Still, it is strange that the animals no longer leap to our spears, is it not?"

I agreed with him that it was strange.

"Although Piero is wrong to blame you, I cannot blame him for blaming you. Can you? And there are others who might observe your strange behavior and come to blame you for their own misfortunes. I myself have no respect for these people, but how can I blame them?"

"How is my behavior strange?" I asked. "Do they blame me for killing the seal, then?"

He held up his scarred hand and shook his head. "It is not that, even though there are few men who kill their doffels. It is this: A wise man takes care not to be left alone in his hut with his sister, especially one so beautiful as Katharine. Then no one can blame him for abominations which bring his people bad luck."

As he said this there was a sudden sharp pain in my stomach. I felt sick; I felt the burn of guilt coloring my cheeks, and I was grateful that the wind through the trees was so icy and bitter that my face must have already been crimson with cold. I turned to Yuri, who was leaning against a boulder and puffing steam as he looked out across the broad, white valley below. I wanted to tell him that whoever had accused Katharine and me of abomination was guilty of slander. And more, I wanted to shout out, to scream into the valley that Katharine was not my sister. I wanted to reveal the ugly tapestry of lies and fakery that had led us to pose as

Alaloi. I wanted to do this for two reasons: to bring this
foolish journey to an end, and so Yuri would know I was a
man of honor. But I said nothing, did nothing. How could I
make this savage, one-eyed man understand the complexity
of civilized ways or the esoteric nature of the quest? I said
nothing, and Yuri shrugged his shoulders. "Katharine, too,
she is a strange woman," he said.

On the tenth day of midwinter spring, I discovered just
how serious the slander against me was. It was a day of ice
flurries and moist, heavy air. The snow was gray and leaden,
and the trees were grayish green beneath the dark gray sky.
The wind, blowing in fits and stops, smelled like wet slate.
The few men who had gone hunting the day before—they
were all Sharailina—returned to the cave in the closing
grayness of twilight when the snow and the shadowed slopes
and the low, dark sky seemed to merge into an impenetrable
sea of gray. They had found meat, they said. Ouray and his
son, Vishne, beat the snow from their gray furs as they
stomped into the cave. They were followed by Olin the Ugly,
a surly man with a great swatch of scar running down his
forehead to his jaw. Olin was grasping the tail of a half-eaten
animal, dragging the carcass towards the Sharailina's huts.
"Sabra meat!" he announced, and his ugly wife, Jelina, and
the rest of his family came out of the huts smiling and eagerly
sniffing the air.

I looked up from the shaft of a new spear I was carving—I
was standing on the snow-packed cave floor outside our
hut—and I saw at once that Olin had little meat to share. I
was wondering how Olin had found the wolf carrion when he
began telling the story of their hunt.

The day before, it seemed, the Sharailina men had tracked
Totunye, the bear, through the southern forests down to the
sea. When the snow began to fall, young Vishne wanted to
return to the cave, but Olin led them down to the beach
where, he said, he had heard rocks cracking and a distant
roar. Ouray, though, thought the cracking was the sound of
the heavy limbs snapping off the trees and the roar was only
the roar of the wind. When they emerged from the forest
they saw a white bear clawing a wolf apart against a mound of
rocks. They rushed the bear, but Totunye, with his long,
black claws and cowardly eyes, saw the scars on Olin's face
(this is the story as Olin told it), and he fled into the storm

because he could see that Olin had long ago been scarred by another bear and was therefore invulnerable. And so they had returned with the meat of the wolf which, as Ouray put it while staring at the face of his brother, "is leaner and tougher than bear meat but not as costly to take."

Several of the Manwelina had gathered around to listen to this story. Wicent's son, Wemilo, and the ever-mischievous Choclo began making jokes. Seif, who looked much like his brother, Liam, except that he was not quite so handsome or large, covered his eyes and laughed at Olin. Then Liam came out of his hut and joined in the fun. "Are you *certain* that it is Sabra, the wolf?" Liam taunted Olin. He licked his red lips and flung back his long, blond hair. "I would want to be *certain* before I ate him, wouldn't you?"

Olin cursed and he ripped the tail from the base of the wolf's carcass. He threw it at Liam, who was laughing and rubbing tears from his eyes.

"Do I not know Sabra when I see Sabra?" Olin shouted.

Liam licked his lips again and cruelly joked, "Do *I* not know Devaki when I see Devaki?" And then he laughed harder.

He was referring to the unfortunate abomination which had fractured the honor of the Sharailina family. Once, years ago in false winter, Olin's great grandfather had cached some shagshay meat for eating the following midwinter spring. When the time came, he and his family had dug up what they thought was shagshay thigh and they had eaten it. The next day Lokni, who was Liam's great-grandfather, had discovered the meat was in reality part of a human corpse that a bear had uncovered from the graveyard above the cave. Apparently, the bear had dragged the human remains down to the snowfield below the cave where the Devaki sometimes store their meat. It was an understandable mistake, but ever after, for three generations the sons of Lokni had made a tradition of ridiculing the eating habits of the Sharailina family.

Liam laughed and licked his lips and rubbed his belly, and he picked up the tail Olin had flung at him. He held it to his open mouth as if he intended to eat it. He made a gagging sound and said, "How I love Sabra's furry tail, there is so much meat!" And then, "It makes me happy that you are certain this is wolf meat. But I must ask you one thing." And here he turned to Seif and shook his head with fake sadness.

He looked back at Olin all the while running his finger through the shredded gray fur. "Does a wolf have gray fur?" he asked. "I myself have only seen white wolves; perhaps the Sharailina know a different kind?"

Olin bent to the carcass and kicked it with his foot. "The fur is white," he said. "It is only the lack of light that makes it seem gray."

"It is as gray as the fur of a dog," Liam taunted.

"No," Ouray said, defending his brother, "it is white. It has been stained gray by dirt and sea salt."

Liam, who thought he was a funny man, suddenly dropped down on his hands and knees, and he pulled his golden head back and let loose a series of barks. "It is a dog," he said as he flopped over and rolled about in his mocking imitation of a dog scratching his back. "You eat the meat of a dog."

I watched this ridiculous scene as I twirled my spear beneath my carving flints. I realized what should have been obvious all along: Olin and his brother had found the cairn of stones that Bardo and I had built over the body of my lead sled dog. The torn carcass lying by Olin's hut was what remained of Liko.

"Dog meat!" Liam said. "The Sharailina hunt dogs!"

Olin protested again that it was indeed a wolf. He moved to flay it with his knife, and I crossed the cave as quickly as I could. "It is a dog," I said. I explained how the thallow had killed Liko, how Bardo and I had buried him. "Don't cut him—he was brave and loyal, and it is not right to eat him."

By this time the whole Devaki tribe had emerged from their huts. They encircled us. The voluptuous Sanya, who was suckling her newborn girl, said, "It is not right for the mothers to grow so hungry their milk dries like puddle-melt in the sun. Mallory forgets that meat is meat; meat is neither brave nor loyal."

All this time Liam was rolling on his back, laughing in between his derisive dog sounds. "Rart, rart, rart," he barked. "Rart, rart, rart, rart." And then he looked up at Olin and said, "I hope the shagshay leap to our spears soon. Or else we will be meat for the hungry Sharailina."

This proved too much for Olin. He shook his long, flint knife in the air, cursed and fell upon Liam. Olin's knees crushed the wind from Liam's chest—I heard the *whumph* of air escape from Liam's lips. Someone called out, "Watch the knife!" and for some reason which made no sense to me at the time, Olin dropped the knife. They wrestled, then. On the hard snow, they grappled and heaved and rolled. Liam managed to trap one of Olin's arms between their bodies. He used this momentary advantage to jab at Olin's eyes with his long fingernails. I was sure that he intended to gouge his fingers into the sockets, to feel for the eyestrings, to blind him. Olin had been mauled by a bear once; it made me sick to see the bearlike Liam mauling him again. "Not his eyes!" I yelled, and I stepped forward, planted my foot, and whacked Liam's temple with the butt end of my spear. He tumbled away from Olin, stunned, holding the side of his head. The blow had cut him; blood flowed from between his splayed fingers, trickling down his thick, golden beard.

He cursed me and spat at my legs. He shouted, "What is wrong with you that you cannot tell sport from killing? Your brains have softened like seal fat—but that is the way with sister-seducers. Did Katharine suck out your brains along with your seed?"

I think I tried to kill him, then. As Olin and Yuri and all the people of the families looked on, I raised my spear back behind my head. I clutched the shaft's leather grip, dimly aware that Bardo and Justine and my trembling mother were watching me from behind a wall of astonished Devaki. "No!" I cried, and straight ahead of me as I sighted on Liam's throat, there was Katharine standing between two Manwelina women. She was staring at me unashamedly as if she knew I would not kill him. "No!" I cried again, and I began to whip my arm forward. But there was a sudden resistance; I could no more cast the spear than I could uproot a shatterwood tree. All at once I felt other hands on the shaft, and someone ripped the spear from my grip. I turned and there was Soli holding the spear as he would a dead fish. His lips were hard against each other, as white as ice. He was holding his breath; beneath his forehead's white skin pulsed a thick vein.

Yuri came forward and grabbed the spear from Soli. He broke it across his knee. His eye flashed on me like a rocket beacon, and he said simply, "Strange you forget we are not hunters of men." Then he turned away from me, leading the rest of his family back to their huts.

Olin came over to me and scratched his scarred face. "It was only a game," he said. "Why do you think I dropped my knife? Do you think Liam would have blinded me, his near-brother?"

He looked at the halves of the spear lying crooked on the snow, laughed nervously and walked away, repeating, "It was only a game."

Soli stood there glaring at me, stiff and cold as a tree. Katharine bowed her head to us and went into the hut. After a few moments Bardo, Justine and my mother went inside, too. Soli and I were alone in the middle of the darkening cave. I thought he might never move or speak again. Then he whispered, "Why, Pilot? Why are you so *reckless*? Tell me, please." With his heel he ground the spear into the snow. "Why do you do what you do?"

I stared down at the spear, biting my lip.

"Why?"

"I don't know," I said truthfully.

"You're dangerous, Pilot. It's been said before. And now, this . . . this *situation*, the expedition, everything we do here— it's all become too dangerous, hasn't it?"

"Perhaps."

"Yes, too dangerous to stay here any longer. Let's hope Katharine has most of her samples because it's too dangerous for her to collect any more. Tomorrow we'll radio the City for a jammer. We'll say our goodbyes and that will be the end."

"Do you think that's necessary?" I asked. "To slink back to the City like whipped dogs, then?" I do not know why I said this—probably just to be contrary. In truth, I was dying to return to the City, to immerse myself in the beautiful but meaningless study of mathematics.

He grew very angry after I said this. I thought the blood vessels in his eye might rupture, leaving him blind. "Yes, it's necessary," he whispered. And then he said the forbidden word, "*I've* decided. We'll leave tomorrow."

He rubbed his eyes, whirled and left me. I stood alone wondering why I was so reckless, wondering why I did the things that I did.

14

The Radio

Preserve art above artifact; preserve memory
above all.
—Saying of the remembrancers

At dawn the next day the Reinalina, Yelenalina and Sharailina families packed their long traveling sleds. Ouray and Julitha of the Sharailina, and their children, Vishne, Namiley and Emily the Younger, tied the binding lashes and harnessed the dogs reluctantly, as if they were uncertain that driving into the storms of midwinter spring would be a wise thing to do. But Olin and the heads of the other families were adamant in their decision to leave. They cited hunger and the scarcity of the animals as their reason for seeking the islands of the west. They cited other reasons, too. "We will journey to Sawelsalia," Olin announced. "There the Patwin will share mammoth steaks dripping with fat. There the men do not raise their spears to one another."

Yuri, who stood there in his worn underfurs shaking his head sadly, said, "This is a bad day for the Devaki. Why do you think our far-cousins on Sawelsalia will have meat to share? Perhaps they will not welcome you with mammoth steaks; perhaps they will not welcome Devaki with the same love Devaki welcome Devaki."

But Olin replied, "Perhaps the Devaki have grown too many to live in this small cave. And if the mammoth herds of our far-cousins are sick and there is not enough meat, we will eat tripe until the sea thaws. Then we will build boats and hunt Kikilia when he comes up to breathe." He turned to me and said, "Goodbye Man of the Southern Ice. Perhaps you, too, should return to your home." So saying he slapped his son, Yasha, on the back of his neck, whistled to his dogs, and then he and his family disappeared into the forest. A little while later, the other families were gone, too.

Yuri scolded his little grandson, Jonath, away from the crackling fire at the mouth of the cave. He said, "It is sad to speak of killing whales. Better to sacrifice the mammoth herds than to hunt Kililia, who is wiser than we and strong as God. But Olin's family is hungry so who can blame him?"

"It is wrong to kill whales," I agreed. I turned to the east where the distant snowfields were flowing with the blood of the rising sun, and I was full of blame and other emotions.

Yuri squinted his eye and mumbled, "Red sky at morning, travelers are mourning—it is a bad day for travel, I think." And then, "I must tell you that there are those among my family—Lilnye, Seif, Jaywe, and of course Liam—who say that you and your family should leave, too. I, myself, and Wicent and Old Ilona, believe you should stay, but the others . . . after you raised your spear to Liam, well, who can blame them?"

I looked at Yuri, with the rancid grease shiny on his face, and I was suddenly sick of him and his little saying: "Who can blame them?" I felt an urge to stumble against him, to "accidentally" push him down into one of the puddles that the fire had melted from the snow, to watch as he splashed in icy water and say, "Who could blame me?" I did not want to hear any more words of wisdom from his thick, chapped, greasy lips.

"Soli has decided we will leave," I said. "So we will leave, tomorrow or the day after."

"Well, Soli is a willful man, and Soli has decided you will leave, and who can blame him?"

But our departure from the Devaki tribe was not to be so simple. Early that morning Soli freed the radio from its hiding place in his sled, and he went out into the woods to find a space of privacy. He tried to radio the City. He failed. He tried all morning and half the afternoon until a fierce storm began covering the trees in sheet ice, forcing him inside the cave. When evening came, we all crowded inside our hut around the oilstones. On the white furs at the center of the hut Soli placed a glossy black box the size of a large man's forearm. He pointed at it and told us, "The radio is dead."

"That's impossible," Bardo said as he toyed with the hairs of his beard. He was half-lying on my bed, eating some nuts he had found. "The radio is dead? No, no, that can't be."

My mother and Justine were busy on the far side of the hut adjusting the furs atop the drying rack. The hut was warm, so warm that the curved walls were gleaming with a glaze of water and ice. My mother brushed drops of water from the silky shagshay fur. Her strong face was yellow in the yellow light, and she tilted her head to the side and asked, "How do you know the radio is dead?"

"If it *were* dead, that would be too bad," Bardo added, as he watched Justine shake out a fur. Much to Soli's annoyance, he liked to watch her whenever he had the chance, and worse, he liked to talk to her, as one friend talks to another. "But whoever heard of a dead radio?" He nonchalantly popped a nut into his mouth, but I could tell he was nervous and worried.

"Of course the radio can't be dead," Justine said. She looked at Bardo and smiled her beautiful smile. "That's quite a thought, isn't it? You might just as well imagine that the sun won't rise tomorrow! It's impossible for these things to die, it really is. The Lord Tinker made the radio *himself*. How could the radio be dead?"

Bardo grabbed his stomach and let out a long groan, which was answered by a whining from the tunnelway. Because two of our dogs were sick, we had brought them inside the hut, sheltering them from the storm. "Tusa," Bardo called out, "Lola . . . do you think the radio is dead? Bark three times if you think it is dead." He waited for a moment, but the dogs were silent in their snow holes, so he said, "You see, everyone agrees, the radio can't be dead."

"Quiet!" Soli hissed, kneeling over the radio. "Restrain yourself, if you can."

"Have you wondered if the radio is only ill?" Katharine asked. She had the crypt beneath her bed open; I could barely watch her sorting her samples. Bent over as she was, her body seemed fuller than usual, and her hair fell in a lustrous black curtain down her shoulders and breasts to the floor. She held up one of the spheres and emptied it. Frothing blue krydda the color of her eyes spilled out over the snow, melting it into indigo slush. I smelled the preservative's pungent, peppermintlike aroma, and she covered the slush with handfuls of fresh snow. "Now that the families are gone, these samples are all..." As she counted her samples one by one, she showed Justine the most precious of them.

Justine said, "If these samples are all we have, well, I'm sure they'll be enough; they'll *have* to be enough because they must have been difficult to collect, and there are no men left to collect samples *from*, except the Manwelina men, of course, and you've... and you've *been* with most of them, haven't you, Katharine?"

I did not want to look at the spheres, at the thick, white glue of the Devaki men. I went to the center of the hut and picked up the radio. To Soli I said, "Perhaps Katharine is right. Perhaps the radio is only ill."

Soli watched me turn the radio over and over in my hands.

"Ah, but if the radio were only ill," Bardo pointed out, "why doesn't it heal itself? Lord Pilot? Have you *asked* the radio if it is ill, Lord Pilot?"

"Yes, that was the first question asked," Soli said. "But the radio is silent; therefore the radio is dead."

"It's this damn cold," Bardo said, playing with his mustache. "It could freeze the bowels of anything."

"Have we considered everything?" my mother asked. "All the possibilities?"

"What possibilities?" Soli asked.

For a while, we debated possibilities: Perhaps the Lord Tinker had forgotten to monitor his radio for our signal; perhaps a sunspot or pulse of radiation from the Vild had at last reached Neverness, distorting the propagation of radio waves through the atmosphere; perhaps the Order had at last fallen into schism and civil war—what if the Tinker's Tower had been thrown down and all the wonderful devices of the tinkers had been destroyed?

As the night wore on, we became tired and crabby, susceptible to wild ideas. I think we had lived too long in those snowy hills, had spent too many nights in the snow hut listening to the wind blow and the wolves howl. For me, at least, all the familiar things of the City seemed far away. The City itself seemed somehow fantastic and unreal, a memory of an earlier Mallory, a buried dream. Looking around at the harpoons, the ripe furs, the oilstones flickering yellow and orange, it was hard to think that a larger world existed. Almost anything seemed possible: What if a new race of aliens had come to Neverness, killed all the humans and taken the

City for their own? What if the Solid State Entity or some other god had changed the laws of spacetime so that radio and other eem waves were either slowed or could not locally exist? What if the City itself did not exist?

All this talk had obviously made Bardo nervous. He twined and untwined his mustache between his fingers, and he massaged his belly. Silently—it was a custom of his when women were present to do so silently—he began breaking wind. The air of the hut began to stink. Justine coughed and waved her hand beneath her nose. Bardo puffed out his cheeks as he pointed at the tunnelway where the dogs slept, and he cursed, "That damn Tusa! Feed him the decaying guts of a seal and he farts like a rocket. By God, it stinks in here!"

So badly did it stink that everyone except Soli was breathing through his or her mouth. (He was intently picking at the radio's casing, oblivious to Bardo's little problem.) My mother wrinkled her nose and covered her face with the edge of her furs. She glared at Bardo. "Men are stinky beasts," she said.

Bardo's face fell into an embarrassed frown while my mother cocked her chin, looking at him with contempt. After a moment the contempt intensified into hatred, both for Bardo and herself. My mother had a tongue as cruel as a double-edged knife, and it was a cruelty which cut two ways: If someone offended her, she would be cruel to him and hate herself for being cruel, and then she would hate him for instigating these twin cruelties.

"Ah, I know what you're thinking," Bardo said to her. "But it was Tusa who farted, or Lola, not me."

In disgust, my mother began putting on her furs. She turned to Soli and said, "If the radio is dead, then it was killed. Tinker-made instruments don't die a natural death." Then she left the hut to take a breath of fresh air. (Or perhaps she went to Anala's hut to drink tea and gossip, an activity she had grown quite fond of during our brief stay in the cave.)

Soli was slicing at the radio's casing with a flint blade, and he said, "There must be a way to open the radio, to find out why it's dead."

"*Open* the radio, Lord Pilot?" Bardo said, rubbing his red cheeks. "Surely you're joking?" Soli might as well have suggested opening Bardo up to determine why his gut produced so much gas.

But Soli was not joking. He was intent upon getting the radio open. Sometime around midnight, he discovered that heated flints applied to the thick, lacquer-like sealant caused the plastic to peel away in flaky layers as thin as a snow crystal. At last he laid the casing bare, but the radio would still not open. He stared at the back side of it for a long time before he noticed four small, round spots, black against darker black, one spot at each corner of the radio's casing. He found that the round spots were in fact holes filled with sealant. He excavated these holes, slowly and painstakingly digging and reaming with hot needles of flint. When he had finished this excruciatingly boring work, he held the radio to the oilstones and announced that he could see bits of bifurcated metal set down into the holes.

"What is it?" I asked.

"That's hard to say."

"Tinker work," I said. "Pilots shouldn't meddle with tinker work."

On their snowbeds, Justine and Katharine were trying to sleep; Bardo was flopped down like a dead bear, snoring loudly.

"Yes, tinker work," Soli said. "But where is the tinker to do the work?" His lips tightened as he inserted a flint needle into one of the holes. He twisted it and it broke. He inserted another needle and twisted the opposite way. It broke as well.

"Damn the tinkers and their arcane arts," I said, and he turned the radio over and shook the flint fragments from the hole.

"Flint's too brittle," he said. He picked up a long sliver of shatterwood shaved from his mammoth spear. "Shatterwood is not quite as hard as flint, but it's not as brittle, is it?" So saying, with a flint carver, he whittled the end of the wood sliver to fit neatly into the bifurcations in the bits of metal set into the four holes.

"Why are you doing this?" I asked. "If the tinkers made the radio to be opened by tinkers only, how do you expect to open it?"

"Where is your famed initiative?" he asked. "It's a mystery, isn't it, how you were able to penetrate and return from the Entity."

"That was different."

"Yes, you were lucky then, but here luck is not a factor, is it?"

He dropped the shaped end of the wood sliver down one of the holes and twisted it to the right without result. He twisted it to the left, but this too accomplished nothing. "Luck," he said, and he twisted harder. "It gives!" he said. He twirled his fingers, and moments later he removed a peg of metal as long as my fingernail.

"What is it?" I asked again.

"That's unknown." He scrutinized the metal peg under the oilstones' light. He handed it to me. There was a thin ridge of metal raised up from and wrapped in a continuous spiral around the length of the peg. "It's obvious, though, that this ridge must work against a similar ridge set into the casing, else the peg would have just fallen out." As the others slept, he removed the three other pegs, and the radio popped open.

"Ha!" I whispered, "a tinker would go mad at the first glimpse of the manifold, but a pilot can unravel a tinker's secrets as easily as—"

"Be quiet! We've unraveled nothing."

I looked into the workings of the radio. There was a jumble of varicolored plastics, claries and metals twisting and joining together in strange and unfathomable ways. I saw immediately why the radio had not healed itself: For some reason, the tinkers had assembled the radio from unusual and archaic components rather than growing it whole as, for instance, they grew the circuitry and other parts of a light ship. The sight of these obviously simple components unnerved me. I made guesses as to how the radio worked, though I might as well have tried to glean esoteric knowledge from a writhing ball of spirali. I realized I no more understood the secrets of the tinkers' radio than I did the Ieldra's secret locked inside the Alaloi's germ plasm.

"It's so barbaric," I said. "Why would the tinkers make a radio from ancient components?"

"Tinkers have their secrets as we have ours," he said. "A device from the past for our journey to the past—that would be their kind of joke wouldn't it?"

I glanced at him and said, "Shake it. Perhaps one of the components has come loose."

"That's not probable," he said, but he did as I suggested,

to no avail. Tinker-made components, I realized, do not come loose.

"Why do you think it's dead?" I asked.

"When this switch is thrown," he said flipping a piece of black plastic on the front of the radio, "nothing happens. There is no flow of electrons. One or more of the components must be ill."

"Which one?"

He poked various components with his index finger and said, "Who knows?"

"Well, it's dead, and there's nothing we can do, then."

"Perhaps, perhaps not."

I looked into the guts of the radio again. Obviously, one or more of the components must have been responsible for receiving our voices, another to encode the information carried in the sound waves, others to modulate the information, and still others to generate and send the radio waves skyward to the satellites orbiting the planet. Which components did which I had no idea.

"It's hopeless," I said.

"Perhaps."

With his long fingernail he scratched the surface of a white crystal. He said, "Perhaps this vibrates at the touch of our voices, vibrates and produces a corresponding vibration in an electric current. Yes, it could cause the electrical resistance to vary, to alter the current. If we could trace the current flow, we might be able to tell why the radio was dead."

I shook my head because there were a hundred components stuck to the inside of the radio. I did not think we could trace the current flow or deduce the purpose of the other components.

"My father," Soli said, "once taught me the theory of radios and other ancient things. He wanted me to know the history of our technology."

"I thought Alexandar was a cantor, not an historian."

"Yes, he was a cantor. And therefore he wanted me to appreciate the limits of technology, or rather, the ugliness of practical theories. He himself hated technology, old or new. The best mathematics, he used to say, is pure mathematics, mathematics that can't be put to use by the mechanics or tinkers. He taught me thermodynamics and hydraulics, the theory of making fusion bombs. Particle theory and hologram theory, and map theory, and information theory, a hundred theories of manipulating things, a thousand. He was a cold, hard, mercilessly precise man, my father. And he wanted me to share his aesthetics, to be just like him." He closed his eyes, rubbed his temples, and turned his head away from me. I heard him whisper, "But I am not; I am not."

I waited a while before saying, "You know about radios, then."

He shook his head. "Once the *theory* of radios was known. But it's all forgotten."

Of course, Soli had not quite forgotten everything. Bits and pieces of his father's teachings came back to him: Eem waves were made up of magnetic and electric fields vibrating at right angles to each other; information could be enfolded into the eem wave in different ways, for instance, by modulating the wave's amplitude or frequency; once the signal had left the radio, it was vulnerable to distortion from sunspots and atmospheric ionization and interference from other electrical sources; and so on. There were a hundred ways to introduce noise into the radio's signal. The elimination of noise, Soli said, was the real problem in transmitting information.

"But if it's coded properly, the signal can be as free from error as we choose to make it. There are ways of adding redundancy to the signal, theorems proving a nearly perfect code exists, if we have the cleverness to devise it. Yes, that must be the trick, encoding the signal and filtering out the noise. Discovering the code."

He stared at the radio and pressed his lips together.

"And if it's not coded properly, the information is destroyed?" I asked.

"No, information can be created but never destroyed—if you believe the holists. At some level, the information always exists. The trick is keeping it together coherently, and transmitting it without noise."

I rubbed my nose, then touched a translucent, blue component. It was as hard and smooth as glass. "But which components encode the information and which filter out the noise? Do you remember?"

He made a fist and ground it against his temple. "Unfortunately, no," he said.

"Too bad," I replied.

"Yes, too bad, but there's always a chance the memories can be recovered."

"A chance?"

We awoke the others, then, and Bardo went to fetch my mother from Anala's hut. My mother ducked into the hut followed by Bardo, who was cursing because he had crawled into a pile of dog dung. Soli motioned for everyone to gather around him. He laid the radio on his lap and said, "Your help is needed."

Bardo shifted his bulk back and forth, in obvious misery. He was still bothered by the nightly risings of his membrum; the furs stretched over his belly almost like fabric over a tent pole. He eyed the radio suspiciously and said, "Too bad, Lord Pilot, too bad." And then he began scraping dung from the knee of his trousers.

"Is that all you have to say?"

"Ah . . . no. What I meant to say was, with the radio dead, we can't leave here until deep winter, can we? And that's too bad because—"

"No, we'll heal the radio," Soli said. "Search your memory. Perhaps you once watched a tinker heal a robot; perhaps there is some bit of childhood lore you might recall."

"Not I, Lord Pilot," Bardo said. "Not I." Then he laughed, and I did too, because on Summerworld where he had spent his childhood, there are neither tinkers nor robots. On Summerworld the lords and nobles despise complicated mechanisms of any sort because they rightly fear the power of tinkers and programmers and others who understand what they do not. And so on Summerworld, men are made to do the work of machines. "I recall," Bardo said, "that when slaves were broken in my family's mines—don't look at me like that Mallory, there was nothing I could do—we used to sell them to the damned cutters. The cutters would scavenge their organs. I never saw the workings of a machine until I came to Neverness."

My mother made a sour face at Bardo and began nodding her head. To Soli she said, "Do you really expect to heal the radio? Even if we remember? The functions of every part? How could we heal even a single part? Where are the tools? Where is the knowledge? Before we had imprinted the art of flaking flint, could we have straightened a chipped spear point?"

"Possibly," Soli said.

And my mother cocked her head, squinted and said, "The Lord Pilot has always been critical. Of certain people who attempt the *impossible*."

Soli's eyes narrowed to blue slits but he said nothing.

All this time Justine had been staring at the innards of the radio. Suddenly her smooth, tan cheeks broke into a smile. "I can't be sure," she said, "how can one ever be sure of childhood memories? Especially memories which seem to be memories of memories, or even memories of what somebody once told us long ago, so I'm not sure I remember correctly, but when I was a little girl—you remember this, Moira, don't you?" she asked my mother. "When we were little girls, don't you remember how Mother used to take us to the museum on the Ruede? You don't remember? Well, I remember, and I once saw a display of ancient electronics." She carefully touched her long finger to a tiny circle of metal inside the radio. "I may be wrong, but I think this was called a diode or triode, I'm not sure which, but I remember there was something called rectifier diodes which shaped the waveform of the radio signal. Or were they called pin diodes? I'm really not sure."

As she spoke, Soli watched her intently, as a thallow watches a snow hare. "Try to remember," he said.

Justine smiled at him, touching the fine hair on the back of his wrist. "But why should *I* try to remember, Leopold, when you've seen similar exhibits in the museums of the City? You used to be interested in such things when we were first married. Don't *you* remember?"

Soli's face suddenly drained of color. He rubbed his eyes, coughed and sighed. "Yes, there is a vague memory," he admitted. "But it was so long ago."

He closed his eyes, wincing as if he had a headache. He held his breath before opening them.

"It's true," he said at last. "Near the Hyacinth Gardens, there is a room full of components like these." He ran his fingers over his narrow lips. It was the first time I had ever seen him embarrassed. "But the names and functions of the components—well, the memory is gone."

"The remembrancers," I reminded him, "say that memory can be hidden but never destroyed."

"Yes," he said, "the remembrancers say that, the remembrancers."

"Their training is not so different from ours," Justine said. "Some of the attitudes are the same, that's what Thomas Rane told me one day at the North Ring, he said, 'Justine,'... well, I won't tell you everything he said, but I remember him saying that all we've ever seen, heard, felt or thought is recorded somewhere in memory, and anyone can unfold her memory if she tries, if she knows sequencing—I think that's what Thomas called it—and imaging, those are two of *their* attitudes similar to ours."

Soli looked at the radio for a while, staring into the past. "Can a pilot think like a remembrancer?" he asked. "Is it possible? Yes, perhaps it's possible."

His eyes closed as he fell into the twentieth of the sixty-four attitudes of hallning, the attitude the pilots call association-memory. From this attitude he passed into imaging, where he remained for a good part of the night. (It was only years later, on the ice of the sea, that he gave me a full account of this grueling labor. At the time, I wondered if he were only sleeping, or perhaps resting in the attitude of open-waiting.) He tried to call up images seen a hundred years ago, but he did not have a remembrancer's skill in decoding the images from chemical memory into eidetic memory. Since the remembrancers teach that the memory of smells is often the key to greater memory sequences, he tried to key off the memories by scratching and smelling the gallium arsenides and germanium of the radio's components; he tried forcing by means of logic-memory; he tried very hard to accomplish a thing he had not been trained to do; he tried all that night, tried everything he could think of to unfold his memory, tried until he was so weary he could hardly hold his head up, but in the end he sat squeezing the radio so tightly that the edge cut his fingers and blood leaked across his knuckles. He did this, Justine whispered to me, because he was furious with himself for failing.

At last he opened his eyes. I did not like the look in his eyes, especially when he began staring from me to my mother. "The radio is dead," he announced. "There will be no healing it."

"Too bad," Bardo said.

"When we return to the City," Soli said, "everyone who's

ever touched the radio will go before the akashics. Moira is right, someone killed the radio, probably to ruin this expedition by stranding us here. And whoever killed the radio will be banished from the City—I swear it."

I exchanged glances with my mother. Surely not even Soli could suspect either of us of risking our lives by sabotaging our own expedition?

In the darkness before dawn we debated who might have killed the radio. Bardo pointed out that there were many—the merchant pilots of Tria, for instance—who would not want our Order to possess the secrets of the Ieldra, whatever those secrets might be. "And there are aliens such as the Darghinni who'd be jealous if human beings proclaimed that the Ieldra favored our race. Also the Scutari, and for the same reason. And on the planets—how many of the religious orders would murder to ensure their mysteries and secrets were not replaced by a greater secret, a higher mystery? What of Heaven's Gate, Vesper, even Larrondissement? And the made-worlds of the Aud Binary, by God? What of—"

"Yes, we have enemies," Soli said. "But we don't let them handle our private things, do we?"

"Ah . . . of course not, Lord Pilot." Bardo chewed his mustache thoughtfully, and he asked the question on everyone's mind, "What will we do now, Lord Pilot?"

We all looked at Soli, waiting.

"Yes, that's the problem," he said, "what to do now, since Mallory has failed to restrain himself. Should we wait for the jammer, or shouldn't we?"

I should mention here that Soli had foreseen the possibility of losing one or more of the sleds (and thus losing the radio) through different sorts of disasters. So he had arranged for a jammer to rendezvous with us at our drop-off point south of the island if we were unable to radio the City. The date for the rendezvous was the first of deep winter, some two hundred days away.

"No, we shouldn't wait so long," Soli said. "We're no longer welcome here, are we? Perhaps we should leave today. We could drive our sleds east to the Outer Islands and wait there during break-up. Then next winter, when the sea freezes, we can make the rest of the way back to the City."

But Bardo did not like this plan, and he said, "What if we

don't find anything to eat in the Outer Islands? What if the sea breaks up early, before false winter? What if—"

"We're Alaloi now, aren't we?" Soli mocked. "We're supposed to be able to do what Alaloi do best—survive. Yes, that's a fine plan, isn't it? We'll leave as soon as the sleds are packed."

"But what if a storm comes up," Bardo protested, "what if we lose our way?"

"We're pilots, too," Soli said. "We'll steer by the stars. We won't lose our way."

All this time Katharine had remained silent. She sat on her bed combing her hair with her fingers, gazing into the flames of the fire, taking little interest in our arguments. But when Soli started gathering his furs together, she went over to him and covered his fingers with her hand. It was the first time I had seen her touch him.

"That wouldn't be wise, Father," she said. "To journey east when . . ."

"When *what*?"

"I mean to say, it might be all right for you and everyone else to journey east and go hungry, but it would be wrong for me and . . ."

"Wrong? Wrong *why*?"

She dug her toes into the snow and said, "Because I'm pregnant, Father."

The silence in the hut was nearly absolute, like the silence of deep space. Soli stared at Katharine while Justine propped her head up on the bed and opened her eyes wide. I stared at Katharine, too.

"Whose child is it?" Soli asked at last.

I, too, was eager to know who the father was.

"Is it Liam's?" Soli asked.

"Who knows?"

"What did you say?"

"How should you expect me to know whose child . . . I've been with so many men, do you see?"

Soli squeezed his bleeding fingers with his other hand and said, "But there were precautions you were supposed to take, weren't there? Methods of . . . these things that women do when—"

"I didn't want to become pregnant, Father."

"How *careless* of you!" Soli whispered.

She smiled and said, "What has happened will happen; what will be has been."

"Scryer talk," Soli muttered, "always this scryer talk."

"I'm sorry, Father."

Again she covered his hand with her own. After a while he turned his head away and spoke into the roof of the hut, "Well, what does it matter who the father is? What matters is that we return to the City so you can bear the child properly. When will the child be born?"

"If one were to pick the most probable day, he would be born on the seventeenth of deep winter."

"Then we'll stay here until ninety-third day in winter. We'll meet the jammer on the first of deep winter. Mallory will apologize for his little crimes. We'll make our peace and live here as peacefully as we can." He turned back to the radio, dripping blood over the components as he touched them. "Yes, Mallory will apologize and restrain himself so we can live here in peace."

Later that day I went to Liam and apologized for raising my spear to him. It was a hard thing to do because he would not look at me eye to eye. I apologized to Yuri; I apologized to Anala, Wicent, Seif and Liluye, all the women and men of the Manwelina. Lastly, I apologized to Soli but I don't think he listened to what I said. He sat in the hut with the radio in his lap, and he whispered, "When we return to the City we'll do a genotyping. We'll find out who the father of the child is."

I tried to sleep after that but I couldn't; I lay awake all that day listening to the storm howl outside, wondering if the child growing in Katharine's belly was my child, too.

15

The Eyes
of a Scryer

If you can look into the seeds of time,
And say which grain will grow and which will not,
Speak then to me, who neither beg nor fear
Your favors nor your hate.
　　　　　　—from *Macbeth*, by The Shakespeare,
　　　　　　　　Century of Exploration Fabulist

And so we lived peacefully among the Devaki, even though it
was often an uneasy peace. Time passed quickly. The storms
of midwinter spring ended, and the clear, dry days of false
winter began. When the ice of the sea broke up and melted,
we hunted migrating cod and coho in the waters by the
beach. We hunted shagshay across the land. We drove a small
herd of them off a cliff, and after that there was no more
hunger. Our life became settled, our days so filled with food
and sunshine and warmth that I paid little attention to the
sullen stares Liam shot me every time our paths crossed, in
the cave or forest. I tried not to worry; I tried to ignore the
feeling of impending doom that gripped me whenever I
looked at Katharine. Each day I watched her belly swell, and
I thought about the seed growing within. A thousand times I
wondered whose child she carried. A thousand times I looked
forward to the day when I could return to the City, deliver
the child to the master splicer and say, "Tell me if I am a
father."

I was not the only one concerned with fatherhood. Liam,
and not a few of the Devaki men, must have wondered who
the child's father would be. But their wonder was different
than mine. They had little knowledge of genetics, and they

did not very much care who the genetic parents of their children were. The Devaki shared so many of their chromosomes that they rightly regarded all the children of the tribe as their near-sons and daughters. To be sure, they acknowledged that only one man could be a child's bloodfather, but what really mattered to them was marriage. What everyone wanted to know was: when Katharine's time came, who would marry her and thus become the father of the newborn child? Everyone thought it would be Liam. Many times during those long days, Yuri came to Soli to arrange a marriage between our two families.

"It is not good for a child to have no father," he said one day after a successful hunt. "Have you seen how Katharine and Liam laugh together? And who can blame them? Katharine is a beautiful woman, and my son is a beautiful man, and they will have many beautiful children, if they are married."

And Soli said, as he said every other time, "Yes, marriage. Well, perhaps; we'll wait and see."

This talk worried Soli so much that he avoided Yuri's shambling approach whenever he could. He spent many nights with the radio, trying to remember how it worked. Often, he would watch Katharine sleeping; he would brood and think his solemn thoughts. One night my mother caught him staring, and she completely misread his look. I was sitting by the oilstones when she came up to Soli and said, "Katharine should abort the fetus. That's what you were thinking. That's what all of us think. Who knows who the father is? She should cleanse herself. There are ways, Alaloi ways. The root of wolf bush—it's a natural abortifacient."

Soli was very quiet then and he did not move. He did not look at my mother. "Go away," he whispered. "Go away."

I think it would have been better for my mother if he had spit on her. Above all things she hated to be scorned. (In this respect, she was exactly like Soli.) I cannot describe how her face contorted when he said this. Usually she made a religion of self-control, but that night her face betrayed shame, rage, fear and other dark emotions that I could not quite name. Her eyes began twitching, and to Soli she mysteriously said, "The Lord Pilot thinks he's holy. But you can't know. You've never known."

To this day I believe we might have avoided disaster, if we had had the foresight to leave as soon as we discovered the radio was dead, or if certain of us had practiced restraint. (Though Katharine would certainly disagree with me: What happened had always happened; as she might say, the seeds of disaster had been planted before either of us was born, perhaps before the stars were born.) How is it that we have an almost infinite ability to delude ourselves, to see the truth before our eyes and proclaim it untrue? Why did I fool myself that the Devaki were a kind, forgiving people, a people who loved peace and harmony above all else? Or rather, why did I think they were *only* that (for they truly were kind, and their forgiveness would one day surprise me to tears)? Why did I conceive of them so simply? Why didn't I see them as they really were?

To believe our own feelings and thoughtways must be universally shared by others is the commonest of mistakes, made by aliens and human beings alike. Despite my experiences inside the Entity—perhaps because of them—I made this mistake. Once, I had entered the reality and smellspace of the alien, Jasmine Orange. How much simpler it should have been to understand a primitive people I had lived close to for half a year. I thought I did understand them. I lived as an Alaloi, and I thought my appreciation of the Alaloi life must be close to theirs. Did they perceive beauty as I did? Surely when hunting through the forest they loved, as I loved, the crunch of cotton cake beneath their skis, the cool air, the barking of the dogs, and everywhere, the spruce trees frozen with white and green, singing with snow loons, swaying in the wind. Certainly they lived closer to life than civilized people; in many ways they were happier, more alive, somehow more fully human. (I, too, found a kind of happiness in the mountains, despite the little evils of lice and dirt and blood tea. It still puzzles me how I became used to these things.) There were moments in the forest, or on the beach by the cold ocean, when I felt alive for the first time in my life. How ironic, I thought, that I had come to the island seeking the secret of life in the tissues of women and men only to find it in the rushing waves, in the cries of the eider and snow geese, in all the wild things of the world. How remote, how meaningless the quest seemed then! What was a god's knowledge embroidered into a man's chromosomes next to the infinitely greater wisdom of the world? I discovered within myself a profound will to live life as completely as I could. I took joy in most of the things I did, in building a fire and watching the snowflakes melt, joy in eating and coupling, joy even in hunting the animals. I came to believe the Devaki shared this joy; sheer joy, I thought, was what they lived for. Harmony, peace, joy—these were the elements of life lived naturally in a natural world.

But there is more to life than joy. The Devaki knew this. In my bones and in my heart, I knew it too, though knowledge and acceptance are different things. This was the essence of my arrogance, my shortsightedness, my mistake; I had forgotten that nature was not only full of joy, but was tragic and violent, too. I did not understand how the Devaki could accept—could even love and embrace—life's violence and tragedies. I underestimated their love of harmony, the true understanding of the World-soul's intention that they call halla. I thought that in the forests of the Thousand Islands, peace and forgiveness were the essence of a people's relations with others. In truth, I knew nothing of the sometimes terrible nature of halla.

The supreme tragedy of life, I have always thought, is that it must end in death. Even for those who die too late, death must one day come. Although it is unpleasant to do so, I must here tell of Shanidar's death because it was this event, and the events that followed, which led to my discovery of what the Devaki would do to preserve their halla relation with the world.

The beginning of winter is usually a time of cool, bright days and spiky cold nights. There is snow perhaps every third day; the light powder falls softly and builds into sparkling, fluffy drifts. But sometimes, once every ten years, winter arrives suddenly, with teeth. The mornings dawn blue cold, with the air so harsh and dry that it does not snow. When we had lived among the Devaki for some two hundred days, the weather turned very cold, and everyone said it would be a long, ten year winter. The Devaki were happy because there was a great harvest of baldo nuts, which they stored in leather barrels. There was frozen coho and sheefish; there was smoked shagshay and eider eggs and roasted silk belly, an abundance of food. The old people who had gone hungry the winter before were very happy, all except Shanidar whose tired body could not hold any more food. On fifty-third day, he began complaining of a hot pain in his belly. During the days that followed, I visited his chamber and tried to feed him soft-cooked eggs, but it did no good. His flesh fell inward; his old yellow skin tightened around his bones. Days passed and I marveled that he remained alive. Often he joked that some men could suck their nourishment from the very air. At other times he coughed for air and could not speak. I wondered what sustained him, what inner fire kept him living long past his time.

The end did not come quickly. On eighty-second day he began vomiting blood. For two days he drank no water, and when the third day dawned it was clear it would be his last. He called for me to carry him from his chamber to the front of the cave. I did as he asked; even swaddled in thick furs he was as light as a child, so light that I thought a good part of him had already gone over to the other side. As I set him down in front of the fires, only his eyes moved, perhaps trying to take in the wisps of clouds high in the sky.

"Mallory Sealkiller is kind," he said, and he coughed.

I threw a few sticks on the fire and asked, "Are you warm enough?"

"You know, I cannot feel my body, so how can I know if I am cold, hmmm?" And then, "Listen, yes, I am cold—so cold. I feel like I've fallen through a hole into the sea."

I built the fire up until it roared. Orange tongues of fire flickered outward, licking the rocky cavefront and melting a circle of snow four feet wide around the firepit. The heat burned my face. With our backs to the warm rock, we sat looking out over the long, snowy slope leading to the forest below.

"That is better, it is good to be warm—Listen, how long will it be before the stars light the sky?"

"Not long," I lied.

We sat there throughout the agonizingly long afternoon, talking of Katharine's pregnancy and other concerns of the tribe. Shanidar loved to talk, even when he was so weak and ill that his breath rattled. He had to pause for long periods in between his words. The Devaki came and went. When they passed, they gave us a wide berth. The women especially, bent low beneath huge blocks of drinking snow, looked at us suspiciously, as if we were wolves intent upon stealing their children. Often during the past days, they had whispered and shaken their heads at my visits to Shanidar, perhaps wondering why I would choose to be with a man who had not died at the right time. As I fed the fire and watched Shanidar's shrunken lips struggle to shape his words, I wondered the same thing.

Darkness fell at last and the stars came out, ten thousand glittering particles of ice against the black fur of night. "*Losas shona*," he said, struggling to look at them with his half-blind eyes. He coughed for a while before gasping, "How I love these lights!—Could you throw some more wood on the fire, it is cold, hmmm? Listen, I think this deep winter will be dead cold early. It is still winter, isn't it?—and already it is so cold. Listen, Mallory, my eyelashes are freezing from my breath. Could you wipe the ice from my eyes?"

I wiped his eyes, and a fit of coughing wracked his entire body. When it was over, he was silent and still. I thought he had died, but no, he gripped my hand suddenly, keeping me there while he grasped at life as a falling climber grasps at the rocks of a mountain. "It hurts," he said. And then, "The lights in the sky are stars, you know. Burning hydrogen fuses into light—my father taught me that when I was a boy."

For a moment I was shocked at his use of the word "hydrogen." I was not, of course, shocked because he knew the word—I remembered that he had journeyed to the stars in his youth—but because he had spoken the word *to me* as if I would know it, too. "Ydroogene?" I said, feigning puzzlement. "You use strange words, Old Man."

He clutched the edge of my fur, and he said, "You have fooled the others, but you have not fooled me, Man of the City. When I was younger—" And here he coughed for a while. "You know . . . I remember what it was like to have strong muscles as you have—when I was a young man who had no legs, I went to the cutter named Rainer, and he grew me new legs, there in his cutting shop in the Farsider's Quarter of the Unreal City. You see, I know a man of the City when I see one."

After much evasiveness and outright lying on my part, after I had looked around to make sure no one was near, I finally admitted that I was indeed a man of the City. "But how did you know?"

"You can wear real shagshay furs and you can learn The Language and you can change your body—You know, I used to have a fine strong body, even though I had no legs—

Listen, you can change everything but the way you think, hmmm? You cannot change your thoughtways—otherwise I would not be an outcast among my own people."

He asked me why we had come to the Devaki, and I told him. I do not know why I trusted him. The night was deepening around us, cold and bottomless as space, and I repeated the message of the Ieldra: "The secret of man's immortality lies in our past and in our future. If we search, we will discover the secret of life and save ourselves." I told him of my journey into the Entity. Even though I no longer believed it, I said that the secret of secrets might be found in the oldest DNA of human beings. I told him all these things as the fire burned low and the stars showered streamers of faint light into our eyes.

"You are a pilot, then? Listen, I am an ignorant man—you know, my father taught me as best he could—you are a pilot, and you might think all the things I have said to you this past year are nonsense, hmmm? But no, you know, it is not nonsense."

His coughing had stopped only to be replaced by a liquid wheezing. Every word forced from his throat was gasped out in between clutching breaths. "Listen, the Devaki have their own knowledge so you must understand that everything I said to you about killing your doffel and standing apart from other men—and do you remember what I said about evil and good, hmmm?—all that I've told you is true."

"I've listened to everything you've said," I told him truthfully.

"Then listen to the plea of an old man. Do not trust the message of the gods. When I was born without legs here in this cave—Listen, this is the saddest story I know—because I was born a marasika without legs, in deep winter they dumped me into the snow where I froze to death. My father brought me frozen to the cutters of the City, but they could do nothing to help me. So my father, my poor father who was Goshevan, son of Jaharawal whose father was Pesheval Kulpak of Summerworld, my father brought me to Agathange. There the men—do you know this, Pilot?—the men are like gods. They brought me back to life so that I could return to the cave of my birth—how kind of them, hmmm? You know, they made me alive again, and they could easily have grown me new legs, but they did not. Why? Listen, this is the truth:

The gods are tricksters, and when they remake a man, they always leave something undone. To humble him. So do not believe this message of your Ieldra about the secret of life because those gods have obviously left unsaid the simplest thing, which is this: The secret of life is more life." And here he tried to lift his body towards the opening of the cave. I turned my head and listened to high-pitched barking and squeals of childish laughter. "Listen, do you hear the sounds of Jonath and Aida playing with the puppies? The secret of life is making children—my father told me this when I was a boy, but I did not believe him."

I thought about fathers and sons, and I listened to him choke for words.

"If you ever have a son, you must be kind to him, Mallory."

I rubbed my nose and said, "You don't know the rule of our Order, but I should tell you: pilots may not marry." I thought of Katharine growing bigger day by day with someone's child. "I'll never have a son," I said.

"Oh, it is very bad to go over to the other side without sons and daughters, I should have believed my father." He coughed and he moaned; he tried to say something that I could not understand.

"Does it hurt?" I asked.

He rubbed his arm weakly and said, "You know, when the Devaki go over they are never afraid because they have sons and daughters to pray for their ghosts." He raised his eyes to the sky and spoke so softly I had to strain to hear him, "But I'm afraid, Pilot." And then, "Oh, it hurts, here in my arm and in my throat—" He coughed hard once and grabbed his chest. "Like ice, oh, listen . . ." and here he began to mumble and groan. I think he said something like, *"Shona los halla; halla los shona,"* and then he closed his eyes and gasped for air. After a while—it was a long time, really—his breathing seemed to stop. I held the corner of his robe under his nose to see if his exhalation would move the silky white hairs. But the fur remained unruffled because he had no breath. I would have felt for the pulse in his throat, but I did not want to touch him. I was afraid he was dead.

I stood up and drew my furs tightly around me. The air was so cold I thought my eyes would freeze. I watched him for a long time, until the skin of his old, shriveled face began hardening like marble. And then for no good reason—for whatever he had been was gone, swallowed like a ray of light down a black hole—I raised my head to the night and prayed for his ghost: "Shanidar, *mi alasharia la shantih Devaki*." His mouth and lips were frozen into a slack mask; his face seemed both too familiar and utterly alien. I could not look at him so I covered him with his fur. I turned my back to his body and went to find Yuri.

I had never before seen a dead human being.

I hurried through the cave, stumbling across the pitted, uneven floor. The oilstones had burned low, and the huts were dim globes lost in darkness. I came to the lava pendant in the middle of the cave. It was the Old Man of the Cave, smiling his dark smile into the cave's black depths. For no reason, I slapped the rock sculpture on its face. The slap cracked through the air. I struck the Old Man of the Cave again, all the while thinking about Shanidar. I wondered if everyone felt as I did upon seeing a dead human being for the first time: I was terrified of dying myself and ecstatic because I was still alive. Later would come mourning and melancholy, but at the moment I was glad that it was he who was dead, and not I. I felt intensely alive; possibly at no moment in my life had I ever tasted life so poignantly. I slapped the sculpture, and my hand stung. I thought the secret of life must be feeling intensely alive.

I woke Yuri in his hut and told him that his near-cousin had died. While he roused the rest of his family—for no event among the Devaki is as important as a death—I went to get Soli and the others. We gathered in the open area behind the Manwelina huts. Wicent and Yuri laid Shanidar's body on a newl skin, and Liam and Seif built six small stacks of aromatic pela wood around him and lit the mourning fires. The warm light bathed Shanidar's naked skin, which Anala and Liluye rubbed from heel to brow with hot seal oil. (The Devaki believe that a man—or a woman—must make the journey to the other side naked, as when he first comes into the world. But since he must journey past the frozen sea, his body must be properly greased against the cold.) The red streaks of light reflected off Shanidar's white body were both ghastly and beautiful. As the women covered him with blue snow dahlia and arctic poppies, I covered my eyes with my hand. The sweet smell of broken flowers stung my nose. Then Yuri, who was Shanidar's nearest near-cousin, picked up a flint knife and sliced the right ear from the corpse's head. Someone wrapped it in feather moss, and Yuri said, "We preserve the ear of Shanidar, and he will always hear the prayers of our tribe. I, Yuri, son of Nuri, will pray for Shanidar's ghost because he had no sons or daughters to pray for him. And my son Liam and his sons, we will all pray for Shanidar, *mi alasharia la shantih Devaki*. Even though it is easy to blame him for waiting so long to go over, we must not blame him because a man must go over free from blame."

When the mourning fires had burnt low and most of our throats were sore from praying and weeping—most of the men were able to weep on command while the women remained dry-eyed and somber—we wrapped Shanidar in the newl skin and carried him outside to the graveyard above the cave. The ground was frozen hard as stone and buried in snow, so we built a pyramid of granite boulders over his body. The boulders were heavy; our stomach muscles strained and our biceps popped, but soon, under the watchful eyes of the stars, we finished our work. Yuri said another requiem and the Devaki yawned and returned to their beds. My mother and the rest of my family, even Bardo, left me there, too.

I stood alone above the grave. The wind spilled down between the black tree trunks, drowning me in cold, muddled thoughts. I stood there all night until the blackness began to soften. How tragic, I thought, that Shanidar had died leaving no particle of himself to grow and taste the bittersweet liquor of life! How I pitied him, pitied myself, pitied anyone who had to die childless and alone! Shanidar was right: To be a link in the eternal, unbroken chain of life—this was the secret of life. There was nothing else, no other immortality, no deeper meaning. I turned away from the wind and slapped some life back into my freezing face. Suddenly, the begetting of children seemed the most important thing in the universe. A son, I thought, could there be anything better than having a son?

I ran back to the cave to find Katharine. I crept through the tunnel of our hut, went to her bed, and I covered her mouth with my hand. I woke her. I whispered in her ear; I told her that I had to talk to her. In silence she dressed, and in silence we sneaked out into the open air. Down into the forest I led her, down to the stream cutting through the hills below the cave. During the night some clouds had come up;

it was warmer but the moisture made everything feel cold as slush. The woods were submerged in the rolling gray of twilight, and snow was falling. The air was marbled with patterns of light and dark. I could barely see my boots slipping against the rounded rocks of the stream bank. At last I stopped and began to talk to her. My words were nearly lost to the gurgling of the stream beneath the ice, but at least no one would be able to overhear what we said.

I took her arm and looked at her. "You told Soli that you didn't know who the father of the child would be. Is that true?"

"Did I say that? I don't think I said . . . you should search your memory, Mallory, what were my exact words?"

I did not remember her exact words, though I remembered that one must listen with exactitude to everything a scryer said. I tried to read the truth from her face, but I could not see the shape of her mouth. It was dark and her lips were hidden beneath the ruff of her hood. She stood with her hands over her belly. She could not hide the shape of her belly. Unlike some women who carried their babies low, as if they had a ball tucked beneath their furs, Katharine's belly was long and ovoid like a bloodfruit.

"Who is the father, then?" I asked. "Do you know?"

"The father is . . . who he is; he is who he will be. The mother . . . the father."

I was desperate to know if I would be a father. I could not bear the thought that Liam might be the father. What would the child look like? Would he have blond hair and thick brow-ridges? Would he be half-Alaloi and half-human? Or—since Mehtar had sculpted our flesh but not our germ cells—would he be wholly human, wholly the fusion of Katharine's and my seed, wholly mine to call "son?" I took her mittened hand in mine and asked her, "Is it our child, Katharine?"

"Is it possible I don't know?"

"But you're a scryer; scryers know these things, don't they? What is the first training of a scryer?—to 'think like DNA,' isn't that it?"

"You're a pilot, you should know," she mocked. Her laughter bubbled out of her in a clear stream. "Mallory, Mallory, sweet Mallory."

"Listen to me," I said. "It's a humiliating thing for a child to be called a bastard." (I should mention that although on many planets the word "bastard" simply means one who is born out of wedlock, I use the word in its broader sense to identify those unfortunates who do not know who their parents or grandparents are. What does it matter if the mother and father are married or not? What matters is knowing one's genetic endowment, the heritage of fine chromosomes, the tracing of one's abilities—and liabilities—back through the generations.)

I think she smiled at me, then. "The child won't be a bastard. I promise you."

Because I thought of myself as a bastard, I took this to mean that I was not the child's father. I was disappointed and my head suddenly seemed as heavy as stone. Next to me the stream ran darkly through a white pipe of ice. In places the pipe had cracked and fallen inward. I stared down through feathery layers of ice to the rushing black water below. "If I'm not the father, then who is?"

"Did I say you weren't the father of the . . . ?"

"Don't play games with me, Katharine."

"I'm not playing; it's just that if I told you, oh, the possibilities, the . . . the *pain*, . . . do you see?"

The wind rose and she drew her hood tightly around her face and crossed her arms over her chest. She began to shudder so I put my arms around her and touched my head to hers. I realized a thing about the scryers then: They do not play games for the love of play; they play to distract themselves and others from the terrible truths they have seen.

"Who is the father?" I whispered in her ear. "Tell me."

"If I told you, it would kill you, don't you see?"

"He's Liam's son, then?"

She began to speak but her voice cracked, revealing an inner core of fear. Her blue eyes were cold with terror. I was aware of this core only for an instant. Then her scryer training took hold and her eyes closed, and her face was as smooth and white as a scryer's robes. She laughed for a little while as she touched her belly. "He's your son, Mallory. *Our* son. He'll be a beautiful boy; he is a beautiful, compassionate . . . a dreamer like his father."

A son! Katharine had told me we would have a son, and true to her words, the news had killed me; I was dying with pride and happiness. I was so happy that I threw my head back and shouted out: "My son! A goddamned son!"

Katharine was dead quiet, staring into the gray, morning woods. I paid her little attention. I listened to the wind sighing through the trees, carrying in from the hills the howl of a wolf. It was a long, low sound full of loneliness and yearning. The wind blew across the snowy white ridges and valleys, and an absurd notion came to me: The wolf's howl was Shanidar's other-soul calling to me, whispering that I should be kind to my son. The wolf howled for a long time. Then Katharine began to cry, and I remembered that Shanidar's doffel had been the seal, not the wolf. I listened to the howling, and I knew the sound for what it really was: just a rush of breath through the throat of a cold, lonely beast. I held Katharine and she sobbed in my arms. With my fingers I touched her wet cheeks. I kissed her eyelids. I asked her why she was so sad, but she could not tell me what was wrong. "A son," she said, and her voice was raw and burning. That was all she could say. "A son, a beautiful boy, do you see?"

To tell of the ruin of our expedition, to give a proper account of the plots and murders leading to the great crisis of our Order and the war that followed, I must here relate events which I did not directly witness. There are those who would doubt such a second-tongue knowledge—I am thinking of the epistemologists—but I myself am sure that Justine's testimony of that day is a close approximation of the truth. After all, what is truth? I can, of course, offer no episteme, for in the affairs of our race, no intellectually certain knowledge can exist. If what I say here sometimes seems illogical, sometimes tainted with chaos and a touch of madness, that is because human life is so tainted and touched.

Two days after Shanidar's burial, on eighty-fifth day in winter, all of the men and most of the boys left the cave early in the morning to hunt shagshay in one of Kweitkel's western valleys. It was a cold day; it dawned blue cold and became colder throughout the day. The air was like a steel mask covering the island. It was so cold that the trees cracked and thundered, spraying splinters into the blue air. Because of the cold, the women and children kept to the cave, gathering around the fires and oilstones wherever they could. Everyone was cold, shivering cold, miserably cold, everyone except my mother. My mother was burning with a fever. But she was not sick. Or rather, she was not sick with disease; she was sick with jealousy and hatred because two days before she had followed Katharine and me down to the stream. She was a good spy, my mother was. She had hidden behind a yu tree and heard me shout with joy. The knowledge of my father-hood had wounded her, and for two days she kept to herself, and her hatred rankled and festered.

When she could stand the burning no longer, on the afternoon of the hunt, she found Katharine alone in our hut. There was a fight, spitting words of poison from my mother and Katharine's infuriating (to my mother) near-silence. I will never know everything that was said, but Justine and the other women overheard bad things, terrible things. My mother called Katharine a witch. "What have you done?" my mother accused. "You've bewitched my son. With your secret ways. Trapped him with sympathy and sex."

These were serious words, so Anala, Sanya and Muliya forced their way into the hut. Justine was out helping one of the dogs deliver her puppies, and when she heard the commotion she ran to join the others inside. In the tight, round space, the four women crowded around my mother and Katharine, keeping them apart.

"Why did you call Katharine a witch?" Anala asked my mother.

At the sound of the word "witch," cross-eyed Muliya mumbled a hasty prayer. Her fat arms jiggled as she rubbed ashes over her eyelids so that the other-soul of the witch would have difficulty seeing her. (I have forgotten to mention that Muliya was an extremely ugly woman. As Justine reminded me, she had a broken nose, and she looked something like a muskox. It is curious that women are often more sensitive to a woman's beauty—or lack of beauty—than are men.)

Sanya nervously rubbed her skinny hands together while she looked from Anala to Muliya. She was a small, intelligent woman with a narrow face like a fox. She licked her stumpy, yellow teeth and said, "We have all wondered why Mallory acts so strange. But witchcraft? Why would Katharine be-witch him?" She smiled at Katharine because she liked her. She clearly did not believe Katharine could be a witch.

"Some women like the shape of their brother's arms," Muliya said. "And they like the touch of their spears even more. Everyone knows Katharine and Mallory were alone together grinding snow."

My mother was aghast at what had happened. She said, "I spoke hastily. Because I was angry. Of course Katharine is not a witch."

All this time, Justine stood between Muliya and the calm, silent Katharine.

To my mother, Muliya said, "I've made blood-tea with you for almost a year. When have you ever spoken hastily? You called Katharine a witch, I heard you."

Anala stood in the center of the hut, looking at the other women. She pulled back her hair, which was as gray as steel. She was the tallest of the women, the strongest, and possibly the most clear-headed. She looked at my mother. "You call her a witch, and those are the worst words a woman can fling at another. If she is a witch, where is the craft of her witchery?"

An argument erupted, then, about the many ways a woman might bewitch a man. (Or, more, rarely, another woman.) Muliya's eyes crossed as she said, "It is well known that the Patwin tribe went hungry because a woman bewitched her near-brother and sucked out his seed. It is a bad thing to bewitch a man."

"But who hasn't thought of doing it?" Sanya pointed out, and she laughed nervously again.

Muliya told of an Oluran woman cursed with a brutal husband who beat her whenever he returned home from the hunt with no meat. One day in late midwinter spring, the woman—her name was Galya—had made a doll of sticks and fur, and had cast it into a pool of snowmelt. The following day her doomed husband stepped on a thin crust of ice and broke through to the sea where he drowned. "And what of Takeko of the Nodin tribe? Everyone knows she fed her lover seeds purple with the araglo mold, and everyone knows how she aroused her lover's rage with her cunning, witch's words. And didn't her lover then kill her husband?"

Anala seemed to grow angry when she heard this. With her hidescraper she shaved a layer of callous from the palm of her hand. She held the yellowed, half-moon wafer of skin between her fingers and said, "How does a woman capture the soul of a man? She must have a part of him so her other-soul can see the other-soul of a man through this part—is this not well known? If Katharine were a witch, she would have gathered tufts of hair or nail parings and the like to work her craft. Where is this craftwork? Who has seen it?"

And Muliya slyly said, "A witch would hide such things, wouldn't she?" She appeared to be staring through Katharine's legs at the bed behind her. Even though her eyes were crossed and weak, they were Alaloi eyes, and they did not miss very much, especially concerning the shape and texture of snow, for which the Alaloi have a hundred words. "Why is there *soreesh*, fresh powder, packed beneath Katharine's bed?"

Sanya shrugged her shoulders and shook her head. "Perhaps one of the dogs yellowed the hardpack and burned a hole with his piss?"

"Who would let a dog piss on her bed?" Muliya asked. "No, I think we should see what is buried beneath the bed."

Neither my mother nor Justine wanted Muliya digging beneath the bed, so they tried to distract her with arguments and denials, and when that didn't work, they asked her to leave the hut. "If Katharine is a witch," Justine said, "of course, I'm sure she's not, but if she is, we can discover the witchcraft for ourselves, and since she's my daughter, shouldn't I be the one to punish her?"

And Anala shook her handsome head and told her, "That would be too much to ask of any mother."

Muliya approached the bed, and my mother stopped her. There was another fight. While Katharine sat on the bed watching, my mother and Justine tried to force the Devaki women from the hut. Justine pushed Muliya, and she tripped and fell through the wall of the hut. There was a crunching and a cloud of snow. Other Devaki women were waiting outside. They picked Muliya up. They kicked in the rest of the hut. They demolished it, crushed the snow blocks beneath their feet, and they swarmed around Katharine's bed. Irisha and Liluye and six others held my mother and Justine from behind.

Anala said, "You see, the mother of the witch always protects the daughter. This is a sad day, but Muliya is right. We must see what is beneath the bed." She squatted, and like a dog digging for a bone, she began hacking at the snow with her hide-scraper. Showers of chiseled snow flew out behind her, covering the furred boots of the other women who were craning their necks, anxious to see what she might find. There was a dull "chink" as of stone against obsidian. "Here it is," Anala said, and she held up a snow-encrusted sphere of krydda.

"What is it?" Sanya asked. "It is so beautiful!"

After Anala had picked off the clinging granules of wet snow, Muliya said, "It looks like a shell, but I've never seen a shell so beautiful or so round." She turned to my mother and asked, "Are there many shells like these on the beaches of the Southern Islands?"

My mother struggled to break away from Marya, Lusa and Liluye. "There are many such shells," she lied.

Anala managed to open one of the spheres. She turned it upside down, letting its bluish-white contents dribble into her open hand. She held the sticky puddle to her nose and sniffed. "Manseed," she announced, and all the women made a sour face.

Muliya dipped her fingers into Anala's outstretched hand. She licked her fingers and gagged and said, "Manseed—but it is sweetened with a juice I have never tasted before. Witchcraft, and here it is: Katharine mixes Mallory's seed with the juice of strange plants to bewitch him."

It was a serious thing they had discovered. Sanya approached Muliya and said, "I have always liked Katharine. She always smiles, even when things are bad. Is it such a terrible thing to have bewitched Mallory? What a wild man he is! If ever a man needed taming, surely he does?" And then she asked the question on all the women's tongues: "Must we send her out onto the ice of the sea?"

"We should smash her fingers off," Muliya said. "Then she could work no more witchcraft."

Justine stood very still, wondering how she could break away from Liluye and the others. She was afraid for Katharine, but she had the coolness of mind to realize that it would be better for her daughter to lose her fingers than her life. Fingers, as she told me later, can always be regrown.

While the women argued over Katharine's fate, Muliya began digging beneath the bed. "Look at this!" she cried as she uncovered two more krydda spheres. "And this! And look, four more, and here, so many of these shells!"

All at once the women fell into silence. One by one, they opened krydda spheres, sampling what was inside them.

"Look, a lock of hair!" Irisha said. "Who has hair so yellow? Liam? Seif?"

Muliya emptied sphere after sphere and called out, "More manseed! And in this one, manseed that smells like tangleroot! Whosever seed this is must have eaten a great mess of tangleroot." A few of the women laughed because it was well known that the bitter tangleroot makes a man's seed stink. "And in this shell, the seed is thin and watery like a boy's. So many, I did not think she had swived so many!"

At last she emptied the spheres containing the nail parings and Jinje's amputated toe. The women moaned and looked at each other; they touched each other's faces to reassure themselves, and Anala stood up straight and pointed at Jinje's rotten toe lying on the crushed snow. "This is very bad, very, very bad. I have never known of anything so bad."

They talked for a while and agreed that Jinje's foot had rotted because of Katharine's witchcraft. "But why would Katharine curse Jinje?" Sanya wanted to know. "To bewitch Mallory is understandable, but to maim Jinje, that is evil."

The women agreed that Katharine was indeed a witch of the worst sort, an evil *satinka* who wreaked harm on innocents solely for sport and pleasure. And when Sanya wondered how a satinka could appear so gentle and kind, Anala said, "That is their art." Then she turned to Muliya and said, "Katharine is a satinka, and that is why this year has been so hard and hungry. We must all blame her for being a satinka, otherwise the Devaki will have no more halla. And that is why we must prepare the satinka's bed."

For a moment Justine was confused. She could not guess why Anala would want to prepare Katharine's bed. Then she looked at my mother, who was almost crying because she knew too much about the Devaki ways. Suddenly, Justine was very afraid. In fact, she was terrified. She began screaming at Anala. She told her everything, told her that we had come from the City to find the secret of life. But no one believed her. To many of the Devaki, the City was only a myth. And even for those few who might have been willing to admit that strange, weak-faced people lived in the Unreal City, Mehtar's sculpture had fooled them too well. As Muliya put it, "Look at Katharine and Justine, are they not Devaki as we are Devaki?"

And Anala said to Justine, "You must not invent tales to

save your daughter. No one can blame a mother for loving her child, but not even a mother can suffer a satinka to live."

So saying, she and the others grabbed Justine, my mother and Katharine, and they began dragging them toward the back of the cave. There, where the floor rose to meet the cave's dark roof, the air stank of oil and smoke and was too warm. The oilstones—there must have been twenty or more—were full of seal fat and brightly aglow. The walls writhed with shadows, and yellow fingers of light wrapped around the black stalactites hanging from ceiling to floor. At the very rear of the cave, the women had made a bed of packed snow. They staked Katharine to this cold bed as if she were a dog. Her arms and legs were splayed, tied to four stakes with leather thongs.

Anala turned to Justine and said, "The mother of the satinka must witness the ceremony."

"No!" Justine shouted. She wrenched an arm free and struck Liluye in the face. "Moira!" she called to my mother. "Moira!" But Marya and two others had their hands clamped around my mother, holding her like an animal in a trap.

"A witch," Anala said, "cannot do her work without fingers." She bent low and grasped Katharine's wrist. "We'll sacrifice the fingers first."

All this time Katharine had remained preternaturally calm. Her eyes were wide open; it seemed she was staring at the whorls and swirling rock patterns of the ceiling. But Justine did not think she was looking at rock. She was looking at her life, reviewing these last moments which she had perhaps seen many times before. How is it possible that she could have accepted her fate so willingly? *Had* she truly seen her own death? Or had she merely seen possibilities, variations on the fatal theme in which Anala decided to spare her, or where she was saved by design or chance? What a hell it must be to foresee the manner and moment of one's death! Others can fool themselves that they are immortal. Or, at least, during every instant of their lives, they can look forward to the sweetness of instants still to come. They never *know*; they never see. But a scryer, she knows and sees too much. All she has in the face of infinity is her training and her courage. Katharine had courage, great courage, but at the end her courage failed her. (Or was it her vision that failed her?) She looked at Anala as if seeing her for the first time.

She struggled against the binding thongs. She began to scream: "No, no, I can't see... please!"

Anala began hacking at Katharine's fingers with her hide-scraper. Katharine thrashed and screamed and balled her fist tightly, and Anala said to Muliya, "This flint is too dull. Bring me my seal knife, please." When Muliya returned with the sharp knife, Anala thanked her politely and began sawing at Katharine's fingers. In a surprisingly short time—for the Devaki are quick and precise at the cutting of meat—she struck off the fingers of one hand and went to work on the other.

When she was done, she stood back and looked at Katharine's still body. "She has fainted from the pain," she said. "Who can blame her?" She looked at Justine and told her, "It is known that a satinka cannot go over to the other side of day carrying a child. Else she would be born a satinka, too." She motioned to Sanya and Muliya and said, "We will take the child while she sleeps." So saying, they cut away Katharine's furs and laid open her belly. As the fetus was torn away from the water sack and its cord was cut, Katharine opened her eyes suddenly. Anala handed the bloody fetus to Sanya and said, "Take care of this," and the younger woman did as she was told.

"No!" Katharine screamed, and she began calling for her mother. She lapsed into the language of the City, calling to Justine to save her baby.

"You see," Anala said to Justine, who had dislocated a shoulder in her struggle with the other women. "She speaks in the satinka's tongue—her witchery is proven."

"She's not a witch!" Justine screamed. "She's a scryer!"

"Strange words," Anala said. "The mother of the satinka has been touched with strange words, too. And that is why we must take out the satinka's tongue." She picked up her knife and continued, "But first we must take the eyes so the satinka cannot watch us from the other side and work her curses."

As quickly as she would shell a nutmeat, she put the tip of the knife in Katharine's eye and twisted her hand with a scooping motion. The eyeball came out neatly, and she gave it into Muliya's care. Somehow, Katharine kept her silence, even when Anala took out her other eye as well. It was only when Anala called for Muliya and Liluye to hold open her jaws that she came alive and screamed, inexplicably, "Mallory, do not kill him!"

All this Justine told me later, after the deed was done. But I was able to verify a part of her story with my own eyes. It was my luck—and Bardo's—to have killed the first of the shagshay earlier that day. It was my fate to be the first to return to the cave. I do not think that anyone except Katharine expected us to return so early. But our sleds were heaped with butchered meat, so we drove the dogs toward the cave even as Anala worked her butcheries within. I remember this clearly: It was so cold that the mass of steaming red shagshay meat had frozen hard along the trail. It was deep cold; the sky itself seemed frozen like a deep, blue ocean. And like water, the air carried sounds, building and amplifying the wind's whisper into a shriek. I heard sounds from the cave. From the distance I thought it was merely the screaming of puppies calling to their mothers. We drew closer, and I realized that the screams were the screams of a human being. Panic seized me. There was a sudden, dreadful knowledge. I grabbed my bloody shagshay spear and ran for the cave.

Several women—I do not remember their faces—tried to stop me from going to the rear of the cave. I knocked them out of the way. (One of them, perhaps the gentle Mentina, gouged my cheek with her hide-scraper. The scar is still there.) Bardo puffed and panted close behind me. Together we fought our way through the women to find Anala trying to pry open Katharine's teeth. There was blood on her lips. There was blood everywhere, blood streaming from Katharine's open belly and from her knuckle stumps, blood burning holes in the snow bed surrounding her; there were pools of blood filling the holes where her eyes had been. My mother started to gasp out the whole incredible story. I knocked Anala away from Katharine, and Muliya and Liluye as well. Bardo freed Justine, clubbing at the women with his spear. He grunted and bellowed and shoved; he stood with his spear pointing at the women. Most of them had grabbed up knives or scrapers or other tools and were glaring at us. No one seemed to know what to do.

I dropped down to listen to the words Katharine was struggling to speak. But I couldn't hear anything because Bardo's voice was booming. "I hope they don't rush us," he said, "because I don't think I could kill them."

"Be quiet!" I said. And then so softly only Katharine could hear me, I whispered, "Neither could I. I could hardly kill a damn seal."

Katharine's lips were moving. "Oh, but you could," she murmured. "It's so easy to . . . but you mustn't kill him, do you see?"

"What did you say?" Her face was anguished; I tried not to look into the pools in her eyepits.

"You choose," she whispered. "The choice is always . . ." She was deep in her scryer's universe, freed from time by Anala's blinding knife. Perhaps she was seeing things in the clear light for the first time.

"I don't understand you."

"You've killed him, but you mustn't kill *him*, because he's your . . . oh, Mallory, stop being such a fool!"

"Katharine, I can't—"

"In the end we choose our futures, don't you see?"

"No, I don't—"

"*Yes*," she said. And then there was no time, and she was a young woman again repeating her final scryer's vows: "Give; be compassionate; restrain yourself because—" and here the words rushed out as if someone had dropped a stone on her belly, "—because you will never die." She panted for a while, then her lips stopped moving, and her chest and her legs and the pulses of blood—everything about her was silent and still. She lay staring through the black stone ceiling into the sky, eyeless in eternity as all scryers hope to be.

That was the beginning of the nightmare. I stood up, and there was blood on my lips and in my eyes. I grabbed Anala's seal knife from the bloody snow. I should have directed my thoughts to Katharine's body—had I done so my life, and hers, might have been very different. But I did not think of her; I did not think at all because I was as full of rage as any beast. I ran towards the Manwelina huts, looking for Anala. A crazy idea had come to me: If I grabbed her by the back of the neck and shook her as a dog would a sleekit, I could make her put the pieces of Katharine's body back together again. I found her coming out of Yuri's hut. She was holding his mammoth spear, and I decided it would do no good to shake her. After all, she was not a cutter; nothing, I thought, could restore Katharine to me or redeem her from death. No, I would not shake Anala; I would cut out *her* eyes so she could see the evil of what she had done.

Confusing things happened. Someone sliced my ear with her knife. Anala threw her husband's spear, which I knocked away with my forearm. Someone drove her knife into the back of my arm. Justine rammed her elbow into Muliya's face while Bardo groaned like a bear. A woman tripped and fell into Anala's hut. Snow crunched. In the light of the sputtering oilstones, particles of snow clogged the air. Anala was terrified—I could see the fear on her broad, yellow face. And then I let my arm fall to the side, and I quietly dropped the knife into the snow. I could no more put it into Anala's eye than I could carve out a seal's eye. I was about to turn back to Katharine when Bardo shouted, "Watch out for Liam!"

I remembered that Liam's sled had been close behind us along the trail. When I turned, he was running at me. His shape was dark and featureless against the bright circle of the cave's mouth. He had his seal knife gripped low. He must have thought I was going to kill his mother—I realize that now. Obviously he had not seen me drop my knife. He shoved the knife toward my belly, and I caught his arm. We kicked at each other's legs, and suddenly we were down, rolling in the snow. He stabbed for my throat but I got an arm up, taking the knife through my forearm. The pain enraged me. I was full of rage and pain, so I got my other arm up in a hold that the Timekeeper had taught me. I grabbed his windpipe. "Sister swiver!" Liam shouted in my ear.

There was a moment. His life pulsed against my finger-tips. There was a moment of crushing strength, a moment of choice. Perhaps I could have let him go; perhaps we could have left the Devaki in peace. But I raged and I squeezed and I crushed his throat until his face grew red with blood and his eyes bulged from their sockets. I killed him. It was an easy thing to do, really, easier than killing a shagshay or a seal.

"By God, he's dead!" Bardo yelled as he helped me stand. "Hurry, we've got to leave before Yuri returns."

"No," I mumbled, "there's Katharine . . . her body. We've got to take her home."

"It's too late, Little Fellow."

"No, never too late."

"No!" Anala screamed. She was kneeling over Liam, feeling his throat, sobbing.

"Oh, too bad. By God, it's too bad, but we've got to hurry!"

We went to find Katharine's body but it was gone. The women must have dragged it outside the cave. I would have searched for it; I would have grabbed Anala by the hair and made her tell me where she was, but my mother came up to me and said, "Bardo is right. We'll leave now. Or we won't leave at all."

I am not sure how we forced our way back to our ruined hut. I remember scrambling about on my knees and hands like a madman, scooping up unopened spheres of krydda while Justine and my mother packed our sleeping furs and other things. Somehow we threw everything onto our sleds. I think the Devaki women could have stopped us if they had wanted to. But they were stunned, and I think they did not want to even look at us. As we pointed our sleds downhill, there was wailing from the cave, the wailing of a mother praying for the ghost of a son who had gone over too soon. It was the most pitiful sound in the universe. So piercing was the sound, so insistent and catching that our dogs lifted their heads and howled and whined. We fled into the cold hills, and the dogs did not stop whining for many miles.

16

The Death
of a Pilot

*If I am fond of the sea and of all that is of the sea's
kind, and fondest when it angrily contradicts me; if
that delight in searching which drives the sails toward the undiscovered is in me; if a seafarer's delight is in my delight; if ever my jubilation cried,
"The coast has vanished, now the last chain has
fallen from me; the boundless roars around me, far
out glisten space and time; be of good cheer, old
heart!" Oh, how should I not lust after eternity and
after the nuptial ring of rings, the ring of recurrence?*

*Never yet have I found the woman from whom I
wanted children, unless it be this woman whom I
love: for I love you O eternity.*

For I love you O eternity!

—fifth death meditation of the
warrior-poets

Somewhere along the stream below the cave, we stopped to
heave shagshay meat off the sleds, to lighten our loads. I took
my mother into the woods, through the yu trees sparkling
with snow. I made her tell me everything. At first, she lied to
me, saying that she had no idea why the Devaki had thought
Katharine was a witch. But then she grew angry and said,
"Wasn't Katharine a witch? What is a scryer, if not a witch?
Why else would my son lie with a scryer? Why would you be
so careless? To rut like a beast and have your fun—how did it
feel? You men! You have your fun, and then we must have the
child. But Katharine wanted the child, didn't she? *Your* child.
Yes, I know, the child was yours. Your seed. I heard Katharine

say so. Your *cousin* and . . . and Soli's daughter, Katharine. She *knew*. She was a scryer and she saw the truth. Willingly, she took you willingly! That witch! And so I went to her and called her a witch. Can you blame me? She should have aborted the fetus. When she had the chance."

It was the second time in my life when I almost struck her. I was sweating and hot despite the bitter cold. I could hardly look at her. "You killed her, then," I said.

"*Who* killed her? Was it I who wanted this expedition? Was it I who went to her bed? My seed? The things you say—my son can be cruel when he forgets to think before speaking."

In silence we walked through the deep snow back to the sleds. The fingers of my wounded arm were numb as I gripped the rails. We followed the stream down through the hills below the cave. We wound our way east away from Kweitkel, where the mountain's many frozen rills and brooks flowed into the stream, swelling it into a small river. Rising up above a bend in the river was a barren hill the Devaki call Winterpock. (The hill is visible from the cave but because of its peculiar barrenness, when the light is poor or diffuse, the hill appears as a depression rather than as a prominence. Hence its ugly name.) The river cut through the woods below Winterpock, a gleaming, white iceway twisting through the trees. Close to the river's south bank we found Soli spearing fatfish through a hole in the ice. He was out on the river, gazing into the water below him, standing over a pile of fish. As we rounded the bend, his dogs started barking at us. He straightened suddenly, looking at us. He had keen eyes, and he dropped his fish spear, grabbed his shagshay spear from his sled and ran to meet us. "Where's Katharine?" he called out. He ran along the river bank from sled to sled. He rammed the end of his spear against the bank. "What happened? Where's Katharine?"

Justine went up to him and began whispering furiously in his ear. His face hardened and he did not breathe. Then Justine sobbed out the whole story of Katharine's death. She did not tell him the complete truth. She did not want him to know that my mother had called Katharine a witch, so she told him that Anala had spied on Katharine, had caught her sorting her samples. "Our girl is dead," she whimpered. "Oh, Leopold she's dead!"

"Why would Anala spy on Katharine?" he asked.

My mother embroidered the lie, saying, "Anala never liked Katharine. We were friendly, and I know. She didn't like Yuri talking. Talking and saying Liam should marry Katharine. A few days ago I heard her mention that maybe Katharine had bewitched Liam. I told her this was nonsense. I thought she believed it was nonsense."

I sat on the bed of my sled listening to this lie. I had my furs off so Bardo could dress my wounds, which were bleeding, painful and deep. How I hated lying and liars! Is there anything more infectious and ruinous than disinformation, the twisted words of untruth? I looked at Bardo, but he seemed more worried about my wounds than the deepness and poison of my mother's lies. He wrapped newl skins around the gashes in my arm. He made a knot and tightened the skins. I was cold and numb, shivering like a naked puppy. I wanted to expose this lie of my mother's, but I was afraid that if I did, Soli might kill her.

"Nonsense!" Soli said. He stood over my mother looking down at her. "Wasn't Katharine a scryer? Wouldn't she have *seen* it if Anala was spying on her? Why would she be so stupid?"

"Who knows a scryer's ways?" my mother said as she twisted her hands together.

"Why? Why?"

"Maybe she wanted to die. She seemed to know. All about her death."

Soli dropped his head, exhaling a cloud of steam. "Why did she become a scryer?" he said, talking to the rocks of the river bank. "And if she saw her death, why not prevent it? Why? No, no, I should never have let her become a *scryer*." He said the word as if it were the filthiest word he knew. He stared at the river while he clenched the shaft of his spear. Then he asked us why we had not rescued Katharine's body. "That was careless. Yes, so careless, wasn't it, Pilot?"

I was gasping from the pain of my bandage. "There . . . was . . . no time," I blurted out.

"You might have saved her," Soli accused.

"Saved her? She was dead."

"*If*," Soli whispered to me, "if you had rescued the body, we might have frozen her in the river and taken her to the cryologists. They might have healed her. But you say there was no time. Wasn't there? Yes, there *was* time. There was a chance—she might have been saved. But you were not thinking of Katharine, you had to have your little rage, your revenge, your stupid murder, and you say there was no time."

In truth, it had never occurred to me to save her this way. Why hadn't it occurred to me? What was wrong with my thinking? Why was Soli quicker to see the possibilities than I, quicker to grasp the main chance? *Could* I have saved Katharine? To this day, I do not know.

"It was too late," I said. "It was warm in the rear of the cave; her brain would have been dead too long. Would you want the cryologists to restore a drooling child to you?"

"She was such a pretty girl," he said as he paced the river bank. "Even when she drooled on me when she was a baby, even when she spat rice cakes in my face. Oh, so long ago, too long—she was so pretty and *innocent*. (I must admit that he said this word as if it were the most beautiful word in the universe.) "So innocent before she became a scryer."

Justine began to cry, and then, unbelievably, he walked over to her and put his arms around her, and he dropped his head down against her black hair and wept like a boy. I watched this unbelievable scene in silence. The great Lord Pilot stood weeping like a novice, and I turned away, put on my furs, and walked out on the river where the ice was clear and blue. The wind cut me to the skin. I was numb with cold, but the image of Katharine alive and whole was more chilling than the wind. I wondered if Katharine could have been saved and resurrected even as Shanidar had once been saved. But saved for what? No cryologist in the City, I thought—or in the universe—had the skill to resurrect dead, disassociated brain cells. It was an impossible thing. Clearly, Katharine had known this. Somehow she had believed in the rightness of her death. Unlike Shanidar—and how I wanted to believe this!—she had died at the right time.

When I returned to the sleds, Soli and Justine were leaning against the gray trunk of a yu tree, holding each other. Their grief had infected Bardo, and he was weeping, too. Huge tears rolled down his cheeks into his beard, which was frozen with ice drops. He looked at me through wet, red eyes; I could tell he was angry at me.

"Katharine's dead!" he shouted. "And look at you! Dry-

eyed as a dead bird! What's wrong with you? What kind of
man are you? She's dead, and you can't even cry like a man!"

How could I tell him the truth? I loved Katharine, and
now part of me was dead; to weep for her would be to weep
for myself, which would have been a cowardly, shameful thing
to do.

Soli and Justine broke apart, and he walked toward me.
The skin of his cheeks was glazed but his eyes were as clear
and dry and sober as the eyes of a pilot should be. He asked
me, "And what of the child? What happened to my *grandson*?"

I was so cold that I didn't immediately understand his
question.

"Did he die when they took him away from Katharine?
Did they smother him?"

"Of course he's dead," I said. "No, it's more than that—
he never really lived. How could he have lived, born thirty
some days too soon? And not *born*. They gutted her like a
seal, Soli, like a damned seal!"

"You're sure?"

I was sure of nothing except my need to build a fire and
stare at the flames, to escape the cold ice of Soli's eyes. "He's
dead," I repeated. "He must be dead."

We talked for a while; everyone except Soli agreed that
the child could not have lived. Bardo kept looking off into the
woods, obviously afraid that the Devaki men would follow us
once they discovered Liam's body. We were all afraid of this.
"We've got to hurry," Bardo said. "Ah, there's so little time
and so far to go."

The light was quickly fading from the hills; the shadows
drew out long and gray and thin across the chalky snow. Like
the sea before a false winter storm, the trees were dark green
and rippling in the wind. Already the sky was darkening,
bruised with purples and dark blues. We hoped the Devaki
would not pursue us through the forest at night. Perhaps they
would not pursue us at all. We decided to follow the river
down to the sea. There, off the eastern shore of the island, we
would turn southward, circling until we came to our rendezvous point. Then we would wait the five days until the
jammer fetched us back to the City.

So began our retreat through the woods homeward to the
City. Bardo and I had the lead sled, followed by my mother.
Soli and Justine, who seemed to need their privacy, took

turns driving the rear sled. Night fell, and it grew very cold. The dogs flung themselves at their harnesses, pulling and panting in the hard air, and we shot along the starlit trail by the river. It was an eerie journey, this nighttime sledding through the nightmare forest. Except for the cracking whips and the dogs' whines and the occasional shriek of a snow loon (and the river's eternal roar), the hills were quiet and deserted. The air flowing down the valley carried the essence of wood dust and pine and other scents I could not quite recognize. For half the night, the starlight was so feeble that it illuminated only the white snowpack and the icicles hanging from the trees; the trees themselves were sunken in darkness and nearly invisible. Behind us and ahead, the dogs and sleds were strung out along the trail like gray pearls on a silver strand. Through the forest the strand twisted and wound and seemed to quiver, and we floated above the silken snow buoyed by the frictionless glide of the runners and by our private feelings of fate and fear. The forest turned beneath the starry sky, and the landscape began to brighten. On the eastern horizon Pelablinka rose, a great white blister of light bursting above the conical yu trees. Although it had been a while since the supernova had exploded, its radiance was still intense. I could almost make out the reds of the yu fruit and the blue-green needles. I stared up at Pelablinka, stared at this most recent of the Vild's exploding stars and wondered how long it would be before the sky was so full of Pelablinka's that there would never be night again? How long before the light, the gamma and the alpha of the supernovas bathed the Civilized Worlds in a radiance of death? How long before human beings had to abandon their planets and flee from the light, flee across the black drears of space to the farthest arms of the galaxy? How long before the stars and the dreams of human beings and a billion billion other living things all died? How long before I died? *Never,* Katharine had said to me, *you will never die.* But Katharine was dead, and I was dying inside, slowly dying as I fled through the shimmering trees of the forest. In the bed of my sled, tucked safely beneath the furs, were the krydda spheres full of life, possibly full of life's secrets. But Katharine was dead, and Pelablinka's light hurt my eyes, and the krydda spheres meant nothing to me, nothing at all.

In this manner, each of us silent and alone with our

separate thoughts, we followed the river down to where it
broadened and straightened a few miles from the sea. We
entered a thicket of yarkona fir. I remember this well. On
either side of the trail, the trees were dense and close, two
walls of gray needles almost prickling our furs as we guided
the sleds between. The wind, what little wind there was,
blew at our backs, urging us forward. The bright nimbus of
Pelablinka was high in the sky; the whole of the forest
seemed made of silver-steel. As we neared the thicket's edge,
the wind died altogether, and it was so quiet I could distinguish the individual pants of the dogs. Tusa was sniffing the
air, lifting his paws high, slogging through the powder. Suddenly the wind shifted; it blew at our faces from the east, from
the edge of the thicket where the shatterwood trees loomed
like straight, black, silent gods. Tusa whipped his head up
and barked. All at once Rufo and the rest of the dogs let loose
a chorus of howls and barks. There was a blur of black against
gray. A spear—it was thick enough to be a mammoth spear—
flew out of the woods and struck Sanuye in the side. So
powerful was the cast that it pinned the dog to the snow.
Instantly there was a tangle of snarled harnesses and yelping,
furious dogs. More spears flew from the thicket. One of my
mother's dogs was hit and shrieked like an old woman.

"*Ni luria-mu!*" came a shout from woods ahead, and
there, stealing from tree to tree like wolves, were men on
skis sliding onto the trail, blocking our way. Their furs rippled
in the starlight, and they each carried spears in either hand.
The Devaki men, Yuri, Wicent, Haidar and Wemilo, and
their near-brothers, Arani, Jaywe, Yukio and Santayana, stood
shoulder to shoulder and spear to spear. Seif, who was
shaking mad, stepped forward and said, "*Li luria, Mallory-mi,*
you have killed my brother, and I have come to kill you,
welcome!"

Some of them threw their spears. Bardo, who was moving
next to me, let out a curse. He pirouetted like an ice dancer
avoiding an unexpected pothole. "Watch your side, Little
Fellow!" he cried out, and he tried to knock a spear from the
air. He stepped in front of me. I will never know whether he
did this by accident or design. He swatted at the air like a
bear swatting at a stream for a darting flatfish, but it was dark
and he had never been good at catching moving things with
his hands, not even as a boy, and he missed the spear. The

spear went into him. All at once he knocked into me and cried out, "By . . . God!" The force of his blow propelled me from the back of the sled down into the snow. Bardo stood facing the Devaki with a red, yu spear sticking out of his chest. I coughed and wiped snow from my eyes, and there was the spear's point splitting his furs exactly at the center of his back. The spear had gone clean through him, but he was not dead, he was far from being dead. He was coughing and cursing, shaking his fist at Seif, staggering, stomping the snow like a wounded shagshay bull. And then the blood came, and the pain, and he bellowed and twisted in agony, and he dropped next to me in the snow. "Little Fellow," he gasped, "don't let me die."

In a moment, I had my spear in hand, and Soli, even my mother and Justine—we all whipped our spears from their holders. There was no room to easily turn the sleds around and no time, so we kneeled behind the bed of my sled, kneeled over Bardo, watching as Yuri slid up to Seif and put his hand on his son's spear. *"Ti Mallory!"* Yuri called me. "This is a bad night, and why did you let Bardo catch your spear for you?"

Seif ripped his spear away from his father's hand. He shouted, "Welcome, Mallory! You have killed my brother, and I have killed your cousin even though I meant to kill you! Welcome, welcome!" He raised his spear and said, "And now I will kill you!"

"No," Yuri said, "Bardo has gone over, and now Liam will have a friend to hunt with on the other side." Some of the Devaki men, Haidar and Wemilo, were weeping; they had always liked Bardo, and he had liked them.

"I will kill him now," Seif said. His face pulled back in a grimace while his arm trembled.

"No," Yuri said, "I am tired of killing."

"He killed my brother."

"And you have killed his cousin."

"My brother!"

"Even so, you must not kill him."

"I have to kill him now."

"No."

"Please."

"No, we would all be to blame if you killed him."

I bent down over Bardo listening to the men who had

killed my pretend-cousin, my brother in spirit, my friend. I
tried to beat his chest back to thumping, tried to breathe life
into his lips. But my frantic efforts were in vain because his
heart had no blood left to pump. "Mallory!" Seif shouted at
me, and Bardo's lips were cold, and because I was dying
inside and still knew nothing of compassion or restraint, I
ripped the spear from Bardo's chest, stood and threw it at
Seif. But it was a poor, blind cast and he dodged it easily.
"Bardo was a warm man, and I am sorry I killed your
cousin," he cried out. "But your soul is hard like ice, and who
will be sorry when I kill you?"

As he said this, I had a sudden idea. I dropped down and
grabbed Bardo by the collar. "Mother, help me!" I said.
"Down to the river, quickly, before his brain . . ." I started
dragging him through the snow. "Justine . . . Soli, we'll freeze
him and take him back with us. The cryologists will save him,
the cryologists. Help me, he's so damn heavy!"

"Let him go!" my mother hissed. She was always the
strategist, always thinking, always planning. "Keep low! If we
expose ourselves, we'll be too easy to hit."

But I wasn't thinking of the Devaki's spears just then. In
truth, they had us trapped and could have killed us whenever
they wanted. I pulled at Bardo; Justine and Soli must have
reached a similar conclusion because they each grabbed an
arm and helped me. Then my mother threw her spear down
in the powdery snow, cocked her head, and asked, "Why is
my son so foolish?"

We dragged him down through the thicket and then
across the ice crusts to the edge of the river, which roared
like black blood through a tube of ice. We eased him out
toward the center of the river where the ice was the thinnest.
The air was full of our quick, steamy breaths; Justine and my
mother were huffing and panting, hopping about like birds.
Soli whispered to himself—it was kind of an apology, I
thought—that he was stupid for not having foreseen the
Devaki would come for us on skis. He ran back to the sled
and returned with the ice axes, and we fell at the ice,
chopping and hacking so fast and furiously that glistening
chips flew up in showers around us. There was crunching and
cracking, and then running water as we broke through ice.
We opened a hole almost as large as a seal's aklia. With each
of us grabbing a part of his body, an arm or a leg or whatever

else came to hand, we lowered him into the hole, submerging
him in the freezing water. The water—it was much colder
than freezing, really—hurt my hands. The cold was sharp and
intense, numbing my fingers to the bone. I could hardly feel
to grip his curly hair. "Hold on!" I said, "hold on!" We held
him as long as we could, and then we heaved and dragged
him up onto the ice. There was a slapping and squishing as
the weight of his body squeezed the water from his furs. I
hurried to dry my hands and put my mittens back on; if I
hadn't my fingers would have instantly frozen, even as Bardo's
body was now freezing. In moments his furs stiffened, encas-
ing him in a glossy sheath of ice. He lay on his back with his
eyes open. I tried to close them but they were as hard as
marble. One of his arms, I saw, had solidified in a crooked
position; his fingers were clenched as if he were shaking his
fist at the stars. I noticed that his furs bulged from his belly as
if a piece of driftwood had washed down his trousers and
lodged there. I remembered that he still suffered his nightly
priapism, and I laughed. It was a harsh sound, which caused
the others to look at me. They must have thought I was
insane. But it was better to laugh than to cry, and wasn't it
ironic that Bardo had died as he had lived, wasn't it funny? I
did not know if the City cryologists could restore him to life,
but if they couldn't, at least he would go to his grave in a
fitting manner.

All this time the Devaki had been watching us from the
river bank. Our "funeral rites" must have appeared incomprehensible to them. After we had chiseled Bardo free from
the ice (his furs had frozen fast to the cold, slick surface), we
carried him back to the sleds. Seif knocked his spear against a
tree and called out, "You see, it is as I have said: The satinka's
witchcraft has touched everything they do. We should kill
them all."

Under the Devaki's pointed spears, we placed Bardo on
the bed of the lead sled. I covered him, then turned to cut
Sanuye away from his harness. It was a bad moment, a whole
series of bad, uncertain moments.

Yuri stroked the shaft of his spear. His eye fixed on
Bardo's body. "We will spear no one," he said. He looked at
Seif and shaggy Wicent who stood next to him. "No man of
the Manwelina will spear any man or woman of the Senwelina.
Liam rests in peace, and there is no need to spear Mallory

even though he has killed his own doffel and has given tender
livers to an old man who lived long past his time. You will not
raise your spears to him even though he raised *his* spear to
Liam and has caused the animals to stay away, and has swived
his own sister, who was a satinka and therefore needed to die.
You will not spear Mallory even though he has killed your
brother. We are not hunters of men; it is bad to be hunters of
men."

We whistled to the dogs, and the sleds inched forward as
the Devaki parted to allow us passage. We moved very
slowly. The trail led across a gully full of smooth stones and
flaky ice crystals as large as knives. We had to partially lift the
sleds and carry them across the gully. As we did so, we
stepped on the flakes, which snapped and crunched and filled
the air with hard, breaking sounds. The Devaki followed us,
whispering among themselves; their strident words rushed
through the forest along with the rustling of the pine needles
and other sounds. I was so full of grief that I stumbled over
ice-slicked stones, little aware of where I was going. Because
I was sorry for all that had happened, because my throat and
eyes and soul were freezing with cold, because I was dying, I
had a sudden urge to explain myself, to apologize, to atone
for my crimes. I would tell them the truth about myself, the
truth about all women and men: that within each of us lives a
murderous beast beyond control. It was this desire to make
things right that ruined me. I emerged from the gully and
turned to face Yuri and Seif. "Liam was a murderer..." I
began, but that was as far as I got. I wanted to tell them that
Liam was a murderer, as I was a murderer and all men are
murderers because life lives off life, and he would have killed
me so that he himself might live. We are all murderers
because that is the way the world is made. But we are all
brothers, too, and sisters and fathers and mothers and sons,
and I would have told them this and a few other simple
things. "Liam was a murderer," I said, and Seif must have
been waiting for just such a slur because he reached back far
behind his head and then whipped his hand forward. A black
rock shot toward me. Had it been a spear, I might have
knocked it away. Unlike Bardo, my hands had always been
quick to follow the movements of my eyes. But it was not a
spear because Seif was obeying the letter of his father's
command not to spear me. It was a heavy black rock, nearly

invisible against the black veil of the forest, even if my mind
had been alert and clear of other dark images, which it was
not. I did not see the rock. It struck the side of my head—I
have reconstructed this event from the story Soli later told
me. All is recorded; all has been and will always be recorded,
so the scryers say. There was a blur in front of my eyes like a
black cloud descending, and the rock struck my head and
pushed part of my skull against my brain. There was an
intense light, a universe of exploding stars. And then I
dropped like a beast to the snow, and all was silent and dark
and cold.

What follows is an account of our retreat across the sea to
our rendezvous point and our return to the City. During
much of this time I was dimly aware of the voices and actions
of Soli and the others around me; just as often, though, I was
comatose or rising or falling through that hellish state of
consciousness in which all the sounds of the world seem at
once overloud, monotonous and confused. Much of what I
shall relate I pieced together long afterward. But I was aware
of the crucial event—revelation, really—and it burns in my
memory still.

When Yuri saw what his son had done, he was aghast and
ashamed. He crossed the gully and placed his hand on my
mother's shoulder as she tried to revive me. He took a single
look at my head and announced, "Mallory will go over now,
and I can do nothing since it is his time to die." He nodded at
Soli and asked, "Do you want us to bury your son by
Katharine's grave? It is unlucky what has happened between
us, and I want no more bad luck."

"No, he's not dead yet," Soli said. "We'll bury him
ourselves when he goes over."

My mother and Justine lifted me onto the second sled and
swaddled me in furs.

"It is a terrible thing to lose a son," Yuri said.

"Yes, it *would* be terrible to lose a son," Soli said,
speaking precisely. "We're sorry for Liam."

"And to lose a daughter, too, even a satinka—that is
terrible. I bleed for you." So saying, Yuri took his knife and
gashed his cheek down to his jaw. And then because he was at
heart a kind man who could really bear no permanent blame
for anybody, he said, "You will go now, perhaps to Urasalia or

Kelkel, and it is good you should go. But if you need to visit your daughter's grave someday, you will be welcome."

"And my grandson?" Soli asked. "Did my grandson live? What about the child?"

Yuri pressed his hand to his slashed face to stop the bleeding. "And who is the father of the child if not Liam or one of Liam's near-brothers? Isn't the child a son of Manwe's sons?" And here he held his bloody hand up for Soli to see, and his voice wavered in a strange way. I do not think he ever suspected that the child was mine. "Isn't the child *my* grandson, too? His blood is my blood, and he will be buried near the cave of his grandfathers."

After that we went down to the sea. A hut was built from sawed snow blocks. For the rest of the night and part of the next morning, I lay in delirium while my mother fussed over me as she had when I was a child sick with fever. She was frantic over my wound. More than once she asked Justine, "What good are the cutters? If not to take the pressure of blood off the brain?"

As the day passed and I grew no better, she almost despaired. "What should we do? The skull is broken. I'm sure of it. Oh, Justine I think he's dying! But what can I do? To take the pressure off the brain? I could drill holes. In his head through the skull, holes. Or I could wait. But it's so hard to wait."

Soli listened to this while he grilled fish over the oil-stones. He stood up and crouched over me, watching my mother gently wrap my head with wolf fur. I did not see the look on his face—he must have been mad over Katharine's loss—but I remember the sizzling of fat, the greasy fish smell, the suffering in his voice when he said, "Yes, Katharine is gone, and soon, Mallory, too. There's nothing we can do; he probably won't live through the night."

"The Lord Pilot gives up hope too easily," my mother said as she dribbled water from a skin into my mouth.

"But there's no hope, is there?"

"There's always hope."

"No, not always," Soli said, and he covered his eyes with his hand. "We should let your son die peacefully. To drill holes in his head, that would be insane, wouldn't it?"

"I won't let my son die."

"You can't save him." And then, the mocking words: "It's his fate. Would you keep him from his fate?"

"If he dies, I'll die."

"Pilots die," he said. "Mallory was told about these things. Yes, he knew his luck wouldn't hold forever. Nobody's luck lasts that long."

"The Lord Pilot is a scryer, then?"

"Don't say that word to me."

"My son is dying. And the Lord Pilot worries about the words I speak?"

"Why speak to me at all? Yes, it would be better if you didn't speak another word ever again." He made a fist and pressed his nose so hard that it bled—so Justine told me years later.

My mother went out to the sled and returned with a bag of flints. She spilled the stones onto her hand, sorting through them with her finger. The brown, fine-grained flints rattled against each other. "I've decided," she said. "We'll make a drill. We'll open a hole and let the blood run free. Will you help me, Justine?"

Justine was beating the ice from our furs and working the inner skin with her teeth to keep it supple. She brushed back her hair, looked up and said, "Of course I'll help, if you think we really have to open Mallory's poor head, but it's such a *dangerous* thing to do, and I'm not sure it will help no matter what we do, but I'll do whatever I have to, even though I'm afraid for him, and what will we do to stop the pain when he feels the drill, and . . . oh, Moira, do we really have to open his head?"

"No," Soli said, and he gave Justine a sharp look, plainly disapproving of her support for her sister's plan. He was angry and his skin was pale; the blood was running away from his face. "The best thing to do would be to wait for him to die. Then we could open a hole in the ice, and there would be that much less weight for the dogs to pull. Yes, drop him down a hole, and his fat friend, too."

"Leopold, you don't know what you're saying!" Justine gasped.

And my mother spat out, "The Lord Pilot *thinks* he knows. What he says with his cruel words. But he knows nothing."

"Do not speak to me."

"The Lord Pilot should be told that—"

"Please do not speak."

"My son is *dying*," my mother said, and her voice thickened into a deep-throated rage.

"Let him die."

I heard these sounds bubbling above me: Justine's piping soprano as she took my mother's side against Soli, and the steel of Soli's deep voice, which rang like a bell about to crack. The argument continued for some time; I remember that there was something in the sound of Soli's words and in my mother's anguished plea that made me pay close attention. And then, after an instant of silence, my mother drew in a breath of air, and she spoke the worst words I had ever heard: "He's your son! Mallory is your son."

"*My son!*"

"He's our son."

"*My son!*"

"To let him die—it would be like killing a part of yourself."

"I don't have a son!"

"Yes, you have a son. Our son."

And then she spoke more words that I did not want to hear, revealing a heritage which I bitterly wanted to deny. Long ago, she told him—and I did not want to know this; I was nearly dead, but I knew I did not want to know this, even though a part of me had always known it, at least ever since I first saw Soli that night in the master pilot's bar—on the day before his journey to the core of the galaxy, my mother had decided that he would never return. All her life she had been jealous of Justine and envious of the things her beautiful sister possessed. Including Soli, *especially* Leopold Tisander Soli. She did not love him. I do not think my mother could have loved a man as a wife loves a husband. But she knew that he was the most brilliant pilot since the Tycho—even she always admitted this. She envied him his brilliance and coveted his chromosomes, which she believed to be the fount of his brilliance. Since she desired a child of her own, a brilliant child like Justine's little girl, why not pair Soli's fine chromosomes to her own? (Because it is a crime, Mother, I thought. Almost the worst crime imaginable.) The stealing of Soli's plasm had been an easy thing to do: a quick, seemingly accidental dragging of her sharp fingernails across the back of his ungloved hand one day in the Hofgarten—that was how it all began. She carefully scraped beneath her fingernails and took the few thousand epidermal cells to a renegade splicer, who split the DNA into haploid chromosomes and fashioned a set of gametes. When Soli did not return from his journey and it seemed he would never return, she used the gametes to fertilize one of her eggs and had the egg implanted in her womb. As a result of this despicable *slelling* I was conceived, and two hundred eighty days later I was born. So my mother told Soli as I worked my lips, listening to her story, struggling to deny what I dreaded was true.

For a while there was silence in the hut. Perhaps I sank down into coma; perhaps the listening centers of my brain were growing deaf. I missed much of what Soli said to her, but I remember his shouting out, "... *not* my son! And when he's buried at Resa, he won't be buried as my son!"

"He is," my mother said. "Your son."

"You're lying."

"Your *son*. Our son."

"No."

"I wanted to have your son—was this so wrong?"

"He's a bastard. He's not my son."

"I'll show you, then."

"No, do not."

"Your son," she said, and while Justine held Soli's elbow and looked on with amazement, my mother drew the wolf fur away from my head. "Come closer and look. He has the Lord Pilot's hair." Gently, she parted the hair on the side of my head opposite my wound. "Such thick black hair. But sprinkled with strands of red. Like the Lord Pilot's own. Like the hair of every Soli male, father and son. I've been plucking the red from the black. Because I didn't want you to know. But now you *must* know. Come here, then, look at your son's hair!"

I remembered my mother plucking the supposedly "gray" hairs from my head in the Devaki's cave when she groomed me for lice, and the riddle of my heritage was no longer a riddle. She had plucked red hairs from my head, not gray. Red hairs, the hairs of the Soli lineage that sometimes do not appear until early manhood. During our expedition, perhaps due to the shocks of hunger and cold, I must have begun sprouting red hair. I was not a bastard, then. I was something much worse. I was—and to this day I have difficulty forming this word even within the most private recesses of my mind—I was a slel-son. I had been called forth to life from Soli's DNA, from his precious chromosomes, from the very stuff of his selfhood. But it had been my mother who had called me, not he. She had used the information bound inside of him to make me, and she was therefore a slel-necker, and who could blame Soli for hating me?

"Look at these red hairs!" my mother said as she ran her fingers through my hair. "Who else but your son? Who would have such hair, black and red?"

"It's only blood," Soli said. "His hair is stained with blood, isn't it?"

"Look closer, then. See? This isn't blood. You can see, can't you? You're his father."

"No," he whispered.

"You must help him."

"No."

"He'll die if you—"

"No!" he shouted, and he jerked his arm away from Justine. It must have been clear to him that if I was really his son, then Katharine was my sister. "You knew," he said to my mother. "All this time, since the City, Katharine and Mallory... *together*! And you *knew*?"

"Oh, no!" Justine said.

"Don't blame my son," my mother said. "Blame Katharine. She was a scryer. She knew Mallory was her brother. And she bore his son anyway."

"What!" Soli yelled.

"The child. It was Mallory's son, not Liam's."

"No!"

Yes, Soli, I wanted to say. I am your son, and Katharine was my sister, and her son was my son, your grandson, and the chain of crime and horror goes on and on. But I could not speak; I could not move. I could only listen.

"Katharine bewitched him," my mother said. She was very angry, and the words spilled out like poison. "She knew Mallory was her brother. Who but that witch of a scryer would mate with her own brother?"

"Why?" Soli asked.

"I asked Katharine why, but she wouldn't tell me."

"You asked her?"

"She was a witch, your daughter. A damn witch."

"You accused her of being a witch? Then you killed her, didn't you? Yes, you killed her."

"She deserved to die."

Soli stood motionless for a moment, and there was madness in his eyes. And then he fell into one of his rare, terrible rages, and he slapped my mother away from me. He tried to kill her. (Or rather, to *execute* her, as he would later claim.) He tried to choke her to death even as she tore his face to meat with her fingernails and nearly crushed his stones with her knee. "Filthy slel-necker!" Soli cried out, "you *knew!*"

I tried to rise, but as in a nightmare, I could not move.

There was horror then, crime heaped upon crime. Justine came to her sister's rescue. She peeled Soli's fingers from my mother's throat. Soli struck out in rage. I do not believe he knew what he was doing. Once, twice, thrice, he struck, smashing my mother's chest bones, breaking Justine's teeth and jaw. My mother collapsed to the packed snow floor, writhing. Justine moaned and gagged and spat out bloody tooth fragments. "Oh, Soli!" she wept, and blood flowed from her lips, but Soli was mad, and he tried to kill his beautiful wife. He broke her arm, broke her nose, and worst of all, he broke the hard, pure love she had always had for him. The mad Lord Pilot, whose face resembled a shagshay carcass after a feast, stared down at Justine as his rage slowly drained away. He pointed at my mother. "You should have let me kill her!" he roared. "This filthy slel-necker!" He came over to my bed and pulled the furs over my head, hiding my hair and most of my face. "He's not my son," he said.

When Soli came to his right mind, he was ashamed of what he had done. He tried to apologize to Justine, tried to help her. But she would not be helped.

"No, no," she said, "leave me alone." Blood bubbled from her nose, and it was very hard for her to speak. However, she managed to force out, "I told you thirty years ago, never again, and I'm sorry for you, sorry for us, I truly am, but how can I trust you now, because if you can do this, you can do anything, and what will I do now?" She covered her face with her hands and cried out, "Oh, Leopold, it hurts, it hurts, it hurts, it hurts!"

"You're still my wife," he said.

"No, no!"

"We've been friends for more than a hundred years."

The presumptuous tone of his voice made Justine angry (and my aunt rarely suffered from that ugly emotion), and she said, "I thought we were friends, but I was wrong."

Soli stared at the wall of the hut. Then he made a fist and punched out one of the snow blocks, and the wind spilled in. He looked out of this makeshift window, pointing at Bardo's sled where his huge body lay strapped beneath the furs. For a long time he had kept his silence concerning Justine's and Bardo's blossoming friendship, but now he was sick with jealousy, so he said, "Yes, now you have new friends. Dead friends."

What happened next is sad to tell. Soli's rage had left him, but the madness had grown worse. He did not realize how badly Justine and my mother were injured. He accused his wife—wrongly—of contemplating adultery. Justine was weeping into her hands, and he took this as an admission of guilt. He told her that he could never forgive her. Since the jammer would be arriving in four more days, he said, it was time to drive the sleds south to our rendezvous, or else a storm might make us miss our ship. When my mother started talking again about drilling holes in my head and Justine would not look at him, he threw his furs onto a sled, harnessed the dogs, and whispered, "Yes, drill if you want to drill, do whatever you want and meet the jammer at the rendezvous if you want to return to the City. What does it matter?"

After he was gone, my mother wrapped Justine's face in newl skins. She set her arm and splinted it. She did this, and all the while her broken ribs rubbed and clicked and scratched at her lungs, causing her great pain. That night she made a flint drill and opened my head to let the blood out. Probably because of her drilling I did not die out on the ice. Somehow—to this day it seems miraculous that my mother and Justine were able to do so—somehow the next morning they lifted me onto one of the sleds. Somehow, they managed to lash Bardo's sled and mine in tandem and drive them across miles of sheet snow. It was a tortuous journey, a killing journey. I remember my mother screaming at every bump or divot in the snow; I remember wind and cold and pain; I remember screaming myself that my head hurt and that Soli was not my father, and many, many other incomprehensible things.

Later the next evening, under Pelablinka's bubbling white glister, we reached the rendezvous point. There was a single snow dome sitting alone on the immense white bowl of the sea. Soli was there waiting, but he would not come out of his small hut, nor would he speak to anyone. My mother and Justine built another hut for themselves and for me. Even though I fell into a deep coma, my mother continued opening my head. "He'll live," she kept telling Justine, "if only we can get him home in time."

We waited three days for the windjammer, three days and nights of wind and pain. Finally it came. The journey back to the City was quick; our return to the glittering spires and the crowds of professionals lining the Hollow Fields was glorious. (At least it was glorious until my mother and Justine stepped off the windjammer and our tragedy became well known.) But I was blind to glory and almost beyond pain. They took me to a dark room beneath the Fields where pilots are brought back to their youth. There the cutters went into my skull. Someone announced that despite my mother's truly delicate and remarkable efforts to save me, Seif's rock had crushed and ruined parts of my brain. After a time, someone else announced that all our sufferings had been pointless because the rescued Devaki plasm had proved to be little different than that of modern human beings. The master splicers had not found the Ieldra's message inscribed within their DNA. The secret of life remained undiscovered, perhaps undiscoverable, veiled and hidden, eternally mysterious. The Lord Cetic proclaimed that it was a pity our search had been in vain. "It's a pity too much of Mallory's brain is gone for us to bring him back. A pity he must pay the final price for nothing."

There must always come a time when our luck runs out, when the ticking of the clock must finally stop. Neither the cetics nor the cutters nor the imprimaturs could help me. To preserve a flawed, damaged brain would have been a crime, and for me it would have been hell, the everness of a life without sound or sight or love or hope. Far better to embrace fate at the right time, and it would be far easier, like falling down a black, spiral stairway longer than the one in the Timekeeper's Tower, the stairway without light, without end. And so in a small, dark room almost within sight of Resa's

Morning Towers, on a cold, snowless day in deep winter, I turned my gaze inward to the deeper darkness and fell. To this day I have not stopped falling.

In Neverness I died my first death.

17

Agathange

*Much of death depends on state of
mind.*
—Maurice Gabriel-Thomas, Swarming
Centuries Programmer

Who can know what it is to be a god? Who can say which
of the carked races of man—the Elf-men of Anya and the
Hoshi, the Newvanian Arhats and all the others—have attained
to the godly, and which are extremely long-lived women and
men wearing bizarre and sometimes beautiful bodies? How
much wisdom must a race acquire before it is deemed worthy
of the godhead? How much knowledge, how much power,
how final an immortality? Are the god-kings of the Eriades
cluster—they who built a ringworld around Primula Luz—
are these human computers merely clever men or something
more profound? I do not know. I know little of the art of
eschatology, of its tidy classifications and endless debates.
Kolenya Mor argues that what really matters is not the status
of a race, but its direction. Are the Agathanians, for instance,
moving godward or have they reached an evolutionary dead-
end? To me, who came as a corpse to the mysterious planet
called Agathange, there was only one criterion upon which to
judge the question of Agathanian godhead, and it was this:
How much of the great secret did they know? Did they, who
swam through Agathange's warm, eternally blue waters, possess the secret of life and an answer to death?

I have said before that Neverness is the most beautiful
city on all the planets, but Icefall, while beautiful in its own
frigid way, is not the most beautiful of the planets. Agathange

is the most beautiful planet. As seen from deep space, she is a glittering blue and white jewel floating in a diamond-etched bowl of black amber. (I should mention that I had my first glimpse of the whole planet only after my resurrection and departure. Upon my arrival, of course, I saw nothing because I was dead.) The stars surrounding Agathange swim with light; looking upward from the luminous, lapping waves the sky is brilliant. Only on cloudy nights is the sea dark, and even then it is the darkness of quicksilver and cobalt rather than that of obsidian or black ink. The sea—the single ocean which covers all the planet except for a few small islands—is warm and peaceful. It teems with fish and other sea life. Schools of taofish and konani numbering in the tens of millions swim through the sparkling waters of the shoals and shallows, while in the deeps of the true ocean, the larger ranita hunt other fish which have no names. Flying fish, perhaps drunk with the sheer delight of racing through the tropical whorls and hollows, school in such profusion that the sea's surface for miles often seems aquiver with a carpet of arching silver. It was this overwhelming abundance of life, I think, which led the first Agathanians to cark their human bodies into seal-like shapes, to escape into the whisperless depths and fill the ocean with their mutable, godling children.

"Properly, the Agathanians are god-men, not gods," as Kolenya Mor later told me. "They do not seek personal immortality; they do not desire to escape the prison of matter, as the Ieldra did, nor do they attempt to remake the universe to their liking." They had come to Agathange, she said, on the first wave of the Swarming. The most common story of their origin—and the one that happens to be true—is this: Long ago, at the end of the Holocaust's third interlude, a group of ecologists fled Old Earth in one of the first deep ships. With them they carried the krydda-preserved zygotes of narwhals, dolphins, sperm whales and other extinct sea mammals. When they discovered a world of fecund oceans and sweet, untainted air, they quickened the zygotes and nursed the baby whales through their childhood terrors of sharks and other predators. When the whales had grown—and grown—and had absorbed the oceans of whalesong preserved within the ship's computer, the ecologists released them into the blue bed of the sea. They saw how happy the animals were, and they held a celebration, drinking casks of centuries-old wine and smoking a seaweed they discovered and named toalache. Days later they came to their right senses. They were envious and sad because they could never know the joy of the whales they saved. The master ecologist said that man, with his monkey hands and desire to own pieces of land and other things, had nearly ruined the Earth. Man was an unfortunate terrestrial species flawed by form and by nature. Ah, but what if that form and nature were changed? And so the ecologists smoked their toalache, and they saw visions of their life as it could be, and they bred their children to have pointed noses and flippers and fluked tails. They named their watery world Agathange, which means, "place where all things move toward the ultimate good." There, for thousands of years, the Agathanians carked and bred their children, whether to ultimate good or evolutionary abomination not even the eschatologists can say.

Perhaps seeking her own ultimate good (or perhaps simply because she had given me life and she loved me), my mother determined to bear my ruined, krydda-preserved body to Agathange. She knew in detail the story of Shanidar. Once, the god-men had restored him to life—could they do less for a *pilot* of our famous Order? She found passage on a deepship traveling out beyond the Purple Cluster. She surrendered my corpse to a group of Agathanians (actually, they were more of a family) who called themselves the Host of Restorers. She was then invited to leave Agathange, to wait in one of the tiny hotels which orbit the planet, while the Restorers worked—or failed to work—their miracles.

She waited a long time. The painstaking repair of my brain lasted the greater part of two years. (I am speaking of Neverness years, of course. On Agathange there is only one season—forever spring—and the many hosts measure time in terms of their degree of advancement toward ultimate planetary consciousness. But I am getting ahead of my story.) For most of the first year I lay suspended beneath the buoyant sea while Balusilustalu and others restored parts of my brain with temporary prosthetics. These clumsy, cortically implanted biochips were only meant to get my heart and limbs and lungs moving again; the tiny computers were too crude to help me regain much of my speech function, nor was I able to remember large portions of my life. My first thought after awakening among a host of a thousand, black, gliding, slippery bodies was that I had

gone over to the other side of day, and the doffels of all the seals
I had killed had come to ask me why I was insane.

It is a truism, a discovery of the ancient scryers, that any
civilization made by gods will appear to humans as incomprehensible and miraculous. How, then, can I describe the
Agathanian miracle when I still do not comprehend all the
details, the complexities of their fabulous technology? I will
tell of what I know: The ocean was full of created organisms,
many of which were one third computer, one third robot, one
third living thing. Most of these tiny tools were microscopic
in size. There were programmed bacteria of every size and
shape, eubacteria, spherical cocci, and spirochetes with their
whiplike tails. They floated among the engineered phytoplankton; the water was rich with flagellates, single-celled
and colonial algae, diatoms with their beautiful symmetry, the
little jewels of the sea spinning out silicates or carbon fibers
or whatever else they had been designed to manufacture.
Mostly though, the Agathanians were concerned with the
manipulation of proteins. The entire ocean was a stew pot for
making, dissolving, and reassembling proteins. It was an
ancient technology: Restriction enzymes, which were nothing
more than protein machines, were used to cut, rearrange and
splice bits of a bacterium's DNA. But the Agathanians, being
gods, had unraveled more of the mysteries of DNA than our
City's splicers ever would. They had created wholly new forms
of DNA. And in the trillions of cells of the created organisms all
through the waters of Agathange, the DNA was transcribed, its
information read and copied into RNA. And the RNA instructed
the cells' natural molecular machines, the ribosomes, to build
proteins: new enzymes, hormones, muscle protein, hemoglo-
bin, neurologic circuitry to weave into the miniscule computer-
brains of new bacteria, protein of every conceivable shape and
function, a potentially infinite variety of protein.

"The variety of life is endless," Balusilustalu would say to
me one day. "What do human beings know of life? So little,
so little, ha, ha! On Agathange even some of the bacteria—
ah, but are they bacteria or are they computers, do you
know?—even the pyramid bacteria are intelligent. There are
infinite possibilities."

As on other worlds, the ocean swarmed with copepods,
salps, annelid worms, sponges, and jellyfish, and with squid,
swallowers, sharks and other fishes higher on the food chain.

But in the water there were other things as well, bizarrely shaped animals which looked like crushing or cutting machines, and there were machines which looked like animals. The Agathanians made these things, or I should say, they designed assembler enzymes to make them. (I will call them assemblers because they were really enzymelike machines.) The ribosomes of programmed bacteria pumped out assemblers designed for specific tasks. Assemblers sifted through the water, constructing large molecules by seizing and bonding bits of carbon or silicon, atoms of gold, copper, sodium, any and every element dissolved into the warm, salty stew of the ocean. Lipid molecules, hormones, chlorophyll, and new twists of DNA—the assemblers welded them into organisms which were half plant, half animal. Assemblers bonded carbon atoms layer upon layer, and so the sea-nymphs spun their networks of diamond fibers, building their beautiful, glittering nests. Assemblers bonded atom to atom, sticking them together like marbles with glue. The Agathanians could—and did—assemble atoms into any arrangement permitted by natural law. They linked molecular conductors to voltage sources within living tissues and shaped electric fields directly and in new ways. If they had wanted to, they could have built a city beneath the waters; I believe they could have made a whale as big as a deepship; perhaps they could have woven circuitry into a whale's nerves and muscles and created a living lightship to sail the cold currents of space. There was nothing they could not fabricate, disassemble and re-create molecule by molecule, neuron by neuron, including a man.

And so Balusilustalu and my host of Agathanians altered my body to breathe both air and water. Somehow they sliced through my brain and managed to keep my cortex free of phytoplankton and seaworms and other muck. For my comfort, they raised up an island from the sea bed. They made the trees to grow and blossom and bear fruit, all within a few days. Other things did not happen so quickly. Inside I was changing slowly, day by day, one cell at a time. By the end of my first year on Agathange, I was spending half my time in the water, half on land. I wandered my little island, wondering who I was and why I was alone. I picked tart fruits from the trees; they tasted like snow apples. But they were more sustaining than snow apples. Indeed, the Host of Restorers had designed a single food which nourished me better than the fish swimming through the island's lagoon would have done. Soon, however, I tired of eating fruit. I began to crave silvery fish, to crave meat, anything that twitched or swam or moved. I longed to shape a tree branch into a pronged trident, to spear a fat wingfish, to fillet it with my overgrown fingernails and suck down the salty meat. But I was forbidden to do so. Balusilustalu had pronounced that I was to enter the water only during those semiconscious moments when my brain was opened.

"You do not understand the sea, and you do not know what you are permitted to eat, and you do not know what is permitted to eat you," she said to me one day after she had restored the perception of the color azure to my visual cortex. (I call Balusilustalu "she" even though she was not entirely female. But she, like almost every Agathanian, was much more female than male.) She was flopped up on the beach of my island, laughing at me so hard that her long torso jiggled, rings of beautiful fat rippling beneath her glistening skin. On her flippers she had claws; she used these claws to draw figures of animals on the wet beach sand. For an Agathanian, her neck was very long and sinuous, as graceful as a swaying seasnake. I should mention that the god-men—the god-*women*—did not all look alike. Some took on the appearance of sea-cows while others were like dolphins, otters or even whales. They bred their children to a thousand different shapes; a City ecologist would swear they were not of a single species. But for all their differences, they shared a common feature: Their eyes were human. Balusilustalu had large brown eyes, intelligent eyes, eyes full of irony and humor. She looked at me with those eyes, all the while speaking to me in her sophisticated language of barks and grunts and clicks. I understood this language clearly. Later, after the translating biochips had been removed from my brain, it would all sound like gobbledygook.

But she knew everything about my human speech. "Meat's meat," I said, not remembering then that I was a man of the City. "A man must hunt meat to live."

"You are a stupid man, ha, ha, not a shark—eat the fruit of the trees; the trees are for you."

She seemed contemptuous of me in the same way a new journeyman feels superior to a novice. Did she expect me to spend my days climbing trees as if I were a monkey? In no matter was her contempt more obvious than at my attempt to understand Agathanian society. "Even if your brain were whole," she said, "you could not hear the sea talking to you. You are a *mathematical* man seeking immortality for yourself, ha, ha! What can you know of the World-soul?" But then, "Wait, wait, we must wait until you remember yourself, and then wait some more to see if you understand the simple things."

After a while, after I had regained the full use of my muscles, I began to remember. Whole pieces of my personal history would come to me, appearing for an instant tenuous and insubstantial, like sea foam, and then churning, vanishing into the breaking crests of memory. It was an unsettling, eerie feeling. Like a child at night, sometimes I would awaken from the sea not quite knowing who I was or how I had come to be there. I would float up and over the dark waves, rising and falling, looking up at the stars. I had dreams. Sometimes I thought I was Mallory Ringess, an innocent novice learning the Boolean algebras; I was teacher, hunter, journeyman, "Little Fellow," father and son, and sometimes, during those lucid moments when I opened my eyes to the dark ecstasies beneath the slipping waves, I was a pilot and I was a fish—I was a pilot-fish—come to learn the secrets of the ageless sea.

One day, when I thought I had remembered all the events of my life excepting the times when I first had murdered and had come to be murdered, and all those moments in between, one day when the sky was full of puffy, white clouds and the sea was quiet and still, Balusilustalu nudged my floating body with her nose and said, "Now we will remake your brain properly; when we are done, you will know you have a brain."

She led me out to the deeper waters where the others of the Host were waiting. The Agathanians enveloped me. A hundred cold noses poked every part of my naked body. Tongues licked my skin. There was a flurry of flippers beneath me and by my sides. Salty foam washed into my mouth. For a moment, Pakupakupaku and Tsatsalutsa and many others lifted me out of the water on their backs. My tiny island wavered in the distance, a speck of gold and green against the sparkling blue sea. There were whistles and barks and puckering sounds. From all around us came answering barks and yodels; the sea was suddenly alive with smooth, black gliding shapes. I counted six hundred and thirty of the Host before I was dunked beneath the water and I had to stop counting. (I later learned that there are about a thousand Agathanians to a host and some ten thousand hosts scattered across the ocean.) Balusilustalu—or perhaps it was Mumu or Siseleka—let loose a series of high-pitched squeaks and clicks. She was talking to the dolphins and whales, I thought, and soon the water rippled with massive shapes. "We are calling the deep gods to witness your rebirth," Balusilustalu said. I marveled that the clever Agathanians had formed their tongues and speech organs so they could articulate not only their own languages, but also whalespeak and whalesong.

All this time they were touching each other and barking; information was passing from nose to nose and from throat to ear. The touching suddenly became friskier, more intimate, more urgent. There in the swirling water some of the host lay up against others, and they opened their slits to deep caresses, and the coupling began. Above me, beneath me and on all sides, many were coupling with gusto and abandon, and then more than many—I watched and listened in fascination while the water filled with their barks and groans. At first I did not understand what was happening. I thought the gods had gone crazy with their sex. But soon I became aware of a knowledge within me. A part of the miracle was revealed to me, whether by telepathy or information stored in my brain's biochips I did not know. The godvoice whispered to me while I floated beneath the water, listening, and this is what I knew: that when an adult of a host is ready to mate, she, the First Mother, creates an egg in one of her ovaries. She finds a partner and a coupling then occurs. (All Agathanians possess membrums, huge ones with triangular red tips bigger than Bardo's, but they do not have testes because they do not need them.) The First Mother thrusts her membrum into the slit of the Second Mother. The egg is squirted into a peculiarly crafted organ called the bakula. In the bakula the egg is partially fertilized. The Second Mother injects the egg with carefully designed strands of germ plasm in much the same manner that a virus infects a host cell with its DNA. Then she passes the egg out her membrum to a third partner where the same process occurs again, and so on many, many times. Finally, when the egg has been passed from bakula to bakula— the Agathanians sometimes refer to this doughnut-shaped protein factory as the "organ of change"—when all the mothers have contributed to the egg's heritage and the fertilization is complete, the Last Mother accepts the zygote into her womb where the fetus grows. Thus each Agathanian is the daughter of the entire host.

"But today we are not making daughters," Balusilustalu said to me as I watched the Host passing their plasm back and forth beneath the sea. "We are making something else, oh, ho!"

What they were making is difficult to describe. In some ways the seed inside the Agathanian's bakulas was like a bacterium, like a "neurophage," since it was designed to consume and replace dead, disassociated neurons. In other ways it was much more like an information virus. Each mother of the Host wove chains of carked DNA, tiny association strings, into the information virus. The mothers moved through the water, touching each other inside, reeling in ecstasy, and they passed the virus from bakula to bakula. And so the impulsive Tenth Mother added association strings according to her inspiration while the wiser Five Hundredth Mother deleted strings and added still others. When the virus was almost finished, Balusilustalu took it into her bakula where she made the final changes.

"We will put it into your brain now," she said. "I invite you to accept the gift of my sisters."

I must admit that I did not want to accept any gift. Even though I was not completely myself, I was aware enough to be very afraid. I am not sure how they opened my brain. I think they used disassemblers to gently split the collagens of my scalp, to dissolve the bone of my skull. I felt as if my whole body were being laid open and spread out tissue by tissue, layer by layer, cell by cell. The water was red and ropy with strands of blood. Parts of me floated in the warm salty sea, unfolding, unraveling slowly. They removed some of the biochips from my brain. When they put the virus inside me, I screamed. There was no pain, but I screamed because I was afraid the virus would destroy rather than heal me. The scream must have carried through the dense, rippling water out to where the circle of blunt-headed sperm whales waited. I heard a series of bubbling groans, which I interpreted as laughter. And then Balusilustalu spoke without moving her mouth, and I heard her voice inside me.

—The deep gods are wondering why apes always scream when they are born? Ha, ha—because they are stupid, I told them.

—No, I'm dying, you're killing me.

—We are restoring you to what you could be.

—To live, I die. The virus will kill me, I know.

—You are so simple, oh, ho! What we have made for you is not really a virus.

—What is it?

—We are gods, are we not, ha, ha! We have made this seed in our bodies to restore you. You may call it godseed.

—Viruses infect, this hierarchy of DNA, the more primitive programming, killing the higher cells—the ecologists taught me this when I was a novice.

—So stupid! The godseed will seek dead brain cells; so many parts of your brain have died.

—Too bad, too bad, as Bardo would say.

—The godseed is intelligent, in a way. It introduces association strings into dead neurons, revitalizing them for a short time. The godseed will take over the programming of the DNA.

—I'm being taken over, too bad.

—Listen, Man, this is the art of Agathange: The association strings reproduce themselves a thousand times over. Replication and life, stupid Man. The new strings organize themselves, clumping together like sea worms, forming thousands of interconnections. And when they grow, the neuron bursts and dies. And the new godseed is born, thousands of godseeds.

—Journeymen die; why don't you leave me alone?

—When the millions of godseeds have migrated across your brain, we will remove the rest of the biochips. The biochips are impossibly clumsy. They are good for moving your legs or so you can wag your stupid tongue but useless for remembering mathematics and other memories that have been enfolded.

—Enfolded?

—The brain is like a hologram; the whole is enfolded within the part.

—No.

—Let me explain.

—No, no, I'm dying and I'm afraid.

For a long time I floated in the water, bobbing up and down in the undulations of the gentle current. Somehow I was fed. In my mouth were the tastes of salt and blood, the rank flavor of seal-skin and piss. (The Agathanians gave as little thought to their excretions as does a baby in a tub of warm water. But the ocean was very large so the clouds of dark, orange piss dissipated quickly.) Long days gradually faded into long nights, and night became day, and the rhythms of light and dark were lost into the deeper rhythms of the sea. And always, the sound of the Host barking and moaning and talking, and the piping of the dolphins as they chattered among themselves, and the huge sound of the sperm whales merging with the long, black roar of the sea—all these sounds surrounded me, beating at my skin in endless waves of sound. I felt the sound in my bones. I felt as if I were swallowing sound, as if the sound of the sea nourished and sustained me. Dark rhythms raced along my blood, and again there was sound in my brain. The Host glided through the water, passing the song and substance of created life back and forth, back and forth as they touched and sang and emptied themselves into one another. Again they opened my brain, and again they touched the deep parts of me with their virus, with their godseed. And again, many times. The Agathanians sang of the stupidity of human beings, and they sang of humans' cleverness, too. They sang of the World-soul and of darkness and light. As the virus did its work, I floated in an expanding ocean of sound. The song of the Host gradually grew clearer. I began to understand things. Sad, mournful notes sounded inside, and I remembered that I had once murdered a seal. Then there was a single high-pitched tone, like the anguished shriek of a shakuhachi. I remembered murdering a man called Liam, and I lived again the moment of my death. The sound of death, the sounds of life: Waves broke over my head, and a seagull beat the air with his wings and cried out above the distant beach, and I remembered things which should have remained obliterated; I remembered learning to count as a child; I remembered elegant theorems and how to knap a blade of flint; I remembered that Leopold Soli was my father; perhaps for an instant I remembered all the events of my life. I remembered things I had never known. Strange, new memories came to me. I knew these memories were the work of the virus inside me. I listened to the song of the sea, the song of the Host of Restorers and all the other hosts. The song of life.

—Why?

—Because it is fun! And too, we restore you because of

who you are, Mallory Ringess, the pilot who will never die,
ha, ha! We give you our memories because you must know.

—I don't want to know anything.

—Oh, ho, listen, Man, and we'll tell you *everything*! Do
you hear the waves whispering the secret? We know you
know, Man. The secret of life is just sheer joy, and joy is
everywhere. Joy is what we were made for. It is in the rush of
the nighttime surf and in the beach rocks and in the salt and
the air and in the water we breathe and deep, deep within the
blood. And the sifting ocean sands and the wriggling silver-
fish and the hooded greens of the shallows and the purple
deeps and in the oyster's crusty shell and the pink reefs and
even in the muck of the ocean's floor, joy, joy, joy!

—No, life is pain, I know. There's a poem; I remember some
of it: "We're born in our mother's pain and perish in our own."

—Life will not perish. We give you these memories so life
will not perish.

—I remember the song of the Host of Restorers.

—All of the hosts are restorers. That is what we are; that
is what we do.

—I don't want to be restored like this.

—It is a great song, isn't it? Do you hear the song?

—I'm afraid.

—Ha, ha!

The song of Agathange is a great song, but it is not a song
most human beings would care to hear. Some parts, of
course, given the wholly human heritage of that mysterious
race, are understandable. Humans and god-men (or even
most gods, I think) share the knowledge that matter and
consciousness are inseparable. The knowledge is old; ages ago
the mechanics found that it was impossible to describe the
behavior of subatomic particles without considering the effects of consciousness on the objects they were studying, just
as it was impossible to explain the disastrous thermodynamics
and poisoning of the Earth, all the while ignoring the conscious and criminal actions of billions of human beings. (This
was, of course, before most mechanics gave up their silly
notion of searching for an ultimate particle. It is an unbelievable fact that the ancients had "discovered," described and
catalogued thirty thousand three hundred and eight discrete
particles—leptons, gluons, photinos, charms, gravitons, quons,
quarks, upside-down quiffs and other figments of their equations—

before they abandoned their hopeless quest.) So, the Agathanians revere the unity of consciousness and matter, and they have pushed their belief to the logical end. The ten thousand hosts of restorers were trying to awaken the whole of their planet to greater consciousness. The song tells of the great restoration: The first ecologists had not trusted their miniscule consciousnesses. Had man's consciousness saved Old Earth? No, and neither would Agathange be saved, because man was man, and someday—even though they made themselves like seals and took to the sea—the natural harmonies would be broken. Only by creating a consciousness far beyond their own, a World-soul, could they sing a song of total joy, which, after all, is what they sought to do.

When my brain had healed sufficiently for me to understand the most ancient harmonies of the sea, Balusilustalu permitted me to hunt the fish of my island's lagoon. I spent long afternoons remembering, and spearing sandfish and shohi and silvertail. I slept on the beach and burnt my fair, Alaloi skin under the bright, pink sun's glare. Often I would swim out away from the lagoon into the offshore current where the migrating whales frolicked and scooped up great mouthfuls of krill. The water churning red with tiny crustaceans, the spouts of the humpbacks and the sei and bluefins, the tang of sea-salt and foam—I remembered the sea as if I had lived in the water for a million years. But I was still afraid of the sharks and predators swimming beneath the waves, afraid, too, of less tangible things. Often I would swim like a pup surrounded by the safety of the Host. And when they opened my brain, the soothing thoughts of Balusilustalu and the others washed through me:

—Do not be afraid of losing yourself. There is the part and there is the whole, and both exist at once.

—I am a *man*! I could never be one of the Host.

—And the wo-men of Old Earth nearly succeeded in creating a planetary consciousness. Ten billion wo-men and children—each one like a neuron in a brain. And all their touching and talking and copulating and writing and fighting and singing—all the instances of intercommunication, just like the interconnecting synapses of a neuron. Ha!

—Why did we fail?

—Why does a manchild pull the wings off flies?

—I don't want to be part of a planetary brain.

—Ha, ha, but *it* wants you be a part of . . . the whole. At least for a time.

—No, no.

—And that is why our ancestors failed. The nascent consciousness of Mother Earth was damaged by its youthful carelessness. In a way, it was never born. The parts were never truly aware of the whole.

—They were afraid, I think.

—Ha, ha, they were stupid! Is a fish aware of the sea, or only the immediate water in which she swims? What does a single neuron in your brain know of mathematics or music or love? We can never be completely aware of the entire dimensionality of the whole, but we can know some of the things it does.

—And the ten thousand hosts—what do you do, then?

—Miraculous things! We're gods, aren't we, oh, ho? We are the brain of Agathange, and when we weep there is rain, and when we sigh the wind blows. When the coral die at the right place, their skeletons form the reefs of the sea. We create new species when there is need, sometimes just because it is fun. And the other things, the higher things, the ecologies and harmonies—we tremble to tell you about these things, we are on the verge of telling you, we want to tell you, we must but . . .

—But?

—But you are too stupid, ha, ha! As even the individual Agathanians, Balusilustalu, Mumu and Pakupakupaku are too stupid. But we at least are aware of the whole; the whole is us, and it is aware of us.

—And the whales?

—As your cortex is to the more primitive parts of your brain, so are the whales to the hosts. You might say the whales are the soul of Agathange. But that would be a simplification, ha, ha!

—So many hierarchies and layers of intelligence; I'd be afraid of losing myself.

—Stupid, stupid man! The hologram is preserved; all is preserved.

—I *am* afraid.

My great fear was not that the planetary consciousness would absorb me. Could a man with hair and fingers and a mathematical brain be absorbed by a host of seal-men? And even if they *could* change my flesh and cark my brain to their whims—and I had to admit they could—why would they want to? What value did Mallory Ringess, a simple pilot of an archaic Order, possess to a race of gods? No, my great fear, what I dreaded above all was losing my selfness to the virus that they had put inside me. The longer I swam among the Host and the more my brain "healed," the more fearful I became.

As the days passed, I gradually realized that the Agathanians had great power over matter and consciousness. (And to complete the semimystical quincunx of the mechanics, over energy, spacetime and information as well. Especially over information.) I noticed that wherever the Host swam, it never rained, nor did the wind blow too hard or the waves grow too steep. Even the sharks were somehow kept at bay. These great, sleek, beautiful murderers ate only a few of the oldest Agathanians, those who were ready to "go on," as they put it. The sharks left the pups—the children—alone. I never understood how Mumu and Siseleka were able to swim right up to a great white shark and impudently touch flipper to fin. It was a mystery why they would wish to do so, unless it was to impress me with their love of nature, and more importantly, of nature's love for them. Only once did I doubt their power. Only once did nature seem as far beyond their control as the sun is to a sunfish.

One day a pod of orcas, with their even-spaced, conical teeth and grim smiles, appeared as if from nowhere. In no time, Siseleka and seven others were torn apart and swallowed piecemeal. The blood was so thick in the water that even the sharks became crazed. There was a slaughter, then. Somehow the sharks died even as they bit at mouthfuls of water. During this confusion one of the orcas forced his way into the center of the Host. He gobbled down eight screaming children as if they were oysters. When he was full—he must have been full, I thought—he whacked his great tail up under a baby, propelling her up out of the water over the backs of her mothers and into the waiting jaws of another orca. Three times this trick was repeated, and each time a hapless child disappeared into the belly of a smiling black and white beast. Then, as quickly as they had come, the orcas were gone, and the red waters grew still.

The Host's sobs, shrieks, cries, whistles and moans continued for a long time. A few of the mothers took me under

the water and engulfed me with layers of seal bodies which
writhed and quivered around me. When it seemed the orcas
had eaten their fill, the song of the Hosts returned to the sea.
Perhaps the Agathanians were taking inventory of their losses or
were merely soothing each other. Perhaps they were busy with
their "higher things." I was terrified by the dangers, without
and within. I wanted only to be back on my island, to pull
myself to safety up the branches of a tree. But after a while the
many singing voices calmed and reached a harmony; the shrieks
and barks flowed into words, the words into thoughts.

—The price, the price, there is always a price, ha, ha!

—But you're gods! When you weep there is rain, you said.

—We're still human, deep inside, and when there is
blood we weep.

—You said the whales are the higher gods. I don't
understand—are they insane?

—Oh, the debts, the sins of our fathers. The consciousness of Agathange is not quite achieved, not quite perfect.
The price.

—Tell me about the orcas.

—Listen to the music of the rising waves.

—Is part of your planetary brain insane?

—Listen to the rush of the drifting clouds.

—Tell me.

—Listen to the sound of your own beating heart.

—No!

—The price, the flaws. The universe is flawed.

—Is my brain flawed? Tell me about the virus—what will
it do?

—The universe is perfect, too, and your brain is perfect
or will be soon, oh, ho! And you must not call it a virus. The
godseed is perfect. The godseed is only for you. The mind of
the hosts has surrounded you and modeled your brain. Our
mind is a computer, like your Order's akashic computers or
the neurologics of your ship. Only much more powerful and
profound, oh, ho! We're gods, are we not? Your brain is like a
perfect hologram. And in a hologram, isn't information about
the whole preserved in every part? And in our bakulas, which
listen to our mind's computer, we make the godseed. The
godseed "reads" the hologram of your brain. It unfolds it, you
are being unfolded now, ha, ha! The godseed knows the exact
order in which your neurons must be replaced. The godseed

"sees" the connections which must be made to the living neurons.

—And my memories?

—Memory is a nonlocal phenomenon. Memory can be created but not destroyed. Every part of your brain contains all of your memories. The godseed preserves memory.

—And myself?

—Ha, ha, you are Mallory Ringess, aren't you?

—Is my sense of selfness preserved? Will I still *be* myself? How will I know?

—What is the sound of the rising sun?

—I feel like I'm drowning.

—Drowning in a sea of information, oh, ho! Information, information everywhere! Information in the conch's spiral shell, and in the song of the hosts: information; information passing beneath the sea, passing from the true information viruses to the mothers, and from mother to virus; and the viruses infect the otters and the octopuses, the sunfish and diatoms. This is what a true information virus is: It keeps our DNA *informed* of the changes of the other species. And it informs us, we inform the life of the sea, passing the information, always passing, back and forth from creature to creature and from plant to plant, under the sea across all the waters of Agathange. Let us open you to the sea of information.

—No!

—Don't be afraid. All will be restored.

—I'm afraid of dying.

—Information is like water, and you are dying of thirst.

There was a moment of stillness, then, hard to remember, impossible to fully forget. They opened me, and the tides of consciousness rushed in. I think I became a part of Agathange, a part of the living mind of the planet. I heard things; I felt the planet moving beneath me. Information passed from me into the sea, while each living creature and plant informed me of its existence. My consciousness was embodied in every clam, whale or starfish—I am sure of it. I was a lobster feeling with my claws through the bottom sand for decaying tidbits; I was the blue-green algae floating on the currents, soaking up sunlight, and I was a diatom and an arrowworm and a kerfer slicing open the soft tissues of a jellyfish. I was a great sperm whale who sang the ecstasy of his mating and moaned the joy of her giving birth. I was many things and one thing, enfolding the world in my tentacles, in my flippers, in my arms. And always information was passing, from plant to animal, from eaten to eater, from virus to bacteria, from mother to daughter. There was a brilliant pattern to this information, a vision as clear as diamond, but now there are only memories of vision; like starlight diffusing through deep blue waters, the memories are tenuous and dim. I was at once myself, a tiny cell with tiny human consciousness, and I was a vast being aware of the information flooding through the universe. I *knew* things. To me as a man, the knowledge was impossibly complex. But as Agathange the planet, when I looked out at the stars, I was aware of the beauty and simplicity. In ways I still do not understand, this awareness changed me and has never stopped changing me, and I am afraid it never will.

When I awoke I was lying on the beach with the heels of my feet stuck down into the wet sand near the water's edge. There was sand in my mouth, sand in my hair, ears and eyes. I moved my parched, gummy lips to speak, and my teeth ground against particles of grit. A seagull cried out. All along the line of crashing surf, the waves were white and foamy. The pink sun was sliding down the western sky, and I wondered how long I had been lying there. My skin was hot, burnt red as a bloodfruit. I clasped my hands to my head and ran my fingers across my scalp, searching for some fissure, scab or scar to prove my brain had been opened. But I found only a few pieces of crackling, black seaweed clinging to the hair. (To the black and *red* hairs.) I closed my eyes, then. I looked inward to the interior of my brain; I looked for memories which might seem unreal. I tested my mathematical powers. I proposed arbitrary axioms and created a logic, and I invented some pretty theorems. I did other things. For a long time I thought deeply, brooding about the problem of identity I had first faced within the Entity. How would I know if my true self had changed? And if it had changed, subtly changed so I never knew, if *I* were somehow different or diminished, would it matter?

Yes, it would matter. My eyes moved beneath shut lids, and I thought of Katharine's last words to me, and it suddenly mattered more than anything in the universe. My great fear was that the Agathanian virus would rob me of free will. It had happened before, to other men. In a way, the fundamental technology was old. The warrior-poets of Qallar and the despicable alien Scutari were known to practice this barbaric art of brain replacement. They call their art "slel-mime," and it is a horrible thing. Tiny slel-viruses—they are computers, really—invade their victim's brain. The viruses first establish colonies at critical locations throughout the cortex. One by one they take over the victim's programs, all of the human habits, beliefs, emotions, thoughts, and mental functions. The victim's brain then runs the programs of his new master. In the end, when the virus has done its work and all the brain has been remade, the man is no more than a machine.

What is inside of you is neither a true information virus nor a slel-virus. We have told you, it is godseed. The hologram is preserved.

I lay there on the beach, listening to the internal rhythms. In truth, I felt as I had always felt—perhaps a little more complex, angrier, grimmer, and too full of the world, but . . . myself. I stood up and looked out across the breakers where the ocean swelled and the Host of Restorers gathered. I heard the Song of Agathange in my blood. Although I remained the proud, vain, murderous man I had always been, I knew I was something more. There was a new truth, a new passion inside me—I could feel it burning somewhere behind my eyes. I almost knew what it was. Something—and not just the Song of the Hosts—had been added to me. I looked out to sea, and I listened to the ebb-sob of the waves, and I knew that the Agathanians had left something unsaid, something unexplained.

I swam out past the lagoon, past the white and pink coral reefs into the deeper waters. Whistling dolphins raced ahead of me, and a humpback breached the surface and landed on his back with a gigantic splash. I found Balusilustalu swimming with the Host. She nudged my stomach as I talked to her in the language of the Civilized Worlds. Once again I asked her about the orcas, and again she answered me in riddles. I was given to understand that the subject was taboo, a thing she could not or would not talk about. (It is curious that for all people—even god-men—there are things which cannot be discussed. The Devaki, for instance, almost never reveal their nighttime dreams, while many of the exemplars disdain any mention of sex or sexuality. And even we pilots may not talk about those things that we may not talk about.)

One final time they opened my brain, but they did not do so physically. They opened me with their thoughts, and with their love. With their need.

—You are restored, and it is time for you to leave.

—There's something inside me, now. Something that I can't quite articulate, can't even think. The key—tell me about the orcas.

—Feel the freedom of the waves inside you.

—Why can't a god give a man a simple answer?

—You're still a stupid man, ha, ha!

—You haven't told me everything.

—We've told you the secret of life.

—No, there's no secret.

—Stupid, stupid, oh, ho!

—Why did you restore me?

—Because it was fun.

—Why?

—Why? Why? Why? Because you are Mallory Ringess, the pilot who has been inside Kalinda, and because she has been inside you.

—Kalinda?

—You call her the Solid State Entity, but her name is Kalinda. And Kalinda knows the secret.

—The secret of life?

—She knows the secret of the Vild. You could say it's the secret to life in this galaxy.

—I don't understand.

—The hosts sing to the life of Agathange and to the ocean, and sometimes we even sing to the sun, but we cannot stop the stars of the Vild from exploding.

—No one can.

—You can, ha, ha!

—No, I'm afraid not. I'm just a stupid man.

—Oh, ho, you're something more!

—What am I?

—Someday you'll know.

—What?

—What? What? What? You're Mallory Ringess, the man whose brain has been made as vast as the sea of Agathange. Do you not feel *vaster*? As the sea swells to wind and rain, so will you rise to the storms of your life. There are *possibilities*, Pilot Man, and they will unfold, one by one. Someday, when

you have been even further *vastened*, you will ask Kalinda
why the Vild is growing. We would ask her ourself, but
Kalinda hates us and there are hierarchies. The lesser gods
must bow to the greater.

—I'll never return to the Entity.

—Someday you will return because it is your fate to
return and because we ask you to return.

—Why?

—Because the stars are dying and we are afraid.

I often think that fear is the worst thing there is. The
Hosts of Agathange said goodbye to me, then. They swam out
into the quickest part of the current. One by one the sperm
whales took in great breaths of air and dived. The dolphins
smiled and whistled goodbye and followed them. And then
the gray whales and the sei whales, the bowheads and blues
and others of the mysticeti disappeared beneath the sea. I
saw no orcas that day, and I never learned their dark secrets.
All around me, from horizon to horizon, the water was blue,
empty and still. In the distance, the glistening sands of my
little island beckoned. I treaded water and shook the long
wet hair away from my eyes, and I looked closer. It wasn't the
sand which glistened in the sun; it was the hull of my
mother's shuttle. Somehow the Hosts had informed her of my
restoration and sent a ship to fetch her. She was waiting to
take me home. As I began the long swim back to shore, I
heard the waves of consciousness swelling and roaring within
me, and I never felt so afraid or so alone.

18

The Tycho's Conjecture

The brain is not a computer; the brain is the brain.
    —saying of the akashics

Some say Neverness is the true Eternal City, the city that will never die. For three thousand years she has stood as a testament to man's ability to endure. In her granite spires and towers, in her gleaming domes, her streets of fire, in the eyes of her pilots and the farsiders burns the cold flame of our immortality, the soul of mankind. I do not know if she will last for thirty thousand more years, as the scryers prophesy, or for thirty million years. Will the planets last that long? Will the stars? As a child of the City, I have always believed her fate is intertwined with man's fate. She is the topological nexus of this brilliant galaxy, and she is also the City of Light to which all seekers someday come. There are secrets buried here; there are wonders; there are glories. Neverness, I believe, is eternal in the way that our dreams are eternal; she will endure as long as the race who made her.

So, she is eternal, and she is beautiful, and she embodies man's very essence. But I must not rhapsodize too strenuously or too long. Our human natures are many-layered. "Verily, a polluted stream is man," as the Solid State Entity once quoted to me. And Neverness, that quintessential city of man, is a stratified city. She is layered with the finest of mathematicians and imprimaturs and phantasts, as well as the sludge of autists, exemplars, and Yarkona slel-neckers. Strange new sects continually change the composition of the City, clogging the glidderies with bewildered (and bewildering) people. She is a beautiful city—I cannot say this often enough—a city of truth. But she is also a city polluted with politics and intrigues and plots; often she is a quicksilver city of sudden change.

On the eighteenth day of false winter in the year 2933, I returned to the streets and spires of my childhood. The city seemed subtly changed. There were the new buildings, of course. In the Zoo, there was a huge balloonlike, purple aerodome which housed the embassy of the new, winged aliens called the Elidi. (I should mention that there was an ongoing, violent debate among the eschatologists and other professionals as to whether the diminutive Elidi were true aliens or were merely one of the many carked, lost races of man. It was a time of violent debates, as I soon discovered.) The College of Lords, those crusty old women and men who ruled our Order, had at last approved and erected the tower celebrating the founding of the profession of phantasts. The phantasts' tower stood among the spires of the Old City; it was a strange building of sweeping curves and odd angles, a disturbing building. Its opalescent facade seemed to catch and hold, at different times, all the colors of the City. Like the compositions of the phantasts themselves, the longer one tried to engrave an image of the tower on the mind's eye, the more it shifted and changed. There were new sects, too, skulking down the back glidderies. Near Rollo's Ring in the Farsider's Quarter, I saw a neurosinger, with his cortically implanted biochips, singing himself unending songs of electric bliss. He made me feel uneasy, probably because he seemed too happy. He accosted me, grabbing the sleeve of my kamelaika, and he claimed a spiritual kinship with me, as all neurosingers did with pilots. After I had explained that we pilots were forbidden to continually interface with our ship's computer (or any other computer), I shunned him as a pilot should. And there were old sects, too: Friends of God off Simoom, and ancient Maggids chanting their histories of what they called the first Diaspora, as well as the ever-present autists, harijan, hibakusha and refugees from the stars of the Vild. There were too many warrior-poets—I noticed this immediately. Of course, one warrior-poet is too many, but on the Street of the Ten Thousand Bars, and along the Way, and in the cafes, ice rings and squares, during one long afternoon, I counted ten of them. Why, I wondered, were there so many of the deadly warrior-poets in my city?

For me it was a time of many questions and few answers. On Agathange, my mother had recounted the disastrous end of our expedition. I remembered, on my own, that Soli was my father. And worse things. Of course, neither of us could know what had happened in Neverness during our two year absence. Immediately upon returning, I asked the Lord Akashic for the news, and there was good news along with the tragic: Bardo was alive! The cryologists had thawed him, healed his ruined heart, and restored him to life. He was off somewhere in the manifold, piloting for the first time since the Timekeeper called his summons for the quest. But others were not alive. I skated down narrow glidderies during the deepest part of night, and I saw Shanidar's toothless face smiling at me from the shadows. Wherever I could, I avoided scryers. The flash of a white robe or white fur ahead of me on the street was enough to send me stumbling through the doorways of strange bars and phantast dens. Once I came upon the false-corpse of a molting Scutari. Its red coils of muscle reminded me of too many things I had seen among the Devaki. Everything reminded me of the expedition. I could not stop thinking of Katharine. I was full of sad, wild ideas: I would return alone to the Devaki and recover Katharine's body; I would take her to Agathange; and when she was healed, I would marry her, and we would leave the Order, find some beautiful, pristine planet and make a new race of our own. In my more sober moments, I admitted that Katharine's body had probably long since decayed and been eaten by bears; it did not exist. She was far beyond the restoring arts of the Agathanians or any other gods.

Because the Agathanian godseed was burning inside me, because I was afire with fear, I went to the Lord Akashic and asked him to make a model of my brain. But he could not help me. (Neither did the cetics, holists, or imprimaturs help me when I went to them.) In his dark, wood-paneled chambers, Nikolos the Elder played with the folds of fat hanging from his little face as he lowered the heaume of the akashic computer over my head. He mapped the base structures of my brain, the amygdala and the cerebellum, the fear-producing limbic system and the folds of the parietal lobe. He mapped my brain from cortex to stem, and then he modeled the synapses of the temporal lobes.

"To begin with, as you must know, Mallory, the virus has

replaced neurons all through the brain. It's magic, of course, and I can't explain it. For instance, in the cluster below the sylvan fissure—it's all new. That's where your time sense is—well, it's really nowhere and everywhere, but it *originates* there do you understand?"

"If I understood what the Agathanians had done to me, I would not have come to you, Lord Akashic. My brain, the hologram, myself—is it preserved or does it change? I need to know."

"Such a miracle!" he said. He shrugged his shoulders and pulled at his pendulous ear lobe. "Well, the hologram *is* preserved, after all. I think. No, no, no—don't worry and don't bother me with any more questions. You'll return here every tenday, and we'll make a new mapping. No, make that every five days—this is a rare chance. The magic of gods! It's too bad we can't detach your head from your torso, arrange a nutrient bath, and model your brain moment by moment— No, no, I'm just joking, don't look at me like that!"

Soon after my arrival, I tried to confront Soli. But he, the vainglorious Lord Pilot of our Order, my uncle, my *father,* would not see me. I wanted to seize his hand in mine, to study the shape and contours of his long fingers for an answer to the riddle of my own. I would make him go with me to the imprimatur for a genotyping. I told myself I wanted proof that he really was my father, but in truth, I was desperate for any evidence at all that I was not his son. For most of a morning I waited in an anteroom outside his chambers at the top of the Danladi Tower. At last a tall, pimply novice emerged from between the arched, obsidian doors, and he told me, "The Lord Pilot is working on a theorem. You may have heard of it—it's called the Continuum Hypothesis. He's sworn to remain sequestered until he proves it."

I was amused at the novice's rude, arrogant manner. Soli was known to choose arrogant novices to serve him. "How long has the Lord Pilot been at his work, then?"

"He's been alone for most of two years."

"Then the Lord Pilot won't see me?"

"He won't see anyone."

"Not even me?"

"And who are you?" he asked. "Dozens of pilots, master pilots such as yourself, have tried to see him, even his friends; but he wants to be alone."

I was glad that he did not seem to know I was Soli's son. Soli would want to keep this a secret, no doubt. The novice was beginning to annoy me, so I stood up and looked down at him. He blushed, and his pimples became even redder. Perhaps he had heard that I had murdered a man; perhaps he was intimidated by the smile on my still-savage face or by the wildness in my eyes, because he suddenly remembered his manners.

"I'm sorry, Master Mallory," he said. "But the Lord Pilot would not want to see you in any case. He hasn't been the same since Justine left him, since your, uh... expedition. And you are Bardo's friend, and Bardo and Justine are, uh... *friends*, and everyone knows it, too, I think. You *have* heard the rumor, haven't you, Master Pilot?"

I had heard the rumor. Everyone said that Justine had left Soli because he was a cruel, wild man. He had broken her jaw one day out on the ice when he had fallen into rage. In revenge, so the rumor went, she had befriended Bardo, and more, she had begun sharing his bed. Some even said they had shared the pit of Bardo's lightship, laying bare their brains to each other, floating together in nude bliss. Could it be true? Had their separate selves joined within the neurologics of the *Blessed Harlot*? Had they shared the same extensional brain, solved the same theorems, viewed the manifold through the same inner eyes, thought the same thoughts? Although there was no proof of this forbidden telepathy, it was the scandal of the Order. Many of Justine's former friends—fine master pilots such as Tomoth of Thorskalle, Lionel Killirand and Pilar Gaprindashavilli—had spoken against her, demanding that the Timekeeper punish her or even banish her from the City, and banish Bardo, too. Others had remained more faithful. Cristoble the Bold had announced that if Justine were banished, he and *his* friends would leave the Order with her. Perhaps, he said, they would flee to Tria and join the merchant pilots; perhaps they would find a new planet and found an order of their own.

Of course, this vicious rumor had quickly reached the ear of the Timekeeper. Immediately that grim, old man had reminded Bardo of his oath to quest for the Ieldra's secret, and he had ordered him into the manifold.

"But your fat friend will return," the Timekeeper said to me at the top of his tower one day. "Even as you've returned

to me. Luck! It's my bad luck that Bardo is run by his lusts.
But aren't we all, eh? Have you heard the talk? So, there
have been changes in the City since your damn expedition.
Some of my pilots—I won't mention their names—are talking
of leaving the Order. Leaving, I said! But no, they won't
leave." He walked over to the chair in front of the window
and gripped the curved back rail as if he would never let go.
"When Bardo returns, you'll talk to him. You'll explain that
it's unseemly for one of my pilots to swive the Lord Pilot's
wife. Now tell me about Agathange. Sit *down*! Tell me how
my bravest pilot returns to me resurrected instead of lost
down the black hole of death."

When Bardo returned thirteen days later, I was faced with
the most painful of changes: The changing of a man who, like
myself, had returned from the black hole of death. I met him
in the Hofgarten, and we drank skotch and beer as we had in
the master pilot's bar four years ago. It was an unhappy,
painful afternoon of angry words and misunderstood silences.
Because that day marked the beginning of *my* great change, I
must record its miraculous events in greater detail.

It is curious that I have made so little mention of the
Hofgarten, for in some ways it is the most important structure
in the City. The Hofgarten, a huge, domed circle of cafes and
bars, sits on the cliffs overlooking the sea. The cafes are built
around the rim of a great ice ring, and they support a
magnificent clary dome, the largest of its kind, or so it is said,
on any of the Civilized Worlds. Each cafe—or bar—has two
large windows: a convex window through which one can
watch the skaters as they make circles around the ice ring,
and a concave window allowing a view of the Old City or the
Farsider's Quarter or—depending on which segment of the
rim the cafe occupies—the icy waters of the Sound. The cafes
are always full of farsiders and aliens who come to informally
meet the men and women of our Order. (And, sometimes, to
skate inelegantly around the ice ring.) It is a festive place
where the haikuists and spelists delight with their quaint
entertainments. But the cafes are also thick with exemplars
trying to persuade eschatologists to the logic of their breeding
strategies, and with warrior-poets and democrats and merchant-
princes and many others who plot, conspire and scheme. In
the cafe nearest the edge of the cliffs I found Bardo hunched

over a foamy mug of beer. "Alark Mandara told me I would find you here," I said.

"Mallory! I knew you couldn't stay killed!" He jumped up from the table, shoved a wormrunner out of his way, and he threw his arms around me. "Little Fellow, Little Fellow," he said as he thumped my back and tears filled his eyes. "We're alive! By God, we are!"

He pulled the iron table closer to the outer window so that we might have a bit of privacy. We sat down on the hard iron chairs. I looked at him, all the while tapping the toe of my boot against the black and gold triangles of the parqueted floor.

"By God, what are you staring at?"

Bardo, my great, strong, mountain of a friend had changed. He no longer looked like an Alaloi. He had been to a cutter who had shaped him back to his old self—almost. Apparently, he had shaven the thick black beard, and loose folds of flesh hung from his cheekbones. Without his beard he looked younger; he also seemed angry, pale and thin, like a great white bear at the end of deep winter. Too, too thin.

"Ah, you see, it's true what they say—Bardo is not well. Am I not? No, I'm not well. Well. I shall drink beer and fill my gut with newl steaks, and I shall be well." So saying, he drained his mug and called for a large plate of meats and kafir and buttered bread. As he stuffed his cheeks, he glanced at me nervously, as if keeping a secret from me.

"I missed you," I said.

The cafe was fetid with people; it was noisy, full of toalache and tobako smokes. The table top was littered with dirty plates and mugs encrusted with sour-smelling beer dregs. Obviously, Bardo had been here for a while, perhaps all day, eating and drinking.

"Two years you've been gone," he said. "The hardest two years of my life. I thought you were dead. Oh, the things I've suffered because of you and your damn quest!"

The novice whose pleasure it was to serve us, a nervous boy with large, too-sensitive brown eyes, brought me a pot of coffee and poured the aromatic liquid into a large blue mug. I sipped the coffee—it was Summerworld coffee, thick, rich delicious coffee—and I asked Bardo to tell me what had happened. As he wiped crumbs from his carmine lips, he looked at me sadly and confided his greatest fear. He tapped his head with his fingers and said, "As a pilot I'm ruined. The finest fruit of this overripe brain—I've plucked it and eaten it and spat out the seeds. My discoveries, my inspirations, my moments of genius, never to come again. It's a terrible thing, my friend, to know that the best has been, and all the remaining days of our lives lead on to rot and decay."

He called for another beer. As the room grew ever fuller, he rubbed his forehead and glared at me. "I am not myself, you see. After your damn expedition—did you know everyone is calling it Mallory's Folly?—after we returned to the City, when the cryologists thawed me, when the cutters healed my heart . . . well, by God, they waited too long! It's my brain that's rotted. Too many brain cells dead and decayed, too bad. I'm not the pilot I once was. It's gone, Little Fellow. The theorems, the associations, the beauty—all gone. I've tried to face the manifold, but I can't. I'm too stupid."

I ordered a tumbler of skotch—Bardo had chosen one of the few cafes in the Hofgarten that served skotch—and I drank it quickly. And then another and yet another. I suddenly did not want to hear his story, his moans of self-pity. I drank quickly to drug *my* brain cells into stupidity, but the skotch seemed to have little effect. Perhaps, I thought, I had drunk too much coffee.

"There's nothing wrong with your mind," I said. "In time, it will all come back. The mathematics—you're a born pilot."

"I am?"

"Soli once said you could be the finest of pilots."

"He did? He said that? Well, he's wrong. My brilliance is dead along with the brain cells, and . . . and other things, too."

"What other things?" I asked him.

"Other things." He stared at the tabletop's etched flower patterns and would not look at me.

"Tell me," I said.

"No, I can't."

"Tell me."

"You'll laugh at me."

"I promise I won't."

"No, I can't tell you."

"Tell me."

"It's too embarrassing, Little Fellow, too, too, embarrassing."

"You've never kept secrets from me before," I said.

"I don't know how to tell you."

"Well, just tell me."

"I can't."

"With your lips, just speak the words, then."

"No, no."

I looked through the spaces between the table's delicate, wrought flowers down at his lap. His wool pants were loose over his belly. "Have you been cured of Mehtar's poison? Tell me."

"Ah, you've guessed it haven't you? But what is there to tell? When the cryologists thawed me, I went to a new cutter who changed my body back to the magnificence of my old self. And he cured me of Mehtar's poison, cured me too well, by God! You should know, I no longer suffer from the nightly risings of my spear; I no longer suffer its rising at night or during the day or . . . or ever. It's gone: Bardo's mighty spear softened like a rotting log. Oh, too bad, too bad!"

Although I wanted to laugh at him, I did not laugh. I did not even smile. "Sometimes," I said, "the cure is worse than the curse."

"Don't repeat banalities."

"I'm sorry."

"Ah, of course you are. Well, I've searched for Mehtar, but it seems he's closed his cutting shop and fled the City." He took a long pull at his beer and continued: "I was so distraught over the loss of my . . . of my *powers*, that I let the new cutter stipple the root cells of my face. 'No one wears beards anymore,' that's what he said, so I let him denude my face. So here I sit, beardless like a boy. I look ridiculous, I know. This is a face to be ashamed of, which is why you see me as I am, sitting here all day swigging beer."

As if to emphasize the poignancy of his story, he gulped his beer and sat stroking his bare upper lip. With his cheeks and lips uncovered for the first time since his novice years, I was forced to consider that most unpleasant aspect of his face: Bardo, my charismatic, ugly friend, had no chin. Worse, his tendencies toward sloth and cowardice had shaped his naked face as time sculpts a mountain. Without a beard, he seemed at once boyish and cruel, saintly and damaged. And unhappy as well, too unhappy for his—or the Order's—own good.

I stroked the beard over my thick jaw, and I decided to

wait a while before sculpting my body back to its old self. In truth, I did not really mind looking like an Alaloi.

We drank our beverages and talked about our glorious journeyman years at Resa and other things not so glorious. I listened to his deep bass vibrating above the chaotic rattle of knives and plates, the low boil of voices all around us. I turned to look through the inner window into the ice ring. There were journeymen in their kamelaikas, master pilots, academicians and high professionals—all of them skating and talking. Bardo pointed at Kolenya Mor as she attempted a waltz double and fell on her plump buttocks.

"Have you heard the gossip?" he asked. "Ah, I'm sure you've heard the gossip. Justine made the mistake of confiding in Kolenya, and now the whole Order knows about us." He drank some more beer and muttered, "They *think* they know."

"Is it true, then? You and Justine? My Aunt Justine? How can that be? Intime, she's a hundred years older than you."

"Time, what's time?" he asked. "Forgive me if I speak poetically, but after a time, ah, after a woman has reached a sort of final maturity, her soul has unfolded like a fireflower and no amount of time can extinguish the flame or attenuate the colors. And Justine's soul is a perfect flower, as beautiful as a violet sunset, as timeless as the sun. It's her soul that I love, Little Fellow. Her soul."

"You love her? I remember you once told me it was wrong for a man to love a woman too fully."

"Did I? Well I was stupid, wasn't I? Yes, it's true, I love her. Bardo has fallen—oh, how I've fallen! I love her deeply; I love her continuously; I love her absolutely; I love her passionately, and I would love her wantonly, if I could."

"But she is Soli's wife."

"No, no, not any longer. When Soli abandoned her, he divorced her in spirit, if not by law."

The smoke in the cafe was dense and irritating; my eyes were stinging, so I rubbed them slowly. "But we live in a city of law, don't we?" I said. "The laws of the Order."

He licked his nude upper lip and said, "Do I hear the Timekeeper's voice speaking through yours? Or is this the voice of my friend lecturing *me* on law?"

"My voice is my own," I said. "I speak for myself, as a

friend to a friend: Listen to me, Bardo, we're *pilots,* aren't we? We've taken vows."

"Ah, you *are* lecturing me on law, by God! I would think that you, of all men, would appreciate the need to go beyond law."

"Why? Aren't I a man like anyone else?"

"Well, you've always been different, even from your ungodly conception—you were born out of law, weren't you? When your mother slelled Soli's—"

"It doesn't matter how I was born; I don't want to speak about this again."

"I'm sorry, Little Fellow. But I was merely remarking on the relativity of law. Wasn't it you who petitioned the Timekeeper to slel plasm from the poor Devaki?"

I gulped my skotch and quickly downed two more tumblers. But I was so drunk with anger that the alcohol had no effect. "There is the law of the City, and of course there is a higher law. I wish I knew what that higher law was."

"And yet you raped the Devaki for their tissues, by God, you did!"

I let go of my tumbler and turned my palms to my eyes. My voice was hoarse as I said, "Once, I thought I could see the higher things so clearly, but I was only seeing my wants, my vanity, my passion for what I supposed was truth. I was always fooling myself that I was an organ, even a part of a higher law, a higher order of things. I could feel it, Bardo; at times I could almost see it. But there are false feelings and false vision, aren't there? What am I, then? I'm a man like you, like anyone else. Once, I placed myself above the law of men, and now Katharine is dead. And Liam. I murdered him with these hands."

"Well, there is the Law of Survival," he said. "That's the highest law of all."

I thought of Agathange, and other things, and I said, "No, that is not the highest law."

"What could be higher than that?"

"I don't know."

Later, after our evening meal, Justine entered the cafe and came straight over to our table. Bardo stood up quickly and took her hand. He seemed at once annoyed yet pleased to touch her. "I thought we had agreed not to be seen together," he said.

She shot him a look which he must have immediately understood, because he nodded his head, then asked, "Ah, what's wrong? What's happened?"

"Haven't you heard the news?" Her voice was raw and breathy, as if she had been skating fast for a long way. And then, "Mallory, I'm so happy to see you!"

We embraced and I bowed my head to her. She had changed since our return from our expedition two years ago. Gone was her Alaloi body, her Alaloi nose, her Alaloi brow, teeth and chin. She had been resculpted. With her pouting, full lips and long black hair, she was the same tall, beautiful Aunt Justine I had always known. If she was not quite so lithe as she had been, if her breasts were a little fuller, her hips broader, her thighs a little too thick with voluptuous fat— well, I thought, that would please Bardo endlessly.

"It's been so long!" she said. She touched the side of my head lightly as if she could not quite believe I had been healed. She took me aside, and in a low, dulcet voice, said, "It's a miracle, you know. Poor Katharine! If only we'd thought to . . . oh, I'm sorry, I shouldn't have said anything, I know it's painful to remember, and I try not to, but I can't help remembering especially at times like these, these public places where Soli's friends—all of *my* friends, too, as I remind myself—everyone looks at me and Bardo as if we're, well, slel-neckers, excuse me for saying that, but the truth is, and I want you to know the truth, Mallory, whatever anyone says to you, you should know that Bardo and I are just friends, good friends, maybe even best friends as I always wanted me and Soli to be, but never could be because, oh, you know what Soli is like, don't you? Of course you know, especially now that . . . well, we won't talk about *that*, but Soli, oh, he's so damn cold, too damn cold, and that's too bad."

I must admit, it bothered me to hear Justine curse because she almost never cursed. It bothered me even more that she had copied some of Bardo's speech mannerisms. "Tell me your news," I said to her.

She sat in a chair next to Bardo's and, without invitation, took a sip of his beer. "You *haven't* heard, have you? Merripen's Star has exploded; it's a second class supernova, that's true, at least according to your friend Li Tosh who was on his way

home when he discovered it, but of course at this distance
even a second class supernova is—"

She stopped in midsentence to look at Bardo. Bardo's
eyebrows were pulled in tight; it was obvious he had never
heard of Merripen's Star. I, too, was unfamiliar with the
name.

"How far?" Bardo asked.

"Merripen's Star is . . . oh, I should say it *was*, well, it's
one of the stars of the Abelian Group."

Bardo and I looked at each other, and I shook my head.
The Abelian Star Group was close to Neverness; the mean
distance of its hundred stars from Icefall was about thirty
light-years.

"How long ago did it explode?" Bardo asked. "How far
away is the wavefront?"

"Li Tosh estimates twenty-five light-years."

Even as we spoke, photons and gamma from the dead star
were streaming outward through space in an expanding sphere.
In six seconds, light would travel more than a million miles;
in some eight hundred million seconds, the sphere's wavefront
would begin to bathe Icefall—and the City—in a lightshower
of hard radiation.

"Ah," Bardo said, "there it is, then, the end of everything.
Too bad."

He nonchalantly sipped his beer. However, I could see
that he was stunned by the news, as I was stunned. Although
we had been waiting for this news all our lives, we were
unready when it finally came.

"What's the intensity?" I asked. "How bad will it be?"

Bardo glanced at Justine and answered for her. "Oh, it
will be bad enough; it will be very bad, sadly bad, probably
even finally bad."

The supernova would melt the ice from the seas; the light
would roast the green plants and dazzle the birds and animals
into blindness. Possibly, it might sterilize Icefall's surface.

Justine took another sip of his beer. She nodded in
agreement. "There is already talk of abandoning the planet,"
she said.

For quite a while we discussed the fate of our city, of our
star, and of our galaxy. At last, Bardo (and Justine) became
bored with this discussion. Most human beings find it possible to concentrate only on those events which will occur in

the near future, and Bardo was preeminently human. Given his innate pessimism, he was usually content merely to be assured of his next meal.

"Ahhh," Bardo said slowly, and in that time, the star's killing light streaked another half-million miles closer. "Why should we worry about *this* supernova when anything might happen, perhaps another, nearer supernova, or an earthquake, or a stroke, or . . . oh, *anything* could happen in twenty-five years, I think, so why should we spend every second talking about something we probably won't be here to witness?" He wiped sweat from his forehead. "Now where's that damn novice—I'd very much like some more beer."

It worried me that certain of Bardo's phrasings sounded suspiciously like Justine's. In truth, it was a much more immediate worry than my worry of the supernova. I thought they were aware of my worry and did not care, and that was very worrisome indeed. Although I was no cetic, it seemed they were in danger of copying, and perhaps running, each other's programs. Such was the danger of sharing the pit of a lightship—if one could believe the warnings of the cetics and the programmers. So far as I knew, no two pilots had ever faced the same thoughtspace at the same time. When I hinted of this danger, and hinted of my worry, Justine smoothed the folds of her robe, straightened her back stiffly, and told me, "You don't understand."

"Ah, you can't understand," Bardo agreed.

"You're not a cetic."

"Of course he's not a cetic."

"He's a pilot."

"Maybe the best pilot that's ever been."

"Well, certainly he's the luckiest."

"Ah, but he's a pilot who's never known what it's like to pilot a ship together with, ah . . . a friend."

"Too bad."

"Oh, too bad, this rule against pilots journeying together."

"It's a foolish rule, really, an archaic rule."

"Rules should be changed to suit the times."

"People shouldn't have to change to suit the rules."

"I'd tell the Timekeeper that, too, if he'd agreed to see me."

"But he wouldn't understand, either."

"No, he wouldn't understand."

"And what's worse, he wouldn't want to understand."

They went on in a like manner for quite some time. Though their faces and bodies were very different, Bardo and Justine seemed too much alike. If I hadn't known differently, I might have guessed they were brother and sister, cut from the same chromosomes. When he smiled, she smiled, and their smiles were the same. They laughed at the same little jokes in the same way; they seemed to anticipate and even to prompt these jokes by some little mannerism or body motion I could not quite detect. Word by word, thought by thought, smile by smile, one of them would originate an idea or a program only to have the other complete it. Or if the program were interrupted midrun, it might play back and forth between them so that it was impossible to tell who was thinking what. They sounded like two brightly plumed Trian parrots squawking empty words back and forth. And when they grew tired of talking and stood looking into each other's eyes, they even breathed together, inhaling and letting out their air in silent syncopation.

"How can we tell Mallory what it's like, this sharing of the same extensional brains?"

"When we're together there is, ah . . . an augmentation."

"Of our selves."

"When we're together outside our ship."

"But when we're together *inside*, well, that's different, there is, ah—"

"There's an augmentation of more than ourselves."

"There's the creation of our *self*."

"One plus one equals—"

"Infinity."

"Aleph two, at the very least."

"By God, there's a mathematics the Timekeeper would appreciate!"

"Our separate selves are infinite, too, so the cetics say, but when we're alone, oh, *you* could say that we're prisoners of a lesser infinity."

"To enter a lightship together, ah, tell Mallory what it's like."

"It's wonderful."

"But frightening, oh, so frightening!"

"It's like falling through a tapestry woven of ten billion threads, and the touch of each single thread is . . . ecstasy."

"It's indescribable."

"It's terrifying, really."

"I can't tell him what it's like, not really."

"Neither can I."

"It's the best thing there is. There's nothing better."

"But there's a price."

"Of course, there has to be."

"The price."

"There's always a price."

The price, I thought, would be the death of the Bardo and Justine I cherished, and soon, if they continued to journey together. I did not like this created Bardo/Justine entity. Their deep, private programs still ran, but new programs superceded them, layered over their old selves like the gold plate of a Trian's goblet. It was their tragedy—and I hoped it would not actually come to *be* a tragedy—that they loved the created luster of their shared-self more than the steel of their truer selves within. They were not really in love with each other; they were in love with the *idea* of being in love with each other. And soon, I was afraid, too soon their deep programs would die altogether and there would be nothing left to love. Should they have a right to kill themselves? Should they have the right, despite their vows and the rules of the Order, to create something new outside themselves?

For reasons of my own, I wanted to talk to them about this, but before I could say anything, Justine excused herself and went off to tell Kolenya Mor her news. After she had gone, I leaned across the table and asked, "What's wrong with you?"

Bardo wiped the sweat from his forehead where it bulged. "What do you mean?"

"When Justine told us about the supernova, you seemed relieved."

"Relieved? No, I'm scared enough to puke my beer."

"In truth?"

He looked over his shoulder at three mechanics sitting at the table next to ours, but no one was paying us any attention. "Ahhh... well, in truth, I *am* scared, but in one way, this supernova is a timely happenstance, don't you agree? It will give us an excuse to flee, if we must."

"You'd leave the Order?"

"I wouldn't be the only one. I can't tell you how many

pilots are tired of the Timekeeper and the other old bones who rule the Order." He waved to the novice and pointed to his empty beer mug. "And we're tired of not having our freedom, too."

I drank some skotch and asked, "The freedom to share your ship with Soli's wife?"

"Don't speak about things you know nothing about. I love her, Little Fellow, by God I do!"

"Then she should petition Soli for a divorce. And—"

"He won't divorce her; he's too damn proud. Just like his son."

"Don't call me his son; never say it again. Never, Bardo, never."

I rested my elbow on the cool sill of the window overlooking the sea. I could not look at him, so I watched the screaming seagulls swoop down to devour the shellfish that washed onto the beach below the cliffs. Across the Sound, the glacier cutting between Waaskel and Attakel was breaking up under false winter's warm sun. Like a great, blunt knife, the glacier splintered, sending a mountain of ice plunging into the sea. The crack and boom of the nascent icebergs reverberated from Waaskel's southern wall so strongly that I felt the window vibrating through the wool covering my forearm.

Bardo's voice boomed and he said, "You've changed, my friend. As have I, as have I."

"Long ago," I said, "when we were journeymen, the horologes and cetics warned us that friendship between pilots would be nearly as difficult as marriage. Because of crueltime, they said, the long absences, the changes."

"Ah, that's true," he said. "But you weren't going to let crueltime—or anything else—come between us. That's what you told me. You gave me your promise, Little Fellow."

"I know."

I was silent, thinking about the inherent fragility of friendship. What is friendship, I wondered, if not a double-faced mirror we hold up between ourselves reflecting those images most pleasing to behold? And when we see images diminished and hardened with the frost of time, and the mirror begins to crack, where is friendship then? There I sat like a hard, cold mirror in front of my agonizing friend, and he must have seen himself as sulky, faithless and confused. And

I, through the reflecting pools of his deep-set eyes—I saw a savage man I did not like.

I will not tell here everything we talked about that night. Although the sun did not set until midnight and rose again a few hours after that, it was a long night. We sat at our little table drinking steadily until the cafe emptied of people. We made half-hearted, obligatory attempts to joke with one another, to recall and laugh at past anecdotes; we talked about every possible thing that two friends could talk about. And all the while, Bardo seemed surly, as if he were blaming me for some unstated thing. At last when morning was almost upon us, after we could drink no more, he stood up from the table and blamed me for killing his faith in his mission as a pilot.

"It's your fault," he said. He banged his fist down on the table so hard that the iron top rattled and bent like the skin covering of a drum. "I'm a defeated man because of you."

"My fault?"

"You and your damn quest! You wanted to know about life, and that's what was too bad. So did I. Your dream, my dream—you'd infected me with your damned enthusiasm. Ahhh . . . We were the breath and soul of the quest, by God! But we killed it, didn't we? It's all gone now. You killed it; you killed me. Bardo is not the man he was, no, no, no, too bad."

He was very drunk, but I was as sober as a cetic. Perhaps the godseed in my head made me immune to drunkenness. I turned to leave but he grabbed my arm and said, "Let's take a circle around the ring."

"You're too drunk."

"I'm not drunk enough."

We left the cafe, clipped in our blades, and skated to the center of the great ring of the Hofgarten. A few yards away, a group of journeymen fresh from their beds were practicing their morning figure eights. I reached out to steady Bardo, who was wobbling on his skates, grasping his beer-bloated belly. "Let go of me!" he said.

"Listen, Bardo, you're still a pilot, still my friend, and—"

"Am I your friend?"

"Listen to me! The quest isn't over, not as long as we're still alive, it goes on and—"

"By God, you *are* a dreamer—too damn bad!"

"And you're afraid of—"

"I'm afraid?" he bellowed. "I haven't seen you in two years, I thought you were dead, and all night long you sit talking about everything but the important thing. Oh, I know you, Little Fellow, too damn well. You like to pretend you're hard as a diamond, but inside you're pissing afraid. Tell me you're not! Pointedly, pointedly, you refrain from discussing Agathange. Do you think I don't know what they did to you? Well, I know. I've seen how you brood, always looking inward, all night, inward through the blue diamonds, through your damn blue eyes like your damned father. Look at me! What are you afraid of? I'll tell you: you're afraid of losing yourself, am I right? Oh, I know you better than you'd guess. You're afraid of losing your humanity. Well, who isn't, tell me, who? For everyone, it all slips away, doesn't it? It rots, cell by cell, bit by bit until it's all gone. So they added parts to your brain, so what? I wish the goddamned gods had made me a new brain. Your brain is your brain! What does it matter if it's made of silicon or bloody neurons or shagshay cheese? It's your brain, by God! When we grow old and our eyes cloud up, what's it matter if the cutter grows us new ones, or builds us jeweled eyes to see up into the ultra-violet, to see the new colors? We're still seeing, aren't we? We see what we want to see—and you with your brain, ah, you'll think what you want to think. You'll think your goddamned wild thoughts because you always have. That won't change. Do you want to know what I'm really afraid of? I'm afraid of you because you're wild as a madman!"

I was furious with him, and I let go of his shoulder. I kicked the ice with my toe pick; there was a shower of snow on ice. "No, you're afraid of yourself," I said. Then I clamped my jaws tight because I knew I was accusing myself, not him.

"What kind of a man are you? I took a spear through my heart for you, by God! Because I knew your secret, because I knew you were afraid of dying, pissing afraid!" His voice dropped and he blinked his eyes, staring at me. "And because I—"

"No," I said, "I don't believe you. You stepped in front of the spear by accident. You're just a limp, drunken coward."

I regretted the words the moment they sprang from my lips. They were terrible words, words that a friend should never speak to another, no matter if they were true. *Especially*

since they were true. I moved my lips silently, seeking words
to negate the words I had so cruelly spoken. But the words
were too slow in coming, and as Bardo's face filled with blood,
he spoke words that were crueler still: "Well, you're a
bastard," he said. "And your mother is a filthy slel-necker.
You're a wild, dangerous, slelled bastard."

I felt as if he had pounded my face with a block of ice. My
muscles trembled, yet I could not move. Bardo disappeared
from my sight, as did the other skaters in their colorful
kamelaikas. There was only the steely glare of the ice puncturing my eyes with hard, white stabs of light. An ocean of
far-off voices engulfed me; I heard skates clacking against ice;
there was a dull wind and the hundred other sounds of the
ice ring, yet I could not see. How long I passed in my blind
rage I did not know. When the reds, blues and greens
returned to my eyes suddenly as flowers come to a snowfield
in false winter, I was standing alone in the middle of the noisy
ice ring. Bardo, my cowardly friend, my oldest friend, was
gone.

I left the Hofgarten determined to stop Bardo before he
found another bar, before he drank himself into a stupor and
collapsed in some dark alley deep in the Farsider's Quarter. I
skated towards the Street of the Ten Thousand Bars. The
early light was streaming through the fragile obsidian hospices and other buildings. The cross streets were deserted,
and to the east, the lesser glienderies were pools of fire. From
the hatch of a hospice, a few Fravashi emerged looking tired
and hungry. They rubbed the nictating membranes from their
eye and whistled to each other with such a high pitch that I
could only make out a tenth of their words. When they
passed a group of sleepy novices, they pitched their whistles
lower so their fluting, piping prayers might be felt and
understood. The novices whistled back with clumsy, inexpert
notes, thanking the aliens. They clapped their hands and
laughed as they hurried off to practice their thought primaries. In their clean white robes, with their white-gloved
hands shielding their eyes against the glare, they looked like
immaculate toy dolls saluting the rising sun.

Down the middle of the street, bright yellow sleds filled
to the rails with foodstuffs, woolens and other goods rocketed

continually past. The sleds, burning hydrogen and oxygen in well-spaced, measured blasts, spewed out an exhaust of water vapor. It was this fine spray from sleds across the City that everywhere settled on cold stone, freezing and silvering the buildings with verglas. I remembered Master Jonath—the historian who had tutored Bardo and me in our second year at Borja—saying that on Old Earth during the holocaust century, the sleds in many cities had been mounted on greased wheels and had burned hydrocarbons inside a steel engine. The resultant fumes, he claimed, had been invisible to the eye and not at all harmful. He, a hater of the cold mists that so often steal over our City, held that we should tear up our beautiful streets and copy the example of the ancients. I remembered him saying this, remembered as clearly as I remembered my multiplication tables. Kindly Master Jonath with his warts and his long, stringy black hair lecturing patiently as Bardo and I traded punches on the ugly gray rug of his apartment—what trick of memory is it that permits us to see our younger selves so clearly? Why are events that happened later in time—important events such as the time Bardo claims I lost my temper and nearly murdered Marek Kesse—why are these memories so often muddy and dim?

Whatever the flaws in my memory, I shall always remember the miracle that happened that morning. I was skating down the Promenade of the Thousand Monuments when my time sense began to dilate. The sliddery divided into two broad bands of orange even as my mind began dividing segments of time into endlessly long infinitesimals. Separating the north and south lanes of the street was a mile-long Promenade of statues, obelisks and other testaments to glories past and glories yet to be. As I passed the immense, mushroom-shaped hibakusha memorial, the nearby novices seemed to be moving with exquisite precision, slowly, slowly, so slowly, as if their limbs were immersed in the slushy, freezing waters of the Starnbergersee. Suddenly, there was a dazzling array of colors. Ahead of me The Tycho's Vanity cut the air with knives of amethyst and diamond and ruby. The monstrous gemstones—some were as tall as a spruce tree—grew out of the Promenade's ice. They joined with one another, red to blue, gold fusing with purple, at strange, twisting angles. To many of our City's pilgrims, the long display must have seemed a bewildering jumble of carelessly

assembled jewels, a fantastically expensive jungle of colors
thrown together at random. To a pilot, the monument had a
different meaning. The thick emerald blocks and graceful
sapphire strands were a physical representation of the ideoplasts
the Tycho had used in the formulation of his famous conjecture. He had commanded that the finest inspiration of his
mind should be made manifest, and so for seventy yards up
and down the Promenade, the first of the twenty-three
lemmas needed to prove the conjecture was captured in hard,
flowing columns of diamond meant to last forever. (The Tycho
had originally called for all twenty-three lemmas to be so
arrayed, one after the other for a mile and a half down the
Promenade. Such a plan, however, had proven too grandiose.
The cost of importing the jewels had nearly ruined the Order,
then much wealthier and more powerful than now.) I was
skating next to the ruby coiled glyphs representing the proof
of the fixed-point theorem, when the moment of slowtime
hardened and time came almost to a standstill. Never before
had I experienced such a profound instantaneity away from
the time-warping neurologics of my light-ship; I did not
believe that it was possible for the unaided brain to stop
time. Engraved on my retina were images of open-mouthed
novices frozen midstroke like white statues. The thunder of
the sleds and the click-clack of steel skates broadened, drew
out long and slow and deep, solidified into a single sound.
With my one arm thrown straight backward and the other
forward, the toe of my skate motionless and pointed, I must
have born a curious resemblance to the Tycho's frozen glyphs.
It was in that moment, with the snow loons suspended low
and gracefully in midflight, with my City stopped all around
me, that I found Bardo.

He was hanging from one of the glyphs. His great hands
were wrapped around a connecting ruby crystal; the bulk of
his body was pitched forward, stretching his long arms,
pulling at his gripped hands. His face was frozen into a mask.
He seemed at once terrified and excited, ashamed and mischievous like a disobedient boy.

How can mind can exist outside of time? How can thoughts
be completed and strategems devised when the brain's
neurotransmitters are quiet and still as blue ice in deep
winter? Is it *possible* to completely stop time? (Katharine
believed that mind creates time. She believed that lovers, in

their moment of joy, exist together in a timeless realm of mind. Once, she taught me a kind of pure instantaneity, but in one way or another, I have been trapped in time for most of my life.) Does time stop—or does it merely dilate so that it seems to stop, a nanosecond into a year, an infinitesimal into an eternity? Most of my brain was still human, I thought, blood and neurons, but parts of me were phased into computer time; the godseed within was electric, processing information in ways I did not understand. The ridiculous image of Bardo swinging like an ape from the ruby spear was fixed in my mind, and I wondered how I could rescue him—and our friendship—from the black amber of time. It came to me, then, all at once what he was trying to do. There, on the ice, as the moment of instantaneity failed and the world came alive around me and rushed in, I knew that Bardo had come here to kill himself.

To my dilated time sense what happened next proceeded as slowly as a seaworm building its shell: Bardo swung back and forth, snapping the crystal with his pendulous weight. The crack of the splintering crystal for a long time hung in the cold morning air. As if he were a slowly deflating balloon, he fell to the ice. In his bleeding hands he clasped the sharp ruby spear. He planted the spear into a mound of frozen slush. The sharp, ragged tip projected upward toward his chest. He looked at me. Slowly, sadly, slowly—and a sad comprehension slowly stole over the tortured features of his face. His eyes moved. He clenched his teeth. A silver drop of water floated from his cheek. He dragged his bloody hands across his black robes. Slowly he smiled. A thin film of beery saliva stretched between his upper and lower teeth. The film bubbled and expanded. It filled with air. At last, as I watched, it popped. He placed his reddened hands on the folds of his robes where they gathered at the neck. He pulled open the layered folds. Red soaked into black. He bared his chest. I saw olive skin covered with thousands of curled, black hairs. He laughed. The low boom took hours to reach my straining ears. Like a mountain of ice slowly breaking away from a glacier, he began to topple toward the jagged ruby spear. Clearly, if he completed his trajectory, the spear would enter the skin of his chest. The spear would slowly make its way through the tightening muscles. Perhaps the spear would push apart the ribs. There would be a moment of eternal pain. It would be cruel. The spear would touch the great heart as it paused between beats. It would go in. And Bardo would cry out, and there would be a sea of blood, and Bardo would be endlessly afraid.

Suddenly, I moved. Around me the world moved with exquisite slowness even as I must have moved with the speed and frenzy of a diving thallow. I am the frenzy, I am the lightning, I thought, all the while repeating mentally the saying of the warrior-poets. And instantly I knew the fiery ecstasy of electric neurons and fast-burning muscles and accelerated motion. Like a warrior-poet in his rush toward his victim's death, I rushed at Bardo, crossing the long stretch of ice between us in a shriveled second, a frozen nothing of realtime. I caught his armpit with my shoulder, throwing him, and myself, to the ice. The red spear missed his chest by an inch.

We lay there stunned, disoriented, gasping for air, I returned to realtime with a wrenching mental snap, and Bardo said, "By God, it's impossible to move so fast!"

I tried to sit up, but the tissues of my body burned and would not move me. "If I hadn't, you'd have killed yourself."

He stood in a half-crouch, leaning with his forearms against his thighs. He looked at me coyly and said, "Well, I wouldn't have, not really. Bardo is too much of a coward to kill Bardo. I saw you skating down the sliddery. I thought you might, ah . . . well, I hoped you'd call out for me to stop."

"It would have been simpler, that's true."

"Well, once again, you've saved me," he said. "Like the time you kicked Marek Kesse in the head when he was choking me, do you remember?"

With his help, I stood up but my shoulder would not work right. There was a fire in the joint as if the bones had pulled apart. "I have . . . a memory of a memory."

He rubbed his bloody hands together and coughed. "There is no way I can unsay what I said, is there, Little Fellow?"

"No."

From behind us came the voices of the novices and the Fravashi. They crowded around us, plainly appalled at Bardo's desecration of the great monument. (And no less appalled, I thought, that I had moved as fast as a warrior-poet.)

"What are you staring at?" Bardo shouted at them.

I tried to raise my arm to steady myself against him, but I

could barely move it. "There is no way I can unsay my words either," I told him. "But I'll say it anyway: You're not a coward."

He looked at the ruby spear which had so nearly impaled him. He gave it such a hard kick that it fell over and clattered to the ice. A thin, freckled novice gasped. Apparently he did not know that, although the huge crystals of the Tycho's Vanity had been ruinously expensive to fabricate, as jewels that might be cut and sold they were worthless. The Tycho, that vain and cunning man, had thought to prevent just such a desecration and theft by ordering that the jewels be impregnated with various impurities and stived with flaws.

"Of course I'm a coward," Bardo said. "But when we were younger, you had the grace never to call me a coward. Even when I *was* a coward."

"I'm sorry."

He kicked the broken jewel again and then looked at my drooping shoulder. He said, "You fell into slowtime, didn't you?"

"It's worse than that."

"Without facing your goddamned ship—you slowed time?"

"I stopped time."

"That's impossible," he said. "No one can stop time."

"I can."

"By God, it's a miracle!"

"Inside, what the Agathanians call their godseed—it's remaking my neurons, and maybe my nerves. Even now, as I speak, the changes . . . how can I know what the changes will be? I seem to still be myself, I believe I am, but—"

"You *are* yourself. Wouldn't *I* know if Mallory was no longer Mallory?"

"I'm sorry for what I said, Bardo. I'm wild and impulsive, and I have no self-restraint."

"By God, that's the Mallory that I know!"

I clasped my hand to my injured shoulder and said, "And I'm afraid."

"Ah, there's nothing worse than fear, is there?"

"I'm afraid of losing myself."

He put his arm around my back and half-lifted, half-carried me to the sliddery. "Little Fellow," he said, "you can never lose yourself. And you can never lose your friends, at least not such a friend as I."

He promised me then that he would never leave the Order of his own choice, even if the sky filled with a thousand supernovas. "In my soul I love this City and my friends almost as much as I love Justine. I would save her if I could. Which is why I'll tell you what I shall tell you. Hold your breath, Little Fellow, because I've some hard news for you."

So I learned that in Neverness, the City of Light, the Last City, the City of a Thousand Plots, there was a plot to remake the Order. It was almost as if the City had been waiting for me to return from Agathange. Since then, a group of pilots and professionals had been plotting to change things according to their designs. And architect of the plot, Bardo told me sadly, reluctantly—the leader of the conspirators who would unmake the Timekeeper and perhaps everything else was my mother, the master cantor, Dama Moira Ringess.

19

The Parable
of the Mad King

*What good is a warrior without a war, a poet
without a poem?*
　　　　　　　—saying of the warrior-poets

Later that day I tried to find my mother. But her little house
in the Pilot's Quarter was empty. I went to her friends,
Helena Charbo and Kolenya Mor, among others, but no one
seemed to know where she was. And no one seemed willing
to admit that there was a plot to overthrow the Timekeeper,
much less remake the Order. Bardo had obviously been
listening too hard to the gossips, Kolenya told me. And
according to Burgos Harsha, who nervously picked at his
bushy eyebrows as I talked to him, there was no plot. "It's
true many of the pilots are unhappy," he said. "But who
would *plot* against the Timekeeper? Who—and I might add
that there *are* pilots and professionals who might be willing to
campaign for certain changes, but changes *within* the structure of the canons, of course, legally, legally—who would be
so stupid?"

When a few days passed and still my mother did not
return to her house, I began to worry. Li Tosh swore he had
seen my mother in the company of a warrior-poet one night
near the Merripen Green in the Farsider's Quarter. This was
proof that she was alive, he said, and I should not worry.
Perhaps my mother had finally taken a lover. But I did worry;
I was ill with worry. I did not believe she had taken a lover.
Then why else would she seek out a warrior-poet? Why do
otherwise reasonable people risk contact with warrior-poets,
if not to have their enemies murdered? And who was her

main enemy, if not Soli? She had slelled Soli's DNA to make
me, and this was a great crime. Soli could even demand that
the Timekeeper have her beheaded, if Soli desired revenge, if
he would acknowledge that I was his son. I *knew* Soli would
never admit this to anybody, not even to himself. But could
my mother be sure? No, she could not be sure, and so she
plotted her plots and hid in the Farsider's Quarter and
consorted with murderers—all without bothering to confide
in me. Obviously, she did not trust me.

If I have given the impression that the whole of our Order
was busy with plots and politics, this was not so. There was
always the quest. Great discoveries were still being made; for
a few, it was still a time of inspiration and daring. Two years
ago, while I hunted silk belly in Kweitkel's forest, a team of
five pilots had proposed to penetrate the Silicon God. Only
one of them, Anastasia of The Nave, had returned to tell of
wild spaces more impenetrable than those of the Entity.
Another pilot, the fabulous Kiyoshi, had come across a planet
believed to be the ancestral home of the Ieldra. Great deeds,
great inspirations: A programmer working with a splicer and a
historian (and what an unholy triad that must have been!) had
retraced the evolutionary pathways and had made a model of
early man's DNA. Master splicers were at work decoding this
modeled DNA, hoping to discover the secret of the ancient
gods. And of course I must mention the fabulist who created
a scenario in which Old Earth was *not* destroyed. This led
Sensim Wen, the semanticist, to reinterpret the meaning of a
Fravashi tone-poem, which in turn inspired a holist to propose
a different model for the progression of the Swarming. A
phantast, who studied the new model, retired to his den and
recreated a hologram of what he called "The Galaxy As It
Might Have Been." Finally a pilot studied this hologram and
journeyed near the inner edge of the Orion Arm where he
expected to find Old Earth. All to no avail, of course. But it
was a gallant attempt, if somewhat ridiculous and bizarre.

Just as bizarre, in its own way, was the memory—the
revelation—of Master Thomas Rane, the remembrancer. Because this revelation ignited a bitter argument among the
eschatologists and was to prove important in the crisis which
followed my return to the city, I record here his famous
words as he remembered down the dark spiral of racial
memory into his distant past.

I am named Kelkemesh, and my arms are young and brown as coffee. I am wearing the skin of the wolf I killed when I first became a man. The skin is wet, I am standing on a ridge high on a mountainside. It has rained, and there are mists in the green valleys below, a rainbow above. The stillness is very real. And then in the sky, at the rainbow's edge, there is a hole. There is a hole in the sky, and it is as black as my father's eye. From the hole comes a silvery light, and then white light; soon the entire sky is a ball of light. The light falls on me like a rainshower. As I open my mouth to scream, the light runs down my throat. My spine tingles. The light runs down my spine into my loins. My loins burn; my loins are afire; my loins fill with burning raindrops of light. It is the god Shamesh inside me and he is burning his image into my flesh. Shamesh is the sun; Shamesh is the light of the world; Shamesh speaks and his voice is my own: "You are the memory of Man, and the secret of immortality is inside you. You will live until the stars fall from the sky and the last man dies. That is my blessing and my curse." And then the light is gone. In the sky the rainbow is fading; the sky is a blue eggshell without holes.

I run down the mountainside to the huts of my father, Urmesh, the shaman. When I tell him I am filled with god-light, he tears his white hair and looks at me in anger and jealousy. He tells me I have been bitten by a demon; the gods do not touch men with their light. He prepares a burning spearpoint to let the demons out of my loins. My brothers are called to hold me. But I am full of fire and light, and I rise up and kill my brothers and kill Urmesh, who is no longer my father. Shamesh the god is my father. I take my bloody knife and wrap myself in my wolfskin and go down into the valleys to live among the peoples of the world.

It was argued that the great remembrancer's memory was a false memory. Perhaps. Or perhaps he really had relived the lives—and deaths—of his ancestors. I myself believed he had re-created the primal myth of the Ieldra and had encoded it as memory. But who could really know? During those chaotic, troubled days, who knew which of us were true seekers and which were merely fooling themselves?

Soon after this, on a day of mashy paste, the kind of snow that usually only falls in midwinter spring, the Timekeeper summoned me to his tower. Although the nature of life is change, there were a few things in my life which seemed to never change. That ageless, changeless man bade me sit on the familiar chair by the glass windows. The chair's black and red inlaid squares of jewood and shatterwood were as hard as they had always been. The clocks were ticking; the room was full of the pulsing, hissing and rhythmic beating of clocks. One of them—it was a glass-encased clock whose visible workings were carved of jewood—chimed. The Timekeeper, who paced back and forth before the curved windows, shot me a grim look as if to say the clock chimed for me.

"So, Mallory, you're looking exceptionally wary today."

He circled my chair so that he stood staring down at my profile. I inhaled the aroma of coffee on his breath. When I lifted my head to examine the spiderweb of lines at the corners of his eyes, he said, "No, don't turn your face to me. Resume the proper attitude—I've questions to ask you."

"And I would question you," I said. "Do I have anything to be wary about?"

"Ha, the young pilot would question *me*?"

"I'm not so young anymore, Timekeeper."

"Just a little while ago, less than four years ago, you sat in that chair and bragged how you were going to penetrate the spaces of the Entity. And now—"

"Four years . . . can be a long time."

"Don't interrupt me! And now you sit here almost as young and twice as foolish. Plots! I know certain pilots plot against me. Your mother—I'm told she's been talking with warrior-poets. Don't try to deny it. What I want to know, what I need to know is: Are you your mother's son or your Timekeeper's pilot?" He rapped his fingernails against the metal casing of one of the clocks. There was a "ping" of ringing chrome. "Tell me, Mallory, where's your devious mother, your bloody, slel-necker of a mother?"

"I don't know," I said. "And don't say that word, no matter what you think she's done."

"I *know* what your mother has done," he growled. "And I know who your father is."

"I don't have a father."

"Soli is your father."

"No."

"You're Soli's son—I should have seen it years ago, eh? Who would have thought your mother would be so bold as to slel his damn plasm? So, I know what your mother has done, and I'm reasonably sure she plans to murder Soli, possibly me as well—your goddamned mother!"

I gripped the chair's curved arms, which were shiny and worn from the hands of a thousand sweating pilots before me. I struggled to say nothing, to keep my hands locked to the chair.

"So, she's betrayed me, but you wouldn't betray me, would you, Mallory?"

"You think I'm a traitor, then?"

"Did I say you were a traitor? No, you're no traitor, I hope, but what about your friends?"

"Bardo has given me his word he won't—"

"Bardo!" he roared. "That tube of blubber, that disobedient mule! Even if I ignored his adulterous ways, his cowardly talk has already infected your friends. It's the younger pilots I'm thinking of: Jonathan Ede and Richardess and Delora wi Towt. And the older pilots, Neith and Nona, and Cristoble. And my professionals. And my academicians, such as Burgos Harsha, a hundred others. There's talk of them leaving the City forever. Schism! They're talking schism, the ruin of the Order!"

"There is talk of change," I agreed.

"Too great a change is death." He stepped over to the window. He pressed his forehead to the frosted glass, then sighed. "Do you think I'm deaf to what's being said? So, the Order has stagnated for a thousand years; so, the professions and professionals have grown rigid in their thoughtways; so, we need new dreams, new problems, new ways. Do we? What do you think?"

I thought what many of my Order thought: that pilots too often fell out against their fellow pilots in jealousy or rivalry, that profession vied with profession, and within the individual professions, different schools fought among themselves to impose their interpretation of the Order's purpose on all the others. The original, unifying vision of a spacefaring humanity discovering its place and purpose in the universe had dissolved into a hundred different philosophies, notions and conceits. "But isn't that the fate of all religions and orders, then? In the end, divisiveness and death?"

"You mean divisiveness and *war*. If I let my pilots go their separate ways, in the end there would be war—a great, filthy, bloody war."

I smiled because I thought the Timekeeper was being overly dramatic. I quoted the historians, saying, "War is a dead art, as dead as Old Earth. There are restraints, aren't there? The lessons of history? I don't think anyone in our Order would wish to reinvent war."

"And what of the war between Greater Cihele and Mio Luz?"

"That was a skirmish," I said. "Not a real war."

"Not a real war! Ha, what do you know of war? The tychists dropped *fusion* bombs on the determinists. How many were killed? Thirty million?"

I shook my head, trying to remember my history lessons. "I don't know," I said. "Thirty something." And then a few moments later, the memory came. "Thirty million four hundred and fifty four thousand—approximately."

"And you call that a 'skirmish?' So, call it what you will, why do you think this skirmish didn't spread into a 'real war?' Restraint, hell! What do you think keeps the Civilized Worlds at peace? It's because war is ruinously expensive to wage—that's the most important reason. Even though the Greater Cihele and Mio Luz are connected by a single pathway, it took the incompetent tychist pilots with their filthy fusion bombs—those few who survived the manifold—it took them thirty years to reach Mio Luz. Our rawest journeyman could make the journey in thirty days."

"Time is mutable," I said, mocking one of his famous sayings. But my smile faded as I accepted his point. If journeying through the manifold became easy, war would become easy, too. And who could journey as easily and elegantly as a pilot of our Order? What could be more disastrous than a war between our Order's different factions? "But even if war were easy," I objected, "it would be too terrible, and no one would go to war against any other, I think. Besides, skirmish or war, the people of the Greater Cihele and Mio Luz were insane. Most peoples and planets love peace."

Unexpectedly, he walked over and stood above my chair. He scowled and said, "Mallory, Mallory, you've been bludgeoned, cut, swived, hated, loved and taught the truth but you're still naive." He brushed back the white hair from his forehead and sighed. "Naive, I say! What's the essence of history? The desire for peace? The desire for peace? Ha! War's the price of our quest for power; war's been the curse of man for twenty thousand years. It's the nature of things that no one can choose peace, but anyone can make all others face war. Why do you think the Earth was destroyed? Shall I tell you a parable of Earth's history?"

I shifted about in my chair, trying to get comfortable. Because I had no choice but to listen to his parable, I said, "Tell me."

He smiled and cleared his throat. "Once a time," he began, "all men lived in tribes and the air was clean and there was food for all, and peace was the law of the Earth. But then one tribe, because they loved themselves more than their mother planet, grew deaf to this law. So they fell into insanity. They grew too large and too powerful. They found that it was easier to steal their bread from others than to bake it themselves. They coveted an empire, a life of ease. They sent their armies westward against the four nearest tribes, each of which had a great love of peace. But peace they could not have. The first tribe faced spear with spear, but they were too few, and the insane tribe slaughtered them down to the last man. The women, of course, were raped and given hoes to slave their lives away with their children in the wheatfields. The second tribe, seeing what had happened to the first tribe, flung down their spears, for the moment, and kissed the feet of the insane tribe's king. They pleaded for their lives. If only the king would allow them to keep their wives and children, they would be good warriors and do as the king commanded. Thus the second tribe was absorbed and the insane tribe grew larger still. The third tribe, who loved their freedom as they loved their lives, fled southward to the desert where the living was hard and there was barely food and water enough for all. The fourth tribe wanted neither to be exterminated, nor to be absorbed, nor to flee. They loved their land passionately. And so their king, who was a visionary man, ordered his warriors to make their spears longer than those of the insane tribe's warriors. When battle came the greater numbers of the insane tribe were checked by the longer spears of the fourth tribe. So neither tribe could prevail. Then the visionary king, who had come to relish the taste of war, realized that in the next battle, the insane tribe

would return with yet longer spears. 'We must have more
warriors!' the visionary king exclaimed. And he turned his
gaze further westward, and his armies enslaved the western
tribes and made still longer spears. And so the fourth tribe
became as insane as the insane tribe. In this manner, like a
disease, the habit of war spread outward to the farthest tribes
of the Earth. The tribes grew into empires which destroyed
the nearer empires, and they lamented that they could not
make war on the farthest empires because the distances were
too great for their armies to cross. At last one king, the
cleverest of all, attached rockets to the butt end of his men's
spears and fusion bombs to their tips. When all the kings of
all the empires of the Earth did likewise, the clever king
observed that war was obsolete and impossible. If any empire
cast its spears at another, he said, it would assure its own
destruction, for against the rain of spears tipped with fusion
bombs even the finest and most costly shields were useless.
And so there was peace on Earth . . . until the court fool of the
clever king reminded him that he had forgotten one thing."

He paused here in his fervid speech to wipe the sweat
from his forehead. He looked at me expectantly to see if I
would ask him what the clever king had forgotten. Although I
did not want to hear the words of an allegorical fool, I asked,
"And what had the clever king forgotten?"

The Timekeeper grinned and replied, "He'd forgotten
that he and all the people of his empire and all the empires of
the world were insane."

I held my breath and asked, "And then?"

"You know the end of the parable," he said softly. "You
know."

I was dutifully thoughtful for a while. Except for the
ticking and clicking of the clocks and our syncopated breathing, the room was silent. Outside the window the snow fell in
sheets. I was cold, but he was sweating. Beads of sweat rolled
down his flat cheeks, down the hard line of his chin. I could
not help smiling and saying, "Timekeeper, it seems that
you've forgotten one thing."

"Eh?"

"The third tribe, the one that fled to the desert where the
living was hard—what ever became of that tribe?"

He laughed then, a deep, rich laugh full of irony and

sadness. I sat in my chair squeezing my forearms. It was one of the few times I had heard him laugh.

"We're the third tribe," he said. "And deepspace is the desert. All the peoples of the Civilized Worlds have fled from war; we're all hibakusha. And there's peace in the galaxy, a fragile, relative peace, but there are always new tribes waiting to fall into insanity. Why do you think we must tyrannize the fallaways? It's because we can't allow these tribes to grow. Our Order and the Order of the Warrior-Poets—for three thousand years we've kept the peace."

"The warrior-poets!" I exclaimed. "They're murderers."

"Precisely. Few know this, but the warrior-poets were founded precisely to exterminate insane tribes and insane kings. Terror was their tool, and they used it well. No king could think of warring against his neighbors without fearing that a warrior-poet would assassinate him."

"You speak in the past tense, Timekeeper."

"So I do. That's because the warrior-poets have been in decline for a thousand years. Now they're not so concerned with preserving the peace. In the process of breeding their assassins—and it took them centuries—they developed a religion to help them face their inevitable deaths. And often, these were suicidal deaths, because kings, mad or not, are hard to kill, eh? This religion has become their reason for existing. Now they seek disciples, not peace."

Again, like a shark, he circled around my chair. He began to rant. Only our Order, he said, could preserve the peace. But if our Order divided in two, there would be no *order*. (This is my word, not the Timekeeper's. He despised puns almost as much as punsters.) Eventually our most precious knowledge would be scattered like pearls beneath the feet of a harijan.

I thought about his words for a long time. Because I disagreed with his fundamental elitism, and because I sensed a contradiction in his beliefs, I said, "But we can't keep our secrets forever. Information is like a virus. It spreads."

"Viruses can be quarantined," he snapped. And then, more ominously, "Viruses can be exterminated, too."

"But it's the Order's purpose to discover knowledge," I said.

His voice grew low and ugly like a wolf's growl. He said, "Knowledge must be cherished and used wisely, eh? Not squandered like a foolish pilot dropping City disks into the palm of a whore."

Because my back was aching and I was tired, I began to reposition myself in the chair. He caught me turning toward him, and barked out, "Don't move, now! Remain in the proper attitude."

I suddenly did not want to remain in the proper attitude. I was tired of him staring at me while I could not look at him. I stood up, turned my head, and caught him unguarded. The look on his face surprised me. His eyes were wide open and his lips set into a shy smile as if he were a boy looking at the firefalls for the first time. He was looking inside himself, remembering, perhaps even remembrancing. At first, I did not know how I knew this. His eyes were black pools as blind as any scryer's. He was looking many places at once, examining future possibilities and dreaming private dreams. Only for a moment did it last, this look of acceptance, of sad innocence and wonder. Then, like a steamy breath on a winter day, it was gone, replaced by harsh vertical lines of defiance and ancient grief. His eyes glowed with dark lights and his lips turned down as he thundered, "Sit down! Restrain yourself and sit down, damn you!"

I did not sit down. I nudged the chair with my foot and said, "I'm tired of sitting."

I stared at him. I could not imagine what had occasioned his lapse into the contemplative. Then I realized—and it was one of the more wrenching realizations of my life—I saw at a flash that this was no mere lapse. He was a man divided, a seeker tortured by an eternal inner war between his dreams and his bitter experience—this I had always known. But suddenly I knew more. I was sensing the minutia about him: the tension of the little muscles above the eyes; his archaic speech habits; his harsh philosophies; his sour smell; and thousands of other things. Somehow, I was processing this rich current of information. I was sure I was reading him. Whereas most such men (and Soli, my moody father is one such) spend their moments vacillating between light and dark like a terrified child being whipped back and forth across an ice ring by two of his schoolmates, the Timekeeper lived within conflicting realities simultaneously. He was truly a man who lived at the top of a frozen, inner mountain above other men. For him evil and good did not exist. Or rather, they existed not as opposites but as different flavors of reality, like honey and black, acid coffee, both of which at any moment must be tasted, swallowed, and if possible, savored. In the terminology of the Entity, he was a multiplex man, part hero, part rogue, heretic, tychist, determinist, atheist and god-worshipper—all of these and a myriad of others at once. If the face he showed to the Order and the ambassadors of the Civilized Worlds was the singular, stern face of a just tyrant, it was the face he chose to wear. And more, it was the persona he chose to *be*. It was wrenching to realize that he had this power of choice. I had always thought of him as a man utterly divided by the reality of dying and death. Now I saw that this was not so. Like all great men, he had a vision. It was what he lived for. It was this vision, the tiny part of which I glimpsed, that terrified me.

"So, young Mallory, what are you looking at; what do you see?"

"What should I see? Am I a cetic, then, to read your programs as I would the poems in your book?"

"I, myself, have often wondered what you are, what you might become."

I rubbed the side of my nose, then said, "I see a man seemingly torn apart by contradictions. But there is a fundamental unity, isn't there? You won't allow farsiders the simplest of our secrets, and you were and are suspicious of the secrets of the Ieldra. I see—"

"No man has ever talked to me like this before! No man!"

"I see this passion of yours to protect, at the same time you—"

"Quiet now! I can't have my pilots—or anyone else—reading me, can I? You see too damn much."

"I see what I see."

"It's dangerous to see too much," he said. "The scryers know this. What's their little saying?—'Eyes once blinded by the light are now truly blind.'"

His eyes were burning stones as he said this, and then he bowed his head and rubbed his snowy temples. I had always supposed that he had a sort of grandfatherly affection for me, but now I saw that the requirements of his private vision would always submerge and drown his kindness. When it had suited his purpose to rescue me from my own impetuousness, he had given me a book of poems and saved my life. If my death would serve his dreams or plans—well, as he had said, viruses can be exterminated.

"Why did you summon me?" I asked him.

"Why must you question me, damn you!" He clenched his fists and the muscles along his neck tensed. It was as if he were hardening himself to make an agonizing decision he did not want to make. I thought that since he had little compassion for himself, he would finally make the harshest of choices. He must have feared that compassion toward another might weaken him and eat away at the steely coil of his being as rust slowly devours the interior mechanism of a clock.

"Why am I here?" I repeated.

He paced to the window and swiped at the glass with his fingernails as if he were a bear digging at a sheet of ice. The nails dragged and scraped, leaving sharp, clear streaks cutting the white frost. He was quiet for a moment, and then the breath rushed out of him all at once.

"It would be the greatest of catastrophes," he said, "if one of my pilots were to solve the Continuum Hypothesis only to have the secret spread like a virus. To fall from any star instantly to any other—so, you understand, only *my* pilots must have that knowledge."

"The Hypothesis may be unprovable," I said.

"It would be better if that were so."

"In any case, I haven't proven it. The Tycho and Dov Danladi, Soli too—they struggled all their lives to prove the Great Theorem. Who am I to prove it, then?"

"Ha, you've changed!" he mocked. "Who *are* you?—this I would like to know. What have the damn gods done to you? We'd all like to know this, eh? You return like a ghost from Agathange, and, suddenly, seemingly, you've gained modesty . . . and other things."

"What do you mean?"

"You know, Mallory, you know. Ten days ago your Bardo ruined part of the Tycho's Monument, didn't he? Tell me, what happened that day?"

"Bardo drank himself into a stupor and broke one of the crystals."

"My novices tell me that you fell into slowtime—is this true?"

"How could it be true? How is it possible to enter slowtime without the aid of a computer?"

He pounded his fist against the window sill and snarled out, "Why must you answer a question with a question, damn you! Tell me, *did* you enter into slowtime?"

"Some say I did," I admitted. "But the truth is, I stopped time."

"*Stopped* time? Ha, I hadn't thought it possible! But you are a truthful man, aren't you? You wouldn't lie to your Lord Horologe. Why, Mallory, why are you so taken with this holy notion of truth?"

"I don't know."

"*Struth!* There's truth and there's truth. Truth's as mutable as time."

"I don't believe that."

He rubbed his eyes and looked at me. "You must promise me a thing, young Mallory. If you should ever discover the proof of the Great Theorem, you must not inform the cetics nor akashics nor the cantors nor your fellow pilots. You must tell no one except me."

I stood motionless while I thought at great speed. If I ever solved the Hypothesis and confided in the Timekeeper, the knowledge would disappear like light down a black hole.

"I've vowed to seek truth," I said.

"You've vowed to seek truth, not to disseminate it and spray it all about like an old man's piss."

"In front of you in the Pilot's Hall, four years ago, I took this vow, to seek wisdom and truth even though the seeking might lead to ruin and death."

"Ruin and death! Whose death, damn you! Is it wisdom to let truth ruin the Order?"

"All my life, I've dreamed of proving the Great Theorem."

"Dreams, what are dreams? Why are you so damn stubborn? Why? Why are you?" And then he groaned out, "Whose death? Whose death will it be?"

"All my life, and to this day, I've dreamed of an Order, a whole universe, where wisdom and truth are one."

"Noble words; naive words—how weary I am of words!" There was an almost unbearable tension in his voice, in each of his steely words. "Either give me your promise or do not."

"I can't give you my promise."

"So."

He spoke this final word mournfully, regretfully, as if he could not bear to shape his lips around the simple consonant and vowel. The sound hung in the air like the low ringing of a bell. For a while he looked at me. And in his eyes, love and hate and another passion I thought of as will, or will toward fate, his fate and perhaps a universal fate, which he must have known was the most terrible and lonely fate of all. Then he scowled and pushed his palms at me and turned away, looking out the window. He dismissed me. Before leaving his tower for what I thought would be the last time, I looked out, too, down at the novices who skated by, oblivious of the judgment that had just occurred high above their snow-speckled heads.

20

The Rings of Qallar

*If ever I spread tranquil skies over myself and
soared on my own wings into my own skies; if I
swam playfully in the deep light-distances and the
bird-wisdom of my freedom came—but bird-wisdom
speaks thus: "Behold, there is no above, no below!
Throw yourself around, out, back, you who are
light! Sing! Speak no more! Are not all words heavy
and made to die? Are not all words lies to those who
are light? Sing! Speak no more!" Oh, how should I
not lust after eternity and after the nuptial ring of
rings, the ring of recurrence?*

*Never yet have I found the woman from whom I
wanted children, unless it be this woman I love: for I
love you, O eternity.*

For I love you, O eternity!
     —seventh death meditation of the warrior-poets

The historians believe that near the end of the second
Swarming Century, the warrior-poets perfected the art of
using bio-computer bits to replace parts of the brain. Unlike
the Agathanians, however, the warrior-poets applied their art
to different ends. Slel-mime, that unspeakable crime in which a
poet's cunningly crafted programs run the brain of his victim,
is only one application. The poets are also known to cark
parts of their own brains. They do this to give themselves
power over their time-sense, so that they can slow time
without the aid of an exterior computer. And for other
reasons. It is said that they alter their own brains' profoundest
programs in order to erase their fear of death. Indeed, the

cetics believe they are utterly devoid of fear. In this respect, the poets are unnatural beings, for fear is as natural to humans as breathing air. To live, to feel the starlight in our eyes and the joy of the deep light-distances, to *be*—this is all we know. To be *not* is unimaginable and therefore terrifying. The birds who spread their wings to the sun, the silvery bottom fish gliding through their world of dark, silent joys, and even the sentient computers, in their ecstatic inward crackling of electricity and lightning information flows—all living things, in some tiniest particle of their beings, must fear the final mystery.

When I began seeking out various of the City's warrior-poets, seeking in the bars, hospices, ice rings and cafes that they frequented, Bardo alternately accused me of being fearless and of having a will to suffer this mystery. "Are you mad?" he said to me a few days after my meeting with the Timekeeper. "Oh, you are mad—I've always known you are. These poets kill because they like death, don't you know?"

"That's true," I said. "They worship death. But I'd like to find my mother—it's worrisome the way she's disappeared."

I was very worried about her plotting with warrior-poets. I planned to find the warrior-poet with whom she had been keeping company these past days. But because I was a novice in the seeking of human beings, he found me instead.

Adjacent to the Hyacinth Gardens, along the Run where it dips south toward the Old City, is a collection of twelve buildings made entirely of exotic woods. Some of the buildings are cavernous structures housing the historians' artifacts and relics; a few are somewhat smaller. Their elegant, polished rosewood rooms are given over solely to the display of art, alien and human, ancient and modern. Although all twelve buildings are called the Art Museum, it is the smaller buildings that hold the Fravashi frescoes and tone poems, the Urradeth ice sculptures and other treasures. The smallest building, a classic rectangular hall faced with shatterwood pillars, is the House of Remembrance. Its four sections are filled with many rooms, but the most famous of them is the Hibakusha Gallery. There reside some of the oldest frescoes depicting unbelievable scenes of chaos and war. There the tone poems build and swirl and fuse, unfolding the epic battles of the Holocaust Century. I had come to view the famous frescoe, "Humanity Rising," which ran along the north wall for a hundred feet. When I was worried, or when I was tired and cold from skating the streets of the City, I liked to sit on one of the Gallery's benches, to breath in the smells of warm wood and flowers; I liked to watch the fresco move, the pretty colors. It was one of my favorite things to do.

It was late afternoon, and I was not alone. Next to me, near the center of the long room, there were a couple of fabulists, no doubt seeking inspirations for work of their own. And at the edge of the carpet behind my bench, near the bubbling fountain, were a group of Friends of God off Simoom. They were each very tall and very thin, and they stank of garlic and goatroot and other exotic spices. They had a habit of twisting the silver chains binding their long, black hair. The habit annoyed me, as did their hissing. As they whispered, they hissed, the sibilant sounds rushing out of their mouths in quick, choked-off breezes. One of them said, "See? Here is evidence the Swarming began during the Holocaust Century, not after. It is as was thought." I looked at the painting's bubbling blues and greens and whites. I watched silvery rockets rising from Old Earth's oceans, but whether or not the rockets were ships launched toward the stars or missiles carrying fusion weapons was difficult to tell. Then one of the rockets divided into two, the two into four and so on, and suddenly there were the bright stars of the Eta Carina nebula, and the four ships had become four thousand streamers of light. The light spread outward in great, glowing balls. In a flash it filled the nebula with a luminous white. For a moment the entire center section of the painting was brilliantly white, and then splotches of gray appeared at random to mar the brilliance. The white darkened to sky-blue as the blotches began to take shape, and a thousand black, mushroom clouds began rising up from Old Earth's atmosphere. I was not at all certain that the painting was the "evidence" that the Friends of God sought. It seemed more likely that for the Fravashi who had made the fresco, the Swarming *was* the Holocaust.

After a while I became vaguely aware of subtle changes in the muffled sounds and odors of the room. The stink of goatroot and garlic had subsided; disturbed voices and the quick rustle of fabric had replaced the whispering. Then there was silence, and I smelled the sudden aroma of kana oil. Warrior-poets, I knew, were famous for wearing efferves-

cent kana oil perfumes. I turned my head, and there stood a
deep-chested man of medium height who was plainly not
interested in watching the painting. He was watching me. He
studied my face as a master player might a chessboard, with
an intense, almost fanatic concentration. Immediately I knew
that he was a warrior-poet; all warrior-poets are cut from the
same cells. He had the curly black hair, the coppery skin and
sinuous neck of his kind. He was beautiful, as the highly bred
races often are. How well-proportioned his fine nose and
broad cheek planes seemed, how balanced his sculpted jaw,
what a beautiful, fearful symmetry! But it was his unique
poet's eyes that possessed the most compelling beauty: His
eyes were deep indigo, almost purple; his eyes were vivid,
clear, soulful, utterly aware—and utterly without fear. Although he looked young, I thought he must be very old, for
only a man who had been brought back to youth many times
could have such eyes. But no, I remembered, warrior-poets
do not restore themselves to youth. Worshipping death as
they do, they believe it is the greatest sin—indeed the only
sin—to prolong one's life past "the moment of the possible."
The warrior-poet, then, was as young as I.

He walked down the edge of the carpet until he stood
almost on top of me. His movements were graceful, quick,
exquisite. "My name is Dawud," he said, and his voice
flowed like molten silver. "And you are Mallory Ringess,
aren't you? I've heard the strangest things about you."

Except for the shifting, throbbing painting and the other
frescoes on the far walls, the room was empty. No one trusts a
warrior-poet, I thought. I examined the black, sable cloak he
wore and the eye-catching, rainbow kamelaika beneath. His
clothes were richly made and beautiful, though the poets
were known to care nothing of riches and but little for beauty.
I turned my eyes to his hands, looking for the rings. All
warrior-poets wear two rings, one each on the little finger of
either hand. The rings are made of various metals and can be
of different color, green or yellow, indigo or blue. There are
seven colors, and in the manner of the spectrum's progression, each marks the level of the warrior-poet's attainments.
A violet ring means he is of the seventh and lowest circle; a
red ring is given to those rare individuals who attain the first
circle. The left-hand ring is the ring of the poet, while the
one on the right hand is the warrior's ring. It is said that no

one has ever been at once a great enough poet and warrior to wear two red rings. On the little finger of his left hand was a green ring. He was of the poets' fourth circle, then; his poetic prowess was not extraordinary. But around his other finger, cut from one of Qallar's artificial metals, he wore a red ring. The ring seemed to glow to match the fiery reds of the painting, and he said, "You have been looking for me, I have been told."

"Do you know my mother? Are you the poet who . . . do you know my mother?"

"I know your mother well."

"Where is she?"

He ignored my question, and he bowed his head politely. "I would have wanted to meet you in any case, to see the son of the mother. I've collected the stories about you. One day, if I live, I'll write a poem. I've heard you stopped time fifteen days ago, saved your friend from dying."

"You shouldn't listen to gossip."

"You shouldn't have saved your friend from his moment. And it isn't gossip, as I know. I know, too, about Agathange. We poets are familiar with—"

"Yes," I interrupted, "you're masters of slel-mime."

"You use that slandered term."

"You create human beings robbed of free will."

He smiled and said, "Do you think you know about free will?"

"You're assassins who kill for pleasure."

"You think so?"

I was confused, distracted by his teeth and nice smile, lulled by his warm, reassuring manner. I said, "You *do* kill, then?"

"Often."

"And your victims are sometimes innocent?"

He smiled and his eyes sparkled. "I have never seen an innocent woman or man, never seen an innocent child—have you, Mallory Ringess? *You* know there is no true innocence. No, don't protest because I can see the knowledge in the furrows of your forehead."

I rubbed back and forth above my eyes and accused, "You poets—you're death worshippers, I think."

"Certainly. But if you please—tell me about worship? Or

shall I tell you? Dario Redring once composed a poem about worship. Shall I recite it?"

"No," I said, "I hate poetry."

"If that is true, then you are crippled in your soul. But I don't think you hate poetry."

"Where's my mother?"

"She is waiting for me."

"Waiting where?"

He again ignored my question and pointed toward the corner of the painting; the interior of the Orion Nebula was lit with stars where some of the first swarms of human beings had made their new homes. "Pretty," he said. And then, "How, would you suppose, the prettiness of this painting is protected?"

"I don't know what you mean."

"If someone were to ruin or steal this painting, what would happen?"

"Why would anyone ruin the painting?" I asked. "And if anyone stole it, the robots would stop him from leaving the museum, I think."

"And if by chance the robots were ruined too, of what crime would our hypothetical thief be guilty? Theft? Desecration? Murder?"

"You can't murder a robot," I said. I shrugged my shoulders because I didn't know where his sequence of thought would converge.

"I am pleased you understand, Mallory—you can't really murder a robot, can you?"

I made a fist and said, "People aren't robots."

He was silent and he smiled at me.

"You carve words to fit your purposes," I said.

"True, I am a poet after all. And you are beginning to see with a warrior's eyes: You can't murder a robot because they are not really alive. They can't program themselves, and they have no true awareness."

I stood up and zipped my kamelaika. "I shouldn't be talking to you. I don't understand why the Timekeeper allows you out on the streets."

"Because Neverness is a free city, and a warrior-poet must have his freedom."

"Freedom," I said, and I shook my head.

"There is another reason, too. Your Timekeeper has his robot-fears just as everyone does. Almost everyone."

"You threaten the Timekeeper, then?"

"I didn't say that, exactly."

"You implied it."

"You must listen to a poet very carefully," he said, and he touched his lips with his green ring. "We speak with silver tongues, and sometimes our words have multiple meanings."

"I'm here to watch the painting, not to listen."

He smiled, bowed to the painting and then said, "If it pleases you, I will listen to you. Tell me about Soli's chambers, and I will listen. Is there an outer chamber adjoining the inner—is that true? How large are the chambers? How many flights of stairs leading to them?"

We talked for a while, or rather, he asked me questions to which I did not respond. He wanted to know the foods Soli preferred, what position he slept in and other personal things. I listened to his words carefully. I immediately understood that he intended to assassinate Soli.

I stood very still before saying, "Go away. I won't help you murder Soli or anyone else."

He touched his red warrior's ring to his red lips. "There are stories told about your journey to the Alaloi—it is said you know about murder."

"What has my mother told you?"

"That Soli is your father; that you hate him; that he hates you."

I stared at him as my muscles tightened; I wondered if my time-sense dilated, if I would be quick enough to kill him before he killed me. I stared at his ring. I did not think I would be quick enough.

He read my face and said, "Don't be afraid to get too close to death. Don't be afraid to die."

"All living things are afraid to die."

"No, you're exactly wrong," he said, and he smiled. "The only truly alive beings are those unafraid to die."

I made fists with my hands and told him, "You imply that human beings aren't truly alive, then. That's absurd."

"Human beings are sheep," he said.

"And what are sheep?"

"Sheep are like shagshay only stupider. On Old Earth, and still on many planets, they are kept in flocks for their wool and meat."

"Human beings are *not* sheep."

"You think not? Have you heard the parable of the cetic and his sheep?"

I looked at the painting, at the progression of exploding stars that was the beginning of the Vild's brilliant chaos. I heard people walking by outside the Gallery, but none of them decided to come in. "The Timekeeper is fond of parables," I said.

He must have taken this as a sign of encouragement for he continued, "Once a time on Urradeth there was a cetic who had a great flock of sheep. But the cetic was very busy fashioning metaprograms which he hoped would control his own baser, more mundane programs. Consequently, he had little time to tend his flock. Often they wandered off into the forest or stumbled into snowdrifts, and worse, they ran away because they knew that the cetic wanted their wool and their meat."

I glanced at the doorway, measuring distances with my eyes as Dawud went on with his parable: "One day the cetic found an answer to his problem. He programmed his sheep to believe that they were immortal. He convinced them that no harm would be done to them when they were skinned; the sheep believed it would be very good for them, even pleasurable. Then he wrote a program to make his sheep believe he was a good master who loved his flock so much that he would do anything for them. Thirdly, through the sheep's dull brains he ran a program which reassured them that if anything bad were going to happen to them, it was not going to happen right away, certainly not that day. Therefore they could get on with their mechanical thoughts of eating grass and mating and lying about in the sun. Last of all—and this was the cetic's most cunning program—he convinced the sheep that they were not sheep at all; to some of them he suggested that they were wolves, to some that they were thallows, to others that they were men, and to a few that they were really cunning cetics.

"After this all his worries about his sheep ended. He devoted all his cunning towards redesigning his deepest programs. The sheep never ran away again. They quietly awaited the day when the cetic would come for their wool and meat. And the cetic—"

"And the cetic," I interrupted, "lived happily ever after. I don't think I like your parable—men are not sheep."

It occurred to me that I was protesting too strenuously, too loudly. The rosewood panels above the painting echoed my words of denial. I tried to understand the warrior-poet's dictum that to really live, one must "live as one already dead." It is a strange, merciless philosophy, but then, the warrior-poets are as strange as the system which breeds them, and they know nothing of mercy. They breed for perfection; it is said that their splicers have tampered with the male and female genomes, completely editing out the extraneous and redundant DNA. On Qallar, each year a million identical zygotes are quickened and a million identical, perfect babies are brought into the light of day. But they are not really so perfect. Some are killed at random immediately after they have drawn their first breaths. This is supposed to be a demonstration that we live in a random, merciless universe. Many are killed because they cannot learn the deadly skills of a warrior or the delicate words of a poet. When they are twelve years old, the warriors-to-be are given knives and grouped together in pairs. Only one of each pair survives this cruel combat, and then pairs are made again and again until perhaps only a tenth of the original million are left. A similar procedure of poetry competitions culls the most poetic of the children. The losers, the stammering children who cannot craft beautiful, clever words in the face of death, are invited to kill themselves. Those who are too cowardly to perform this "noblest" of actions are tortured to death by the others. The torture, Kolenya Mor once told me, is not meant as a punishment. It is supposed to induce the unfortunate child to reprogram his death fear at the last moment, to enable him to ultimately savor his ephemeral life even as it slips away. There are other, worse trials that the warrior-poets must endure as they grow older. There are alterations of body and brain, the subtle molding of a man's soul. No one, not even the eschatologists, knows very much of these trials. Two things, though, seem certain: that every moment of a warrior-poet's life is meant to smoothly lead him to his death, and that of the original million, only a hundred or so survive to wear the rings of Qallar.

Dawud smiled and he looked at me intensely, as if he could read my deepest programs. He was a man who smiled too often, but I must admit he had a beautiful, intense smile. In a way, he was the most intense person I have ever known.

"The cetic who founded the Order of Warrior-poets," he said, "did not live *happily* ever after. What is happiness, after all? The cetic, after much hard work, finally decoded his death program, or, I should say, his fear-of-death program. He purged it from his brain, from his very neurons. And lo! —there are many poems written of this—the cetic discovered that it is the fear of death which enslaves us. You might say the dread of the dying self sends us stumbling blindly about our daily tasks as if we are nothing but sleepwalking robots programmed to feed and drink and copulate. Fear is the drug which makes us sleep. But when the fear is gone—no, Pilot, please don't leave quite yet—when fear is extinguished it is like plunging into a pool of cold water. To awaken is wonderful. To see clearly, to taste the intensity of each instant of life—this is what the warrior-poets teach; this is why we live; this is why we die."

I made a move to leave, then. I did not want to listen to a murderer tell me how life should be lived. But Dawud held up his large, square hand and said, "Please don't go. There is much of the poet inside me that speaks to the warrior in you. And inside of you—such secrets! Tell me, Pilot, because I have come so far to know: What is it like to die?"

"What can I tell you that you don't already know?" I asked him. "Have I died? Some say I have, but what is death, then? Now, I live, and that's what matters—I'm tired of thinking about life and death, ill with worrying about meaning or the lack of meaning. You, with your need to embrace your own death, to live intensely—or die—no matter the pain you'd bring to yourself or others—you think pain can wake a man up to intensity, but there's a hell of being too awake, too aware, isn't there?"

And he said simply, quoting his masters, "He who would hold light must endure burning."

I rubbed my temples, looking down at the edge of the carpet against the glossy floor. "Give me darkness, then," I said.

"What is it like to live again?"

Because his questions irked me, because I was suddenly feeling contrary and as mischievous as a young journeyman, I said, "To live, I die."

"You like to mock people, don't you? Please don't mock me; it would be senseless to mock me. I would like to know about the Agathanians, about their designs, about their programs, about you."

"Isn't the art of Agathange similar to the art of the warrior-poets?"

"It is similar but not the same."

"You poets—when you reprogram your victims—"

"They are not 'victims,' Pilot. They are converts to the Way of the Warrior."

"But you rob them of their free will, it's said."

He flipped back the edge of his cloak, exposing his muscular arm. "This question of free will is subtle and treacherous, and we won't solve it here. Better men than we have enslaved their minds wondering about free will. Let us say that a living thing is free, relatively free, the greater its independence from its environment. The more it depends on other living systems, the more its activities are necessarily shaped by its environment. Independence increases with complexity; the greater the complexity, the greater the amount of free will. A virus, for instance, must largely do what it is programmed to do. A man is more complex."

"Then you imply that men have free will," I said.

"Men are robots and sheep."

"I can't believe that."

"*Some* men have free will some of the time," he said as he smiled.

I reached into the leg sheath of my kamelaika and removed one of my skate blades. I held it flat in my hand. "I believe I have the freedom to drop this or not, as I wish."

"Free will is illusory."

"I will *not* drop it," I said, sliding it back in the sheath. "A free choice, freely made."

"But not so free, after all, Pilot. Why did you choose not to drop it? Because this fine, wood floor is polished so nicely? You wouldn't want to scar the fine floor, would you? You have a respect for finely made things—I can tell. But from where did this respect come? Who programmed it into you? You can't tell me, but I can tell you: It was your mother, years ago when you were a boy. She taught you about beauty in the unspoken ways she appreciated beauty, with the silent language of her eyes and hands. Your mother loves beautiful things, even though she doesn't know of her love, even if she would deny it if you asked her."

I pulled the skate blade back out and pointed it at him. "I'm afraid to ask how you know so much about my mother."

"Your mother is a complex woman, confused sometimes, but I have helped her see things more simply."

"Tell me."

"Your mother came to me freely. Of her own free will she asked for my help. It is this way with everyone we help."

"You've helped her lose herself, then. You poets—"

"We poets replace useless programs with new ones. To help them run their—"

"My mother is not a robot, damn you!"

He took a step back and smiled at me. Although he must have known I was trembling to kill him, he seemed quite relaxed. "Your mother's metaprogram has been rewritten," he said almost casually. "Her master program, her defining program—it is the same way with all converts, religious or otherwise."

"Tell me what this new program is, then."

"Will you tell me the code of *your* new program, Mallory Ringess? The program that the Agathanians wrote into their virus?"

"Is that why you've come here?"

"The program, Mallory, the metaprogram—you tell me. What makes you run? What runs you?"

I squeezed the skate blade and the edges cut into the callouses on my palm. "If I knew, if I knew—how can I tell you what I don't know, damn you!"

"We should all know the code of our programs," he said. "Otherwise we can never be free."

So saying, he turned to face the painting and let out a sigh. "The Fravashi are very clever with their living paintings. This is a pretty picture—I always enjoy watching the bacteria colonies move across the painting. The programs are so elegant, controlled, and yet unpredictable."

As if the frescoe had been listening to his words (or perhaps Dawud had timed his words with exquisite precision), just then, at the center of the painting a star cluster flared into prominence. The most brilliant of the stars was the Poet's Glory; orbiting that hellish, blue binary was a small, ocher speck representing the planet Qallar. As the perspective shifted and magnified, the planet grew to the size of a snow apple. Dawud looked at me, smiled, then plunged his hand into the folds of his cloak. He removed a knife; it was a double-edged murderous, shining thing. He held it in front of me. "Is my will free?" he asked me. "Can I let go of this knife or not, as I will?"

I was suddenly aware of the pungent pepperiness of kana oil, the dreadfully slow inrushing of my breath. He closed his fingers around the knife. He moved very fast. He was balanced and fluid as he entered into the slowtime state of the warrior-poet. My own time sense began to dilate and slow, otherwise I could never have tracked his motions. Between his thumb and forefinger he held the knife. He whipped his arm forward. The knife tore through the painting's clear outer membrane into the heart of the red sphere that was Qallar. There it quivered. A thick soup of red and orange paints bubbled from the wound, coloring the knife with liquid rust. The bubbling subsided and slowed to a pulsing ooze and then stopped altogether. Like a quickly hardening lava, the paint had completely covered the haft of the knife. It looked like a volcano uplifted from the painting's surface.

"Look at the painting, Pilot."

I stared at the desecration, horrified. As I stared, I noticed a peculiar thing: The painting was healing itself. Dawud, whatever his intentions had been, had failed to destroy it. There was a violent surge of scarlets and bursting orange as the colors reorganized themselves, revealing the most startling pattern of design. I had seen the fresco many times before, but never had I watched the drama which played itself out in front of us. From Qallar's running surface a red blob of paint broke loose and began migrating across the length of the painting. As it drifted, it glowed and divided and grew. The blob—it began to look more and more like a twentyday fetus—fell through a black pool of living paint until it reached a small yellow star that I recognized as Darrein Luz. Then there were many stars, and for a moment the red blob disappeared into a shower of light. Suddenly, in the spaces beyond Darrein Luz, between the white stars, round, red moons began to coalesce. There were many of them. The moons had embedded themselves in a nebula I knew well. They had chosen the stars of the Solid State Entity. The moons began to pulsate, and red streamers of light projected out from their surfaces, touching each other, joining moon to moon in a web of red filaments. I realized, of

course, that the moons were meant to represent the brains—
the brain—of the Entity. But I could not understand why and
how the Fravashi fresco could hint (if a painting could indeed
hint) that there was some connection between the planet of
the warrior-poets and the Entity's mysterious origins. Perhaps Dawud's knife had permanently warped the painting's
patterns; perhaps there was no connection.

"The programs, Pilot, what controls the programs?"

I rushed him, then, hoping to catch him in my arms, to
hold him until the robots came to take him away. But while I
had been watching the painting, he had removed a needle-
dart from his cloak. I grabbed him and tried to wrench him
down to the carpet, but he stuck the dart in the side of my
neck. The dart must have been tipped with a drug because
almost instantly my muscles began seizing up and I could not
move. He unlocked my hands from around him and pushed
away. I stood there paralyzed, frozen. I could not even blink
my eyes.

He smiled, reached out and touched my eyelid, pressing
on my eye, testing. His fingers were hard, skilled and gentle.
He said, "This is an elegant drug. It will edit your bio-
programs—for a time. Your muscles will still listen to your
brain, but you will not control the brain's signals. Can you
control the beating of your heart? No, and for a few hours,
you will have no control over yourself. Where is free will
now, Pilot? Who programs the programmer? Can you tell
me? No, you can't move your tongue, even though you can
feel it pressed into the cracks between your teeth. Now,
Pilot, I must go to your mother. Goodbye."

He left me standing there, silently and freely cursing my
lack of freedom. I could not help watching the painting. The
colors were beautiful and they did not stop moving.

21

The Eyes
of a Child

*The first and hardest teaching of our profession
always must be to view the world as through the eyes
of a child.*

— Marinar Adam, Twelfth Lord Cetic

*We do not see things as they are; we see them as we
are.*

— saying of the cetics

The effects of Dawud's drug lasted not a few hours but a few
minutes. Soon, I could move again of my own free will, and I
was immediately afraid of the implications of this freedom.
Did the godseed in my head seek out and neutralize—devour—
invasive drugs, much as it sought out and replaced dead brain
cells? Or had it altered certain of the neurotransmitters,
leaving me immune to the actions of drugs? I had no time to
wonder at the drug's ineffectualness, not if I was to follow the
warrior-poet to my mother. I staggered out of the room and
ran down the empty hallway adjacent to the Gallery of the
Thousand Ice Glyphs; by means of this shortcut I hoped to
reach the street in time to catch sight of him. When I passed
between the gleaming entrance pillars, I found that he had
already descended the fifty-four steps and disappeared into
the crowds skating along the glissade below. A horologe that I
stopped told me this. When I began sprinting down the
steps, he waggled his long finger at the glissade to the west
and called out, "You'll never catch a warrior-poet—are you
mad?"

I was very mad, or at least very angry, so I pushed

through a group of fabulists. One of them, a skinny, delicate woman with pale, blue-veined skin and fearful eyes, told me that the warrior-poet had recently passed the Darghinni Rotunda. And as I rounded that huge, cylindrical building, a wormrunner muttered a few sullen words. The warrior-poet, he said, had entered the Hyacinth Gardens. I sensed a note of fear in his voice as he rubbed his beard and asked, "But why would you want to find a warrior-poet? Where's the profit in dealing with those madmen?" In this way, by stopping and questioning people seemingly at random, I made my way down the long band of ice into the Hyacinth Gardens.

It was a tortuously inefficient manner in which to proceed—I realized this almost at once. The glissade was crowded with exemplars and harijan come to view the blue snow dahlia and other flora of the Gardens. In the patchy, uneven light of late afternoon, the crowds seemed hungry, whether for the flaming red beauty of the alpine fireweed or for their evening meals it was difficult to tell. The wind came in spurts and gusts, and the sky was full of dense clouds which intermittently blocked the sun; snow flurries blew with a chill intensity and then, a few moments later, would cease, and there would be a moment of calm and sudden sunshine. As a result of this fickle weather, without warning people would come to an abrupt, grinding stop in order to open or readjust the folds of their robes. (Or to zip or unzip their kamelaikas.) Here a Friend of God would pause to wipe the rancid, garlicky sweat from his forehead and there, a quarter-mile later, he would shiver, whisper a silent supplication, and hunch down in his robes as he tried to appreciate a grove of yu trees. Many were skating in and out of the warming pavilions; the normal flow of traffic had degenerated into hundreds of turbulent pockets of men and women in search of thermal comfort. I had to push and dart to make any progress at all. To my right were fields of yellow litlits and alien trees, and beyond them, the broad, blue glimmer of the Run where it curved along the edge of the Pilot's Quarter; to my left, the twisted, beautiful shapes of the winter bonsai grew according to the whims of the splicers who had designed them; straight ahead as I skated were people, a surging river of people, too damn many people.

Near the middle of the Gardens, where the ice sculptures

glittered and the air smelled of snow dahlia and a sweet, minty alien scent, I noticed the imprint of fear stamped on the face of an astrier. I paused to ask her if she had seen the warrior-poet pass. I had this notion that a warrior-poet sailing quickly by might leave a track of fear in his wake. She was a stout, pretty woman, and she stood like a rock between me and her fourteen children, half defiantly, half in fear. She denied that she had seen the warrior-poet. At first I did not believe her. I wasted precious moments while she stood with her hands on her hips and shrilly informed me that the strictly celibate, death-seeking warrior-poets were as different from astriers as night from day; if she *had* seen the warrior-poet, she said, she would have pulled the hoods over her children's eyes, to shield them from evil. I moved closer to her, the better to read her face, and she stuck her chin out, as if to warn me away. I drank in the thick, womanly musk emanating from her woolens; I listened to the subtle tremulo of her voice. I heard fear in the tenseness of her vowels, the quick, stuttering sounds of nervousness and doubt. Faintly I smelled her fear. All at once—and I did not know how I had come by this skill—I realized it was not a fear of the warrior-poet, or at least, it was not a fear of warrior-poets in particular. It was a more general fear that I detected, in a way, a fear of all things or anything that might harm her children. She, who had no doubt left the hundreds of her youngest children safely in the care of her husbands on Goodrest, was quietly, if subliminally, afraid of every person on the glissade. If she had seen a warrior-poet, her fear would have built to a roar and screamed from her eyes. Perhaps she would have clenched her hands and sweated a profuse, acrid sweat as her bio-programs prepared her to flee or fight. With excitement I realized that fear has many colors, shades and tones. I would have to be careful to distinguish the cool blue of wariness from blind, crimson panic, if I hoped to find the warrior-poet.

I apologized for disturbing her, and I pushed off down the glissade. I saw an autist who was clearly afraid of something. I began to ask the ragged, filthy, barefooted man if he had seen "Death sailing by on silver skates." (One had to translate words into the autists' peculiar idiom or they would pretend not to understand the simplest things.) Then, once again, I found myself spontaneously practicing the skills of a cetic. I found I could read the autist's fear program. I saw that his was not a fear of pain or death at the hands of a warrior-poet. Indeed, he did not fear his suffering, and he scarcely feared death. As all of us do, he feared losing what was dearest to him. I was surprised to see that autists—if this rotting, miserable, stinking wretch of a human being was a typical specimen—live solely for pleasure. I could see this in his smiling, constantly moving lips as plainly as I could see the vacant smiles of the ice sculptures lining the street. But the pleasure he sought was not the fullness of gut after a fine meal or of sexual ecstasy; it was not even the toalache afficionada's euphoria or the number-storm of those many pilots who love their mathematics too well. What pleased the autist was to exist wholly within a world of his own creation. His was the pleasure of fantasy and delusion; to him his thoughtscapes were as beautiful and as real as the ice castles of Urradeth appear to a child. And the thing he feared above all else was the intrusion of external reality—what the autists would call the lesser-real—and the ruin of that perfect thoughtscape he sought, the realreal. (It is an irritating fact that the autists claim spiritual kinship with pilots. What is the manifold, they will ask, if not a creation of the ship's computer and the mind of a pilot in fugue? It does no good, of course, to explain that a pilot's mathematics is a vision of the deepest structures of the universe. They will just stare into your eyes and babble, "Brother Pilot, the realreal is one of the manifold beauties inside the godhead when the good god is inside the real head.") An autist will suffer every sort of bodily degradation rather than lose sight of his precious realreal.

I examined the autist's slack facial lines, and I saw that for him death was merely an abstract thought to be filed at some arbitrary address of his awareness; death was the never-real. Since he did not believe that *he* really existed, he could not fear losing himself to death. There was no fear of death in his milky, diseased eyes. There was only a hint of quiet regret and sadness that the beauty of his thoughtscapes would dissolve into nothingness when his mind ceased to be. And of that final tragedy he had little fear because he would not be in-the-real to witness it. Then, too, it is the faith of autists everywhere that: "In the realm of the real, the almost-real becomes sometimes-real according to the realness of the real head. The sometimes-real is a realness to be reborn into the realreal. In the realm of the realreal, there are many layers of reals; the realreal can be created but not destroyed."

All of this, I should emphasize, I saw in an instant. I think I was reading most of his programs; possibly I was reading his mind. I never talked to him (if one can really talk to an autist), nor did I dally to appreciate the subtleties of my new powers. I skated down the glissade trying to distinguish the different tones of fear on the hundreds of faces. Warrior-poets notwithstanding, we all fear something, and in some part of our being, we fear it every moment of our lives. I quickly became adept at reading people's fear programs. I passed a merchant-prince afraid of losing his jewels and silks. A hibakusha, a wizened, little brown-skinned woman dressed in patched woolens, approached him begging for the means to pay for the expensive procedure which might restore her to health. But the merchant could not see the desperation (and fear) in the beggar's eyes because he would not look in her eyes. He would not look at her pained face, at the bald head where only a few wispy filaments of hair hung above her high collar. He coughed loudly and hurried by, careful not to let any portion of his robes touch the poor woman. I saw: an aphasic who feared that the mental use of words or any sort of symbol would bind her thoughts and therefore ruin her freedom of mind; an eschatologist lost in fear of his fear; a dozen men off Lone Jack fearfully avoiding all aliens, even the gentle Friends of Man; a cowardly pilot by the name of Dixon Dar; a seemingly blissful arhat covered with soft snowflakes and stinking of sihu perfume. (I did not need a cetic's powers to perceive that the arhat was afraid of being thought a fake—as in fact she was. It is an ill-kept secret that sihu oil is absorbed through the skin and induces the artificial nirvanas of which the arhats are so falsely proud); a frightened, lonely novice who had just entered Borja; hundreds of men, women and children all betraying their fear. I stroked by fearful, heaving bodies, and I passed into a bubble of warm, almost tropical air. The crowds grew so thick that I had to walk my skates across the ice. There were maggids and nimspinners and exemplars bunched together, gawking at the fields of hyacinths on either side of the glissade. The air was sick with flowery fragrance. It was suddenly warm and humid so I unzipped my kamelaika down to my belly. One of the maggids exclaimed that it was a miracle that tropical flowers could grow on an ice planet. I looked through the shifting throng at the ten thousand delicate, hanging curlicues of pink and white and blue. They were beautiful. I caught the eye of a fat historian and shook my head silently, sharing our mutual fear: that the expense of maintaining an exterior microclimate and other like extravagances would one day break the Order— if indeed the imminent schism did not do so first.

After I had broken free into the cooler air at the western edge of the Gardens, I began seeing on the faces of the thinned-out crowd that particular kind of fear indicating a near encounter with a warrior-poet. I will call it fear of madmen, for most people regard the warrior-poets as being truly mad. When I was a young child I had often noticed that adults were inexplicably afraid of the many babbling madmen who roam the City streets. Most of the madmen, of course, were—and are—quite harmless. How then to explain why *master pilots*, for instance, could be so afraid of them, they who had mastered their fear of the manifold? I had never understood this phenomenon, but all at once the answer seemed obvious: A madman's jerky motions, his aimless words, the wild glint in his eyes—everything he does seems to bubble up from some private well deep within his being. It is a well which spouts actions seemingly beyond his control. And why does a madman appear to have no control? It is because he appears to have no fear; that is, he lacks a certain kind of fear. He is unafraid of embarrassing himself or others with his animal screams and mumbled prophecies. This fearlessness is very threatening to the typical civilized person because he understands, in some portion of his self, that it is only the fear of what others think that keeps *him* from skating naked down the street and howling at the moon when the miseries of life are more than he can bear. (If indeed he lives on one of the eighty-six civilized planets which have moons.) Fear is the glue that keeps civilization together. Without the fear of consequence, men would take forcefully the women of their choice, elidi children would pull the wings off their younger siblings and women would tell their husbands their innermost thoughts. And that would be the end of the world, the end of all the worlds on which human beings live. Without fear we would fly about at random like billions of unpredictable atoms. I must repeat that one does not fear a madman because he is dangerous; a madman is feared because he appears to have no fear, and therefore he is unpredictable and might do anything. And it is the same with warrior-poets. One does not fear them because they are dangerous; the sun, after all, is dangerous. But the sun is predictable (or it used to be before the Vild began to explode), and the warrior-poets, those fearless fanatics of Qallar, are not. Often they act at random. Their passage through a crowd leaves a trail of fear, the fear of fearlessness, which is really a fear of randomness. To live in a universe which does not listen to our plea for order and meaning is our most basic fear, and we fear it more than death. It was this trail of chaotic fear left by the warrior-poet Dawud that I followed across the Great Circle outside the Hofgarten and down an orange sliddery deep into the Farsider's Quarter.

Near the Merripen Green, where the streets narrow and the many fine, three-story blackstones shelter the richer of the farsiders, I talked to a cetic fresh off Melthin. He had the harrowed, somewhat bitter look of an itinerant professional; my first thought was that he had traveled among planets such as Orji and Yasmeen teaching his art to the backward novices of the Order's lesser schools. He stank of travel, and of fear. In front of his hotel I stopped him and quickly explained what I was seeking.

"Yes, it's true," he said, wiping the sweat from his forehead with his orange sleeve. "A few minutes ago, the poet in the rainbow kamelaika—but how did you know?"

Because I wanted to make certain that it was Dawud I pursued and not some other, I asked, "His warrior's ring—was it red? Did he wear the poet's green ring?"

"His rings?"

"Quickly, then, what color were his rings?"

"I didn't notice his rings; I was looking at his face."

"Damn!"

I quickly, breathlessly explained that I was following the warrior-poet's track of fear; being a cetic, I thought he would appreciate my little quest. But like many of the lesser professionals he was overly proud and chary of anyone—a pilot no less—who might challenge his meager authority. "One must be careful in reading the fear programs, very careful. How many types of fear do you think there are, Pilot?"

How many types of programs animate the flesh and brain

of a human being? I stroked up the street and turned onto a
sliddery, wondering about this. The sliddery led past the
Winter Ring. Here were obsidian blackstones eight stories
high, curving walls of chipped glass inside which the apartments were tiny and stacked one atop the other like a child's
blocks. I had seldom been in this part of the City before, and
I marveled that so many strange people could live so closely
with one another. I made my way toward the edge of the
Ring. There were many skaters resting on the dilapidated,
splintery benches set around the Ring. Between the benches
and the orange band of the street, which circled the Ring
around its northern half, every hundred yards or so, stood
the ice statues of our Order's famous pilots. There were
fifteen of these white monoliths. Wind and sun and freezing
mists had worked at the statues' features; it was nearly
impossible to distinguish the pitted, imperious face of Tisander
the Wary from the Tycho's jowly frown. I skated backward
into the Ring, absorbed for a moment with the silly notion of
reading the Tycho's programs from his statue's deformed
features. But it was impossible to do so. Even if the sculptor
had once captured the Tycho's essence and chiseled it into
ice, even though the faces were resculpted once every year
or so, the slow melt of time had degraded any information
bound into the ice crystals and had rendered the programs
unreadable.

Almost unreadable. For a moment, I struggled with my
perceptions, without and within, and I was dizzy. I looked
out and up, and there was the dizzying effect of concentric
circles: the satiny, whitish circle of the Winter Ring where
the farsiders laughed and spun and ground their toepicks into
the ice, the circle of blue and red benches, and the ice
statues surrounded by the curving orange street, and above
the street, the tenements gleaming like mountains of glass,
and far above, the marbled crown of the sky. I turned my
head, looking for the warrior-poet, but he was nowhere in
sight. Although I very badly wanted to find him, I felt that I
must pay attention to this new perception of mine, this new
way of seeing.

Near me a harijan was flopping about on skates too big for
him. He was a savage, jowly man dressed in a purple parka
and yellow pants so tight that his membrum bulged beneath
the dirty silk. Because his boots provided too little ankle

support, he had no feel for the edges of his blades. He stumbled about grasping for the arms and the support of nearby farsiders. In a way, he reminded me of Bardo. I looked more closely and saw determination and the stamp of cruelty on his thin lips. In another way he reminded me of the Tycho, of the Tycho's imago that I had encountered inside the Entity. I stared at the harijan, and it was like staring at Bardo and the Tycho. Each of them, I thought, bore a streak of cruelty, of self-love and brazen sexuality. I knew well how these traits—these programs—had been shaped in Bardo's case. But what of the Tycho and the comicly dressed harijan? I was dizzy as I turned and stared at the Tycho's icy, half-melted face. Suddenly I knew a thing: The Tycho's cruelty and the harijan's (and Bardo's, too), had been programmed by the cruelty of their fathers. I do not mean to imply that all men who are cruel have cruel fathers. The fount of cruelty is as deep and turbid as an ocean. But certainly it was so with the harijan; I could read his cruelty program as plainly as I could read his fear.

I bent over, resting my arms on my knees. I gasped for air. All around were children, men and women, and the statues of my father pilots, and I saw in each the set of muscles and nerves which betrayed their programs. A woman with a slender chest and great, streamlined thighs clumsily landed a waltz jump, and I understood—I "saw at a glance," as the cetics say—the many years of practice and the slightly mistaken programming causing her to catch the outside edge of her skate and nearly stumble. Here a pretty boy cried in frustration because he couldn't cut a decent eight, and there another laughed to hide the very same emotion, a program he had probably learned from his stoical father. How many programs command the muscles and thoughts of a human being? There are one million, twenty-seven hundred and six such programs. (I am joking, of course. I record this only because an infamous cetic once set himself the task of counting and classifying all possible programs, and he gave up after reaching this number. The number and variety of programs is potentially infinite, as is man.) There are programs determining the fluidity of our speed strokes, and there are programs which lead us to lather our bodies in precisely the same manner every time we bathe. We are programmed to fear darkness and loud noises, and we program ourselves to fear a

thousand things, failure and poverty, for instance. I saw these
programs on the farsiders' faces: the sex programs, the men
lusting for women, the dark women and the plump, the
skinny or the tall; the women with their subtle body language, initiating and often running the men's sex programs,
the different shades and manifestations of lust; and more sex
programs, the children programmed with dormant, powerful
urges, completely unaware of their own programs; the love,
dread, pride, shame, sympathy, grief, melancholy and joy
programs, the programs of hate and rage; there were beliefs
and belief programs in the eyes of a Summerworld Buddhist,
a belief in cyclic universes and rebirth of the soul and many,
many stranger beliefs; there were programs to control beliefs,
and occasionally, on certain naked faces, the imprimatur of
beliefs which controlled programs. I saw one woman, a wise,
strikingly beautiful woman wearing the embroidered gown of
a Urradeth neurologician, who bore the burn of self-mastery
in her brilliant eyes. A few, rare people, it seemed, were
sometimes able to master their beliefs and run their own
programs. How this fascinated me! These belief programs
which can write, edit and command other programs are
called master or metaprograms. I wondered at the origin of
the programs which run our lives. Why is one man quick and
another slow? Why will one woman smile knowingly as she
speaks of ananke and ultimate fate while her sister denies
meaning, and drugs herself with toalache and sex? Could it
be, as the splicers claim, that our initial set of programs is
wholly written by our chromosomes?

I do not believe so. Ah, but from where does this disbe-
lief, this program of skepticism arise—from my chromosomes
as well? And how were my chromosomes programmed? By
chance evolution? By God? And who, then, wrote the deity
program, or the programs of the natural universe? Who
programs the programmer? One could go mad pondering
such infinite regresses of cause and effect. I do not believe
there can be a simple explanation. Some programs—an in-
fant's crying, defecating, sucking and sleeping modes, for
example—are certainly written in our chromosomes. Other
programs are copies of our parents' programs; sometimes the
world we live in writes programs into our nerves with pleasure and, too often, with fire and pain. The origin of certain
programs is a secret which will perhaps always remain un-

known. Does the brain hold the secret in the way it molds itself to fit its tiny corner of the universe, the billions of neurons weaving together, forming trillions of interconnections? The akashics believe so, yet they have never realized their dream of mapping and understanding man's soul. It is a commonplace that each human being possesses a unique set of programs. Each of us takes great pride in this uniqueness; we often justify our existence by looking up at the stars and observing that in all the universe, there is no other being quite like ourself. We are special, we believe, and therefore uniquely valuable. In a way, we are our own unique universe, as worthy of existence as the greater universe surrounding us. I, too, had always believed this; I had always regarded my arrogance, vanity and rage programs as endearing faults without which the bright jewel I knew as Mallory Ringess would somehow shatter inward and cease to shine, like a diamond with only a single, cracked face. Now I looked around the ice ring at the faces of my fellow human beings, and I was no longer so sure. I saw arrogance as an exemplar completed a difficult axel, and vanity in the carriage of a pretty, black-skinned matron off Summerworld. All the programs which drove me to change my flesh, to love, to joke, to murder, to seek the secret of life—each particle of myself was somewhere duplicated within the selfness of another man, woman or child. My programs were not unique; only their seemingly random arrangement within me was. Why should I take pride in programs which sprang from the coil of inherited chromosomes or from my mother's painful pinches as she programmed me not to lie? Why should I be aware of myself as a separate being at all?

For me the problem of uniqueness was really worse than I have stated. I was full of my new power of reading people's programs; when I looked inside myself I could almost read my own. And I saw a horrible thing: Not only were my programs not unique, but in many ways, I was no more in control of my programs than a dog was of its own wagging tail. Even the best of human beings—such as the Urradeth neurologician—could control only some of their programs. And as for the others, the harijan, whores and wormrunners that I saw, well, the warrior-poet had been right, after all. We are sheep awaiting the butcheries of time; we are clots of brain tissue and bundles of muscle, meat-machines that jump to the touch of our most immediate passions; we—I have said this before—we react rather than act; we have thoughts in place of thinking. We are, simply, robots; robots aware that we are robots, but robots nonetheless.

And yet. And yet we are something more. I have seen a dog, Yuri's beloved Kyoko, a lowly beast whose programs were mostly muzzle and hunger, growls and smell, overcome her fear and flight programs to hurl herself at a great white bear, purely out of love for her master. Even dogs possess a spark of free will. And as for humans, within each of us, I believe, burns a flame of free will. In some it is tenuous and dim as an oilstone's flame; in others it burns hot and bright. But if our will is truly free, why do our robot programs run our bodies and minds? Why do we not run our programs? Why do we not *write* our own programs? Was it possible that all women and men could free themselves and thus become their own masters?

No, it was not possible. I looked at the faces of a tychist and a Jacarandan whore, and their ugliness overwhelmed me. How ugly the set of bitter experience, the lines and etchings of time! In their terminal adulthood, how ugly and tragicomic grown human beings really were! With eyes for a moment freed of the distorting lense of my own programs— with the eyes of a child—I saw a tragic thing: We are prisoners of our natural brains. As children we grow, and new programs are layered down, set into the jelly of our brains. When we are young we write many of these programs in order to adapt to a bizarre and dangerous environment. And then we grow some more. We mature. We find our places in our cities, in our societies, in ourselves. We form hypotheses as to the nature of things. These hypotheses shape us in turn, and yet more programs are written until we attain a certain level of competence and mastery, even of comfort, with our universe. Because our programs have allowed us this mastery, however limited, we become comfortable in ourselves, as well. And then there is no need for new programs, no need to erase or edit the old. We even forget that we were once able to program ourselves. Our brains grow opaque to new thoughts, as rigid as glass, and our programs are frozen for life, hardwired, so to speak, within our hardened brains. *And this is how we were designed to be*. Evolution has made us to grow, to grow up, to have our children, to pass on our programs, and then to die. Life goes on this way. And so the flame burns weakly but freely, trapped inside a sphere of glass. We burn with sufficient light to illuminate the code of our programs, but we lack the means. We don't know how, and we are afraid, utterly terrified to break the glass. And even if we could master our fear, what then?

If *I* could find courage, I wondered, what would I see? Would I be ashamed of the arrangement of programs—of my very self—beyond my control? Ah, but what if I could write new metaprograms controlling this arrangement of programs? Then I might one day attain the uniqueness and value that I found so lacking in myself and the rest of my race; as an artist composes a tone poem, I could create myself and call into being wonderful new programs which had never existed within the rippling tides of the universe. Then I would be free at last, and the flame would burn like star fire; then I would be something new, as new to myself as the morning sun is to a newborn child.

Where does the flame go when the flame explodes?

On the ice of the Winter Ring, surrounded by people skating, laughing, jumping, grimacing and shouting, as I stared at the frozen, mutilated Tycho's face and at the face of the harijan in the yellow pants and at the faces of all the people on the ice and on the worlds of man, as I stared at my own face, in an instant, I had this dream of being something new. But it was only a dream. When I looked up and out across the Ring, I saw Dawud skating toward a woman who looked like my mother, and my dizziness gave way to anger, and I became a robot once again.

I accelerated across the ice, dodging the people as best I could. The wind whistled in my ears and stung my face. I dropped my shoulder to pass a half-naked courtesan. When the shivering, blue-skinned woman saw me approaching madly at speed, and saw that I was skating straight toward a warrior-poet, she made an "O" of fear with her tattooed lips. She jumped out of my way. Dawud saw me, too. I was perhaps thirty yards from him, but I could see him smile. It was a smile of admiration, and faintly, of surprise. He bowed his head to me. The muscles jumped in his throat, and his curly black hair rippled in the wind. My mother opened her fur collar, and he immediately stuck one of his needles in her neck. Then he sped away toward the eastern half of the Ring. My mother, probably following his smile, turned, saw me, tilted her head, and pushed off in the opposite direction.

I could follow only one of them, so I sprinted after my mother. I caught her at the edge of the Ring as she passed beneath the milky, gleaming statue of Tisander the Wary. I grabbed the hood of her furs and yanked her to a stop. She didn't struggle. I pivoted just in time to see Dawud, in his rainbow kamelaika, disappear down one of the eight streets giving out onto the sliddery circling the Ring.

"Mother," I gasped, "why did you run away from me?"

A few fearful arhats near us snapped their tangerine robes and kept their distance, although they looked at us with the awe which farsiders so often have of pilots. (And what is awe, I suddenly realized, if not a blend of love and fear?)

"Where is the poet skating? What did he do to you?"

"Mallory," she said, and she shut her eyes. Her eyelids fluttered as if she were passing through dream-sleep. She was breathing heavily, and her eye was twitching, slightly. It was an old program. I had thought Mehtar had cut it from her muscles when he had sculpted her face, but apparently the program ran deep. She opened her eyes and squinted as she cocked her head and asked, "Why were you tracking me?"

"Where have you been?"

"And why must you answer a question with a question? Haven't I taught you? That it's disrespectful?"

I told her of my meeting Dawud in the Hibakusha Gallery and of what had followed. I propped my boot up on a nearby bench, digging at the old wood with my blade. "Why were you meeting a warrior-poet, Mother?"

"It was a chance meeting."

"You don't believe in chance," I said.

"You think I'm lying? I'm not lying; my mother taught me. Not to lie."

She laughed then, a disturbed laugh as if she had a private joke with herself. There was a deep tension in her laughter. I detected the subtle strains of untruth, and I found—amazingly—that I could read this particular program of my mother's. She was, quite simply, lying.

"What did the poet put in your neck, then?"

"Nothing," she said. She reached up and touched the ugly

wood collar pin fastening her furs. "He was returning the pin.
It had come off. He found it lying on the ice."

I looked behind me at the streets which radiated away
from the Ring, cutting between the circle of glass tenements.
I considered pursuing Dawud, but I was afraid I would lose
my mother. And clearly she knew what I was thinking.
Clearly she planned to lure me away from him.

"The warrior-poet could have killed you," I said.

"The warrior-beasts can kill anyone they choose."

"And who does Dawud choose to kill?" I asked. "Soli?"

"How would I know?"

Lies, lies, lies.

Her eye twitched then, and I saw what I should have seen
long ago: My mother was addicted to toalache—the facial tics
were the result of her hiding this shame from her friends, and
from herself. I saw other things, too, other programs: The
layers of fat girdling her hips, which betrayed her compulsive
eating programs and love of chocolate drinks and candies; her
arrogant speech patterns, the clipped sentence fragments
hinting at her belief that others were too stupid to understand any but the briefest bursts of information (and hinting,
too, at her basic shyness); the way she had programmed
herself to squint in place of smiling. The cetics call these
program-revealing body signs "tells." I searched her face for
the frowns, eye-rolls and blinks that would tell the tale of
herself. I saw. . . shocking things. I had always known—even
if I had not been aware of the knowledge—that she possessed
a sort of slovenly voluptuousness. Now I saw something else;
now her omnifarious sexuality was revealed. To my vast
embarrassment, I saw that she was capable of coupling with
an exemplar, boy, woman, alien or beast—or even with a
beam of pure radiant energy, if that kind of union between
flesh and light were possible. (The arhats, of course, believe
it is.) If she was chaste in everyday practice, it was not
because she didn't have her desires. It is from my mother, I
believe, that I have inherited my wildness.

My hands were numb from squeezing the wood slats of
the bench, so I rubbed them together. Around the Ring, the
flame globes began to flare. The ice was shiny with hundreds
of lights. The skaters were deserting in mass for the nearby
cafes. Only a few groups of harijan were left near the edge of

the Ring. In the dropping darkness, their shouts seemed harsh and too near.

"I think there's a plot to kill Soli," I half-whispered. "What do you know of it, Mother?"

"Nothing."

From the tightness of her lips I saw that she knew everything.

"If Soli is assassinated you'll be the first person the Timekeeper will suspect. He'll drag you before the akashics, lay your brain bare."

She squinted and said, "There are ways. Of fooling the akashics and their primitive computers."

For reasons of my own I was very concerned with any limitations of the akashic computers, and I asked, "What ways?"

"Ways. Haven't I taught you that there are always ways of outwitting your competitors?"

"You also taught me that it's wrong to murder."

She tilted her head and nodded. "A child must be taught certain . . . certainties. Otherwise the universe will engulf her. But when she is a *woman*, she learns what is permitted."

"You'd murder Soli? How blithely we speak of murder, then."

"*You* speak. I've never killed a living thing."

"But you'd send the poet to do your killing. Is that *permitted*?"

"Everything is permitted. To those who see the need. Certain few people are chosen. For these few, the laws of the many don't apply."

"And who chooses them, Mother?"

"They're chosen by fate. Fate marks them, and they must leave their mark."

"Murder Soli and you'll leave a bloody mark."

"The great acts of history," she said, "are written in blood."

"You see Soli's murder as an act of greatness?"

"Without Soli, there would be no more talk of Schism. The Order would be preserved."

"You think that?"

She smiled her disturbed, conceited smile, and the wind began to blow. It was a bitter wind carrying in the first cold of night. My mother pulled her collar tightly around her throat.

Her robe was drab and ill-fitting; I realized that she habitually wore these plain garments as a kind of camouflage. People would look at the lumpy folds and conclude that here was a selfless woman caring little for style or ostentation. But appearances, I thought, lie. In truth, my mother gloried in herself as if she were still a little girl.

"How I hate Soli!" she said.

I kicked my blade into the ice and said, "And yet you chose him to be my father."

"I chose his chromosomes to make yours," she corrected.

I took off my glove and ran my fingers through my hair feeling for the strands of red, which were coarser and stiffer than the black hairs. But my fingers were too cold and numb to feel much of anything. "Why, Mother?" I asked suddenly.

"Don't ask me these questions."

"Tell me—I have to know."

She sighed and sucked her tongue as if it were a ball of chocolate. "Men are tools," she said. "And their chromosomes are tools. I slelled Soli's chromosomes to make you. Lord Pilot of our Order."

I rubbed the side of my nose and looked at her. She was squinting at me, biting her lip and pulling at the fat skin beneath her chin. I thought I saw the skeleton of her plan. She would connive to make me Lord Pilot, and then she would manipulate me from behind as if I were a phantast's puppet. When I accused her of this, she asked me, "How could I manipulate my own son? You manipulate yourself. I have no desire to *manipulate*. The future Lord Pilot."

As she laughed to herself, I thought that I had been blind to the essential conceit of her plan. I looked at her eyes, which were dark blue pools against the deeper darkness of her hood, and I saw overweening pride and ambition. I said, "But it's the Timekeeper who rules the Order, not the Lord Pilot."

"The *Timekeeper*," she agreed.

And then I knew; then I could perceive the full flesh of her grand strategy. She said the word "Timekeeper," and there was an unbearable stress in the syllables of that word. My mother was an ambitious woman. She would have the Timekeeper killed, too. And more—she would plot to make herself the Lord of the Order.

Vanity, vanity, vanity.

"No, Mother," I said, reading the tells on her face, "you'll never rule the Order."

The air escaped her lips in a quick "whoosh." She clasped her hands to her belly as if I'd punched her beneath her heart. "My son has *powers*," she said. "You can read me, I think. Your own mother."

"I can read some of your programs."

"What have they *done* to you?" She looked at me as if she were seeing me for the first time, with horror tightening her anxious squint. (And what is horror if not a blending of hate and fear?)

"What has the poet done to *you*, Mother?"

"Don't answer a question with a question! Why were you always so disobedient? I thought I'd taught you. Obedience long ago."

I did not like the turn of our conversation. I hated the way she pronounced the word "obedience." It was an ugly word; the way she said it, it was a word rife with strange connotations and terrible meaning. I remembered that the warrior-poets were infamous for instilling in their victims an irreversible and total obedience. What poisons had Dawud planted in her brain? Genotoxins to combine with her chromosomes and to subtly alter her deepest programs? Had he introduced into her blood a slel-virus that would devour her brain and replace it, bit by bit, with preprogrammed neurologics? With *obedient* neurologics? Had he slel-mimed her brain? My mother stared at the dark circle of the Ring, and I wondered what portion of her free will had already been dissolved and replaced by the will of the warrior-poet.

"This poet is very dangerous," I said. "He'd kill you like a flea, if he wanted."

"Everyone dies."

"He'd kill your soul."

"I'm not afraid of dying."

"I always thought you were afraid, Mother."

"No, I'm not afraid. Doesn't the acceptance of death free us from fear? And if we're free, isn't everything possible? No, I'm not afraid."

I rubbed the ice from my mustache and said, "Those are the poet's words, I think, not yours."

She pulled her hood more tightly around her head. She began speaking in a slow, even voice, as if she were explaining ring theory to a novice. Even though she kept her voice calm, I could hear the rhythms of new programs in her voice. Her words, the ways she emphasized and articulated certain sounds (she overaspirated the consonants made by stopping the flow of air with the tongue), the choppy phrasing of her sentences and thoughts—everything about her was the same yet slightly different. I could read her, but I could not tell if the new programs originated merely from Dawud's ideas and beliefs, or if he had in fact mimed her brain. I trembled when she said, "You think Dawud manipulates me? No, it is I. Who manipulates him. He thinks he has found a way. To eventually control my programs. Call it slel-mime or call it what you will. He *thinks* this. But from where did this thought come? *I* gave him these thoughts. It's the most subtle kind of manipulation; my mother taught me about manipulation."

Had Dawud rewritten her software or carked the hardware?—I trembled to know this.

"Perhaps the akashics could help you," I said.

"I think not."

"I could take you to them. But you must tell me how I can find you."

"Haven't your friends told you? That I've become a student of the warrior-poet's?"

"Where can I find the poet?"

"And why would my son want to find a warrior-poet?"

"Perhaps I want to warn him that he's being manipulated." In truth, I wanted to trap him before he had a chance to mime my mother's brain, if he already hadn't. I wanted to kill him.

"It's the nature of my manipulation," she said, "that to inform him he's being manipulated will only work to manipulate him into believing he can manipulate the manipulation by manipulating me into believing *I'm* manipulating him. It's a complicated thing. Do as you will." She smiled and nodded her head, turning into the light. Her shadow lengthened into a black spear, then shortened, back and forth across the glossy ice. "After all, no one is manipulating *you*."

"Oh, God!"

"Haven't I taught you not to blaspheme?"

"Where is the poet, Mother?"

"Am I my master's keeper?"

"Where, Mother?"

"If you can read me, then you tell me."

"You've sent him to murder Soli," I said.

"Soli," she repeated. She closed her eyes because it must have been finally clear to her that I could read her.

"Why would the poet murder for you, then?"

"It's an exchange, of course. Of devotion. The warrior-poets seek converts, don't they? Therefore, I devote myself to becoming. Like a warrior-poet. And in exchange, Dawud will—"

"When, Mother? Oh, God, it's too late isn't it?"

"How I hate Soli!"

"Mother!"

"Don't look for a warrior-poet," she said, "you might find him."

"I'll kill him."

"No, Mallory, don't leave me. Let him do his work. Why would you want to save Soli? As we speak, the poet is most likely climbing Soli's tower. Or sending Soli's guards over. Or asking Soli the poem."

I kicked my skate against the ice in an attempt to knock some blood back into my numb feet. I was cold and confused, and I asked, "What poem?"

"It's a tradition of the warrior-poets," she said. "They trap and immobilize their victims. And then they recite part of an ancient poem. If the victim can complete it, he's spared. Of course, no one ever knows the poem."

I pushed away from her and began stroking across the Ring. I could not believe her. She was mocking me. Surely a warrior-poet would not risk failure by taking the time to ask his victim a poem.

"Where are you going?" she called out before I had skated a dozen yards.

"To warn Soli of a madman!" I shouted.

"Don't leave me! Please!"

"Goodbye, Mother."

She tilted her head from side to side and shouted back:

Because I could not stop for Death—
He kindly stopped for me.
The tower held but just Ourselves
And Immortality

"That's the poem," she said. "If the warrior-poet traps you, too."

I bent low and drew in deep breaths of air as I waved goodbye and pushed against the ice. I did not intend to let a murderer—a master of slel-mime, a madman—trap me. It was my intention to trap him.

22

The Hanuman-
Ordando Paradox

To be fully alive is to be fully aware.
To be fully aware is to be full of fear.
To fear is to die.

—saying of the warrior-poets

I raced eastward through the nighttime city streets. I took a
shortcut through the heart of the Farsider's Quarter. The poet
had a lead on me, but he could not know the City as I did.
Neither, I hoped, could he skate as fast or as far without rest.
The dimmed colors of the glissades and lesser glidderies
seemed to flow and blend, red into orange, purple into
green. The pretty buildings lining the extremely narrow
Street of the Neurosingers, with their balconies and lacy
stone grillwork, were hung with dripping icicles. Directly
below, the drips had frozen into a jungle of icy bumps,
tubercles and miniature volcanoes. The skating was treacherous so I turned down the Street of Fumes. There the ice was
not quite so irregular, but there were dangers of a different
kind. A myriad of odors wafted out of the half-open doorways
of the remembrancer dens. The air was redolent with the
bubble of hot tar, with the fragrance of hair oils and new
woolens and a thousand other smells and smell-drugs. Instantly I recalled sprinting down the street the day of the
pilot's race. (It did not seem possible that three years had
passed since that day.) Memories consumed me. I could
almost see Soli smoothly stroking fifty yards ahead; I could
almost hear the click-clack of his long, shiny racing blades. I
was passing one of the larger dens when a couple of common
whores opened the door. Their lips were stained red and

their breath stank of alcohol. They stood holding hands beneath the cold flame globe, which was one of the clear types, with the plasma crackling along its colors within. They blocked my way and immediately sidled up next to me. The taller of the two—her hair was like dark, red wine—flung open her furs. She wasn't wearing any under-robes; her skin was naked and white. She offered to take me down one of the alleys off the street, to spread her furs and lie back in the snow, to perform an immediate coupling without charge. She was very drunk. No doubt she was remembering previous, impulsive pleasures she had experienced while under the hot wash of alcohol. That is the limitation of that particular drug: It brings clear memories of other times passed while drunk, but little else. I smelled the heady esters of skotch and remembered the night in the master pilot's bar when I had first met Soli. I hated Soli, I remembered, so why should I hurry to push the two whores aside, to rush halfway across the City to warn him? Why not stay to take my pleasure with the whore? (She was quite beautiful—one of those rare whores who loved whoring because she loved men.) Why not let Soli die?

Although I made fast progress, crossing the broad, milky ice of the Way before the nightly swarms rushed into the Quarter, I worried that Dawud would reach Soli's tower ahead of me. In truth, I did not want Soli to die. He was my Lord Pilot, my uncle, my father; it would have been wrong to let a warrior-poet kill him. Also—and this was wholly selfish of me—I thought I might earn his gratitude. If I could soften his heart, he might forgive Bardo and Justine (and me), and I might stop the schism before it really began. I considered calling for a sled. However, on the narrow, twisting streets of the Old City through which I had to pass, a sled would only have been a hindrance. It was one of the few times in my life when I wished for the convenience of a fone. Then I could simply, and instantly, warn him that Death was on his way. But, as the Timekeeper would say, if we permitted fones people would forever be foning each other with their most immediate and frivolous thoughts. They would make appointments to meet each other at a certain place and time, and they would demand the use of timepieces, and of private sleds to carry them at whim about the City. The streets would fill with explosive, noisy machines and other noisome things, because once the technology beast was uncaged, people would want squawking private radios and private sense boxes and a host of other things. When I was a novice, I had often sniggered at this domino theory of technology, but later, when I had seen Tria and Gehanna and other hellish planets which chose not to limit their technology, I decided that in this one matter the Timekeeper's edicts were justified.

And yet when I reached the entrance of the Danladi Tower, I cursed the Timekeeper and his edicts. The wind spilled down from Urkel's ghostly foothills, down over the deserted Hall of the Ancient Pilots and the Chess Pavilion, whistling through the dormitories and lesser buildings at the edge of Resa. It whipped clouds of ice-powder into the Tower's open doorway. There was a dreadful sucking sound as of air being forced through a tube. The rectangular wooden door, which was as plain and severe as the illustrious Lord Danladi had been, creaked as it swung back and forth, and it was smeared with blood. There was blood everywhere. Inside the doorway, corpses littered the hallway. There were six of them. A journeyman lay crumpled with her throat cut open like a second red mouth; next to her—half on top of her—slumped the corpse of Tymon the Equivocator, a pilot who had graduated the year before Bardo and I. The line of corpses progressed down the cold, quiet hallway to the stairwell. Clearly, the pilots and journeymen had tried to stop the warrior-poet, and he must have fallen on them with his quick, killing knife like a madman among children. The fresh-scrubbed body of a novice blocked the stairwell, hugging the first few steps; his pink lips pushed against the stone lip of the fourth step. I had to jump over him. His once-immaculate woolens were stained. There was a red circle above his heart. It looked like a sign above a cutting shop. There was a fresh, soapy smell in the air, as well as the smells of blood and fear.

I climbed the winding stairs as silently as I could. And then through the short hallway to Soli's chambers, and all the while my boots slapped against the stone and my breath exploded from my lungs like rocket gases. I was afraid my noise would have warned the warrior-poet, if indeed it wasn't already too late for warnings. The white furs of the inner chamber were drenched with the blood of Soli's journeyman, Markoman li Towt, who was kneeling backwards on dead legs

with his arms splayed out and his head thrown back like a
doll's. The neck was cut and broken, and his thin lips were
pulled back against his fine, white teeth. The rest of the
room—the tapestries on the wall, the low couches and tables,
the prayer books, chess set and the coffee service—was
undisturbed. The door to Soli's inner chamber was ajar so I
pushed it and stepped inside. Into chaos. I had never been
inside his sanctum before, and I was surprised to see that Soli
kept plants. Green plants and flowers were everywhere;
there were potted plants, plants on shelves, plants hanging
from the slanting, black slab of the obsidian ceiling. (The
Danladi Tower, I think, is the only building in the City made
entirely of that glassy substance.) Everywhere there was
wreckage. Plants and pots had been smashed into the fireplace; a stringy mass of charred vegetable matter was roasting, entangled between the andirons and the crackling logs.
Loose black dirt and shards of clay ground beneath my boots.
I smelled the perfume of crushed shira flowers. And then,
through the foliage of a half-overturned bush I saw them.
Near the window the poet had bound Soli to the bole of a
spinnaker tree. A cocoon of sticky, steely protein filaments,
the kind they grow on Qallar, was wrapped around Soli's
chest, biting into the bark of the tree behind him. He was
struggling as furiously as a netted fish, pulling at the cocoon,
jumping from side to side, trying to overturn the tree. But
the tree was huge. It grew from a huge pot set into a recess
in the floor. Its branches spread out beneath the skylight
twenty feet above us. Leaves shook and rattled, and a few of
the tree's triangular, yellow flowers spiraled lazily to the floor.

"Don't come any closer, please, Mallory."

This came from the warrior-poet, who was standing half
behind the tree. The colors of his kamelaika were dirtied with
blood; blood stained the tree where his clothes had touched
the gray bark. He held the point of his thin killing knife
pressed to the corner of Soli's eye. He called out, "I was just
about to run this up his optic nerve, but once again you've
surprised me."

Soli's drugged eyes were open wide and twitching. Almost every muscle in his face was locked, and sweat globules
ran off his forehead. He stank of fear.

"Let him go," I said.

I stepped closer and Dawud held out his hand. "Your

mother was not supposed to have revealed our plans. How
did you get her to speak?"

I pointed at Soli and repeated, "Let him go."

"But we haven't reached the moment," Dawud said. "And
in any case, my Order has been paid for his death."

"Yes, I know. Tell me what you've done to my mother."

He laid his hand gently on Soli's head. He ignored my
demand. "Your mother has paid well for this *possibility*."

"Possibility?" I did not know what he meant. Soli stared
emptily as if he knew nothing at all. His face was blanker
than an autist's. There was nothing to read except pain and
fear.

"What type of poison is this, then?" I asked. "That can
rob a man of his self-awareness and render the programs
unreadable?" I was trembling to rush over to Soli, to slap the
anger back into his face. I did not like to see him like this.

"No, Pilot, don't move! We've almost reached the moment of the possible." He said this by way of explanation.
(Perhaps he could read *my* curiosity program.) "Soli is almost
alive; in moments he'll be reborn."

Suddenly Soli screamed and bit through his lip. Blood ran
down his chin and neck. The bloody flap of his lower lip stuck
to his teeth; his incisors were visible through the ragged tear.
All at once every muscle in his body seemed to fire and
contract. His body was a knot of spasming muscles. I thought
the spasms would break his bones and burst his tendons but
Mehtar had sculpted him into an Alaloi, after all, and sculpted
well.

"He's in agony!"

Dawud smiled at me and said, "Please stay where you
are, or the Lord Pilot will have to die before his moment."

"You're torturing him!"

"Yes, of course; how else to awaken him? Pain is the
lightning that will illuminate his mind and wake him up." He
ran his thick fingers through Soli's sweat-drenched hair. He
made a fist, clamping the hair in his fingers, holding Soli's
head tight. His red ring gleamed through the black tangle
like a burning pool of blood. "You see, Soli is living intensely
now. I've given him the drug. As I speak, the sound waves
are striking his skin like fists. Do you smell my perfume? The
pungence of the kana oil? To Soli it is acid eating away his
nose and lungs. You can't imagine his pain: The light of the

flame globes is like knives through his eyes. He wishes he
could close them, he prays. And in a short while, I'll run the
tip of this knife into his eye, right up the optic nerve. And
then there will truly be a frenzy, then the lightning will split
his head. And then, the moment, Pilot. A single, clear
moment, brighter than lightning, and a moment without fear.
I'll take the lesser life of the robot and give him the greater.
Soon—you see he's almost ready."

"But he'll be dead!"

"No, he'll have truly lived for a moment, and in the
endless rings of eternity, his perfect moment will live again
and again."

"That's madness!"

"He's ready! Look, can you see the fear in his eyes, like
an ocean! He hears my every word, though he understands
nothing but fear. The fear; the ring of eternity; the pain."

"No!"

I did not want to know any more about the warrior-poet's
bizarre religion; I did not care if Soli overcame his master
fear program and lived his perfect moment. The poet's need
to carve his beliefs into Soli's flesh sickened me. Why, I
wondered, must fanatics always infect others with the virus of
their beliefs? Why must beliefs always seek to invade its
victims, to fill them with fever, and then to infect yet others
like a plague? Why this madness, I wanted to know? I
watched the knife dip towards Soli's waiting eye, and I
screamed, "No!"

I moved across the room. I fell into slowtime, and I
moved in a frenzy of speed. It was this rash, lightning
movement, I think, which saved Soli's life. (The lesser life,
that is. The simple life of mathematics and westering that a
pilot was born to live.) (The poet had no more time for torture.
He could have killed Soli immediately, but then there would
have been no "moment of the possible." To his skewed
system of belief, the assassination would have been in vain.
He watched me jump over an uprooted bush, and with his
full, red lips he made a sour face. It was plain he did not want
to kill me. But he shook his head and his voice poured forth
like wine. "You almost could have been one of us," he said. "A
lover of eternity."

He accelerated into slowtime; he was all precision and
exquisite motion, a blur of flashing red and green rings and

swirling cape and flickering steel. I knew my only hope was
to avoid the finger knives and poisons and needles secreted
within his cape, to dodge or block the edge of his fist, and
above all, to slip beneath the scythe of his killing knife. I had
to close with him. Then I could grapple, hand to neck and
arm to arm. I could apply the art the Timekeeper had taught
me and bring the power of my Alaloi muscles and bones to
bear.

But it was not so easy to close with him. He must have
immediately guessed my strategy. He lunged at my belly in
diversion and then slashed at my fingers. There was a heat in
my fingertips as if the displaced air of the lightning knife had
burned me. I looked down. He had cut through two of my
fingernails into the soft tissue beneath. The blood was welling
up—slowly, slowly, everything appeared to move so slowly in
slowtime—beneath the nail. We whirled and thrashed about,
crashing through the plants. I knocked my head into the pot
of a hanging fern. I made a fist and squeezed; blooddrops
rained onto the leaves of a fairy moss, slow red splashing
against veinous, green lace. I punched at his throat. He easily
blocked my arm, stepping aside as gracefully as a ballerina.
Although we were both deep in the amber of slowtime, it
seemed that he was moving more quickly than I. Either that
or he was reading my programs and anticipating my moves.
The arts of a warrior-poet, I thought, are devious and deadly.

There is one art, however, which the warrior-poets have
never mastered. They, who live every moment so intensely
on the brink of death, can never know the passive, melancholic, secretly fearful mindsets of the scryers. And who,
after all, can truly comprehend the mysterious dance of
future dreams which plays before the inner eye of a scryer?
From where do these images come? In what manner are they
made manifest within the mind? Some say scrying and
remembrancing are parts of a single phenomenon. If it is true
that the universe eternally recurs, like a poet's drama playing
over and over again with the same actors acting precisely the
same way during each performance, then isn't an ancient
memory also a vision of the far future? It may be so. As
Dawud aimed a thrust at my eyes—a thrust I barely avoided—I
smelled the thickness of kana oil, and I began to remember.
Or so I thought. At first the images that came to me *seemed*
like recent memories. There Dawud lunged and cut my

hand; there he stabbed at my temple; there he reached inside
his cape and removed a dart enamelled with purple bo
poison. But they were not memories, I realized, but something new. For a moment I thought I was not *seeing* these
images at all; in one instantaneous particle of time, I conclud-
ed that I was reading the subtle shifts of weight and muscle
that betrayed Dawud's fighting programs. From these tells I
was reconstructing in my mind the sequence of killing moves
he would choose to make—so I thought. He lunged and he
stabbed and he plucked a purple dart from his cape; I
watched the skin on the palm of my hand opening like a
fireflower. The sequence of moves was exactly as I had
envisioned. I suddenly knew I was not reading his programs,
or rather, I was not *just* reading his programs. There were
images, precise colors and motions, a new mode of vision.
Dawud lunged and feinted and flicked the dart at my neck.
Something new: I had time to block and counterfeint and pull
my neck out of the way. Was I reading his programs? I did
not think so. I knew that a warrior-poet is trained from
childhood to mask his programs. For a warrior to telegraph
his moves is a sin. And there is more to it than that. It is a
basic result of the theory of games that a warrior must
introduce a number of random elements into his moves, else
his enemy might figure out his strategy. Thus some of the
slashes and feints that Dawud aimed at me were made at
random. His muscles and nerves had been trained—programmed—to fire of their own will at certain instances. He
might plan a lunge and a groin kick only to find his arm
pulling up short and the kick delivered to the throat instead.
I could not be reading these random programs because they
originated so quickly, so impulsively; I could not read his
other programs because they were masked. But if I could
not, how did these vivid images come to me? How did I avoid
his killing knife?

I was scrying—I knew it immediately although I tried to
deny it. I entered into that peculiar, melancholic mindset
where one's life (and death) is seen as a slow, almost abstract
picture about to be made real. There was a moment of
instantaneity, and then, a brilliant flash as if the interior of a
vast, darkened chamber had suddenly been illuminated. My
eyes were open yet I was momentarily blind to the colors and
textures of the chamber. There were images, a bright mosaic

of pattern and possibility. The various objects of the room, the dividing branches of the spinnaker tree to my side, the red-streaked rug, the green and yellow and red plants, the rainbow colors of Dawud's kamelaika, his cruel, killing, knifeblade of a nose, and his intense eyes so calm and so aware—all these things seemed to shimmer, to dissolve into a sea of color, to shimmer again as they flowed and formed and rearranged, and reformed into the angles and shadows and curves of a warrior-poet in motion. I "saw" his arms and legs and cape coalesce into a blur of light. There were images and futures to choose from: He slashed at my eyes; he slashed at my throat; he planted his foot and slashed my hands. The possibilities stunned me. I was blind because he had slid his steel across the blueness of my irises; I was struck dumb because my throat was in pieces; I could not feel to grip his neck because he had hacked the fingers from my knuckles. But only one future would come to pass; his knife could not be in a thousand places at once. He moved, had moved, will always have moved. The tapestry of events that would in moments come into existence twisted together. The silver thread of his thrusting knife, the bright, decorative green and red bands of his rings, the black, curling threads of his hair, and the red and black threads of my own, his kamelaika's gold and purple and orange threads, all the threads of my life were tightening, weaving. *But in the end we choose our futures,* as Katharine would have said. As she did say, as she always will say. The futures formed within me, and without, and Dawud was about to move. I was scrying—it was a wonderful and terrible thing. I looked into Dawud's eyes, and the purple fibers and flecks of blue within his irises shimmered. His pupils dilated. There was vision. With a scryer's sight, I saw the muscles of the iris diaphragm uncoil, the long, purplish protein fibers untwisting, and deeper, the vibrating carbon atoms, the hydrogen, oxygen and nitrogen of protein. Dawud's eyes and the fabrics of the wall tapestries, the blooddrops on his knife, were alive with proteins. And the atoms of the proteins were composed of yet tinier particles which possessed charge and mass, color and spin and charm, and all was movement, oscillation and energy. And deeper still: The chamber melted into a brilliance of light, and the tiniest of particles unraveled like balls of gaudy silk. There was an infinity of meshing, polychromatic, silken threads made of . . . but it is impossible to singularly describe the deepest structure of reality. The threads were flaming crimson; the threads were molten gold; the threads were the standing wavefronts of the mechanics and the theorems of the cantors and the conscious choices of a pilot in slowtime. I followed this thread of consciousness, staring blindly at the patterns all around me, and I suddenly knew, as all scryers know, that I was looking at the very tapestry of the universe as it formed. I watched the threads of the universal hologram unfold. In a way, I was uncoding the hologram, looking ahead to read the code, for what is scrying if not the reading of the master program of the universe? *But in the end we choose our futures.* One forming pattern seemed brighter than the others. It was embroidered with beautiful (and terrible), irridescent threads. The threads wove, and the greens were glowing emerald, and the purples brightened to burning indigo. There was a rainbow-colored kamclaika, a warrior's crimson ring, and a killing knife made of steel. And choice, there was always choice. Dawud chose to plunge the knife into my unguarded belly. He came for me. But I saw the motion before he moved, and when he lunged, I twisted out of the way. He slashed at my throat. I blocked his arm and locked it, and it snapped. And when he shifted the knife to his other hand, I jumped away from him and rather clumsily kicked his groin.

The kick would have maimed a civilized man. But, as I later learned, when the warrior-poets pass into puberty they undergo a cutting which enables them to retract their testes into their abdomens at will. (The slander that the warrior-poets are smooth between the legs is untrue. Nor is it true that they do not feel the urge to couple with human females. The poets, of course, worship passion even though they do not allow its physical expression. Chastity begets intensity, they say.) Dawud staggered for a moment, then flicked an orange-tipped dart at me. It missed my head by an inch. I heard it scrape along the individual follicles as it passed through the long hair hanging over my ear.

"Very good!" he gasped out. "So good, now."

"Damn you!"

"Help me, Pilot."

"Put your knife away, then."

"Help me with Soli."

"No, no, you're mad."

As we continued our deadly game, it must have become clear to him that something was wrong. In truth, he should have killed me at the first pass of the knife. Something was very wrong—he must have known this because he began to talk to me, to try to distract me. And then I caught his other arm in my hands and broke it, too. The knife went spinning out of his hand into a clot of roots and dirt. I grabbed his biceps and drew him closer. Although I expected him to cry out, or to look down in horror at the sharp prongs of bone ripping through his kamelaika, of course he did not. He smiled. With his tongue he fumbled about in his mouth as if he were trying to pry loose a sliver of a baldo nut from his teeth. But it was not a nut; it was a tiny dart, and he spat it at me even as I jerked his arm up in front of my face. The dart went into his own hand. In the moment before the poison paralyzed him, he gasped, "Scryer-pilot, warrior-pilot—I should have known."

His entire body spasmed and went rigid, like Soli's. I searched inside the compartments of his robe until I found the golden, tubular spinneret all warrior-poets carry. I shook it against my ear listening to the liquid proteins slosh inside the tube. It was nearly full. I held the tube over the poet's chest, and as I squeezed the pressure-sensitive end, an exceedingly fine jet of proteins squirted from the tip and hardened into a steely strand. It took me a few moments to circle and recircle his body—I had to half-lift him off the floor—and I bound him in a sticky cocoon.

I had defeated a warrior-poet!

My moments of scrying passed, and I returned to realtime. I sat back against the bole of a rubber tree. I was exhausted, elated and afraid. Dawud slowly regained the use of his muscles as I watched. He must have absorbed much less of the poison than Soli had, either that or his accelerated metabolism had burned it out of his body. Soli, I saw, remained as stiff and unmoving as a robot.

"How do I go about cutting him free?" I asked Dawud.

"You must cut me free first," he said as he worked his jaws. "Please."

I looked at him to see if he was joking. I could not think of a single reason why I should cut him loose.

"Warrior-pilot, scryer-pilot—are you listening? On Qallar

there is a code of honor. Cut me loose and give me back my
knife. Or kill me yourself. I need to die."

There was not the slightest hint of deception in his voice.
A warrior-poet cannot live with the shame of defeat and
capture. I am sure that if I had immediately freed him, he
would have plunged the knife through his eye and into his
brain, which is how a warrior-poet must kill himself when it
is time. There was an excitement about his whole being. If he
had been Devaki, he might have employed the *uswa* tense of
"exalted impatience" to indicate his eagerness for the coming
moment.

I bent over and picked up the knife. The steel was sticky
with black dirt. There was a spot beneath the olive skin of his
neck where the great artery pulsed. I could kill him easily, as
a Devaki kills a wounded shagshay bull. Why should I deny
him his supreme moment?

"I could kill you," I told him.

"Please, Pilot."

"I *should* kill you."

"You know about killing, it is said."

I hesitated, prying dirt-chips from the knife with my
fingernail. There was fear in the warrior-poet's eyes.

"Kill me quickly," he said.

"Is it that easy to kill, then?"

"It is easy, Pilot. You should know. The knife, now, quickly
before the moment passes."

I was afraid to kill him, and he was afraid of my fear. He
feared that I would not kill him. Thus he would lose his
perfect moment. He would be doomed to the crushing
mundaneness of quotidian life, and this, I saw, was the single
thing that all warrior-poets feared. And if I helped him over
to the other side, as he wanted, what then? He would be as
dead as dirt, and there would be no more possibilities, then
or forever.

"I can't kill you," I said.

"To live, I die—you've heard our saying before, haven't
you, Pilot? And when I die, I'll live again and forever."

"Damn you and your paradoxes!"

"Yes, the Hanuman-Ordando paradox."

I let the knife dangle carelessly and asked, "You have a
name for it?"

He nodded his head. "The warrior, Ivar Hanuman and

Nils Ordando, the great poet, when they founded my order, they were aware of the essential paradox of existence. And they found a way out."

There came a groan from the spinnaker tree. Soli's voicebox was bobbing up and down but he could not speak. I turned back to the poet. "What is the way out?" I asked.

"If the universe eternally recurs," he said, "then there is no true death. There is nothing to fear. The moment of the possible lives again and again, forever. Give me the knife, and I'll show you. We'll relive this moment a billion times."

"I do not believe in eternal recurrence," I said.

"Few do."

I did not want to tell him that a whole school of scryers and remembrancers believed that eternal recurrence is the rhythm of the universe. "It's an absurd philosophy," I said.

"Yes," he agreed, "but it is the only way to resolve the paradox, which is why we choose to believe in it."

My eyes itched so I rubbed them and managed to irritate them further with dirt. I blinked rapidly as the tears ran down my cheeks. "You choose to believe in a philosophy which you admit is absurd? That's even more absurd."

Soli moaned and worked his lips. He was struggling to say something. I did not think he could see either of us because he could not move his head.

"Yes," Dawud said, "when fear is gone, we can choose our beliefs."

"But an *absurd* belief? Can you really do that? In truth? Why?"

"Because it is the only way out of the paradox. Because it enables us to live and die. Because it is comforting."

I felt the knife's edge with my thumb. It was very sharp. I said, "I don't understand how you can choose to believe the unbelievable, all the while *knowing* that it's unbelievable."

"But I do believe—as all warrior-poets believe—that this moment, as we remain here arguing, will recur an infinite number of times. When you kill me, or allow me the honor, my same death will occur again and again. As it has already happened a billion billion times."

"That isn't even close to infinity," I said.

"It isn't? Well, I'm a poet, not a mathematician."

I swung the knife against one of the rubber tree's branches. With a dull "thwack," the entire limb came off. I felt instantly guilty and pressed my thumb against the wound where the sap oozed out.

"I can't share your belief," I said. "If I let you die, I let die what you say is the most wonderful thing—this intensity of yours."

"No, the moment will live forever."

"No," I said. "When the light goes out, it's dark."

"Don't be afraid, Pilot."

"We're circling each other's words like double-stars," I said.

"Kill me," he said.

"And if I did, what would happen to my mother, then? If she's been mimed? No, you'll have to live so you can tell me how to heal my mother."

I rubbed the bridge of my nose. There was another reason I did not want to kill him: I wanted to know what happened when one's brain had been infected with a virus, to ask him about the knifeblade edge between life and death.

"There's an old haiku written by Lao Tzu," I told him. "'A man with outward courage dares to die; a man with inward courage dares to live.'"

When I said this, the smile on his face told of humor and irony. "You are clever, Pilot."

I pointed at Soli, who was struggling against the tight jacket of his cocoon, and I said, "When a warrior-poet traps his victim, doesn't he recite a poem before killing him? And if the victim can complete the poem or stanza, he *must* be spared—isn't that right?"

"That is so."

I bent over him as he lay with his mouth half-open, smiling. I smelled oranges on his breath, and I said, "Listen. Do you know this poem?"

Because I could not stop for Death—
He kindly stopped for me.

"What is the rest of it," I asked. "The poem, Poet?"

"You mock our tradition," he said. And then, reluctantly, he recited:

Because I would not stop for Death—
He kindly stopped for me.

The tower held but just ourselves
And Immortality.

At last Soli found his tongue and began shouting, "It hurts! It hurts! Kill me—I can't stand the pain!" His face was shiny with grease and sweat, and he was working at his lip. There was madness in his eyes.

"How long will it be before the drug metabolizes?" I asked Dawud.

"You don't understand, Pilot. The drug is not like the drug that immobilized me, or you. The drug will never completely metabolize. Most of its effects will attenuate after an hour, if he lives, but he will always bear a special sensitivity to his . . . moment of the possible."

I went over to Soli and tried to stop him from chewing at his lip. I tried to cut the fibers binding him, but they were tougher than steel. "Lord Pilot," I said. "My . . . Lord Pilot." But he did not seem to understand me.

"He hears your every word," Dawud said. "But he cannot comprehend the meaning. The pain, that's all he knows."

From the stairwell across the outer chamber came a faint clanging, as of metal against stone. The Timekeeper, then, must have sent robots into the tower.

"Soli, it will be all right . . . the robots will cut you free."

"Yes, it hurts," he said. "It hurts."

The clanging grew louder. There was the ringing of many tactors against obsidian steps. It sounded as if an army of robots were banging up the stairwell. And on the poet's face, a look of resignation tempered with irony.

"Soli will be all right, then," I said.

Just then two immense, red, tutelary robots crossed the outer chamber. They did not pause at the doors to the inner chamber. Two other tutelary robots followed them closely, and behind them were two more. Stamped into the metal of their base clusters was the outline of a standing hourglass. They were the Timekeeper's robots, "the long hand of the Lord Horologe," called forth on those rare occasions when order must be restored to the City.

"I've captured a warrior-poet," I said. "He tried to kill the Lord Pilot."

I stood there waiting for the robots to say something, perhaps waiting—absurdly—for them to congratulate me or

to inform me that the Timekeeper was grateful I had arrived
in so timely a manner. But they said nothing. Then all was
motion and hard metal, the lightning sweep of metal append-
ages, grinding, clamping metal. The first robot swept me up
and caught me in its cold, metal clamps. The second robot
hoisted up the warrior-poet and dropped him into the open
clamps of the third robot. It clicked its pincers, waiting. The
other robots scanned the wrecked chamber. I struggled, but
it was useless. I quickly told the robots what had happened,
but it was like explaining the opening theory of chess to a
radio. They did not listen.

"Can't you tell a pilot from a murdering poet?" I shouted.

Dawud laughed and the smile never left his face. "They're
robots," he said. "You must forgive them their actions."

As the robots dragged us away, I raged because the
Timekeeper was not there in his person. I could not wait to
inform him of his robots' error, to tell him that I had saved
Soli from torture and death. I banged my fist against the
robot; I bruised my knuckles and twisted and cursed, and all
the while, Soli stood staring, shouting, "Yes, it hurts; it hurts;
it hurts; it hurts!"

23

Plutonium Spring

The good Kristian should be aware of mathematicians and all those who make empty prophecies. The danger already exists that the mathematicians have made a covenant with the devil to darken the spirit and to confine man in the bonds of Hell.
—Saint Augustine of Hippo

Why should man seek justice in a universe which is manifestly unjust? Are we so insignificant and vain that we cannot look upon the raw, naked face of randomness without praying it will smile upon us merely because we have been righteous and good? If indeed vanity begets the desire for justice, then I believe the Timekeeper is the vainest of men. As I have said before, he is famous for his punishments. Someday, no doubt, the sculptors will engrave his commemorative busts with glyphs meaning "Horthy the Just." It is a sobriquet he has earned. When that grim old man learned of Soli's near assassination, he ordered the cleverest of justices. His robots dragged Dawud and me to the basement of his tower where we were locked into identical, adjoining cells. Our cells were stone cubes one hundred and one inches on each side. (The end joint of my little finger is exactly one inch long. For no good reason, it amused me to measure the dimensions of my cell.) The walls were stone and the floors were set with cold flagstones; the ceiling, as far as I could determine, was a seamless square of black stone. The robots pushed us through the doorways of our cells, and the doors rolled shut. Darkness swallowed me. The blackness was total. With my fingers I pried at the crack between the door and the jamb but it was useless. The door was a single slab of heartstone, impossible to move.

I had defied the Timekeeper, and therefore he would falsely blame me for Soli's near assassination—this was the conclusion logic forced on me. Surely his robots would have informed him I had captured the warrior-poet. Surely he knew I was innocent. Would he ever call me before the akashics so I could explain my innocence? I did not think so. In the cell's darkness, a hundred questions plagued me: Where was my mother? Where was Soli? Did he believe I had been part of a plot to assassinate him? Had the poet's drug destroyed his mind, then? Had the Timekeeper told everyone I had tried to murder Soli? Had he told *anyone*? Were Bardo and my friends at this very moment pleading for my release? How could they if they did not know where I was? *If the Timekeeper wanted me dead, why was I still alive?*

While we awaited the Timekeeper's judgment, we passed the time by talking to each other. Near the ceiling there was a narrow tunnel of an air duct connecting our two cells. By jumping up and clutching the smooth lip of the duct, I found I could chin myself and converse through the thick walls without shouting. Our conversations, however, were always interrupted because I could only hold myself up for a few minutes before my arm muscles cramped. We recited short poems to each other; we made puns and played with words; we argued over those few beliefs that our two orders held in common. I lost most of the arguments. The warrior-poets, I am sorry to say, are sly with their words, even more so than the neologicians or the wily semanticists. Although Dawud *seemed* to speak precisely, one had to listen carefully to what he said, or the meaning would slip away like a wriggling, wet fish from greased fingers. One time, when I observed that it was strange beyond probability that the warrior-poets and the Solid State Entity would practice the identical custom of asking their victims poems, he remarked, "Oh, yes, Kalinda of the Flowers. She has always . . . taken an interest in warrior-poets."

"Kalinda?"

"That is what we call the goddess."

That was what the Agathanians called Her, too.

"But why Kalinda *of the Flowers,* then?"

"Perhaps because the Entity is perceived to be female, and the association with flowers has always been perceived to be a feminine thing. Who knows the origin of names?"

"But you say she knows about you poets?"

"Of course," he said. "Once, long ago, my order tried to breed female wa.rior-poets but . . . it was a disaster. Kalinda—the Entity—made us stop."

"I hadn't thought the gods take an interest in the affairs of man."

"What do you know of gods, Pilot?"

"'As flies are to little boys, so are we to the gods,'" I quoted. "'They kill us for their sport.'"

"Of course, The Shakespeare. Very good."

"Gods are gods. They do as they please."

"You think so?"

I thought of my journey to Agathange. I clung to the lip of stone and gasped out, "The gods make us in their image. Or remake us."

"No," he said, and his voice came roaring through the air duct, "that is exactly wrong."

"I didn't know you poets were masters of eschatology, then."

"Why are you always so sarcastic, Pilot?"

"Why must you poets answer a question with a question?"

"Did you *ask* me a question?"

After perhaps a few days of this arguing—in our dark, featureless cells time was hard to measure—the poet grew silent and would not answer when I called out to him, which I did at intervals for hours. I was sure that he had been executed, beheaded at the Timekeeper's command. Then, finally, he answered back. My relief that he was still alive surprised me.

"I've been before your Timekeeper," he said. "He's clever, isn't he? Should I tell you my sentence? He contrives my death in a way which won't offend my order. He is a just man."

"No," I huffed out as I strained to keep myself from falling back to the floor. I kicked out to obtain leverage, but my boots skidded against the smooth walls. "He's just a man."

"He is merciful; his punishment is sublime."

"It's barbaric."

"I can't expect a pilot to understand."

"You warrior-poets are mad."

"What *is* madness?"

"Only a madman would know."

"Only a stubborn pilot would refuse to appreciate the genius of his Timekeeper's sentence."

In a way, the Timekeeper's punishment *was* clever and perhaps even sublime, though I hardly thought it admitted of genius. Quite simply, he had contrived an ancient and barbaric means of execution: In the empty cell adjoining the warrior-poet's (we were the only prisoners in the Tower, the only prisoners for many, many years), the tinkers had placed a mechanism which, upon the reception of a certain signal, would release a cloud of poison gas. Inside the mechanism they had placed a minute quantity of plutonium. The signal for the release of the gas would be the random decay of any of the plutonium's individual atoms. Dawud might live for years or, more probably, he might die the next instant—he wouldn't know until he heard the hissing of the gas and smelled its vinegary acridness. It is bizarre, but true, that his order could blame only a random, quantum event for his death, which for the warrior-poets was no blame at all.

"Certainly," I said, "the Timekeeper will have placed a large enough piece of plutonium in his damn machine so that the probability of your living more than a few days approaches zero."

I did not tell him how shocked I was that the Timekeeper possessed stores of plutonium. It was the most barbarous of all barbarities.

"Of course," Dawud agreed. "There will be a sufficient quantity of plutonium. But you miss the point."

"Which is?"

"Imagine for a moment, Pilot, that you were *my* lord—his name is Dario Redring. When Dario comes to your city and asks for me, asks, 'Is he alive?' your Timekeeper can respond truthfully that he doesn't know. *Am* I alive? No one can know. From the point of view of others, I am inside a sealed cell. I am in limbo. Has the plutonium decayed? There is a probability. The degree of my aliveness is represented by a wave function which contains probabilities of life and death. Only when my cell is opened and Dario and your Timekeeper look inside will one of the probabilities actualize, while the other vanishes and the wave function will collapse. Only their act of observing my state of being will cause my aliveness or deadness to become manifest. Until then, as far as everyone outside my cell is concerned, I am neither alive nor dead. Or rather, I am both dead and alive. And that is why I don't think your Timekeeper will ever permit my cell to be opened. Until then, your Order will remain blameless for my fate."

"But that's absurd!"

"My order relishes absurdity and paradox, Pilot."

"You gave me the impression that you were ignorant of mathematics."

"I speak of philosophy, not mathematics."

"The probabilities—"

"Of course," he interrupted, "the *possibility* exists that the plutonium will never decay and I will never die."

"But you *will* die. The Timekeeper has seen to that."

"Of course! And it will be a sublime death. I must compose a poem to celebrate it."

"To never know one moment if it will be the last—that's hell!"

"No, Pilot, there is no hell. We are creators of our heavens."

"Madman!" I said. I pushed off the air duct, and landed on the floor with a slap.

Dawud's response, when it came, was so faint I could barely hear it, muffled words lost down a black tunnel of stone: "You're just afraid the gas will kill you, too."

From Dawud I learned little pieces of news he had gleaned during his audience with the Timekeeper. The news was not good. Apparently, the Timekeeper had loosed his tutelary robots upon the City. Warrior-poets had been captured and banished. The robots had "accidentally" pinched the heads off of three pilots—Faxon Wu, Takenya the Fearless and Rosalinda li Howt—who were ready to desert the Order for Tria. (I later learned that hundreds of autists had mysteriously vanished from the Farsider's Quarter at this time. The Timekeeper, I knew, had always hated autists.) When the pilots, high professionals and academicians had learned of the Timekeeper's violation of canon law, there was talk of taking a deepship and leaving in swarm for some new planet on which to start an entirely new Academy. Somehow, the news of my imprisonment had spread, and Soli had called for my beheading, while Justine and the Sonderval had called for a convocation of the Pilot's College. They would ask the other master pilots to remove Soli and elect a new Lord Pilot—so the rumor went. Nikolos the Elder, the Lord Akashic, had surprised everyone by asking for a convocation of the College of Lords. Would that plump, hitherto timid little man really call for a new Timekeeper, as Kolenya Mor warned he would? No one seemed to know. No one—especially not the Timekeeper— seemed to know where my mother was, or what she was doing. And all the while, Bardo was petitioning the Timekeeper for my release, petitioning, blustering, threatening, and bribing various masters and lords to add their names to the petition. He had called for me to be tried before the akashics. I was innocent, he argued, and I should be allowed to establish my innocence. But Soli, who hated Bardo for stealing away his wife, invented a counter-argument. I should not go before the akashics, he said, because their computers were made to model only *human* brains. Who could know whether or not my brain—my Agathanian-carked brain—could fool the akashic computers? (Who could have suspected that Soli was my father, that he feared the akashics would unfold this fact and make it known? Who knew what anyone's motives were during that maddest of times in our City?)

Ironically, the Timekeeper's judgment filled Dawud with joy. He was so excited that he could neither eat nor sleep. He would pace his cell for days at a time, composing poems and shouting the verses out until his voice grew hoarse. "Imminent death is the spice of life," he quoted. "It is true, of course. Pilot? Are you listening? Tell me your thoughts—are you thinking about the possibilities?"

I am not by nature a meditative man. I dreaded being left alone in a moist, dark cell with nothing to hold my mind other than my own fearful thoughts, thoughts of painful possibilities. Most of the time, I slumped against the freezing walls; I stared at the blackness in front of my face, waiting. I listened to the warrior-poet as he paced and howled out his ecstatic verses, and when the pacing ceased and he was quiet, I listened to the plip-plop of the condensation droplets spattering against the floor. I listened to my heart beat. Often, usually after I had just awakened from a fitful sleep against the hard, moist flagstones, I was stiff and cold. I ate the nuts and bread dropped at intervals through the slit at the base of the door, and I slurped down water from a large bowl. Into that same bowl I dropped my dung and piss, hoping that the robots had been programmed to clean it before refilling it. (I have always, incidentally, disregarded Turin's Law, crudely put that any robot sufficiently intelligent to clean dishes is too intelligent to clean dishes. That may be true of human beings, but the cold, soulless tutelary robots guarding us possessed only those 'specific intelligence functions required of them. Such as killing the Timekeeper's enemies should they try to escape. I cannot believe they were self-aware.) I am ashamed to admit that I fell into long spells of self-pity. I thought about myself too much. I tried to concentrate on externals, but sensa of any sort were weak and few. The clanging of the robots beyond the door, the muted words of Dawud's poems—these sounds I listened to, but as I contemplated a robot's self-awareness, or lack thereof, and judged the quality of the poet's verses (they were not extraordinary), I was led ever inward to my deepest worries and fears.

After a while, I found that my sleeping habits were being destroyed. I would sleep for long periods of time, perhaps as long as a day, escaping myself. Then would come fits of anxiety, surges of mania. I paced my cell and my muscles knotted and relaxed, over and over, rhythmically rippling like the waves of the sea. I had thoughts. I tried not to think about the origin of my thoughts. I tried not to think at all. I scratched my dirty beard and felt along the slick wall for cracks or weaknesses, but I could not stop thinking. I brooded, wondering what I was becoming. How I dreaded this *becoming*! There was something new inside me—when I thought about it and tried to conceive its shape and direction, I was as excited as I was terrified. I tried to sleep, and sleep would not come. Whole days must have passed in which I did not sleep. These spells of sleeplessness were punctuated by instances of micro-sleep when my brain would deaden for a moment or two. And I would awaken to cold, rank air, the sound of dripping water and the smell of my fear. Sometimes I would test myself to see if I was going mad. Could I still do the calculus of free sets? Did it feel just the same as always to scratch my itchy, greasy scalp? Could I open and close my fingers at will? In this way, and in a thousand other ways, I

tested the cavern of my mind for hidden fissures and flaws,
and for new, crystalline formations of ability and thought.
What thoughts, what actions, what dreams could I *will*, if my
will were truly free? Could I will my brain to change as I
wished, or were there restraints, natural rules of develop-
ment which could not be violated? In the deepest part of my
mind, where the universe runs like a cold, black stream, I
searched for the fount of free will. There was a moment when
I could almost see the ultimate impulse guiding my actions,
could almost taste the cool deliciousness of pure freedom.
The moment lingered like a water droplet flung into the air.
And then it was gone, sucked down the whirlpool of my
thoughts. There was a black hole at the whirlpool's center,
and within that hole, another, blacker still. There was an
infinity of holes within holes waiting to swallow the sanity of
anyone who contemplated himself for too long.

For me, my prison became a hell. I have always feared
darkness; when I was a novice, I had irritated Bardo by
keeping my light burning all night. And silence is the darkness of sound, the death of the everyday vibrations, rhythms
and tones that give song to the soul. We are creators of our
heavens, the poet had said, but lately he had grown ominously
quiet. Perhaps the plutonium had decayed; perhaps the
poison gas had seared his lungs and liquefied his brain. Or
perhaps he had tired of ecstasy, tired of balancing on the
knifeblade edge between life and death. Had he flopped to
the floor of his cell in an exhausted stupor? I did not know.
There was silence inside his cell, silence in the still air
currents, the silence of stone. Even the water on the ceiling
had stopped dripping. My body no longer seemed to stink. In
front of my eyes the blackness was fuzzy like wool, and my
fingers were so numb that the texture of the walls felt waxen,
and there was no smell or taste, no sound at all. I hallucinat-
ed. For a moment I imagined I was floating in the pit of my
lightship. I dreamed there were stars. But then, when I
reached out with my mind to face the ship's computer—
nothing. There was neither the torrential rush of the number-
storm, nor the white light of dreamtime, nor any hint of the
manifold's splendid music. I realized I was alone within a real
stone cell as black and empty as deadspace. I was alone inside
my mind, and I was in hell.

As the days passed the hallucinations grew stronger, more

total. Since my sensory nerves were quiescent, my brain supplied its own stimulation. My visual cortex began firing of its own accord. There were colors. Showers of purple sparks cascaded through the air. The air itself sparkled like a flowing robe of green and blue silk. I saw pulsating, concentric circles of red light turning inside each other, and yellow and orange wavy lines flashing and quivering. There were a hundred different smells: spices and perfume, incense and feverbalm and musk. I heard bells ringing and crunching ice, the sound of a howling wolf. Such hallucinations, of course, are common among those who are robbed of contact with the external world. Journeymen often see visions the first time they float within the Rose Wombs. And the Alaloi, too, tell of hunters trapped out on the icepack in endless snowstorms who lose their sense of up and down, right and left, and begin to see bright bands and streamers of light splitting the swirling clouds of snow. I *knew* the colors and sounds I sensed were not real, but I also knew that if the hallucinations continued for too long, I might end up more brain-damaged than a pathetic aphasic.

For a long while I distracted myself with pure mathematics. I conjured up the bright, violet ideoplasts for the Axiom of Choice, and I lost myself in the beautiful Theory of Sets. I invented (or perhaps discovered) theorems that might someday be useful in proving the Continuum Hypothesis. There was a moment when the luminescent, many-shaped ideoplasts appeared so rapidly and vividly that I thought the number-storm might begin of its own, without the aid of my ship-computer. And what a wonder that would have been! To enter into the manifold at will, to face the universe with nothing more than mathematics and will and naked brain—how often during those hellish days I prayed for this ability! But prayer is the signpost of helplessness and failure. The freedom of the manifold was denied me, and I soon found that in my prison of darkness, mathematics seemed all too arbitrary and unreal.

I might have emulated the autists and created fantasies and thoughtscapes in which I could dwell for as long as I lived. To dream lucid dreams, and all the while, to be aware of the dreams, and more, to change their shape and texture at will—this was a possibility. I might have experienced clear, rippling, aquamarine water, the warm, rushing waves of an otherworldly beach, the sticky clutch of a woman lying beneath me on the hot sand. But—despite what the autists say—it would not have been real. I would be lost in the unreal, devoured by images and events which could never and had never really occurred. If at last the Timekeeper gave me my freedom, I would be as mad as any autist.

I do not know how long I could have stood the silence had I not chanced to recall a rather pretentious saying of the remembrancers. One day as I was dragging my long, curling fingernails across the slatelike flagstones, I was thinking of the master remembrancer, Thomas Rane, turning over in my mind the implications of his memory of the god-man, Kelkemesh, and the primal myth. These words came of their own to my inner ear: *Memory is the soul of reality.* Within me were years of memories, a whole lifetime of memories. Memory, then, would be my salvation. I would dwell in the past. I would take refuge in my memories like a wounded seal seeking safety in his aklia. I would live again the crucial moments of my life, and if I lived them too passionately— well, at least I would remain within a reality which had actually existed.

At first all went well. As time dripped on, I found I had less and less need of physical distractions. I stopped singing to myself, which was a great relief because I have never been able to keep a tune. I had little need to lick my kamelaika's scratchy wool, or to taste the salty blood of my gnawed lip, or to press my eyes with my thumbs in order to induce phosphenes, those bright pinpoints of light we sometimes see when our eyes are closed. My memories were more stimulating than mere sensation; my memories were gleaming jewels suspended in ice water; my memories were the soul of my distant and recent past. I remembered learning to tie the laces of my skates. How frustrated I had been when the looping of the knot had eluded my childish fingers! How I had raged when my mother tried to help me! I remembered other happier events, such as the first time Bardo and I had taken a yellow-sailed ice schooner out onto the frozen Sound. Bardo had been reluctant to borrow the schooner and had pointed out that we knew nothing about sailing. But I had ridiculed him into recklessness. (Journeymen often think that because they have survived the manifold, they can master any form of transportation.) A fierce wind had come up unexpectedly, nearly smashing us against the rocks of Waaskel. Still, our rush across the Sound had been exhilarating, a few moments of pure fun. In the darkness of my cell, there were other memories, each more vivid than the last. Like an old man, I remembered, and I wondered what different memories I might have had if only I had made different choices when I was younger. Why had I decided to become a pilot instead of a cantor? Why did I love Katharine? Why did I murder Liam? *Why were my memories growing ever more burningly real?*

he remembrancers, it is said, must overcome a difficult problem when they are younger. To remember too well is to forget only with great difficulty. As my memories grew more and more vivid, they seemed to linger, burning themselves into my inner eye. I might conjure up the first time I had seen a Friend of Man, and the blue trunk of the alien would wriggle like a sleekit and obscure more important memories. I began to have trouble forgetting. I recalled reading the poems of the Timekeeper, and whole pages of print were indelibly stamped onto the white tissue of my mind. I could "see" every bend and twist of each black letter as if I were reading an open page of the book. This was the memory of pictures I had heard so much about from childhood friends who had gone on to become scryers or remembrancers. I remembered that there were tricks for forgetting. In my mind, I built a long black wall and superimposed lines and words, whole stanzas and pages of poetry onto the wall. The squiggly black letters disappeared, black into blackness— a time. Other memories, such as Katharine's smile, were harder to banish. I had to resolve the pale tones of her skin into a million dots of primary colors. Each red and green and blue dot I then intensified until it flared and swelled and exploded like a tiny star. A million points of light burst inside me and then coalesced into a blinding haze, like that of an icefield on a false winter day. Most difficult to forget were sounds. The memory of music persisted despite my efforts to drown it out with the boom of rockets or with other noise. I was surprised to hear entire symphonies with a clarity almost hyperreal. Again and again the melody of the Takeko's Madrigal of Sorrow played inside, the round tones of the adagio forming up like beads of gold. I heard and reheard Bardo singing love songs to Justine, and I listened to the keening of the shakuhachis

and the gosharps that my mother used to play. I do not mean
to say that I heard each of these things simultaneously, for I
did not. One sound gave way to another only with difficulty.
For instance, the music of seagulls and the drumbeat of the
sea I could not forget until I had taken the component sine
waves of the sounds through a Fourier transform, enfolding
them into a hologram. I could then "drop" this hologram into
a black, soundproofed box where it would remain until I
wished to remove it and *unfold* the sounds of memory. Thus I
created millions of mental boxes for the memories that haunted me. In this way I made room for other deeper memories,
memories I did not know I possessed.

Everything is recorded; nothing is forgotten.

I do not know exactly when I became aware that I was
remembrancing. Many people, of course, are cursed and
blessed with nearly perfect memory, but they are not remembrancers. They can see only the faintest spark of racial
memory. To remember the lives of our fathers and of our
mothers' grandfathers and their great-grandfathers and so on
down the branching tree of our descent, to unlock the
memories of our race's distant past encoded within our
chromosomes, to "think like DNA," as Lord Galina would
say—this is the higher art of remembrancing. It is an art
which consumed me.

With a dizzying speed, images of my ancestors' lives
flickered before me. I saw slick blood and an uncoiled umbili-
cal cord as my grandmother, Dama Oriana Ringess, screamed
and pushed my mother from within her into the light of day.
How my mother cried in her pain! I saw Soli. He was, in
truth, my father. There were memories from Soli's childhood;
I understood, finally, what I had remembered inside the
Entity, the memory of Alexander Diego Soli teaching his son
mathematics. And deeper and back, generation fell from
generation; faces formed and changed, as mutable as clay.
There was the long, broad Soli nose and the ice-blue eyes;
there the full lips of a Ringess pressed together and then
parted to reveal the twenty-eight thick Ringess teeth. Further back, a Soli tampered with his chromosomes to strength-
en his mathematical abilities. (It was from this Soli, Mahavira
Andreivi Soli, that I inherited my strands of red hair.) And
deeper down the roots of time: There were poets, scryers,
whores, pilots, katholiks, shepherds (of sheep), slaves, kings,

warriors, and even an astrier named Cleo Reiness, half of whose five hundred children went on to populate the moons of Durrikene, half of whom carked their DNA and eventually came to be known as the alien Fayoli.

One day when I was remembrancing, I heard Dawud stir within his cell. It seemed he was still very much alive, if exhausted from his long wait for the plutonium to decay. He recited a short poem to me—the first in a long while—and one couplet rang in my ears and pulled at the cords of my memory:

> *Only bone remembers pain;*
> *Only pain and bone remain.*

Then there was a long silence followed by a long, convoluted poem he had entitled "Plutonium Spring." I stood to chin myself up to the air duct, the better to listen to his strident words. I heard him intone:

> *The rhythm in my blood is the dancing of blinded locusts*

And then, "Pilot, are you still alive? Can you hear me?"

"Yes, I was . . . remembering."

I wanted to tell him a thing that I had seen, that Eva Reiness was the great-grandmother of Nils Ordando. The warrior-poets shared a portion of my chromosomes. We were near-brothers, I wanted to tell him. All men are brothers.

"Do you believe in chance?" came his measured words through the black duct.

"I . . . sometimes I believe in chance, sometimes in fate. I don't know what I believe."

"How long do you think it has been? What are the chances that the plutonium would not have decayed?"

"Perhaps it was just a joke," I said. "Perhaps there is no plutonium and no gas. Perhaps the Timekeeper is trying to destroy your sanity—what little a warrior-poet has."

There was a silence, and I had to let go of the duct. After a while Dawud gasped out, "Fate and chance, the same glad dance."

To a warrior-poet who believed in eternal recurrence, of course, that would be so.

"Pilot, can you hear me?" After I had pulled myself up to

the duct, I could hear him plainly. "These past days have been such an ecstasy," he said. "I find I no longer want to die. I have made poetry, and I have thought... such thoughts, and dreamed and... Can you hear me?"

"Yes," I said into the darkness.

"The gas is coming soon. The plutonium is about to explode. There are hot gases, dying hydrogen—how delicate the falling violets are!"

"Is this part of a poem?"

"Life is a poem that we compose. This is the faith of the warrior-poets: that we can capture life's essence, the moment of the possible, in words."

I said nothing because it is my faith that the essence of the universe lies far beyond the realm of human words.

"I will die soon, of course. There are killing vapors in the granite darkness."

"Are you a scryer, then?"

"No, a poet. And I have composed my death poem. Will you promise me something? When I am dead, my body must be brought back to Qallar in a black marble casket. If you live long enough, you must find a farsider who knows the art of writing. The words of my death poem must be chiseled onto the casket's facing."

My fingers began to cramp, and my forearm muscles trembled. I made him a promise I had no intention to keep. For no good reason, I told him of my remembrancing. I tasted gummy old food and blood in my mouth as I said, "Nils Ordando was a son of the Ringess line."

"Yes, that is known," he replied instantly. "The founders of both our Orders were hibakusha. They fled the Agni nebula during the computer wars. When the hydrogen—"

"We're almost brothers," I said.

"All men are brothers," he said. "And all men are hibakusha. And fraticide is the rule of the species." And then, "Can you smell the gas, Pilot?"

Here he recited his poem, the last stanza of which was:

I am sodden beneath wrappings of flesh;
I am golden beneath the morning sky;
I am holy beneath my evaporating flesh;
I am naked beneath the plutonium sky.

I shouted to him but there was no answer. I listened for the sound of hissing gas. I pulled up and tried to get an elbow into the air duct as I wedged my head and shoulder into the stuffy, tight tunnel. Would I hear the whine of an airlock grinding shut? Would the poet scream and thrash as he gasped for clean air? With my head ridiculously squeezed into a dark hole in the wall, I listened for any sound at all, but in the poet's cell there was silence.

After a while, I pushed off the wall and began pacing my cell. A madman, a murderer, a lover of words, my near-brother—I called out to him, but he did not answer me then, nor during the days that followed. I repeated the words to his poem, "Plutonium Spring," and I memorized them. It was an easy thing to do.

Everything is recorded; nothing is forgotten.

Again I fell into racial memory. I fell far back, seeing archetypal images, smelling primal smells, hearing the heartbeat of ancient poems. I remembranced Old Earth. There the sky was a lighter blue than that of Icefall, light blue like a thallow's eggshell; there the land was warm and the valleys were green, and there were orchards of real apple trees, fields of golden wheatgrain. There my far-grandfather lived in a whitewashed cottage in a city by the sea. He was a pilot and a boatmaker. His hands—my hands—were yellow with callous, and wood splinters stung his fingers. He had a wife, and there was a coupling, thousands of joyous couplings, and there was a son, and they were happy. And then the robot armies came and burned his boats, burned his city with a hellish, glowing mineral that exploded and shattered his windows and fused the glass, fused and flared, and then there was light everywhere, the unbearable flash of memory.

I heard the clanging of robots, steel denting steel, and a high-pitched whine of metal shearing apart. The smell of burning steel. And more sounds: robots banging against stone walls, ringing steel, humming, shouting, cursing, and a curious "pinging" sound I could not quite identify. "Mallory!" a voice from the past called to me. "By God, let's have this door open!" the voice boomed.

Bardo, I remembered, had such a booming voice. *But this was no memory!* "Open, now!" Then the heartstone door rolled open, and there was a brilliant flash, and I covered my eyes. "What's wrong, Little Fellow, are you blind?"

I moved toward the sound of his voice. "Not . . . blind," I said. My eyes burned and hurt. It felt as if someone had stuck the tip of a heated knife through my pupils and wiggled it back and forth. Then I realized the brilliance was only the dim flicker of the flame globes. My eyes were adjusting to the feeble light, slowly. "How did you get in, then? What day is it?"

Bardo's arm went around my back, and I smelled his flowery, sweet scent, and the smell of his fear. "We've got to hurry," he said. "Can you walk? By God, you stink! Didn't they let you have a bath? Look at your goddamned filthy beard! Hurry, now. We've got to hurry. Justine and the others are waiting. Ah, I shouldn't have done this—what have I done?"

"It was necessary," someone said. "We should never have allowed the Timekeeper *robots*."

I covered my brows with my hands, squinting. Bardo's face, inches from my own, was dripping blood. There was a cut on his nose, a gash near his earlobe. Nikolos the Elder, the Lord Akashic, stood close by. A master akashic and a couple of journeymen carrying a computer accompanied him. Then I saw the robots. Up and down the long, stone corridor were robots of two different kinds: the large, red, Timekeeper's robots, with their pincers and clamps, and black robots of a type I had never seen before. All of the tutelary robots—there were four of them—lay inert against the gray floor, a twisted, burnt, metal wreckage. The black robots were smaller, but obviously deadlier. Like an ant, each had six legs; each had metal drills and plasma torches and guns and killing lasers mounted on black steel. Four of these robots lined the corridor. At the far door, where the row of cells ended, were four more.

As we made for the door, Bardo huffed out, "Look at my face! Stone chips—I think a bullet hit the wall. Oh, what have I done? This is madness!"

"*Not* madness," Lord Nikolos said. He screwed up his round, little face. "It's a well-organized plan—try to remember that."

Lord Nikolos hastily informed me of recent events. The College of Lords, he said, had threatened to censure the Timekeeper for keeping me a prisoner in his Tower. (And for his misuse of his tutelary robots. And for other reasons.) They had forced the Timekeeper to allow Lord Nikolos and his subordinate akashics to examine me, to establish my guilt or innocence. And so the plan: When the Tower doors were thrown open to Lord Nikolos and his akashic computer, Bardo's robots had rushed in to rescue me.

"Goddamned robots!" Bardo cursed. "My entire fortune, five hundred thirty thousand City disks—I had to bribe the tinkers to make the robots. It cost me everything. But I had to—"

"*How* many disks? No one has that much money."

"What else could I do? The Timekeeper would have executed you, by God!"

"What about the warrior-poet?"

"Dead, maybe still alive—why do I care?" He grabbed my arm and pulled me up the stairs. "Come on, Little Fellow, we've got to leave *now*! Escape—that's the only way."

We went through the doorway and up the stairs to the street. It was cold and blustery with a wet wind off the Sound. It was dark; no one was in sight.

"This way!" Bardo said. He urged me toward a sled waiting by the curb. "To the Fields—we've got to hurry!"

"What about Lord Nikolos, then?"

"I'll remain in the city," Nikolos said. "I think the College of Lords will have to censure or even remove the Timekeeper, in the end. Either that, or there will be full schism."

"What do you mean, *full* schism?"

"Ah, I should have told you immediately," Bardo said. "Li Tosh, the Sonderval, all our fellow pilots—we're leaving the City tonight. Because of you, my friend, in protest, and because we're sick of the Timekeeper and the other old bones who rule the Order."

We rocketed through the streets, and at various places along the sliddery, all the way to the Hollow Fields, the windows of the surrounding buildings were lit, hundreds of bright, yellow squares against black granite. It seemed that the eyes of the City itself were watching us. It was an eerie feeling. I knew that I had seen this moment before. In my prison, then, I had been scrying, as well as remembrancing.

"What's wrong, Little Fellow?" Bardo shouted above the roar of the jets and the wind. "Doesn't it feel good to be free?"

I looked up at the glowing sky above the runs and pads of

the Fields, up at the rocket tailings of the ships escaping the City. I had seen that sky before, too, and other even brighter skys soon to come. I said nothing, and we went down to the Caverns where we found a hundred other pilots waiting their turns by their ships, and one by one we fled into the plutonium sky.

24

Deus Ex Machina

Through wood and dale the sacred river ran,
Then reached the caverns
measureless to man,
And sank in tumult to a lifeless ocean:
And 'mid this tumult heard from far
Ancestral voices prophesying war!
            —from "Kubla Khan" by Samuel Taylor
            Koleridge, Century of Revolution Scryer

The hibakusha say that war is hell, and they should know. The Pilot's War, as it came to be called, at its beginning was mostly fun. Of course, there need not have been war at all, but when the Timekeeper discovered our escape from the City—as I later learned—he was wroth. His pilots, he declared, could not leave the Order without his first dissolving their vows. Bardo and I, he proclaimed, must be returned to the City to face our punishments. Failing that, we should be executed in space at the soonest possible moment. He sent Leopold Soli to carry out this sentence. And Soli was glad to obey him because he was even more wrathful than the Timekeeper. He was mad with pain (the after-effects of the warrior-poet's drug continually tortured his nerves), and mad with jealousy, too. He vowed to capture Justine and Bardo— either that or kill them. And I am sure that he wanted to kill me. He left the City in his lightship, the *Vorpal Blade*. The lightships of his friends, Tomoth, Seth, and Neith of Thorskalle, and the lightships of one hundred and twenty-five pilots loyal to him and to the Timekeeper rocketed after him. And so it began.

We really had no plan for war. Our plan—Lord Nikolos'

and Bardo's plan—was simple, and it did not include violence. We ninety-eight schismatic pilots would escort a deepship full of men and women representing our Order's every profession. Pilots, eschatologists, mechanics, and tinkers—we would journey to Ninsun, which was a star near the Aud Binary. We would found a new academy. And the Timekeeper would be forced to either accept us as rivals, or to accept the changes that the College of Lords was demanding and call us back to Neverness in forgiveness and peace.

But peace we could not have. As the Timekeeper had once observed, it is the nature of things that no one can choose peace if his enemy chooses war. Soon after our escape, we rendezvoused around the fixed points of a star near Icefall's, a white dwarf ridiculously named Milky Minikin. By light radio we talked ship to ship. We held a conclave, of sorts, to discuss what we should do. (At the time, of course, we did not know that Soli intended to pursue and execute us.)

I remembered seeing the imago of Bardo's bearded face come into my ship's pit. And hearing his voice: "We're free, by God! Can Bardo outwit an old tyrant who never leaves his Tower?" he asked rhetorically. "By God, does tangleroot make your seed stink?"

"Was it necessary?" I said this into the black air of the pit. It was hard to imagine Bardo hearing my words, seeing my face in the pit of *his* ship—and at the same time, floating naked with Justine while she listened to my words, too. "Wasn't there any other way, then?"

"No, there was no other way. The Timekeeper would have had you beheaded."

"Bardo, has it occurred to you that our escape was too easy?"

"Easy!" he exclaimed. "Easy for you, because you didn't have to spend a fortune to get robots made. You didn't have to coordinate—"

"I didn't mean that the planning was easy," I interrupted. "I meant our actual escape. Why did the Timekeeper permit the akashics into his Tower, if he knew they would find me innocent? Why didn't he try to stop the pilots from leaving the Caverns? Why didn't—"

"You are beginning to worry me, Little Fellow. Well, in truth, I've worried about these things all along. I can only guess that the Timekeeper was pissing afraid that the College of Lords would censure him."

"I have another hypothesis," I said.

"And what is that?" He—his imago—wiped sweat from his eyes.

"What if the Timekeeper *let* us, all of us, pilots and professionals, escape?"

"And why would he do that?" he asked. "No, no, don't tell me—I don't like bad news. I think I see where your sequence of thoughts is converging."

Because I was crabby from my long imprisonment, I voiced the obvious anyway. "I think the Timekeeper let us escape so he could murder us, everyone who has openly gone against him. Here, in space, far from the city, so he could hide his crime."

"Murder us, ah . . . *how*?"

"Perhaps he'll send Soli to do his work."

"And how would Soli track us?" he asked. "He can't know our destination, nor any of the fixed-points of our mapping sequences. And no, I don't think Soli would work the Timekeeper's murders; no, no, that's not possible, is it?"

I did not answer him. After a while, I asked, "Is Justine really there with you, in your pit? Why can't I see her, then? Can I talk to her?"

Bardo's face reddened, then disappeared. His imago did not return. There was a spell of silence. And then his voice—only his voice—filled the pit of my ship: "Justine will talk to you but she's, ah . . . unclothed, so she doesn't want you to see her; she's your goddamned aunt, after all, isn't she?"

I did not tell him that when I was a boy I used to peek between the crack in the door while Justine took her morning bath. At least I had until my mother caught me and pinched my nose until it bled. Justine had a beautiful body, long and voluptuous like Katharine's. I could not really blame Soli for being jealous of Bardo.

"I'm so glad you're alive," Justine finally said.

"Where's my mother—do you know?"

"We tried to find her, of course, but we couldn't. After you were imprisoned . . ."

"Ah," Bardo's voice broke in, "did you know that another warrior-poet tried to assassinate the Timekeeper?"

"Of course, the tutelary robots killed *that* poet before he ever reached the Timekeeper's chambers."

"Your mother is in hiding, Little Fellow. Probably somewhere in the Farsider's Quarter. We couldn't find her."

And Justine continued, "After the Timekeeper saw how close he'd come to dying—well, Moira couldn't very well come out of hiding, could she?"

"She's still in the City."

"Of course she is."

"I'm sure she's still alive."

"There's always hope."

Once again, I noticed how alike they sounded. Except for their intonations and the timbre of their voices, they spoke their words in the same manner. Their programs were similar, much too similar. When I told them how this worried me, their response was immediate: "Ah, of course, Mallory is a cetic."

"Cetics are known to worry."

"But you shouldn't worry about us."

"No."

"We'll be all right if—"

"If only Soli would leave us alone!"

"If only Soli weren't so damn mad!"

"Ah, Soli's the real worry."

"Soli."

"If he comes after us—"

"Well, of course he will and—"

"That's too bad."

"Too damn bad."

Bardo and Justine, of course, weren't the only ones worried about Soli. Other pilots voiced similar fears. Li Tosh, the Sonderval, Jonathan Ede—I talked to each of my old friends separately, in private. But we could reach no consensus, so we sent our imagos ship to ship, and the other pilots did the same. In each pit floated the glowing, shrunken heads of ninety-seven pilots. It was a strange, crowded, confusing way to hold a conclave. I talked to these pilots simultaneously. They talked to me. The finest young pilots of our Order: Delora wi Towt, Richardess, Paloma, Zapata Karek, Matteth Jons, and Alark of Urradeth. And others who were not so young, Justine's friends: Veronika Menchik, Helena Charbo, Aja, Ona Tetsu, and Cristobel the Bold in his famous ship, *The Silver Thallow*. And others, eighty-five other talking, jabbering, arguing pilots.

"This discussion is useless," the Sonderval said. His head

was the longest and narrowest in the circle of heads. He had a long upper lip and a dimpled chin. "We must have a strategy."

"By God, there can be only one strategy," Bardo said. I was pleased to see that Justine had agreed to let the imago of her head appear next to his. I smiled at her, and she smiled back. "We'll go on to Ninsun, as planned."

"And what if there is war?" Zapata Karek said in his high, squeaky voice. "Should we leave the deepship to be captured? Would you abandon the professionals?"

"And what of the professionals?" Delora wi Towt asked. "Shouldn't they have a vote in what we decide?"

Each of the heads turned toward hers, staring at her round, pink face, as she twirled her braids. Obviously no one wanted to let the professionals have a vote. "If Soli comes after us," the Sonderval said, "it will be a war between pilots. We *pilots* should decide what to do."

Cristobel the Bold nodded and said, "If there's really to be a war, we should try to surprise Soli, take the war to him."

"War!" Bardo cried out. "Why do we have to have a goddamned war?"

Richardess blinked his tired, red eyes (he was an albino, with white hair and dead, white skin devoid of any pigmentation, and he was very old, the oldest of us pilots), and he said, "The Bardo is right—why should we have a war? Have we forgotten our vows to quest? Why not scatter across the lens of the galaxy? Why should we wait for a *war*?"

All this time Li Tosh hadn't spoken. He looked from face to face as he smiled his bright, gentle smile. Finally, after Richardess had finished cataloging the horrors of war, he found his moment and said, "Whatever we do, if we do it together as brother and sister pilots, we must have a single plan. The Sonderval is right." He looked at me, and his almond eyes were smiling, always smiling. "A single plan— therefore we should elect one of us to be Lord Pilot, at least temporarily."

"A Lord Pilot," the Sonderval agreed, "it's necessary to elect one."

"Ah, but who will it be?" Bardo asked.

"Who are the master pilots among us?" Justine replied. "Who may we choose from?"

"Well, there's yourself," Bardo said. "And Li Tosh, of

course, and Richardess, Cristobel, Veronika Menchik, Helena Charbo and Aja—master pilots all."

"And there is Thomas Sonderval," the Sonderval said, most unhumbly, I thought. "Don't forget—I was made a master pilot on ninetieth day last midwinter spring."

Li Tosh smiled at our old rival and said, "For myself, I would not want to be Lord Pilot."

"Nor I," Bardo admitted.

"Nor I," Justine said.

"And who else is a master pilot?" Li Tosh asked, almost innocently. "Tetsu? Matteth Jons? And, of course, I almost forgot . . . Mallory Ringess."

He looked at me, and all of a sudden, the head of every pilot and master pilot was turned my way. "The Ringess," he said, "is perhaps the finest master pilot that's ever been."

"He *is* the finest, by God!"

"The Ringess found his way in—and out—of the Solid State Entity. The Ringess," and here he recited a long list of my qualifications, among which were the rumors that I was a hidden cetic, a remembrancer, and maybe even a scryer. Above all, Li Tosh told them, I was a lucky man, lucky to be alive after dying such a seemingly final death. And who wouldn't want to elect such a lucky Lord Pilot?

I won't record here everything that was said after that. I suspected that Bardo, Justine and Li Tosh together had orchestrated their dramatic little speeches. They must have planned from the first that I should be the Lord of the schismatic pilots. Had they, before they ever left the city, cajoled their friends and fellows into voting for me? I think they must have. Fifty-four of the ninety-seven pilots bowed their heads to indicate they favored my elevation. Twelve of them, for one reason or another, declined to vote. Thirty-one pilots—and I was sorry to see that Richardess was one of these—shook their heads vigorously. Each of them denied that I had any right to be Lord Pilot over anyone. I was tempestuous and too bold, they said. (Paradoxically, some people fear bold leaders while most others value the quality of boldness above all else.) To a pilot, they immediately deserted us. Some left for Tria; some of them returned to the City. A few decided to honor their vow to quest and followed Richardess, perhaps out into one of the arms of the galaxy.

In this way, I became Lord Pilot of sixty-six rebellious

pilots; if there was war, I would be a warlord responsible for sixty-six lives.

"Congratulations, Little Fellow!" Bardo said to me in the privacy of my ship. He looked at me as he pulled at his mustache. He began naming names of pilots who had remained loyal to the Timekeeper, and to Soli. "What will you do now? If Soli moves against us, there will be at least two of Soli's ships to our one."

"What a fine mathematician you are!" I said. "At least you can still count."

I assured him we would win against Soli despite our numbers. If he fell against us, we would maneuver and strike and fall away into the manifold; we would lay cunning traps and make double attacks; we would tempt the enemy into spreading his forces too thinly, and then we would turn and pin ship against ship and win all the pieces, and the game would be ours.

I knew nothing of war. War, as I would soon discover was not a game, though I could not help thinking of it as a game. Real war was really not much fun. I found that I had no liking or genius for war. In truth, I was surprised and somewhat ashamed to find myself leading pilots to war. I consulted the library of my ship-computer and discovered that my understanding of the elements of strategy was based solely upon games such as chess and ko that I had played as a child. Real war, it seemed, was much more chaotic than any game. Real war had no rules. I studied the annals of ancient warlords and strategists. Sun Tzu, Liddell Hart, The Tolstoi, Julius Caesar, Musashi the Sword-Saint, the First Richard Ede—all the great authors of war. I hurried my brain with slowtime, and their words were like photons illuminating a lightsail. I learned the axioms of war. Never divide your forces; choose your own space and time for battle; never be predictable— these fundamentals, so often ignored by princes and generals who had led millions to their deaths, I learned as quickly as I could. I studied the ancient campaigns of Aleksander, and classic battles, and the tragic Man-Darghinni wars, which were not so ancient. I was like a slightly talented novice forced to learn the rules of chess and study the games of the grandmasters all in a single night. My computer made simulations of history. I relived Caesar's genocide of the Tencredi and watched Hannibal Barka's horse warriors roll up the

Roman flanks at Kannäe. And then there was slaughter; then the murderous Karthaginian infantry closed and killed sixty thousand legionnaires so crushed together they could not lift their swords nor cover themselves with their shields. Their shields failed. I followed this theme of failing shields ahead two thousand years. As if I were standing with a telescope on the cratered surface of Old Earth's moon, I watched the brilliant, terribly beautiful First Exchange of the Holocaust. I marveled as the space shields were overwhelmed and the northern continents flared with ten thousand balls of expanding white light. From Taddeo Astoreth's *The Way of War*, I learned that all battles, no matter how complex, are decided according to four simple elements: force, space, time, and intelligence. Although Soli might outnumber us two to one, Aleksandar had overcome odds of five to one at Gaugamela. If I were to defeat Soli at real war, I would have to lead my pilots into familiar spaces of my choosing and fall against him when he was not ready. Most important, in this strange, unprecedentedly mathematical war we might wage, would be intelligence, for we would have to predict the mappings of Soli's pilots almost as they made them.

If Soli fell against us; *if* he could track us through the manifold.

Every ship, of course, when it opens a window perturbs the manifold slightly. If two ships are far from each other, these perturbations are impossible to detect. But if the ships are close enough, if they are within a well-defined region, the radius of convergence narrows, and a probability mapping can be made. Any ship, with a degree of probability, can track—can "predict"—the mappings of any other. If we could flee far enough and fast enough, the probability of Soli finding us would approach zero.

And so we fled along the fallaways toward Ninsun. Stars streamed past like snowflakes in a storm. We fled fast and far. Finally we fell out around Ninsun, which was a small white star orbited by a single planet. And Soli and his pilots were there, above the planet, waiting for us. I counted one hundred and twenty-nine lightships. The *Vorpal Blade*, Tomoth's and his brothers' *Time Past*, *Time Present* and *Time Future*—like diamond knives they hung poised above Ninsun, reflecting the light of that feeble star and the glowing, dusty lights of the Aud Cluster. Immediately I called out to my pilots. (How quickly I thought of them as "my" pilots! How quickly and finally we fall to vanity!) I called out a ten-star sequence beginning with Shima Luz. We made our mappings and disappeared into the fallaways. And Soli and his pilots, I am sorry to say, because they were well within the region defined by the Aud Cluster's gravity field, had no trouble tracking our perturbations of the manifold.

"By God, we've been betrayed!" Bardo's voice boomed. "Who could have told Soli we would choose Ninsun, of all the damn stars in the damn galaxy?"

I, too, wanted to know this. I tried to contact Soli by light radio, and it surprised me that he agreed to talk to me.

"How far do you fall, Pilot? Not far enough—no, never far enough, isn't that true?"

This was Soli's voice, and it was speaking to me in the pit of my ship. We had fallen out above a star with a number but no name, one of the blue, supergiants at the edge of the Cluster. It was the first time we had talked since the day I murdered Liam. His imago appeared before me. He was thinner than I had remembered, his cheeks gaunt, sunken. His hand covered his eyes as if he were agonizing over a deep loss and did not want to look at me. Everywhere else, on his face, and in the tremors of his starved body, I read the tells of anger and pain.

"Who betrayed us?" I asked. "How did you know we'd journey to Ninsun?"

"The Timekeeper knew Bardo's plan all along. He's always been good at spying."

"And so he sent you to murder us, then?"

"Essentially," he said, "that's true. But is there need for more murders? No, there's no need, not if you surrender and return to the City."

I think he must have known I would not surrender because he was not at all surprised when I said, "No, Leopold, I won't go back."

"You call me by my given name?"

"Should I call you 'Father,' then?"

When I said this he grabbed his belly and dug his fist in. He winced as if his stomach acid were eating up through his throat. "No," he told me, "you should say instead: 'Yes, Lord Pilot, I will return to face my punishment.'"

"You're not my Lord Pilot anymore."

"Yes, you've been elected Lord Ringess—isn't that what *your* pilots are calling you? Let us hope none of them lose faith in your leadership and try to assassinate you."

I pressed my knuckles up to my lip, then said, "I didn't try to kill you; I tried to save you. The warrior-poet—"

"Who are you to save anyone?" he asked. He clearly didn't believe that I had saved his life.

"Don't you remember anything?" I asked.

He took his hand away from his eyes. The whites were shot with ruptured, red capillaries. He looked as if he hadn't slept for a long time. His hand was shaking like that of a palsied, old man. "The Timekeeper said his robots captured you and the poet as you were about to murder me. What else should I remember? What was seen . . . was seen."

"No, that's not true! I'd tracked the poet through the City. And I—"

"Yes, you're a liar, aren't you? But even if you were telling the truth . . . it's too late, isn't it? There are all your other crimes to pay for."

In a way, he was right; it was too late. Our private enmity had festered and infected the Order, and now many would have to pay. Neither of us, however, was eager to see pilot murder pilot. (At least, I think we both wanted to keep our murders in the family, so to speak. Once, when I informed him—and this was sheer cruelty on my part—that Bardo and Justine would never return to Neverness unless the Time-keeper forgave them and permitted them to marry, he whispered, "Justine, how was I so stupid . . . Justine?" and there was murder on his lips.) And so, by unspoken consensus, we began a war of maneuver. At first it was more of a game than a real war. Like any good general or warlord, Soli hoped to win as much as possible with as little loss as possible. He sought to demonstrate by maneuver that our position was hopeless, that we should surrender without battle. Following his lead, pilots such as Stephen Caraghar and Salmalin would cut across our pathways, fall out, and harry the fat, whalelike deepship. They would then demonstrate the finesse of their predictive mappings, a warning meant to say, "You see, we pilots of the *Order* can find you wherever you are and destroy you."

Soon our tactics became more provocative. When one of Soli's pilots fell out above the deepship, Delora wi Towt, for instance, might fall out of the manifold near both ships. The two lightships would dance in and out of the manifold, two lightning slivers of silver seeking an advantageous probability mapping. The "victorious" pilot would be the one who best predicted the mappings of her "enemy." She—or he—would fall out into realspace, into inky blackness and prepare the ship's spacetime engines while she lay in wait. If her enemy fell out at the predicted point-exit, the soon-to-be victorious pilot would demonstrate that she could have destroyed the other. As the victorious pilot's spacetime engines fixed on a point-source near her enemy, the realspace near the enemy ship would begin to buckle and distort, to bubble like a sheet of hot clary. And when the bubble burst and the window to the manifold was open for an instant, the victorious pilot would spin her lightship along its axis in a gesture of triumph as if to say, "Therefore I could have made a mapping into the core of a nearby star, and hurled your ship into hellfire. If this were real war, you'd be annihilated."

Given our red, dripping, human natures, as Bardo reminded me, inevitably, this war of maneuver could not last. One day, as we segued into the August Cluster, Tomoth of Thorskalle murdered Jonathan Ede. Of course, Jonathan's death may have been an accident. Perhaps Tomoth—that murderous blond giant with his murderous mechanical eyes—"accidentally" opened a window to the manifold too near the *Ship of All Ships*, and sent Jonathan into the core of a star. But what exactly is an accident? Was it an accident that the brilliant, and usually calm Li Tosh sought vengeance for his best friend's murder? Was it an accident that he sought out and outmaneuvered Tomoth's brother, Seth? That he destroyed him as Jonathan had been destroyed? I do not believe so. And when pilot began falling against pilot with frenzy and abandon, that was no accident either.

(Was it an accident that I had punched out and broken Soli's nose? Was the composition of my chromosomes an accident, too?)

I remember Soli's final words to me before we ceased our communications for good and fell into real battle. "Why, Pilot?" he asked me. "Why did you make it come to this?"

And just after Jonathan had fallen into his death, Bardo's imago appeared before me. "It's unbelievable!" he roared. "What a crime! Perfidy! Abomination! Sacrilege! By God, I'm running out of words!—Barbarity! Catastrophe! Oh, what a tragedy this is! Oh, too bad!"

Because I was grieving over Jonathan's death, because I could not bear the thought of causing anyone else to die, because I was grieving, I was too cautious. Let me repeat that: I, Mallory Ringess, was too cautious. I led my sixty-four lightships across the stars of the Triffid nebula with the fearfulness of an old chessplayer moving his pieces across his sixty-four squares. I sought to maneuver my force from Veda Luz to Karanatha and on to the Danladi Thinspace at the edge of the Triffid. There, where the pathways were few, we might trap Soli's ships. As they fell out of the manifold and desperately sought to map one of the few point-sources, we would surround them (in a topological sense, we had to find a set of point-sources both closed and bounded, that is to say, compact) and destroy them one by one.

But we never reached the Danladi Thin. Soli must have guessed my strategy because he surprised me. I remember well the instant I came to question caution. I—and my other pilots—had just fallen out, and the light of Veda Luz dazzled me. The interior of the nebula glowed a soft, ice-blue from the reflected light off the particles of interstellar dust. Veda Luz itself was a burning blue, a hot blue supergiant as bright as Alnilan or the First Spica. It was a huge star. So massive was Veda Luz that the manifold in its neighborhood was vulgarly distorted. I had difficulty leading my pilots through its windows in an orderly manner. There came an instant when six of my pilots had to wait while the others found their windows and fell through to Favasham, which was the next star in our sequence towards the Danladi Thin. In that instant, Soli's old friend Lionel Killirand in his *Infinite Sloop* fell out, fell upon Cristobel the Bold and destroyed him. And in that instant, thirty-two master pilots fell upon Olafson Jons and Nashira and Ali Alesar of Urradeth and Nikolos Korso and the inimitable Delora wi Towt. Probably it was Lionel who actually killed her. There was a snarling confusion as lightships slipped in and out of realspace, thirty-seven diamond teeth darting at each other through blackness into starlight as if they were a pack of Alaloi dogs fighting for position close to the fire. I was aware of this battle as hundreds of quick, vanishing-point deformations of the manifold, hundreds of glinting ripples on a shimmering, nighttime sea. I tried to turn our main body of lightships back, kleining along our pathways, but by the time we returned to Veda Luz, the battle was over. Lionel and the others had fled. And six of our pilots were lost.

Like a team of beaten sled dogs with their tails between their legs, we retreated across Jonah's Star Far Group almost to the edge of the Orion Nebula. I floated in the pit of my ship as I briefly talked with my pilots. Bardo especially was wounded by the battle's outcome. We touched the hulls of our ships, and his voice and thoughts propagated through my ship-computer and formed in my mind. For a moment, the neurologics of his ship were faced with my own. We shared the same thoughtspace. Because we were stunned and whipped with defeat, because we were grieving, we allowed ourselves a few moments of this forbidden electronic telepathy.

—Little Fellow, can you hear/feel/see me?

I could see his intelligent, brown eyes, hear his voice, smell his fear and farts as he floated within the pit of the *Blessed Harlot*. It was something of a mystery how Justine could stand to be near him inside such a tiny enclosed space.

—Where is Justine, then? Why can't I hear her thoughts?

—She's here asleep, next to me. When she saw what happened to Delora . . . ah, well, she's faced away, for a while.

—I've blundered, Bardo. I should never have . . . tried to meet Soli that night in the bar. You remember. That's where it all started, this sequence of bad chance.

—You should think about the pilots we've lost instead of your life's mistakes.

—I can't *stop* thinking about them. If we . . . why did Delora have to die, then? Why should anyone have to die?

I thought about all of the billions of people who had died in wars, and I discovered one of war's many perversities and ironies: The hell of war is not multiplicative. Or rather, it is inversely multiplicative. The pain of losing someone you know is a thousand times greater than the deaths of a thousand people unknown.

—By God, I loved her once, did you know that, Little Fellow? Delora was my first lover, and she was patient with me. At Borja. I needed patience back then.

—She was a brilliant pilot.

—Ah, you don't understand. She was a *woman*. And now she's gone.

—War is hell, the hibakusha say.

—"War is hell!"—what a thing to think! "War is hell," *you* say with ice in your damn cold breath, but I know how you really feel; so don't think you can hide it, because you can't.

It was true. I was trying to turn a diamond face to the deaths of Ali Alesar and Cristobel and Delora, but it was not working. Bardo, who was listening to my thoughts almost as they formed, reminded me that I should be full of hot rage; I should ball my fists and curse and swear vengeance against Lionel Killirand. Aloof compassion, he whispered in my mind, was the emotion of a saint. And bitter self-doubt was childish.

—You're not a child and you're no saint.

—What am I, then?

—You're a man, by God! I loved you better when you used to rage like a man. You almost snapped Kesse's head off his goddamned neck, by God you did! I can't forget that.

—Neither can I, Bardo. I can't forget anything.

—Ah, too bad.

—I'm changing, now . . . so fast.

—I know, Little Fellow, I know. Sometimes I don't understand you anymore.

—If I could make you see the probabilities . . . the possibilities. Soon, there will be a battle, the beginning of the end. I can see it coming. I'm—

—What's wrong?

—I'm afraid. I'm afraid of losing everything. Sometimes I'm even afraid of losing you.

—But you can never lose your friends, Little Fellow. Haven't I told you that before?

—Will we still be friends, then, after it is finished?

—By God, I swear we will!

Bardo was still my friend, and as we entered the Orion Nebula, he began to examine the tactical implications of his infamous Boomerang Theorem. We fell among the stars of the the Trapezium, which glowed with the lovely green of interstellar ionized oxygen. We fell among stars so young that they had been born when man was still half an ape roaming the grasslands of Old Earth's mother continent. Near the Chu Binary we fought a skirmish with Soli's main force. Bardo and Justine—and Charl Rappaporth and Li Tosh—discovered they could fall instantly back along their pathways to a window and thereby surprise any pilot who might have followed them. In this way they sent eight of Soli's pilots into stars. It was a clever trick, but it could not be so easily duplicated. To defeat Soli, who copied and used our tactics against us as quickly as RNA copies and spits out protein, we would need more than tricks.

At last we made our way past the Tycho's Thick into the Rosette. Surrounding us was that glorious star-making machine I had passed through on my journey into the Entity. Here were stars and mappings I knew well. We were close to the Vild—perilously close—and I could not help wondering what it would be like to fall out among the ashes and degraded light of that star-blown hell. As we passed through the spaces of Rollo's Rock and Farfara and Nwarth, we lost Duncaness and his *Riggersworm*. To be sure, in revenge we destroyed Alhena Ede. (This huge, sardonic pilot was Jonathan Ede's older sister. Of all the tragedies of our tragic war that might have occurred, I am at least glad that brother never killed sister. But both Edes died, and that is too bad. They were the last of their famous line, and their talents disappeared along with their bodies, chromosomes, and lightships.) For every pilot we lost we took one of Soli's. But we could not keep on this way forever. Every pilot we lost increased the odds against us, and Soli had more pilots to lose than we did. When three of my pilots vanished into the Northwest Thick, I knew I had to close with Soli in one, final, decisive battle.

It was wholly my decision to lead my pilots into the spaces surrounding Perdido Luz. I cannot apologize for that. Having failed to use time and intelligence successfully, I had only the element of space left to offset Soli's greater force. We fenestered past Kaarta and New Earth on to the stars of the Fayoli because I was familiar with those mappings and those spaces. Because I was seeking a particular thickspace in which to trap Soli, we segued into the manifold near Darrein Luz. There the stars are small and burn with yellow and orange lights; there time is a little strange; there the Entity has distorted the manifold beyond probability. According to our star maps, Perdido Luz was not a part of the Entity. Had it been, no pilot (except perhaps Bardo and Justine, and Li Tosh) would have followed me there. But star maps are sometimes out of date and just plain wrong. Star maps take little account of a nebular brain's rapid growth. I guided my pilots through the thickspace I had mastered years ago, and we fell out near

Perdido Luz. None of us—not even I—guessed we were perturbing the space, the very essence of the Solid State Entity.

Of course I knew it was a wild risk to seek battle within that thickspace. But what choice did I have? Ages ago Hannibal Barka had shocked a nation called Rome by driving his army of men and hairless mammoths across a range of mountains. All the mammoths and many of his men had frozen to death in the snow-drenched passes, but his army had survived to destroy the Romans at Lake Trasimene. I was no Hannibal, but I could still choose my space for battle. Soli would know nothing of the Perdido Thickspace, and if he followed us there, I would surprise him as Hannibal had the Romans.

In Neverness, journeymen and novices were trudging through slushy streets on their way to dinner; and in the heart of the Entity, She was thinking Her great thoughts; and the killing radiations of Merripen's Star and other Vild stars were rushing towards Neverness, always rushing; and Leopold Soli and a hundred lightships fell out of the manifold. They hovered above Perdido Luz's fourth planet, a gas giant encircled by ghostly rings of ice. We caught them at a point-exit near the silvery center ring. My pilots used the prepared mappings I had shown them, and we fell upon Soli through the thickspace as if we were a pack of hungry wolves.

I now understand what the ancient warlords meant by "the fog of war." Although I could not place each of my pilots as I would stones upon the interstices of a ko board, I had hoped at least to observe and control the tide of the battle. I found I could control nothing, not even my sweating palms nor the throbbing of my heart. I fell out into realspace for less than an instant, and the sparkling center ring of the fourth planet hung like a glacier above me. I made an instant mapping. My ship-engines opened the manifold near Gregorik Smith's *Rose of Earth*. I made another mapping and again my ship-engines opened the manifold. Blackness split, like a rent in a pilot's kamelaika. And then we were both gone, he into the heart of Perdido Luz, and I into the point-rich pathways of the thickspace. There was a rush of theorems, the sparkling ideoplasts of the number-storm. I flowed through the dense mesh of the thickspace as if my lightship were an information virus finding its way through the dark red veins of a man's brain. There was a branching and then a joining of tunnels. The manifold opened again. There was light, the weak yellow light of Perdido Luz. One of Soli's pilots—it was Neith of Thorskalle in his distinctive, wingless ship—was waiting for me. But I had fixed a sequence of mappings. Before he could drive me into the star, I escaped, back into the throbbing arteries of the manifold. In and out of the manifold we danced until Neith made a mistake. He entered a pathway which, in its looping through the manifold, intersected with only one other. For him and his *Time Future*, there could be only two possible point-exits into the realspace near Perdido Luz. I calculated the probabilities, and I was waiting for him when his ship silvered the blackness. Waiting to murder him. He never had a chance.

Be compassionate, Katherine had said to me.

But what place could compassion have when it came time to make war? No, sometimes there could be only cold, murderous *passions*, and so all around me like a winter storm at night the battle raged. The lightships were glittering ice slivers, and they tore through the dark of realspace and disappeared into the manifold. The complexities of the battle overwhelmed me. There was slowtime, rushing time, theorems to prove, mappings of point to point, and the ever-present acid of pure terror. At first the burning yellow point of Perdido Luz was below me, and then it was above. (And by above, I mean that it was between me and the Canes Venatici cloud of galaxies. The stars of the Canes Venatici, by ancient convention, are said to be above all the stars of our galaxy.) As I made a mapping and eluded Lionel's *Infinite Sloop*, I realized I had fallen out on the far side of Perdido Luz opposite the fourth planet. I was a mere billion miles from the battle. And then the manifold engulfed me, and I mapped through to the thickspace beneath the planet's rings, and there was a haze of light, as of the sun through a dense ice-fog in Neverness. There were a hundred dancing lightships. I had no idea who was winning the battle. I tried to talk ship to ship with my pilots but there was no time. I escaped one of Soli's pilots only by making a desperate mapping through a finite tree. I escaped into the manifold, but I could not immediately return because the tree's branchings were numerous and complex. I seemed to fall forever. Time flowed as slowly as glacier ice. For a while I was sick with battle lust; I was sick with myself. How easily I had again become a murderer! How easily the virus of war had

infected us all! Even as I proved a minor result of the
Inclusion Theorem, pilots were murdering pilots. It was
unbelievable, really. This is what battle is, I thought. Battle is
not merely a word; it is organized murder. I balled my fists
then in the darkness of my ship, and I cursed. I remembered
a thing which should have been on all our minds before we
ever decided to schism and fall against our fellow pilots: War
is the worst thing that human beings do. To think of it abstractly
or treat it as a game is worse than barbaric.

And yet it is true that murder is as natural to humans as
making flint axes or suckling babies. And humans are noble,
tragic, splendid beings around a core of barbarity. When I at
last returned to the battle, I had a moment to observe the
ripple and flux of the lightships as they murdered each other.
Although the battle seemed utterly chaotic, as if a cloud of
madness had overcome the pilots on both sides, it was not so.
To murder may indeed be madness, but the pilots did not
murder at random. No, my brother and sister pilots were
men and women of passion, if not compassion. I watched as
certain pilots seemed to seek each other out. Bardo and
Justine in their fat, sleek, *Blessed Harlot,* pursued Lionel's
needlelike *Infinite Sloop* into the manifold. In vengeance for
Delora wi Towt's death, they murdered him. It was revenge
that impelled Tomoth to fall against Li Tosh and sent them
plunging through pathways I would have warned them against.
All around me, beneath the cold yellow light of Perdido Luz,
the battle degenerated into tens of vengeance combats. My
pilots quickly abandoned my strategy and our prearranged
mappings. Soli's pilots, as I later learned, were poisoned with
old rivalries and hatreds. They ignored Soli's master plan.
Salmalin, who had always been jealous of his most brilliant
pupil, the Sonderval, fell against his *Cardinal Virtue*. Madness and murder; murder and madness. There was one awful
moment when two of Soli's pilots went mad and turned
against each other. And then an even more awful moment
when Tomoth fell out into realspace, and by sheer bad
chance, caught me unmapped. To this day I can still imagine
how his ugly, red, jeweled eyes must have gleamed when he
realized he could at last avenge my insulting him that night in
the master pilot's bar, and moreover—a thousand times
moreover—he could have his vengeance for my murdering
his brother, Neith. But vengeance, like a Devaki spearpoint,

cuts two ways. Li Tosh, and Bardo and Justine, fell on
Tomoth in the instant before he murdered me. They murdered
him; they opened a window into the manifold and sent him
down a dark tunnel into the hell of a nearby star.

I come now to perhaps the saddest part of my story.
When Soli saw that Tomoth and Lionel were dead, he fell
into a rage. I might have hoped that he had learned compassion, but no, he fell against Bardo and Justine without mercy
or restraint. For a moment their ships floated like thallows
beneath the fourth planet's icy rings. Soli's elegant, lithe
Vorpal Blade glistening behind the *Blessed Harlot*—this image burned through my telescopes into the neurologics of my
ship. I was close enough—a hundredth of a light-second—to
meld my ship's neurologics with those of the *Blessed Harlot*.
In a frantic effort to help Bardo and Justine find a mapping, I
did so. But they ignored the mapping I showed them.
Probably Justine did not believe Soli would really murder
them. Certainly, as I realize now, they were intent on making
a particular mapping of their own. Although I "listened" to
their final interior dialogue, I listened only for a moment. I
understood only a part of their private thoughts. Here, for
the sake of history and the preserving art of the remembrancers, is what I heard:

—There, see the curve of Soli's *Vorpal Blade*?

—He always was a romantic man, really, and I—

—Think now, beneath the ring's thickspace, the point-
source where if alpha is a statement scheme then there exists
a solution class such that—

—A cantor once told me, he said he'll destroy you because—

—Therefore the universal class and every other class is a
subclass of—

—Of course I'm ready to define the cardinal, but I can't
stop thinking about Soli and the cantor. He said, Justine,
your husband is a tychist in his heart who'd chance almost
anything to prove his theorem, and he said between love and
hate there's nothing and . . .

And they were gone. A window to the manifold opened,
and they were gone.

I have seen this moment before, I thought. In my time of
scrying, in my stone cell, I had seen many futures. In one of
them, just before Soli destroyed them, Bardo and Justine
opened a window to the manifold and fled the battle. In

another, Bardo and Justine held each other in each other's
arm and in each other's thoughts as Soli himself opened the
window and thus became a murderer. Which future had come
to be? Which event was now already microseconds past?

In the end we choose our futures, the scryers are fond of
saying. I made my choice. I chose that Bardo and Justine
should live. And so I waited. How long I waited for them to
return to the battle! How long must a Lord Pilot wait before
he must turn his attention elsewhere? I waited vast, endless,
countable, whole seconds; I waited an eternity. But Bardo's
ship did not return.

I fell against Soli, then. Or he fell against me. In truth,
we fell against each other. Our two lightships so different in
design, my *Immanent Carnation* with her swept-forward
wings and Soli's *Vorpal Blade*—we were like streaks of lightning splitting the night. We maneuvered for advantage in and
out of the windows we opened. At last, I thought, at last. I
made a simple mapping. I fell into an open loop which was
partially bounded by a Danladi sequence. As the manifold
opened before me, I was sure I would fall out into the
thickspace and ambush Soli. But he had guessed my strategy
and was waiting for me. I was helplessly unmapped with
none of my fellow pilots near enough to save me. I am sure
he would have murdered me. My Lord Pilot, my uncle, my
executioner, my father.

I believe the pilots of both sides would have fought and
murdered down to the last ship if the voices had not begun.
Everyone, even Soli—especially Soli—heard the voices, although they were not really voices at all, but word plasts that
we interpreted as voices. Each pilot's ship-computer began to
manufacture the ideoplasts for words and idea structures. In
the pit of my ship, the neurologics enveloping me began to
quiver with subtle rhythms not entirely their own. Immediately I sensed the handiwork of the Entity. I was trying to
escape Soli (or was I really trying to murder him?) when the
bright, snowflake ideoplast representing the Axiom of Plexity
shattered into fragments. My mathematical thought array was
completely ruined. Then the ship-computer produced the
orange, multipronged ideoplast for "the categorical impera-
tive to prove." This plast connected to a red cylinder
representing the specific solution set. The red cylinder joined
with a black torus, the ideoplast of universal negation. To-

gether these plasts formed a word plast which I understood to mean: *You must discover the answer to death.* In a like manner, other word plasts formed and joined to the central word plast. A black torus appeared again and merged with the first plast of universal negation. There was a spearlike green plast representing a specific type of mapping, and automorphism, and the thought: *Death lies within me* grew from the central concept. In a few moments other ideoplasts formed and swirled about each other and fell into place as the little word-storm quieted and cleared. I wondered why She did not appear to us as an imago of the Tycho as She had when I first penetrated Her. Perhaps She wanted to stop the battle by interrupting the number-storm within each ship. If that was Her intention, She succeeded. One hundred and twelve lightships hung motionless in realspace, and these words played through each of us:

How far do you fall, Pilots? How do you like war? Do you still seek the secret of life? Then you must discover an answer to death. Death lies within me. Death is a star I will call Gehenna Luz. If you seek an answer to the dying stars of the Vild, you must quit your war and journey to Gehenna Luz. I will help you. But you must hurry because Gehenna Luz will die very soon. The way is far but not too far; the secret of life is near. The first pilot to reach Gehenna Luz will be told the secret.

I cannot wholly explain why this simple message destroyed our will to war. I cannot—and could not—look inside the minds of Li Tosh and Carman of Simoom and Leopold Soli and proclaim: "See, this is where the cool stream of devotion extinguished the flames of madness." Why should we have even believed Her, that inhuman, capricious goddess? Perhaps our warring inside Her and our rape of the manifold had outraged Her; perhaps She wanted only to lure us on to our doom. I can only say that we did believe Her. We needed to believe Her. One hundred and twelve ships floated above the rings of the fourth planet, and we believed that the secret of the dying Vild (and perhaps the other secret) was close at hand. There came a moment, I think, when we looked out over the array of ships, and at the coffee-black spaces where the *Infinite Sloop* and the *Blessed Harlot* had recently been, and we were ashamed. We were not warriors; we were Pilots of the Order of Mystic Mathematicians and Other Seekers of the Ineffable Flame—I cannot explain why we each should suddenly remember this.

We held a conclave, there near the thickspace. We sent our imagos ship to ship, listening to the voices of our "enemy" pilots, watching the lips of pilots we had known all our lives. It was as if we had awakened from a terrible dream. The sad Li Tosh, the anguished Sonderval grieving for Delora wi Towt, Soli with his death-ruined eyes and silent face—almost all the pilots agreed we must call a truce.

"This has been a waste," Soli's imago spoke to me later in the privacy of my ship. "What fools we've been."

"Bardo is dead," I told him.

"So many dead."

"And Justine. How could you have killed them?"

"I don't know," he said.

Inside my pit I floated and rubbed my nose, which was so congested from filtering dry, recycled air that I breathed with difficulty. "You would have killed me too, wouldn't you?"

"I don't know," he said. And then, after a moment's reflection: "Yes."

"But the war is over," I said. "These murders diminish us. They're barbaric. They make little men of all of us. I can't kill anymore; I will not."

"Yes," he said, "it's over. The war." He pressed his eyes, then said, "But between you and me, the race goes on, doesn't it, Pilot?"

"How could it not, then?" I agreed. "It goes on."

Because we were both Lord Pilots, Soli and I said a requiem for all the pilots that had died that day. Then each of us faced our ships and made our mappings. The stars vanished and the lightships fell through their windows into the manifold. So began our race to find the star Gehenna Luz before it exploded, into the lonely, deceptive heart of the Solid State Entity.

25

The Great Ocean
of Truth

*God created the integers, and all the rest is the work
of man.*
—Leopold Kronecker, Machine Century Constructivist

*The knowledge at which geometry aims is the knowl-
edge of the eternal.*

—The Plato

*Mathematics is a game. Its pieces are the axioms we
create, and its rules are logic. That mathematics is
occasionally useful to mechanics and pilots is accidental.*

—Mahavira Lal, third Lord Cantor

*I do not know what I appear to the world; but to
myself I seem to have been only like a boy on the
sea-shore, and diverting myself in now and then
finding a smoother pebble or a prettier shell, while
the great ocean of truth lay all undiscovered before
me.*

—Isaak Newton, first Lord Mechanic

It is the strangest of phenomena that intelligence can shape
the deep structures of the universe. How often I have had to
admit this; how often I have had to contemplate this mystery.
As I fenestered into the heart of the Entity, as I again
penetrated that fathomless brain, I wondered again and again
how Her great, rippling waves of intelligence created the
wild, segmented spaces, the infinite loops (not to mention the

omnipresent infinite trees) and the other dangers of Her interior manifold. She, Herself, strange to say, could not tell me. She did not know. She was not aware of every bubble and topological transformation which occurred within Her. When I learned this, I was surprised, though I should not have been. Is a pilot in dreamtime aware of the firing of each individual neuron within his brain? Can he ever fully understand the flow of blood through arteries, diffusing cell by cell through millions of capillaries, the hot rush of electrochemical impulses which is the fount of his pleasure? What is this thing we call intelligence? If intelligence is the result, the cumulative effect of billions of quantum and electrical events within the brain, how can intelligence turn itself outside-in to understand itself? It is an old problem with a simple solution: For any brain to be entirely aware of itself, it would have to be vastly larger than itself. Within the bounds of simple matter and energy, this is impossible. (Though our eschatologists have theorized that the Ieldra, and the mythical Elder Ieldra, have an infinite intelligence. And since infinite sets may contain subsets of themselves which are themselves infinite, they say it is possible that such godly intelligences can fully understand themselves. I do not know. Intelligence is not a set, and it is wrong to analagously apply the theory of sets in this manner. One would think the eschatologists would appreciate this simple fact.) And if we truly possess a free will, the problem grows worse, much worse. If I freely concentrated on a particular question—for instance, why would the Entity encourage one hundred and twelve pilots to enter *Her* brain?—if I thought this thought freely, I would be the *cause* of the fear and doubt which crackled through me. I would *cause* particular neurons within my limbic brain to fire. If I should somehow attempt to understand these impulses, the very act of my understanding would interfere with them. And then, at the very moment I thought I knew the shape of my fear, it would be gone, evaporated like snow crystals in the noonday sun.

The Entity, of course, understood this as clearly as a pilot understands that two times two is four. Although She apparently wanted us to find the star Gehenna Luz, She did not really care about discovering the shape of the manifold within Her. We pilots could do that. She wanted only—at least this is my understanding—to think and be. If this tremendously concentrated thinking caused the manifold to distort into a series of infinite trees or to warp into a Danladi bubble— well, that was interesting, but not nearly so interesting as the openness or closure of realspace, and the other problems of the universe. To be sure, much as a man is aware that his visual cortex lies beneath the bone at the back of his head, She knew that certain pockets of the manifold were distorted in certain ways. This knowledge saved some of us pilots from stumbling into infinite trees, as I once had. She warned us away from the worst dangers. She provided us mappings, when She could, and She provided us with the fixed-points of Gehenna Luz. Had She not helped us this way, I believe few pilots would have dared to go on.

For me it was terrifying to find myself once again journeying through the dark nebula that was the Entity. The dense, interstellar dust, the glowing hydrogen clouds, the cancerous black bodies, and always those goddamned mysterious moonbrains, as Bardo would say—whenever I fell out into realspace, I had difficulty imagining why I had once again, despite myself, returned to this strange hell. I was still full of the horror of war, and the afterimage of Bardo's *Blessed Harlot* as it disappeared haunted me. I wondered where he was, almost moment by moment, wondered how he would face his death? I wondered where my fellow pilots were. I could not track their lightships across the Entity because the manifold was like bubbling, black mud. Too bad. Often, I wondered at the Entity's purpose. Did She really want us to witness the death of a star? Or was it all just a cruel trick, Her way of exterminating the soul of an Order which had grown stale, obnoxious and bellicose?

If She—this goddess whom the warrior-poet had once called Kalinda of the Flowers—if it was important to Her that we quickly reach Gehenna Luz, why didn't She give us more help? Specifically, I wondered why She didn't show us the solution to the Continuum Hypothesis. If we could prove the Hypothesis, we could have mapped from Perdido Luz to Gehenna Luz in a single fall, in almost no time. Why had She provided us laborious mappings through Her twisted interior if a much simpler solution existed? Ah, but what if there was no solution? Or what if a solution existed, and She did not know—or care—what it was? (As a historical note, I should mention that there is an ancient, unrelated theorem of the same name. The Old Continuum Hypothesis states that there is no infinite set with a cardinality between that of the set of natural numbers and the set of points in space. For a century, this remained impossible to prove or disprove, until one of the first—and last—self-programming computers discovered the axioms of Generalized Set Theory and decided the question once and for all.)

Of course it was arrogant and foolish of me to suppose that I might prove what the Entity perhaps could not. But for all my pains and adventures, I was still an arrogant man. I wanted badly to prove the Hypothesis. I needed to prove it, and to prove it before another pilot such as Soli proved it. All my life I had dreamed of proving it, and now great secrets lay before me if only the pure light of inspiration would illumine this most famous of theorems. I floated naked within my ship's pit, all the while wondering where this inspiration might come from. From slowtime I passed into the white light of dreamtime, and the manifold opened to my mind. Strange are the pathways of a goddess's brain: I entered a rare Lavi torsion space and began in-folding through what I prayed would be a finite set of folds. Time slowed. I seemed to have forever to think my thoughts. My thoughts were like the dull glow of an oilstone; my thoughts were as weak as the light of a coldflame globe through a drifting cloud of snow on a winter night. I did not know where to seek inspiration. The great brain of my ship lay before me; its neurologics surrounded me in a web of electric intelligence, but it had been designed to compute, to reason by symmetry and heuristics, to manipulate logic structures, to store information, to do a million things which complemented and added to the mental powers of a human brain without replacing it. I could face my ship forever and be forever lost to the ecstasy of the number-storm, and still tremble for the fiery touch of inspiration. The sheer size of a brain, I thought, did not necessarily determine its talent for creating mathematics. Perhaps even the Entity—and here I was being utterly foolish—had little real interest or talent for pure mathematics. And then I had another thought as clear as the Timekeeper's glass: If I were to prove the Great Theorem, the inspiration would have to come from somewhere within myself.

I am a mathematical man. I am a curious man. I have always wondered at the nature of mathematics, and at my own nature as well. What *is* mathematics? Why should mathematics describe the laws of the universe so exactly? Why should our minds' seemingly arbitrary creations and discoveries fit so well this mad, swirling blizzard we call reality? For example, why should gravity (to use the model of newtonian mechanics) act between two objects according to the inverse of the *square* of the distance separating them? Why doesn't it act according to the second and a half power, or the two point zero one five and so on power? Why is everything so tidy and neat? It may be, of course, that the human brain is so puny that it can discover only the simplest, the most obvious of universal laws. Perhaps there remains an infinity of laws so hopelessly complicated that they would be impossible to state. Had gravity acted more complexly, The Newton probably never would have found an equation to describe it. Who knows what wonders will forever remain hidden from the mathematical sight of man? This explanation, however, favored by the eschatologists, still does not explain why mathematics works as it does, or why it even works at all.

What is mathematics? I have turned this question in my mind, turned and returned to this mystery all my life. We create mathematics as surely as we create a symphony. We manipulate our axioms with logic as a composer arranges musical notes, and so the holy music of our theorems is born. And in a different sense we also discover mathematics: The ratio of a circle's circumference to the diameter remains the same for human minds and for aliens of the Cetus cloud of galaxies. All minds discover the same mathematics for that is the way the universe is. Creation and discovery; discovery and creation—in the end I believe they are the same. We create (or discover) undefined concepts such as point, line, set and betweenness. We do not seek to define these things because they are as basic as concepts can be. (And if we did not try to define them, we would make the mistake of The Euclid and say something like: A line is breadthless length. And then, using other words we would have to define the concept "breadthless" and "length." And so on, and so on, until all the words in our finite language were eventually used up, and we returned to the simple concept: A line is a line. Even a child, after all, knows what a line is.) From our basic concepts we make simple definitions of mathematical objects we believe to be interesting. We define "circle"; we

create "circle"; we do this because circles are beautiful and
interesting. But still we know nothing *about* circles. Ah, but
some things are obviously true (or it is fun to treat them as if
they were true), and so we create the axioms of mathematics.
All right angles are congruent, parallel lines never intersect,
parallel lines *always* intersect, there exists at least one infinite set—these are all axioms. And so we have lines and
circles and axioms, and we must have rules to manipulate
them. These rules are logic. By logic we prove our theorems.
We may choose the natural logic where a statement is either
true or not, or one of the quantum logics where a statement
has a degree or probability of trueness. With logic we trans-
mute our simple, obvious axioms into golden theorems of
stunning power and beauty. With a few steps of logic we may
prove that in hyperbolic geometry rectangles do not exist, or
that the number of primes is infinite, or that aleph null is the
smallest infinity that exists, or that . . . we may prove many
wonderful things which are not obvious at all; we may do this
if we are very clever and if we love the splendor of the
number-storm as it rages and consumes us, and if we are
filled with the holy fire of inspiration.

What is inspiration? From where does it come? As I
fenestered through the torsion space, the Lavi Curve Theorem and the Second Transformation Theorem were as beautiful as diamonds, and I was full of wonder. Where does
mathematics come from? How is it born? Yes, we have
axioms and logic and concepts such as "line," but where do
these abstractions come from? How is it that even a child
knows what a line is? Why do the Darghinni, who are as alien
as aliens can be, think according to the same logic as human
beings? *Why should this be so?*

I segued through the last fold in the torsion space; my
ship dropped into realspace, like a flea popping out of the
shaken robes of a harijan. I looked at the veiled stars of the
Entity, and I thought of the age-old answer of the cantors.
Mathematics is a special language, and language is born
within the brain. Our brains have evolved for fifteen billion
years from the brains of man-apes and back, from the simpler
mammalian brains, from the ganglia and nerve clusters of
creatures slithering or swimming through the warm salt water
of our distant past. And back still further to the bacterial
spores which carried life to Old Earth. But from where did

these spores come? Did the Ieldra create them? Who created the Ieldra? What is life? Life is the information and intelligence bound within DNA, and life is the explosive replication of protein molecules, and life is the carbon, hydrogen, oxygen, and nitrogen which exist or are born with the cores of the stars. And the universe gives birth to stars; the universe is a vast, star-making engine; the universe brought forth Bellatrix and Sirius and the blue giant stars of the greater Ede Cluster; from stars such as Antares and the First Canopus the stuff of life is made. Every atom of ourselves was assembled in some faraway, heavenly fire. We are the children of the stars, the universe's creation. If our star-born brains conceive "line" and the other elements of language, should we be surprised that "line" is a natural and meaningful concept within that universe? Is it a wonder that the logic of the universe is our logic, too? The cantors are fond of saying that God is a mathematician. They believe that when we create the special language of mathematics we are learning to speak the language of the universe. We have all of us, we pilots and mathematicians, uttered the sounds of this language, in however an infantile and primitive form. Once or twice, while contemplating the wonderful *fit* of mathematics to the contours of spacetime and to the undulations of the manifold, I have felt that the universe was talking to me in its special vocabulary, if only I could listen. How could I learn to listen? How could I learn to speak more elegantly the pure tones of mathematics? What *is* inspiration?

I journeyed on, and my ship seemed like a dark, stale tomb imprisoning me, darker by far than the Timekeeper's stone cell. As a germinated seed seeks its way out of the ground into the light of day, I longed to break free of the old thoughtways that stifled me and restrained my inspiration. How I longed to prove the Great Theorem! But at the same time that I had longings, I had a certain dread, too. I wondered, again and again, at the nature of my own intelligence. From where did my powers of scrying and remembrancing spring? What other powers might I someday gain? If I did somehow prove my theorem, would the proof really be my own? Or would it be merely the creation of the Agathanian's information virus? Could I dare to call forth the seed of inspiration within me, to try to shape that seed as it grew, to taste the bittersweet fruit it might bear?

I followed the Entity's mappings across a series of thickspaces. Once, I fell out into realspace as dark and empty as the intergalactic void. I nearly panicked, then. But I found that I was actually in the middle of a thickspace! The point-sources were stived as closely as the black eggs in the belly of a jewfish. How this could be so I did not know. Only stars or other matter (or intelligence) can deform space to create a thickspace. I quickly opened a window, and I segued into the manifold. I fell into dreamtime as I thought about this odd thickspace. If the brain of the Entity could contain such wonders as a starless thickspace, what wonders might lie within my brain? Suppose I really tried, tried so hard my eyes burned like coals and my brain's blood surged like an ocean—suppose I tried for the thousandth time to prove the Continuum Hypothesis?

As soon as this thought hardened, the number-storm intensified. A tide of ideoplasts began to build and flow and rage before my inner sight. I was excited almost beyond control. For the thousandth time I contemplated the deceptively simple statement of the Hypothesis: that between any pair of discrete Lavi sets of point-sources there exists a one-to-one mapping. I broke the statement apart and examined the pieces. What, exactly was a Lavi set? What was a point-source? Was I sure I understood the difference between a Lavi set and a *discrete* Lavi set? How could I show the mapping was one-to-one, and more importantly, how might I construct the mapping to begin with? At first I fell into old thoughtways and rediscovered my old attempts to find a solution. Often I found myself reasoning in circles. I grew discouraged at the shallowness of my thinking. How could I prove this? How could I prove that? How could I break the rusted chain of my habitual, uninspired thoughts?

I tried to restate the problem in a different form, hoping that a new way of looking at it might enable me to see the obvious. And though I did find an equivalent statement, it proved even more opaque than the original. I decomposed the Hypothesis, recombined it into a slightly different statement— all to no avail. In my mind, I represented the pieces of the Hypothesis with pictures in order to "see" relations that I might have overlooked. I generalized the Hypothesis to include all Lavi sets, and I played with mappings of specific Lavi sets which were quite well known; I tried proof by contradiction; I dissected related theorems (Bardo's Boomerang theorem, incidentally, is closely related, though simpler to prove); I followed long, dark corridors of reasoning down thousands of steps; I cursed and I rubbed my eyes and temples, and finally, when my beard and hair were rimed with crusts of dried sweat and I had nearly abandoned hope, I began to make wild guesses.

I do not know how long I tried to prove the Hypothesis. Days, seconds, years—what did time matter? And yet it did matter. At any given time, Soli might be close to *his* moment of inspiration. The race went on, and measureless moments passed into endless days, and I began to think the Hypothesis was unprovable. For a long while I tried to show that it was unprovable, even though I did not really believe it could be so. My intuition—and a mathematical man should never ignore his intuition—something within me whispered that the Hypothesis was indeed provable, and more, that the proof would seem embarrassingly obvious once I had found it. *If* it could be found. If *I* could find it. If. . . If one mapping between a pair of discrete Lavi sets of point-sources exists, then there are an infinite number of mappings; if one covers an n-dimensional cube with finitely many sufficiently small closed sets, then there are necessarily points which belong to at least $n + 1$ of these sets; if one stirs a bowl of blood tea for a thousand years, there will exist at least one point—one corpuscle of blood—which will remain fixed in its original position, undisturbed by the stirring; if/then; if I examined the ideoplasts of the Tycho's Conjecture and the Tiling Theorem and the Fixed-Point Theorem, if I broke down the brilliant crystalline arrays into the simple shards of proof steps instead of clumping the arrays together, then I might better understand the inspirations leading to the proofs of these famous theorems. If I understood the proofs better, then I might better use the theorems to prove the Great Theorem.

If. . . If a pilot dwelt too long in dreamtime, then he must withdraw from the thoughtspace and sleep. I was suddenly tired of the interplay of ideoplasts flooding my mind; I dreaded thinking ever again a single mathematical thought. I bit my lip and cursed and despaired. Finally, I slept. I closed my eyes and mind to the number-storm, and I floated like a corpse in a deathship. I slept a long time. When I at last

awoke my eyelids were stuck together; my mouth tasted of
blood. Probably I had ground my teeth while I dreamed. My
mind was dark and cold, like black ice. I was as empty as an
abandoned snow hut on the shelf of the deep winter sea. And
yet the cold was not total. There was a flush of warmth inside
me as if I had been rescued from a capsized sled and fed a
bowl of hot tea. The faint flame of an idea burned in my
mind. Where it had come from I did not know. For no
particular reason I thought of an obscure theorem, the Justerini
mapping theorem. The flame grew brighter, as if I had
breathed on the glowing embers of a woodfire. I was very
excited. How elegant, I thought, was the collapse of the
omega function by which Olaf Justerini had proved his neglected
theorem! How beautiful!

I began thinking in a general manner of the whole structure of the Continuum Hypothesis. I saw, in a general, hazy
way, how the same idea leading to the collapse of Justerini's
omega function might be applied to collapse the Lavi correspondence scheme. I trembled with excitement and with
fear, too, because I had had a thousand such hazy ideas to
collapse the correspondence scheme. But this idea was
different—I could almost see the difference. Somehow my
idea felt right; somehow it fit and completed the holes in my
pattern of thinking. I reached out to my ship's neurologics,
and there was light. Ideoplasts swirled around the still point
of my mind, and the manifold opened. I entered again into
dreamtime. I had an anticipation of *rightness* as I translated
my idea into the diamond crystal of a new ideoplast. The
flames of my thoughts grew hotter. I built up the array of my
proof. The Lavi correspondence scheme could be made to
collapse *if* and only if the Justerini subspace was embedded
within the simple Lavi space. Could I show it was embedded?
It must be embedded; there must be a simple series of steps
to show it was embedded; even a novice could show it was
embedded. My thoughts burned like lava in my brain. My
brain itself felt electric and different, vastly more capacious,
as if it could hold an ocean of molten thoughts. I felt that I
was thinking in a way I never had before, not even when I
faced my computer and hurried my thoughts with slowtime.
Now my thoughts came much faster. Whole new concepts
came to me and fell into place, all in a flash. I understood
things. How can I describe the exquisite pain and pleasure of

this understanding, this wonderful vision of orderedness? My thoughts seared me; my thoughts were flaming crimson; my thoughts were burning raindrops of light. The subspace *was* embedded within the simple Lavi space! And then the correspondence scheme collapsed, almost as the layers of a stars collapse around the core when it becomes a supernova, and there was a choosable mapping. *There was a choosable mapping!* There was elegance, beauty and starlight. I made a mapping. The white light of dreamtime swept by in brilliant streamers, then collapsed into a single point of starlight which burned and expanded and brightened until it filled all of my mind.

Oh, Soli, I thought, the race goes on, but *this* race is over.

I fell out into realspace above the hot white star that the Entity had named Gehenna Luz. I had proved the Great Theorem; I had journeyed far at a single fall, and now all the stars in the sky were finally mine.

26

Kalinda
of the Flowers

*When Man took to his bed the Computer, there was
great rejoicing, and great fear, too, for their children
were almost like gods. The mainbrains bestrode the
galaxy at will, and changed its very face. The Silicon
God, The Solid State Entity, AI Squared, Enth
Generation—their names are many. And there were
the Carked and the Symbionts, whose daughters
were the Neurosingers, Warrior-Poets, the Neurolo-
gicians and the Pilots of the Order of Mystic Mathematicians. So beautiful were these daughters that
man longed to touch them, but touch them he could
not. And so was born the Second Law of the Civilized Worlds, which was that Man could not stare
too long at the faces of the Computer or her children, and still remain as Man.*

—from *A Requiem for Homo Sapiens,*
by Horthy Hosthoh

Gehenna Luz was a beautiful star. It was a massive star, white
and scintillant and hot. I was ravished by its beauty. Why
stars, I wondered? Why was there anything at all? Why do
we breathe, suck in sorrow, joy, pity and pain? Why is—

*You have proved your theorem, my Pilot, and still you ask
these questions.*

It was the godvoice of the Entity inside my mind, a voice
which I had hoped I would never have to hear again. But She
had prophesied that I would return to Her, and return I had.

The stars are *that we might glory in their beauty. And we
exist to worship light.*

459

I remembered how the Entity loved her riddles and her games, and I thought:

—Do you have such a simple answer for every question, then?

I am here to answer your questions.

—Well, I have a thousand questions. Where's Bardo? Why, if you could have stopped the battle whenever you wished, why did you let him die? Is he dead? Do you know? No! Do not speak to me . . . like this. I don't want to listen to your voice, here, inside. How can I guard the privacy of my mind, then?

Human beings do not really want privacy.

There was silence for a while, and then inside the pit of my ship, appeared the imago of the Tycho, with his walrus jowls and savage grin. He was so close I could have reached out and plunged my hand into the phased light waves that were his bristly face. When he spoke, real sound waves washed my ears: "Would you rather speak as a human being? Then we will speak thus."

"Where is Soli? The other pilots? What was the result of the battle?"

The Tycho licked spit from his yellow teeth and said, "You have fallen far, no pilot further. The others are worming their way through the manifold. Only you have proven your theorem; only you will be told the secret. Fix your telescopes on the asteroid cluster twelve degrees above the solar plane."

I oriented my ship's telescopes according to his/Her directions. I looked out into the space a billion miles from Gehenna Luz, at a great cloud of asteroids, rocks, dust and other debris. Some of these fragments were huge, cratered and pocked, red with silicates and iron; some were a darker dun color, probably rich with carbon and water compounds. At first I had no idea why the Entity had bade me look at such a bone-heap of pulverized matter. Then, as the ship-computer analyzed the carbon, hydrogen, nitrogen and oxygen proportions of one of the smaller asteroids my stomach tightened. I felt an overwhelming apprehension—no, that is not the right word—I immediately knew that something, in a cosmological sense, was very wrong.

"This used to be Gehenna's single planet," the Tycho said. "It was twice as massive as Icefall. Now it orbits Gehenna in pieces. Human beings did this. The manswarm tore the planet apart."

I could hardly believe that She would permit human beings to enter Her brain, to tear planets apart. Then I thought of the decadent human beings I had encountered on my first journey inside the Entity, and I was not so sure.

"How many human beings?" I asked. "Where are these human beings?"

"Fix your telescopes on the long, crescent-shaped asteroid. There, do you see? Look how they shimmer!—their hulls are spun diamond, the same as your lightships."

I looked through my telescope and saw the terrible image of many man-made worlds. Each world was a spinning cylinder about thirty miles long and ten miles wide. I wondered how many people lived inside each world. I counted the worlds. There were ten thousand four hundred and eight of them. They were like a colony of rod-shaped bacteria spread out against the black blood of space. My first thought was that human beings must have colonized Gehenna Luz before the Entity had grown into this part of the nebula. Perhaps they had even come from Old Earth. A deepship had fallen out, I thought, and the human beings had made a world into which they could increase their numbers. They had mined and smelted and metabolized the elements of the planet to grow habitats and food, to reproduce themselves ten thousand times over. If that was true, they would be among the oldest peoples of the galaxy. (I mean the oldest *human* peoples.) They must have been here for thousands of years.

When I told this to the Tycho, he pulled his jowls and laughed until the spit ran down his chin. He said, "You know your first thought is wrong. Why don't you examine your second thought? You must know where these human beings come from."

"Tell me."

"Think, Mallory."

I rubbed my knuckles across my chin and asked, "How long did it take for them to dismantle the planet?"

The Tycho smiled his humorous (or humoring) smile. "Okay, you can calculate how long they've been here from the doubling time one of their worlds needs to reproduce itself. It's an exponential growth. A mathematical man should be able to calculate such things."

My head hurt, and I pressed my eye and the side of my nose with my fist. I did not know why the Tycho would want to tease me. "What is the doubling time, then? How many years?"

The Tycho's smile was savage as he said, "Do you mean, how many *days*?"

"Days!"

"The manswarm breeds quickly, doesn't it, Pilot? Ten Neverness years ago the first world fell out from the Vild."

"Ten years ago!"

"They were lost, you see, and they had hungers."

"Ten years!"

"Shall I show you what human beings can do when they hunger for growth? Are you ready to watch a star explode?"

"Why," I whispered, "why would they explode their sun? Is it possible?"

I closed my eyes for a moment to watch the telescopic images my ship infused into my visual cortex. I stared at the sifting dust and rocks and ten thousand made-worlds. I wondered again how many people lived in each world. "Mallory," a voice called out to me. "Mallory, listen."

I threw my hands over my ears. "No," I shouted. "The dead don't have tongues, so they shouldn't speak."

I did not want to listen. I did not want to open my eyes. I did not want to hear the dulcet voice or look at the lovely, eyeless face that the Entity was pulling from my memory.

"Oh, Mallory, Mallory!"

At last I could stand it no longer. I opened my eyes and looked at Katharine. She floated before me wearing her white scryer's robe. Her skin was white as marble, and her eye hollows were deepest black. She smiled at me. "It was foreseen long ago," she said. "What is has been."

I wanted to reach out to her, to grab her up in my arms and kiss her full red lips. But I told myself that she was nothing more than light and memory, and dispassionate words hanging in the air. I would not try to touch her, I promised myself. No matter what happened, I would keep my fist pressed against my cheek.

"Why do you torture me, then? Are my crimes so great?" And I cursed and shouted to the Entity, "Bring back the Tycho, damn you! I can talk to him."

But the Tycho, it seemed, was gone. Katharine's imago—

it was only Katharine's imago, I reminded myself—answered me: "Long ago the first scryers saw the painful future of... Do you understand the pain of this vision, now? Oh, sweet Mallory, with your sweet brain and your sweet life, it hurts more than a man can bear, and so I'll show what man and woman can... Do you see what I've seen? Will you see it if I show you? Look! What has been will be, again and again until all the stars... Do you see?"

In my mind a picture formed. There was a hot white star orbited by a lifeless, frozen planet. Suddenly, from the thickspace close in towards the sun where the photons and radiation spilled out into space like a waterfall of white light, there came the hazy foreimage of an object falling out of the manifold. The image hardened. A clear, diamond cylinder thirty miles long spread its lightsails in a thousand-mile-wide umbrella to capture Gehenna's profuse radiations. Slowly the light-pressure of trillions of particles against the gossamer, silvery lightsails imparted momentum to the cylinder. It accelerated. In a short time—perhaps only as long as a long deep winter on Neverness—it reached the planet. The cylinder opened. Clouds of tiny disassemblers (or perhaps I should call them programmed bacteria) fell down like a meteor shower through the airless vacuum and gathered over parts of the planet in great patches of shiny dust. Then the disassemblers did their work. They tore loose oxygen atoms from water molecules; they concentrated masses of carbon and other elements. They ate away the very ground. They concentrated hydrogen. In vast reservoirs carved out of the planet's crust, clouds of hydrogen were stored. Again the cylinder opened, and an army of robot-lasers fell to the planet. They found the hydrogen reservoirs. Optical crystals in the hearts of the lasers converted infrared light into short wave beams aimed at the hydrogen pockets. The hydrogen grew hot and glowed; it heated to a hundred million degrees and fusioned and exploded. In seconds, great balls of fire and light erupted from the surface. The crust of the planet was vaporized, pulverized, blown into hot dust. Rocks and fused sand fragments were flung out into space. Ice became steam and boiled away. Later, when the dust had settled, the cylinder opened and released still more disassemblers over the chewed-up surface of the planet. In this way, layer by layer, the planet was stripped crust, mantle and core, torn apart like a dirty snowball and scattered into space.

More pictures formed inside me. I was fascinated with this vision of assembler technology gone wild, so I closed my eyes and watched the disassemblers mine the floating planetary fragments for silicon, mercury and helium, and every other natural element. I watched a cloud of assemblers escape from the cylinder into the newly created asteroids, watched as they bonded carbon atom to atom until they had assembled the gleaming, diamond hulls of many more cylinders. The assemblers built other things. Telescopes, sulki grids, neurologics, flame globes, shakuhachis, flying wings, chopsticks, gossilk, trees, houses, glucose pellets, fields of grass—there was no end to the things that the assemblers made. Assemblers made more assemblers, and so the process of converting a planet into ten thousand cylinders did not take very long. Assemblers bonded carbon to hydrogen and oxygen; assemblers had been programmed to fix nitrogen, to build up amino acids and string together proteins. Assemblers could even make human beings. A manswarm of human beings, billions and billions of human beings.

How many human beings?

"Do you see, sweet Mallory?" the Katharine imago asked me. "So many, who could have foreseen that life would have made so many?"

"Are the images you showed me—this history—is it real?"

"Reach out with your telescopes. Are the ten thousand made-worlds real?"

I rubbed the side of my nose and said, "Can I know what's real when I'm inside your brain and you're inside mine? You can make me see anything you want me to, I think."

She smiled as she dipped her hand into her robe's pocket of concealment. When she removed it, her finger was smeared with blacking oil, which she daubed into her eyepits. She said, "You see well enough these pretty . . . You must know they are real."

I pulled at my beard and asked, "How many people live in each cylinder?"

"It's not the same number for each . . . It will take me a segment of time to recite the exact numbers. And the numbers change as we speak. It's so funny, the way you can't help counting all the time, this fetish for exact numbers."

"*Approximately* how many people, then?"

She nodded her head as she spoke. "Ten million human beings live inside each world."

"Human beings—" I began.

"Human beings," she said, "are so wonderful! Half animal, half..."

I pressed my lips together (I couldn't help thinking that my face must have looked as tight-lipped as Soli's), and I said, "It's impossible for ten million people to reproduce like that in ten years."

But even as I spoke, I knew very well that it was not impossible. Assemblers could be used to ripen infants into adults in a few years. But what kind of humans would these be? It was impossible for a human mind to bear its full fruit in the span of a couple of years. I did a swift calculation. If the number of worlds doubled every three-fourths of a year, most of the worlds and the people living inside had not existed three years ago. (Assemblers could even build a fully grown human being in a few days. During the second dark age, the imprimaturs had performed many such forbidden experiments. It was true, a woman or man could be grown like a joint of cultured meat. She would have working arms and hair and hot red blood pumping through her arteries. She would even have a brain. But the brain would be as barren as the upper slopes of Mount Attakel. Assemblers could make a woman or man, but they could not make a mind. *They could not make a human mind*.)

"You still don't *see*," Katharine said, and she brushed her hair away from her forehead. She turned towards me. If she had had eyes, I would have guessed she was reading my face for tells. "How can I make you see?"

And then there were sights and smells and sounds. As if I were a thallow soaring on a mountain thermal, my mind's eye—my ear and my nose—floated across space and pierced the hull of one of the cylinders. There was warm, moist air, the rich smells of life. Below me and above, curving out and around and down on all sides for miles was a jungle of encompassing green. There were trees and chess-board lawns and ponds and apple orchards hung with sweet-smelling red fruits. And everywhere I looked, circling forward and aft, left and right, there were babies. Babies were everywhere. Naked babies, their bodies as wrinkled and soft as spirali, crawled and squirmed through the long green grasses of the lawns. A small army of domestic robots watched over them. Some of the robots nursed newborn babies from plastic teats which they stuffed in their moist, toothless mouths. Everywhere babies were crying, sucking, sleeping and defecating in the grass. The air was rank with the smells of spit-up milk and mustardy baby dung and fresh, new baby skin. A few of the older babies—they were children, really—climbed like hairless monkeys through the spreading branches of an apple tree. They plucked ripe, red apples and bit off chunks with a crunch, and flung the fruit to the grass below. The lawns were littered with half-eaten apples. I was appalled at the waste. It almost reminded me of a Davaki meat-orgy. I wondered if the apples were riddled with worms. Why else would the babies throw away so much fruit? One of the babies lay cradled in the crotch of a tree while he picked over an apple as carefully as a novice would study a hologram of the galaxy. He smiled, then sank his little white teeth into the apple. The apple was full of worms. Worms swarmed through the meat of the apple. With another smile, the boy-baby held the apple to his lips and sucked out a couple of worms, which he gulped down like milk. I was puzzled why he did this. I wondered why all the other babies carefully sought out apples full of worms. Then I heard Katharine whispering in my ear, and I knew the answer: Baby children—and all human beings—need protein to grow, and worms are nothing but water, fat and protein.

I closed my eyes, and when I opened them, I was back in the pit of my ship looking at Katharine. "So many," she said, "the worlds are full of new ... Oh, yes, there are adult humans, too, a thousand for every world. The ultimate astriers, do you see? But the babies know the real ... They're so sweet and eager to live—and they're so hungry!"

"Worm eaters," I said, thinking of Shanidar's ghastly smile and the many horrible things he had eaten. "It reminds me of certain things I'd rather not be reminded of."

"Don't be afraid of your memories. Memory is everything."

"This careless fecundity. It's so damn barbaric!"

"Be compassionate, Mallory."

"They're barbarians."

"And that is the problem with human beings, do you see? Oh, these poor people *are* uncivilized! They're so... Their hunger is so limitless. They've consumed the elements of the planet, but they've run out of one crucial... The planet was nitrogen-poor—did you know that? This limits their growth. How can they make protein without nitrogen? So now they must look for more food. Other planets around other stars: food for human babies, do you see?"

"No, I'd rather I was blind."

Katharine pointed her finger at me. The oil-smeared tip was invisible. She spoke, and her words were slow and grave. "The ten thousand worlds are like enormous deepships—only not so like. How is it possible, you wonder, to open a window for such a massive object as a made-world? The deformations would have to be so... *enormous*. When Gehenna has fallen into supernova, the deformed spacetime in the star's neighborhood will suddenly unbend, like a sheet of rubber—isn't that the analogy pilots always use? And like our pilots, the pilots of the made-worlds will make their mappings. Just before the light incinerates them, the worlds will be flung into the manifold like... like stones through an open window. It's the only way."

"They're barbarians!"

She shook her head hard enough to whip her long, black hair from ear to ear. "No, they are women and men, like us. Like, but not the same because the lack our pilots' artistry. Their mapping theorems are so crude. Rarely do they find a one-to-one mapping. Most of the time, they must map from a point-source to an open set of... You see, most of the worlds will fall through a window and scatter at random throughout the galaxy. Eventually they will fall out around other stars. Which stars these will be, none of the lords of the manswarm can know."

"Barbarians!"

The Vild was nothing but dead stars murdered by human beings.

I understood, then. I thought I understood everything of human beings and their terrible fate within the limiting lens of the Milky Way galaxy. The blood was hot in my face because I was terribly embarrassed. What have we done, I wondered? Why *human beings* at all? Human beings had at last abandoned all restraint. Human beings would destroy a star because the urge to new life and new niches for life was greater than reverence for the life of any star; in a way, paradoxically, it was greater than existing life itself. Ten thousand worlds full of human beings would fall through the windows of the manifold to the galaxy's distant stars. Some worlds might fall *into* stars; some would dwell too long in the manifold and run out of food; a few worlds would be lost in infinite trees or other topological traps. Perhaps only a half or a third of the worlds would survive—who could calculate the probabilities? But that would be enough. The seed worlds would reach bright new stars, and they would make billions of new human beings. Nothing would stop the wreckage of whole planets and the transmutation of simple elements into human beings. Human beings in their billions would become trillions of trillions, and the stars would die one by one, and thousand by thousand, and the Vild would grow until all the stars and planets and interstellar dust were used up, and the galaxy, from the dead Alpha Crux to the burned-out Antares, was nothing but a swirling spiral of diamond-hulled worlds full of hungry human beings.

To the glowing imago of Katharine, I said, "You must hate us."

"Sweet Mallory, no, I don't hate you."

"How can they reproduce and journey thus, knowing they'll destroy everything?"

"But they don't know *anything*, don't you see? These ten thousand worlds—the human beings inside believe they sacrifice a few stars so their children can bloom and prosper. Because starlight . . . because they cannot journey as our pilots do, they lack perspective. Because the light from most of the supernovas hasn't had time to reach much of the galaxy, they can't *see* it. In truth, even though they are its creators, they don't know the Vild exists."

"But they must know that sooner or later all the stars will be dead!"

She smiled and said, "They hope that event will occur later, not sooner." And then she added, "If all the stars fell into supernovas, the galaxy will flare with wild . . . The star fire will create an abundance of new elements, and so their childrens' children will find new, if dangerous, possibilities for life."

Despite myself, I could not help smiling, too. I was

dreadfully ashamed that my fellow human beings were destroying the stars, yet perversely proud that we were clever enough and powerful enough to do so. Even a goddess, I thought, must be helpless before a galaxy-wrecking swarm of human beings.

And then pride gave way to guilt, and I repeated, "You must hate us."

"Sweet Mallory, I don't hate you, I . . . Oh, don't you see? We scryers, all who learn the art . . . this new ecology, it was foreseen so long ago. Even the Agathanians, they saw this moment in its becoming."

"Why wasn't I told, then? If I knew—"

"Don't you see? If you had known, you would have despaired, because it is one thing to know, another to . . . What could you or anyone of our Order have done to stop the Vild's growth?"

"Am I so different than I was? What can I do . . . *now*?"

"You will stop the pain because that is your fate. The Vild is *torturing* the galaxy. My sweet Mallory, you brought yourself here to cure the pain . . . and for other reasons."

Although I dreaded hearing these "other reasons," I said, "Tell me, then."

Katharine smoothed the flowing folds of her robe and said, "I can't tell you. It's not for me to . . . No, I must leave you now, Mallory. For the time, for an eon of time, until I am remembered. Kalinda will tell you what you need to know. Kalinda of the Flowers."

"Katharine, I never told you the most basic thing which is—"

"Goodbye, sweet Mallory, goodbye."

"No!"

Katharine shimmered as she disappeared. I knew it was a ridiculous thing to do, but I reached out to touch her. I touched air. I floated with my arm outthrust and my fist clenched, and I stared into the sudden blackness.

"I remember you too well," I said aloud. "Goddamn my memory!"

A moment later, a new imago I had never seen before came alive and floated above my head. I looked up. She was a beautiful girl. Her skin was as brown as a baldo nut, and she wore a red robe from neck to knee. Her eyes were almost as black as the Timekeeper's; they were shaped like almonds and seemed too large for her head. It occurred to me that I had never seen eyes so wise and intelligent in a human face. Around the little finger of each of her quick little hands she wore a red ring, and her dark hair was decorated with tens of little white flowers. Her name was Kalinda of the Flowers.

I would bless your memory and help you remember, if I could.

It is impossible to describe her voice. Certainly it was high and sweet like the piping of a snow loon. At the same time, it was rich, measured, and calm. When she spoke, she enunciated each of her words clearly, in a very unchildlike manner. In a godly manner. Her voice was the godvoice, and it sounded inside me in deeper tones that perfectly harmonized with the music pouring out of her girlish throat. There was whimsy in her voice, and there was poetry. She gave me a knowing look as she recited:

Dear, beauteous death! the jewel of the just,
  Shining nowhere but in the dark;
What mysteries do lie beyond thy dust,
  Could man outlook that mark!

There were more poems after this, ancient poems and modern, poems of Fravashi origin and poems that I thought she must have composed herself. I was given to understand that this too-wise little girl was a part of the Entity in a way that the Tycho, and certainly Katharine, were not. Had she lived on one of the worlds which fell out into the Entity's dark interior long ago? Had she been killed, encapsulated and absorbed into one of the Entity's oldest and deepest memory spaces? Why did the warrior-poets and the Agathanians refer to the Entity as Kalinda? I looked at her fingers, at the rings, the rings of a warrior-poet. Was it possible? Was this the girl that Dawud had spoken of? Had she been the result of an experiment in breeding female warrior-poets? *And she wore two red rings!* I had a terrible suspicion. I felt—and probably the goddess was quite pleased that I felt this way—I somehow guessed that this poetry-loving child was alive within the very core of the Entity. Perhaps the Entity had taken pity on the young warrior-poet; perhaps she had honored the only human being ever to have worn the poet's and the warrior's red rings. I thought of the image of an onion, and my eyes burned with tears. The Entity must be very like an onion, layer upon layer, whole moons of her brain built up over an inner self who loved flowers and poetry.

Don't be afraid of the death, my Pilot.

Aloud I said, "But every star in the galaxy, every poem that's ever been written, everything—it will all be lost."

Kalinda plucked a flower from her hair. She placed it in the palm of her hand, pursed her lips, and blew it at me. The flower floated in the air and drifted toward me.

You still don't understand. Nothing is lost. I picked this hyacinth thousands of years ago, but smell it—isn't it still fresh?

"I've tried to understand, thought about this all my life. The decay, the entropy—"

Entropy is missing information; entropy is a measure of uncertainty. When entropy is maximum, then all messages are equally probable. The greater the uncertainty, the greater amount of information conveyed in the message.

"The message of the Ieldra, it's—"

From the moment the universe was created it moved away from the disorder of the primal explosion. Macroscopic information is continually created.

"But I—"

Gods seek perfect information about the universe. But information can never be perfect. Consider one of your exhalations, your carelessly bitter words of warm air. If a single gram of matter as far away as Shiva Luz were to be moved a single centimeter, it would change the microscopic state of your breath. Even the universe itself can never create enough information to know its own future.

"'What has been will be,' Katharine used to say."

You cannot even dream what the future of this galaxy will be.

"We're all doomed and damned, aren't we?"

No, it is just the opposite, my Pilot. There are infinite possibilities.

She plucked another hyacinth from the garland around her forehead and placed this little flower of light in my hair. She told me many things, then, wonderful things. Much of what she said I did not understand, or understood only poorly, as a novice who has been given numbers to play with has only the vaguest notion of transfinite arithmetic. When I asked her why she would *allow* the ten thousand worlds to murder Gehenna Luz—for clearly the goddess had the power to destroy every world inside Her, if She so desired—she hinted at the existence of certain unalterable ecological "laws." (If I confuse the pronouns referring to Kalinda with those of the goddess, it is because I was confused. In some sense, I am still confused.) Her words were almost gobble-dygook: There was something about the decisions of every entity in the universe determining what she called the "ecology of choices." It would be a great crime, she said, to needlessly interrupt the natural flow of choices. And it was an even greater crime not to restore the flow if it had been interrupted. It seemed that there were other ecologies, too. There was an ecology of ideas and an ecology of prophesies, and an ecology of information. She told me about the ecology of determined actions and the ecology of fundamental paradoxes. There were many, many of these ecologies; there was a hierarchy of ecologies. The study of the interplay between ecologies, she said, was her art. When I admitted that her art was as apprehensible to me as probabilistic topology was to a worm, she said, "Worms know enough about transformations to become butterflies."

She told me something else. All of our communications, all of her manipulations of the manifold that I had found so disturbing, the inexplicable phenomena inside of the Entity—everything that I had so far witnessed, she had accomplished on an unconscious level. No being, she said, could afford to be aware of life processes which she could make automatic. Could a man take the time to consciously adjust his heartrate to the many and varying needs of his environment? To speed up his metabolism and bodily temperature in order to fight a bacterial invasion? To be *aware* of each individual bacteria? No, and neither could a goddess afford to be aware of a mere man, nor even ten thousand worlds full of women and men. The true concerns of the goddess, it seemed, were far beyond my concerns as to man's fate within the galaxy.

As we had talked, millions of black bodies had fallen out around the star. She told me that they were a form of manufactured matter as dense as black holes, but not nearly so massive. The black bodies—I might as well call them gamma-phages—stored energy; she had made the gamma-phages to absorb and hold the light of the supernova. Why she should need such enormous quantities of energy she kept a mystery. She hinted that I must trust her, that there was a vital reason why stars must die. But how could I trust this godchild with her goddamned, godwise eyes? Kalinda smiled so sweetly, but she had devoured the brain and mind of the Tycho, and the minds of Ricardo Lavi and other pilots, and who could know what other feasts she might someday require?

Do not brood so, my Pilot. It would be unpoetic if all the stars died. You won't let them die.

Because she was lonely, because she could read the fear and wild anticipation in *my* eyes, because she was at heart a compassionate goddess, this child with flowers in her hair promised to help me if only I would promise her a simple thing. Although it was reckless of me to do so, I made her this promise, a promise which I shall tell of presently.

And now it begins.

If I had possessed a millionth of the Entity's powers, I think I would have stopped the murder of Gehenna Luz. But I was just a man, and there was little I could do. Kalinda twisted the ring around one of her fingers and told me to watch the swarm of worlds through my telescope. I did as she commanded. I watched one of the worlds nearest the sun open. It looked like two halves of a gigantic oyster opening to an ocean of sunlight. And inside was a pearl of a machine, a great jewel of a spacetime engine.

It is pretty, isn't it? See how it sparkles. Face your ship, my Pilot, and let your computer model what is to come.

I watched human beings accelerate the natural life cycle of a star. The lords of the manswarm—or somebody, or some computer—oriented the spacetime engine on points within the plasma core of Gehenna Luz. It took fourteen hundred fifty four seconds for the probability waves to propagate through space to the star. At the points near the core, where the temperature was one hundred million degrees, the zero-point energy of spacetime was suddenly converted to thermal energy. In the neighborhood of the point-sources, the plasma was a molten sea, and there was a series of explosions. The core of the star grew even hotter. The hydrogen plasma began burning at an accelerated rate, faster and faster, four hydrogen atoms slamming into each other to yield each helium atom plus a bit of energy, plus a raging maelstrom of energy ripping across the red sea of hydrogen.

Do you burn to return home, my Pilot? There is always a returning. I will descry a part of your future: One last time you will return to me.

At an accelerating rate, zero-point energy was converted to heat. At one hundred and fifty million degrees, helium fusioned to form carbon, the element of life, and it grew hotter still. A million years of stellar evolution occurred in perhaps a tenth of a year. When the core fire reached six hundred million degrees, carbon fused into neon. And time contracted even as the star's core contracted, pressing inward, generating temperatures greater than a billion degrees. Thus the atoms of oxygen were born, and oxygen burned to form silicon and iron, and the core of the star was very, very hot. The star—this is how I saw it through the thoughtspace of my ship—the interior of Gehenna Luz was like an onion with a core of iron plasma. Enveloping the core was a silicon shell surrounded by burning sulphur, and skins of oxygen, carbon, and helium. The core was now hot enough to finish its own evolution in a few days, and so the spacetime engine grew still, and the manswarm inside the made-worlds prepared to make their mappings.

Life and death; death/life.

Because iron will not fuse spontaneously into heavier elements, soon the entire core had burned itself out. The core grew too massive, too dense. Without the electron pressure of gushing energy to oppose the gravity of the star's interior—at the Chandrasekhar limit—the core collapsed at a quarter of lightspeed. In less than a second, it fell inward like a crushed thallow's egg. It grew hellishly hot, eight billion degrees hot. The core matter broke down into protons and neutrons and was compressed to such densities that it rebounded with a snap. An enormous shock wave ripped through the onion skins to the surface, blowing off the star's outer layers. Gehenna Luz exploded in a fire of hydrogen plasma and gamma rays and bright, hot light.

The secret of life.

I did not actually see the ten thousand worlds fall in. My ship modeled the manifold, though, and I watched it twist like a roasted worm, twist and distort. I saw millions of huge, gaping windows open in the neighborhood of the worlds.

Then, in a moment, the worlds were gone, flung out into the galaxy where new and virgin stars awaited.

You have wondered at the Ieldra's secret, but I may not tell you because I am what the greater gods would warn you against. When you return to Neverness, you must ask your Timekeeper why this is so. He is very old, and in a way, wiser than you could believe. And for now, goodbye, my Pilot.

I did not remain to watch Gehenna's wavefront of light blow across my ship. I had seen enough. I was eager to find my brother and sister pilots, wherever they might be. I was eager to do other things as well, so I found a window and made a mapping. As I fell into the manifold, into the timeless realm where the only light was the light of mathematics and dreamtime, Kalinda clapped her hands together and sang out, "But it's so pretty!" Then she, too, was gone. However, I could still smell her flowers, and the sound of her last poem rang in the air:

> Stars, I have seen them fall,
>   But when they drop and die,
> No star is lost at all,
>   From all the star-sown sky.

27

Kelkemesh

It may be fairly asked why animals, who live by talon and beak and their most immediate and savage impulses, do not devour each other down to the last writhing worm? And why do the gods not shatter worlds when they tremble with godly wrath? Why is man uniquely cursed with war? The answer to this question is both historic and evolutionary: We walk the brink of racial suicide because we were smart enough to make atomic bombs and stupid enough to use them.

—from A *Requiem for Homo Sapiens*,
by Horthy Hosthoh

Deep within the Entity was a planetless star which has come to be known as the Pilot's Star. It was a small, yellow star of no particular distinction except that it was closest—topologically closest—to Gehenna Luz. When I fell out above the Pilot's Star I found that of all the lightships racing through the manifold, only one had arrived. It was Soli's *Vorpal Blade*, shining in the starlight like an Old City spire on a winter night.

I sent my imago into his ship's pit, which was a warm, dark sphere much like my own pit. I talked to him. His long, hard Alaloi muscles knotted beneath his hairy belly, and he greeted me. "How far do you fall, Pilot?" And then, "Do you remember the race the day after you became a pilot? There was my lead the whole way then, too. But now neither of us will cross the finish line, will we? Your goddess's star has fallen supernova too soon—the deformations were point to

476

zero-point so there can't be any doubt that it was a supernova. There'll be no more mappings beyond this star, will there?"

"Only mappings homeward."

"Yes, the race—"

"The race is over, Soli." I told him then that I had just witnessed the death of a star. I told him about the hundred billion homeless people who had helped cause the growth of the Vild.

There was sweat on his forehead, sweat in his beard. He didn't want to believe I had reached Gehenna Luz before him. "No, that's impossible," he said. "My mappings were tight and elegant. Yours couldn't have been tighter."

"Perhaps I didn't need to make as many mappings," I said.

"Why not, Pilot?"

I wanted to shout out my proof of the Continuum Hypothesis. Would the news that I had proved what he had struggled vainly for three lifetimes to prove ruin him? Very well, let it ruin him.

"How should I tell you, then? It's the simplest reason: that between any pair of discrete Lavi sets of point-sources there exists a—"

"It's proven!"

"—one-to-one—"

"You've proved it, haven't you?"

"—mapping."

"Yes, the bastard Ringess and his reckless dreams—not entirely reckless after all." He held his chin up proudly and asked, "What's the proof, Pilot? Tell me your proof."

I told him nothing. I was tempted to blurt out my collapse of the Lavi correspondence scheme, but I said nothing. For the first time in my life, I began to truly understand the Timekeeper and his secretive ways.

When I didn't answer him, he tapped his long nose and asked, "Are you ashamed of your proof? How could you be ashamed? Ah, but was it entirely *your* proof? Yes, there's a little shame, now, in your reckless, carked brain, in everything you do. You're not to be envied, no; you should be pitied instead."

"It's not your pity I want."

He said, surprisingly, "Pity these lost peoples of the Vild.

You say they've lost their sense of wrong and right. Isn't that the worst fate? To lose that which is necessary to live happily within . . . within the bounds of . . ."

He did not finish his sentence. He closed his eyes and strained to speak. I thought he might want to tell me something about Justine, or perhaps, about pity and forgiveness, but he seemed to have lost his voice. The apple of his throat jumped up and down as he swallowed empty swallows of air.

At last he rubbed the muscles of his neck and said, "Yes, your goddess has told you secrets. When we return to the City, we'll have to call a new quest. The Timekeeper will be spoken to. We'll have to send a mission to the Vild, to educate the poor people in the rudiments of mathematics, the rules of civilization."

"The Timekeeper," I said, "will call no more quests."

"Do you speak as a scryer, or as a criminal afraid to pay for his crimes?"

"Soli, I have to tell you about the Timekeeper."

"Yes, you'll tell me the words of your goddess."

"Words of truth. In truth—"

"Tell me the truth, not lies," he said.

"I'll tell you what I know, what I've deduced. And what I've *seen*. I'll tell you everything."

He opened his eyes, and they were as wet and blue as the icy sea. "Tell me how to make love last. Isn't that the secret of the universe?"

Soon after this—it was actually many days of realtime—the other lightships began to fall out near us. Li Tosh, the Sonderval and Alark of Urradeth—at least some of my old friends had survived. And Soli's pilots, Salmalin, and Chanoth Chen Ciceron in his segmented *Nimspinner* fell out as well, and we waited some more. Of the one hundred and twelve who had set out for Gehenna Luz, forty-one fell out around the Pilot's Star. The others, we presumed, must be dead, killed in battle or lost in the manifold. (At the time, of course, no one knew that not all the pilots had tried to reach Gehenna Luz. Five pilots—Kerry Blackstone, Gaylord Noy, Tonya Sam, the Katya and Sabri Dur li Kadir—for mad reasons of their own, had fallen back to Perdido Luz and had continued to war until only Sabri Dur was left. And later I discovered that at least twenty-eight pilots had abandoned the quest for

Gehenna Luz at the outset. They had beheld the freakish manifold within the Entity, and, to their shame, they had fled back to Neverness.)

We held another conclave. Soli surprised me by quickly spreading the news that the Great Theorem had been solved. I think this must have excited my fellow pilots more than the discovery about the Vild. "This will change everything," Li Tosh said to the imagos of the other pilots. He brushed his lank brown hair out of his eyes, and I read the beginnings of awe there. "We should honor the Ringess for his brilliant discoveries."

"Yes, and how should the Ringess be honored?" Soli asked the forty pilots gathered together in his ship's pit. And again he surprised me, saying, "Never again should pilot fall against pilot. War demeans us, doesn't it? If, to end this war, my time as Lord Pilot must end, then none of you should call me Lord Pilot again." He turned to his old friend Salmalin. Salmalin was fingering his warty skin along the edge of his jaw, looking from Soli back to me. There was awe in his eyes, too. "You may call the Ringess, 'Lord Pilot,' if that is what you decide," Soli said.

Salmalin puffed out his old, withered cheeks in surprise, in awe that Soli would abandon his lordship to me. And then, like a wave, the awe washed the faces of the other pilots. It swept the reason from them. I have never understood this virus of servitude that infects human beings. Most of them idolized me a little and I hated that. They projected their own dreams and desires onto me. Somehow I was to be a vehicle for their collective wills. I saw—and this realization sickened me—I suddenly knew that to them I was no longer just a man. I was something else, or rather, many things at once: dreammaker, pathfinder, a leader of men. They bowed their heads to me, and thirty-five of them, even Soli, voted that I should be Lord Pilot. I looked at their awe-stamped faces with that uneasy mixture of emotions all leaders must feel towards those they lead: love, contempt, irony and pride.

Later, when we were alone together in the pit of my ship, Soli said to me, "Congratulations... *Lord* Pilot. It's what you've always wanted, isn't it?"

"Why, Soli? I don't understand you. Why this sudden humility, then?"

He looked at me, but there was little awe in his eyes;

there was only sadness and exhaustion. "The race is over, but the race goes on," he said. "Yes, you are Lord Pilot now, and you wonder why. Should you be told why? Yes, you'll be told because soon enough you'll know of your own: To stand like a god above your fellow pilots—there's no glory there. There's only the continual temptation of arrogance. And arrogance demeans us, doesn't it? All my life, fooling myself that . . . but now, after all this, there is a certain—it is hard to use this word—*enlightenment*. Yes, arrogance is the worst crime. And that is why my vote was for your lordship. It's my revenge."

In this manner, far above the saffron, hydrogen bomb that was the Pilot's Star, I became the Lord Pilot of our Order. It should have been a happy moment, a moment full of pride and exultation, the greatest moment of my life. But it was a bitter moment, as bitter as the pit of a yu fruit. I was truly Lord Pilot at last, but Bardo was gone, and I had promises to keep.

I returned to Neverness on the second day of deep winter in the year 2934. It had been nearly a year since my escape from the Timekeeper's cell. Intime, I must have aged ten years; I felt older, deepened by my crimes, changed. I half-expected my City to have changed as well. But she greeted me with the same, eternal, cold face that I had always known. It was the face of stone frozen with snow-swirls, a white, icy face veined with red and purple streets. It was cold that year, even the historians admitted it was cold. Some of them jokingly dubbed it the Year of the Dead because—they said—the dead days of deep winter had begun so early. But we all knew their real reason: On sixday, the Pilot's College made plans to chisel the names of the lost and dead pilots onto the Tomb of the Lost Pilot, which stood beneath the foothills of Attakel near that lovely, granite outcropping known as Our Lady of the Rocks.

One thing in the City had changed. The Timekeeper was no longer preeminent. Even as we pilots had fought our battle around Perdido Luz, the lords of the Order had waged a battle of a different sort within the Academy's cold towers and halls. Nikolos the Elder had finally persuaded the College of Lords to place restrictions on the Timekeeper's powers. As the days passed, the lords had changed certain of our Order's oldest canons. With the replacement of the seventh

canon some thirty days before my return, the Timekeeper
must have guessed that he might himself soon be replaced.
The lords had broken with a millennia-old tradition. They
had decided that the Lord of the Order could be retired
while still alive, and more, that any lord, even one such as
the lowly Lord Phantast, could be Lord of the Order. There
were other changes, too. For instance: The Timekeeper
would not be allowed to ground a pilot, nor to strip any
master of his or her rank; never again would the Timekeeper—
or any Lord of the Order—be allowed to keep a private army
of tutelary robots.

When we surviving pilots dropped our ships down into
the Lightship Caverns, the whole Academy (and many farsiders
and aliens) turned out to welcome us. There was a parade as
if it were a festival day; there were horns blaring away, and
eiswein and kvass, and gossilk streamers blowing in the wind.
The schismatic professionals in the deepship returned with
us, and they immediately skated forth to heal the wounds of
our Order. We endured a few wild, anxious days as the
various colleges held their conclaves. Old rivalries and dis-
putes still rumbled within the bowels of a few of the professions, particularly those of the eschatologists and mechanics.
But when the professionals and academicians learned the
outcome of Perdido Luz, they were horrified. And when the
news of the Vild's origin spread, they were filled with raw
terror. They made their peace. They agreed to let the College
of Lords convene, to decide a new "order for the Order," as
the historian Burgos Harsha joked. In truth, the Timekeeper
had gambled sending Soli to capture or kill the schismatic
pilots, and he had lost his gamble. Instead of gaining time in
which to win over the lords, he had alienated them. Nikolos
the Elder called for an inquest into Soli's near assassination,
and into the causes of the Pilot's War, and then he called for
the Timekeeper's abasement.

By the time tenday dawned clear and deep cold, even the
most cantankerous and crusty masters and lords realized that
great changes were imminent. We lords (and it felt strange
for me to include myself among them) met inside the College
of the Lords, a stately, square building made of slabs of
white-grained granite. From a distance it looked like a shining white box neatly placed down into the blue and white
folds of land beneath the Elf Garden, almost like a huge,

square snow-hut. And it was as cold as a snow-hut. The lords of the Order huddled inside the drafty sanctum, and we shivered in our formal robes. Lord Kolenya with her moon face, and Lord Nikolos, the Lord Akashic and the Lord Cetic—all the lords except the Lord Horologe were there. We sat at a cold table devoid of decoration or veneer. It is curious how great a part climate and discomfort can play in the affairs of human beings. We drank our steaming mugs of coffee and rubbed our hands together. We made a quick, cold decision. We decided that the Timekeeper would no longer be Timekeeper. For the time, there would be no Lord of the Order. And then we adjourned and went out on the streets of the Academy to tell the waiting masters, journeymen and novices the news.

Lord Harsha met me on the slick steps outside the College. Looking to the right and left at the other lords and professionals, he bowed his head politely and said, "Congratulations, Mallory, I always expected you to do great things." And then he asked me the question everyone must have been wondering. "Who will tell the Timekeeper? I would not want to be there when he is told."

"I'll tell him," I said. "And it would be better if the lords were present when I tell him."

"Now, Mallory," Lord Harsha said as he pulled the ice from his nose hairs. (He was the same Burgos Harsha who had directed the infamous Pilot's Race five years ago, my mother's friend. He had been elevated to Lord Historian when old Tutu Lee, who had always been one of the Timekeeper's most faithful admirers, had slipped on the ice, cracked her head open and died.) "Now, Mallory, just because it was an irksome thing for the Timekeeper to imprison you—yes, yes, an irksome thing, but that was a bad time, do you remember? What choice did he—"

"The Timekeeper must be told," I said.

The next day some of the lords gathered at the top of the Timekeeper's Tower. Other prominent pilots and professionals had been invited to witness the formal ceremony by which we would "honor" the Timekeeper's many years of service. The Sonderval and Li Tosh came at my request. I did not expect Soli to suffer this final humiliation, but he surprised me and announced that he would attend. There was another surprise waiting for me when I arrived by sled outside the arched doors. My mother skated out of the crowd of curious professionals circling the Tower, and she came right up to me.

"Lord Pilot," she said, and she touched my hair where Seif's stone had crushed my head. "My son, we've made you. The Lord Pilot."

"Mother, you're still alive!"

The Tower doors were open. Li Tosh and Rodrigo Diaz, the Lord Mechanic, stood inside the doorway, watching. It was dusk, and the hundreds of brothers and sisters of our Order lined up beneath the gliddery's numerous coldflame globes. Their furs—it was almost too dark to make out their colors—were flapping in the wind. Everyone, it seemed, was watching me.

"I was worried you'd been killed," I said.

"Haven't I taught you? To worry about *worrisome* problems? There's no need for worry."

But I was very worried; I was horribly worried. I read my mother's face, looking for the tells of fear, of worry. But there was no fear there. In a way, the woman who held my shoulder for support as she ejected her skate blade was not my mother; in a way, my mother had been killed the day she first met the warrior-poet.

"Will you come up the Tower with me?" I asked.

"Of course I will," she said. She smiled a calm smile. Gone from her face were the nervous tics that had always afflicted her. And in their place, nothing. "Haven't I prepared for this moment all my life?"

Indeed, she had prepared too well. Later that day, I heard a rumor that my mother had spent the last year trying to persuade certain of the lords that the Timekeeper must be deposed. She had persuaded them by threat of assassination. Many believed that old Tutu Lee's slip on the ice had not really been a slip after all. Burgos Harsha, after all, was my mother's friend, and now he was Lord Historian. But how could I blame my mother for being a murderer? Parts of her brain—perhaps her whole brain from amygdala to cortex—had been mimed. I was sure of it. And therefore she was not my mother. I told myself this over and over: She is not my mother.

Soli arrived, then, wearing nothing more than his formal black robes. When Salmalin asked if he had forgotten his furs, Soli knocked the ice from his skates and said, "My body must get used to the cold." He took pains not to look at either my mother or myself. He turned to greet the Lord Mechanic and their old friends.

It was blue cold, shivering cold, too cold to stand there talking, so we went up to the top of the Tower. The Time-keeper received us with a gracious head bow and invited us to stand next to the curving glass panes of the southern windows. I squeezed between my mother and Knut Osen the Emancipated, the Lord Ecologist. There were twelve of us lords and masters, and we looked at the Timekeeper, who paced the white furs at the center of the room as he looked at us.

"So."

The Timekeeper, in his loose, red robes, seemed as gaunt and restless as a starved wolf. His white hair was not so thick as I had remembered. Beneath the skin of his neck, his muscles vibrated like the strings of a gosharp. His face, with its sharp angles and scowl, had subtly changed. Perhaps it was his eyes, those shiny black marbles rolling right and left as he defiantly stared at us. His eyes were cool, soulless and peaceful. I should have been immediately suspicious of this. I could not read his eyes, nor could I read any feature of his face. To be sure, there were tells in the measured way he growled out his greeting, and tells, too, in his quick glances through the glass towards the plain of the Hollow Fields gleaming in the distance. But I could not interpret these tells. He was a ruined man, I reminded myself, and ruined men will run new, desperate programs. Probably his blood was singing with a nepenthe or some other euphoric. I watched him as carefully as a Devaki watches a seal's aklia. I silently vowed that as long as I remained in his Tower, I would not turn my eyes away from him.

He stood next to one of his grandfather clocks as he alternately stared at Nikolos the Elder's jiggly belly and grimly smiled at Soli. The clock's brass pendulum swung back and forth, and I heard the ticking. The room, as always, was full of ticking clocks. I listened to the ticking of steel and wood, the pulsing, pings and beeping of the clocks around the room. My heart was beating like a drumclock as the Timekeeper's eyes fixed mine, and he asked, "Do you hear the ticking, Mallory, my brave, foolish *Lord* Pilot?"

Without waiting for an answer, he stepped over to the

Fravashi driftglass glowing in one of the clock cases. He abruptly turned to us, addressing us all at once: "*My* Lords and Masters," he began. He emphasized the word "my" as if we must still submit to his will, as if he were still Lord of the Order. "So, it's time, is it? You are come to tell me my time has run out?"

Nikolos screwed up his soft, intelligent face as if someone had just gouged his shin with a sharp skate. He looked at me, silently imploring me to say something. I stepped forward and took a breath. "It is the decision of the College of Lords," I said, "that you be forgiven your crimes. You will not be banished. Surrender the Seal of the Order, and you will be permitted to remain in your Tower."

"You'd forgive *me*?"

I wanted to tell him that I would forgive him anything because he had once saved my life and shaped my fate when he had given me the book of poems. A part of me—the boyish novice he had once taught the art of wrestling—was still somewhat in awe of him. "We'll forget that Bardo and eighty other pilots are dead because of you."

"Pompous, young pilot! What do you know about my crimes? What do you *know* about anything?"

"Surrender the Seal," I said. Behind me Burgos Harsha and Lord Parsons mumbled that the Timekeeper should hand us the Seal formally, without delay. I looked across the room at the Seal of the Order where it sat ticking atop its polished stand. Even thirty feet away, I could smell the wood's bitter, newly applied yu-oil polish.

"The Ringess asks for the Seal of the Order," he said. "And if I gave it to him, what then? You lords think to change the Order! Ha, how will you do that?" His voice lowered to the timbre of a gong. "So, I've seen change in my time, but man always remains the same."

I thought of the godseed alive inside my head, of the Great Theorem and other things, and I said, "No, not always the same."

"A man and his crimes," he said.

I let his words echo from ear to ear. The way he said "crimes" was a tell. A memory began to form up, and I had the nagging feeling I should know exactly what crimes he was referring to.

The Timekeeper's eyes wandered over us, lingering a

moment too long on Soli. "So, Mallory, if I'm to be Time-keeper no more, who'll do the hard things, eh?"

"Who will murder, is that what you mean?"

"Was it I," he asked, "who tried to assassinate Soli?"

There were more tells in the sibilant sounds of "assassinate," and suddenly I knew. "Yes," I said, "the first time Soli was nearly murdered—that was your crime, I think." I turned to Soli, who was staring out the window at the City lights. I finally caught his eye, and I explained, "It was the Timekeeper who tried to assassinate you the day of the Pilot's Race."

"Is that true?" Soli asked. He stood still as a hunter, and he looked down at the Timekeeper. Although he pretended to a cool detachment, a journeyman cetic could have seen he was furious. "Why did you do that?"

My mother caught his elbow and said, "I've lived long enough. For you to know I'm innocent. Now it's too late."

Soli wrenched his arm away and spat out, "Yes, you are innocent of *that* attempted murder."

"So, it's true," the Timekeeper said. "It's too late."

"Why would you want to have me assassinated?" Soli asked him.

I rubbed the side of my nose and said, "Tell us about the Entity. Why would the gods warn man against Her?"

"Is it true?" Soli asked him.

The Timekeeper suddenly whirled, and his words lashed Soli like a whip. "Of course it's true! I'll say it now as I've said before: Piss on the Ieldra and their damn secrets! When you returned from the core, all your damn talk of the Elder Eddas—you forced me to call the Quest. There are some things we're not meant to know, but you wouldn't listen to me." He stepped close to Soli. He clenched his fists and asked, "Why wouldn't you listen to me, Leopold? So, it's your damn pride. How you talked of your damn discovery, talked and drank your filthy skotch in your damn bar! You had every novice in the City dreaming of your Ieldra and their Eddas. I asked you to keep your silence. I told you; I warned you, but you wouldn't listen. You had to argue with me. 'The truth is the truth,' you told me. So, damn your truth! Leopold, why wouldn't you listen?"

"Yes, it's true," Soli said sarcastically. "You tried to assassinate me because I wouldn't listen."

"What is there that man shouldn't know, then?" I asked the Timekeeper. "Tell me, I need to know."

Soli smacked a black-gloved fist into his open hand. He bowed to the Timekeeper and said, "Who should judge you? Yes, who judges the judge? You and I, we've had a long run, haven't we? But it's over. It's time you surrendered the Seal, isn't it?"

The Timekeeper glanced at one of his clocks and smiled grimly. "So, it's time," he said. He circled the room and stood before the Seal of the Order. He placed his hands on the clock's steel casing.

Behind me Nikolos muttered, "Carefully!" as Burgos Harsha drew in a quick breath of air. Many of the lords were whispering to each other; the room was hissing with their whispers.

The Timekeeper approached us holding the Seal close to his body. I heard its rhythmic ticking. Inside the Seal's glass window, I watched the blue and white imago of Old Earth orbiting the Sun. The Timekeeper stopped in front of me, and the ticking grew louder. I half-suspected that the Seal was a fake, a replica clock made into a weapon of some sort. I was afraid it might explode.

"Who shall I surrender it to?" he asked. "So, will the Lord Pilot accept this?"

I had to remind myself that I was now the Lord Pilot. I opened and spread my hands. As he held out the Seal to me the ticking grew even louder. I was very aware of the ticking of every clock in the Tower.

"The Seal of the Order," the Timekeeper said. He paused a moment, and then held the clock tightly to his chest, as a Devaki mother suckles her baby. He seemed to be waiting for something. I could almost hear him counting to himself.

"My Lords!" he said. "You say I must surrender the Seal of the Order. So. Here it is."

"Mallory!" my mother shrieked.

My eyes were frozen on the Timekeeper's as he dropped the Seal into my hands. It was heavier than I had thought it would be; I nearly dropped it.

"'Send not to ask for whom the bell tolls,'" the Timekeeper said, quoting one of his infamous poems, "'it tolls for thee.'"

The Seal chimed one single time, and then it grew silent.

I had one of those foolish, irrational fears that I had done something wrong, perhaps grasping it too hard and somehow damaging the interior mechanism. I shook the Seal beside my ear. Nothing. Suddenly I noticed that the Tower had grown disturbingly quiet. I heard my heart thumping; other than the breathing of the other lords and masters, it was the only sound I heard. All of the clocks in the room had grown silent at the same moment. The ticking had stopped. The pendulum clocks were still, and the bio-clocks were dead, and the cobalt sands of the hourglasses had run out.

"It's time," the Timekeeper said. He aimed a gnarled finger at the southern window behind us and growled, "Look!"

I did not look. This, among other things, saved me. But Jonath Parsons and Nikolos the Elder and Burgos Harsha—they and many of the others looked out the window. Burgos later said that he saw a dazzling flash and a glowing gout of clouds billowing outward above the Hollow Fields, but that would have been impossible. We all felt the Tower shake, however. Up through the foundations came a rumble which felt like an icequake. All at once the brittle Tower windows shattered inward. There was a cracking and a roar, a rainshower of glass. Flying shards were everywhere. Tiny glass spears stung the back of my neck and head. Burgos and a few others screamed out, "My eyes!" while the Timekeeper covered his own eyes with his forearm. There was a hot wind while the glass storm blew through the room. When the shockwave had passed, the Timekeeper threw his arm away from his eyes, and there was a knife in his hand. It was as long and silvery as a blade of glass. At first I thought it *was* glass, so quickly did its gleaming edge whirl towards my face.

"So, it was too old," the Timekeeper said cryptically. Then he moved toward me, and he was as fast as any warrior-poet. I dropped the Seal of the Order. I accelerated, too. As my inner clock began ticking furiously and time slowed, I began to scry.

"Mallory!" my mother cried out.

I saw the future pattern of the Timekeeper's knifework even as he dropped the knife toward my stomach. I saw another thing. I saw my mother jump between us. I watched the Timekeeper's knife split the wool beneath her breast and bury itself up to its hilt. When I saw this future, I moved quickly to make sure it would never be. But although I scryed, I was not quite a scryer. I saw the future imperfectly. To this day, I *see* it imperfectly. I tried to knock my mother aside, but I had not foreseen everything. The Seal struck the fur carpet and rebounded at an odd angle. I barely avoided tripping over it. This caused me to knock her forward, slightly, rather than to the side. I drove her into the Timekeeper's knife. As the blade dipped into her chest she smiled—perhaps it was really a grimace of agony—and she plunged a shining, warrior-poet's needle into the Timekeeper's neck. There were cries and shouts behind us. Dead cold waves of air slashed through the blown-out window jambs into the room. Soli, with puffs of steam escaping his cut, bleeding lips, rushed the Timekeeper. My mother fell back against me, and I eased her down to the soft furs. The Timekeeper almost fell on top of us. The needle's poison froze his nerves, and he toppled like an ice sculpture; he lay dead against the glass fragments on the floor.

"Look!" someone cried out. But I did not have time to look because my mother was bleeding to death as she lay across my lap. Her hot blood soaked the wool on the top of my thighs. She did not speak. Her eyes were open, watching me. I saw she had no fear of death. Perhaps she was so driven by the warrior-poet's programs that she even welcomed death. I thought she had saved me not out of love but because she was programmed to seek her moment of the possible. I should be no more grateful to her than I would be to an obedient robot. And yet I was grateful; as the life flowed out of her, her racking coughs tore me apart. Perhaps all sons are programmed this way. Bright arterial blood burst from her lips, and I wanted to believe she was dying as my mother rather than a warrior-poet. I looked for the spark of humanity which I believed must burn within each of us, the eternal flame, the shining point of clear light.

"The Timekeeper is dead," Soli said. He was standing above us holding his own hand, which was bleeding. A piece of glass had cut his fingers. He glanced at the Timekeeper's body. "A warrior-poet's nerve poison wasn't it? Your mother knew about these things." And then, looking down at her, he said quickly, urgently, "If we hurry, maybe we can carry her to a cryologist before her brain dies."

I was shocked that he said this. I hadn't thought he was capable of forgiveness or compassion. I realized that I did not know him at all. I felt for a heartbeat in my mother's chest, and then I closed her eyes. "No," I said, "there will be no cryologist. She's dead, you see; she died at the right time."

I stood up and turned toward the window. I saw a terrible sight. Most of the lords were kneeling or hunched up on the floor, bleeding from wounds. Nikolos the Elder was rubbing at his eyes, irrationally rubbing the glass into his eyes. Flying glass had shredded Burgos Harsha's face. He screamed and writhed on the floor while Mahavira Netis, whose firm brown face was gouged and bleeding, bent over him and picked out the longest of the glass splinters. And this was horrible but not terrible. "Look!" someone cried, and pointed out the window. "Look!" I looked and saw the terrible thing. Above the Hollow Fields rose a mushroom-shaped cloud. I had never seen a mushroom before, but I knew very well what a mushroom was; all human beings had learned that sometimes clouds will rise in the shape of mushrooms. The cloud boiled up almost black against the blue twilight sky. It rose and billowed outward, a dark mushroom mountain joining the circle of real mountains around the City.

"It's an atomic bomb, isn't it?" Soli asked as he joined me by the window. He saw what I saw: All the towers of the Fields and many of the buildings in the most southern part of the City had been ruined, blown down to their foundation stones. "Why are we alive? Why wasn't the whole City destroyed? It couldn't be—who could believe it's an atomic bomb?"

But it was an atomic bomb. I somehow knew this, as indeed, Soli must have known, too. There was a roaring and thunder, and the mushroom cloud seemed to glow. More, specifically, it was a hydrogen bomb, as I later learned from the tinkers and mechanics who explored the fused crater where the Lightship Caverns had been. It was a small, laser-ignited hydrogen bomb, an old, old bomb which had leaked away much of its deuterium in the thousands of years before it exploded. The fireball had been hardly hot enough to destroy the Caverns. That was why we were alive. That was why the whole City was alive, because it was a weak, old bomb, and it had exploded underground in the heart of the Caverns. But I did not know this as we watched the mushroom cloud growing over the southern part of the City. I thought of the Timekeeper's words: "So, it was too old," and

I knew only that he had tried to destroy everything with an atomic bomb.

"Why?" Soli asked. "Was he so bitter?"

I bent to help Mahavira pick the glass out of Burgos' face, but there was little I could do. I went over to the Timekeeper. Many of the lords—fortunately, few of them were badly injured—gathered around me. I touched the Timekeeper's face, which was locked and hard from the nerve poison. I told them what Kalinda of the Flowers had told me: "He's old," I said, "and Horthy Hosthoh was not his birthname. He's been Timekeeper for a long, long time."

"For hundreds of years," Soli said quickly.

"No, for *thousands* of years," I said. "If the Entity is right, this Timekeeper is the very same Timekeeper who founded the Order. He's been Timekeeper for 2934 years."

Soli gasped out, "Rowan Madeus? You say that this is *he*? There have been eighteen Lord Horologes—it used to be easy to remember all of their names. You ask me to believe that all this was *faked*?"

"Faked, in truth," I said. "The Timekeeper has faked the histories. He must have kept a slel-clone. Seventeen times, he has let one of his slel-clones die in his place. Seventeen times, he has gone to a cutter to restore the appearance of youth and begun his career anew. But there will be no eighteenth time." The freezing wind rushed through the room, bringing in the solemn ringing of the Old City bells. I had not heard their tolling since I was a boy, when the great blizzard had buried the City and a thousand people (most of them poor harijan) died. I thought of the Entity's solemn, rolling words, and I said, "He's *written* history. And I believe he's even older than the Order. Rowan Madeus was just one of his names."

"It's impossible," Soli said.

I took a deep breath of air. I was full of horror and hope. I was very excited. "Soli, I believe he was of the line of Thomas Rane, the remembrancer. He's immortal—he *was* immortal. His name was Kelkemesh." I stood up and half-shouted, "Don't you see? The quest, our expedition, it's all been for nothing. The Timekeeper, this Kelkemesh, he's the oldest, so damn old. We've journeyed across half the galaxy with our questions when the answer was here all along."

But the answer—the secret of life I had sought for so

long—proved not to be so close at hand. During the nightmare days which followed, days of digging through the rubble
of collapsed buildings for the thousands of buried corpses and
sorting out the bodies for burial, the Lord Imprimatur,
Nassar wi Jons, worked over the body of the Timekeeper.
Nassar was a gnarled, lump of a man, a man who had been
born marrow-sick with so many diseased bones and deformations of flesh that the cutters and splicers had needed all their
ingenuity merely to sculpt him into the bent—but brilliant—
little gargoyle who attempted to uncode the Timekeeper's
secrets. I had told him: "As you did with the Alaloi plasm, as
you tried to do, search along his DNA for the Ieldra's
imprimatur."

On eleventh day he made his disappointing and shocking
pronouncement: The Timekeeper's DNA was no different
than my own, or any other man's. (Any other man, that is,
who had not been born marrow-sick.) And this Timekeeper
was not really *the* Timekeeper.

"He was a slel-clone," Nassar explained to the College of
Lords as we sat in an emergency session. With his mismatched
eyes—his blue eye was larger than his half-closed brown
eye—he glanced at me and shook his lumpy head. "A double,
a fake . . . a robot, if you will. The pathways, excuse me, Lord
Pilot, the *neural* pathways were etched with the imprint of
new, robot programs. A double, you should know."

Another slel-clone! A double, with those too-peaceful eyes
that were not the Timekeeper's eyes—why hadn't I perceived
this immediately? No doubt he had brought this slel-clone to
maturity and programmed it with enough of his own habits,
speech patterns and memories to fool us. He had programmed it to murder. Not all the Timekeeper's robots had
been destroyed, then. This last robot, this scowling, breathing mockery of a man, had lived long enough to murder my
mother, to almost carry out the Timekeeper's revenge.

"Where is the Timekeeper, then?"

"Who can know?"

I made a fist and rapped my knuckles against the table. "If
it was a slel-clone," I said, "its DNA should be identical to
the Timekeeper's."

"No, Lord Pilot," Nassar said, confirming my fears, "if the
Ieldra's message really is imprinted in the Timekeeper's
chromosomes, if he knew this and wanted to keep the secret,

if he had the services of a master splicer, then he could have carked the slel-clone's DNA to edit out the Eddas, you should know."

"Goddamn him!"

"You should know something else, and I as Lord Imprimatur am the very one to tell you. I don't believe in your Elder Eddas. Few do. The Timekeeper made a slel-clone to do his killing while he escaped the City—not to hide a nonexistent secret. Forget the Timekeeper, Lord Ringess. You'll never see him again."

But I could not forget the Timekeeper. Even as the College of Lords made plans to build a new Cavern to house the new lightships which were being designed (the bomb had destroyed every lightship, shuttle, and jammer in the City) I thought about him all the time. The Entity had not lied to me, I told myself. Why would She lie? The message of the Ieldra *was* buried within the Timekeeper, wherever he was. If he had fled to the stars in a lightship, the secret had fled to the stars with him. If he was hiding within the City, perhaps in some hibakusha tenement in the Farsider's Quarter, then his secret was hiding there, too.

Later that day we buried six thousand two hundred and six people on the Hill of Sorrows beneath Urkel. It seemed that most of the city had endured the cold to attend the funeral. On the broad, snowy south side of the gravepit huddled a mass of harijan, aliens and farsiders come to honor their dead. (Most of the victims, of course, were horologes, cetics, tinkers, and the various journeymen who attended the lightships. A few were pilots.) Across from them, where the robots had excavated a narrow plain abutting the Hill's vertical, scooped-out walls, were the men and women of the Order. We stood in our professions, row after row, lined up on the black, frozen earth. We pilots stood nearest the grave. There were too few pilots. We—the Sonderval, Salmalin, Li Tosh and the other survivors of Perdido Luz—we were a thin, black line pressed from behind by the eschatologists in their blue furs, and from behind them, by the rows of the mechanics. Because I was Lord Pilot and Soli was Past Lord, we stood together at the very lip of the grave. It was there, even as the pit was flooded and the icy waters began to rise over the stacked bodies, that I learned of the Timekeeper's fate.

"He's fled the City," Soli said. He was wearing a black,

hooded fur. He threw back his hood so I could hear his words
better above the wind. How fierce he looked, with his
thallow-beak of a nose, his sculpted brows and glittering eyes!
How angry, how vengeful! "The night before the atomic
bomb, he stole a team of dogs and a sled from the kennels—
the master of the kennels told me this. Like a thief in the
night, he fled out to sea. Why, Pilot? Did he seek death? Or
does he hope to live, among the Devaki or some other tribe?
Or is it solitude and forgetfulness he wants? Yes, solitude,
until a hundred or a thousand years have passed and he
returns to become the Lord Horologe once again."

I dropped my head and looked down into the cubical pit.
I looked for my mother—I had been told she was somewhere
among the top layer of bodies. But the water froze quickly,
and I could not find her.

"If he returns a hundred years from now," I said, "he may
return to a dead city." I pointed skyward in the general
direction of the Abelian Star Group, where Merripen's Star
had exploded. "The supernova may soon accomplish what the
Timekeeper's bomb did not."

Soli nodded his head, then muttered, "Your mother should
have been interred in the cantor's mausoleum," Soli said
sadly. "She was a cantor, after all."

"No, she was a hibakusha. She couldn't help herself, you
see. Let her be buried as the victim she was."

"The Timekeeper killed her, didn't he? His clone? You
should want the Timekeeper dead."

"I hope he lives," I said, trying to be compassionate for
once in my life. "If he does, the secret will live with him."

Soli bowed his head and said, unexpectedly, "It was the
Timekeeper who murdered our radio. It's all so clear, now.
He wanted our expedition to fail, didn't he? Yes, and there-
fore he murdered Katharine. If we had been able to radio the
City before . . . But no, we had no radio and Katharine is
dead."

"I loved her, Soli. Oh, God, I loved her!"

"The dead," he whispered. I had never seen anyone look
so bitter. "So many."

I began to grieve openly for my mother, then, and I
covered my eyes because I was ashamed for Soli to see me
weeping.

"There's nothing left for me in Neverness," Soli told me.

"No, nothing, and therefore my vows must be renounced. It's time for me to leave the Order."

"Where will you go?" I asked. Despite myself, I was curious to know his plans.

"I'm weary of the stars," he said. "And I hate this city. There is a sled and dogs waiting for me at the Quay. I'm going out on the ice, possibly past Kweitkel. I'll track the Timekeeper— it shouldn't be hard. When I find him, I'll spear him like a fish. For what he's done to the Order." A little clod of dirt, disturbed by his boot, plummeted outward and down, into the grave. When it struck the ice, it broke into pieces. "I'll never come back," he said.

"The Timekeeper's body must be returned, then."

"No, I'll go on to the Devaki. Perhaps Yuri will honor his word and still welcome me."

"If you live as a Devaki," I said. "There will be no cutters and cetics to bring you back to your youth. In the end, you'll die."

"Yes."

His entire body stiffened up, then. He worked his mouth against the cold, trying to say something. At last he forced the words out. "You could come with me," he whispered. It must have been the hardest thing he had ever said. "We could take two sleds. You could bring his body back to the Lord Imprimatur. You'll have your secret, and I'll have . . . I'll have what I have."

I caught him staring beyond the City to the west. His face was long and dark in the shadow of the Hill of Sorrows, but I saw there an unmistakable glimmer of reverence. He did not hate Neverness; he loved her. He felt driven by bad chance from the Order and from his city. If he had to leave—I read this in his eyes, and he later told me so—he wanted to send back what he thought of as a gift. Perhaps the Lord Imprimatur would decode the secret from the Timekeeper's frozen body. Perhaps the secret would save man from the Vild and from other dangers. Because he loved the Order, and in the end because he loved life more than he hated me, he restrained his anger and his spite, and he told me, "The Timekeeper has a lead, but we both still wear our Alaloi bodies. And two can travel faster than one, the Devaki say. We'll catch him, won't we? Out there . . ." He pointed west where the edge of the sea sparkled beneath Attakel's glaciers.

It took me only moments to decide. As the pilots and professionals bowed their heads to say a requiem for the dead, I lifted my head up. To the west lay open air and hard, endless ice.

"I'll come with you," I said into the wind that cut between us. "To find the Timekeeper."

The memory of the last and holiest of my pilot's vows was more chilling than the wind, which was dead cold, cold enough to harden the grave ice into an opaque, blueish-white crypt around my mother's body. I listened to the wind blowing down through the City and across the miles of the empty sea. Once, long ago, I had vowed to seek wisdom and truth even though the seeking should lead to my death and the ruin of all that I loved and held dear. Very well, I told myself, out on the sea, within the body of an old, old man, was wisdom. Out there I would find truth at last.

28

Ananke

It lies not in our power to love or hate,
For will in us is over-ruled by fate.
  —Cristopher Marlowe, Sailing Century Poet

So we went out onto the sea. Early the next morning I went
down through the Farsider's Quarter and met Soli at the
Quay, where the western edge of the City meets the ice.
There was really nothing else to do. Every jammer in the
City—even the wormrunners'—had been destroyed; therefore we could not pursue the Timekeeper from the air. In the
dark and quiet we loaded our sleds. We did our work quickly.
Onto their wooden frames we heaped skins full of baldo nuts
and our sleeping furs, and the ice saws, harpoons, bear
spears, hide-scrapers, oilstones and other tools we would
need to survive the air-shattering cold. Much of this equipment was familiar, leftovers from our first expedition. In my
old sealskin boots I trudged along the wooden boardwalk set
into the snow of the beach. I smelled the dry, cold, salt wind
blowing off the Sound. When I hefted my old harpoon,
memories began to ripple. The icy stiffness of the leather
harnesses, the clouds of spindrift swirling low across the dark
ice, the eager whines of the dogs as the sledmaster led them
on leashes down from the kennels—it all seemed so familiar,
so natural, so achingly real. I harnessed my seven dogs to my
sled, all the while filled with a sense of urgency and longing
to be off. The sledmaster, a burly farsider from Yarkona,
worked his smooth jaws furiously as he chewed a wad of
feverroot to keep warm. In between his spitting gouts of fiery
juice into the snow, he lectured us about the dogs: "Your lead

is Kuri," he said to me, "and your second is Arne, and that's Hisu, Dela, Bela, Neva and Matsu," he said, pointing down the line of the harness. He spoke the names of the other dog team to Soli, who was bent over stroking the snout of his lead dog, Leilani. "You'd better be gentle with them. They're not used to long runs. And watch out for the ice schooners, please, because they like to chase them."

I smiled as I peered through the darkness at the mooring slips where the bare-masted ice schooners vibrated and groaned in the wind. It was much too early for anyone to hoist a bright-colored sail and go schooning about the Sound. (Too, with part of the City in ruins, it was not a day for recreation.) My dogs were biting their traces and sniffing each other, and I couldn't help wondering if Soli and I wouldn't do better to sail off west in a schooner. But of course that would have been disastrous. Out on the deep sea, the ice would be cracked and fissured, shagged with ice pocks and crevasses. A team of dogs, even such soft, playful dogs as these, was our only hope. I wished we had more time to train *real* sled dogs, like Liko and our other old dogs. But we had no time. Already the Timekeeper was days ahead of us somewhere to the west.

At first light we drove down the sled runs to the sea. The ice of the Starnbergersee glowed golden orange before us. We looked for the Timekeeper's tracks in the wind-packed snow, and we found them. Patches of spindrift partially covered the pawprints and runner grooves, but there had been no snow for the past ten days, so the tracks were straight and easy to see. We followed them out around the lip of Attakel, out where the ice is naked and white, where everything the eye can see is either snow or sky or ice, and the colors are the colors of ice or the reflected wavelengths of light off the ice: the distant purples of the iceblooms growing in ever widening circles around us; the milk-glazed, turquoise icebergs frozen fast into hundreds of motionless pyramids; the iceblink's yellowish glare flung up into the cobalt sky.

We traveled fast the whole day. By late afternoon the mountains of Neverness were a blue and white haze behind us. They wavered in the air, seeming more insubstantial than the air itself. With every mile we crossed, as I breathed through my frozen mustache and listened to the scrape and glide of the sled runners and the dogs' panting, my memories of the City became more insubstantial, too. I was taken with the world and the sensations of the world. How I loved the silky, musty smell of my shagshay furs, the stinging salt air against my greased face, even the ache of cold fingertips inside cold mittens! The slow, steady west wind murmured its music in my ear, and I was once again full of fear and fate. In truth, I was a driven man, as driven as the poor dogs yelping at the crack of my whip. But I was also being pulled *by* something, something that was as outside myself and separate as the light of the stars. This something I thought of as fate, not my own fate in particular, but a higher fate, the fate to which all things in the universe must submit. I felt this fate—and it was the fate of Soli and the Timekeeper and my City, the fate, too, of the flint tip of Soli's bear spear—I felt the long, urgent sound of ananke roaring in my blood. I kept my eyes fixed on the vibrating circle of the western horizon. Even as darkness fell over us, I wanted to go on. I was exhilarated, breathless with the thrill of our first day's run. I felt I could go on into the night, on and on westward following the Timekeeper's tracks by starlight. But the dogs were tired and hungry; their paws were chafed and crusted with ice. We could not go on. Far from the City, and still too far from our fate, we stopped to build a snow-hut on the sea. In the dark we cut blocks of snow with our saws and shaped them into a hut. Into the hut went our oilstones, food and sleeping gear. We fed the dogs chunks of cultured fat steak; we fed ourselves and sipped our coffee and slipped down into our furs to think our private thoughts and dream our dreams.

I did not sleep at all that night. For a long time my patterns of sleep had been changing as I changed. I lay listening to the muffled breathing of the dogs in the tunnel and to the wind working through the chinks between the snow blocks. The hut was aglow with the light of the oilstones, which I kept full and burning until the morning. On his snow bed next to me Soli stared up at the flickering flame shadows on the ceiling. He lay still and quiet; it seemed as if he were sleeping with his eyes open. But he was not sleeping. Without looking at me he began discussing the little problems of our day's run. "That sledmaster knew nothing about dogs. Well, he was a Yarkonan, wasn't he? Tomorrow you should leash Arne in Neva's place. Put him between the bitches, that way he'll leave Kuri alone and Hisu won't snap at him." He fell back into silence, then continued, "We'll have to cut socks for Bela and Matsu, won't we? Did you see their paws? Yes, we'll have to cut socks for both teams before the Outer Islands. The wormrunners say the ice there is ragged as an autist's robe."

It was sad that the only time Soli and I seemed to understand each other was when we struggled together to solve a problem, either a mathematical problem or the much more immediate problem of staying alive in temperatures cold enough to freeze the carbon dioxide in our breath. We talked of hunting seals when our food inevitably ran out; we talked of the fine quality of the *saffel*, the fast snow. Toward morning our talk began to turn to mathematics. He wanted to hear my proof of the Great Theorem, but he was too proud to ask. His bitterness hung between us like a frozen cloud.

"My life has been given to mathematics, and what has it given me?" he muttered into the hut's curving walls. I told him, then, the proof of the Continuum Hypothesis. Without the stimulation of my ship (and his *Vorpal Blade*), blinded of the visual spaces in which to conjure up the ideoplasts of the Hypothesis, it took a long time to make him see the proof. At last, when I had worked my way through the demonstration that the Justerini subspace is embedded in the simple Lavi space, he sat upright so quickly that he nearly smashed his head through the snowy ceiling. He exclaimed, "Stop! I see it now! I should have seen it before, it's such a sharp trick: The Lavi correspondence scheme collapses now, doesn't it? It's a beautiful proof, an elegant proof." And then his voice died to a sigh, and I had to strain to hear him say, "Oh, I was so close."

I said, "It's a constructive proof, you see." I bent over and trimmed the oilstone's wick with my knife. A constructive proof: Not only was it possible to fall from any star to any other with a single mapping, but there existed a way, inherent in my proof, to construct such a mapping.

"A beautiful proof," Soli repeated. "Yes, and now your dilemma. Anyone—even the merchant pilots and the like—will be able to fall where they will."

"Perhaps," I said.

"War, real war between planets will be possible."

"That was the Timekeeper's theory."

"The Order will never be the same, will it? All the Civilized Worlds?"

I drew the hood of my furs around my head. I said, "That was the Timekeeper's fear. He tried to kill me—kill us both—because he was afraid."

"Yes," Soli said. "We used to talk about such things all the time. He warned me against change, and punished me many times for not listening. Change—if it hadn't been for your reckless first run to the Entity, we might have had change without..." And here his voice hardened and cracked, "... without disaster."

I knew he was thinking of Justine so I said, "I'm sorry."

"What will you decide?" he asked me. "About the Hypothesis? What will you do?"

"I don't know," I told him.

He fell into silence, and much later, passed into a fitful sleep. I lay awake watching him shift about and twist inside his furs. I wondered if I should and would show the proof of the Hypothesis to the other pilots. I began to play the proof over again in my mind. When I reached the complex exposition of the first Danladi Lemma, I mourned the loss of my ship. Reflexively—almost instinctively—I found myself mentally reaching out as I would toward my ship's neurologics. I faced myself. My eyes were tightly closed; I seemed to float within the dark covering of my furs. Outside the hut was blackness and cold, but inside, inside my head, there was fire and light. For a moment the diamond ideoplasts of the Lemma stood out as clearly as anything I had ever seen. Then there was a blizzard of ideoplasts as the proof took shape. I did not know exactly how these ideoplasts infused my visual cortex. There was no ship-computer, no neurologics to create the visual spaces of dreamtime and the other spaces of a pilot deep within the manifold. There was only my brain and my changing self, whatever that self and brain really were. And there were mappings, a whole sequence of mappings. The thickspace above Neverness appeared, dense, twisted and impenetrable. Suddenly it unraveled like a ball of silk, and I saw thousands of new mappings, new pathways to the stars. To Vesper and Darghin, and on, to the Takeko Double and to Abrath Luz where she burned hot and blue and bright, and further on to the stars which have no names, the doomed and lost stars of the Vild. There were an infinity of interconnections between the stars of the universe; every star was connected to every other. I saw this in a moment,

and I was more deeply aware of the manifold than ever
before. When I thought of the source of this vision I fell into
fear. Then, as suddenly as it had come, it was gone. The
manifold closed in like a winter sea. There was darkness. I
opened my eyes to the shadows of the hut. Soli was snoring
in ragged spurts as he ground his teeth. Even though I was
close enough that the icy dew of his breath beaded up on
my furs, I felt very alone.

The fear stayed with me through the night, more intense
than it had been since I had returned from Agathange. I
wondered again at the evolution of the Agathanian's godseed.
Had it completed its work? Was my brain dying, replaced bit
by bit with preprogrammed neurologics? I did not know, but
I felt something terrible and wonderful was happening to me.
I conjured up this image: I saw millions of neurons, with
their fat, irregularly shaped cell bodies, swelling and bursting, the myelin sheaths coating the long axons dissolving,
being absorbed. Throughout the hideously complex weave
and mesh of the millions of millions of threadlike dendrites,
the neurologics were replicating and growing. There would
be new connections, crystal sheets of protein computers
linking up. And all this occurring, or so I imagined, inside my
cortex, in that wondrous red jelly above my eyes. And here
was my fear. The frontal lobes would be disconnecting with
my limbic brain, or perhaps connecting in strange new ways.
My control of myself would be changing. There would be
new programs, perhaps profound, new, hidden programs.
And now it was done, or almost done. How I knew this I
could not say. I knew only that when I closed my eyes and
mastered my fear program, the manifold opened to me, as
splendent and deep as ever the manifold from within my
lightship had been. And here was my wonder. Within me was
a fathomless, shining, crystal sea flowing outward in every
direction. I felt intimations of infinity, that all things were
possible. I lay awake watching the light of dawn come streaming through the cracks between the snow blocks. Then the
dogs began to whine and bark as Soli stirred and knocked the
ice-powder from his furs. I rubbed my eyes and blinked, and
I heaped a few handfuls of snow into the pot above the
oilstones so we would have some coffee to face the new
day.

*   *   *

For ten days we followed the Timekeeper's tracks due west. Twice we lost them where the spindrift was thick and heaped up into gleaming white dunes half a mile long. But we easily found them again by driving our sleds in a sinusoidal wave pattern along the western axis of our run: First we would curve out to the north and then bend back south, cutting across what would have been our straight line westward. And then south, curving back north, and so on, wriggling across the snow like a sleekit until we found his tracks. As long as the Timekeeper ran westward—and what other way could he run?—this little technique would be infallible. Unless it snowed. If it snowed mile after mile of ice would be furred with unmarked whiteness, and we would waste too much time moving in undulating waves. But it was much too cold to snow. We depended on the cold, even though the cold knifed through our furs and chilled us to the core. In truth, the cold nearly killed us. It was so cold that the snow was dry and gritty like sand. The air held no moisture, and the sky was deep blue, almost blue-black like an eschatologist's folded robes. The dry, chill air worked at our noses until they began to bleed. We sucked in air hard as icicles, and we felt ice points crystallizing in our nostrils, freezing and cutting our warm, tunneled flesh. Soli suffered more than I. Frozen blood encrusted his mustache and beard, and the collar and chest of his white furs. He looked like a great white bear who had thrust his muzzle into the bloody carcass of a seal. But the blood was all his own; he was weak from cold and the steady loss of blood. Once, during a windstorm as he stumbled behind the snow wall we had hastily flung up, he stupidly removed a mitten to warm his nose with his hand. The tips of three of his fingers—and they were the same fingers which had been cut by glass in the Timekeeper's Tower—quickly froze. Because he was cold and shivering I loosened my own furs in the Devaki fashion, and I warmed his iced fingers against my stomach. It was strange to feel his hard fingernails and skin against my own, strange and disturbing. As soon as his fingers thawed, I thrust his hand away from me and covered it. "Make a fist inside your mitten," I told him. "And try to keep your hand out of the wind."

He looked at me through eyelashes frozen with tears (the cold made our eyes run with tears), and he said, "You're not the only one who remembers how to heal frozen fingers, are you?" And then he made a fist and tucked it beneath his armpit. "Thank you," he said.

During the whole time of our run we rarely spoke to each other unless it was to convey some vital bit of information. Even then we would often communicate by shaking our heads at a quick, grunted-out question, or by pointing at the Timekeeper's tracks where they veered slightly northwest, or by smiling our thanks as one or the other brewed the morning coffee. Our cold, painful lives soon settled into a rhythm. At the end of the day's run, we would build the snow-hut and shovel over and patch the chinks from outside. After this we would bring in our cooking pots and food, our stiff sleeping furs which we rolled out across the snowbeds we built, everything we would need for the night. While Soli tended the oilstones and the hut filled with light, I would bring in blocks of snow to be melted for coffee and a single block to stop the tunnel against the wind. When the dogs had been fed and we went through our furs with the snow-beater, it was time to drink our Summerworld coffee, to eat our stewed baldo nuts and boiled meat. Time to warm ourselves and think. Later, with our furs hanging from the drying racks, as we lay abed sipping our last mugs of coffee, Soli would read to me from the Book of Silence.

Most people think of silence in the negative, as the mere absence of sound. But this is not true. Silence is a real thing, almost as palpable and hard as stone. Those nights inside the hut when the wind had died and the dogs were asleep, Soli would sit propped up in his furs silently staring into his blue coffee mug. Once, when the air warmed slightly and ice crystals hung in the sky like a yellow veil over the sun, we argued about what we would do if a front passed through and it snowed. After we were comfortable (and I use this word in a very relative sense) inside the hut, I insisted that the Timekeeper would run for Kweitkel. I was very sure of myself. Soli pressed his fingers tightly against his coffee mug and shot me a look which might have meant: "You're just like me, too damn stubborn and arrogant!" Then he was still and silent as stone, and the Book of Silence opened. His cold eyes and face were the key; upon his face was written the first page of the Book, and what was written there was hatred.

He hated himself. All women and men, of course, being human beings find some part of their all-too-human selves to hate. But he took this hatred further; he made an art of hating himself. His pride, his anger, his aloofness from the sufferings of his fellow man—he hated these weaknesses just as he hated his lack of imagination and failure to prove the Hypothesis. And more, he hated himself merely for having weaknesses of any sort. I watched him place his white, blistered lips above the rim of his mug and blow on his coffee, and it occurred to me that he hated being human. He, that broody, inward-looking man who had so often ventured down the dark, icy glidderies of his soul, had discovered that we define our humanity—our very selves—more by our weaknesses than by our strengths. And here was the trap which held him like the enclosing freeze of the winter sea: He loved being human as much as he hated it because it was the only thing he knew how to be. The greater Soli, the Soli who might someday emerge from the flawed, bitter, old Soli if only he would relinquish his icy grip upon himself, this Soli he feared (and therefore hated) above all things. And he knew all this. He saw himself more clearly than I ever could through my naive cetic's eyes. It was this self-knowledge and self-vision which sealed the tomb of his self-hatred. If he could really *see* the spiral of hate and fear binding him, shouldn't he be able to break free? No, he could not. He was only human, after all, wonderfully, tragically human. Human beings, he had tried to tell himself for three lifetimes, must accept their own humanity.

By the time we reached the first of the Outer Islands, he had to accept the weakness of his human flesh, too. Thirtyday dawned even colder than it had been. Ten miles to the south of our hut—and it seemed even closer in the clear morning air—the ancestral home of the Yelenalina family was a green and white hump above the sea. Soli was coughing at the harsh air (so was I), all the while stealing quick looks southward as he fumbled with the dogs' harnesses. At first I thought his clumsiness was due to his distracted thoughts; perhaps he was wondering what had happened to the Yelenalina family these past few years. When Leilani unexpectedly dug his claws into the snow and began barking at a horde of snow loon making their way toward the island, the leather straps came up tight around Soli's fingers. He winced and bit his lip.

"Are they frozen again?" I asked as I stepped through the

crunching, squeaking snow. I helped him untangle Leilani and his second dog, Gita, who had leaped into the air in her futile effort to get at the birds. "Let me see your fingers."

"No, they're fine," he said with steam puffing out of his bloody nose. "Yes, cold but fine."

"Let's get them warm," I said. "It will be hard going from here to Kweitkel. We're about forty miles from the Fairleigh ice-shelf, I think." I reached for his hand. "Here, I'll warm them for you."

"No."

"Your damn fingers are frozen, aren't they? You should have kept them warm, as I said."

"No, they're not frozen."

"Let me see."

"Go away, Pilot."

I was shivering in the morning half-light while the wind drove snow down my neck. I wanted to be off on our day's run, to let the rising sun and my exertions warm me. I turned west, looking into the hazy whiteness for the folds and crevasses of the ice-shelf. I said, "Let's go into the hut. I'll heat some water and we'll thaw your fingers that way."

Despite the cold, Soli's forehead was covered with sweat. "We don't have the time, do we?"

I thumped Arne's side, and I tied a leather sock over his sore paw. "If you lose control of your sled and drive it into a crevasse, we'll lose more than time."

Then he shook his head and kicked the snow and said, "Yes, time." And, unexpectedly, he went into the hut.

I followed him through the tunnel. When we had gotten his mittens off, I saw that he had not lied. His fingers were not frozen. They were worse than frozen. His flesh had died and run to rot. His fingertips were black with bacteria, stinking with gangrene. They smelled worse than year-old, decayed fish heads. I could barely stand the stench so I backed up until my head bumped the wall of the hut.

He held his fingers away from him as he would a dead sleekit and said, "The healing primaries haven't helped, have they?"

"We could return to the City," I said. "Even if the gangrene got your whole hand, the splicers could grow you a new one in half a hundred-day." In truth, I did not really want to return to the City.

"No, there's no time, is there? We'd lose the Timekeeper."

"Would you rather lose your fingers?"

"Better that than my returning to the City like a beaten dog."

I looked at his ruined, swollen fingers, which were puffy with diseased gases, and I told him, "I'm no cutter."

"You have a knife, don't you? Therefore you may cut."

I rubbed my nose and said, "It won't be easy."

"Are you afraid?" he asked me.

"It won't be easy to live among the Devaki without fingers."

"No, it won't be, will it?" he said.

His face was somber as I took his hand in mine and turned to examine his fingers. I did not really want to touch him, much less cut his fingers off, but there was nothing else to do. Onto a newl skin I set out a needle and thread from my sewing bag. I unsheathed my seal knife. I held it over the oilstone until it was hot and black with carbon. Then I cut off his fingers. As he ground his teeth and groaned and attempted his pain primaries, I took his middle and forefingers off at the second knuckle, and I cut the finger next to them all the way down to the palm. Quickly I stanched the bleeding with the hot knife and sewed the stumps closed. All the time that I held his hand, I could not help noticing how closely its shape matched my own. (For all his professed bitterness with the Order, he still wore his pilot's ring around his little finger. I did not think he would ever take it off, unless I had to amputate that finger, too, and the ring fell off on its own.)

When I finished binding his fingers, I brewed him a mug of cha tea to quicken his body against infection. He looked at his hand with disgust written across his lips. He was giddy with pain and curiously talkative. "A piece of glass lacerates my fingers, wrecking the circulation, and this is the result, isn't it? One happening begets another, on and on, as the Timekeeper used to say. This chain of logic, as inexorable as a proof: If Justine hadn't made me . . . if *I* hadn't hit her, what would our lives have been? It's hard to stop thinking about that, Pilot; there's no help for the thoughts. She's dead, because of me. And now, almost home, but . . . but, no, the Alaloi do not die from lost fingers, do they?"

During the next few days we made slow progress while he learned to manage his sled with one hand. His fingers healed quickly, and by fortyday he could manipulate the traces between his thumb and stumps with a fair skill and without real pain. One night as I was rationing out the last of our baldo nuts, he admitted that sometimes he felt a ghost pain where his fingertips used to be. He hated these pains. "It's too bad we didn't bring any skotch," he said. "Don't look at me like that, Pilot! It's not that the ghost pain is so hard to bear; it's that it reminds me of the tricks our nerves and brain play on us. It's all so *uncertain*, isn't it?"

I knew about these tricks of the brain. I, myself, as we threaded across the ice-shelf's crevasses, was tormented by such tricks. Why do we see what we see, hear what we hear? How is it that nerves can drink in information from the outer world? How do our brains make sense of this information? Is it true, as the ancient akashic Huxley once claimed, that our brains are no more than reducing valves which limit our reality, reducing our perception of the universe so that we are not driven mad by an endless wash of sensa, data, sights, colors, smells, sounds, thoughts, feelings, heat, cold, bits and bytes, a swirling, soul-swallowing ocean of information?

One afternoon—it was on forty-second day, I think—as I stood with my yu rod probing the snowcrust over what I believed to be a crevasse, the changes in my senses overwhelmed me. I realized that the godseed must have worked on parts of me other than my brain. Like a drillworm it had chewed its way up my optic nerve into my eye, redesigning and replacing the nerve ganglia with neurologics. My vision was different, subtly different at first, and then very different. I blinked my eyes against the metallic glare of the iceblooms. I saw new colors and strange new hues and shades embedded within the old colors of green and red and blue. I looked up the spectrum into the ultraviolet where the colors—I named them brillig and mimsy and high purp—were seething with an indescribable fire. That night, when the sun had fallen out of her golden robes, and the scarlets and pinks bled from the sky, I beheld the colors of heat, the gloze and flush of infrared. The jagged peaks of Urasalia to the south were stony crimson, much cooler than the glowing flush of the surrounding sea ice. The air was marbled with different colors: with glore and high gloze and the lava of ruby running off the warm bodies of the dogs as Soli unharnessed them. My eyes (and ears) had newly come alive to radiations

of many sorts. I was afraid to look skyward, afraid I might
drink in the gamma murmur and radio whisper of the distant
galaxies. With difficulty I made sense of all this information.
The normal eye—the human eye—reacts to a single photon,
a single "ping" of radiation striking the retina, the tiniest of
quantum events. But the brain ignores these reactions, reducing the noise of its own nerve cells so that it takes at least
seven photons to make the brain see light. My new brain was
sensitive to single photons. It was sensitive to much else, too.
When the wind died and all was quiet, I heard the back-
ground hiss and rustle of individual molecules colliding,
rebounding, rushing past, and colliding yet again. All about
me, in my eyes, nose, and ears, was noise. It took me many
days to integrate this noise; it was many days before the
damping gates of my new brain cut off the noise and allowed
me to lay back in my furs and think in peace.

Despite these distractions, with each mile we sledded, we
drew closer to the Timekeeper. Every day we came across
one of his abandoned nightly camps, and we searched the
gnawed thallow bones (evidently he had killed one of these
great, elusive birds), the dog dung, and knocked-in snow
blocks of his huts for signs of age. The Timekeeper's lead—
four days when we had set out—had dwindled to no more
than a day. Given our average sledding speed, he was probably twenty-two miles ahead of us, out where the world
curved into the sky.

On forty-seventh day we paused to hunt seals. As once
before, I was lucky. We killed three small seals. We quickly
butchered them and stowed the meat in my sled.

"The Timekeeper hasn't been so lucky," Soli said. "Why
are you so lucky every time you hunt your doffel? How many
times has the Timekeeper opened an aklia—six times? And
not one seal. He's losing time. He's probably hungry and
weak. We'll trap him soon, won't we?"

But we did not trap him as soon as I would have liked.
The next day it was much warmer than it had been, too damn
warm. A mass of warm air had moved in from the south. The
low sky was a solid, seamless expanse of white clouds hanging
over the grayish-white sea ice; the hut and the dog's gray
coats and Soli's frosted furs as he bent over to ice his sled's
runners, were lost into the enclosing whiteness. Even though
I was close to his sled—perhaps ten feet away—it seemed like

half a mile. In the whiteness, distances were strangely expanded or shrunken. The ice around us was dented with fissures and folds, almost like a Fravashi carpet after a journeyman pilot has walked across it wearing steel skate blades. But it was difficult to make out its individual features because there were no shadows to highlight the icescape's undulations and sudden cleavages. I smelled tingling needles of moisture in addition to the normal morning odors of seal blood, dung and coffee. After Soli tightened the traces of his rear dog, Zorro, he came over to me and pointed at the sky. "Snow," he said. "Before morning is over."

"We can go five miles before it snows."

"It's too dangerous. What's five miles?"

"Five miles is five miles," I said.

"It's impossible to see five miles ahead. The damn clouds."

"We'll take the run mile by mile."

"It will snow before we've gone a mile."

"We'll take it foot by foot until it snows, then."

"You're a tenacious bastard, aren't you?"

"You should know," I said.

We had gone about one mile when large flakes of cotton cake began fluttering down from the sky. Soli was just ahead of me, and his playful dogs jerked this way and that, sneezing and snapping snowflakes from the air. I should have paid more attention to the dogs and called an immediate halt, but I was taken with the colors of the six-sided crystals as they tickled my nose and stung my eyes. Through the snowstorm came a bellow, as of a great white bear who had cut his paw on an ice splinter. All at once Leilani and Soli's other dogs began a tremendous chorus of barking. And then they were off into the swirling storm, pulling their sled and a cursing Soli over the ice. I could not help thinking that these soft, city dogs had never seen a bear before, or else they would have tucked their tails between their legs, turned and fled instead of running blindly into the wind.

My dogs needed no encouragement to follow Soli's. Wind and ice pelted my face as Kuri and Neva and the others lunged against their harnesses. In no time at all we were whipping across the snow almost as fast as an ice schooner. I gripped the sled rails and dug my boots into the snow. This slowed us a little. In vain I whistled to the dogs. We probably would have run on top of Soli's sled if Leilani hadn't let loose a high, pitiful yelp. Soli's other dogs cried out in panic as the snowbridge over a crevasse crumbled. Leilani and Zorro— and Finnegan, Huchu, Samsa and Pakko along with Soli and his sled—plunged over the rim downward, one after another, pulling each other like connected stones, disappearing into a crack in the ice of the sea. My lead dog, Kuri, saw this happening, and he pulled up short before he too went over. He crouched belly low to the snow, barking as he sniffed the open air of the crevasse.

I jumped out of the sled and looked down. Twelve feet below me, at the bottom of the crevasse, there was the black, churning sea. The heavy sled quickly sank, pulling the frantic dogs one by one down into the water. At first I thought Soli must have caught himself up in the sled. He was dead, I thought, the great pilot dead at last. I looked for his body in the floating mound of what had been the snowbridge, but I did not see him. Then I heard him shout, "Mallory, help me!"

He was clinging to the jagged wall of the crevasse just beneath me. Somehow he must have freed his bear spear even as he went down into the crevasse. He must have jumped from his sled at the last instant and thrust his spear into the rotten, cracked, ice wall, levering himself out of the water.

"My legs . . . it's so cold."

I threw a rope to him and heaved him up. It was harder than pulling a two-man seal from his hole. He had soaked his legs and half his torso in the killing water. His legs were so numb he couldn't use them to kick away from the wall, to help himself up and out of the crack. My shoulders were popping in their joints, but at last I got a hand on his collar and hauled him over the edge. He nearly fell on top of me. He lay there gasping as the snow fell in waves and I stripped his sodden furs away from his skin. "It's so cold, let me die." I unlashed my sled's binding straps, burying him in my unrolled sleeping furs. The snow was thick as the fur of a bear, and I turned the dogs and drove back toward our hut. Like blind lice we felt our way through the snowstorm. We were very lucky to find our hut half-buried under a mound of snow. (We were lucky, too, that we never came across the unseen bear. Perhaps Totunye had fallen into the crevasse along with Soli's poor dogs.)

How fragile is the life of a man! Let his core temperature drop a few degrees, and he will begin to shiver. Let it drop a little further, and he will begin to die. I dragged a dying Soli into the hut. I laid out his furs, lit the oilstones, and set the water to boil. If I could get a little hot coffee into him, I thought, I could warm him from core to skin. But I did not have time to make the coffee. His violent shivering stopped abruptly as he fell into unconsciousness, into the coma of hypothermia. His skin was blue; his breathing shallow and ragged. I touched his forehead. It was cold as ice.

Because he was dying, because he was, in truth, my father, I stripped to the skin and squeezed down into the sleeping furs with him. There was nothing else to do. Against my neck was the softness of shagshay fur; my naked chest pressed his hairy back. His cold, stiff legs were next to mine. I was so close to him that I did not dare open my mouth, else his long hair would have gotten in. I threw my arms around him. The Devaki, when they need to warm a frozen hunter, fall into just such a disgustingly intimate position. I could not bear to touch him, yet I found myself hugging him tightly, pressing him close, letting my body's heat flow into him. For a long time I held him that way. The furs trapped the heat, and he began to shiver. That was good because he had come alive enough to make his own heat. While half inside the furs, I prepared the coffee. I held his mug to his lips, encouraging him to drink. We lay there for most of a day, and at last, when he could finally eat, I cooked seal steaks, which we dipped in liquid seal blubber. The food revived him enough so that he looked at me and said, "It wasn't you who tried to assassinate me, was it?"

"No, Soli."

"Then Justine's death, my part in the Pilot's war—it was all madness, wasn't it? A stupid mistake?"

"It was a tragedy," I said.

"Yes, it's ironic." His fingers were working the heavy brows above his eyes. "After Justine was abandoned, after *I* hit her, there was no going back, not for us, not for me. That was the worst moment of my life. So, this Alaloi body of mine—it could have been resculpted but it was kept to remind me. As a penance, you see. And now, if not for this thick body and your help, well, the water would have killed me."

Although each of us had slid towards the opposite edges of the furs, we were still very close. I smelled his breath, which was rank with coffee and ketones, the stinking result of our all-meat diet, of our bodies burning protein for glucose. I smelled other things about him, mainly anger, fear, and resentment. "You shouldn't have helped me," he said, "but you couldn't help helping me, could you? It's your revenge."

"No," I said.

"Yes, you love feeling holy about yourself, don't you?"

"What do you mean?" I asked, though I knew exactly what he meant.

"Even before you had the slightest reason... Do you remember that night in the bar? When Tomoth called you a bastard? You couldn't help your temper, could you?"

"I had no self-restraint, then."

"'Heredity is destiny,'" he quoted.

"I don't believe that," I said as I held a spitted sweetbread over the fire.

"What do you believe?"

"I think we can change ourselves, rewrite our programs. Ultimately, we're free."

"No," he said. "You're wrong. Life is a trap. There's no way out."

He was quiet while he sat up munching the crusted organ meat. He was deep in thought. His lean, hairy stomach rose and fell, rose and fell, as he sucked in the relatively warm air of the hut. He swallowed and said, "Let's talk about the Fravashi, this favored alien race of yours. The Timekeeper would have banished all of them from the City, if he could. Their alien teachings, this notion of ultimate fate, of—what do you call it?—of ananke. You've listened to them more than a man should, haven't you?"

I had never heard Soli wax so philosophical before, so I let him continue: "*Free will?* Have you thought about that term, the way the Fravashi use it? It's an oxymoron, as self-contradictory as a 'cheerful pessimist' or a 'happy fate.' If the universe is alive and conscious, as you believe, if it moves itself toward... if it has a purpose, then we're all slaves because it moves *us* towards that purpose as if we were pieces on a chessboard. And we don't know anything of the higher game, do we? Yes, and so where is the freedom? It's fine to talk of ananke, of this merging of our individual wills with the higher—is that what you believe?—but for human beings, ananke means hate, desperate love, despair, death."

"No," I said, "you don't understand."

He spat a piece of gristle against the packed-snow floor and said, "Enlighten me."

"We're ultimately free, not totally free. We're free within certain bounds. In the end, our individual wills are a part of the will of the universe."

"And you believe that?"

"It's what the Fravashi teach."

"And what is the will of the universe?" he asked as he dumped a handful of snow into the coffee pot.

Outside, the storm was drowning the hut in snow. The north wall, the only uncovered wall, glowed grayly with the light sifting through the snow blocks. "I don't know," I said.

"But you think you can discover what it is?"

"I don't know."

"That's an arrogant thought, isn't it?" he said.

"Why else are we here? Discovery or creation—in the end it's the same thing."

"Yes, why are we here?—the cardinal trivial question. We're here to suffer and die. We're here because we're here."

"That's pure nihilism."

"You're so arrogant," he said, and he shut his eyes and ground his teeth together, almost as if he were asleep. "You think there is a way out for yourself, don't you?"

"I don't know."

"Well, there is no way out. Life is a trap, no matter at what level you live it. There is always a crescendoing series of traps. The Timekeeper was right: Life is hell."

"We're creators of our hells."

He jumped up off the snowbed and stood naked on the floor. Beneath his skin his muscles were long and flat, like leather straps wrapped around wood. His lean shadow cut the curving, white walls. "Yes," he said slowly. "Half my hell was created by me, and the other half you created for me."

My lips and cheeks were burning in the warm air, and I mocked him, saying, "Heredity is destiny."

"Damn you!"

"We're creators of our heavens," I said softly. "We can create ourselves."

"No, it's too late."

"Never too late," I said.

"For me it's too late." He rubbed some seal fat on the red scar tissue of his finger stumps. He said, "Arrogance, everywhere such arrogance—it makes me ill. But soon there will be no more of this arrogance." Here he shot me a look of resentment, of awe, of hate. "In the whole Devaki tribe, there's not one man who is tired or ashamed of being a man, who wants to be more than he is. And that's why I'll never go back to the City."

That night I had dreams of the future, of Soli's future and my own. I scryed until dawn, and I drank some coffee and scryed halfway through the snowy day. I wanted to show him what I had seen, to tell him that life is not a trap, at least no more of a trap than we make from the sharpened ends of our cold bones and the sinews of our twisted hearts. I wanted to tell him the simplest of things. Instead I stood up and began pulling on my furs. "It will stop snowing soon," I said. "Before nightfall."

Soli sat inside his furs as he fitted his spear with a new blade of flint. (The old point had snapped in the wall of the crevasse.) He looked at me with the loathing he held for scryers and said nothing.

"The Timekeeper is close," I said. "He's fifteen miles northwest; three of his dogs are sick inside his hut, and the aklia he opens today will be empty."

"Scryer talk."

"If we sled all night, we'll surprise him in the morning."

"If we sled all night," he said, "we'll drop down the first crevasse, won't we?"

From a piece of newl skin I began cutting socks for the dogs. "No," I told him, "I know where the crevasses are."

"We'll sled circles in the blackness."

"No," I said. "The stars will be out. We'll steer by the stars."

He smiled at this old saying and bowed his head. "All right, Pilot, we'll steer by the stars, if they come out."

When night fell the wind was blowing from the north, blowing the last of the warm air and snow clouds away. It was very cold. The sky was as black as a rippling pilot's robe, and it was full of stars. In the north Shonablinka lit the rim of blackness; westward the hexagonal array of the Fravashi Ring twinkled high above the horizon. We drove the sled northwest through the silky, new snow. The dogs must have thought we were crazy, sledding through chest-high powder at night (chest-high to them, that is), skirting the crevasses that they must have feared lay beneath their covered paws. Far into the night it turned deep cold. The air was like frozen oxygen; my lips were so numb that I could not whistle, nor could I speak. We sledded silently across the seascape that I had seen in my scryer's vision, every gleaming fold and drift. We did not stumble across any crevasses. We stopped only once, to boil water for coffee. I kept my eyes fixed on the stars and on the horizon beneath the stars. In the twilight, just before morning, I saw a tiny hump of snow raised up from the immense white hump of the world. "There it is," I huffed out and pointed, "The Timekeeper's hut. Do you see it?"

"Yes, there it is. You were right."

He whistled to Kuri—and how I marveled at his beautiful whistle, his way with dogs—and with the wind lashing our faces, we slid over the snow-drowned sea.

29

The Secret of Life

When the Fravashi first became a people, the Dark God came down from the stars and spoke to the First Least Father of the Adamant Mindsinger Clan. "First Least Father," he said, "if I promise to tell you the secret of the universe at the end of ten million years, will you agree to listen to my song?"

The First Least Father was thirsty for new music so he told him, "Fill my windpipes; sing me your song."

So the Dark God sang his song, and ten million years passed while the Adamant Mindsinger Clan warred against the Faithful Thoughtplayer Clan and the other clans, and in all this time on all of Fravashing there was only this single, dreadful song.

When the Dark God returned he told the First Least Father the secret of the universe. "I don't understand," the First Least Father said at last.

Whereupon the Dark God laughed at him and said, "How did you expect to understand? Your brain hasn't changed at all in ten million years."

The First Least Father contemplated these words and sang out: "My God! I didn't think about that when we made the bargain!"

—Fravashi Parable

We came at the Timekeeper from the south in the very first part of the morning. He had built his hut fifty feet away from a newly opened crevasse. Fifty miles away, Kweitkel stood revealed by the dawn; the holy mountain was like a great

blue and white pillar holding up the western edge of the sky.
When the Timekeeper saw us sledding toward his hut from
the south, he must have thought we were Devaki hunters
returning home. We wanted him to think this. We had
circled south just so he would think this. In truth, even if he
had guessed who we were, we gave him no time to ice his
sled, to load his furs and food (what little food remained), to
harness his dogs and flee. We slid into his camp just after first
light, and he was outside his hut politely waiting for us in
Devaki fashion with steaming mugs of blood tea.

"*Ni luria la!*" he called out, "*Ni luria la!*" In his white
furs, which covered almost all of his face except his black
eyes, he seemed as watchful as a wolf.

"*Ni luria la!*" I answered.

All at once three starved dogs bounded from the tunnel of
his hut and ran among our dogs, barking, sniffing and licking
each other's black noses. The Timekeeper must have recognized my voice immediately; he must have seen that our sled
was a city sled, that our dogs were city dogs who greeted his
dogs with wagging tails and red tongues lolling. He set the
mugs of blood tea down into the fluffy snow, ignoring the
largest of his dogs when he began lapping down our welcom-
ing drink. He threw back the hood of his furs. His smooth
brown face was shiny with grease, set with the stamp of grim
humor and fate.

"So, the bastard Ringess has tracked me. Or should I call
you, 'Lord Ringess?' Ha!"

Before we had come to a stop, Soli was off the sled with
his spear cocked behind his ear, aiming the point at the
Timekeeper's belly.

"Leopold," the Timekeeper said. "Have you made your
peace with your son? Tell me, does the City still stand? How
did you escape my old bomb?"

Soli ground his teeth so hard that blood ran from his nose.
I could see that he trembled to spear the Timekeeper, so I
said, "Wait!"

"Yes, wait," the Timekeeper repeated.

Quickly I told him that part of the City had been destroyed,
that my mother and six thousand others lay frozen in a mass
grave. I told him how my mother had died trying to save me
from his slel-clone's killing knife.

"I knew the bomb was old," he said. "So old."

"You're a murderer," Soli said. He kicked up a shower of snow as he planted his rear foot.

"So, here I stand, a murderer tracked and trapped by murderers."

Soli's fist tightened around the spear. I felt certain he was about to kill the Timekeeper. I watched the murder programs begin to run. But he surprised me. He stared the Timekeeper up and down and asked simply, "Why the City? The City you founded three thousand years ago? Is that true?"

The Timekeeper let out a puff of steam and turned to me. He said, "So, you've been inside the goddess, and she's talked to you. What did she tell you about me, eh, Mallory?"

"She said you were the oldest human being, that you've been alive for thousands of years."

"How old am I? What did she say?"

"She said you've been alive at least since the Holocaust Century."

"I'm old, it's true."

I climbed out of the sled and stood by Soli. He stepped closer to the Timekeeper; the Timekeeper stepped backward in the direction of the crevasse. "How old?" I asked.

"So old," he said. "Very old. Older than the snow. Older than the ice of the sea."

"You'll have to pay for your murders," Soli said.

For no good reason, the Timekeeper quickly looked up into the sky. I saw the old hell bubbling in his black eyes, and I knew that he had already paid for the murders with pieces of his soul. He was paying still; he would never stop paying.

"It's so quick," the Timekeeper said. "All human lives happen so quickly, a few hard seconds, no more. Is it murder to mercifully end their lives a few moments before the ticking stops of its own and they die a natural death? Tell me!"

But neither Soli nor I had anything to add about the nature of murder so we said nothing.

"The City's had its time," the Timekeeper said. "The Order, too. You know why I did what I did."

"Did you have to kill my mother, then?"

"It was my double that killed her, not I."

"No, you killed her."

He made a fist and growled out, "Your mother and you,

the bastard Ringess with your carked brains, your wild new ideas, all of you, the doom of the human race."

I wiped ice from my eyelashes and said, "You would have killed me."

"Once I tried to save you—do you remember?—saved you because I loved you like a son." He glanced at Soli, then quickly turned back to me. "Do you still have the book of poems? I wanted to save you from the goddess. I saved you too well, goddamn me for trying!"

I stepped closer to him. He was scratching Tusa's ear, pointedly not looking at Soli's raised spear. Jets of steam billowed from his nostrils in slow, even spurts. In the morning air I smelled his sour skin, his sweat, his carnivorous breath. He was afraid of something. His face was as hard as any human face I had ever seen, but there was fear cut into it. I moved closer, stepping between him and Soli. Soli cursed and began circling in order to have a clear line of sight should he decide to spear him after all.

I rubbed my cheeks, trying to warm them so my words wouldn't be slurry. I said, "When the Lord Imprimatur unraveled your slel-clone's DNA, he found nothing."

"So? There's nothing to find."

"The Elder Eddas," I said. "The secret of the Ieldra."

"Gobbledygook!"

"The Entity told me their secret was embroidered in your chromosomes."

"Gobbledygook!"

"What do you know about the Ieldra?"

"Piss on the Ieldra!"

"Why would the Ieldra warn me—warn all of us—of the goddess?"

He smacked his fist into his mitten and yelled out, "Why this? Why that? Why, why, why?"

"How old are you?" I asked.

"Old as stone."

"What did the Ieldra do to you? I need to know."

"Piss on you!"

I stepped closer; he stepped back. "Tell me, Kelkemesh," I said. "I've come so far to know."

He closed his eyes and grimaced. With his mouth open he threw his head back as if he were about to scream. It was the first time I had ever seen his eyes closed. "So, you know my name; then you know everything. What's left to tell you, eh?"

"The secret."

"How old?" Soli asked.

He pointed his chin at me and opened his eyes. He held his palm pushing out toward Soli. "I was born thirty thousand years ago," he said. "Old Earth years. Do you need to know exactly how many years? One hundred forty-two years more than thirty thousand years ago. One hundred forty-two years, eighteen days and five hours more." As he said this he pulled a flat, gold clock from his furs, opened it, and said, "And fifteen minutes more, twelve seconds, thirteen, fourteen, fifteen seconds . . . how many more seconds do I have? If the Ieldra would have had their way, I'd live forever. They *made* me to live forever, damn them! It's my purpose, they would say. *Their* purpose."

"That's impossible," Soli said. He circled back the other way so the Timekeeper stood between him and the crevasse. "No one could live that long."

"Ha, Leopold, you're wrong! Shall I tell you? One day, long ago, when the forests of Old Earth were green and seamless as a mechanic's robe, they came down from the sky and told me they had chosen me to carry their message. The damn gods! I never saw their bodies; I don't think they had bodies, maybe they had never had bloody bodies. Do gods have bodies like men? They appeared as balls of light, bright blue balls like the hottest flames of a wood fire. They told me this: They said that the Earth—even my Earth of thirty thousand years ago—they said it was too full of men. The lights in the sky were stars, they said. Soon men would leave Earth and wander among the stars. I thought I was going mad. No, they said, I was not going mad; I was one of one hundred and twenty-five immortals chosen to carry the Ieldra's message through time. To carry their damn message so human beings, when we learned to burn the fuel of the stars, would listen to the voice of wisdom and not go mad, and we would not burn ourselves with starlight or other heavenly fires. The Ieldra—damn their faceless faces!—they said their spirits were ready to live within a sky so black and vast that not even the starlight could escape the blackness. A black hole, they said. I didn't understand a word of their gobbledy-gook, of course. They told me they were sad to leave the human race alone, naked in our ignorance. 'Naked!' I said to them. 'Ignorant!' Why, I wore the skin of the wolf that I killed with my own hands, and I knew the name of every plant and animal in the forest! The Ieldra didn't laugh at me because they had no mouths, but I heard them whispering and laughing inside me, all the same. Then they opened me, the bloody gods. They filled me with their crewelwork, every bit of me, embroidering every cell of my body, down to the last strand of DNA. They carked my seed, my goddamned soul! I didn't understand what they were doing. I was so pissing afraid that I knocked my own teeth out with my fist. I was burning from inside out. It felt like I'd swallowed hot tallow, like I'd eaten the magic mushroom and lay dying of fever, all at the same time. After that they left me to my fate. They carked their consciousness into the core singularity and left me to wander Old Earth for most of thirty-thousand years. My teeth soon grew back, of course, once, twice, many times, my damn teeth, every time I wore them out. They left me with these fine white teeth, to chew the bitter root of immortality, to taste the fruit of the world over and over until I was so sick of the world I could have died. But I couldn't die, and that's the hell of it. So now you know."

I looked down for a moment, thinking about gods and immortality. The snow was up to my knees; it was so powdery and dry I could see each ice crystal tumbling down the holes I made as I stepped closer to the Timekeeper, closer to Soli.

To the Timekeeper I said, "The message inside you— don't you want to know?"

"No."

"Embroidered in your DNA."

He grimaced again, revealing his long, white teeth. "No, there's nothing there but disinformation and noise."

"They're gods! Why would you doubt the message of the gods?"

"Because they lie," he said. "The gods, they lie."

Soli pushed through the snow, circling right, then left. His hand was hard over the leather grip of the spear while he wiped his bleeding nose with the other. He was backing the Timekeeper toward the crevasse.

I held a naked hand to my chapped lips, then asked, "The other immortals, what happened to them? Where are they?"

"They're dead," the Timekeeper told me. "The Ieldra

made us immortal, but we could be killed. A stone through the forehead, a knife . . ." and here he looked straight at Soli, "a spear through the heart—there are ways."

"All of them? Dead by accident?"

"Old Earth was a very violent place."

I saw that he was lying, or at least, he was keeping part of the truth from me. He watched Soli circle, watched the tip of his spear glowing golden as it caught the light of the rising sun. "You killed them, didn't you?" I asked suddenly.

He jerked his chin up and caught me with his eyes. "So quick, Mallory. Always too damn quick. So, I hunted them down like sheep, now you know, all of them, one by one, even the five of them—shall I tell you their names?—even the five immortals who escaped the Holocaust and fled into the manifold."

"Too bad," I said.

"They'd lived too long and the secret had to be kept, eh?"

"And you're the keeper of the secret?"

"So, I'm the Timekeeper and I've kept it all this time."

"You've decoded the Eddas—am I right? Tell me what they say."

"Tell yourself."

"You've no right to keep this secret," I said.

His eyes grew hot as coals and he shouted, "Rights? You talk of rights? The damn Ieldra took apart my *soul*! Not even gods have such a right."

I held up my fist to show him my pilot's ring. I said, "The day I received this, you called the quest for the Elder Eddas. The quest is over, then."

"No, Mallory, it's not over."

"The imprimaturs could decode the Eddas from your insides if—"

"There's nothing to decode."

"—if we brought you back to the City."

"So, you'll bring me back dead. Can the noble Ringess and his nobler father slaughter me like a sheep? Ha!"

Soli *could* kill him, I thought; he and I had raced across the sea just to kill him. I knew he blamed the Timekeeper for Katharine's death, so when he moved his spear, I thought he was about to kill him. He was aching to kill him, but struggling to restrain himself. He licked blood from his mustache and said to me, "If you want this old killer to live, we don't need his whole body. Yes, cut a few fingers off and freeze them. The imprimaturs can decode the Eddas from the DNA of his fingers."

He stared at the Timekeeper, and the Book of Silence opened. I read a whole chapter of the Book. He, the proud Soli, was well pleased with himself for rising to his humanity and not spearing the Timekeeper. He *loved* the idea of being merciful and gracious at the last instant.

The Timekeeper's lips pulled back in what could have been either a snarl or a smile. "Ha, is this all you want?" So saying he snapped his arm like a whip, and a long steel knife fell from his sleeve into his hand. He shook off the mitten from his other hand. As easily as I might trim the wick of an oilstone, he stretched out his little finger and lopped it off. The finger dropped into the fluffy snow and disappeared down a hole rimmed with blood, which quickly froze into little ruby crystals. He held his splayed, four-fingered hand in front of Soli's face. White bone gleamed in the dark, red suck of the wound, but strangely there was little blood.

"Take my finger," he said. And then he bent down, retrieved the finger from the punched-in hole. He flung it at Soli's face. Soli moved his head aside, and it went sailing past him, sailing past me, and it fell again into the snow.

Such a little gesture of scorn, but the Timekeeper had read the Book of Silence, too. He must have known about Soli and scorn. Soli went mad, then. He fell into rage; every bit of humanity and graciousness fell away from his mad eyes. He ground his teeth and snorted, and blood sprayed out of his nose. His spear arm drew back behind his ear, far back with his forefinger straight along the spear shaft, pointing behind him at me.

"Read the book, Mallory," the Timekeeper suddenly called out. I had no idea which book he was referring to. I tried to step closer, to stop the tide of violence beginning its surge, but I was already beginning to remember, and I could hardly move. "The book is for you."

I think he wanted very badly to die. But life was too much of a habit, and he could not die so easily, not the Timekeeper, so he charged Soli and tried to put his knife into him. Soli threw his spear. With his spear he had once killed a great white bear, and now he would kill an old, old wolf of a man.

Even though the Timekeeper tried to twist out of the way, Soli's spear caught him in the chest.

"So!" the Timekeeper howled out in pain. He stumbled and fell into the snow, ten feet from the edge of the crevasse.

Then Soli was all over him, kicking him in the face and throat, grabbing the spear shaft and jerking it back and forth, the better to ruin as much flesh as possible and to work the tip deep into the Timekeeper's heart.

When I began to move forward, Soli shouted, "Stay away!"

I took a step closer to them, the last step, the fateful step, the step I had seen myself take a thousand different times as I lay scrying in our silent snow-hut. I did not know why I took the step. I only knew that I must, that if I stepped closer to Soli, somehow the secret I had sought for so long would be revealed to me. My foot seemed to hang in the snow as it settled downward. My muscles were nearly frozen. The cold air hurt my eyes. My vision of the future—the future that was now, had always been and would always be—had taken me this far but no farther. Beyond this time, nothing. I was as blind to future moments as a child floating in his mother's womb is to light.

"Bastard!" Soli shouted. "Stay away!"

He ripped his spear from the Timekeeper's chest. There was a hole in the Timekeeper's furs as big as my fist, an ocean of blood. With the strength of an Alaloi—or the frenzy of a madman—Soli bent low and lifted him straight up over his head. He staggered over to the edge of the crevasse.

"No, Soli!" I cried out. I moved across the snow as fast as I could, but I was remembering too much to fall into slowtime, and therefore I moved too slowly.

"Soli, no!"

I grabbed at Soli as he heaved and pitched the Timekeeper's body into the crevasse. I fell against him; both of us nearly followed the Timekeeper over, too. There was a crack and a splash as the body broke through the thin, new sea ice twelve feet below us. The Timekeeper plunged into black water; he sank like a stone and disappeared. The secret of life.

"Damn you, Soli!"

The seals and fishes would scavenge the Timekeeper's body, and the secret of life would pass into them and be lost forever somewhere in the icy deeps of the sea. I clung to Soli's furs waiting for the Timekeeper's body to rise, but it did not rise; it would never rise again.

"Bastard!" Soli shouted this ugliest of words as he caught his good hand up in my hair and tried to snap my head back. Then I went mad, too. How thin the line between love and hate, reason and rage! Soli and I went down into the snow, tearing at each other as if we were mad dogs. I blindly grabbed for his throat. I punched his nose. With his two-fingered hand he must have found his spear because the bloody, frozen point dipped toward my face. I am sure he would have shoved it into *my* throat, but he did not have a very good grip on it. I dropped my chin to cover my throat and jerked suddenly. Somehow the flint tip glanced across my forehead over my eyes. There was a hot pressure and a ripping sound and blood. The flint was in my blood, and his blood, the Timekeeper's blood frozen to the sharp spear point, melted into my blood as Soli sawed the spear across my skull. I had the eerie sensation that my blood recognized the kinship of the Timekeeper's blood, that inside me his blood was whispering to me, calling forth my deepest memories. Or perhaps it was the shock of the spear or the brilliant glare of the sun off the eastern ice that set me to remembrancing—I do not know. I grappled with Soli hand to two-fingered hand, and the cold tide of memory (and rage) swept me under.

I remembered a simple fact of genetics; I remembered that all human beings shared a common ancestry. The kinship of blood: Soli rolled against me, and his chest came up against mine, pressing me down through the layers of snow. I opened my mouth to scream, but the blood dripping out of his nose got in and gagged me. I swallowed his blood, my blood, the blood of his father and grandfather, who was the Timekeeper, the grandfather of Bardo and Li Tosh, too, perhaps even Shanidar's grandfather, the grandfather of the entire human race. For thirty thousand years the Timekeeper had wandered the continents of Old Earth, all the while filling the women he took with the flood of his loins. Filling them with godseed. How many children he had fathered across the centuries I could not guess. Perhaps tens of thousands of children. And in each one of them girl and boy, the secret of the Ieldra coiled and was passed on to *their* children and their children's

children, on and on, father to son, mother to daughter year
after year so that on all the continents and oceans of all the
planets of man (and on the made-worlds, too) no woman or
man lived in whom the great secret did *not* live, lying
dormant, waiting inside. Inside me.

We rolled over and over in the snow as Soli tried to stab
his spear into my neck. But I locked his arm—it was a lock
the Timekeeper had taught me as a child—and I felt the joint
stiffen up as he grunted in anger and pain. Soli, too, had once
taken wrestling lessons, and he broke my hold. He got a knee
up and spun about. There was snow in my mouth and down
the collar of my furs. I was swimming in snow. The ice points
stung my naked shoulders and froze my neck. Rivulets of
snowmelt and sodden clumps of icepaste chilled my chest.
We punched and gouged and wrestled through the clean
snow, trying to kill each other.

"Should I kill him?" Soli suddenly screamed. But, no, the
scream was inside of him, not in his mouth. I was reading his
face; perhaps I was reading his mind. The scream was inside
me.

The brain is only a tool . . .

Something else called to me, and I shut my eyes to Soli's
clawing fingers, turned my head and listened to the voice of
memory. In a way, it was like a song. There were harmonies,
microscopic motions, and rhythms. I looked into my blood,
looked down the dark squiggle of my chromosomes where the
Elder Eddas was hidden. I looked into a place where the
imprimaturs had often looked, into that useless collection of
"junk genes" making up much of every cell's genetic material. I listened to my blood telling me that the junk genes *did*
have a purpose. They coded for and produced the proteins of
chemical memory. They were nothing but memory. The
Ieldra had not meant for their message to be decoded into
something so crude as human language. Their secret, the
secret of life, was to be remembered.

*The brain is that instrument for running and reading the
programs of the universe.*

Each of us carries inside the key to memory. I felt a
rhythm in my blood, and it was the precise dance of adenine
and guanine, thymine and cytosine, and the threads of memory encoded within my chromosomes began to unravel. Somewhere deep inside me, strands of DNA were coding for

alanine and tryptophan and other amino acids, building up
the proteins of chemical memory for my brain to read. Or
perhaps the memory of my DNA had already been encoded
within the neurologics of my new brain; perhaps I was
remembrancing to the fervid touch of electrons instead of
forming images called up by protein sequences. Protein/
electrons—in the end, did it matter how information was
stored? No, what mattered was the voice of the Ieldra
whispering those few parts of the Elder Eddas that I could
understand. The memories of the gods. The secret of life,
they said, is simple; the secret of life is . . .

"Should I kill him? Decide, then!"

Man is a bridge, they said.

The simplest things are the most difficult to understand. I
grabbed Soli's beard and jerked his head back and forth. I felt
my awareness spreading outward from our thrashing bodies,
outward in circles through the cold powder, spreading outward like a blanket of snow over the frozen seascape of the
world. I was aware of many things at once: of the morning
wind as it hissed and hugged the ice; of Kweitkel's white
summit poking into the blue belly of the sky; of Soli's hot
breath exploding in my ear. I remembered many, many
things. I remembered myself as I really was. Usually our
awareness flickers from the inner to the outer and back again
like a thallow cocking its head from side to side. We spend
our lives being aware of objects and events, and occasionally
we are even aware of ourselves, but to hold both points of
view at the same time is a very rare thing. I remembered that
I was a man who hated Soli; I remembered this hatred as if I
were watching myself hate him. It was stupid of me to hate.
My rage and hate programs were ruining me, imprisoning
me, robbing me of my freedom to think and feel and be. I
hated that my hatred was ruining me, and yet I could not
stop hating.

Human beings must free themselves, whispered the Eddas
in my inner ear, *they must be free.*

"Decide, then!"

Soli gouged my cheek with his fingernail; it parted the
layers of my skin one by one. I gasped in pain, and I
remembered there was a way out, the way I had once seen on
the ice of the Winter Ring, the way of creation. Many had
crossed the bridge of creation before me. I remembered the

first female warrior-poet, Kalinda, she who had loved flowers and life so greatly that she had fled the death-worshippers for the healing oceans of Agathange. There the god-men had remade her brain as they had mine. She had fled the worlds of man, fled far into the manifold. She had laid her brain naked from its surrounding coffin of skin and bone. With the elements of asteroids and planets that she consumed, she had added to the neurologics of her brain. She had created her brain and watched herself grow, century after century, growing and creating until her brain had become as large as a moon, and then many, many moons. The misnamed Solid State Entity, I remembered as I heaved against the churning snow, had once been as human as I; she had been a little girl who liked to put flowers in her hair.

The voice of memory, of an old, dying man: *The gods are tricksters, and when they remake a man, they always leave something undone.*

Soli began to reach back to grab his spear lying half-buried in the snow. It was the wrong thing for him to do. I felt his body's programs pulsing beneath his powdered furs, running along the length of his hard muscles into his arm. I coughed at the bitter air as I whirled and wove my arm beneath his arm up over the back of his neck. *The half-nelson is the first hold I'll teach you*, the Timekeeper whispered in my ear, and I was a novice once again grunting on the white furs of the Timekeeper's Tower. And younger: I was the boy Kelkemesh wrestling with his father, Shamesh, on a mountain glade on Old Earth. *It's a good hold, but the full-nelson is a deadly hold*. I forced my other arm up into Soli's armpit halfway to his neck. "Bastard!" he screamed, and I remembered then the thing that the Agathanians had left undone: the determination of my fate. I *could* choose. I could edit and rewrite my programs; I could create myself, here, in this very moment of rage and cold, rolling over and over in the snow.

But the price of birth is death, the Ieldra whispered.

Yes, I could create myself, but to create, I must un-create first. To die is to live; to live, I die. Could I be a murderer? My life, myself—and there could be no returning that way ever again; there could only be the great journey, on and on toward the infinite things, the quest without boundary or end. I remembered my promise to the Entity. How, I wondered, would I find the strength to sacrifice my fear?

There are infinite possibilities. And infinite dangers, too.
"Should I kill him? Decide now!"

I joined both my hands in the dense, wet hair at the back of Soli's neck. His sweat was freezing as I locked my fingers and began to pull downward, forcing his head toward his chest. And in my fingers, a great strength, the strength that Soli and my mother, and even Mehtar the Cutter, had put there. I must break his neck, I whispered to myself, I must snap it as I would a piece of shatterwood because he had murdered Bardo and was murdering me, because the universe was cold and unfair, because, after all, more than anything else I loved being human. I must choose a death. Never mind that a few wild chances had led me to this moment wrestling in the snow. In the end, weren't chance and fate two sides of a single face? I stared into the face of fate and found that it was my own. Does a man have free will? *Can you read the programs of the universe, the infinite possibilities?* There, on a cold, windy morning in deep winter, I remembered myself and saw a sad, windburnt, finally compassionate face smiling back. Yes, I can, I whispered. I *will*—a choice freely made beneath the freedom of the deep sky.

And so, a moment of letting go, of disengagement and freedom. I heard the snap I had been waiting for all my life. Soli crouched a few feet away from me holding the pieces of his spear on either side of his bent knee. He threw them spinning far out into the snow. He rubbed the back of his neck and said, "We could have killed each other, couldn't we? What's wrong with us, Pilot?"

I pressed my hand to the cut on my forehead to stop the bleeding. I was panting and I said, "Listen, Soli, this . . . trite tautology, not so trite: The secret of life . . . is life."

Soli got up and went over to the crevasse. He looked down. "The Timekeeper is dead," he mumbled half to himself. He seemed not to have heard what I told him. "Your secret, dead too. Why couldn't you have stayed away from me? Yes, why this cycle of . . . why does it go on? But no, it won't go on, I swear it, never, never again."

I stared west at Kweitkel as the memories thundered within me. I listened and I watched the light refract in colors off the sparkling snow. Everything—the pink granite of the mountain's northern pinnacle, the fresh white powder, the blue air itself—seemed newly created. I stood like a man stupefied with skotch, drunk with the beauty of the world. There was no more rage or fear. I turned east where the endless sheet of ice was burning with the light of the morning sun. Somewhere out there, beneath the red ball of fire boiling low on the horizon, was Neverness. *Infinite possibilities,* she whispered to me.

Soli knelt suddenly, going down on his hands and knees, systematically beating the snow near him. I remembered that the Timekeeper had hurled his finger into the snow.

"No, Soli, don't bother trying to find it. There's no point, now."

"Why not, Pilot?"

Quickly, as my body heat melted the snow that had gotten down my furs, I told him about my memories.

"But it makes no sense, does it?" Soli said. "Why were the Eddas encoded as memory? If the Ieldra wanted to tell us their message, why didn't they choose a simpler means?"

One of the Timekeeper's skinny dogs trotted over to me and I patted his side. He sniffed the air in the direction of the crevasse and began to whine. "What could be simpler, Soli? The Ieldra shared their wisdom with everyone. In truth, it's ironic: They relied on our intelligence to remember their intelligence. They must have thought it would be the simplest thing for man to learn the true art of remembrancing. And we should have, thousands of years ago. They never dreamed we'd be so stupid."

Infinite dangers. I glanced north at the blue-black curtain of the sky hanging over the frozen icebergs. I listened to the Eddas whisper.

Soli stood up and whistled to the rest of the Timekeeper's dogs. When he was done going over them with his hands and eyes, he asked, "Is this how it ends? The quest?" Then he, too, was staring off, blinking against the fresh wind.

I turned my head. To the south, the ice was smooth and white as an Alaloi baby's skin. There was no end to the southern ice of the Starnbergersee. "It goes on and on," I said.

We went into the Timekeeper's hut, and Soli boiled water for coffee. He bathed the wound on my forehead with hot, soaking cottons; he thawed it, cleaned it, and, with a strand of seal sinew, sewed it closed. After we had drunk our coffee, he fed and tended the sick dogs while I explored the inside of the hut. I searched through the Timekeeper's things until I found the book. Along with a few steel pens and a glass sphere full of ink, it was wrapped in an oilskin, shoved between the pillowed furs at the head of his bed. It was a fat, leather-bound book which closely resembled the book of poems he had once given me. I opened it and smelled the thickness of old leather. An icy gust blew through the chinks in the wall, rattling its white pages. It was not a book of poems. The Timekeeper had painstakingly—agonizingly— covered the pages of the book, line after line, with letters he had inked and drawn (and composed) himself. It was an exquisite work of calligraphy, the work of a man who cared not at all if he spent an hour penning a single word. The work of a lifetime. I turned to the title page of the book. There, in black letters as thick as a dog's claws, I read:

A REQUIEM FOR HOMO SAPIENS
BY
HORTHY HOSTHOH
TIMEKEEPER AND LORD HOROLOGE
OF THE ORDER OF MYSTIC MATHEMATICIANS
AND OTHER SEEKERS OF THE INEFFABLE FLAME

I turned the page and found that the book began with the following words: "These are *my* Eddas." I ran my eyes over the other pages of the book, reading continuously. The last page, I saw, was unfinished. The Timekeeper's sequence of words ended midsentence, and at least one hundred of the book's pages after that were blank.

Soli, who had never learned the art of reading, came over to me and asked, "Why would the Timekeeper want you to have this book?"

I closed the book and rapped the cover with my pilot's ring. I said, "This book, these words—it's his Eddas."

"Tell me about the Eddas," Soli said. "Not the Timekeeper's Eddas. That would make me too sad. Tell me about *your* Elder Eddas, the message of the gods."

I told him all that I knew. This is what I said: The Eddas were the Ieldra's instructions to human beings on how to become gods. Man is a bridge between ape and god, and the Eddas were a design for a bridge which would not crumble into snow dust. Men must be gods because that was how we were built. The god program runs deep in our race, as deep as the primitive DNA from which we sprang billions of years ago. We must learn how this program runs because that is our fate. I told him this simple thing as he pressed a mug of hot coffee into my hands. But there are infinite dangers, I said. When man looked godward with insane eyes, the very stars would explode and drop from the sky. Insane god-men, insane gods—the universe is full of insanity; insanity lurks everywhere, like a mad, cannibalistic thallow waiting to gobble up any godling who attains great intelligence and power. The more complex the programs of an organism, the greater is the danger of insanity. It is very, very hard to be a god. I breathed in the rich fumes of the coffee, and I said that it was the gift of the Ieldra to help man cross the bridge. Because they were compassionate beings, yes, but also because it was part of their purpose to save the universe from insanity.

"Of course, man is already part god," I said. "And we're part insane, which is why we're arrogant enough to tamper with the natural life-cycle of the stars. And therefore: the Vild. Because we're ignorant, Soli, because we don't know. We don't *see*. There are rules; the Eddas *are* rules, rules on becoming, of determining our place in the ecology."

The deep structure of the universe is pure consciousness.

Soli nodded his head and sipped his coffee as he listened to me talk on through the day into the night. The beginning of everything, I said, is the reprogramming of our brains. Even our antiquated human brains can be reprogrammed. We *can* write our master programs; there are techniques for doing so; the Elder Eddas lay down the rules for these techniques. In the end, we can remake our brains, and if we aspire to greater consciousness, then we must, for what is the brain but a small lump of matter that concentrates consciousness? Matter/energy; space/time; information/consciousness—consciousness; there are fundamentals describable by the Ieldra's beautiful, simple mathematics. In a way, matter is merely frozen energy floating in an icefield of spacetime. And consciousness is matter's way of organizing itself; consciousness is immanent in every snowflake, atom, blooddrop, photon and grain of sand, every neighborhood of spacetime from the Virgo Cloud to Perdido Luz. *Consciousness inheres,* I whispered; consciousness orders everything. The mathematics of order: There are rules for quantifying the involvement/ duty/identification among all the living organisms and inorganic matter in the universe. *Tat Tvam Asi*, That Thou Art, and what do I owe a stranger or an alien? My father? A bloodworm? A distant star? What is man's place in the universal scheme? The great danger, I said, is in falsely perceiving the otherness of all things. Then we will pull the wings off flies, or murder seals, or other human beings; then we may destroy the stars.

"There's help for the Vild, Soli. A solution, a way out. There's a unity of . . . consciousness. In a way, matter is just a standing wavefront of consciousness, and energy, every bit of gamma radiating from the Vild stars, every photon, this moving wavefront—it was all created by human action, and therefore it can be uncreated. Or, I should say, *re*-created. Made over in a different form, do you see? It's part of the ecology, now."

"You keep saying *the* ecology," he said, sipping more coffee. "What ecology?"

There is an ecology of information. Stars will die; people and gods will die, but information is conserved. Macroscopic information decays to microscopic information. But microscopic information is eventually concentrated. Nothing is lost. Gods exist to devour information. The lower intelligences sort, filter, concentrate and organize information. And the gods feed.

"Pilot?"

"I'm sorry, I was . . . remembering." I licked coffee from my teeth and said, "There are natural rules for determining our place in the ecology. If we could decode the universal program, read the intention of the universe, then—"

"You're not answering my question."

"I'm trying. The Vild—it's not the intention of the universe. What do human beings know of ananke? There are always imperfections and insanities. The orcas—"

"The *what*?"

"On Agathange, the orcas may or may not be insane, but they play a crucial role in *that* planet's ecology. And so, consider the Vild: an ocean of energy to be used."

As the Entity had made thousands of black bodies to store the energy of Gehenna Luz, so could we use the energy of

the Vild. Information could be coded into signals and sent
anywhere, given enough energy. Sent *everywhere,* this interflow
of information. We could speak with the nebular brains in our
galaxy. We could extend our galaxy's information ecology.
We—every human being, Fravashi, oyster, sentient bacterium, virus, or seal—we could drive our collective consciousness across the two million light-years of the intergalactic
void to the information ecologies of the nearer galaxies,
Andromeda and Maffei and the First Leo—all the galaxies of
the local group were alive with intelligence and vibrated with
the thoughts of organisms such as ourselves. Someday the
time would come to interface with the ecologies of other
groups of galaxies. Within ten million light-years off the
supergalactic plane of the local supercluster were many groups
of galaxies. Canes Venatici, the Pavo-Indus and the Ursa
galaxies—these burning, brilliant clouds of intelligence and
others enveloped our own small galaxy in a sphere of light
four hundred million light-years in diameter. To speak with
such distant galaxies would require the energy of a supernova, perhaps many tens of thousands of supernovas.

"*La ilaha il Allah,*" I said, "and we're all a part."

"Listen, Pilot, I don't understand you."

I listened to the night wind whispering outside the hut,
and to the quieter whispering inside. In truth, most of the
Eddas I did not understand, either. Most of it was—there is
no other word—gobbledygook. I did not yet have the brain to
understand it. For a moment, the whole, vast architecture of
the coming information ecology unfolded before me, layer
upon layer of ideas, biological systems and information structures spreading out, opening like the pages of a book. It was
overwhelming and wonderful, but I was like a worm crawling
across the first page of the book, trying to read it letter by
letter by the feel of the ink across my belly. I understood
perhaps a single page in all the millions of pages of the
Eddas. And the Eddas themselves, the collected wisdom of
the gods, were only a tiny part of the secrets that the
universe held, as insignificant as a single snowflake in a
blizzard.

I tried to tell Soli all this, but I do not think he really
wanted to understand. "You say that these memories are in
each of us? The whole of the Eddas?" He was staring straight

ahead as he knelt on the floor, roasting a baldo nut over the oilstone.

"Yes," I said, "passed down from father to son. That's why the Timekeeper killed the other immortals. He didn't want anyone telling people what was inside them. Because he knew."

"Knew what?"

"That the bridge can only be crossed one way. And he knew that if we listened to the memories, we'd want to make the crossing."

"It's not so easy to remember," he said.

"You could remember the Eddas, if you wanted to."

"Is that true?"

I watched the flame's reflection in his eyes. It must hurt him, I thought, to stare so long without blinking. "I could show you how to remember," I said.

He chewed his baldo nut a long time before he swallowed. "No," he said, "there are enough memories already. It's too late, isn't it?"

"Never too late," I said.

"Yes, too late."

I drank the last of my coffee and wiped my lips. "What will you do now, then?"

He sucked on his fingers a moment to warm them. He said, "All my life—and it's been a long life, hasn't it?—I've spent every moment trying to figure out why I was alive. My own private quest, Pilot. Now you say the Eddas are inside me; you tell me I have only to remember and . . . and what? You say I'll learn the secret of life on a higher level of existence. But life's life, isn't it? There's always misery, yes; and the higher the level of existence, the greater the misery. I've had enough—do you understand? I, Leopold Soli . . . I. I, like the Timekeeper—enough. How can there ever be an answer?" He rubbed his nose and looked at me. "All my life I thought I was learning how to live. But I knew nothing, did I? Justine knew everything. Yes, I'll sled on to Kweitkel and live with the Devaki, if they'll let me. We were happy there once, Justine and I. Do you remember?"

Later we heard the bawl of a bear far out on the ice. Soli thought it might be the same one who had led his dogs to their deaths in the crevasse. He went out to look for the pieces of his bear spear that he had cast into the snow. When

he returned, he held the broken end of the spear by its point.
"It was reckless of me to break the spear," he said. "But at
least the flint can be saved. It's a good piece of flint."

I ran my finger lightly along the cut on my forehead. "A
good piece of flint," I agreed. "It nearly killed me."

"Yes," he said, and he punched out and knocked away
part of a snow block from the roof. For a while he watched
the spindrift curling through the opening before he began to
shiver. He stood up to patch the hole and said, "Ever since
we first met, I've wondered: Why?"

He cut a new block of snow, trimmed it and tapped it into
place. He sat across from me on the Timekeeper's bed. He
tried to meet my eyes, but he could not. His face was hard
with emotion, the muscles locking as two contradictory programs began to run. He wanted to tell me how much he
hated me, how he resented my very existence. The words
were almost on his lips. His eyes were bright blue, as shiny
as the sea. He opened his mouth. He wanted to say, "Yes, I
wanted to kill you; I was ready to kill you; I would have loved to
have killed you." And then a long moment slowly passed as
his face softened, and he rubbed his eyes, and he said the
other thing, the thing that he thought he did not want to say:
"No, I couldn't kill you. How can a man kill his own son?"

I stared at the fire as the hut filled with silence. He threw
his hand over his eyes, rubbing his temples.

"Why *you*, Pilot?" he asked at last. "What will happen to
you?"

I sat there with him eating baldo nuts, and I told him one
last secret. Then everything seemed to be beating: my heart,
his heart, the air molecules outside beating against the frozen
snow. I listened to the beating of the Vild stars calling me,
then I told him, as compassionately as I could, that it was his
son's fate to be a god.

30

Neverness

A day, whether six or seven ago, or more than six thousand years ago, is just as near to the present as yesterday. Why? Because all time is contained in the present Now-moment.

To talk about the world as being made by God tomorrow, or yesterday, would be talking nonsense. God makes the world and all things in this present Now. Time gone a thousand years ago is now as present and as near to God as this very instant.

—Johannes Eckehart, Mongol Century Horologe

The next day Soli rubbed his red-rimmed eyes and announced that he would take the Timekeeper's sled and dogs and go on to Kweitkel. I could turn around immediately, he said, and hunt seals all the way back to Neverness. However, the Timekeeper's poor dogs were in no condition to pull a sled. Three of them were sick with frostbite, and all of them were starving.

"I'll come with you as far as Kweitkel," I said. I adjusted my snow goggles and looked out at the mountain. In the pristine air, its gleaming cone seemed much closer than it really was. "It would be best to leave the Timekeeper's sled here. The sick dogs can ride in our sled; the others can follow after us."

In truth, neither of us felt very sure that the Devaki would welcome Soli, and I did not want to leave him stranded with a team of sick dogs. So I accompanied him for this last part of his journey. It took us two days to reach the island. We built a hut thirty yards from the rugged shoreline. Yuri had told me three years ago—it seemed like three lifetimes—that I would never be welcome on Kweitkel. Very well, I would not touch foot to land. (Unless, of course, a bear clawed open my hut and chased me into the pretty yu trees above the beach.) Soli set out into the forest on skis. He would tell the Devaki some made-up story of tragedy and woe, of how Justine and Bardo, and my mother, had each gone over to the other side. He would return the next day, he said, with skinfuls of baldo nuts for my return home, and with meat for the dogs, if it had been a good year for the Devaki and they were feeling gracious.

I waited three days and three nights while the wind blew and nearly buried my hut. I was worrying fiercely when, on the afternoon of the fourth day, several sleds appeared at the edge of the forest. One of them slipped down the beach to the sea. I stood with my hand shielding my eyes against the noonday sun. I looked closely at the sled. Soli was driving it, and he was not alone.

"*Ni luria la!*" I called out. I did not know what else to say. I squinted and stared at the sled. At first I thought that Soli had a little bear cub riding atop the stacked skinfuls of baldo nuts. Then I looked more closely. It was not a bear cub; it was a Devaki child bundled in shagshay furs. I could not guess why Soli had a child with him.

The men at the edge of the forest did not greet me. They stood by their sleds, half behind the yu trees, looking out to sea. Because of the glare, I could not make out their faces.

"*Ni luria la,*" Soli answered, and he drew closer. I squinted and saw that the child was a boy, perhaps three years old. In his lap he held a stick doll. As the sled scraped to a stop, he looked down, studying the doll with a shy intensity.

Soli left the boy on the sled. He walked over to me, and in the language of the Devaki, he said, "It's too bad you had to wait."

"Who is the boy?" As soon as the words were out of my mouth, I knew who the boy was.

"He is the found-son of Haidar and Chandra," he said.

At the mention of his found-parents' names, the boy looked up and smiled. "*Haidar mi padda moru ril Tuwa,*" he suddenly said without any prompting, and he told me the story of how his found-father had killed a mammoth the preceding winter. "*Los pela manse, mi Haidar, mi Haidar lo li wos.*"

He was a handsome, strong-looking boy with an easy smile and quick, blue-black eyes the color of the twilight sky. He did not really look much like other Alaloi children I had seen. When I smiled at him his shyness melted instantly. He boldly stared at me as if he had known me all his life.

The color of Katherine's eyes, I whispered to myself. "What is his name?" I asked in a raw, uneven voice.

The boy smiled, showing me his straight, white teeth. *"Padda,"* he said, *"ni luria la; ti los mi lot-Padda?"*—"Welcome, Father; are you really my blood-father?"

"It's impossible," I said, although I knew that in this strange universe we inhabit, there is very little that is impossible.

Soli crunched through the snow closer to me and grabbed my arm. I whispered in his ear, "He can't be my son. Anala cut the fetus from Katherine a good forty-days before her time. Do you remember? He couldn't have lived."

"Couldn't he?" he murmured as he turned to look at the boy. "He's tough as a diamond. He's my grandson. All the Soli line—we're hard to kill, aren't we?" And then, "Look at him! The cutter sculpted your face but he left your chromosomes alone. How can you doubt it?"

He picked some ice from his furs and told me what had happened: "When they saw me approaching the cave, the Devaki were surprised to see me. And they surprised me by holding a feast in my honor. They roasted mammoth—they've been having luck with the mammoth herds these past years, even though a big bull trampled Yuri two years ago and crushed his skull. But everyone remembered what Yuri had said that day, so they welcomed me. They forgave me, can you believe that, Pilot?"

"Tuwa wi lalunye," the boy said as he licked his lips, watching us. Obviously he thought that Soli was telling me about the mammoth feast.

Soli rubbed the back of his head and continued. "It was Anala who told me. About the boy. None of the Devaki women expected him to live, even Chandra, who nursed him after Katharine . . . after we returned to the City. But he did live. It's a miracle, isn't it?"

I watched the boy as he fidgeted and slipped a tiny bone spear into the doll's curved fist. His long chin, I saw, could have been my own chin before I had been made into an Alaloi; his wavy hair was black and shot with red.

"But they murdered Katharine!" I said. "They called her a *satinka*. Why didn't they smother the baby and bury it in the snow?"

"That's not their way, is it?"

"I never thought he could have lived. I never *saw* it. I never guessed."

Soli scratched at the blood beneath his nose and coughed. "He was a tough little baby, they say. Chandra told me he rarely cried, not even when he burned his hand in the oilstones."

I blinked my eyes and said, "Katharine, before she died, she would have *seen* it if he were to have lived. Why didn't she tell me?"

"A scryer's ways."

"What's his name?" I asked, forgetting for a moment that the Devaki do not name their children until they are at least four years old.

"They haven't named him yet," he said. "But Haidar talks of naming him Danlo the Younger, after his grandfather. After Haidar's grandfather, that is."

I closed my eyes and shook my head. "No," I said, "he'll be a pilot, and people will call him Danlo Peacewise because he'll lead a mission to the Vild. He'll learn numbers and geometry, and he doesn't know the names of the stars yet, but he'll—"

"No," Soli said softly. He turned to the boy, who dug into one of the skins and popped a baldo nut into his mouth. He cracked it between his hard little teeth and smiled at me.

"He's my son!" I shouted.

"No, he's Haidar's son, now. His found-son, yes, but he loves him as much as his other sons. Haidar is the only father he knows. He'll be a good—"

"No!" I took a step toward the sled. "He's my son, and when he sees the City for the first time, he'll cry out, 'Father, I'm home!'"

Soli shook his head and pointed toward the line of thick-ribbed ice above the beach. Haidar, Wemilo, Seif, Jonath and Choclo stood on the blue whorls and crusts, watching us. They were dressed in their hunting furs, and each of them held a shagshay spear. I raised my open hand to them, but

only little Choclo—he was no longer very little—smiled back,
I had always liked Choclo.

Soli said, "When I entered the cave and Anala showed me
the boy, she said Haidar had gone with Wemilo and Choclo to
hunt shagshay. That's why it took me so long to come back,
because Haidar had to be asked. When Haidar returned from
his hunt, he said that *I* could carry the boy back on the sled.
To say goodbye—that's what Haidar said, do you understand?
He said that the boy should see his blood-father once before
saying goodbye forever."

I stared down at the snow, knowing what Soli would say,
yet stunned when he said it. I walked over to the sled and
picked the boy up. He was heavier than he looked.

"*Padda*," he said. A curious look crossed his forehead, and
with his long fingers he picked through my beard, examining
the red strands he found there. "*Padda*," he said again. But
there was no emotion in his voice. He said the Devaki word
for father as if it were an abstraction, as if he had learned the
name of a strange new animal.

"Danlo," I said, and I kissed him on the forehead that was
shaped as mine used to be. "My son."

I set the boy down on the snow, and he ran over to the
hut and crawled through the tunnel to see what he might
discover there. I looked up into the sky, silent and blue above
me. I swallowed hard, once or twice. My eyes were burning
with pain; I was surprised that they were as dry as the frigid
air swirling around me. Perhaps, I thought, my damned,
carked soul was no longer capable of tears.

"I can't take him with me," I told Soli.

"No."

"My son—he'll grow thinking he's a misshapen Alaloi."

Soli rubbed the side of his nose, saying nothing.

From inside the hut came a giggle of delight. I crawled
through the tunnel and smiled at Danlo, who was sitting at
the head of my bed. He had found the Timekeeper's book.
He was turning the pages one by one, picking at the black
letters as if he thought they were worms.

I looked through the hut's shadowy, freezing air at *infinite
possibility*, and I bit my lip. Gently, I pulled the book back
away from his lap. "*Li los book*," I forced out.

He was angry because I had taken his new toy from him.
He glared at me for a long time. I was afraid of the rage I saw

in his eyes, the rage that cut me like a spear. Then his curiosity returned and he smiled. *"Ki los buka?"* he asked me.

"A book," I explained, "is just a bundle of decorated leaves tied together. It is nothing important. Nothing at all."

Later, when I had packed the sled and Soli stood holding Danlo's hand for the short trip back to the beach, I whispered in Soli's ear, "Don't let my son grow up in ignorance. Tell him that the lights in the sky are not just the eyes of the dead. Tell him about stars, will you?"

I turned the sled in a circle eastward, and I gripped the hard, frozen rails.

"Yes," Soli said, "I'll tell him."

"Goodbye, Danlo," I said as I bent and lifted him into the air. Because his long hair smelled so good I kissed his head again. I grasped Soli's naked hand and told him goodbye, too.

"Yes, goodbye," he said. Then he did an astonishing thing. He pulled hard on my arm and leaned over suddenly as I nearly stumbled. He kissed me once, fiercely, on the forehead. I felt his chapped lips burning my cold skin; to this day I can feel the burning still. "Fall far and fall well, Pilot," he said.

I called to the dogs and drove the sled downwind into the gleaming plain of snow which opened before me. I never looked back with my eyes, though in my thoughts and dreams I have often looked back. I did not think I would see either of them again. *Never,* came the whisper, *never again.* The air was so cold and bitter that my eyes were full of tears before I had covered half a mile of the distance towards Neverness.

I am coming to the end of my story. There is little to tell of my journey homeward. The dogs and I ate our baldo nuts and mammoth meat, and after that we were hungry. Although I opened many aklia to hunt seals, they no longer leapt to my spear. Most of the time it was very cold. Twice my toes froze; to this day my toes have trouble with the cold. When I was almost within sight of the City, a blizzard caught me unprepared. For fifteen days I lay huddled with my half-frozen dogs in a hastily made snow-hut, reading the Timekeeper's book and listening to the storm. Arne and Bela died next to me, from frostbite and hunger. I left them buried in the snow.

Somewhere it is recorded that on the ninety-first day of deep winter in the year 2934, Mallory wi Soli Ringess, having failed in his quest to find the Elder Eddas, returned to the city of his birth. (I am told this is how the Sarojin's famous fantasy, *The Neurosingers*, ends.) I returned to one of the most bitter ironies of my life: The lords and masters, and most others, did not want to believe I had "remembered" the Elder Eddas. A few of them, the Lord Imprimatur in particular, ridiculed me. At least they did until, on the last day of the year, the greatest of our remembrancers, Thomas Rane, stripped off his robes, closed his eyes and floated in one of the tanks of the Rose Womb Cloisters. He remembered far into the murky past. He called up the memories that are within each of us, and he listened, as I had listened, to the whisper of the Elder Eddas. With joy (and too much pride) he taught many others of his profession to remember them, too. The word of this great remembrance quickly spread through the Academy. For days, I could not skate down the most out-of-the-way gliddery without some novice tugging on the sleeve of a schoolmate and pointing at me in awe. Even certain of the exemplars, who stand in awe of no man, could scarcely meet my eyes when they talked to me. It was very embarrassing. In truth, I much preferred ridicule to awe.

Soon after this the College of Lords made me Lord of the Order. I immediately took charge of the rebuilding of the Lightship Caverns and the surrounding, bomb-ruined City. I sent robots into the mountains beyond Urkel to cut great quantities of stone. By twentieth day in midwinter spring, the foundations of a grand spire (some said grandiose) had been laid. As the gray, snowy days passed, a needle of pink granite rose above the newly built Hollow Fields, above the halls and towers of what came to be called the New City. In a year, when the spire was completed, it would be the tallest in the entire City. I named it Soli's Spire, to the surprise and consternation of everyone who thought they knew how much I hated my father.

During this time I led a miniature expedition into the sealed-off Timekeeper's Tower. I trudged up the stairs to the Timekeeper's sanctum. Snow had blown through the ruined windows and accumulated, covering hundreds of the Timekeeper's clocks. I rescued the clocks. I ordered the snow removed and the windows rebuilt, of glass. The entire Tower, I decided, would be a museum.

In the basement of the Tower, I discovered many, many ancient books, a whole library of musty, leather-bound books.

I read the books; to this day I continue reading them. I walked through the long, stone corridors winding down into the deepest levels of the Tower. I came to my old cell and looked within, remembering. I opened the heavy door of the adjacent cell, the cell in which the warrior-poet had composed his death poem. There was a smell of dust and animal droppings and death. I found his white bones picked glisteningly clean by the sleekits whose burrows tunneled deep beneath the ground. His red warrior's ring and his poet's ring gleamed against the long, curled finger bones. So, I thought, the warrior-poet had really died. Then I remembered that he had made me promise to send his body back to his planet of birth. In all the confusion of the War, I had forgotten him. I ordered his bones removed and wrapped in his warrior's cloak. Robots cut a black marble casket and polished it until it shined like a mirror. I, myself, chiseled the words of his death poem into the facing. The novices who watched me working in the dark basement—and perhaps everyone else as well—must have thought that I was two-thirds insane. When they supposed I wasn't listening, they laughed at me. But they did not yet understand how vital it was that the dead, any dead, must be honored and, more, remembered.

I must now tell of the promise that I made to the goddess, Kalinda, and of the miracle which caused me to keep that promise. The miracle: On the fifty-sixth day of false winter, Bardo's *Blessed Harlot* fell out of the manifold and was brought down to the newly built Lightship Caverns. For many days the Hollow Fields had been reopened to the stream of shuttles from the deepships and longships which are the lifeblood of the City. And one by one, the lightships of pilots who had journeyed far across the galaxy during the quest began to return. (Many pilots, of course, had remained true to the quest and had not seen Neverness since the day the Timekeeper issued his summons. Their names are honored above all others.) At first it was thought that the *Blessed Harlot* was one of these ships. But then a journeyman tinker recognized her great, drooping wings and blunt nose and sent a novice to inform me. I met Bardo at the Caverns, but he refused to immediately explain the miracle of his existence.

"Bardo!" I cried out when he stepped from his ship's pit. "How is it possible?"

"Little Fellow!" We embraced and he thumped my back,

as usual. He felt as massively solid—as real—as he always had. He was weeping freely. Fat teardrops ran down his cheeks. "Little Fellow!" he said. "Little Fellow. By God, it's good to be home!"

"Tell me what happened to you. Are you alone? Where's Justine, then—may I ask?"

He smiled sadly as he grabbed his belly and shook his head. Except for a slight graying of his temples and beard, he looked much the same as I remembered. "Oh, you may certainly ask," he said. "But not here. I'm so thirsty—I haven't tasted beer for a long time. I'm dying for the taste of it. Will you come to the Hofgarten with me so I can drink some beer?"

On a day of brilliant sunshine and warm mountain breezes we went to the Hofgarten to drink beer and skotch. We sat at a polished wooden table in our favorite room overlooking the sea cliffs. The outer windows were open to let in the air and the hot rays of the sun. We sat by the window, drinking our drinks, and talking.

"Ah, this is good," he said as he held the mug of beer to his lips. He licked foam from his mustache and then took a few more gulps. "So good. I should tell you about Justine. She is well. She has gone to Lechoix, to visit her mother and to teach at the elite school. She won't be coming back to Neverness, too bad."

I sipped my skotch, but there was little pleasure there. The taste of it distracted me from the important thing I had to ask Bardo. "Begin at the beginning," I said. "How did you survive the battle? The star?"

"Shall I tell you of the battle? How am I still alive? There is a simple explanation, my friend. We were rescued. The Entity saved us, somehow—I don't know how. One moment we had fallen out in the heart of the star and we were being fried like meatworms in a fire. We were dying, you see. The next moment—well, we were free."

He finished his beer and called for another. His fat cheeks were very red, whether from the beer or from embarrassment, it was hard to tell.

"And then?" I asked.

"And then we fled, by God! There, now I've told you. 'Bardo the Coward'—that's what you're thinking, I know. We found a mapping back to the fallaways, and then on to Lechoix. We couldn't stay together that way, Justine and I.

Sometime I'll have to describe it, the hell of losing yourself in someone else. Sometime. The Timekeeper was right. It's not good for pilots to share the same ship. Oh, you must hate me, Little Fellow, for being the coward that I am!"

In truth, I did not hate him; I loved him for being a coward. "I'm glad you're alive," I said.

He would not say anything more about Justine, so I told him everything that had happened since the battle. He was glad that the Timekeeper was dead, and gladder still that I was Lord of the Order. Of my discovering the Elder Eddas he was not so glad. Bardo, my irreverent, profane friend, had come to mistrust the gods.

"Why aren't you drinking your skotch?" he asked as he slapped the table. "Drink, Little Fellow, and I shall tell you about the Entity and what she's done to me. She's talked to me! I, Bardo, a prince of Summerworld and soon-to-be master pilot, that is, if the *Lord* Pilot finds me worthy—I've talked to the goddess and returned to tell you!"

I picked up my tumbler of skotch. I put it to my lips and sniffed, but I did not drink it, because of the memories. "What do you want to tell me, Bardo?"

He belched, and a sour, sick look came over his face. He was already a little drunk. "Ah," he said, "I haven't been entirely truthful to you. Forgive me. The goddess didn't tell me that she had rescued me from the star. She said that she had *created* me. Remembered me, by God! Justine and I—we were dead, she said. Our beautiful ship destroyed. Oh, too bad! This is what she told me, Little Fellow. She said that she remembered the configuration of every atom, every synapse of our goddamned bodies and brains. She recreated me, she said, from hydrogen gas, from carbon molecules and stardust. She saved me from death. A resurrection, she said, a second chance. Is it possible?"

"I don't know."

"*Is it possible?* By God, tell me, Little Fellow!"

I took a sip of skotch and let the liquid amber roll across my tongue. I listened to the crosstalk between sense and memory, the memory contained in each molecule of skotch. The alcohols and ethers burned their way through the pink papillae into my blood. The taste of esters and the pungent, fufural aldehydes recalled the planet Urradeth where the skotch had been made forty years ago. I smelled the crisp grains of barley roasting over a peat fire, and barley mash fermenting, its essence being distilled into the golden liquor of memory. I swallowed and saw the man who had cut the barley, his steel scythe reflecting the harsh, blue light of Urradeth's sun. In the body and germ of the barley were atoms of carbon, bits of countless exhalations of the people who had colonized Urradeth. Bits of Old Earth and her yellow sun, the hydrogen of the stars, and the oxygen made in a distant stellar fire which had no name that I knew—the tree of memory and being was infinite, and the contemplation of its interconnecting branches made me dizzy. *The memory of all things is in all things*. I coughed and spat a mouthful of fiery skotch over the table. The droplets beaded up on the oiled wood, the shatterwood which had been poached from Alisalia's forest by a wormrunner long-since dead. Yes, I thought, She, a goddess had made a man as easily as a man might carve a favorite stick doll he has remembered from his boyhood.

Through consciousness, gods create; creation is everything.

"It's possible," I said at last.

"Oh, that's too bad," he said. "That's the very worst thing. So bad, too damn bad. Perfect information is impossible, I think, and therefore Bardo is not the man he once was. What am I, then? How will I ever know?"

It was the old problem, the old fear. But finally, here in the body and soul of my old friend, the possibility of a new solution.

"You are who you are," I said. "You're Bardo, my best friend. That's enough, then."

Beads of sweat shined on his bulging forehead. "And who is Mallory Ringess?"

"I am that I am."

He licked his red lips and banged his mug on the table. He shook his head, rapped the window with his pilot's ring, and he said, "The Entity told me that I was to bring a message to you, that I would be both the messenger *and* the goddamned message. To remind you of your promise. What did she mean?"

"I've promised to return to Her, Bardo."

"Why?"

I pushed the tumbler of skotch away from me. It slid almost frictionlessly across the wet table. "This will be hard to explain but I must try. Kalinda was a warrior-poet before she was ever a goddess. The poets, in *their* quest for the perfect human, they long ago embroidered their chromosomes. And worse, they edited what they thought was useless information, up and down the genome. In their ignorance, they edited out a vital thing. And that's the tragedy. Each warrior-poet, even Kalinda—especially Kalinda—they can't remember the Eddas. Because, inside them, where it whispers in us, there's nothing."

"That's too bad."

"Kalinda—the Entity—she's what the Ieldra didn't want: a goddess who grew into herself without the benefit of their wisdom."

He leaned over the window sill to take a breath of fresh air. He belched and said, "But the Entity must have known how to decode the Eddas. Think of the pilots who have been lost inside her. Ah, think of me. If she could . . . well, if she could really *create* me, then she must have been able to read every bit of my DNA."

"In truth, I believe She knows everything about the Eddas . . . *now*. But it's too late, do you see? For all Her power, for all Her glory, She's a little insane."

He belched again and said, "Well, I still don't understand."

I stood up and pushed my chair away from the table. "It's a beautiful day," I said. "Let's take a walk on the beach."

Because he was drunk, he threw his arm around my shoulder and half-stumbled, half-dragged me outside. We walked down the icy path cutting through the cliffs to the beach. I told him of my plans to send a mission to the Vild. Our Order's finest pilots, I said, would lead the mission. There would be many lightships, and a seedship carrying historians, programmers, mechanics, eschatologists and remembrancers, above all, remembrancers—a full complement of masters representing our Order's every profession. We would civilize the Vild. Or rather, we would civilize and teach the wild peoples of the Vild not to destroy the stars. I would show the pilots the proof of the Hypothesis, and they would teach the barbarians the art of mathematics. And somewhere in the ruins of the Vild, the masters of the seedship would establish a new Academy, perhaps many Academies to teach new pilots. To learn, to journey, to illuminate, to begin—that is the motto of our Order, and it would remain the motto no matter how far our pilots fell.

"But the Vild's radiation—it propagates, does it not? And what about Merripen's Star? And all the others? Eventually, the light will sear the entire galaxy."

"No, we won't allow that future to be." I closed my eyes and said, "We'll make new life forms that live on light. Half-bacterium, half-computer, half-photoelectric cell—a swarm of new life throughout the galaxy, feeding on photons, shielding, becoming a part of the ecology. Such an intelligence—you can't imagine."

"And then?" Bardo asked.

We were standing on the beach, looking out at the Sound. There was the smell of salt and old snow, the rich, ageless ferment of the sea. The sea ice had mostly melted; waves were swelling up, cresting and crashing against the rocky shore. In the air above us, a couple of snowgulls were screaming. They dove and swooped and skimmed across the foamy shallows.

"Someday," I said, "too soon, I'll leave the City. I'll go to Her, as I've promised. And then I'll grow. There will be a . . . a union, of sorts. A marriage, if you will. If I will. She's lonely and a little insane and therefore: this new ecology of information. We'll make something new, something that has never been before, never within this universe. And there is something else. This—it is hard to explain—this *becoming* that I've been afraid of for so long, now no longer. Because of you, I see it now. We are what we are. Everything, every woman, man, child, seal, rock, thought, theorem, and speck of dirt—it's all preserved, all created. That's what gods do, Bardo."

We picked our way across the rocks and sand, trying not to step on the pretty pebbles and smooth shells washed up along the high tide line. Bardo was puffing and panting; he leaned over with his hands on his knees. His face had gone as pale as an autist's. I thought that he was about to be sick. "Oh, my poor belly," he groaned. "I've drunk too much beer." Then he remembered his dignity, straightened up and leaned on my shoulder. His weight was very great, very comforting, very familiar.

He stared out at the water mournfully, then turned and

examined my face. "Look at you! A man wearing a caveman's body, and two-thirds a god inside your head!"

Give; be compassionate, Katharine had told me.

"No god is there but God, and we're all a part," I said.

He was quiet for a moment, and then he picked up a stone and whipped it out into the water. As boys, we had often played this game of skipping stones. "Three skips," he said. He dropped a gritty, wet stone into my hand. "We'll see if you can get four."

"No, Bardo, I didn't come here to skip stones."

His face flushed into anger, and he scooped up a pink spirali shell and dashed it against a rock. It broke into pieces. "Why do you always do what you shouldn't do?" he shouted. "Where's your sense? Oh, too goddamned bad!"

"I'm sorry."

"No, you're a god, and gods aren't sorry, I don't think."

"I'm your friend."

He glanced up and down the beach, first at a couple of novices holding hands by the water's edge, and then out at the seals on their rock. There were nine gray seals, and they were basking in the sun with their black noses pointed straight up towards the sky. He dropped his voice low, as if he were telling me a secret. There were vapors on his breath, the sour-sweet smell of beer. "No, Little Fellow," he said. "Can a man be friends with a goddamned god?"

I looked out at the waves washing the shore rocks. There was light off the sparkling water, colors that he could not see. "To live, I die," I whispered.

I thought that he hadn't heard me because he was petulantly kicking at the wet sand. His chin was dropped down into his neck, and he would not look at me. And then, "No, you'll never die—isn't that what Katharine prophesied?" He smoothed the folds of his kamelaika over his belly. "But, I, Bardo—I'm just a man, and if I don't feed this fine body of mine soon, I *will* shrink away and die. Let's forget these painful eschatologies for the moment and dine like men before we evanesce completely. I'm going back up to the Hofgarten to order a meal. And then I'm going to become not just a little drunk, but gloriously drunk. Are you coming with me, Little Fellow?"

For in the end we choose our futures, the scryers say.

"Perhaps later," I told him. "I'm not hungry right now."

He shrugged his shoulders, bowed his head formally, and

began the hike back up to the Hofgarten. I watched my best friend—this messenger of the gods, this miracle of creation—stumbling among the black, sea-sculpted rocks.

It is true, I now know, that creation *is* everything. Kalinda had sent Bardo to remind me of that. She had created him from memory, and someday, I, too, would learn the art. Someday, I would remembrance Katharine and bring her back into being, because creation is what gods do. That is what we all do. Each of us—gods, men, or worms in the belly of a bird, in our every thought, feeling and action no matter how trivial or base—we create this strange universe in which we live. We create God. At the end of time, when the universe has awakened to itself, the past will be remembranced, and everything and everyone who has suffered the pain of life will be redeemed. This is my hope; this is my dream; this is my design.

I stood upon the beach dreaming, with the cold ocean in front of me. I squeezed the flat, smooth stone Bardo had given me and hurled it side-armed at the waves. It hit the water spinning, and then skipped four times. There was only a moment between the last two skips, before it sank beneath the water, and in that moment, the spinning lens of the galaxy took me a thousand miles through space. And the galaxy itself continued its journey outward from the still point of creation, and I fell through the universe. To this day I continue to fall, not into that negative eternity of neverness and despair, but through that other universe where the stars are bright and uncountable, and the quest for life, if not the secret of life, goes on.

Each moment, I believe, we die, but each moment too, we are reborn into infinite possibilities. And so on a lovely day in false winter, I paid the final price and turned my face to the wind. As it usually did, the salty spray off the water made me hungry. I walked back up the beach toward my shimmering City to join Bardo for dinner, to be gloriously human again for a little while.

About the Author

David Zindell's short story, "Shanidar," was the winner of a Writers of the Future award. He was also nominated for the John W. Campbell Award for best new writer. *Neverness* is his first novel. He is currently at work on his second.

"The trilogy is an epic exercise in imaginary world building that ranks with Frank Herbert's *Dune*."
—*The Oregonian*

West of Eden
by
Harry Harrison

☐ Volume One: **West of Eden** (26551-2 • $4.50/$4.95 in Canada) In a world where dinosaurs still exist, the young human Kerrick grows to manhood in the midst of the Yilane—cold blooded, intelligent reptiles—and uses his knowledge of their ways to become the humans' leader, and the dinosaurs' most feared enemy.

☐ Volume Two: **Winter in Eden** (26628-4 • $4.50/$4.95 in Canada) In this sequel to **West of Eden**, Kerrick must embark on a quest to rally a final defense against the Yilane, who have discovered that a new ice age is coming and are attempting to reconquer human territory.

☐ Volume Three: **Return to Eden** (27700-6 • $4.95/$5.95 in Canada) The stunning conclusion to the *West of Eden* saga. Kerrick leads his people to a safe haven only to discover that without effective weapons they are terribly vulnerable. His dinosaur enemy, the Yilane Vainte, outcast from her people, stalks him as well, seeking his death.

Buy these books now on sale wherever Bantam Spectra books are sold, or use this page for ordering: